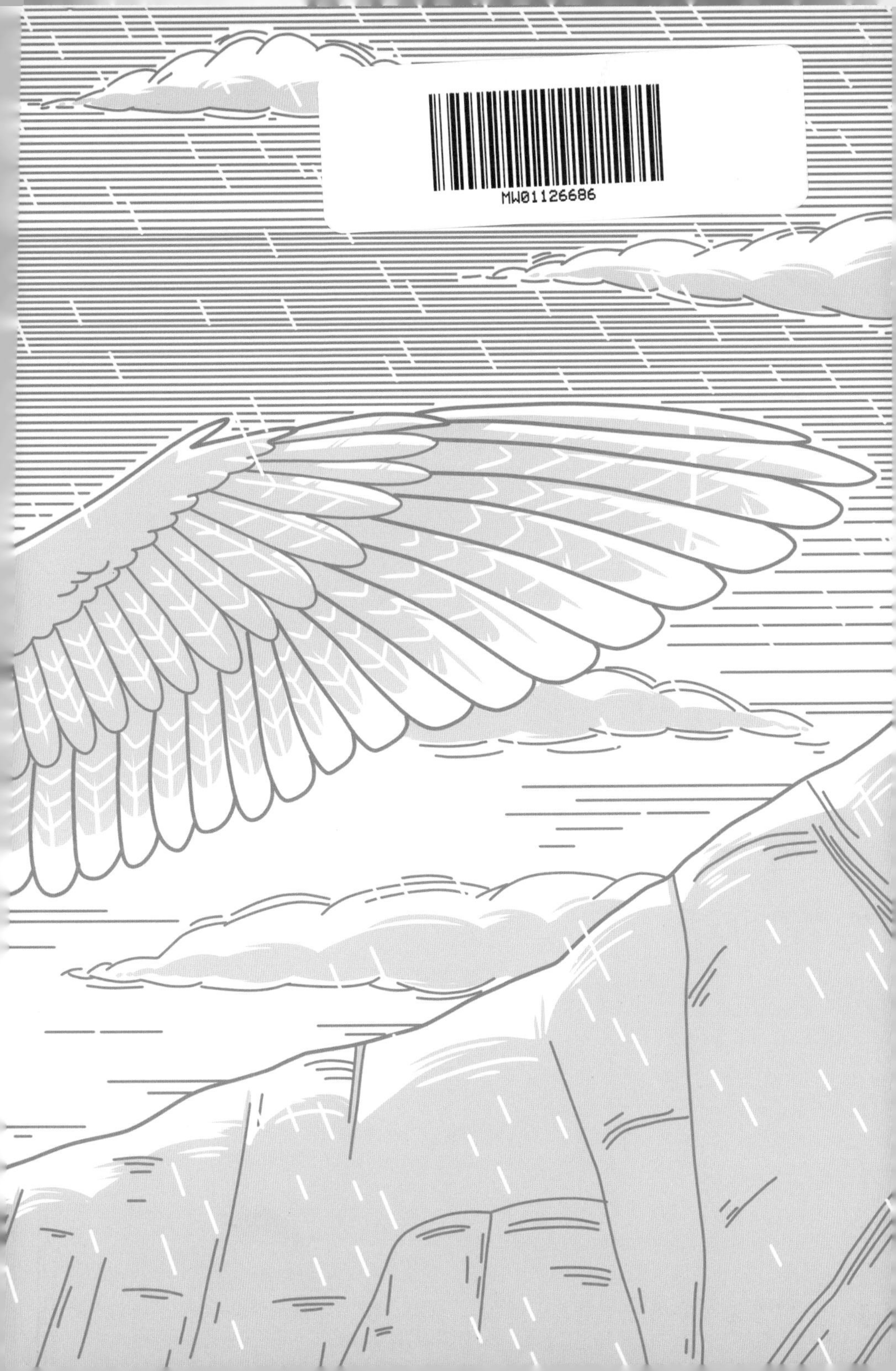

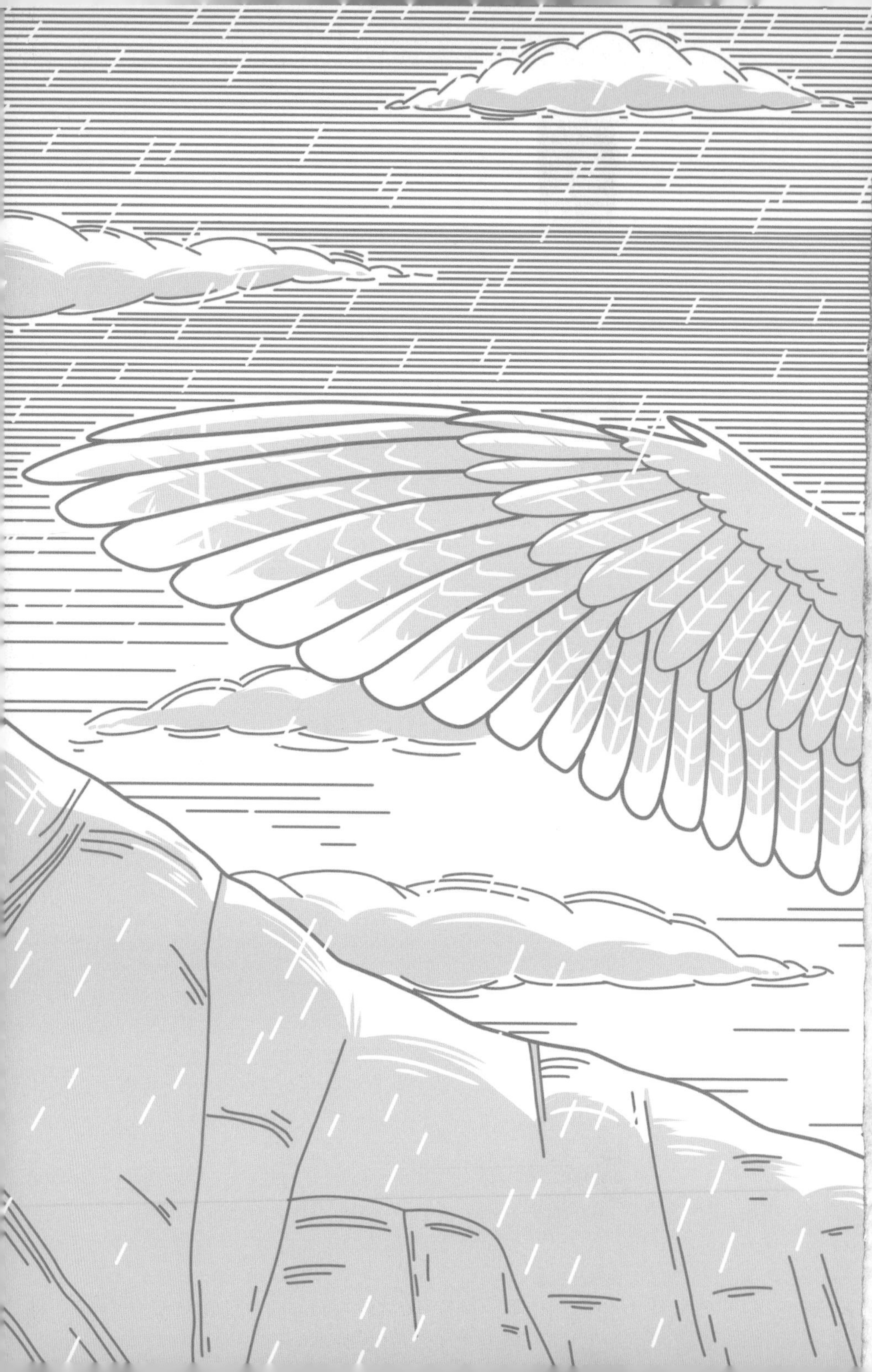

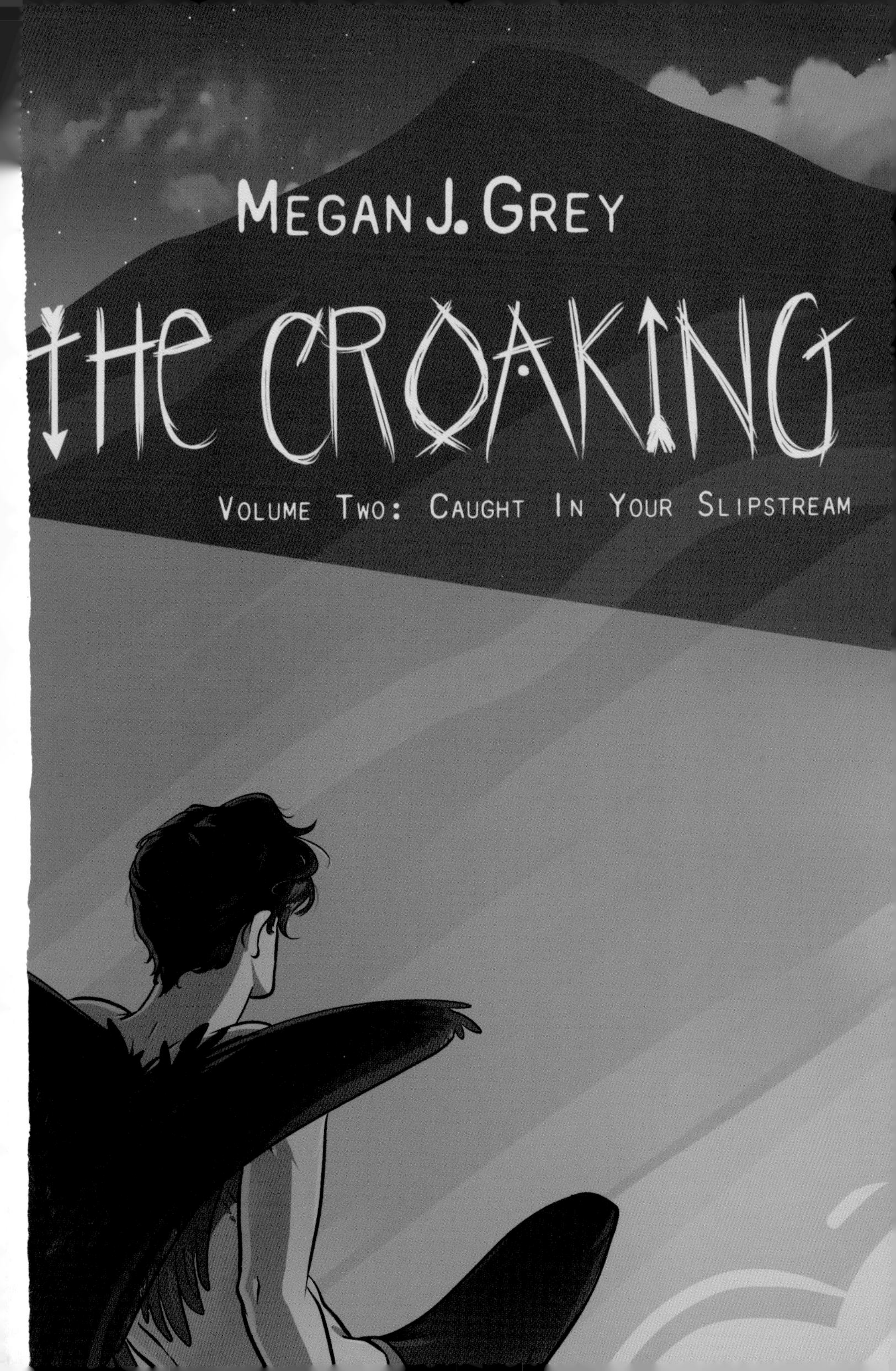
Megan J. Grey
The Croaking
Volume Two: Caught In Your Slipstream

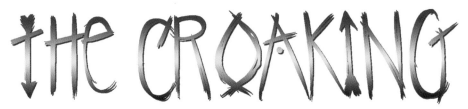

THE CROAKING

VOLUME TWO: CAUGHT IN YOUR SLIPSTREAM

by

MEGAN J. GREY

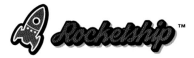

Rocketship™ Rocketship Entertainment, LLC
rocketshipent.com

Tom Akel, CEO & Publisher • **Rob Feldman,** CTO • **Jeanmarie McNeely,** CFO
Brandon Freeberg, Dir. of Campaign Mgmt. • **Phil Smith,** Art Director • **Aram Alekyan,** Designer
Jimmy Deoquino, Designer • **Jed Keith,** Social Media • **Jerrod Clark,** Publicity

The Croaking volume 2 | Softcover Edition ISBN: 978-1-962298-01-8 | Hardcover Edition ISBN: 978-1-962298-02-5

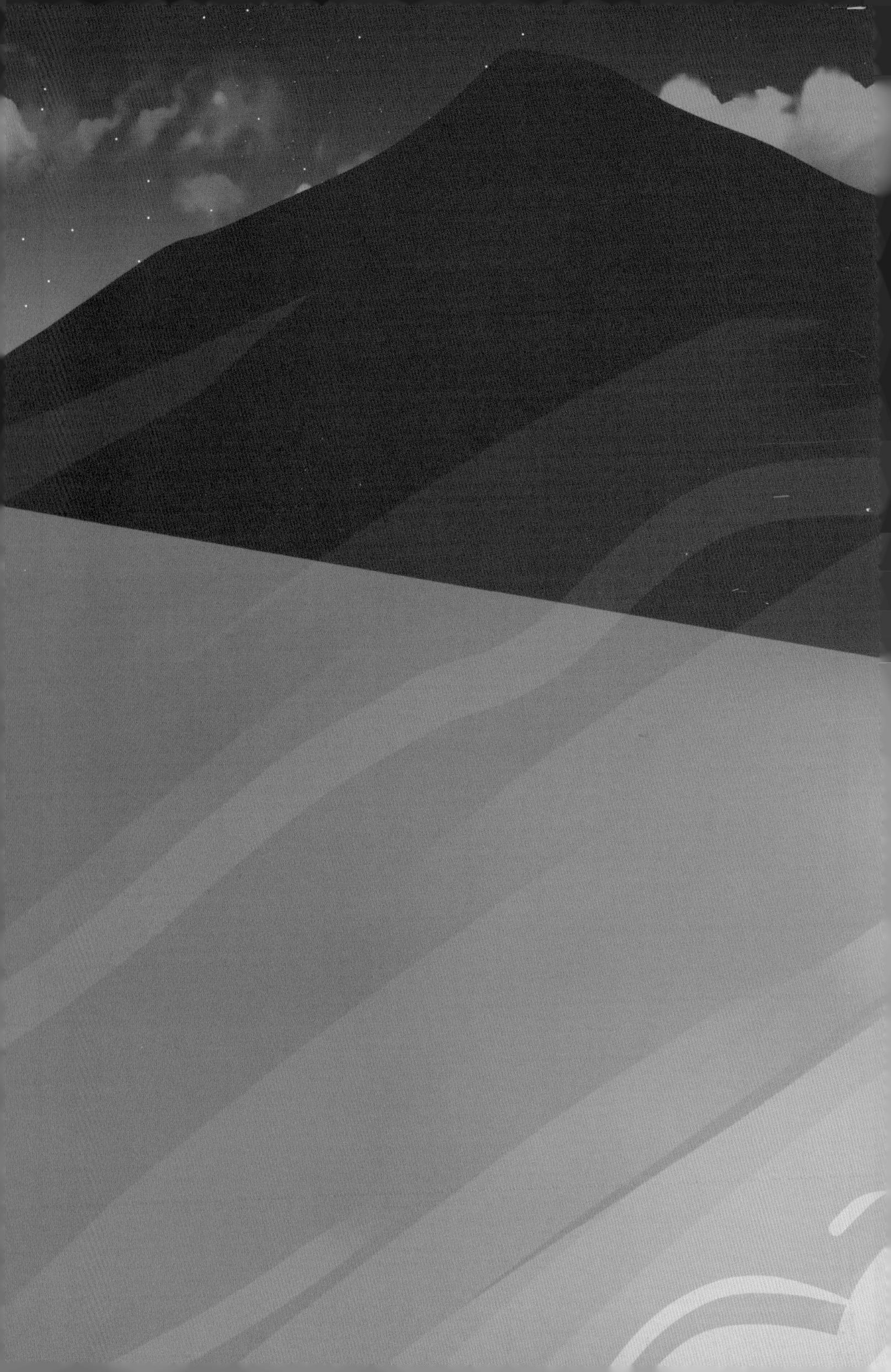

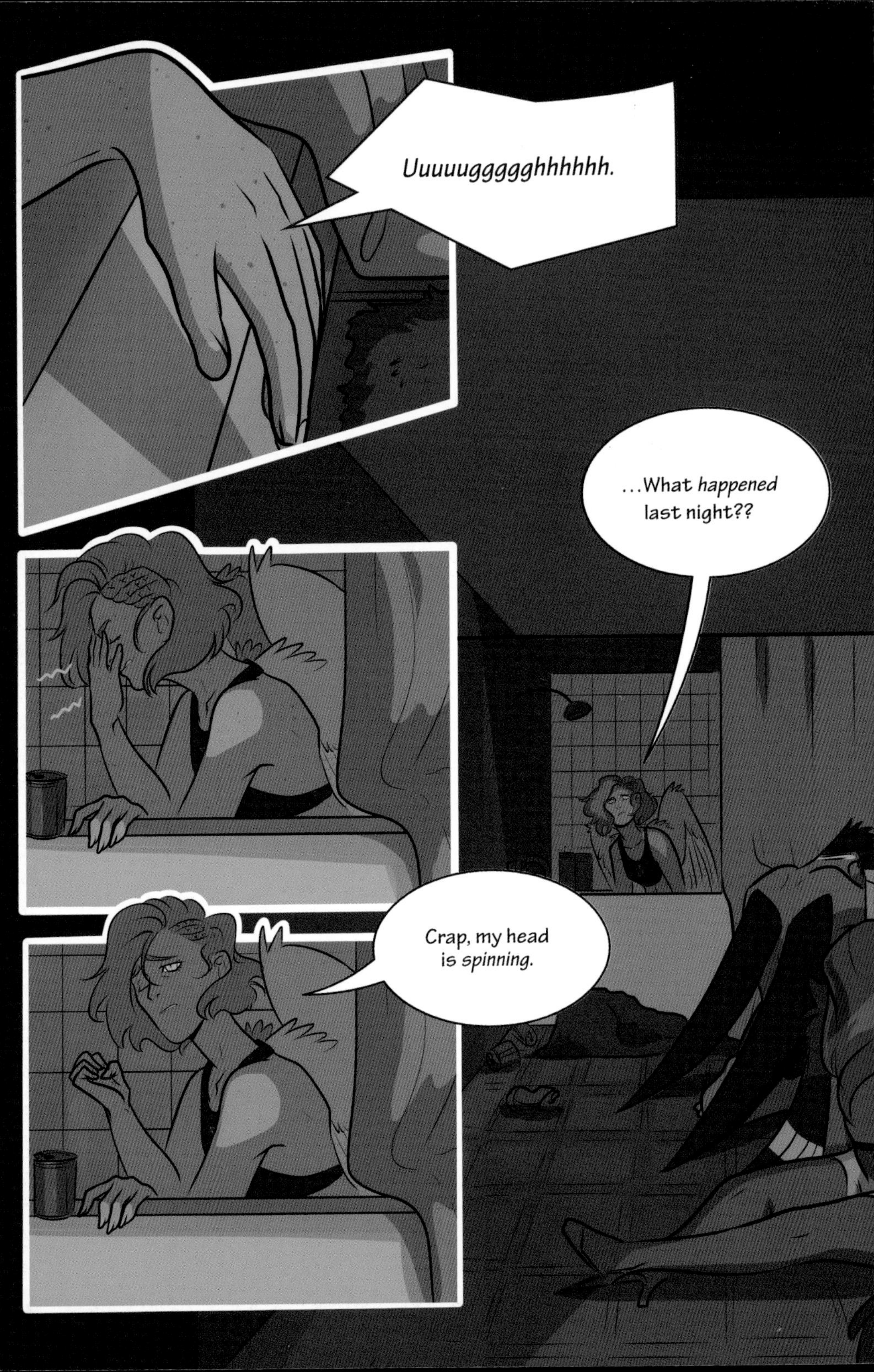
Uuuuugggghhhhhh.
...What happened last night??
Crap, my head is spinning.

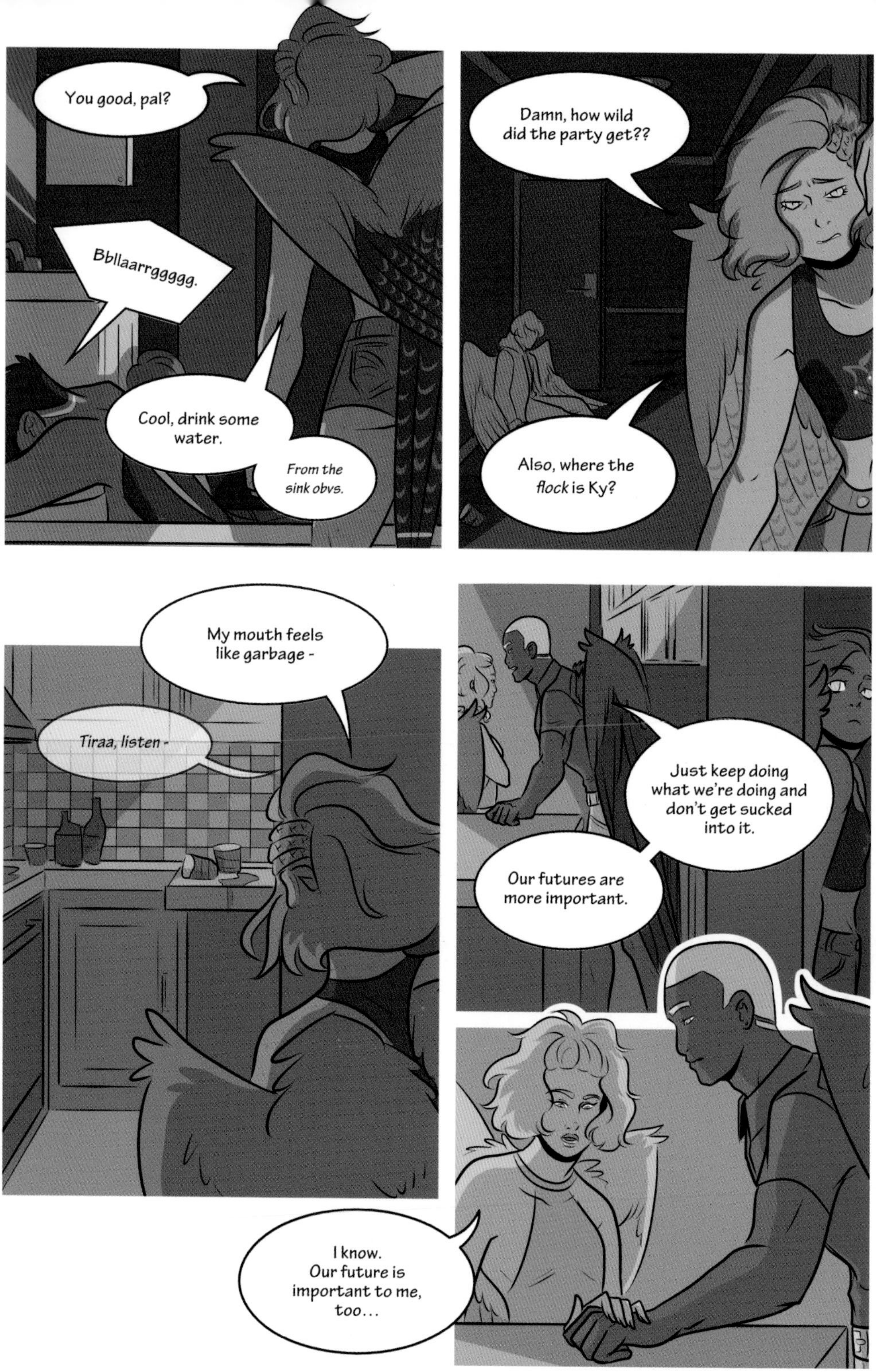
You good, pal?
Bbllaarrggggg.
Cool, drink some water.
From the sink obvs.
Damn, how wild did the party get??
Also, where the *flock* is Ky?
My mouth feels like garbage -
Tiraa, listen -
Just keep doing what we're doing and don't get sucked into it.
Our futures are more important.
I know. Our future is important to me, too…

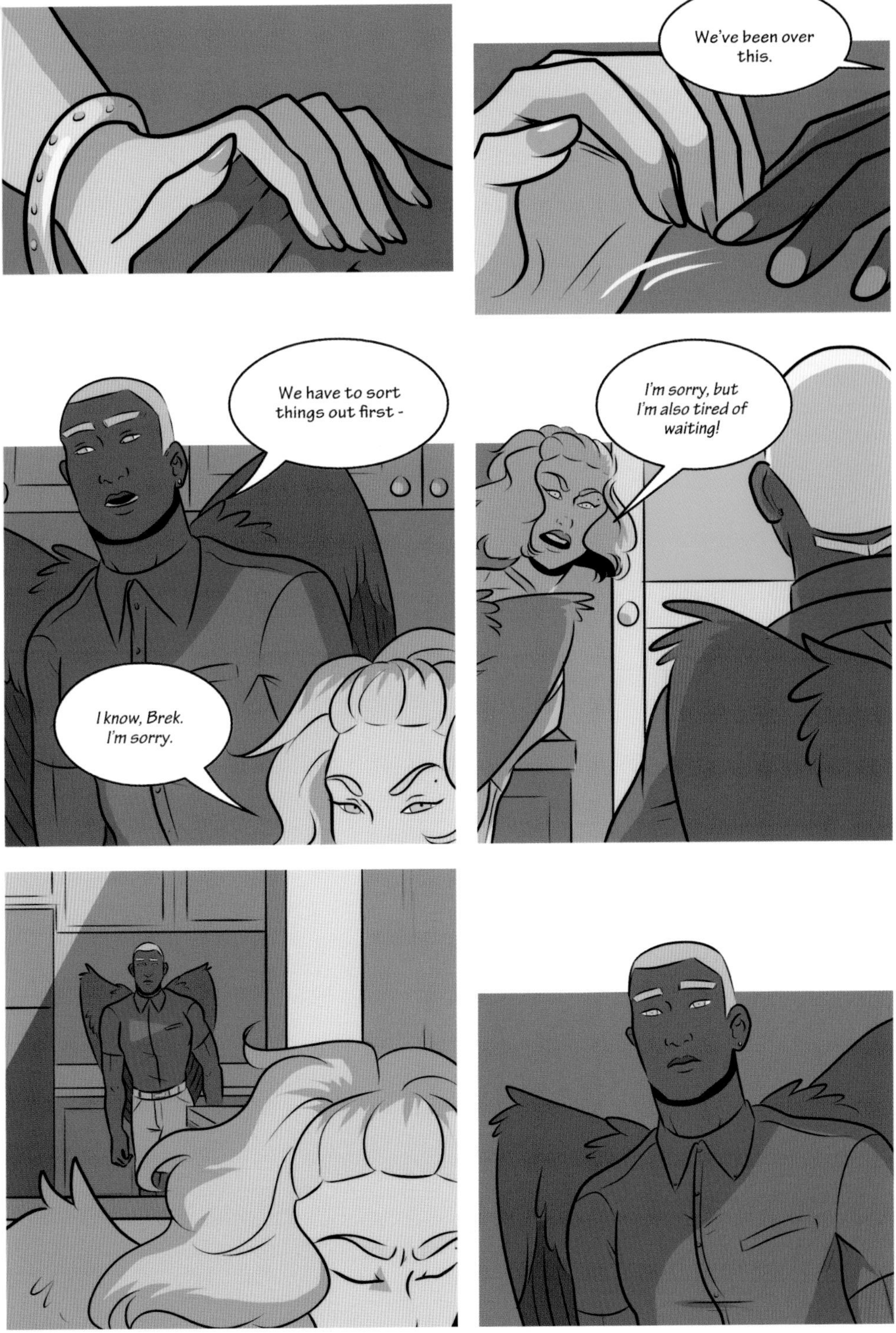
We've been over this.
We have to sort things out first -
I know, Brek. I'm sorry.
I'm sorry, but I'm also tired of waiting!

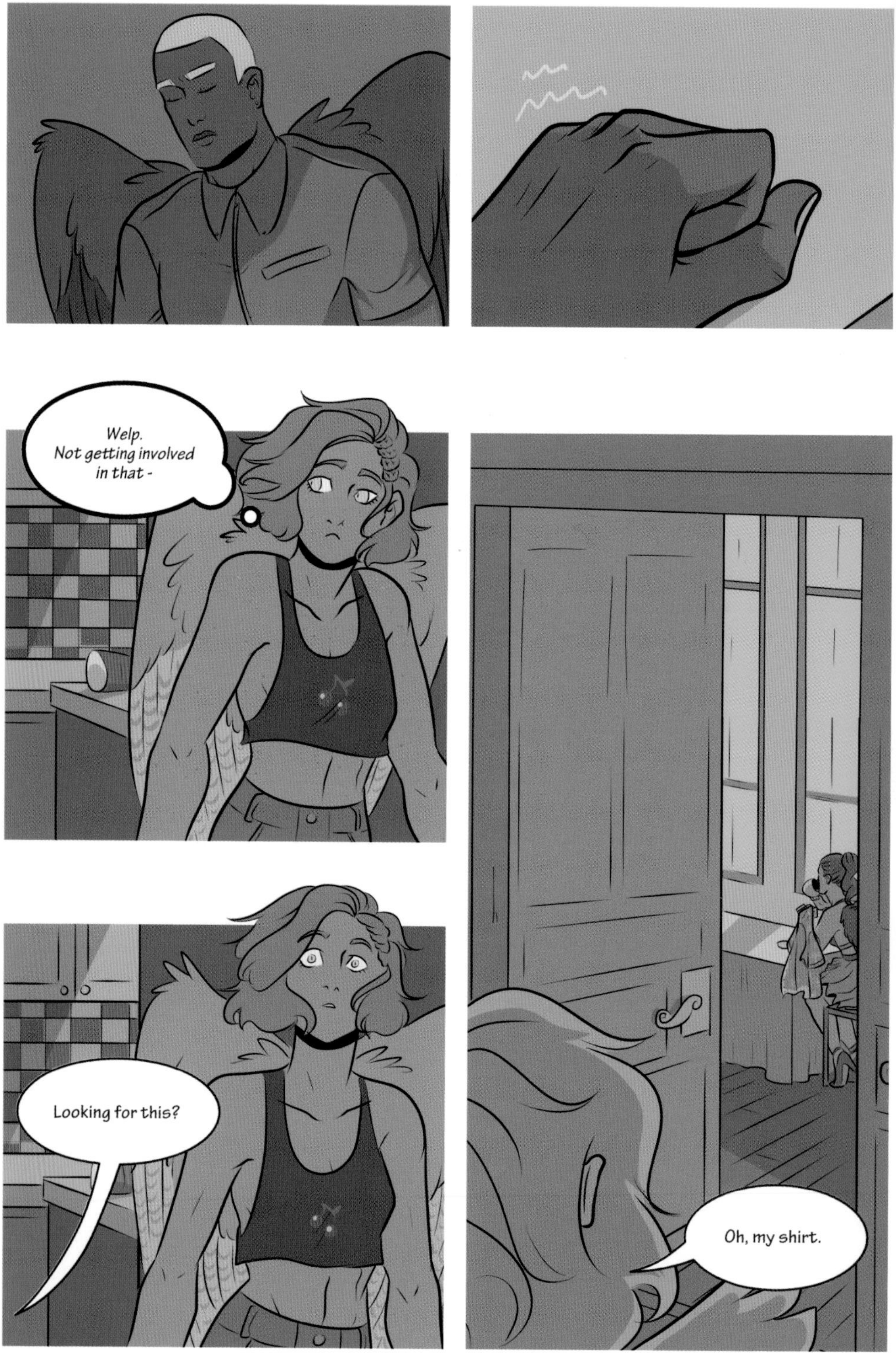
Welp. Not getting involved in that -
Looking for this?
Oh, my shirt.

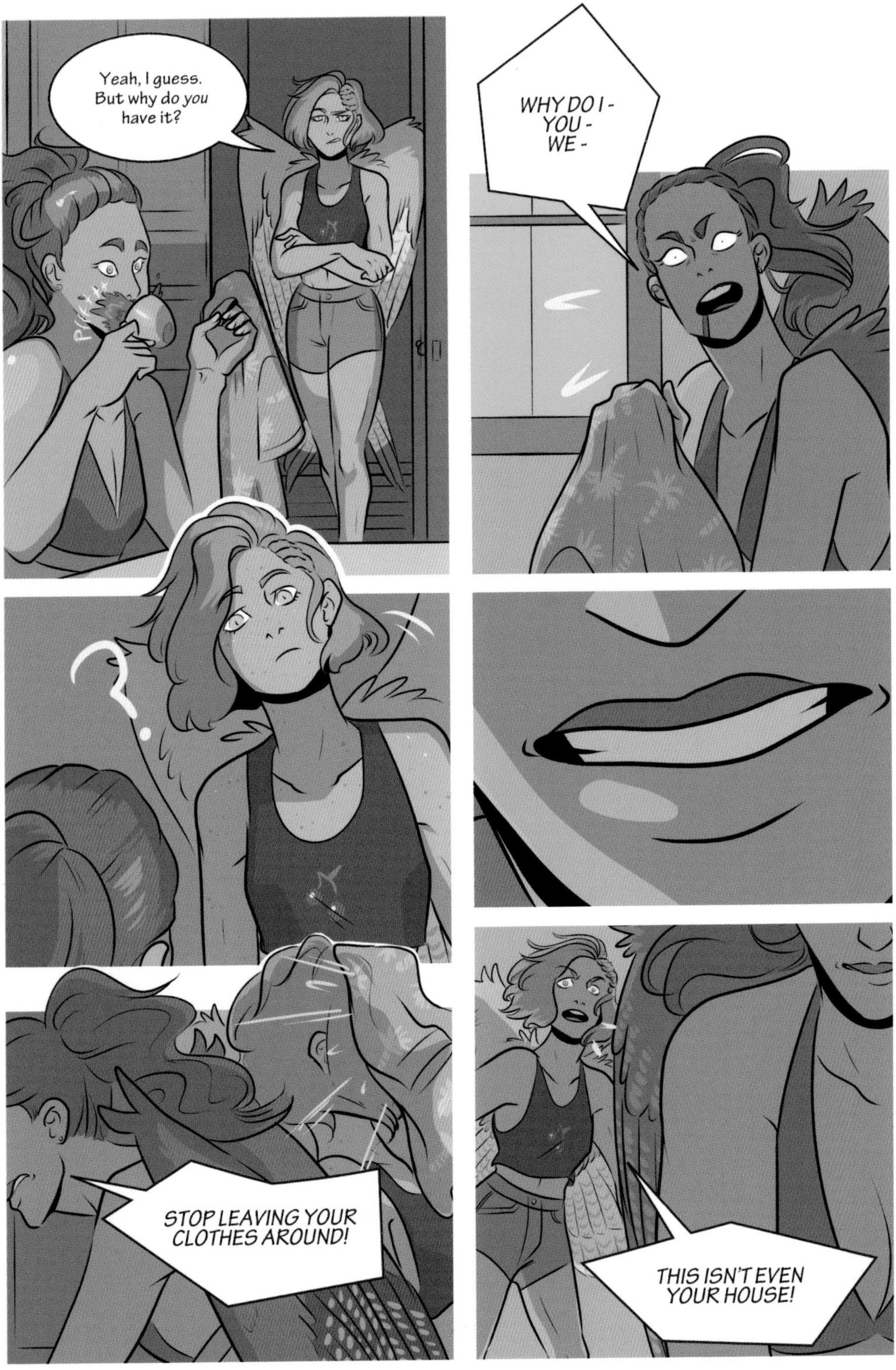
Yeah, I guess.
But why do *you* have it?
PFFT
WHY DO I -
YOU -
WE -
STOP LEAVING YOUR CLOTHES AROUND!
THIS ISN'T EVEN YOUR HOUSE!

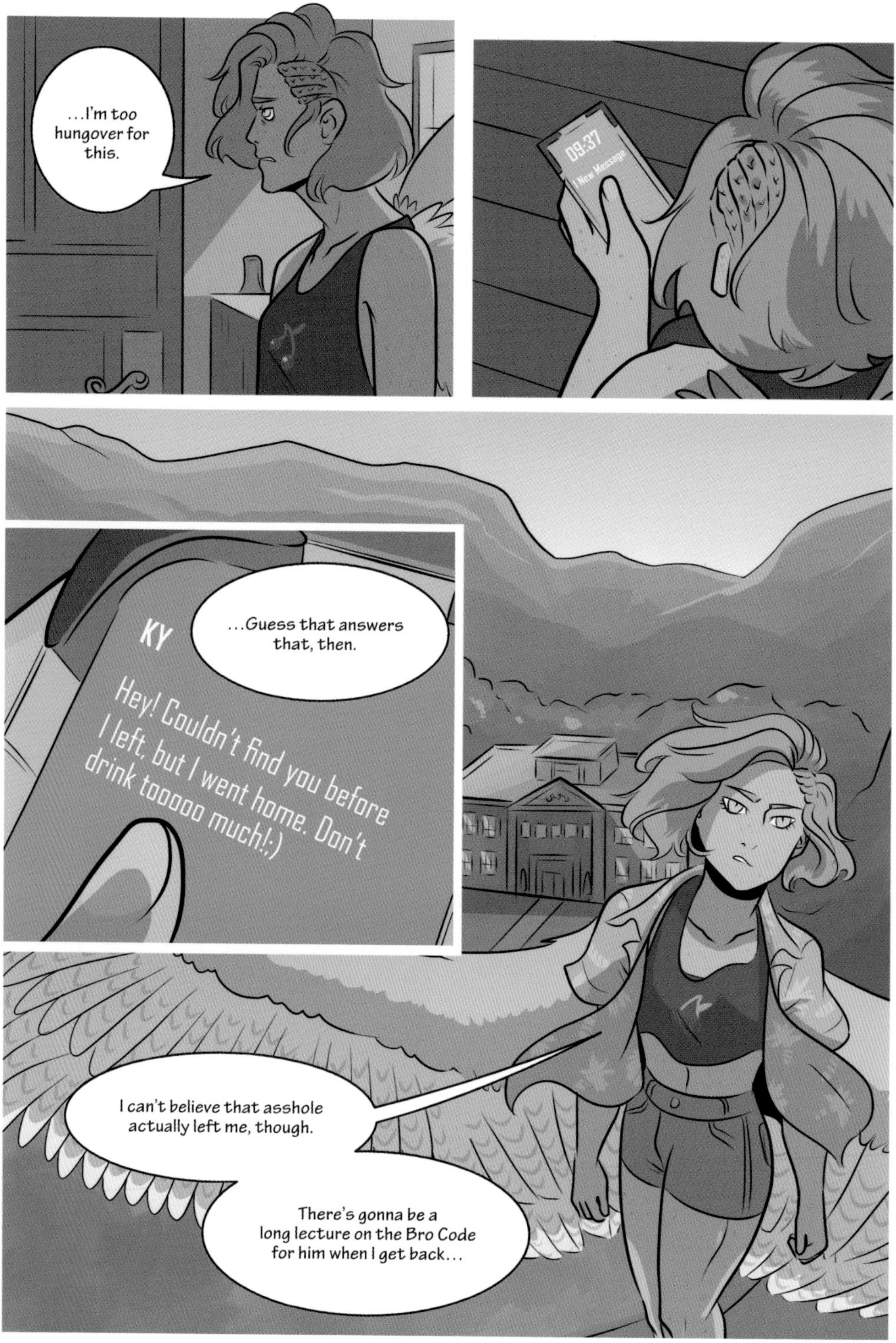
...I'm too hungover for this.
09:37
1 New Message
KY
Hey! Couldn't find you before I left, but I went home. Don't drink tooooo much! ;)
...Guess that answers that, then.
I can't believe that asshole actually left me, though.
There's gonna be a long lecture on the Bro Code for him when I get back...

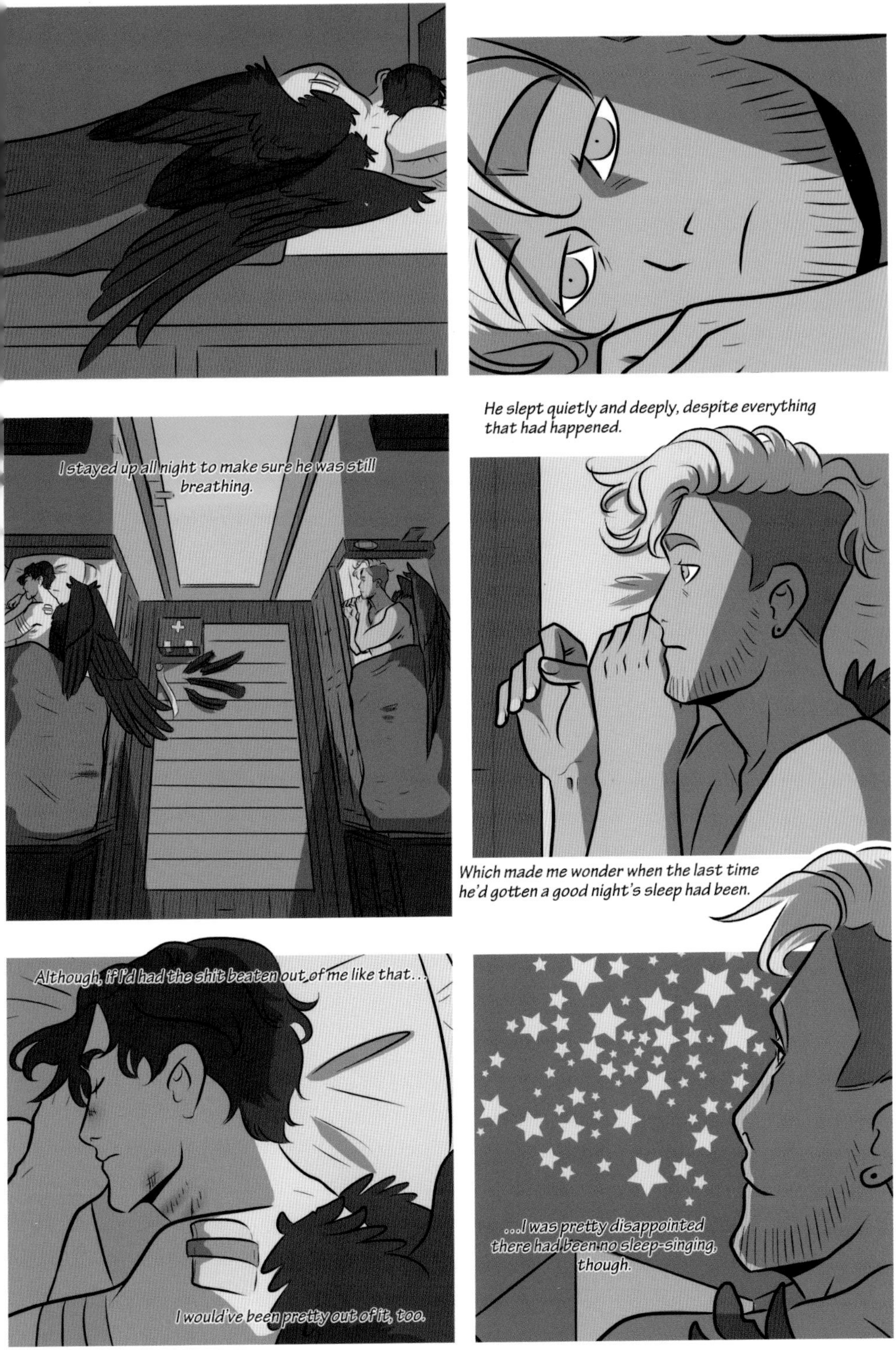
I stayed up all night to make sure he was still breathing.
He slept quietly and deeply, despite everything that had happened.
Which made me wonder when the last time he'd gotten a good night's sleep had been.
Although, if I'd had the shit beaten out of me like that...
I would've been pretty out of it, too.
...I was pretty disappointed there had been no sleep-singing, though.

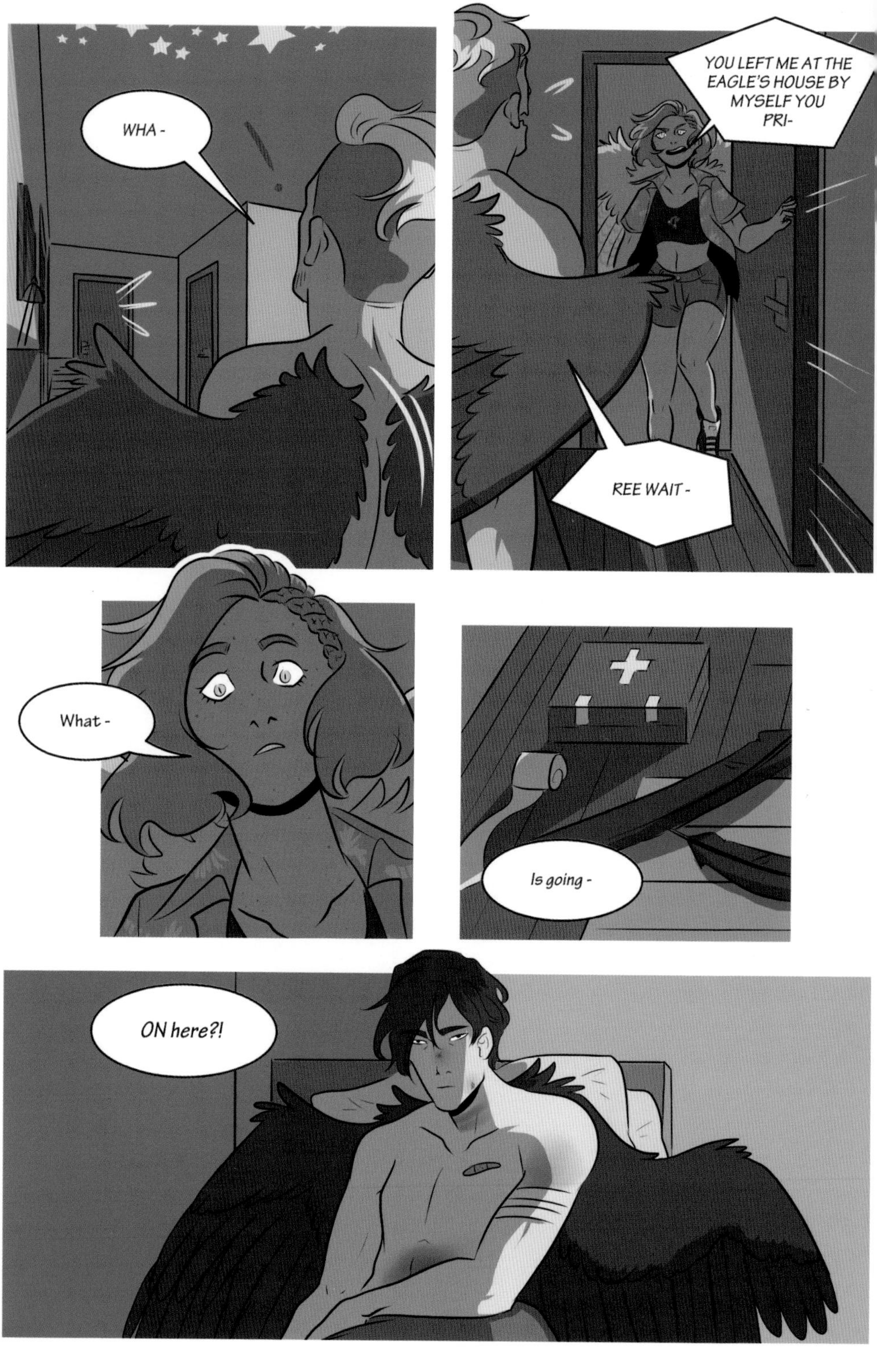
WHA -
YOU LEFT ME AT THE EAGLE'S HOUSE BY MYSELF YOU PRI-
REE WAIT -
What -
Is going -
ON here?!

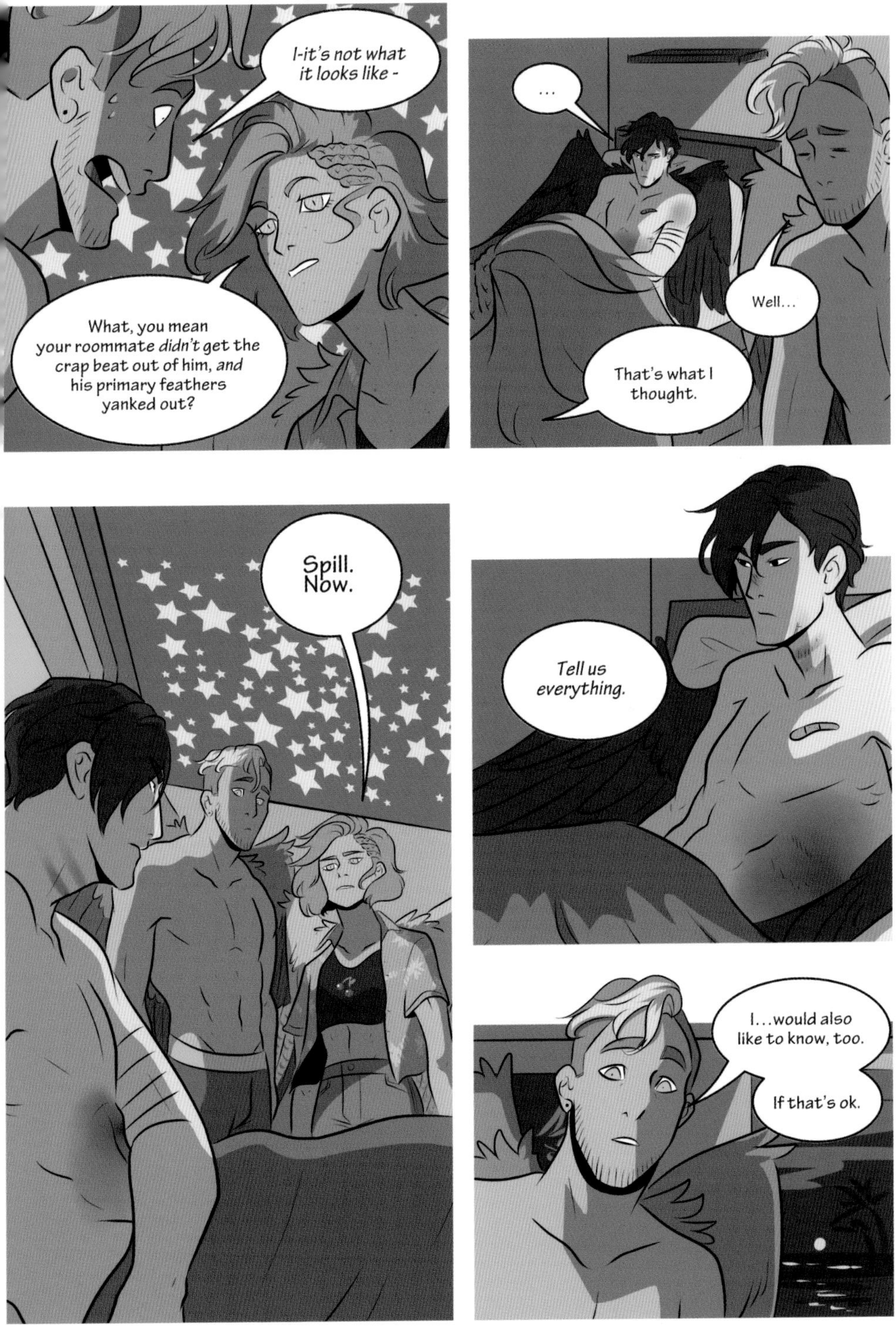

I-it's not what it looks like -
What, you mean your roommate *didn't* get the crap beat out of him, *and* his primary feathers yanked out?
...
Well...
That's what I thought.
Spill. Now.
Tell us everything.
I...would also like to know, too.
If that's ok.

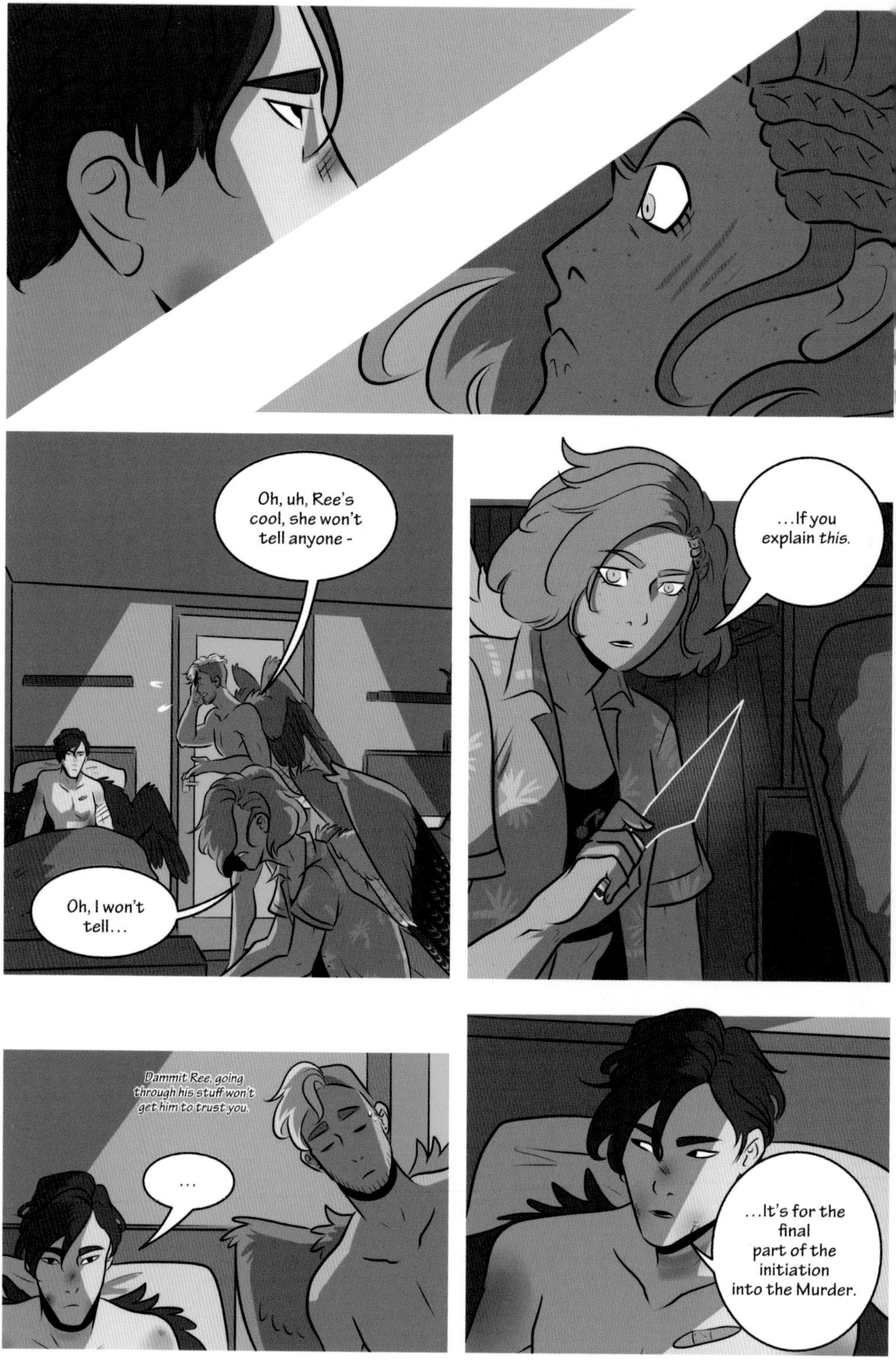
Oh, uh, Ree's cool, she won't tell anyone -
Oh, I won't tell...
...If you explain *this*.
Dammit Ree, going through his stuff won't get him to trust you.
...
...It's for the final part of the initiation into the Murder.

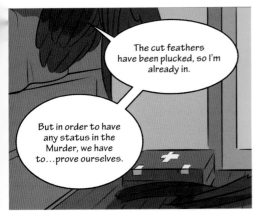

The cut feathers have been plucked, so I'm already in.

But in order to have any status in the Murder, we have to...prove ourselves.

Kill someone, you mean.

But you just want protection from the Magpies, and you've got that now!

So you don't need status, right?

He might not have a choice.

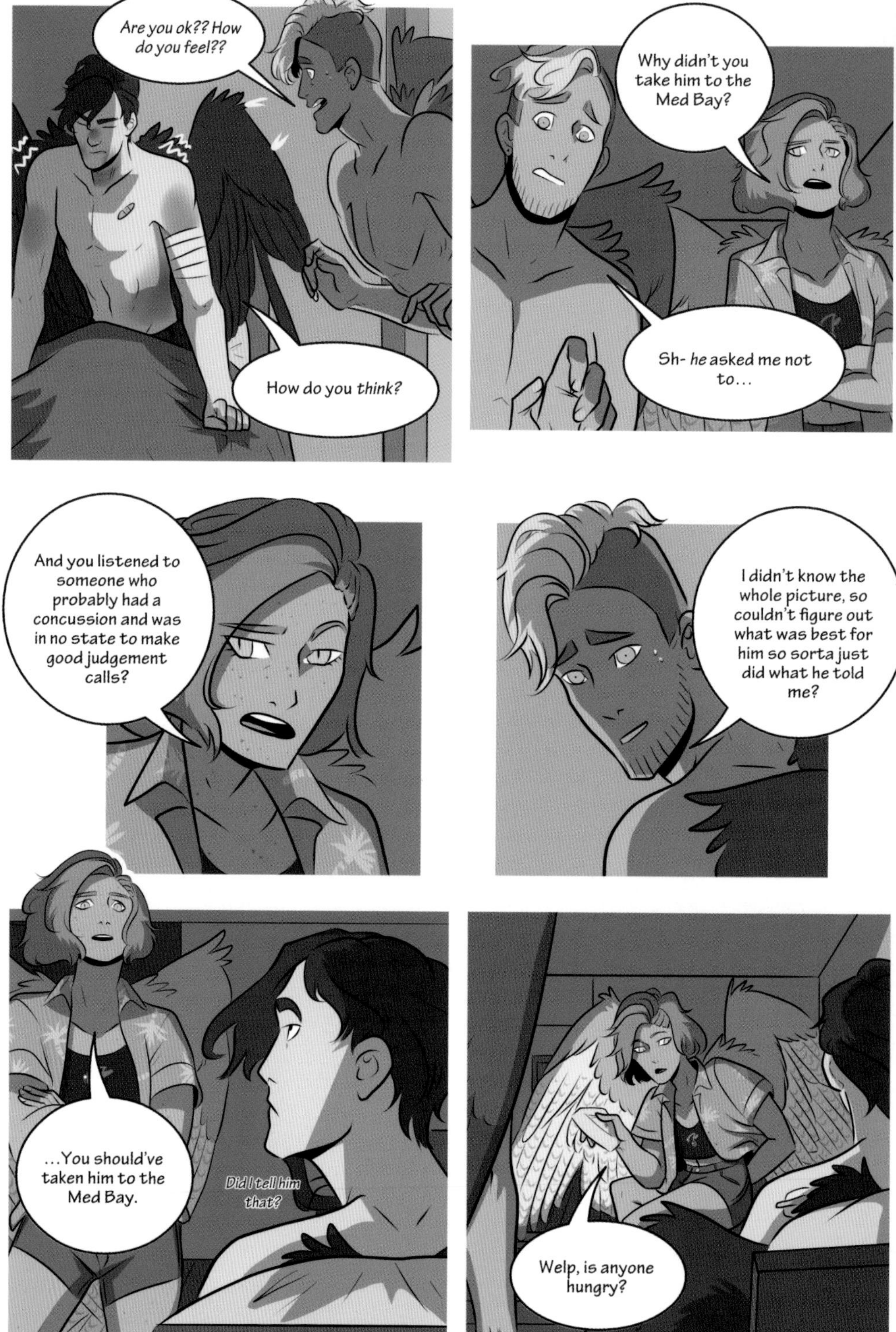
Are you ok?? How do you feel??
How do you think?
Why didn't you take him to the Med Bay?
Sh- he asked me not to...
And you listened to someone who probably had a concussion and was in no state to make good judgement calls?
I didn't know the whole picture, so couldn't figure out what was best for him so sorta just did what he told me?
...You should've taken him to the Med Bay.
Did I tell him that?
Welp, is anyone hungry?

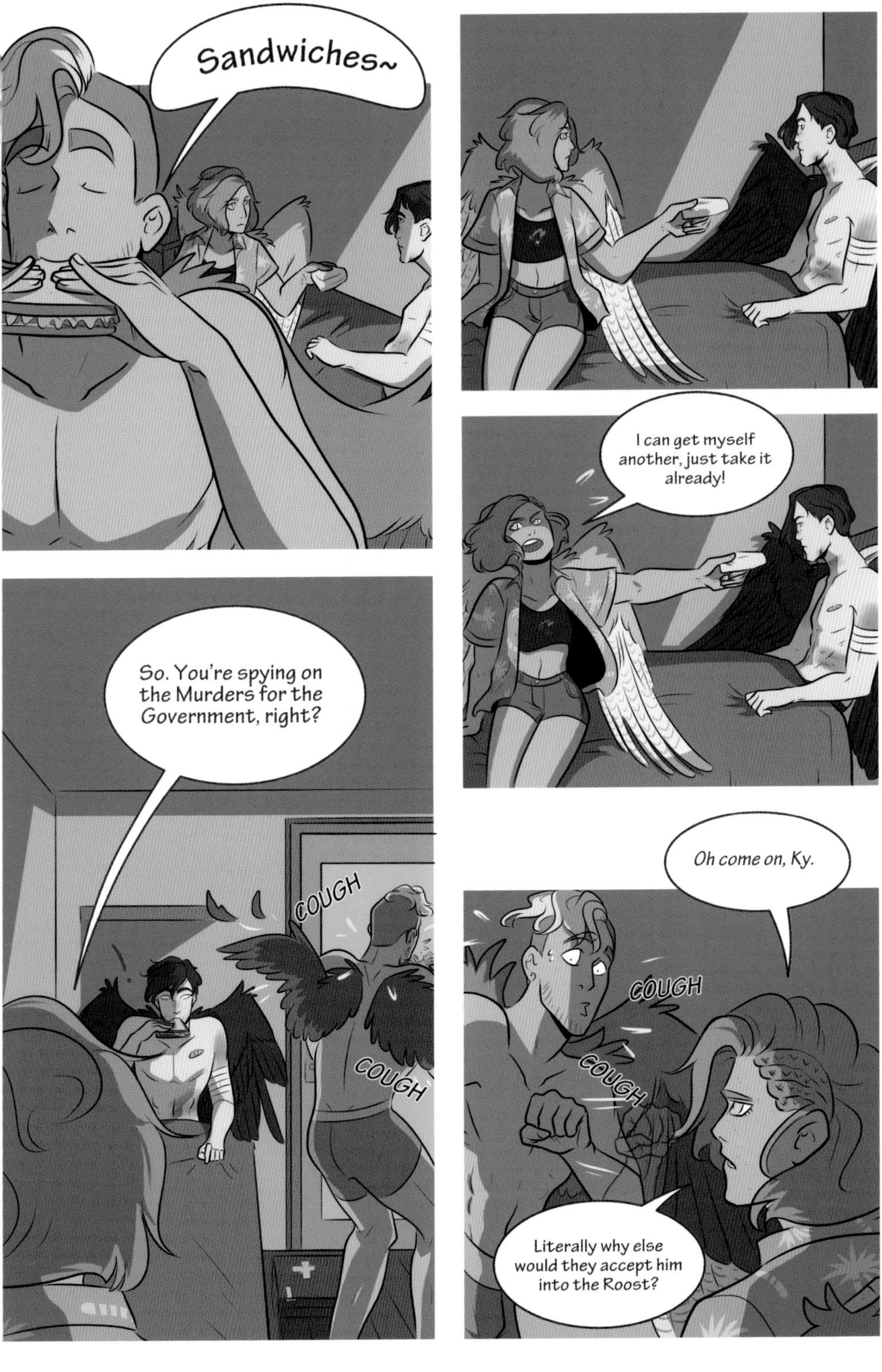
Sandwiches~
I can get myself another, just take it already!
So. You're spying on the Murders for the Government, right?
COUGH
COUGH
Oh come on, Ky.
COUGH
COUGH
Literally why else would they accept him into the Roost?

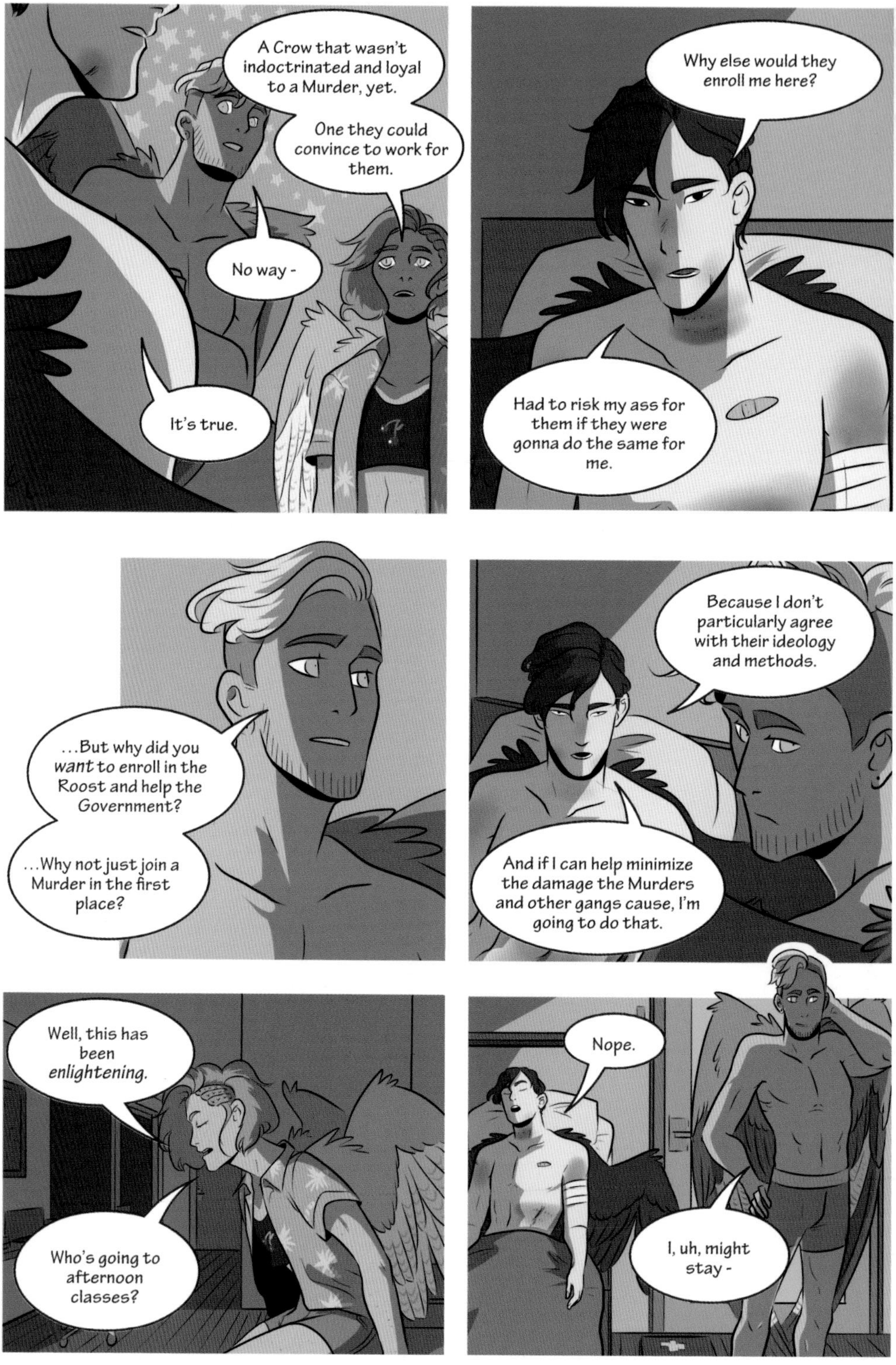
A Crow that wasn't indoctrinated and loyal to a Murder, yet.
One they could convince to work for them.
No way -
It's true.
Why else would they enroll me here?
Had to risk my ass for them if they were gonna do the same for me.
...But why did you *want* to enroll in the Roost and help the Government?
...Why not just join a Murder in the first place?
Because I don't particularly agree with their ideology and methods.
And if I can help minimize the damage the Murders and other gangs cause, I'm going to do that.
Well, this has been *enlightening.*
Who's going to afternoon classes?
Nope.
I, uh, might stay -

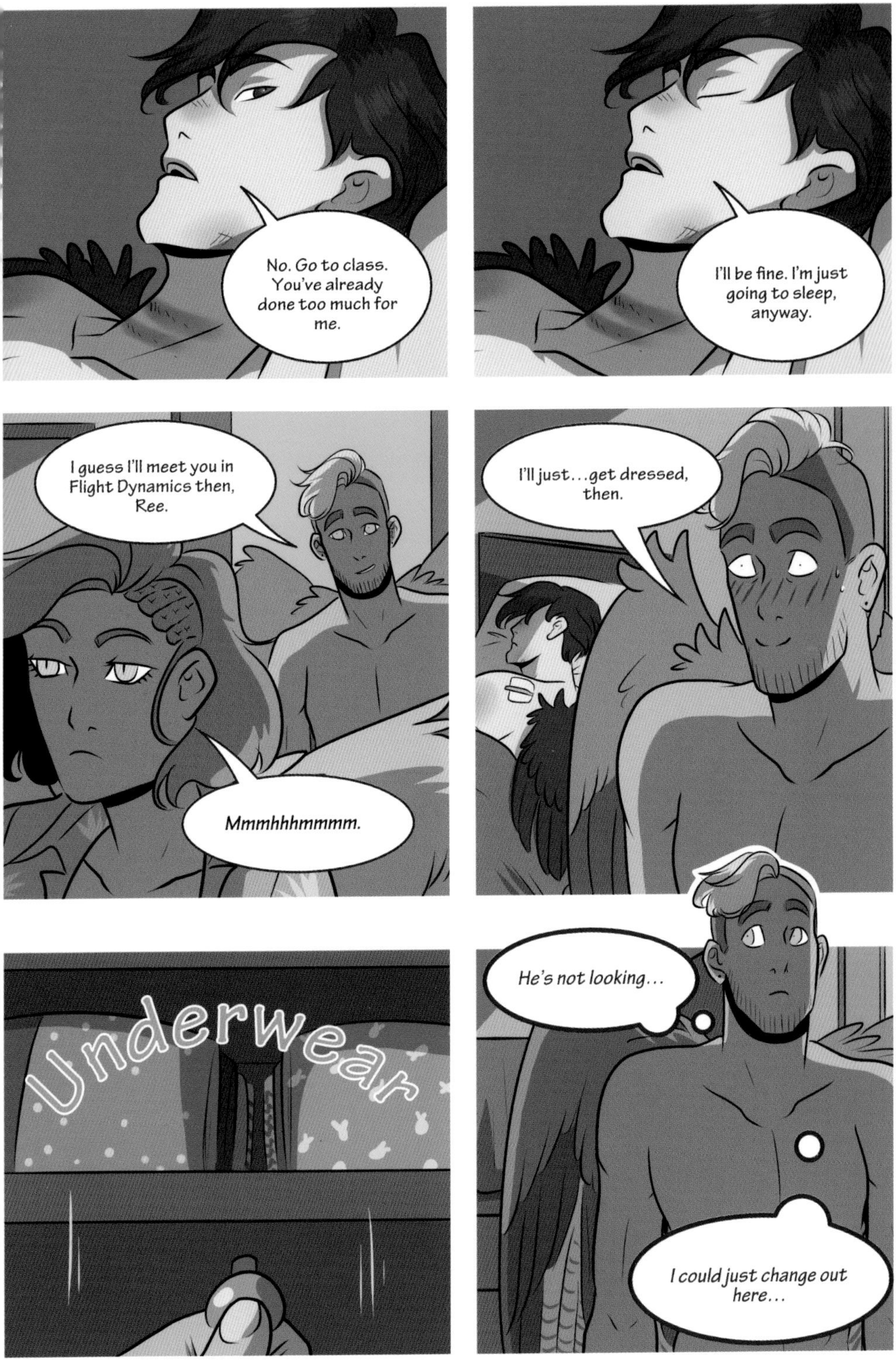
No. Go to class. You've already done too much for me.
I'll be fine. I'm just going to sleep, anyway.
I guess I'll meet you in Flight Dynamics then, Ree.
Mmmhhhmmmm.
I'll just...get dressed, then.
Underwear
He's not looking...
I could just change out here...

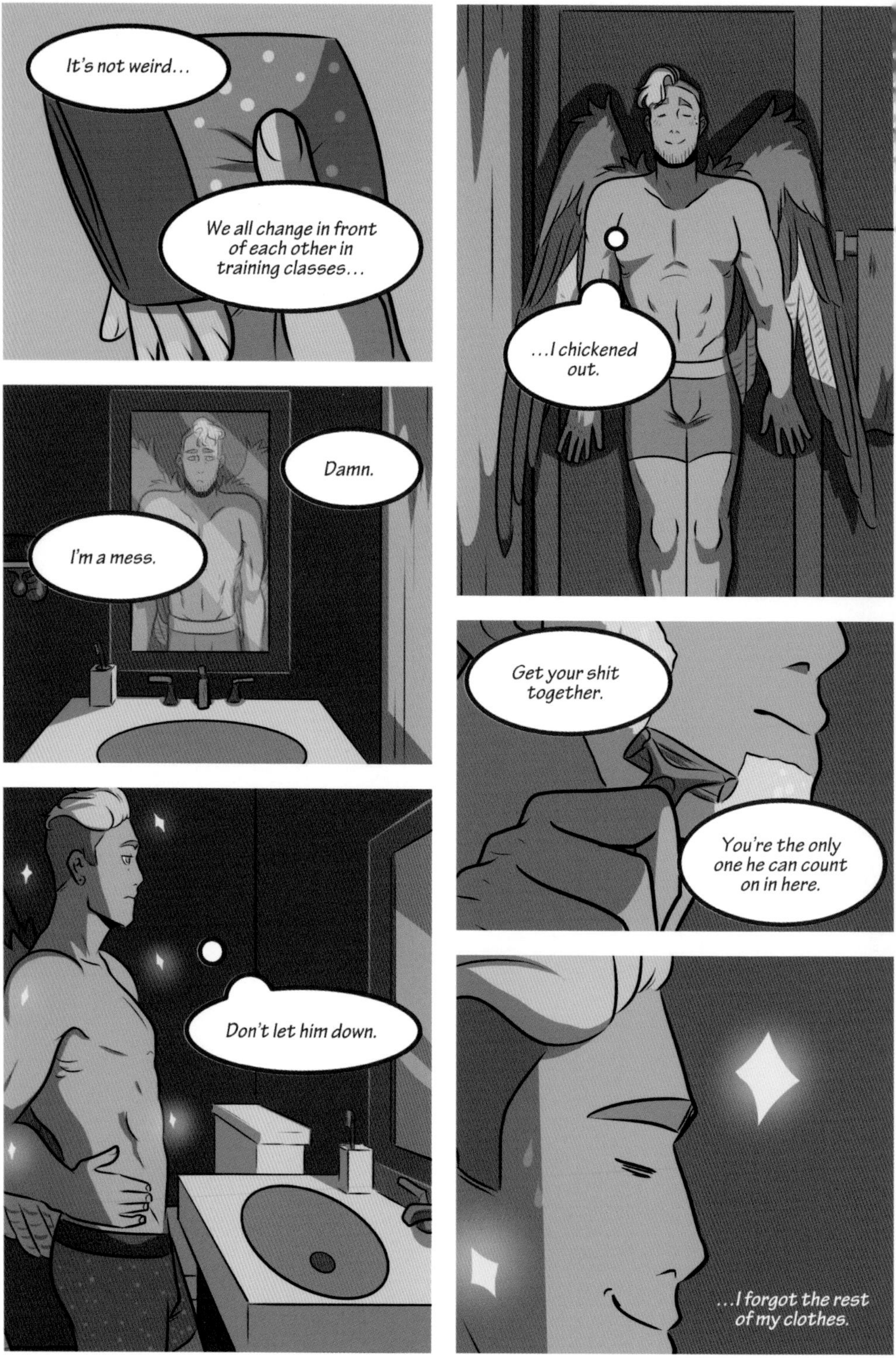
It's not weird...
We all change in front of each other in training classes...
...I chickened out.
Damn.
I'm a mess.
Get your shit together.
You're the only one he can count on in here.
Don't let him down.
...I forgot the rest of my clothes.

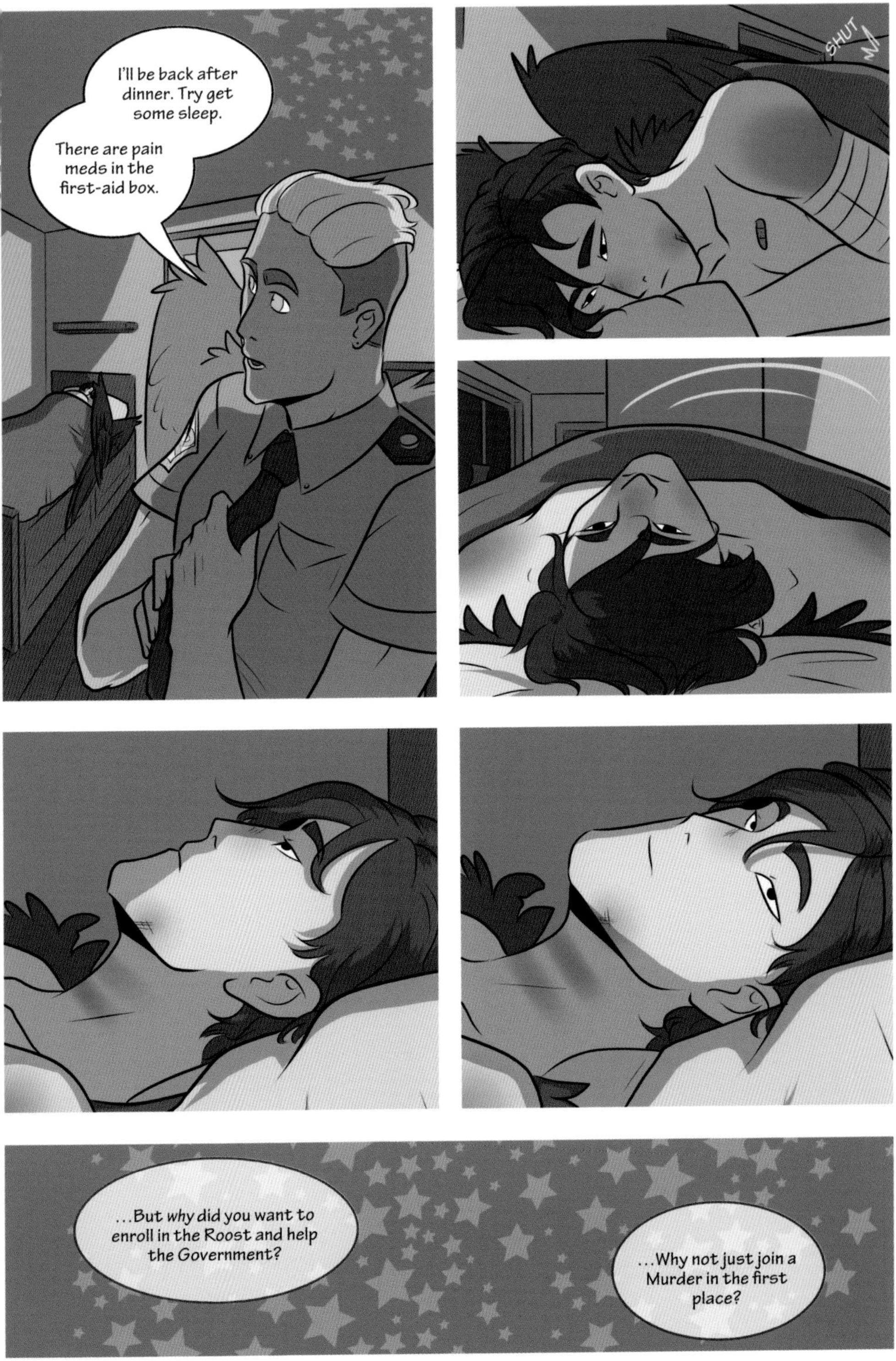
I'll be back after dinner. Try get some sleep.
There are pain meds in the first-aid box.
SHUT
...But why did you want to enroll in the Roost and help the Government?
...Why not just join a Murder in the first place?

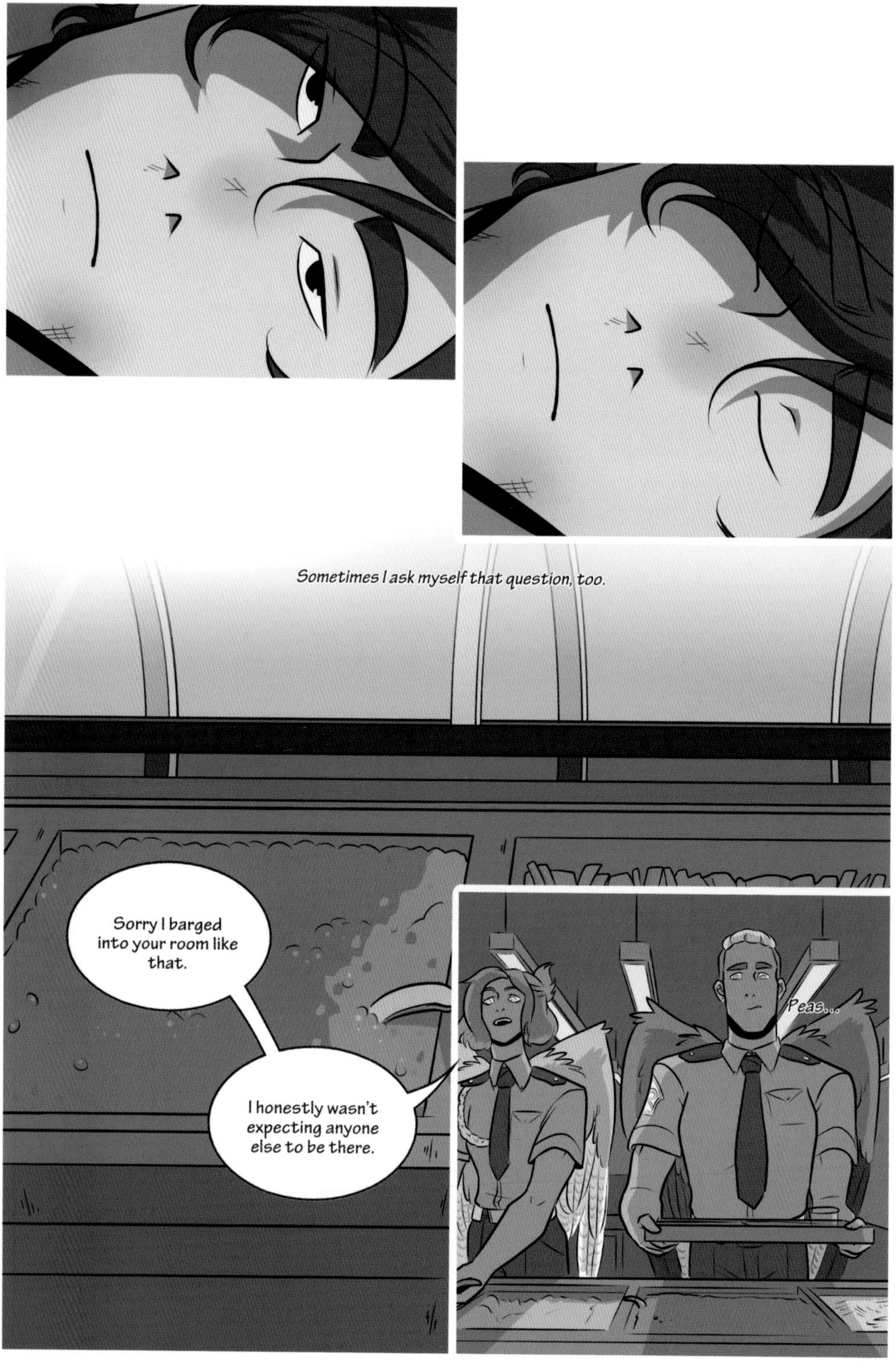

Sometimes I ask myself that question, too.
Sorry I barged into your room like that.
I honestly wasn't expecting anyone else to be there.
Peas...

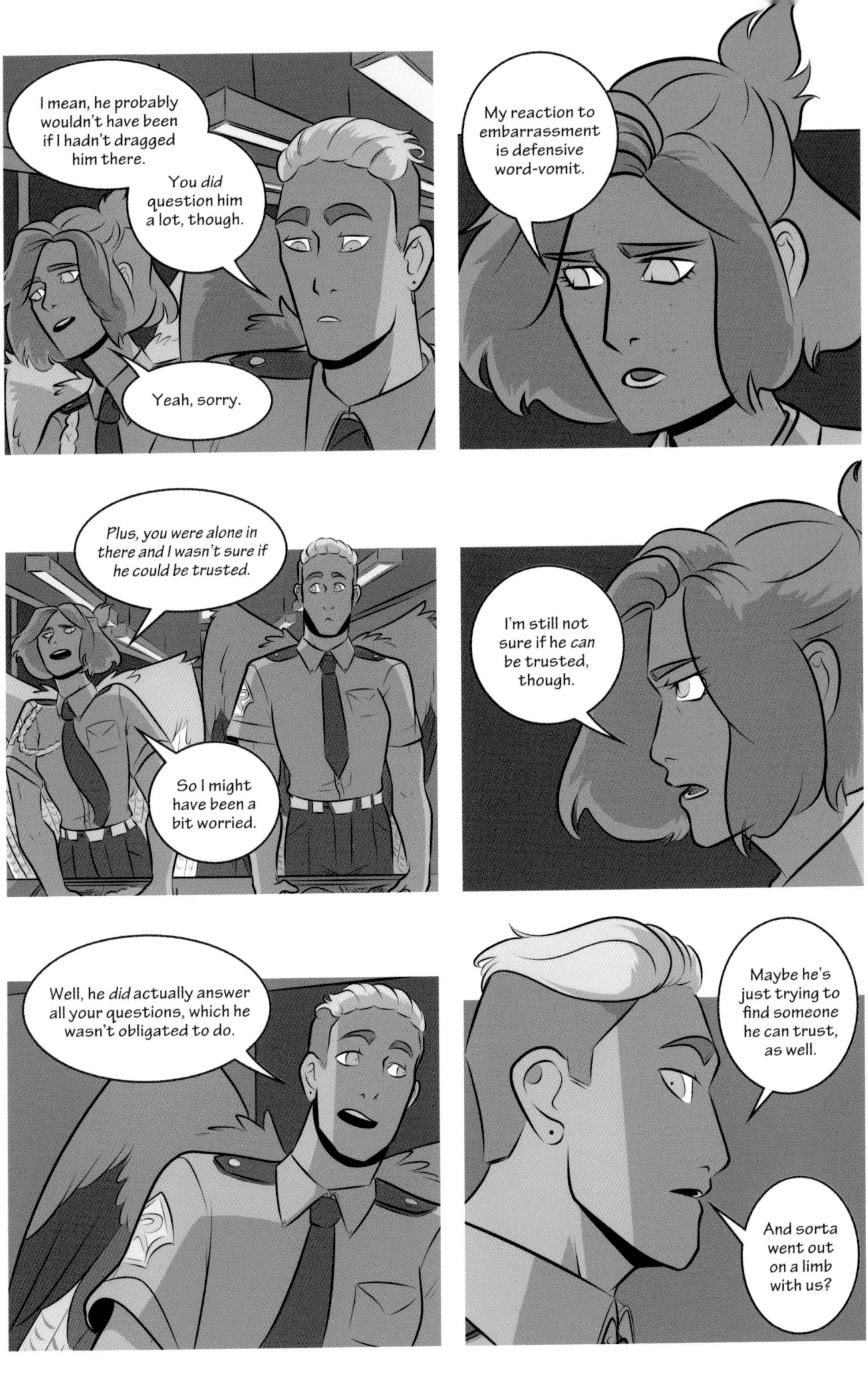
I mean, he probably wouldn't have been if I hadn't dragged him there.
You *did* question him a lot, though.
Yeah, sorry.
My reaction to embarrassment is defensive word-vomit.
Plus, you were alone in there and I wasn't sure if he could be trusted.
So I might have been a bit worried.
I'm still not sure if he *can* be trusted, though.
Well, he *did* actually answer all your questions, which he wasn't obligated to do.
Maybe he's just trying to find someone he can trust, as well.
And sorta went out on a limb with us?

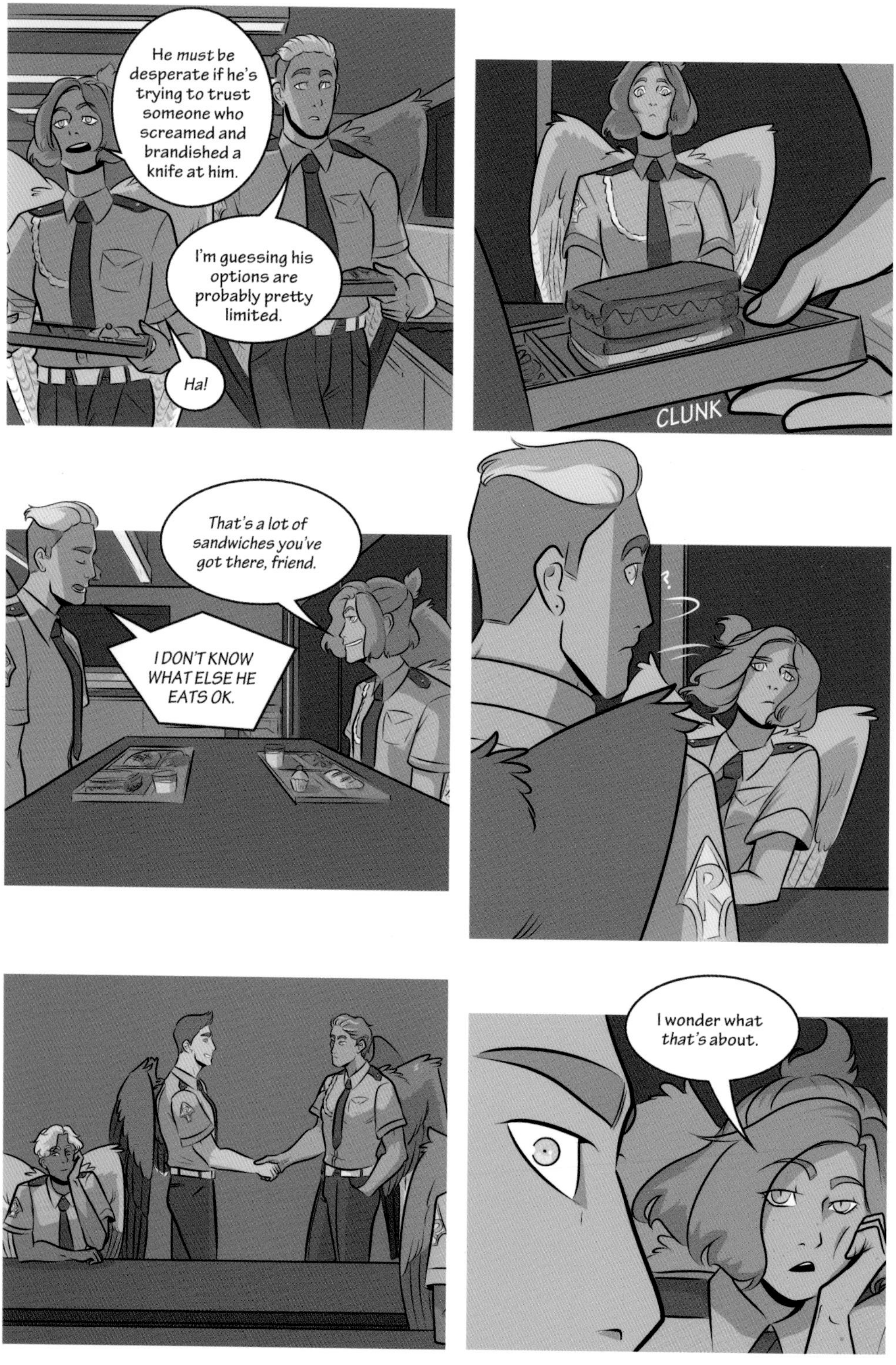
He *must* be desperate if he's trying to trust someone who screamed and brandished a knife at him.
I'm guessing his options are probably pretty limited.
Ha!
CLUNK
That's a lot of sandwiches you've got there, friend.
I DON'T KNOW WHAT ELSE HE EATS OK.
?
I wonder what that's about.

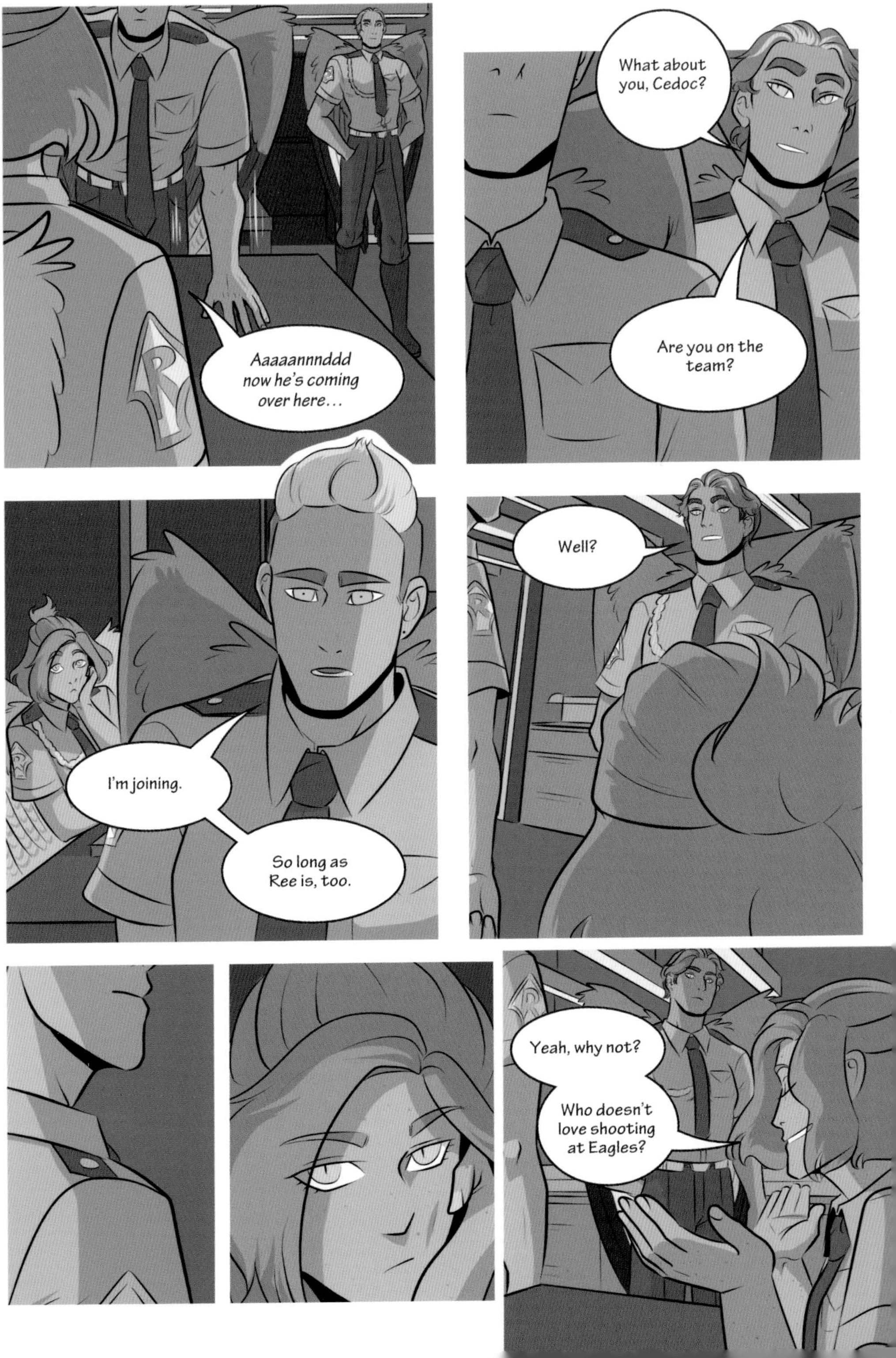
Aaaaannnddd now he's coming over here...
What about you, Cedoc?
Are you on the team?
I'm joining.
So long as Ree is, too.
Well?
Yeah, why not?
Who doesn't love shooting at Eagles?

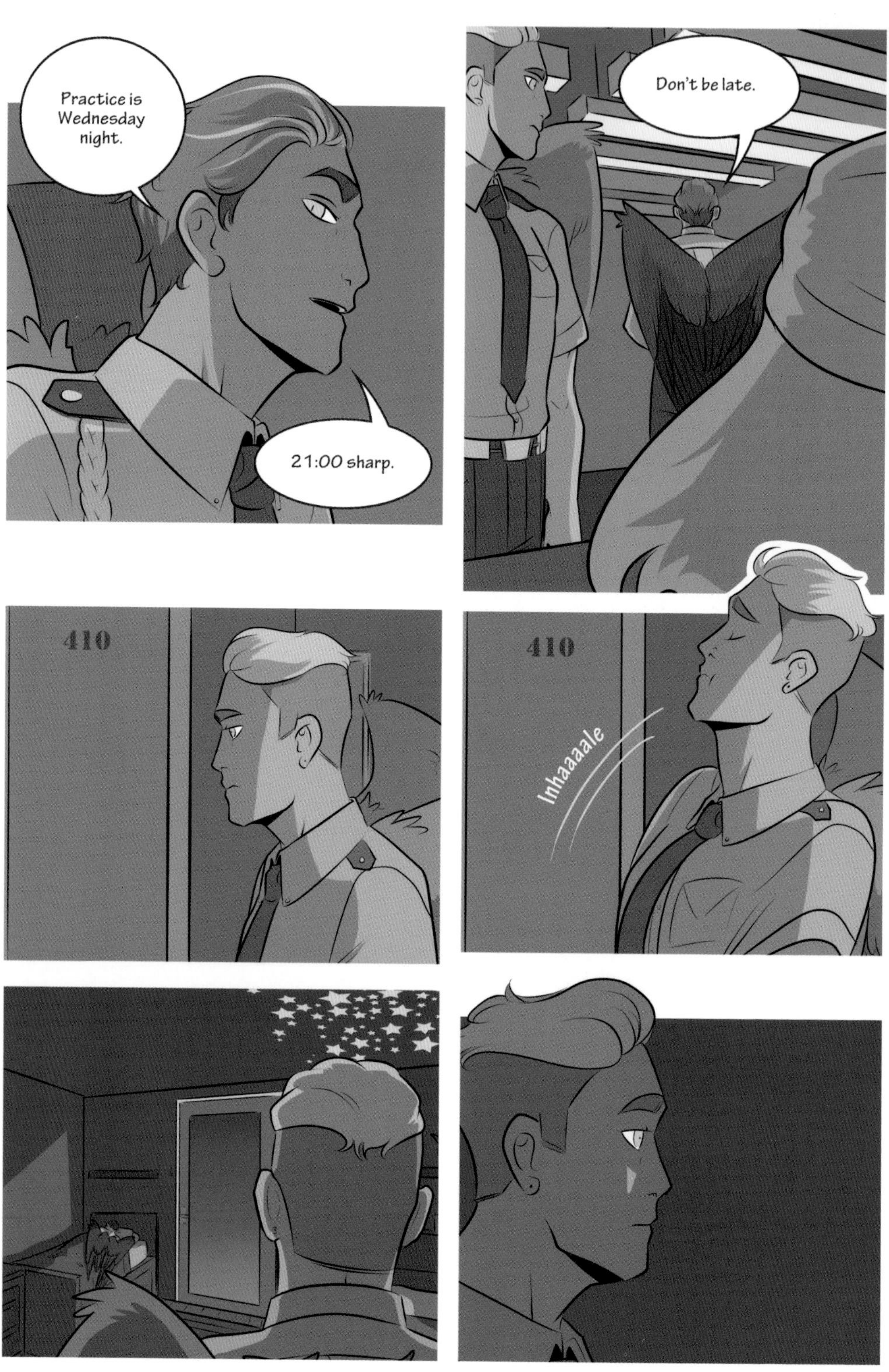
Practice is Wednesday night.
21:00 sharp.
Don't be late.
410
410
Inhaaaale

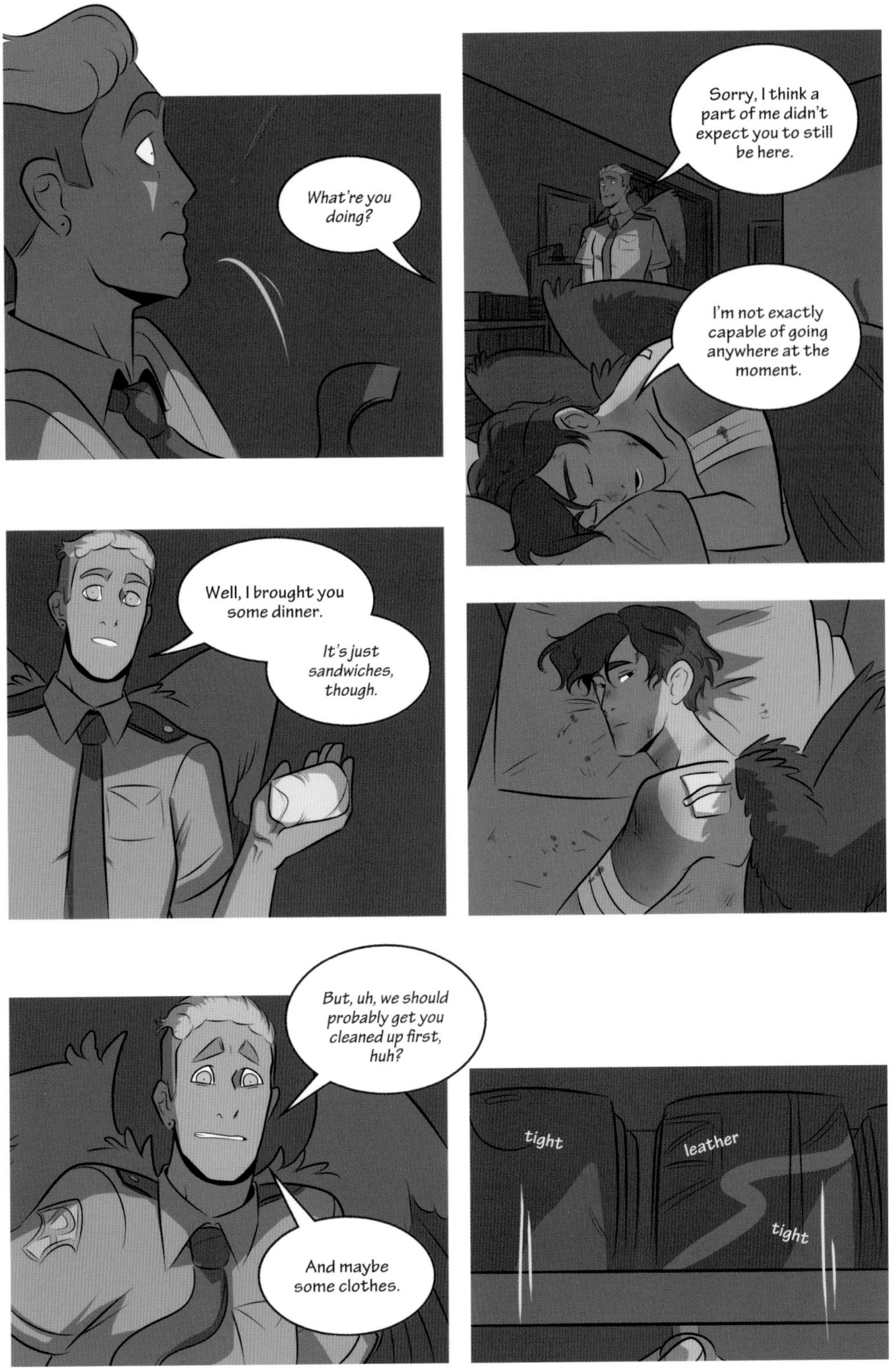
What're you doing?
Sorry, I think a part of me didn't expect you to still be here.
I'm not exactly capable of going anywhere at the moment.
Well, I brought you some dinner.
It's just sandwiches, though.
But, uh, we should probably get you cleaned up first, huh?
And maybe some clothes.
tight
leather
tight

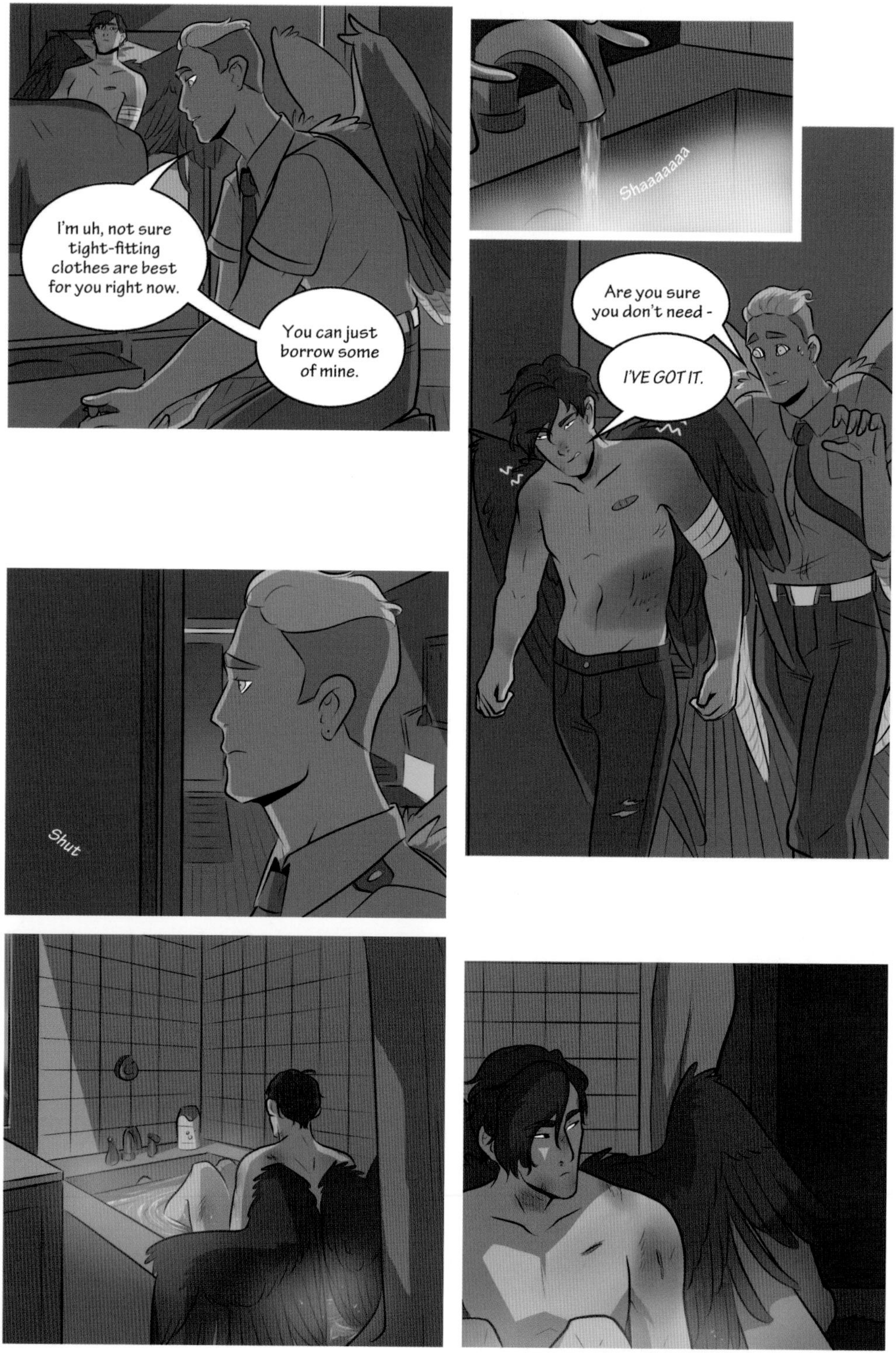
I'm uh, not sure tight-fitting clothes are best for you right now.
You can just borrow some of mine.
Shaaaaaaa
Are you sure you don't need -
I'VE GOT IT.
Shut

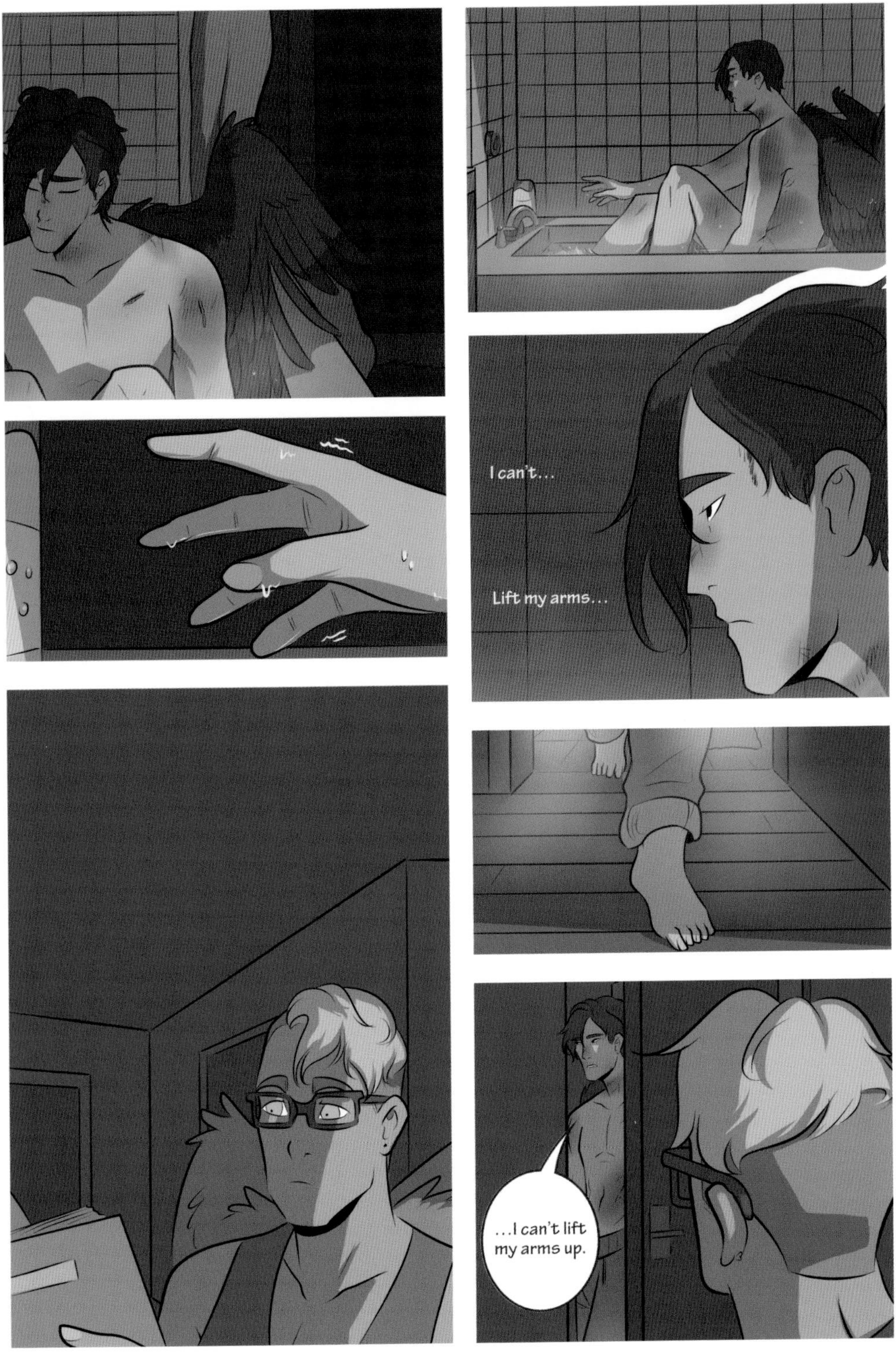
I can't...
Lift my arms...
...I can't lift my arms up.

Do you need me to wash your hair?

...The dried blood is kinda itchy...

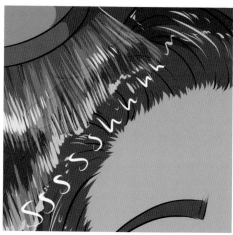

Sssshhhh

His hair is soft, too.

Sssshhh

Like down feathers.

Alright, you're done.

Although, you could use a trip to the dust baths, too.

I don't really feel like having people see me right now.

The Crow girl that helped me rescue you –

She said you're looking for something, and that's why the Magpies attacked you?

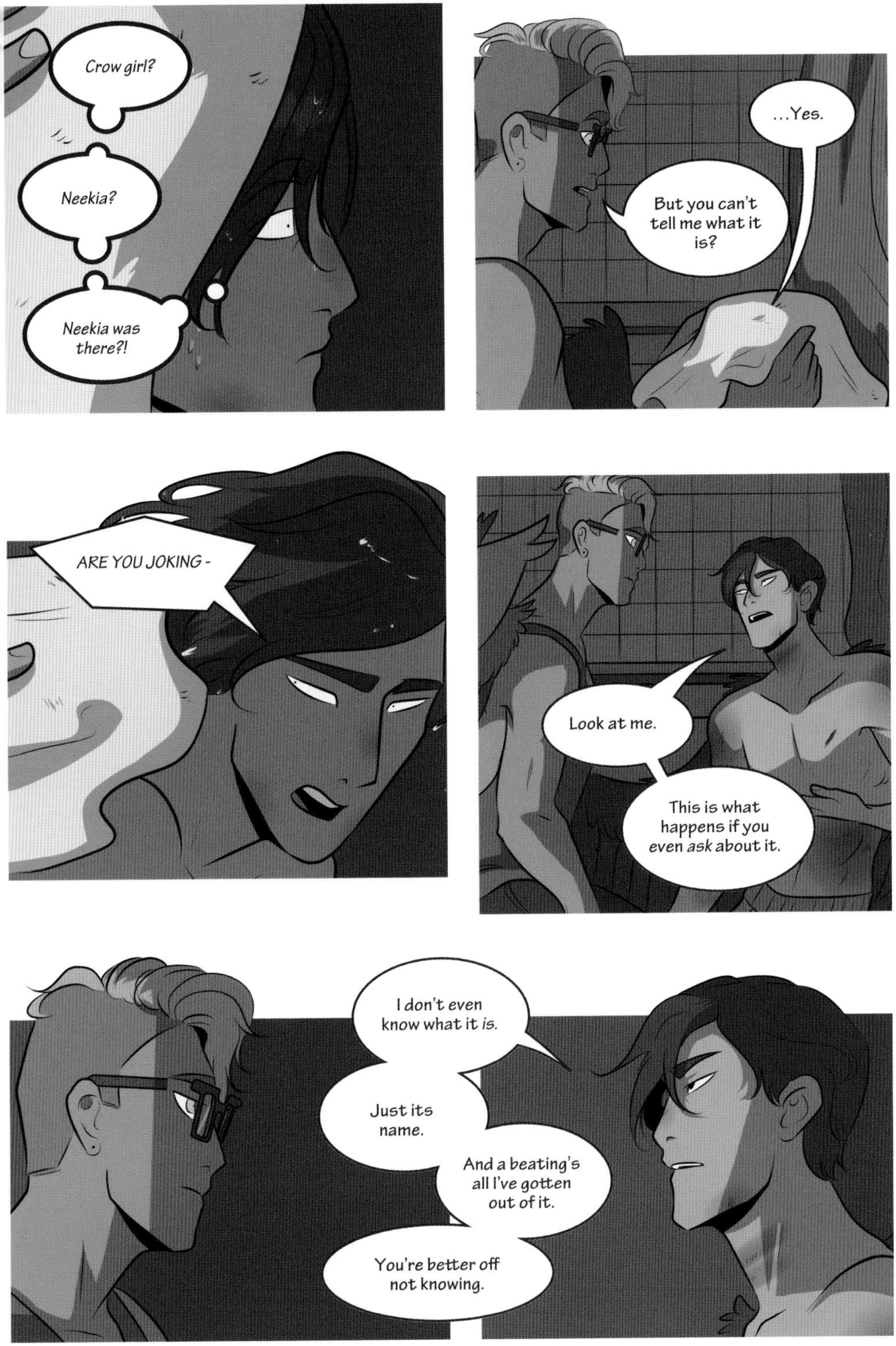
Crow girl?
Neekia?
Neekia was there?!
But you can't tell me what it is?
...Yes.
ARE YOU JOKING -
Look at me.
This is what happens if you even *ask* about it.
I don't even know what it *is*.
Just its name.
And a beating's all I've gotten out of it.
You're better off not knowing.

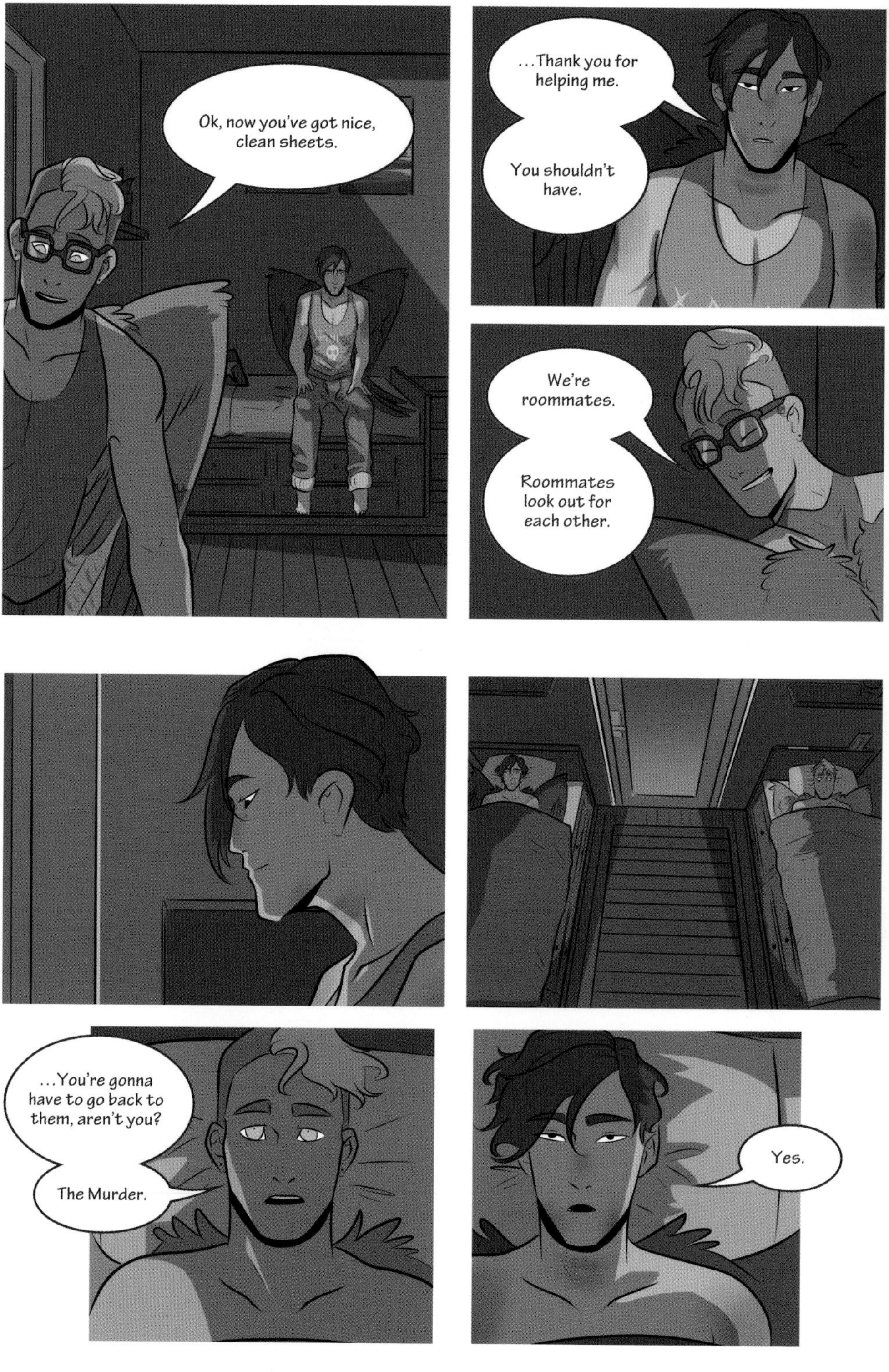
Ok, now you've got nice, clean sheets.
...Thank you for helping me.
You shouldn't have.
We're roommates.
Roommates look out for each other.
...You're gonna have to go back to them, aren't you?
The Murder.
Yes.

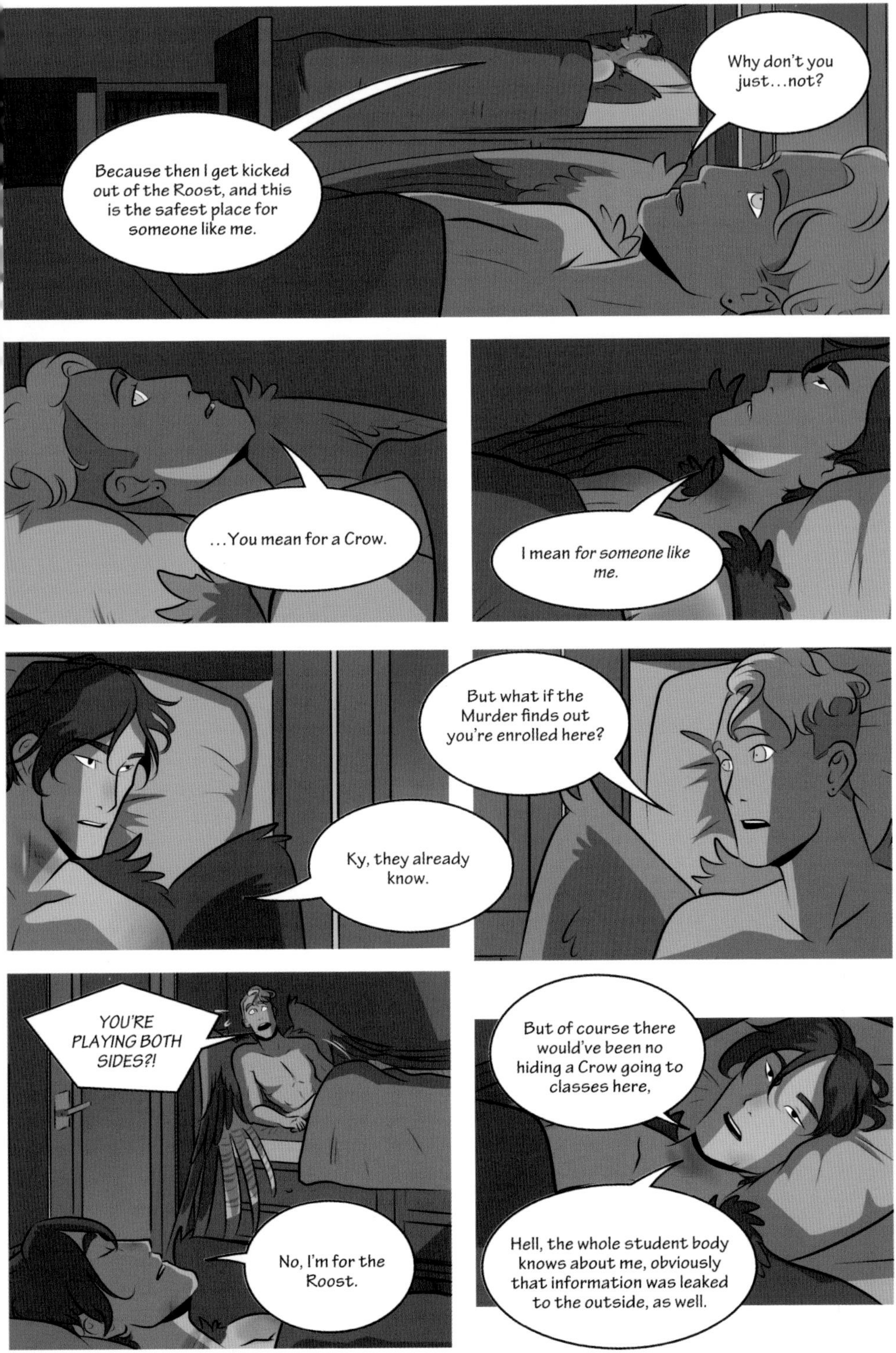
Why don't you just...not?
Because then I get kicked out of the Roost, and this is the safest place for someone like me.
...You mean for a Crow.
I mean *for someone like me.*
But what if the Murder finds out you're enrolled here?
Ky, they already know.
YOU'RE PLAYING BOTH SIDES?!
No, I'm for the Roost.
But of course there would've been no hiding a Crow going to classes here,
Hell, the whole student body knows about me, obviously that information was leaked to the outside, as well.

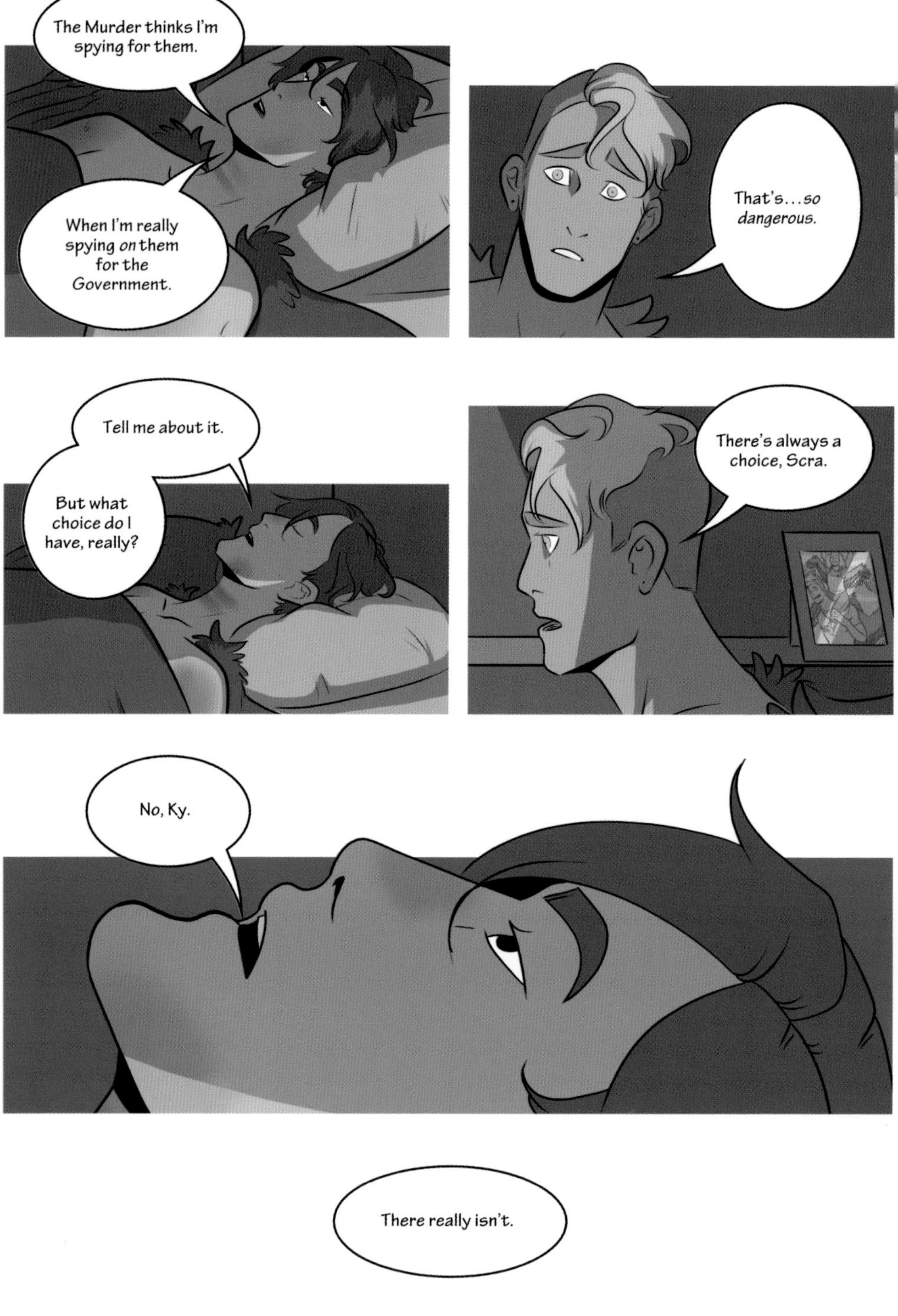
The Murder thinks I'm spying for them.
When I'm really spying *on* them for the Government.
That's...*so dangerous.*
Tell me about it.
But what choice do I have, really?
There's always a choice, Scra.
No, Ky.
There really isn't.

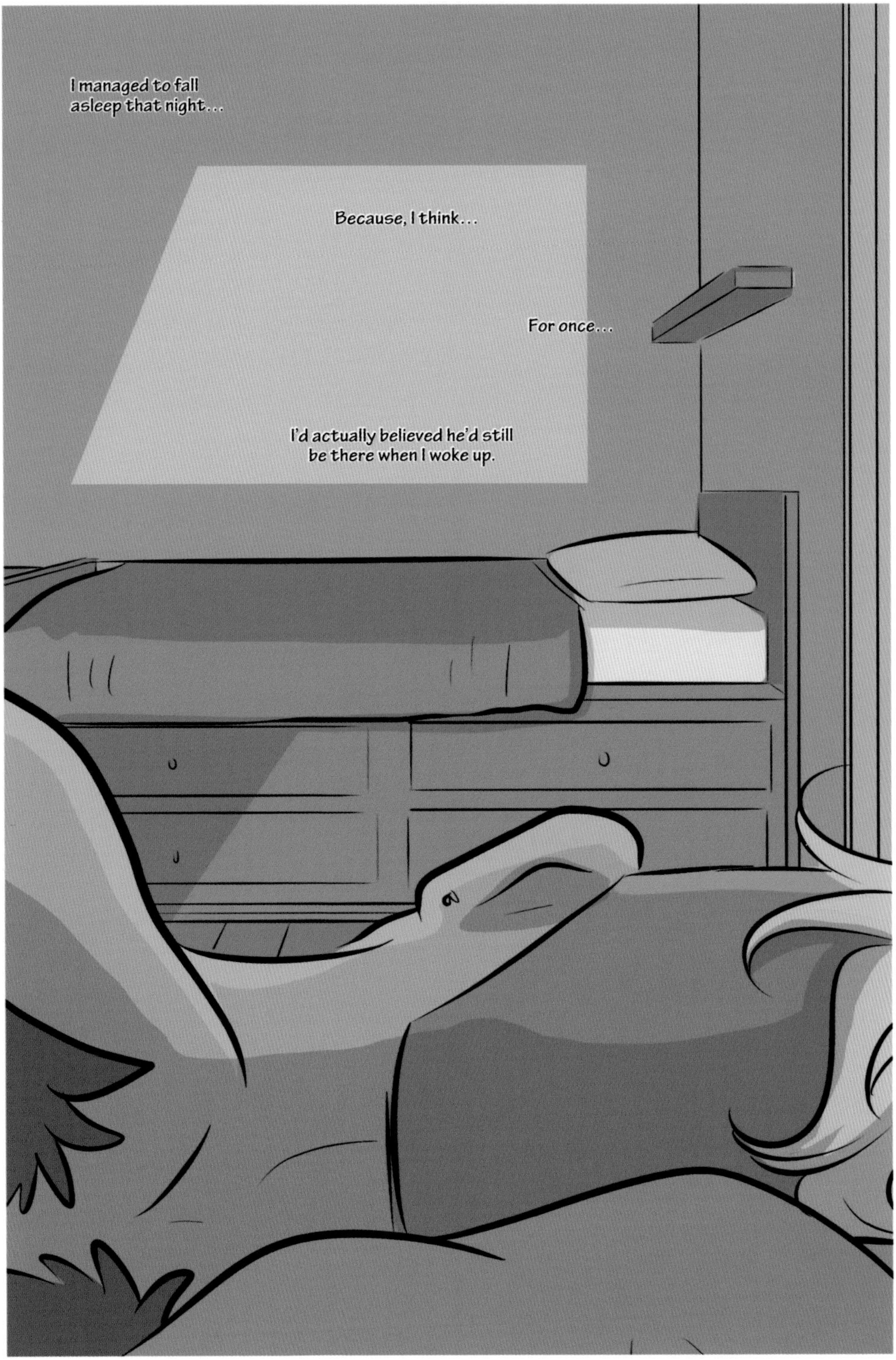
I managed to fall asleep that night...
Because, I think...
For once...
I'd actually believed he'd still be there when I woke up.

THE CROAKING

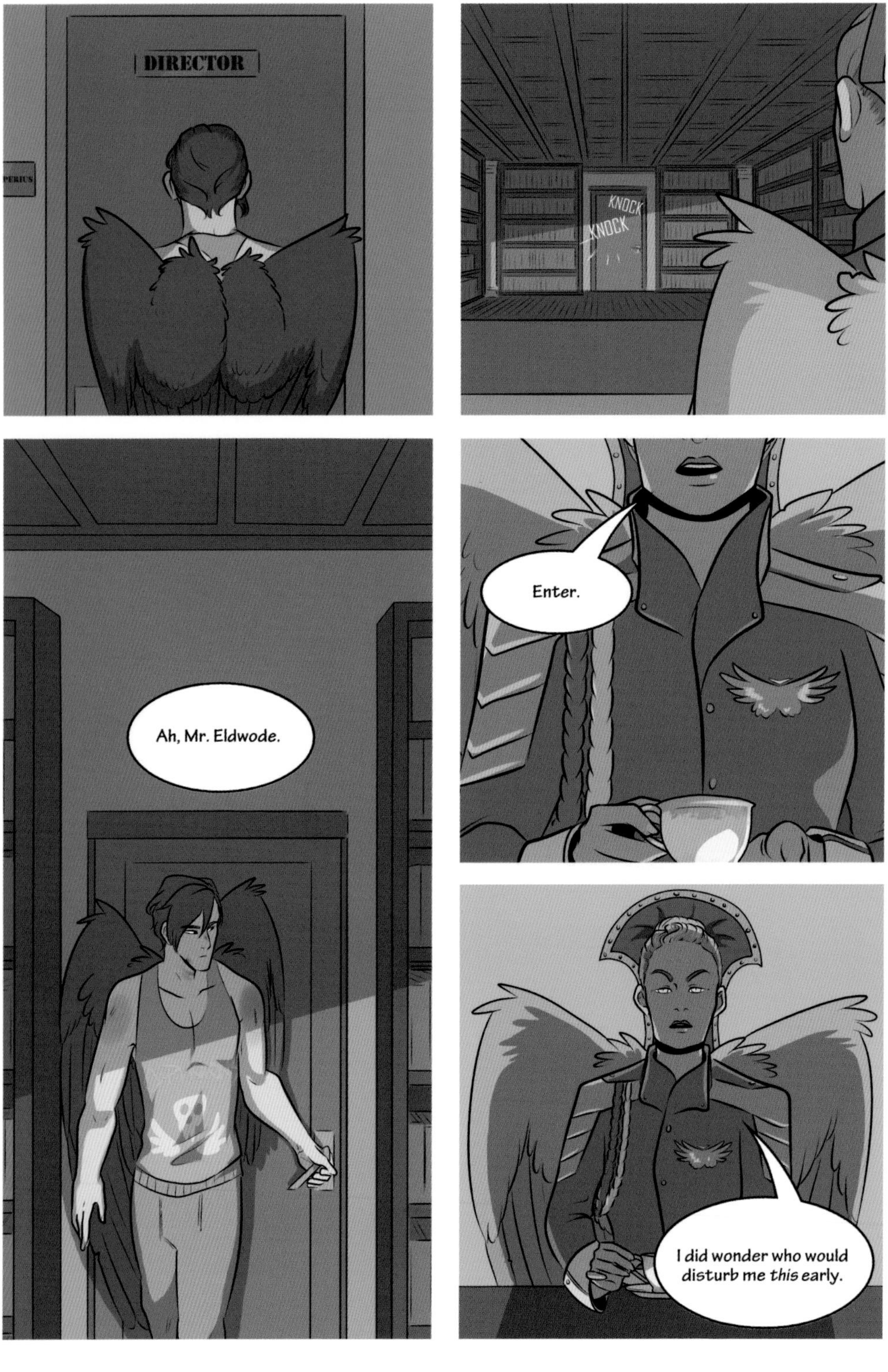
DIRECTOR
PERIUS
KNOCK
KNOCK
Enter.
Ah, Mr. Eldwode.
I did wonder who would disturb me *this* early.

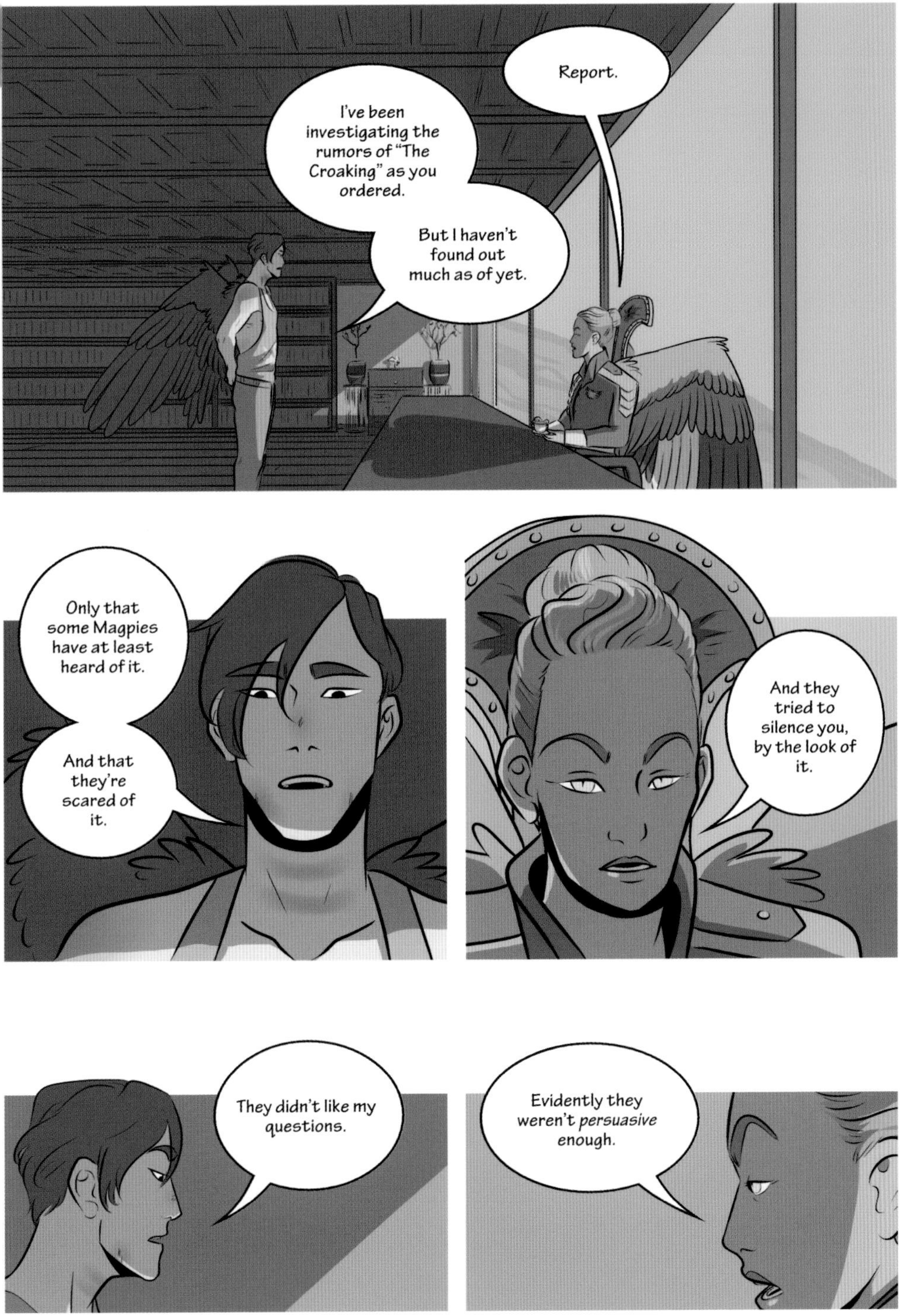
Report.
I've been investigating the rumors of "The Croaking" as you ordered.
But I haven't found out much as of yet.
Only that some Magpies have at least heard of it.
And that they're scared of it.
And they tried to silence you, by the look of it.
They didn't like my questions.
Evidently they weren't *persuasive* enough.

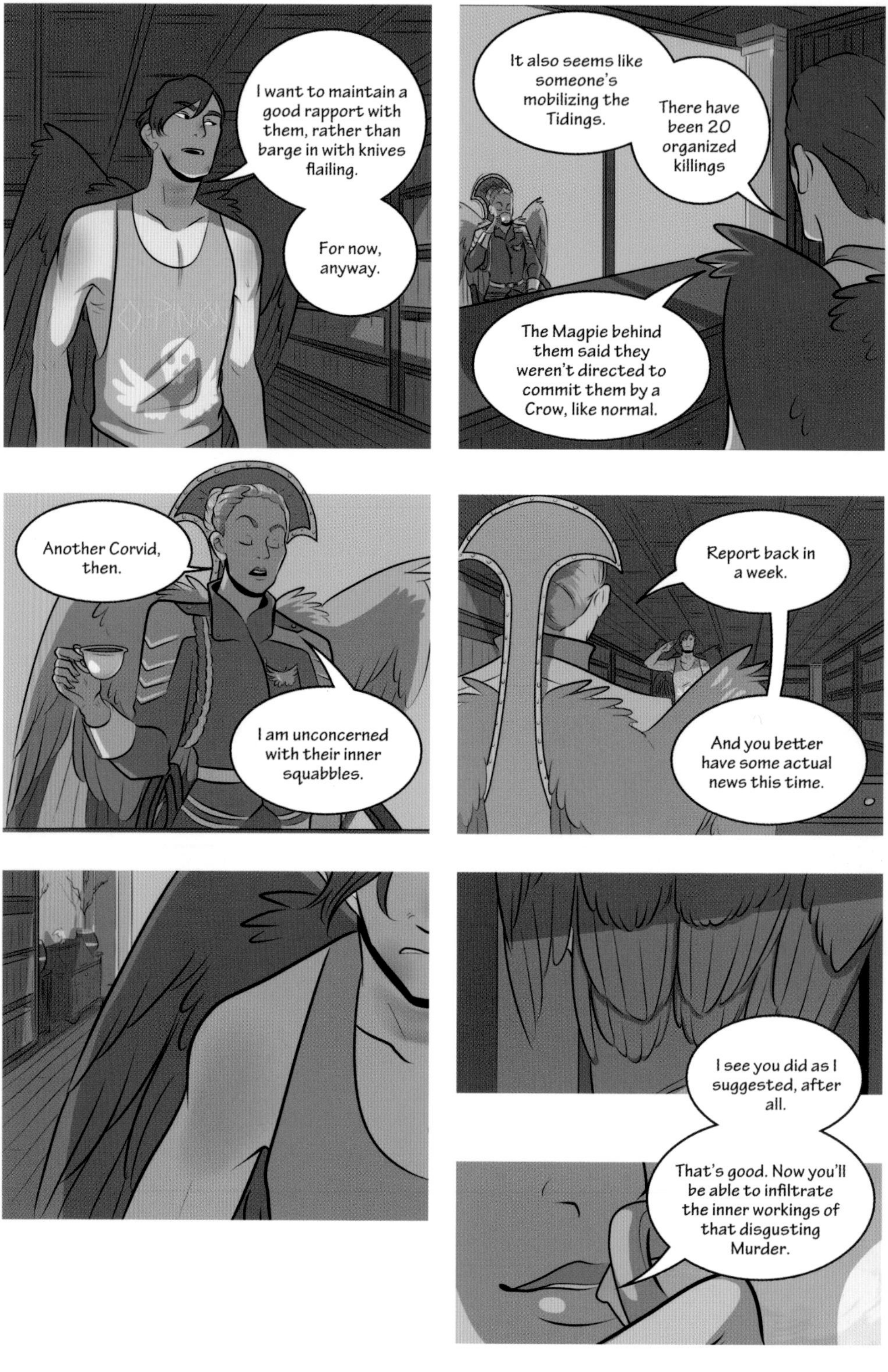

I want to maintain a good rapport with them, rather than barge in with knives flailing.
For now, anyway.
It also seems like someone's mobilizing the Tidings.
There have been 20 organized killings
The Magpie behind them said they weren't directed to commit them by a Crow, like normal.
Another Corvid, then.
I am unconcerned with their inner squabbles.
Report back in a week.
And you better have some actual news this time.
I see you did as I suggested, after all.
That's good. Now you'll be able to infiltrate the inner workings of that disgusting Murder.

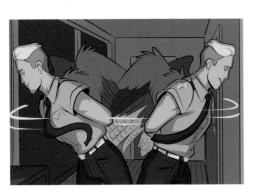

Oh, thank Icarus!

I thought you'd been kidnapped again!

I'm fine? I just had to go report to the Director.

Ah...Right.

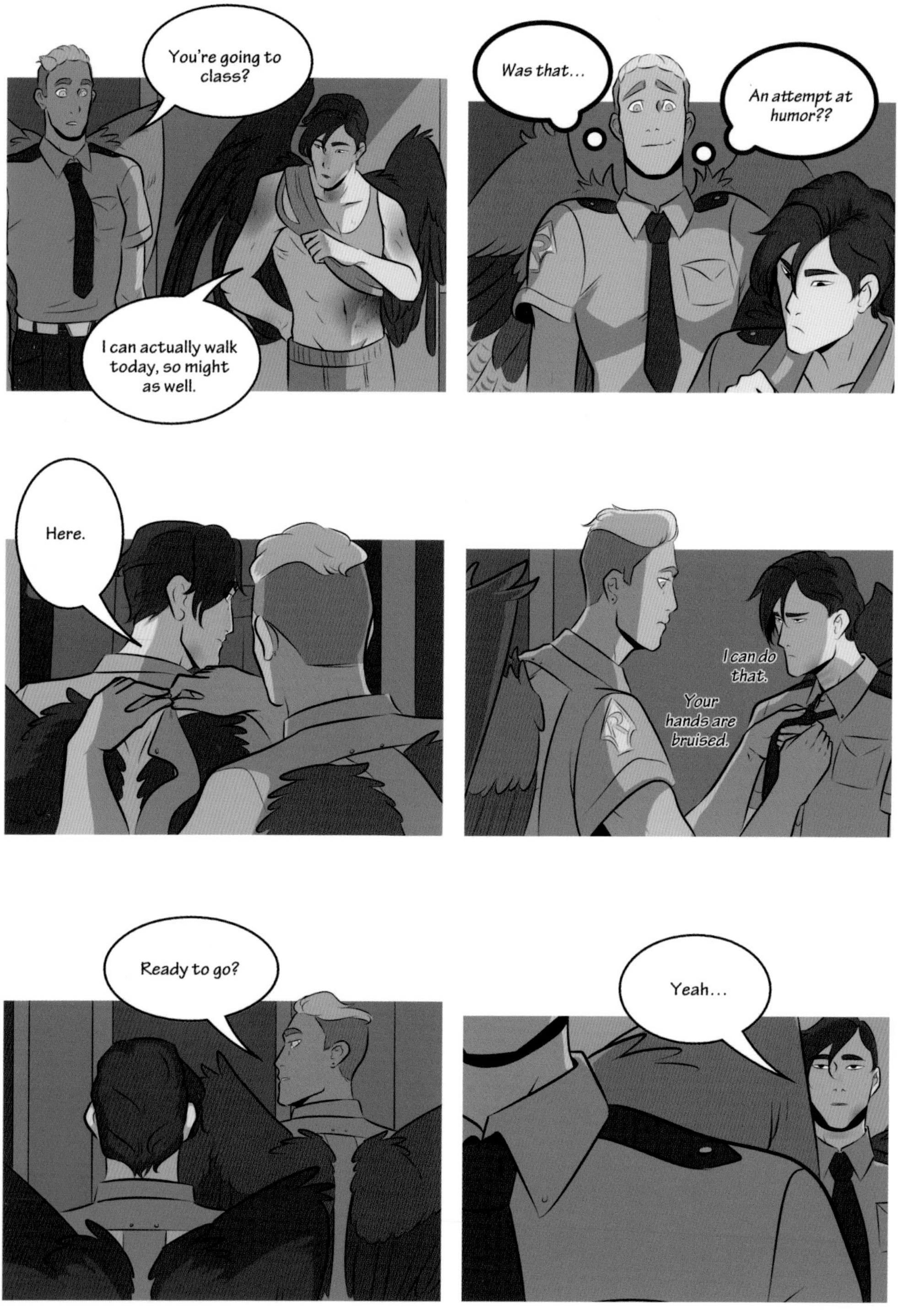
You're going to class?
I can actually walk today, so might as well.
Was that...
An attempt at humor??
Here.
I can do that.
Your hands are bruised.
Ready to go?
Yeah...

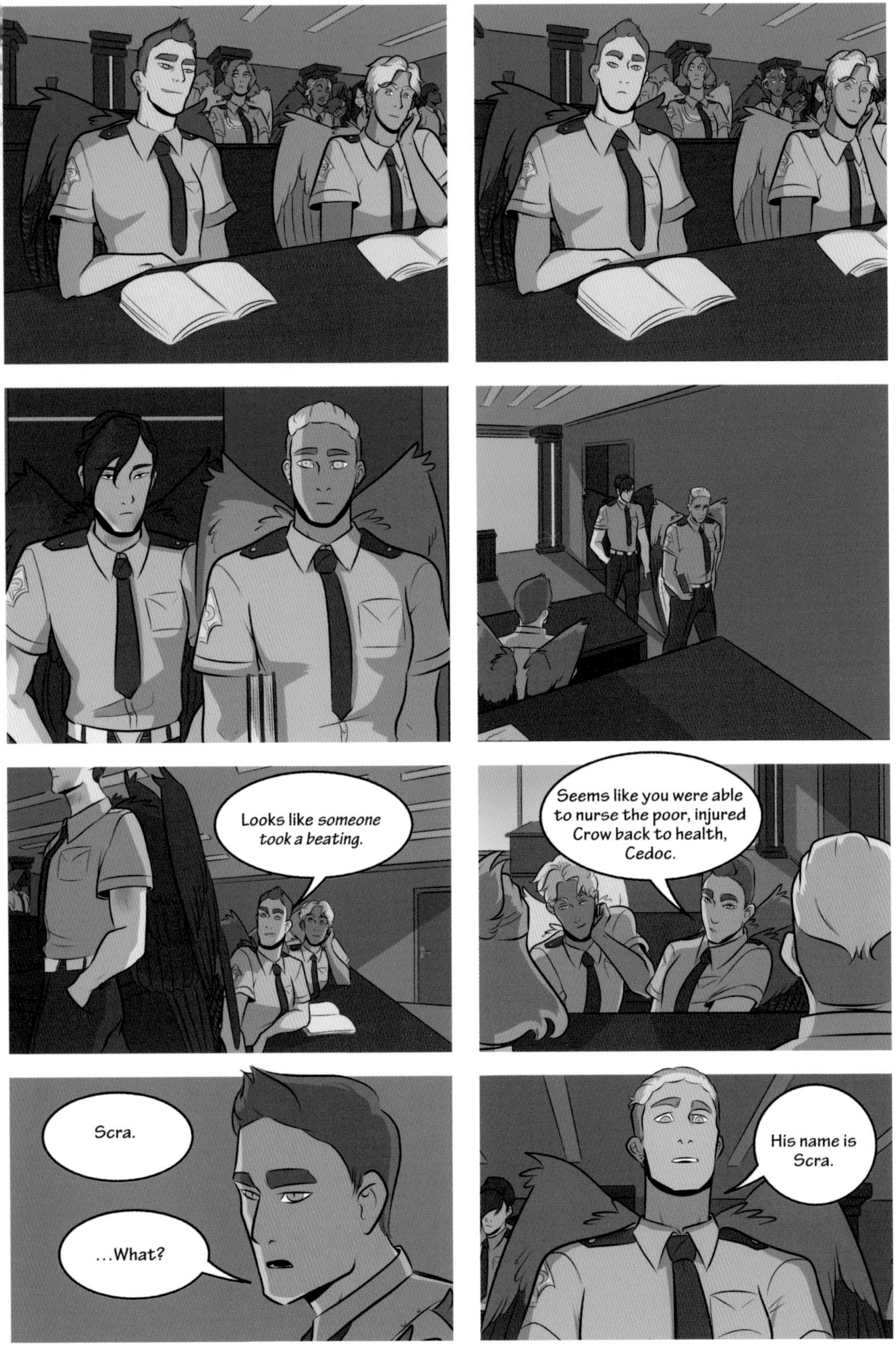
Looks like *someone* took a beating.
Seems like you were able to nurse the poor, injured Crow back to health, Cedoc.
Scra.
...What?
His name is Scra.

Che - whatever, man.

Withheld #

Meet at border 23:39

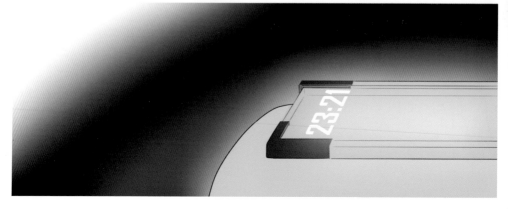

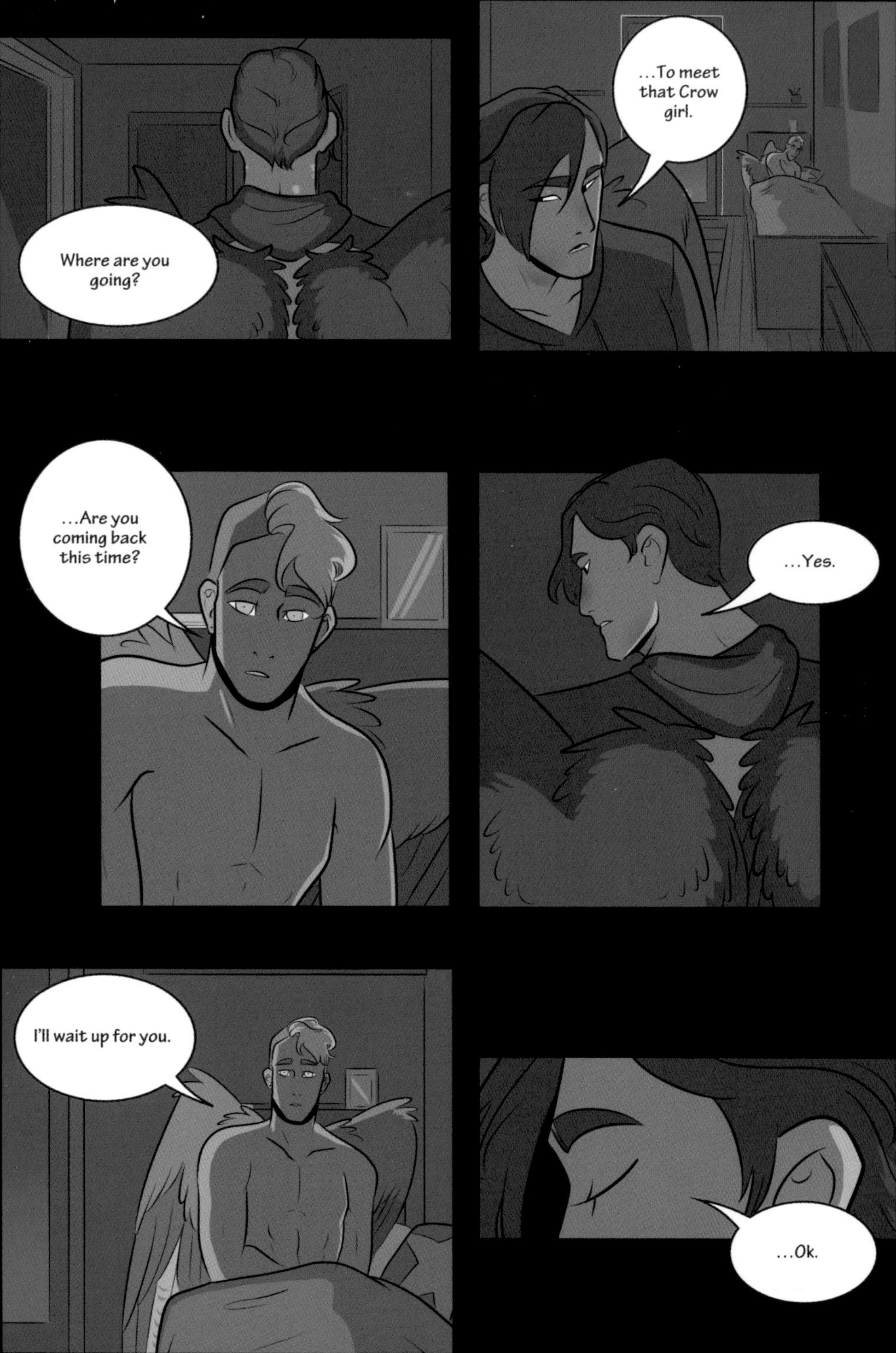
Where are you going?
...To meet that Crow girl.
...Are you coming back this time?
...Yes.
I'll wait up for you.
...Ok.

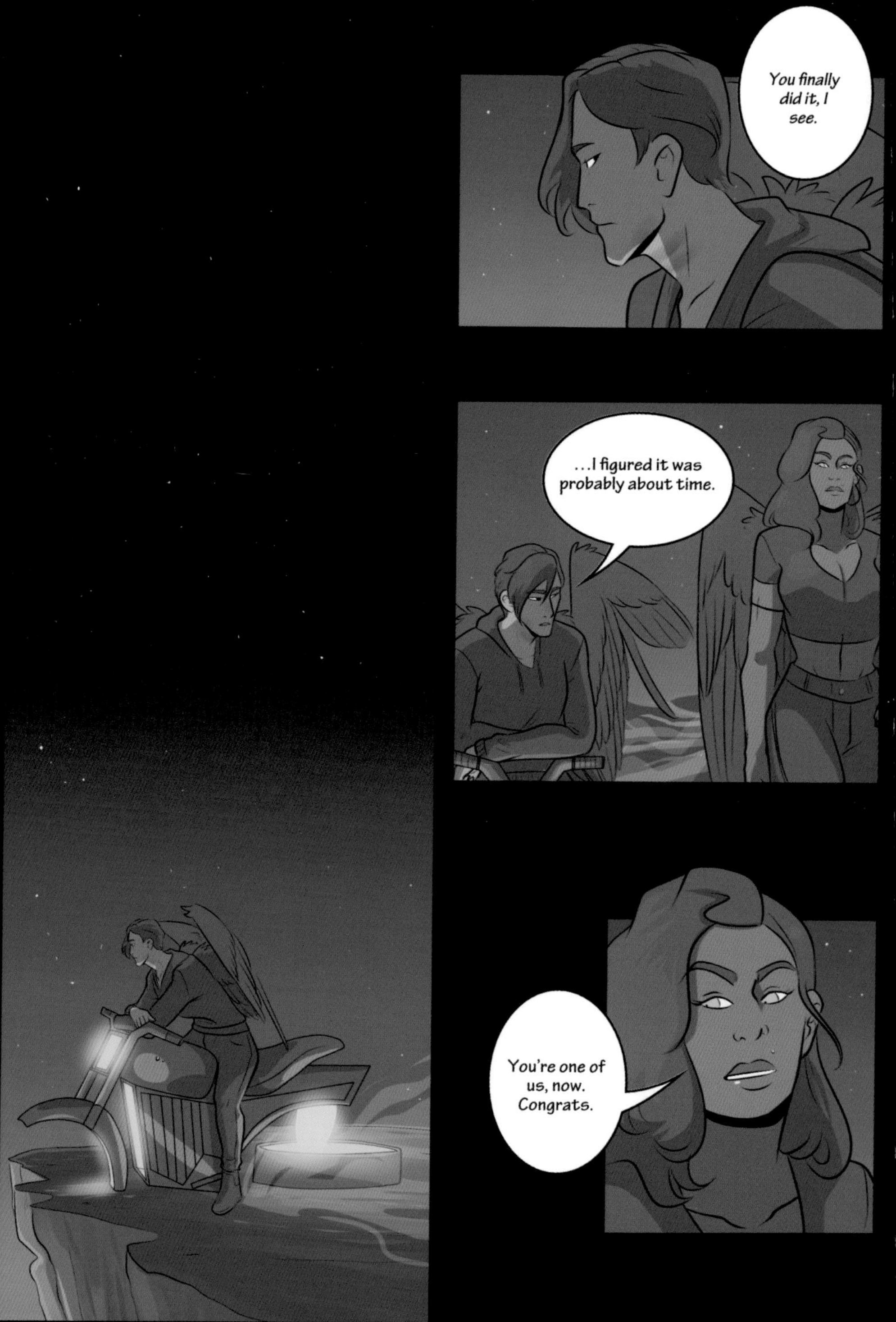
You finally did it, I see.
...I figured it was probably about time.
You're one of us, now. Congrats.

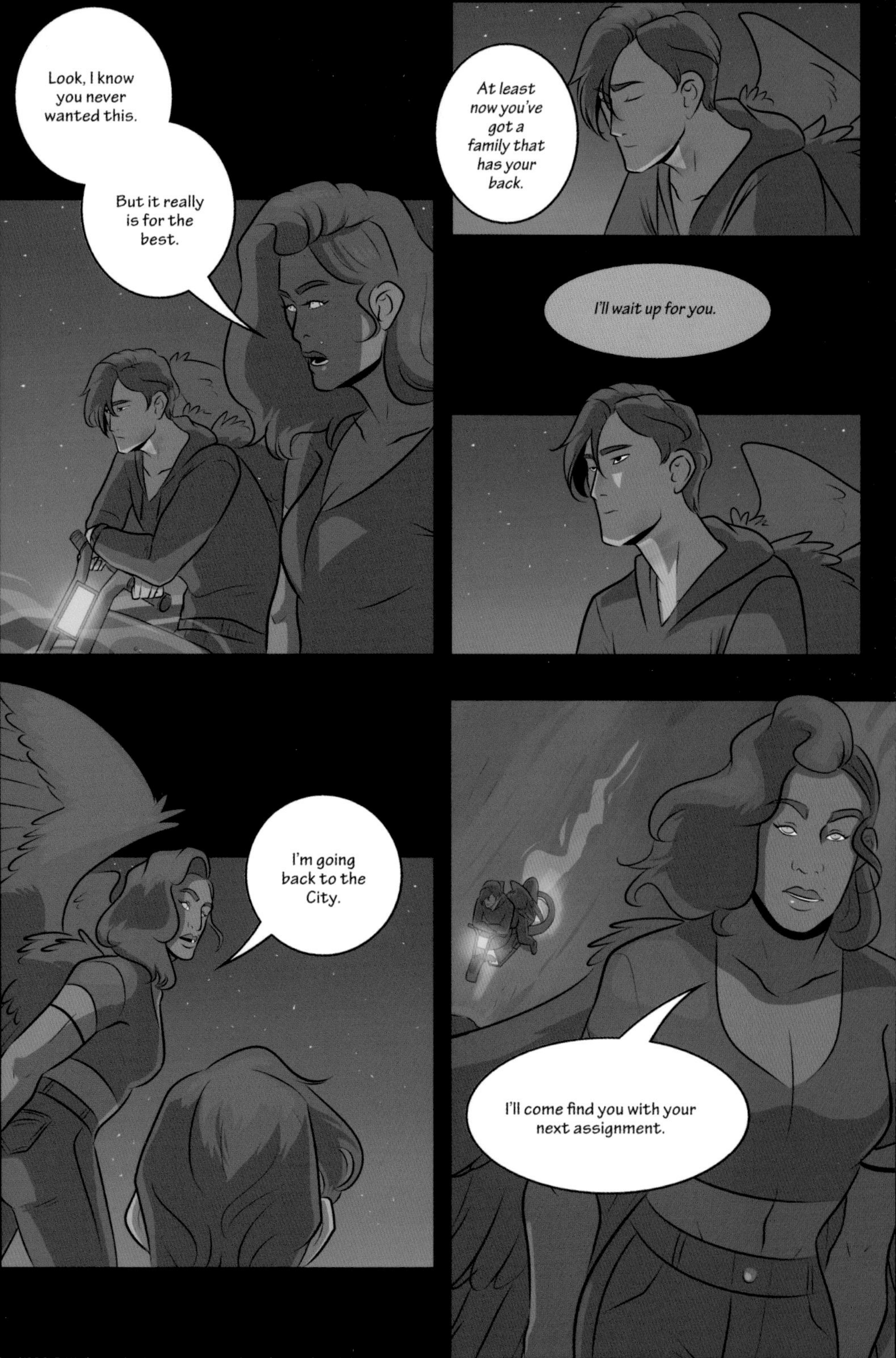
Look, I know you never wanted this.
But it really is for the best.
At least now you've got a family that has your back.
I'll wait up for you.
I'm going back to the City.
I'll come find you with your next assignment.

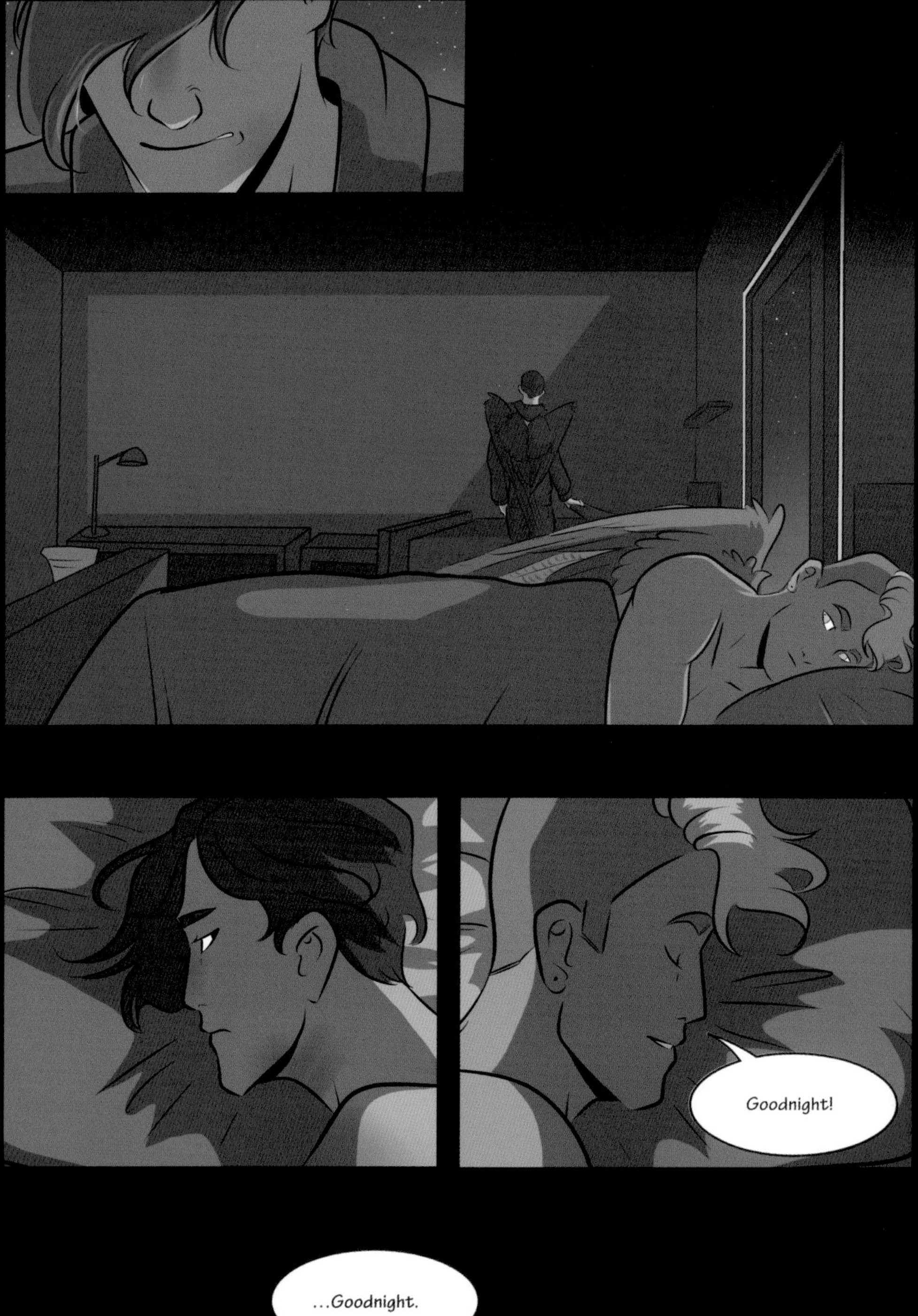
Goodnight!
...Goodnight.

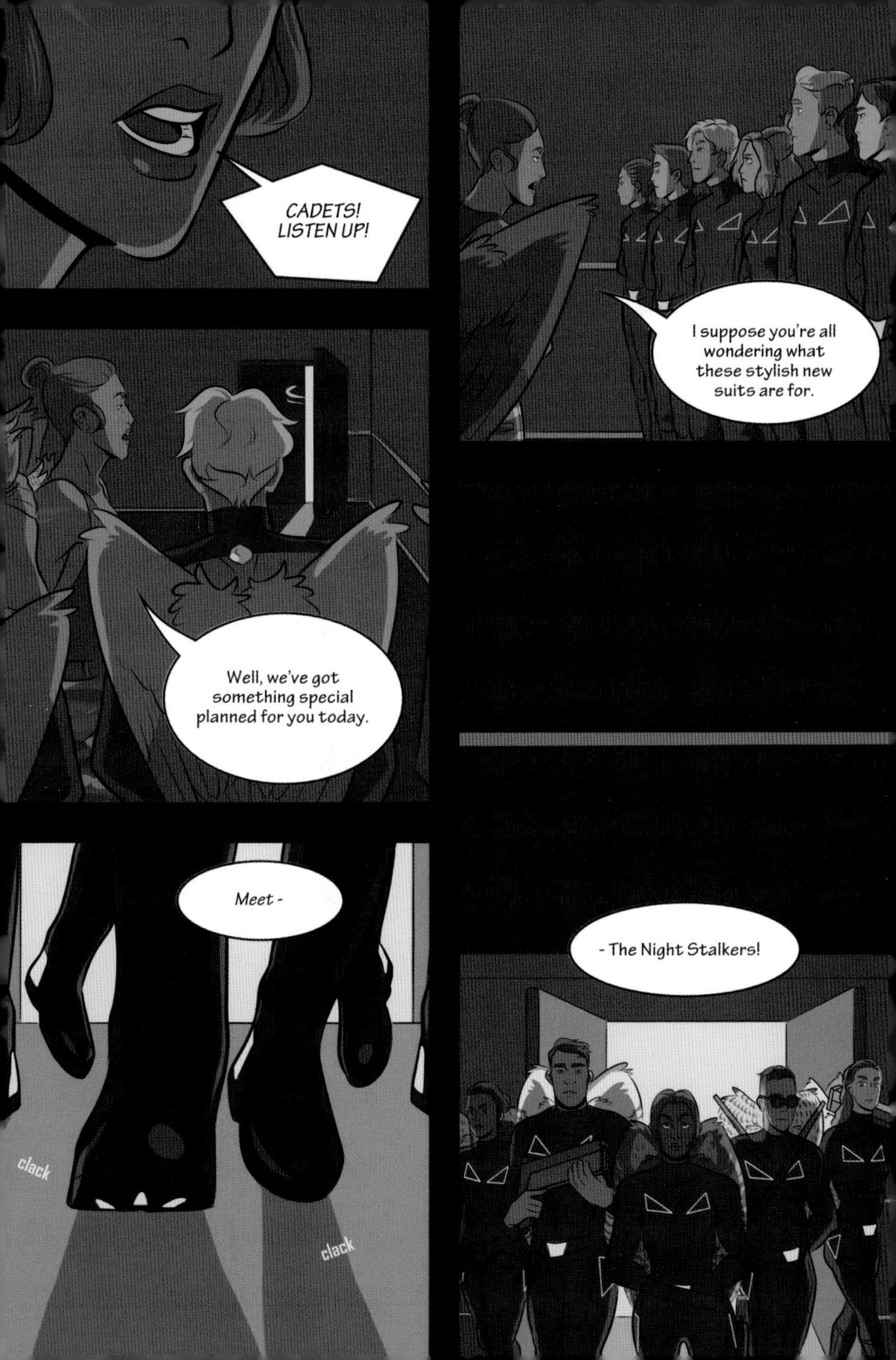
CADETS! LISTEN UP!
I suppose you're all wondering what these stylish new suits are for.
Well, we've got something special planned for you today.
Meet -
clack
clack
- The Night Stalkers!

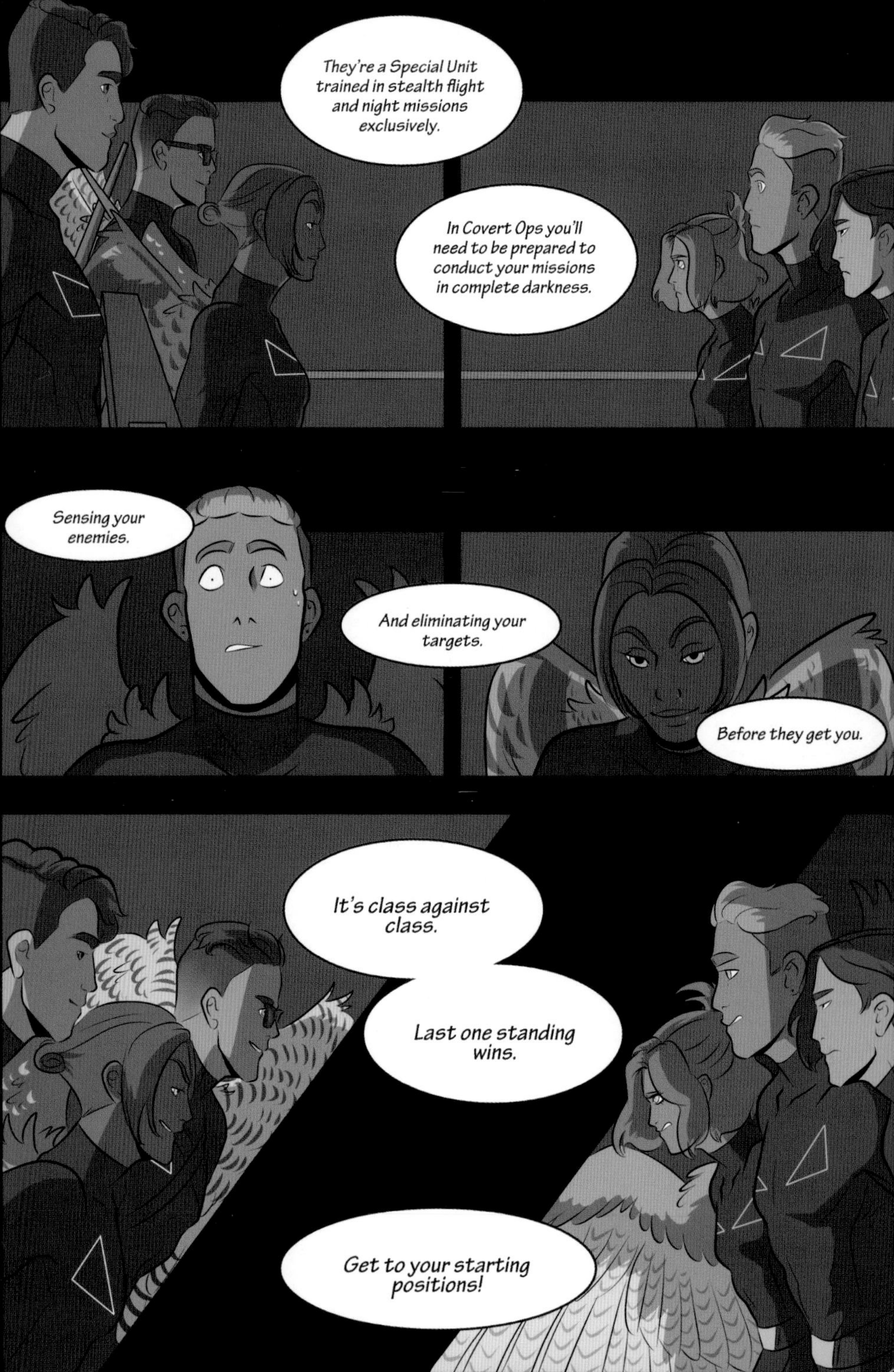
They're a Special Unit trained in stealth flight and night missions exclusively.
In Covert Ops you'll need to be prepared to conduct your missions in complete darkness.
Sensing your enemies.
And eliminating your targets.
Before they get you.
It's class against class.
Last one standing wins.
Get to your starting positions!

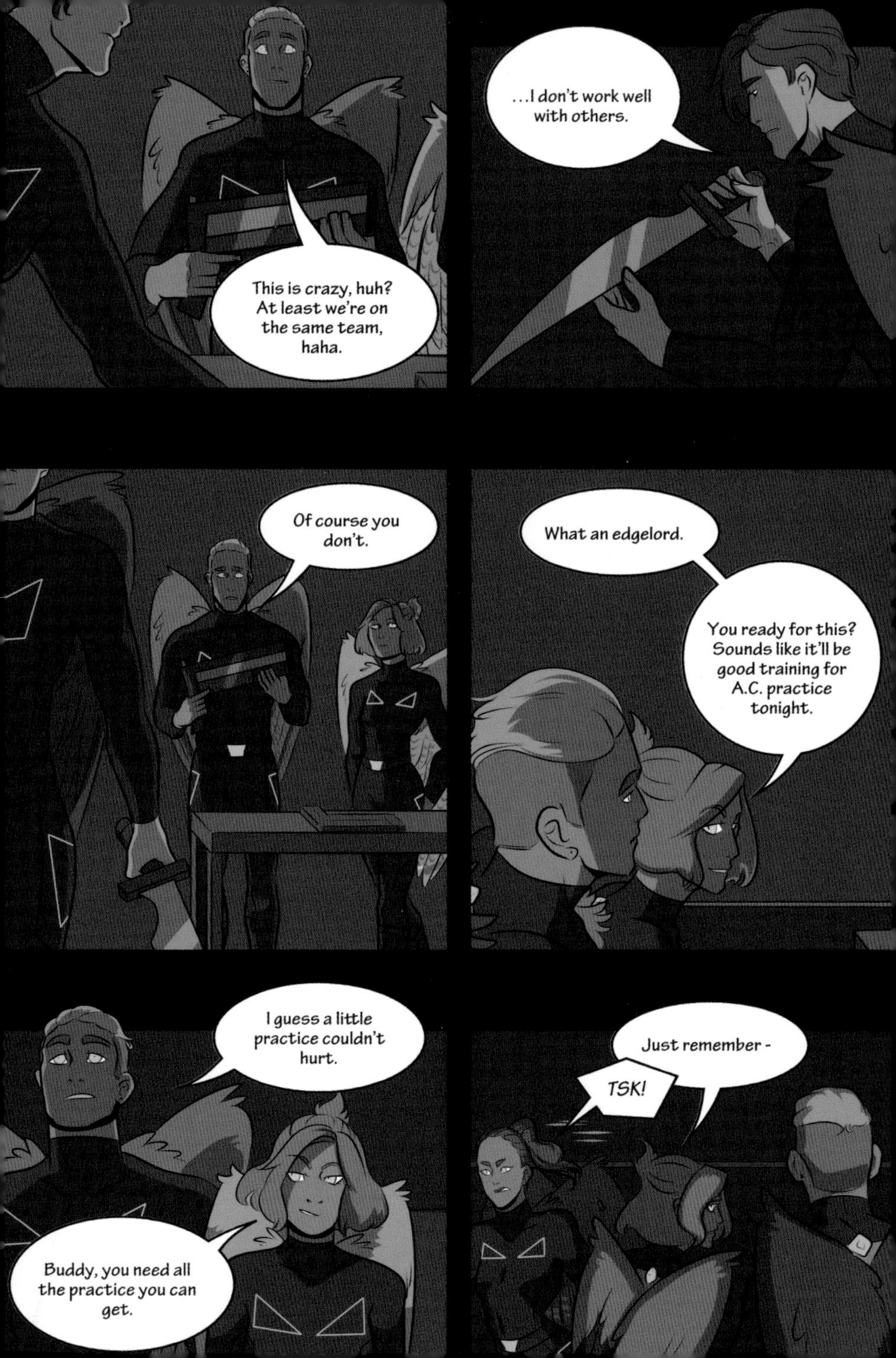

This is crazy, huh? At least we're on the same team, haha.
...I don't work well with others.
Of course you don't.
What an edgelord.
You ready for this? Sounds like it'll be good training for A.C. practice tonight.
I guess a little practice couldn't hurt.
Buddy, you need all the practice you can get.
Just remember -
TSK!

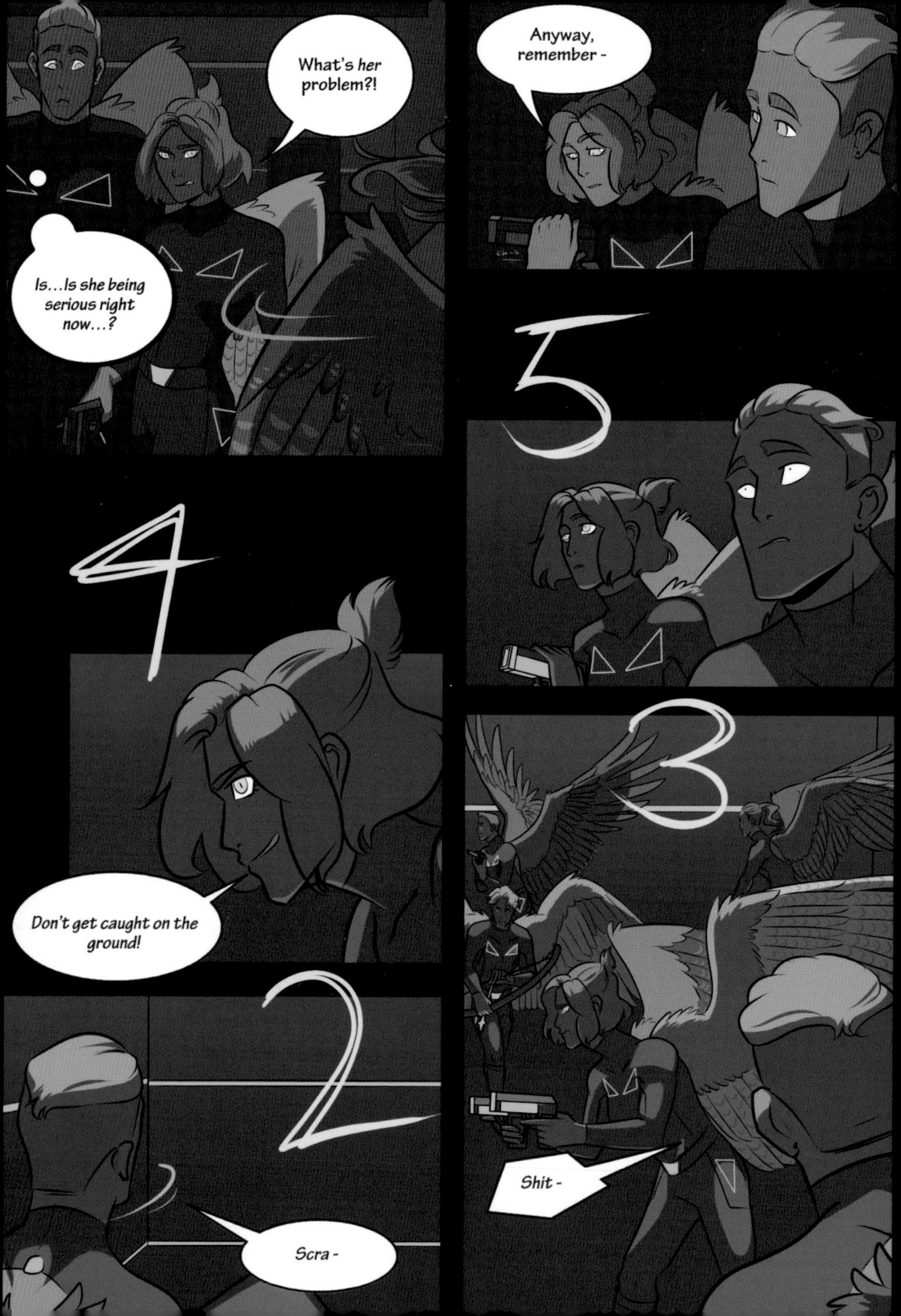
What's her problem?!
Is...Is she being serious right now...?
Anyway, remember -
5
4
Don't get caught on the ground!
3
2
Scra -
Shit -

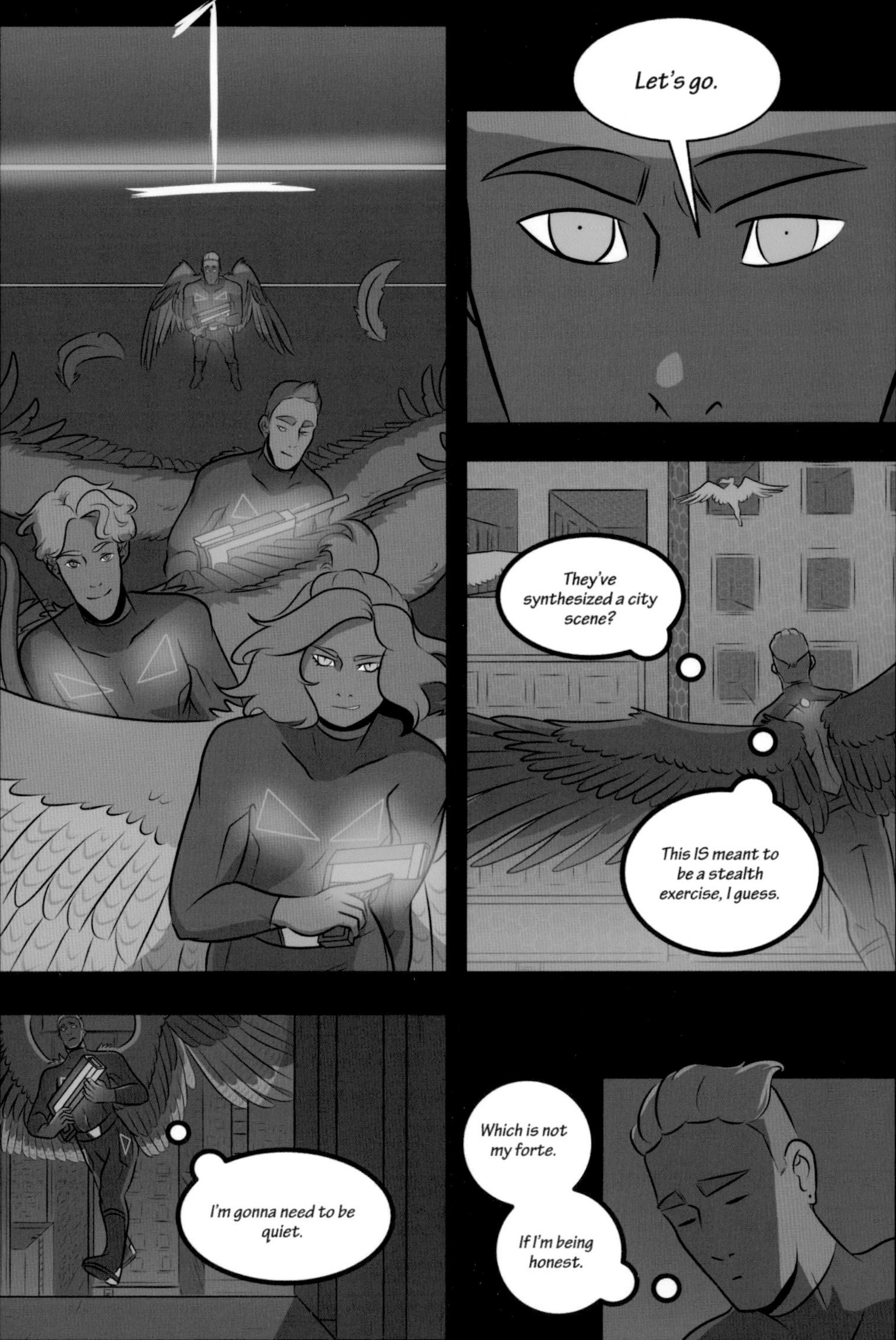
Let's go.
They've synthesized a city scene?
This IS meant to be a stealth exercise, I guess.
I'm gonna need to be quiet.
Which is not my forte.
If I'm being honest.

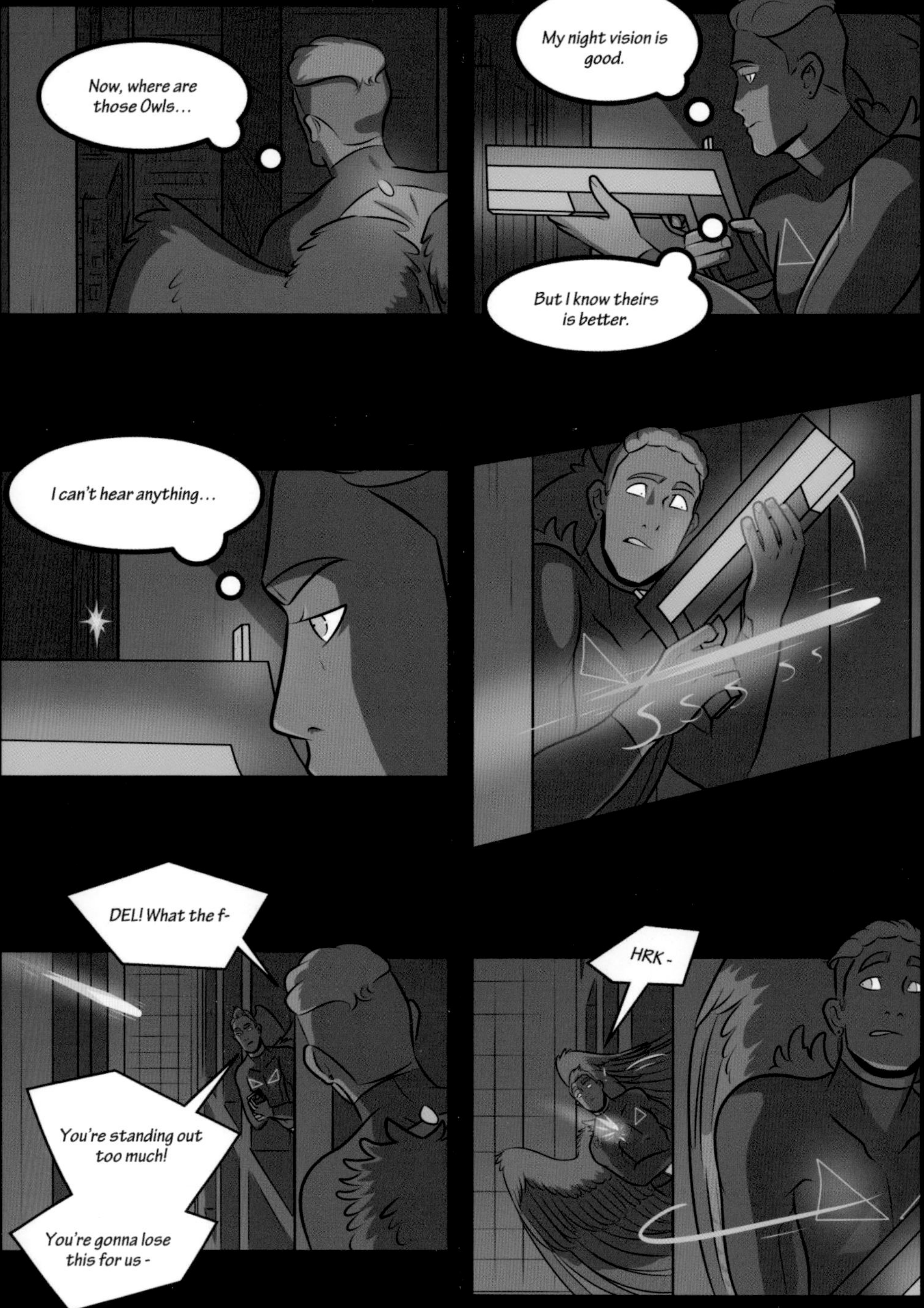
Now, where are those Owls...
My night vision is good.
But I know theirs is better.
I can't hear anything...
DEL! What the f-
You're standing out too much!
You're gonna lose this for us -
HRK -

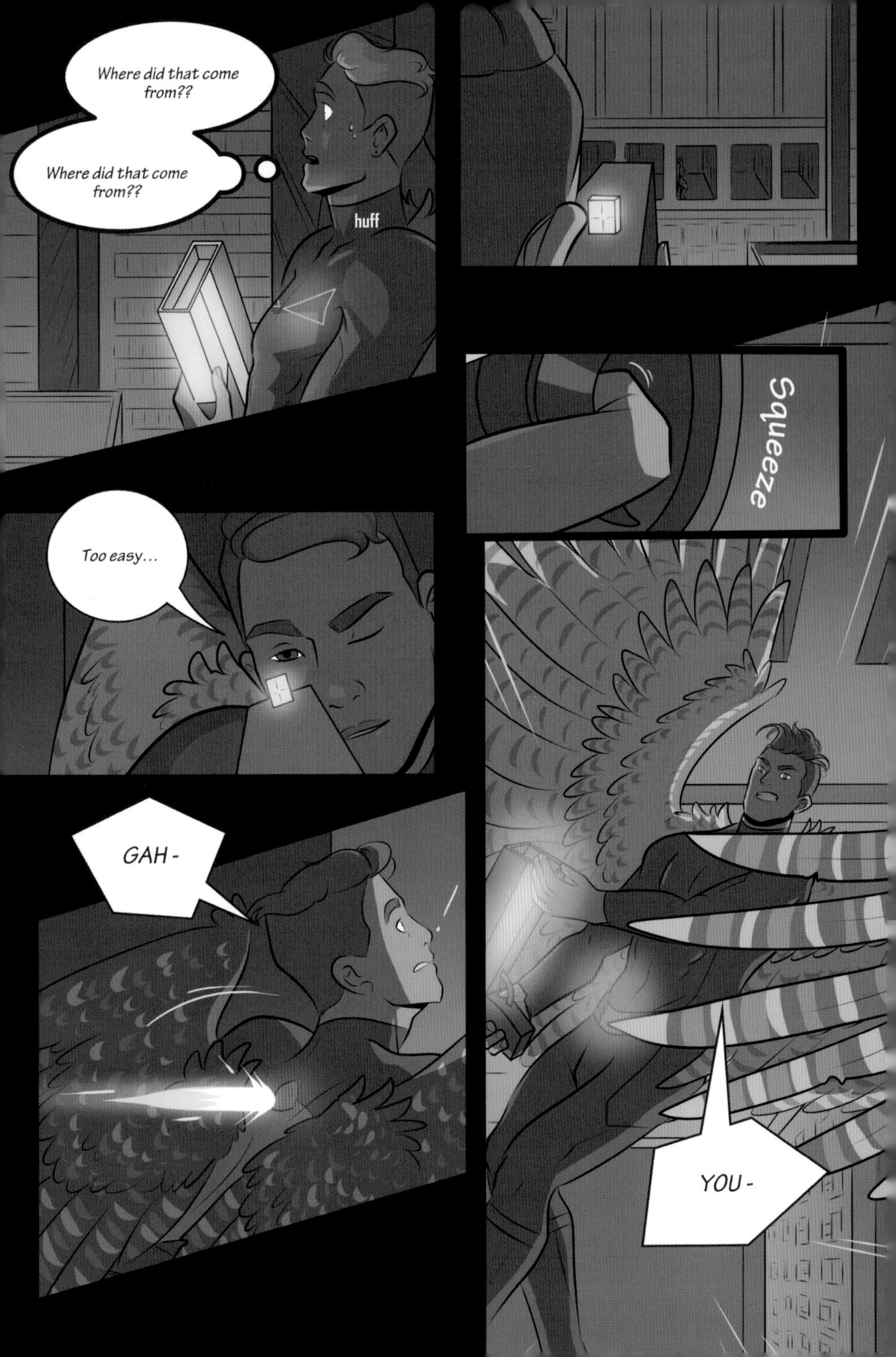
Where did that come from??
Where did that come from??
huff
Squeeze
Too easy...
GAH -
YOU -

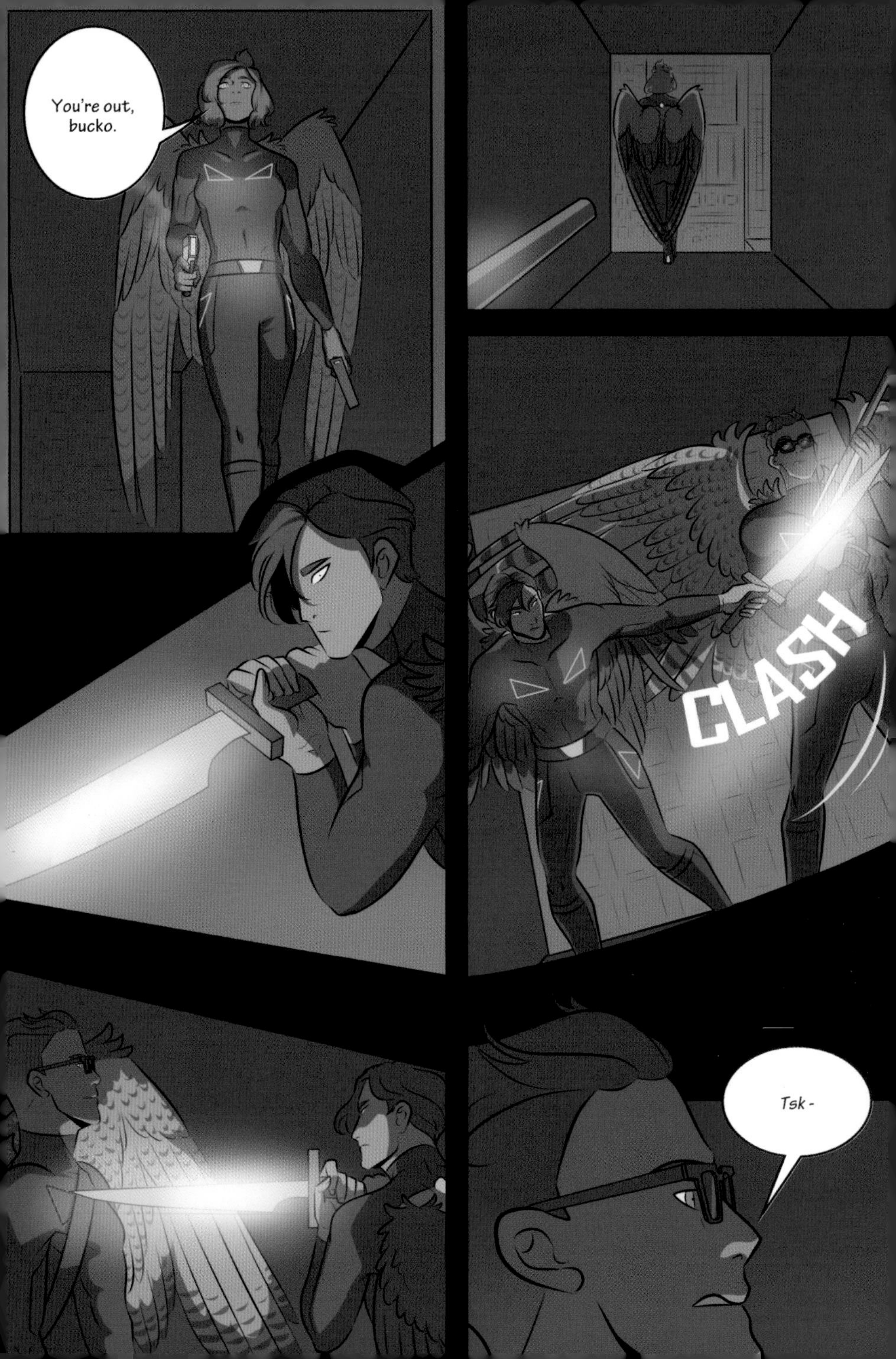
You're out, bucko.
CLASH
Tsk -

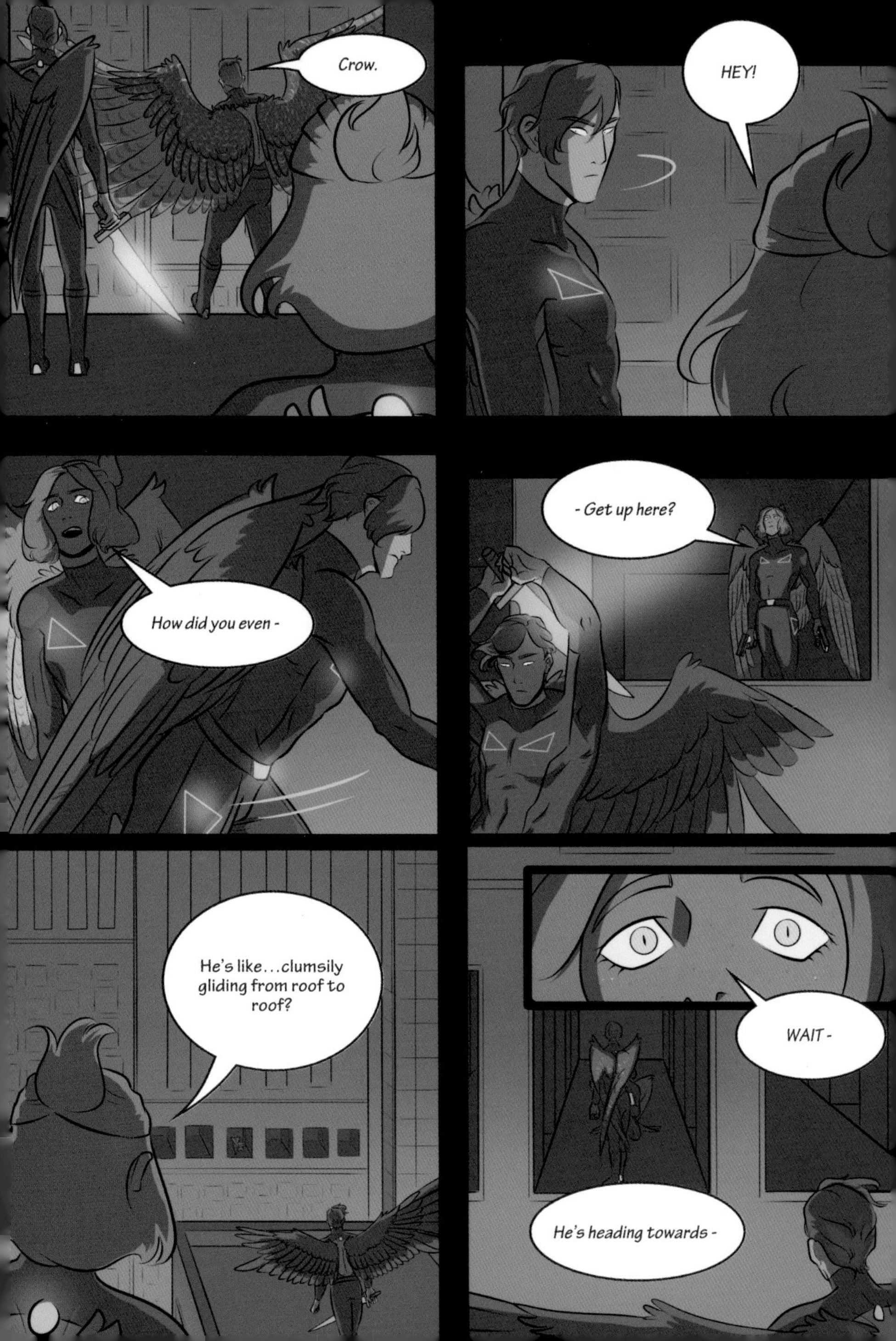
Crow.
HEY!
How did you even -
- Get up here?
He's like...clumsily gliding from roof to roof?
WAIT -
He's heading towards -

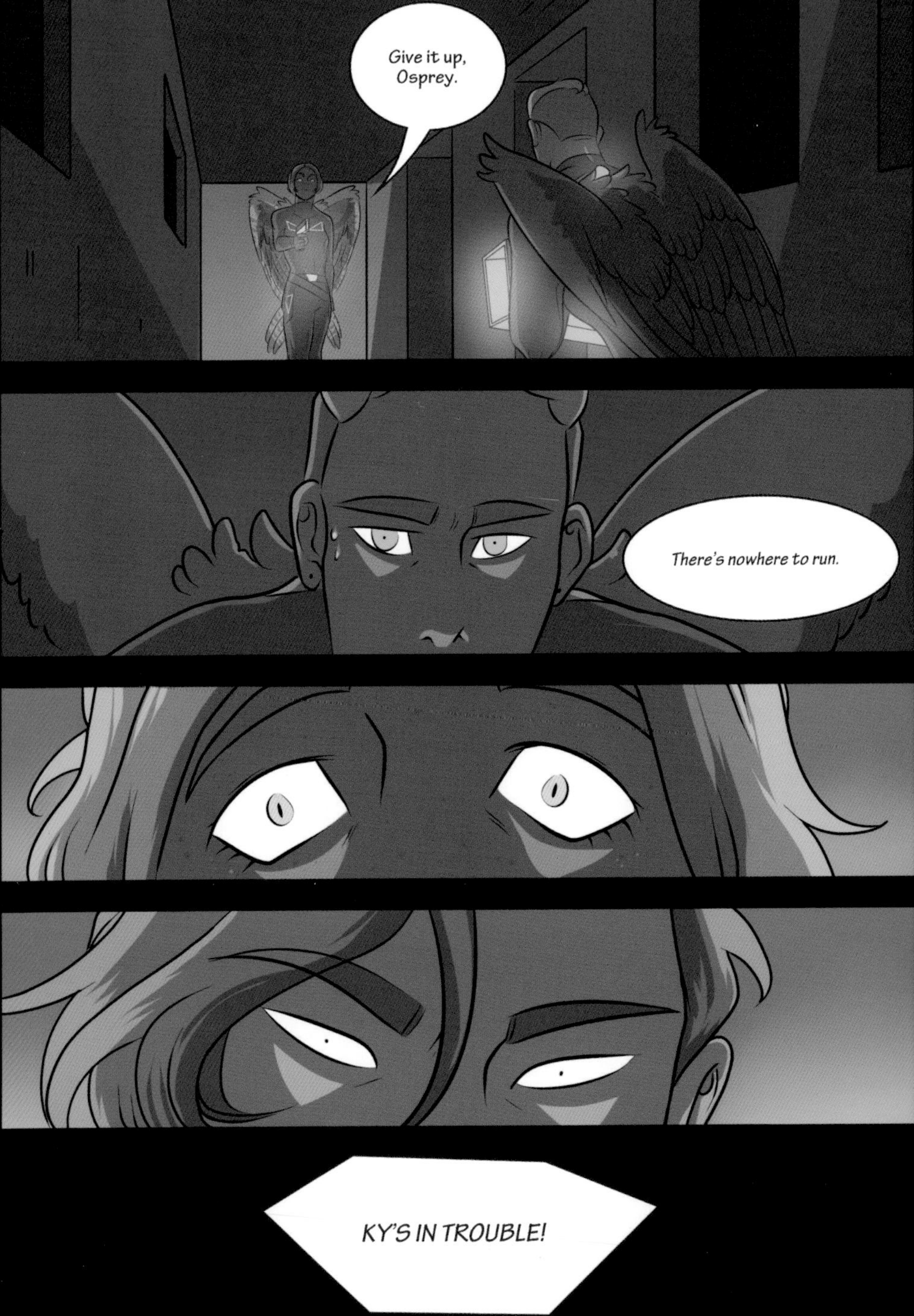
Give it up, Osprey.
There's nowhere to run.
KY'S IN TROUBLE!

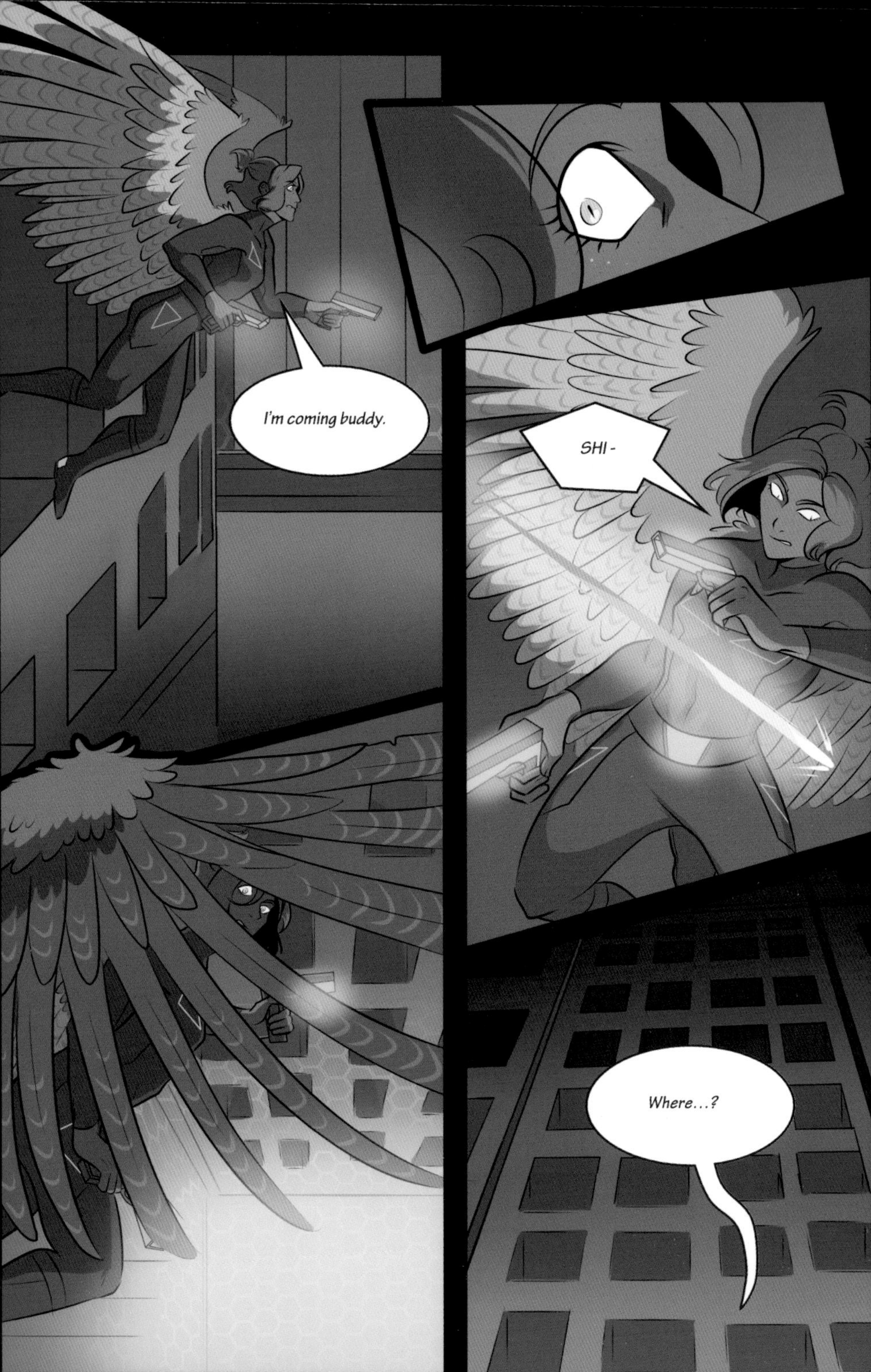
I'm coming buddy.
SHI -
Where…?

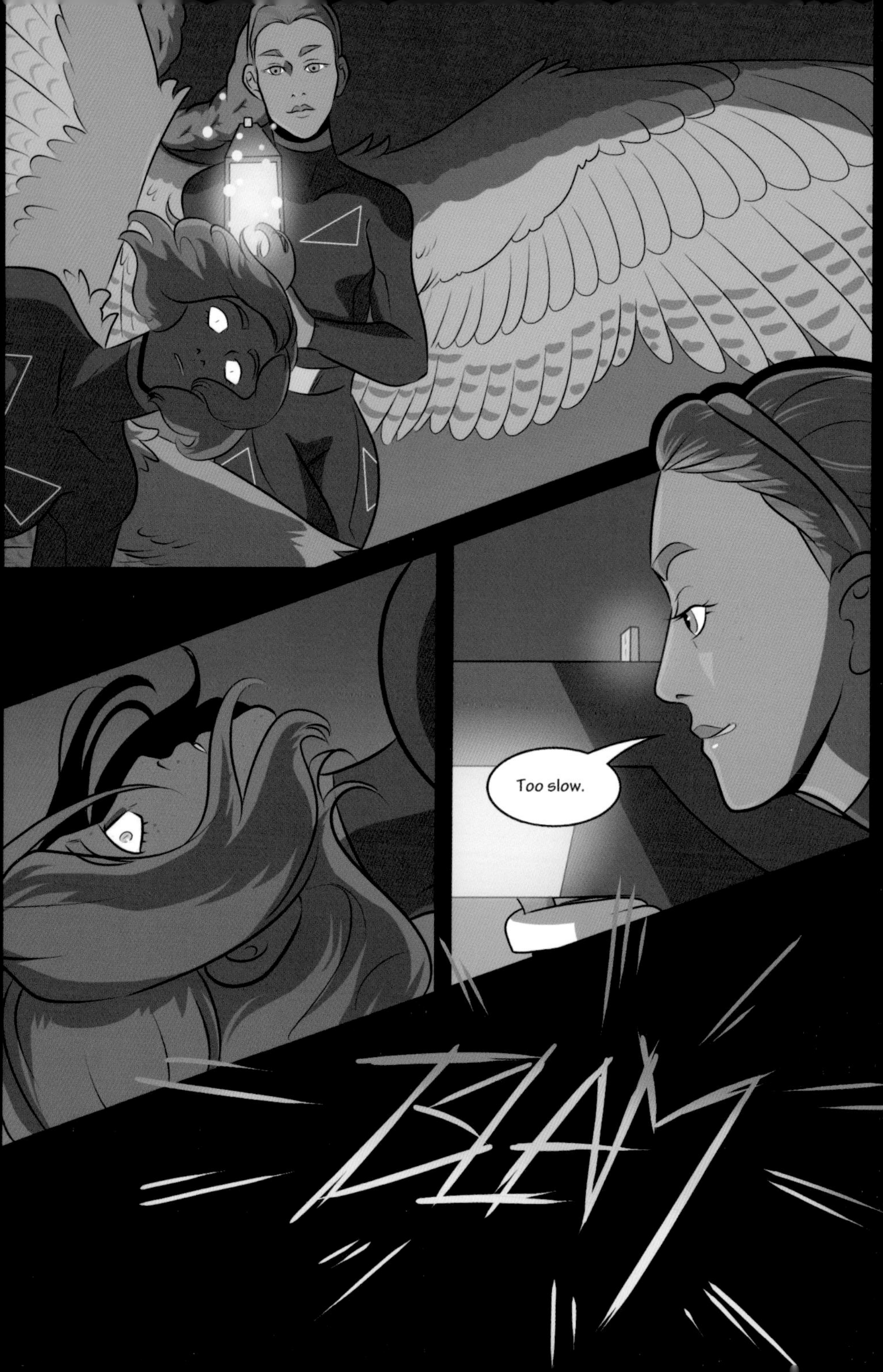
Too slow.
BLAM

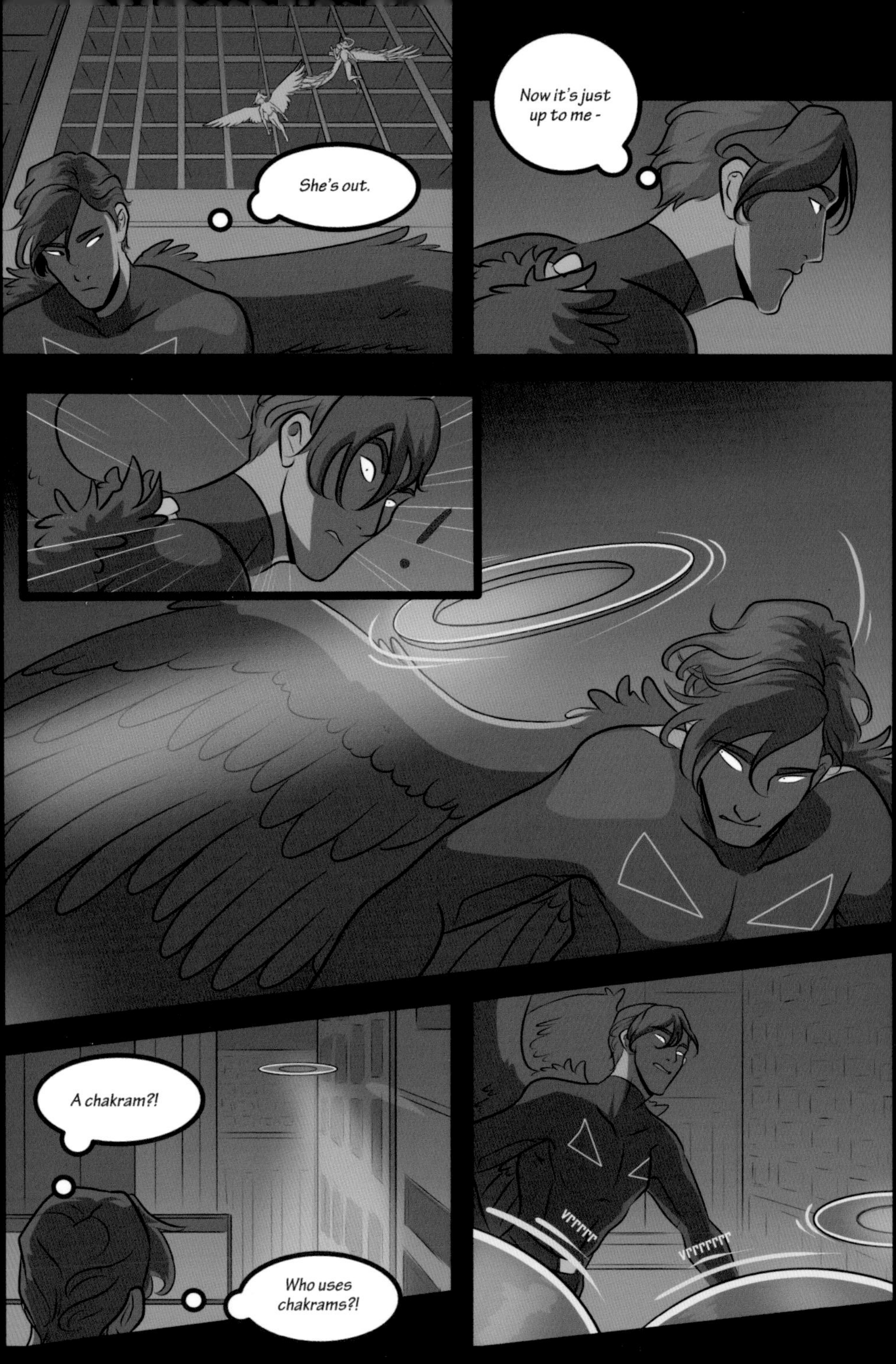
She's out.
Now it's just up to me -
A chakram?!
Who uses chakrams?!
Vrrrrrr
Vrrrrrrr

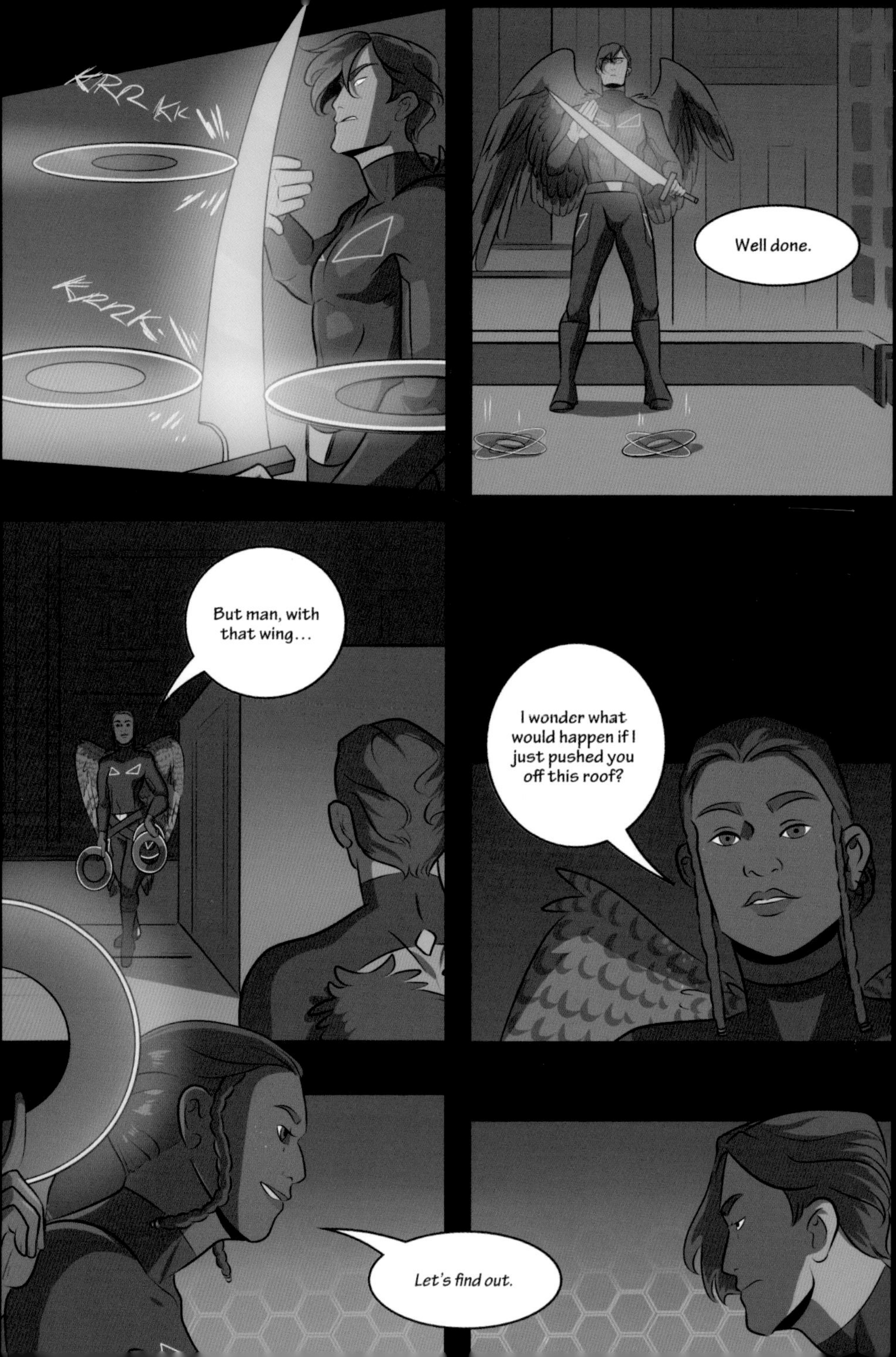
KRRKK
KRRK
Well done.
But man, with that wing...
I wonder what would happen if I just pushed you off this roof?
Let's find out.

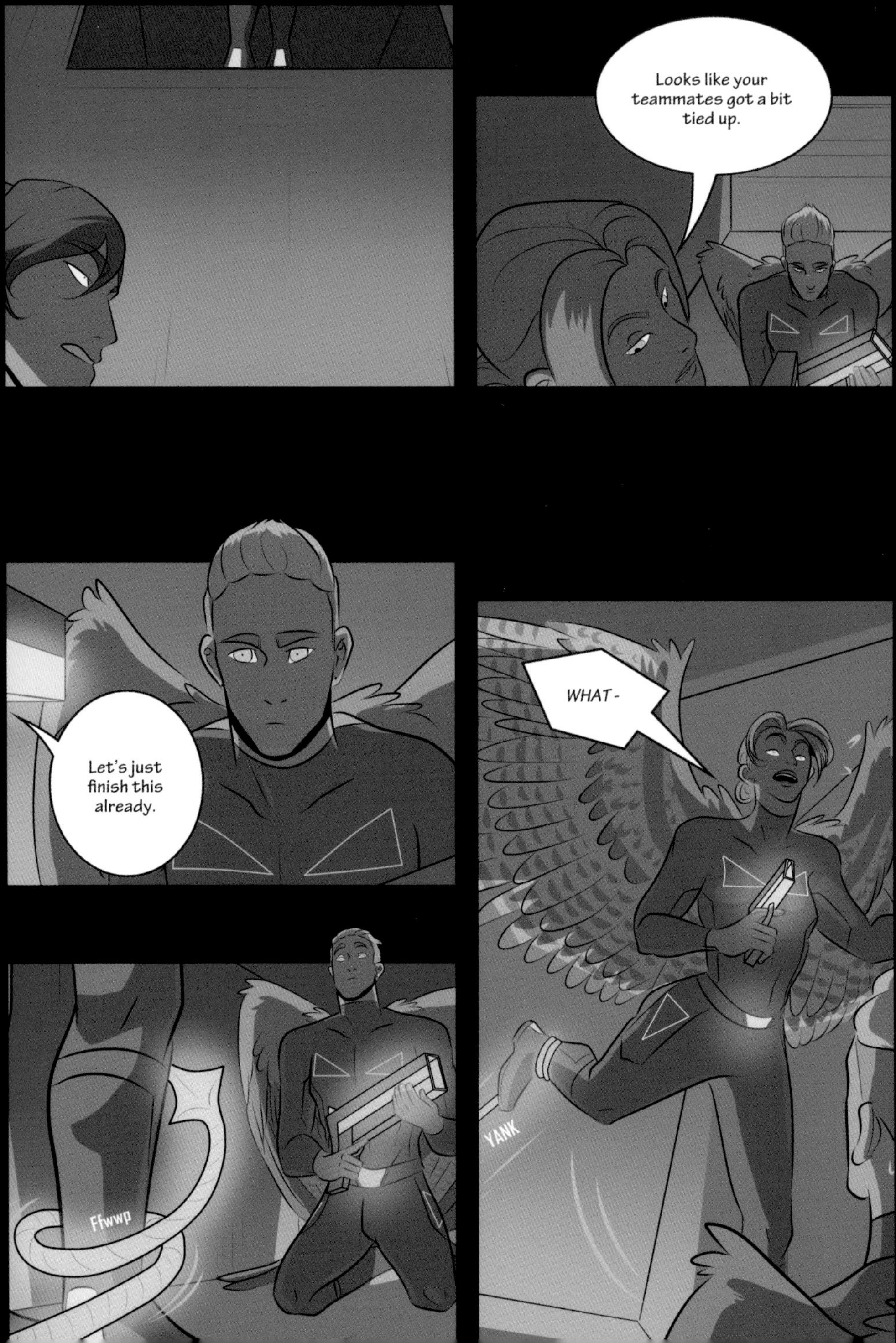
Looks like your teammates got a bit tied up.
Let's just finish this already.
Ffwwp
WHAT -
YANK

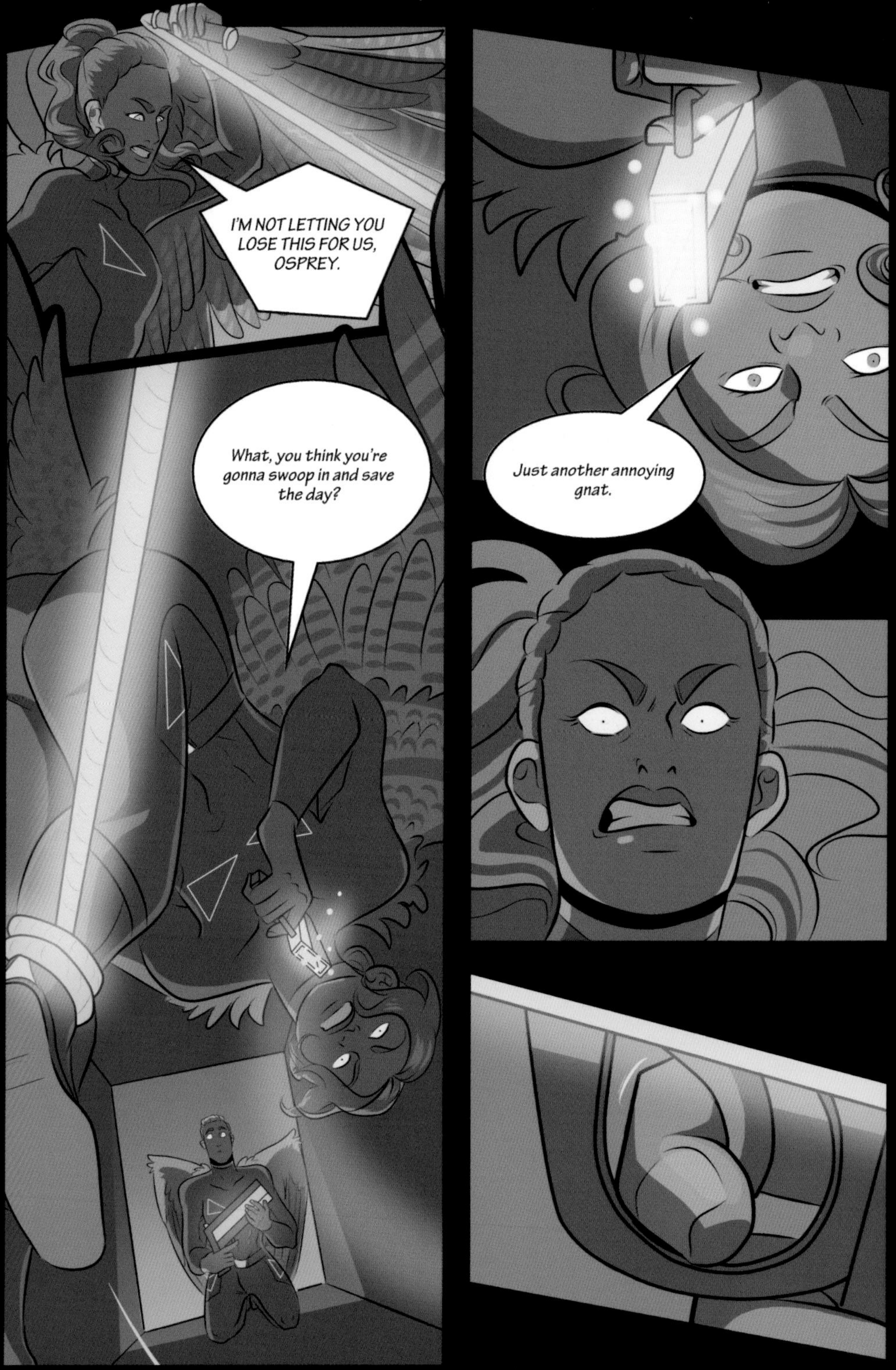
I'M NOT LETTING YOU LOSE THIS FOR US, OSPREY.
What, you think you're gonna swoop in and save the day?
Just another annoying gnat.

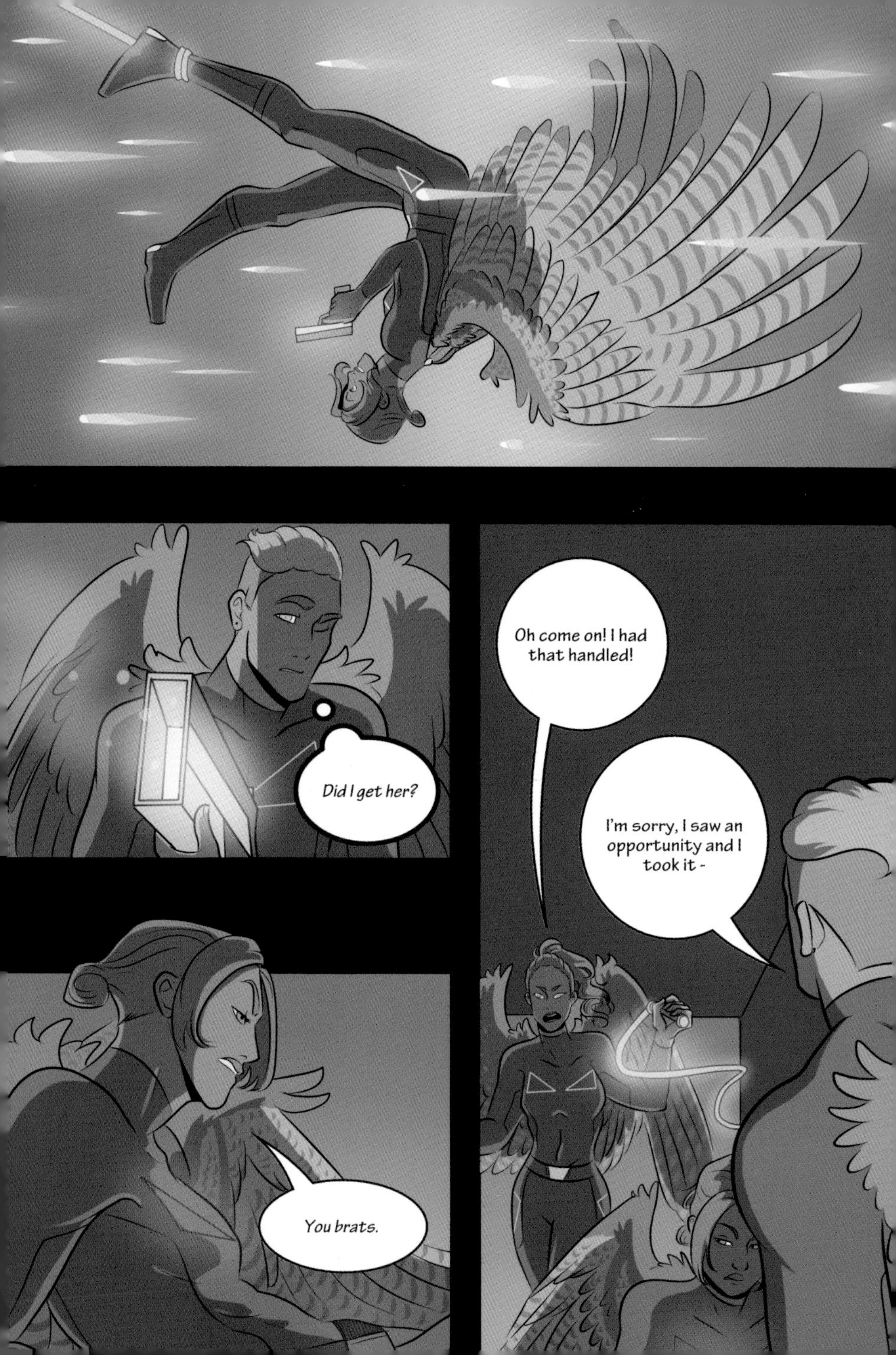
Did I get her?
Oh come on! I had that handled!
I'm sorry, I saw an opportunity and I took it -
You brats.

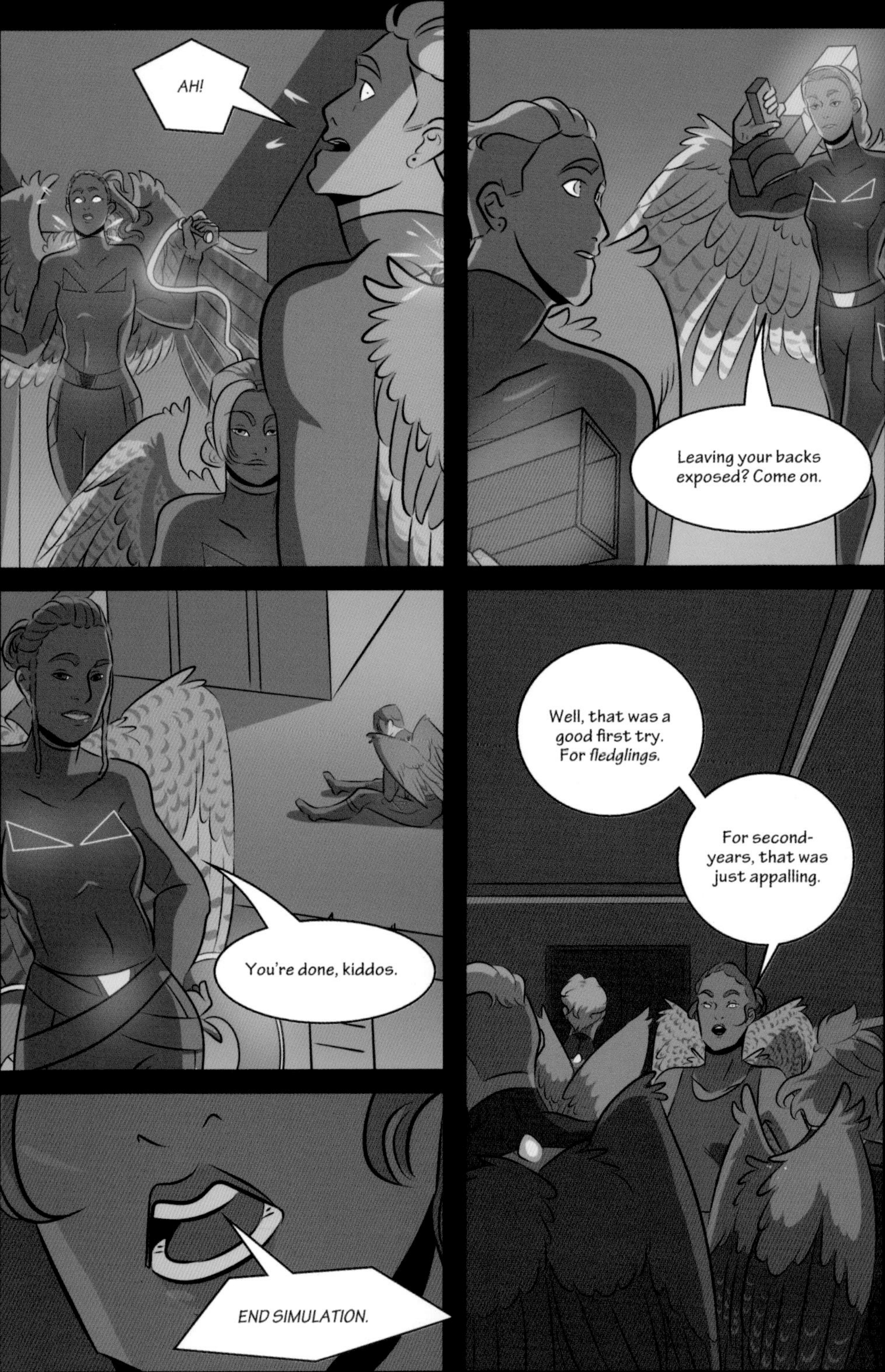
AH!
Leaving your backs exposed? Come on.
You're done, kiddos.
END SIMULATION.
Well, that was a good first try. For *fledglings*.
For second-years, that was just appalling.

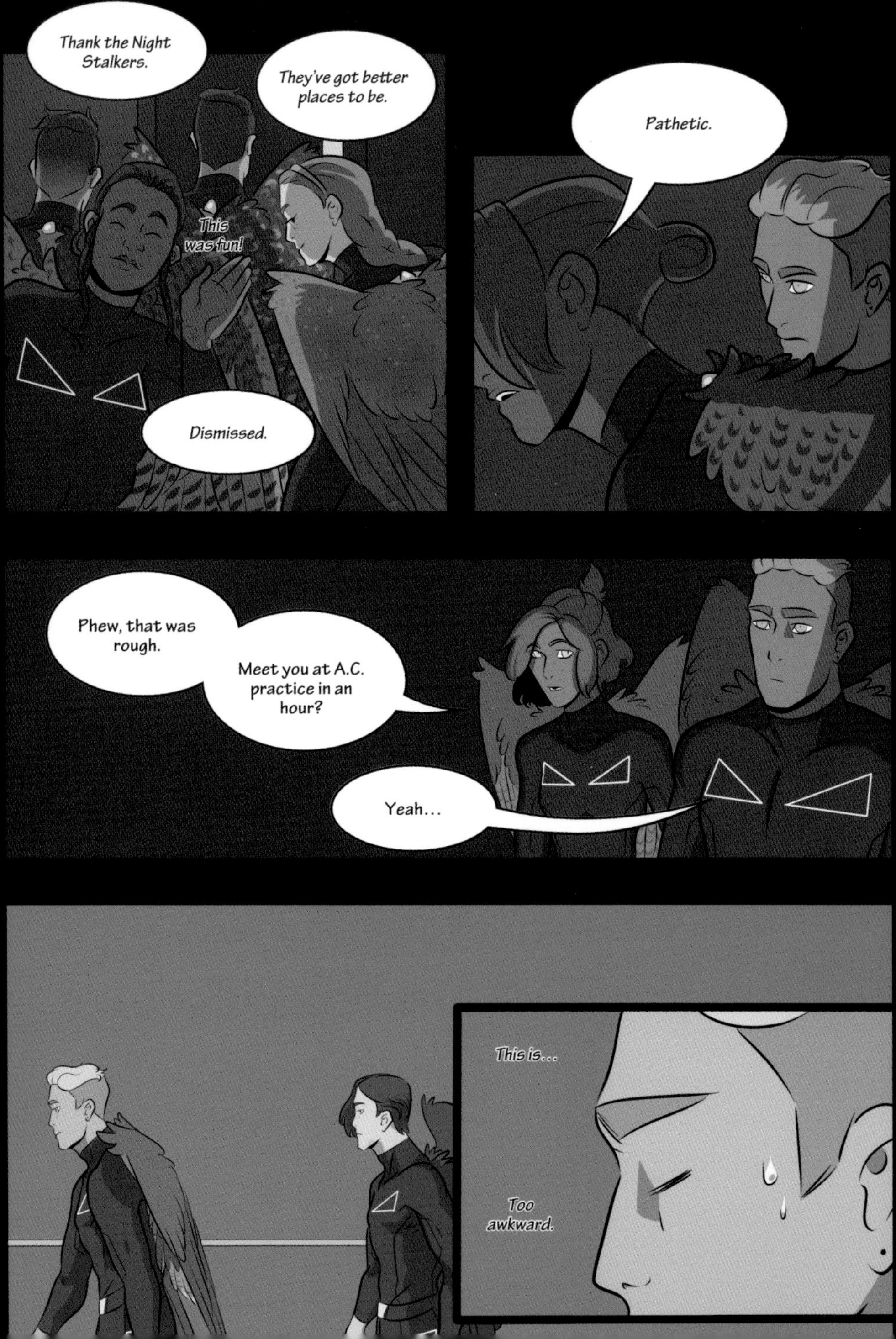
Thank the Night Stalkers.
They've got better places to be.
This was fun!
Dismissed.
Pathetic.
Phew, that was rough.
Meet you at A.C. practice in an hour?
Yeah...
This is...
Too awkward.

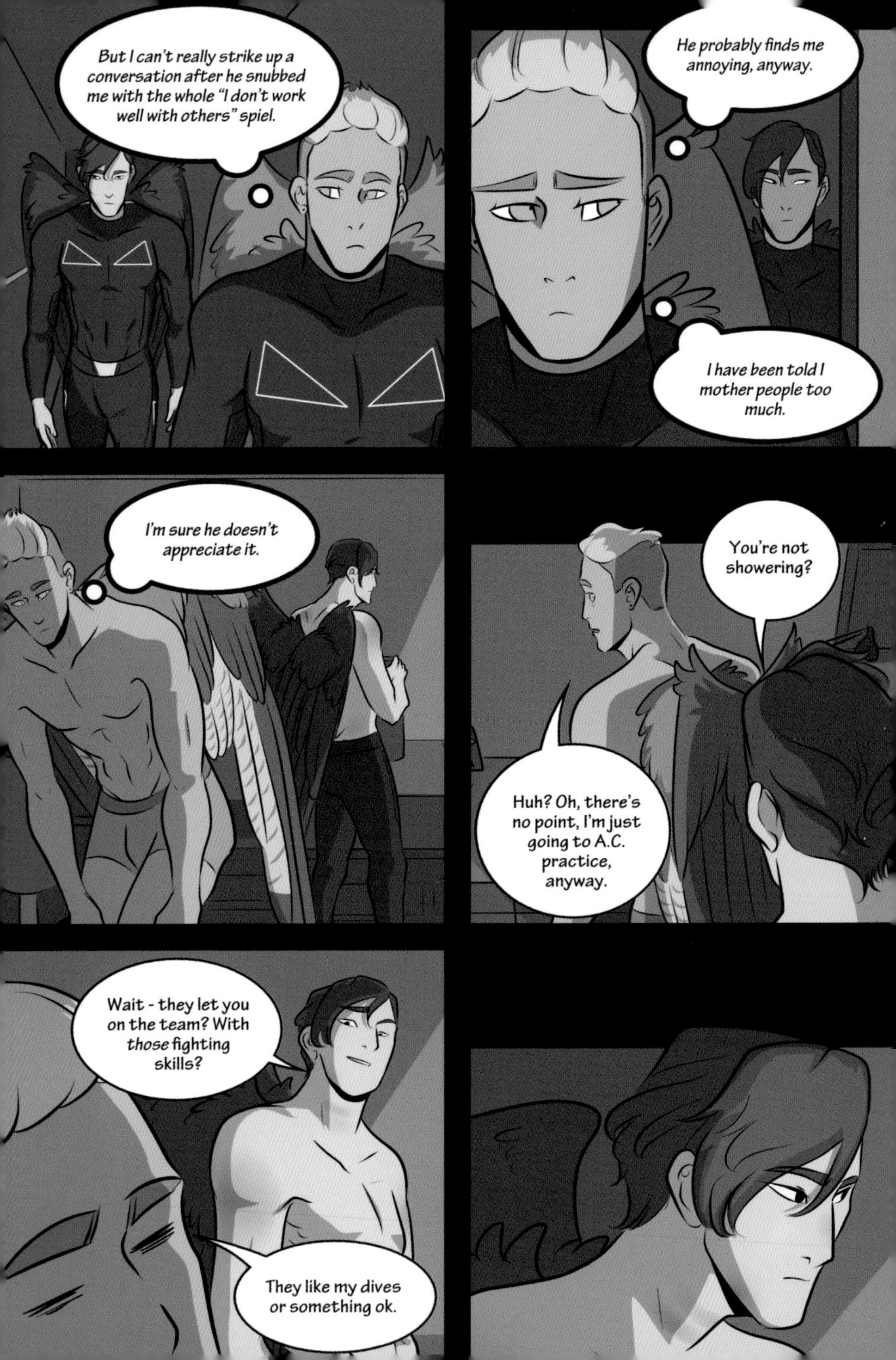
But I can't really strike up a conversation after he snubbed me with the whole "I don't work well with others" spiel.
He probably finds me annoying, anyway.
I have been told I mother people too much.
I'm sure he doesn't appreciate it.
You're not showering?
Huh? Oh, there's no point, I'm just going to A.C. practice, anyway.
Wait - they let you on the team? With *those* fighting skills?
They like my dives or something ok.

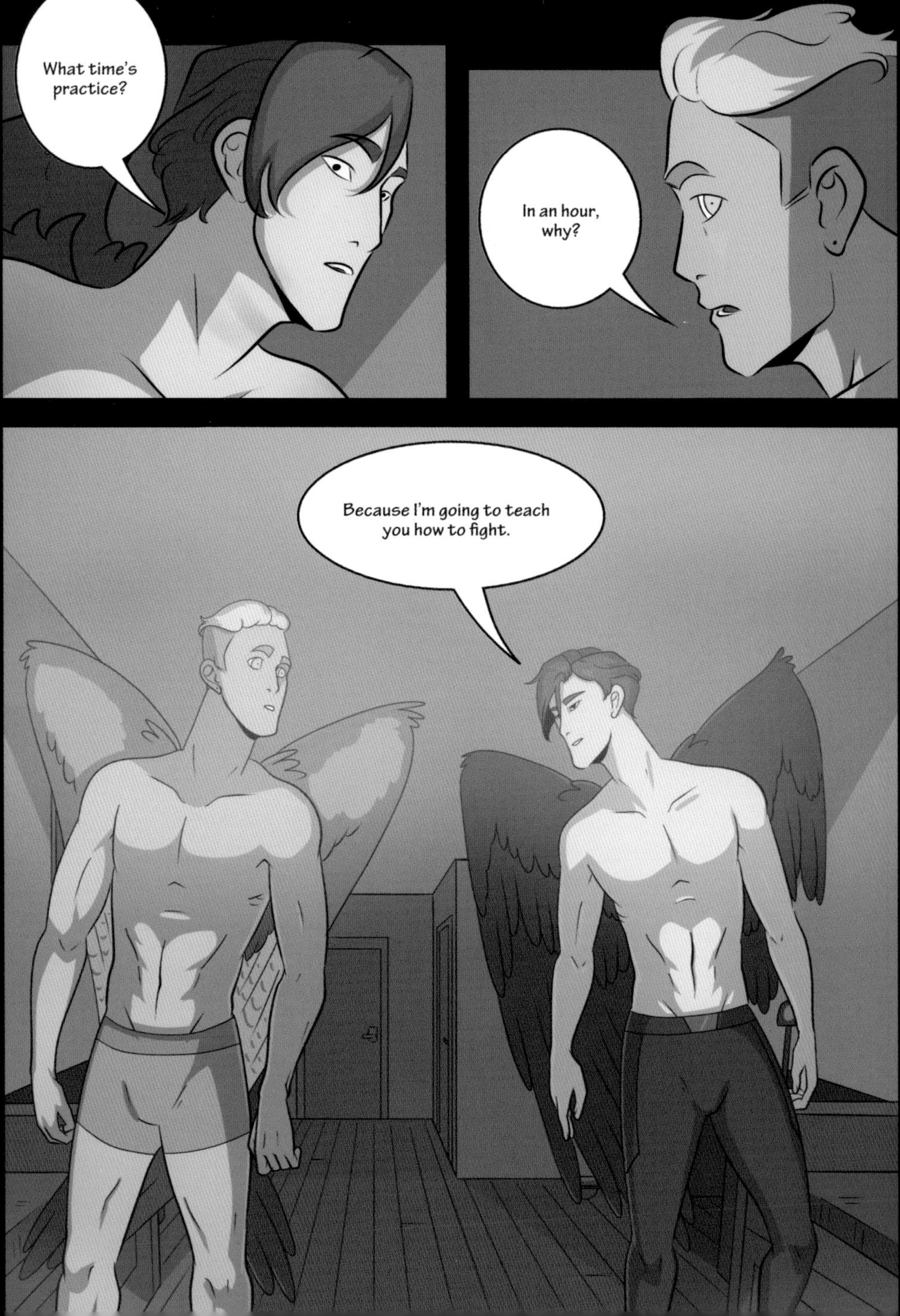
What time's practice?
In an hour, why?
Because I'm going to teach you how to fight.

THE CROAKING

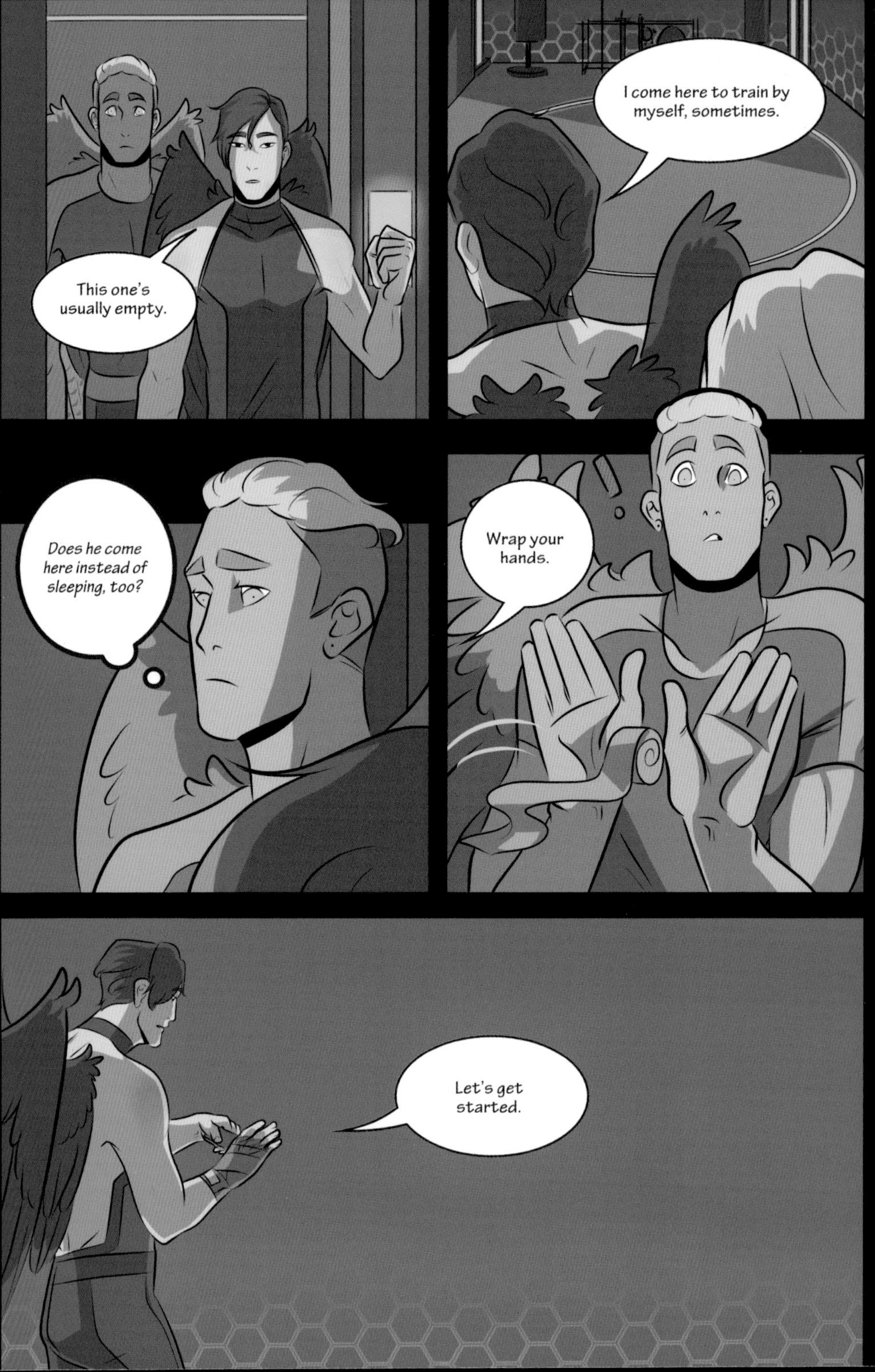
This one's usually empty.
I come here to train by myself, sometimes.
Does he come here instead of sleeping, too?
Wrap your hands.
Let's get started.

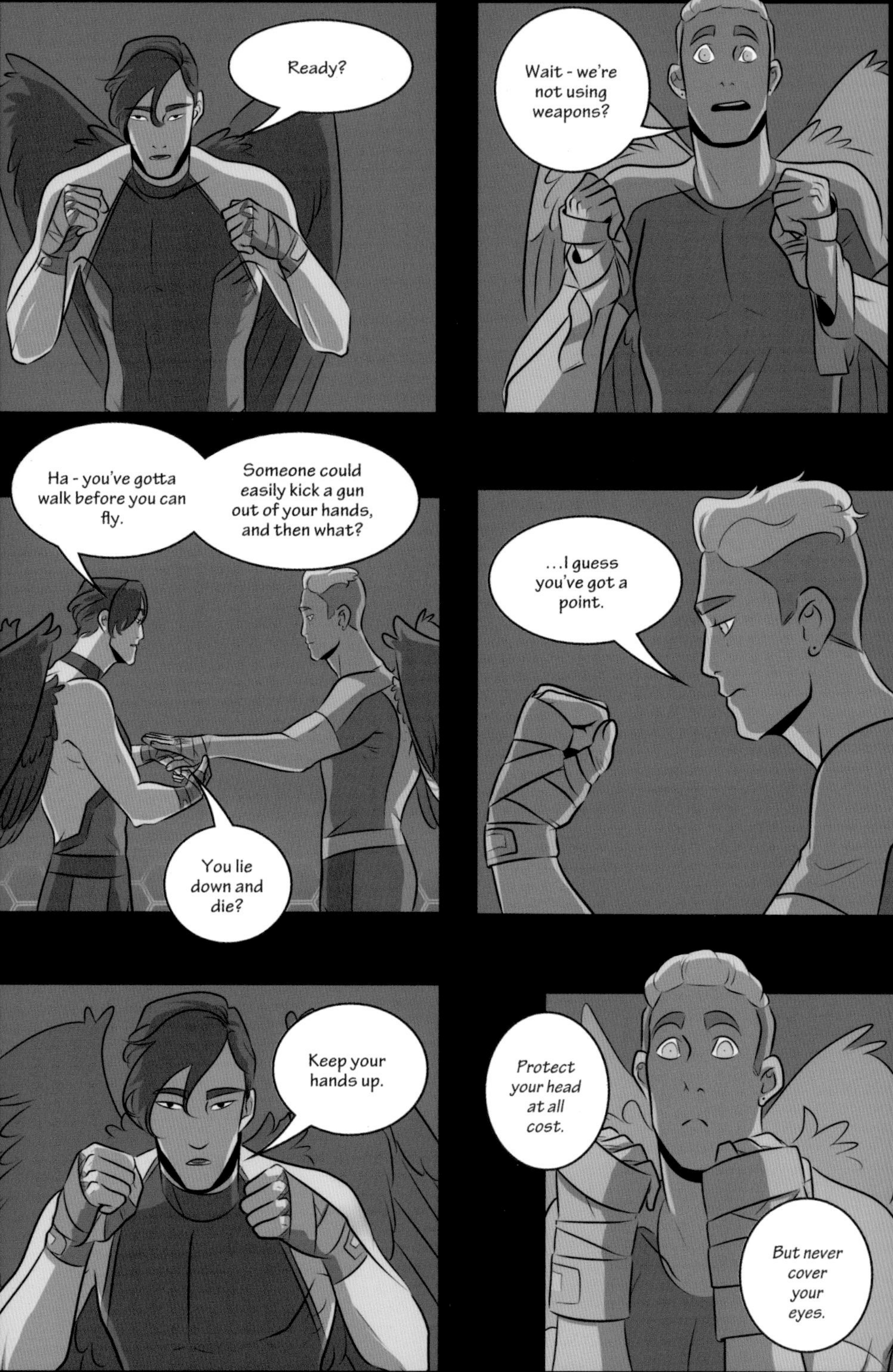
Ready?
Wait - we're not using weapons?
Ha - you've gotta walk before you can fly.
Someone could easily kick a gun out of your hands, and then what?
You lie down and die?
...I guess you've got a point.
Keep your hands up.
Protect your head at all cost.
But never cover your eyes.

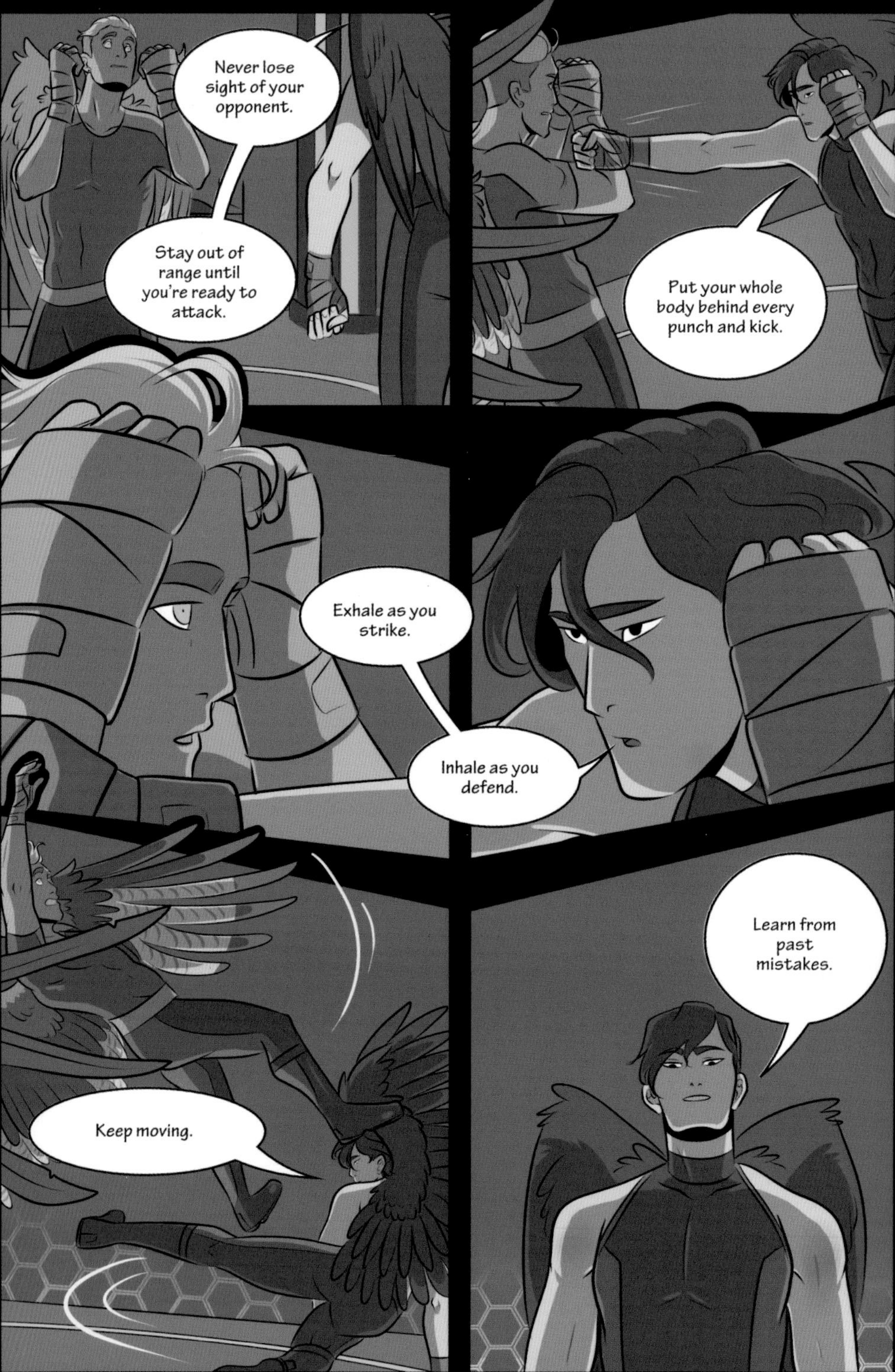
Never lose sight of your opponent.
Stay out of range until you're ready to attack.
Put your whole body behind every punch and kick.
Exhale as you strike.
Inhale as you defend.
Keep moving.
Learn from past mistakes.

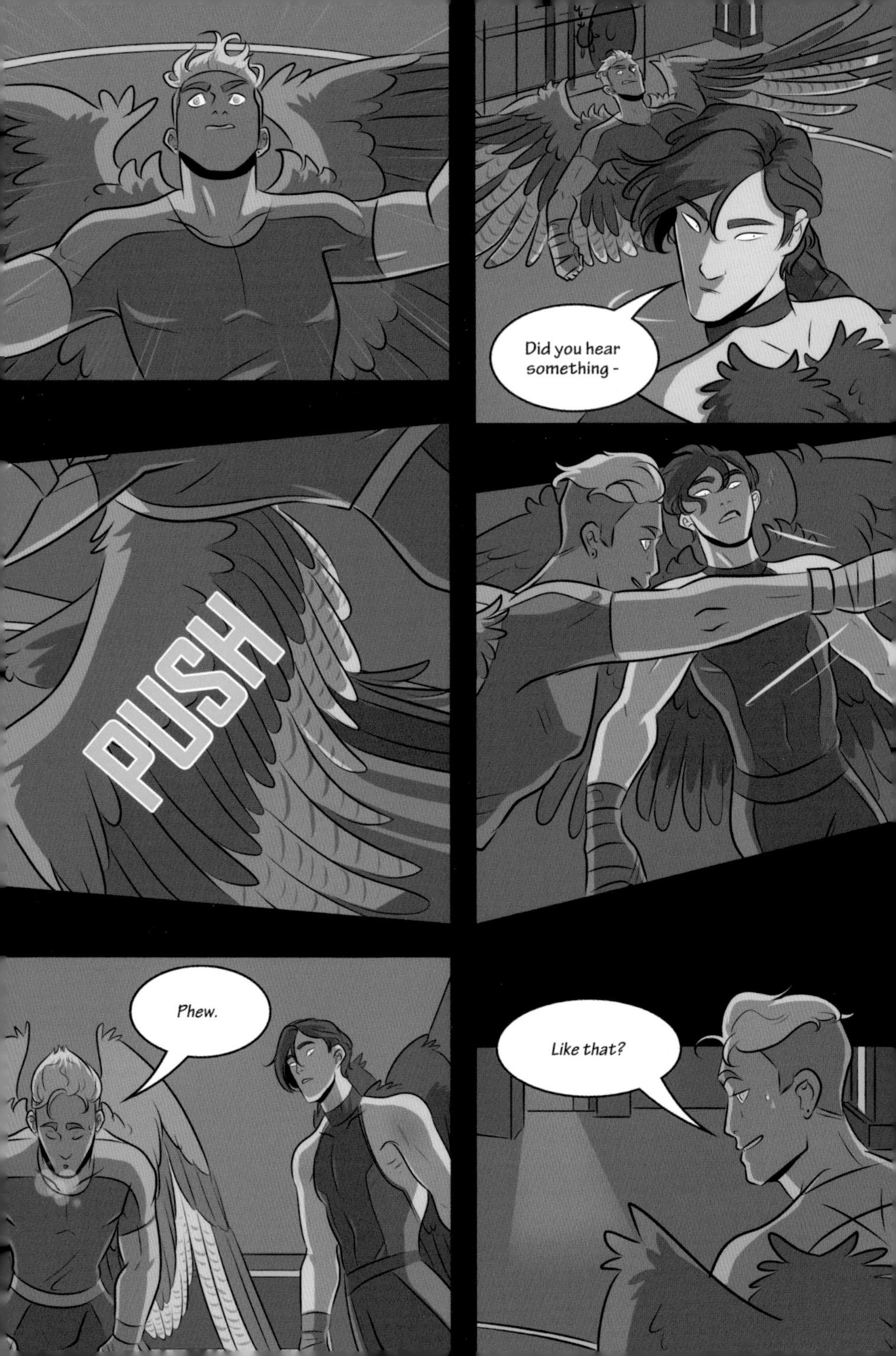
Did you hear something -
PUSH
Phew.
Like that?

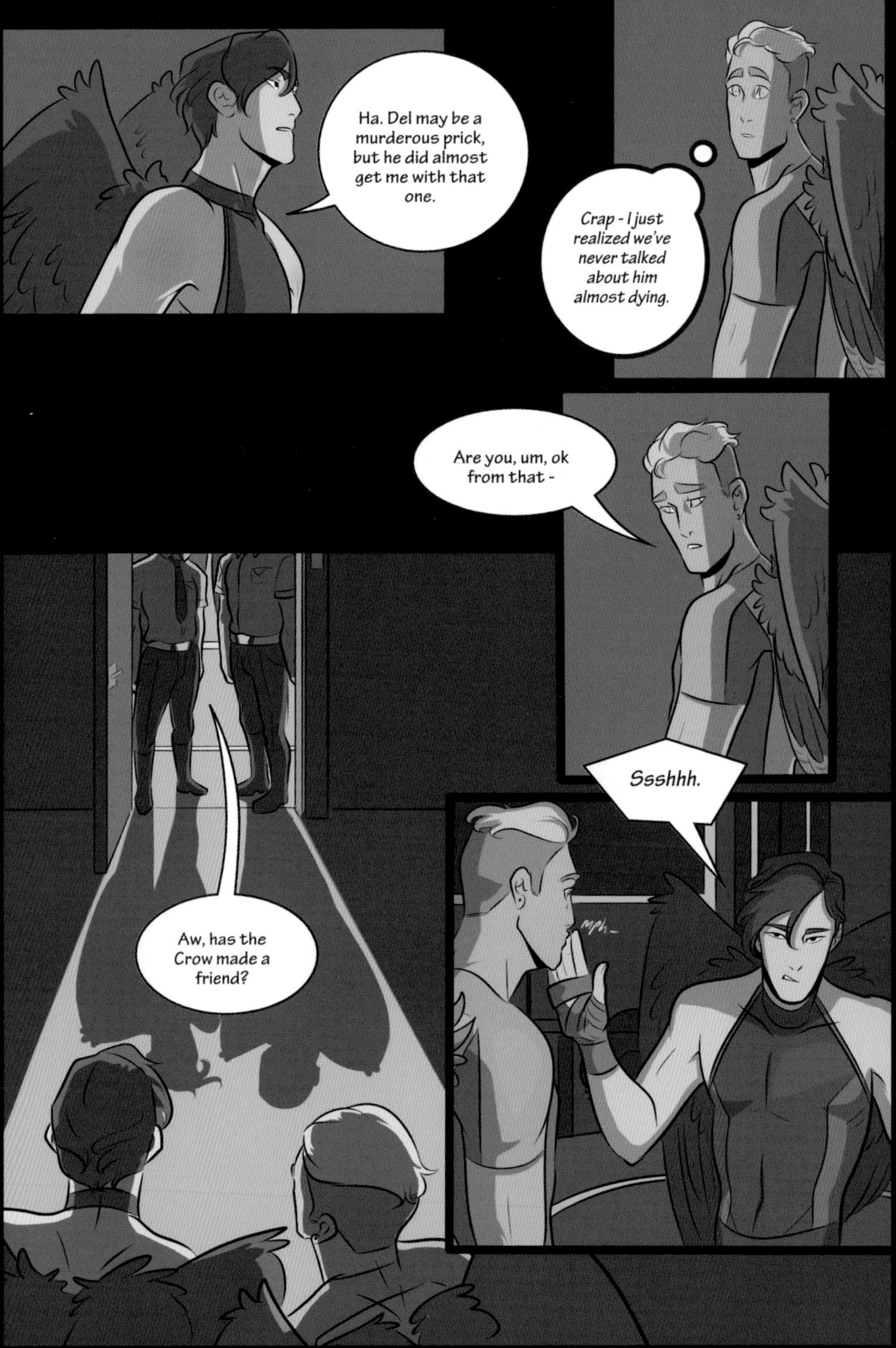
Ha. Del may be a murderous prick, but he did almost get me with that one.
Crap - I just realized we've never talked about him almost dying.
Are you, um, ok from that -
Aw, has the Crow made a friend?
Ssshhh.
mph-

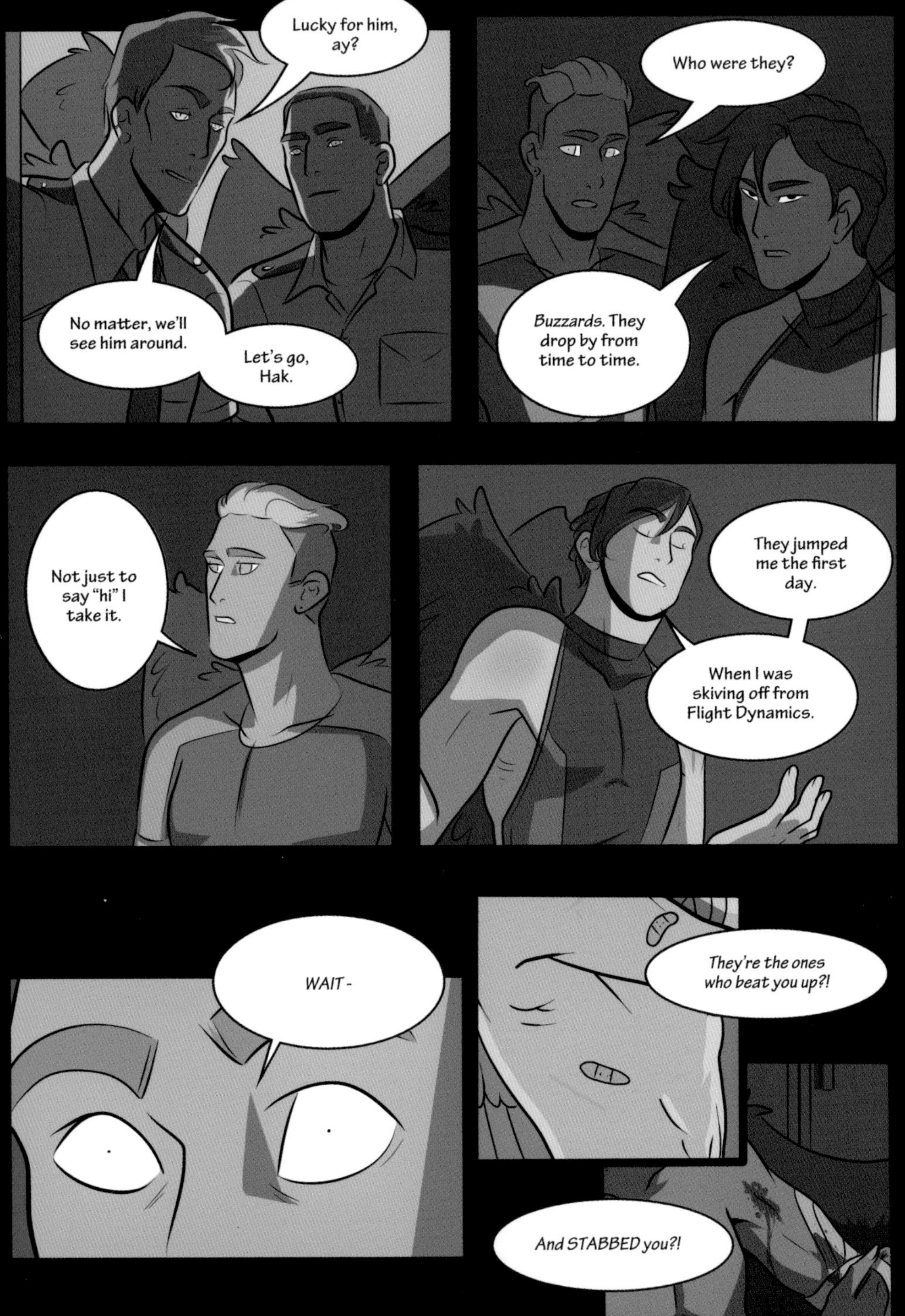
Lucky for him, ay?
No matter, we'll see him around.
Let's go, Hak.
Who were they?
Buzzards. They drop by from time to time.
Not just to say "hi" I take it.
They jumped me the first day.
When I was skiving off from Flight Dynamics.
WAIT -
They're the ones who beat you up?!
And STABBED you?!

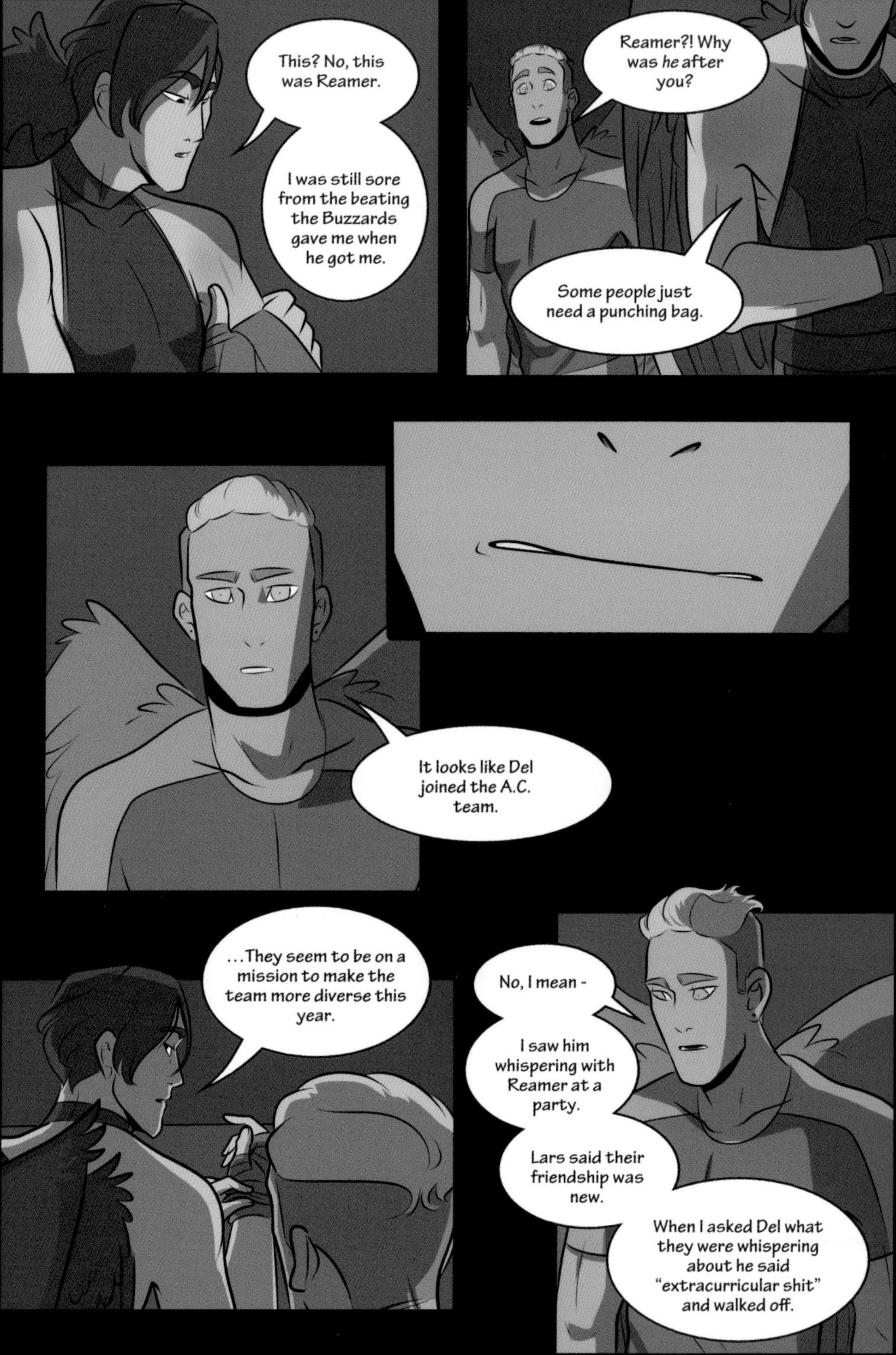
This? No, this was Reamer.
I was still sore from the beating the Buzzards gave me when he got me.
Reamer?! Why was *he* after you?
Some people just need a punching bag.
It looks like Del joined the A.C. team.
...They seem to be on a mission to make the team more diverse this year.
No, I mean -
I saw him whispering with Reamer at a party.
Lars said their friendship was new.
When I asked Del what they were whispering about he said "extracurricular shit" and walked off.

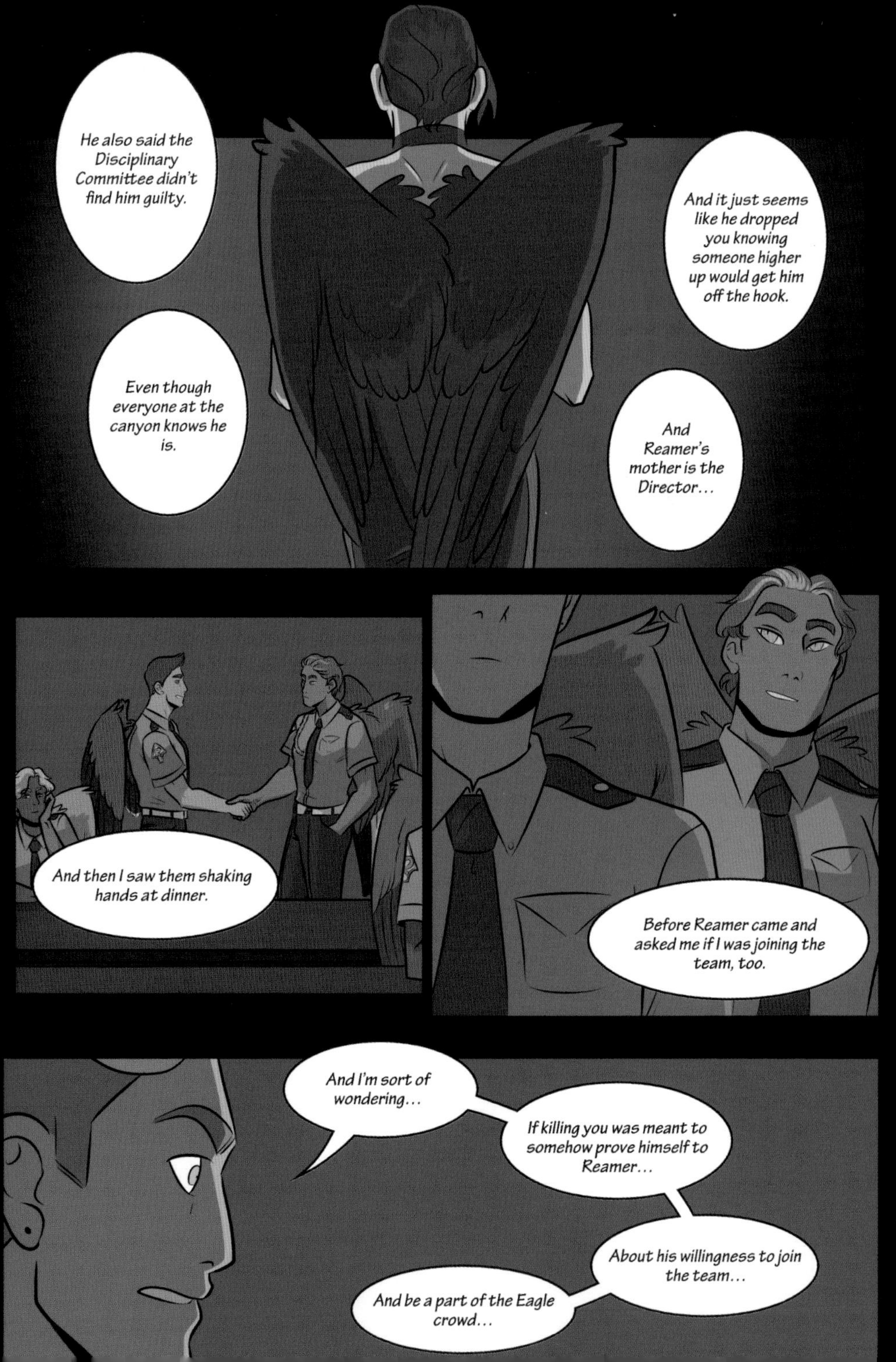
He also said the Disciplinary Committee didn't find him guilty.
Even though everyone at the canyon knows he is.
And it just seems like he dropped you knowing someone higher up would get him off the hook.
And Reamer's mother is the Director...
And then I saw them shaking hands at dinner.
Before Reamer came and asked me if I was joining the team, too.
And I'm sort of wondering...
If killing you was meant to somehow prove himself to Reamer...
About his willingness to join the team...
And be a part of the Eagle crowd...

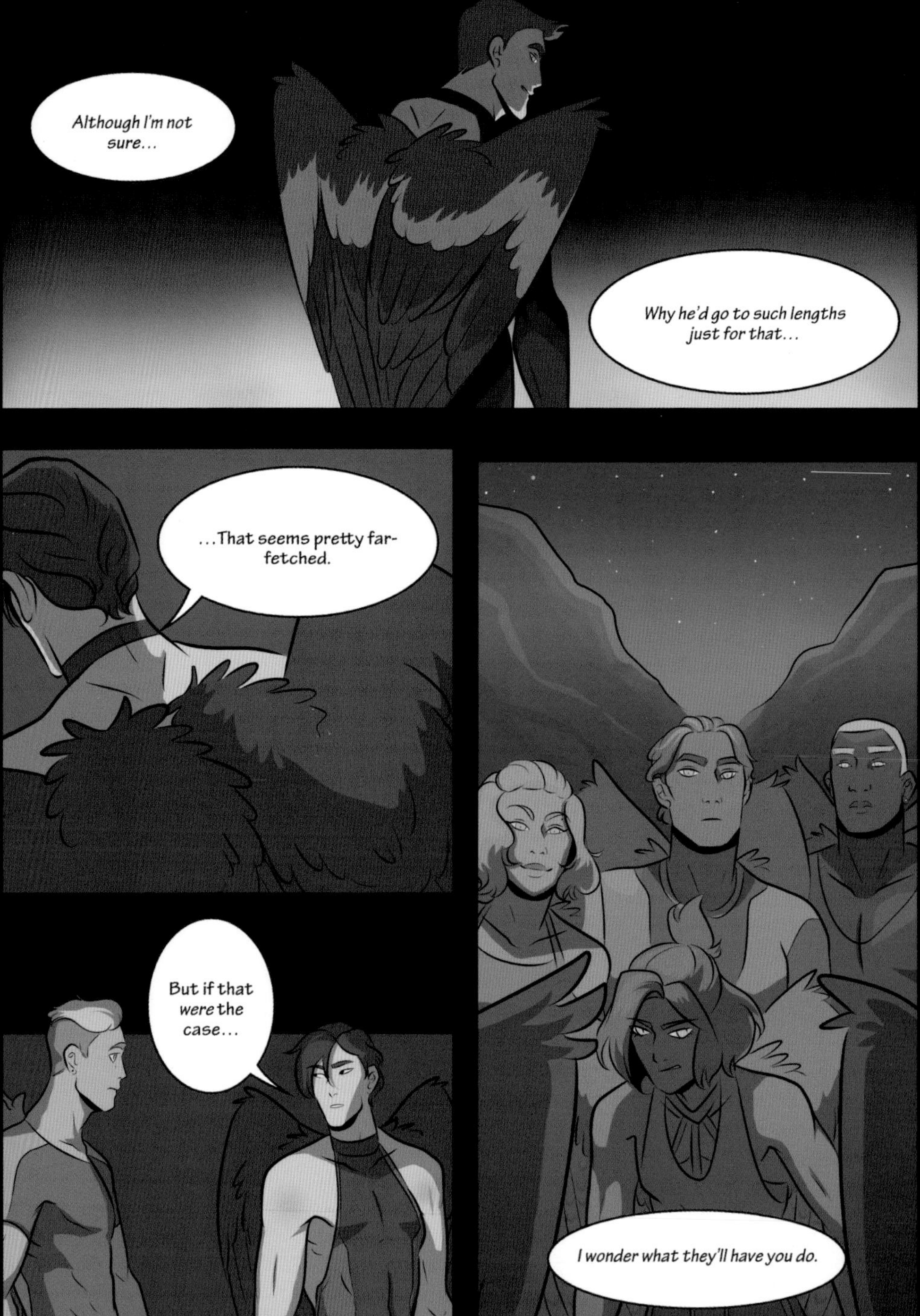
Although I'm not sure...
Why he'd go to such lengths just for that...
...That seems pretty far-fetched.
But if that were the case...
I wonder what they'll have you do.

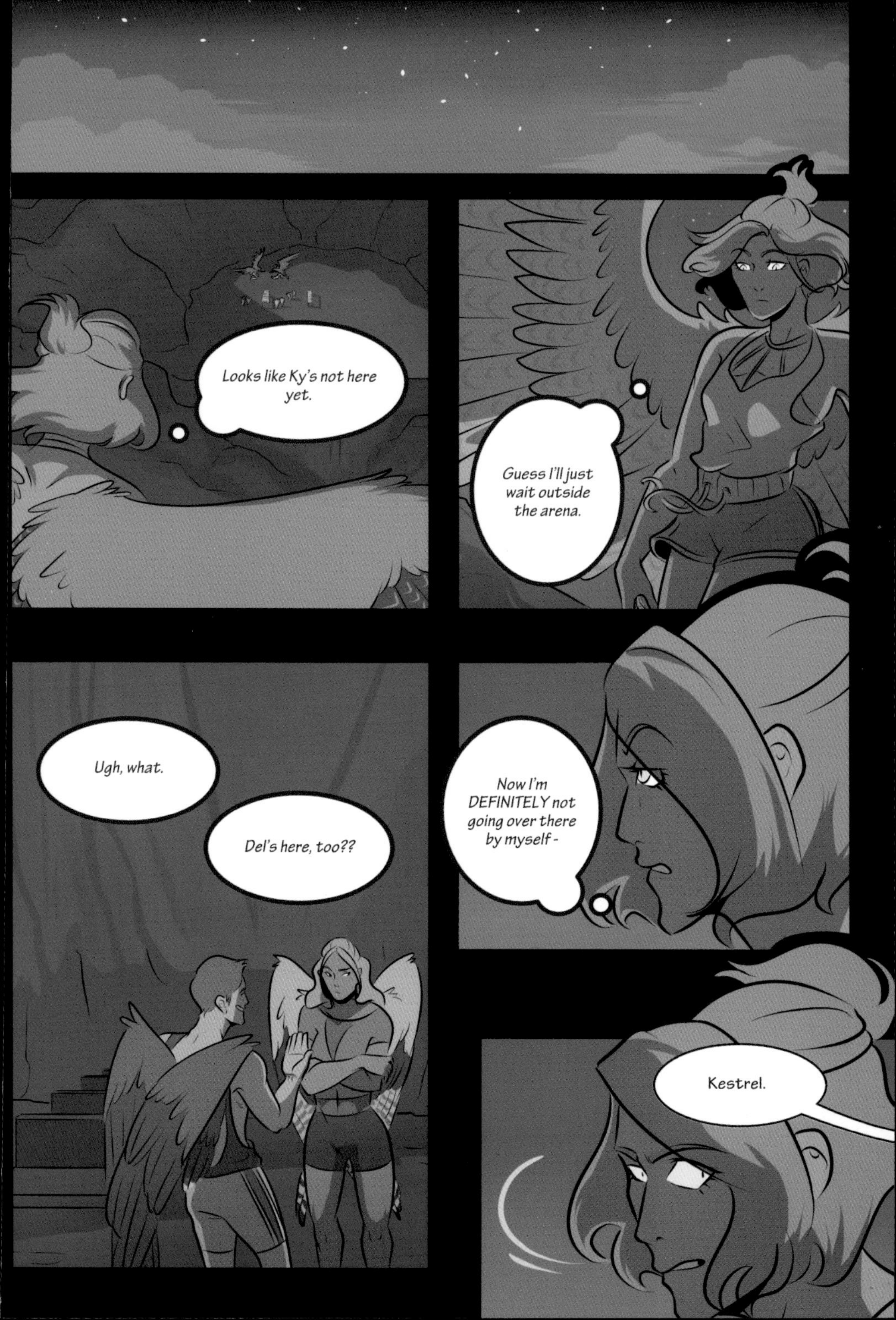
Looks like Ky's not here yet.
Guess I'll just wait outside the arena.
Ugh, what.
Del's here, too??
Now I'm DEFINITELY not going over there by myself -
Kestrel.

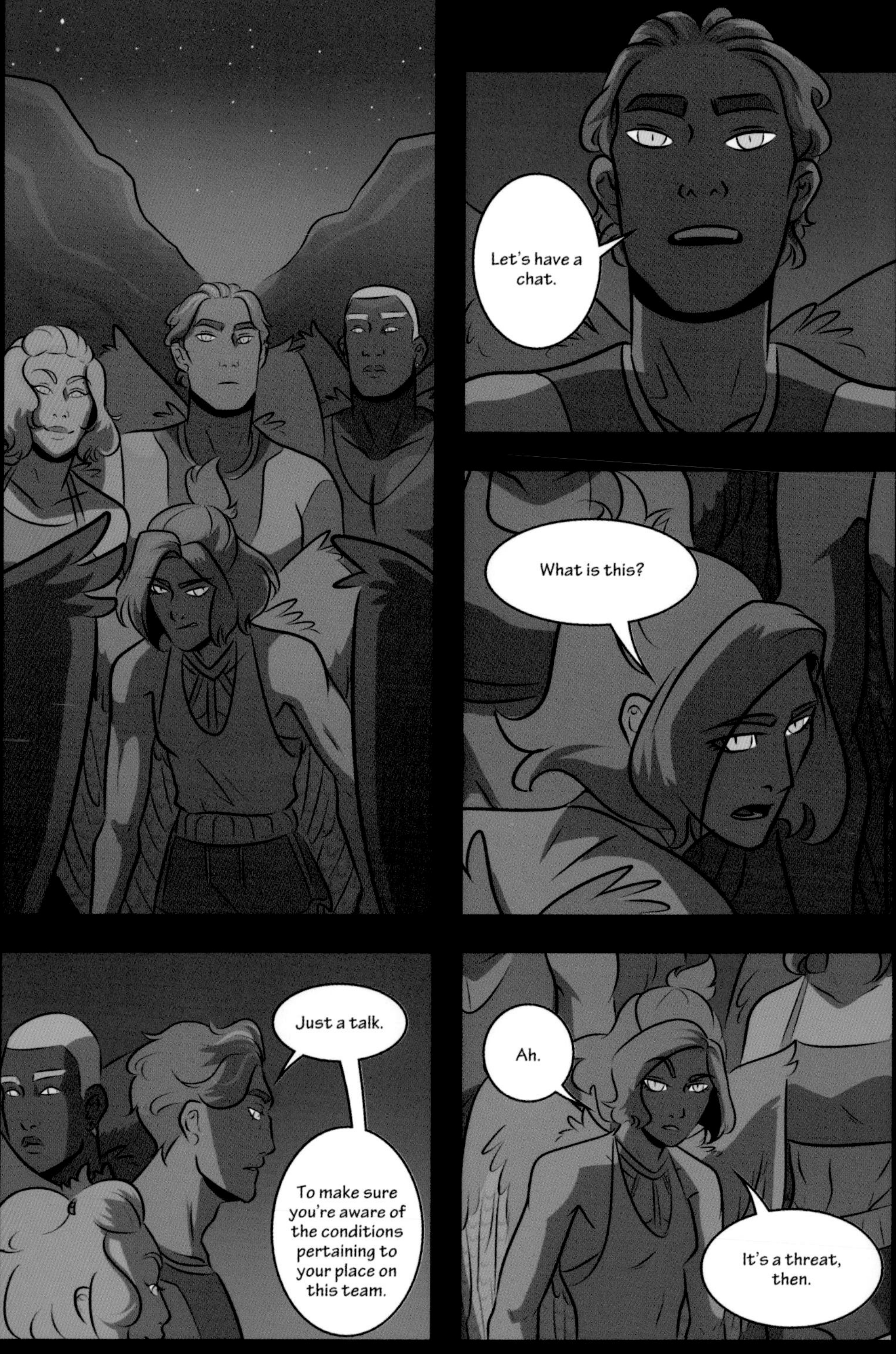
Let's have a chat.
What is this?
Just a talk.
To make sure you're aware of the conditions pertaining to your place on this team.
Ah.
It's a threat, then.

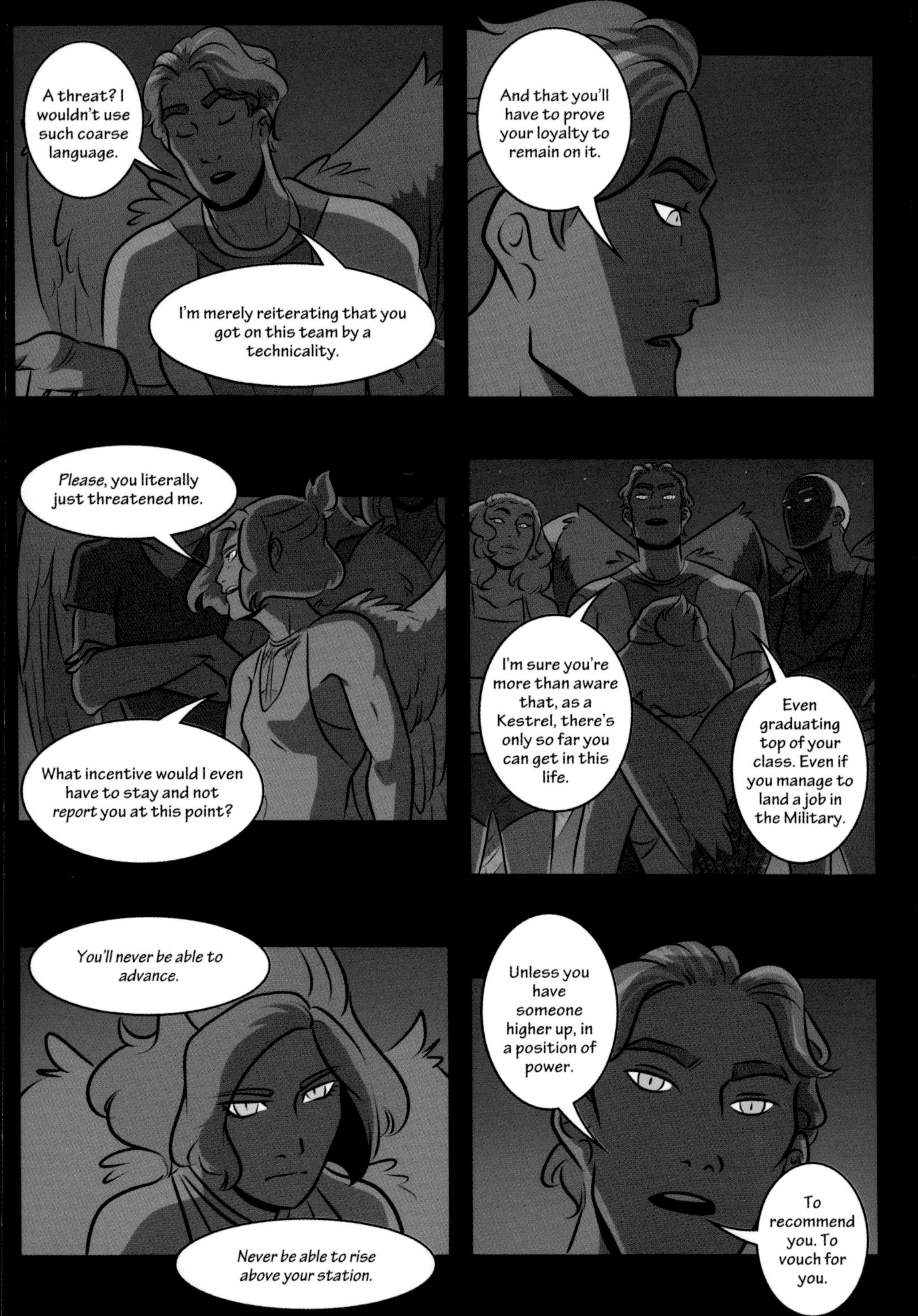
A threat? I wouldn't use such coarse language.
I'm merely reiterating that you got on this team by a technicality.
And that you'll have to prove your loyalty to remain on it.
Please, you literally just threatened me.
What incentive would I even have to stay and not *report* you at this point?
I'm sure you're more than aware that, as a Kestrel, there's only so far you can get in this life.
Even graduating top of your class. Even if you manage to land a job in the Military.
You'll never be able to advance.
Never be able to rise above your station.
Unless you have someone higher up, in a position of power.
To recommend you. To vouch for you.

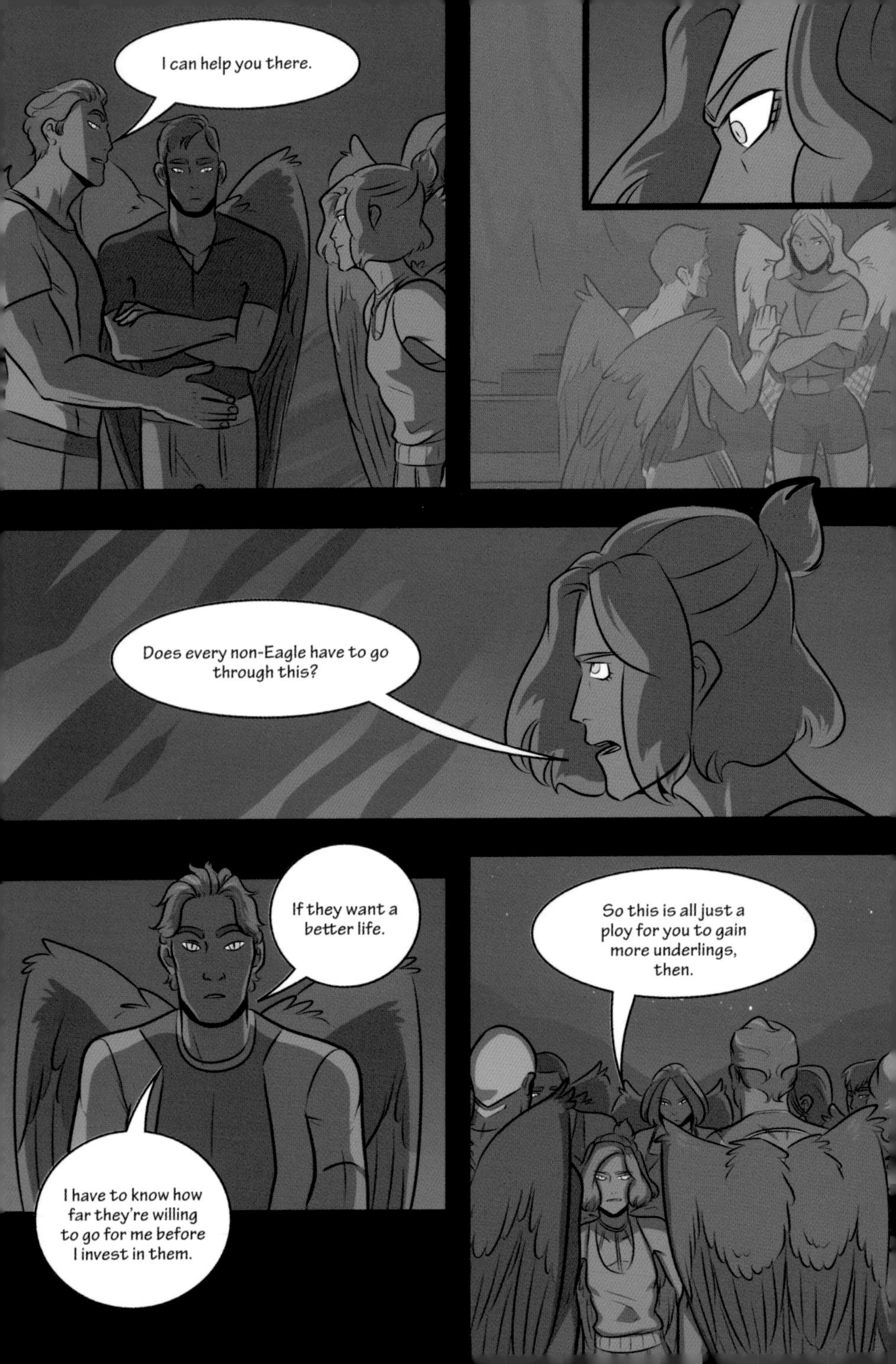
I can help you there.
Does every non-Eagle have to go through this?
If they want a better life.
I have to know how far they're willing to go for me before I invest in them.
So this is all just a ploy for you to gain more underlings, then.

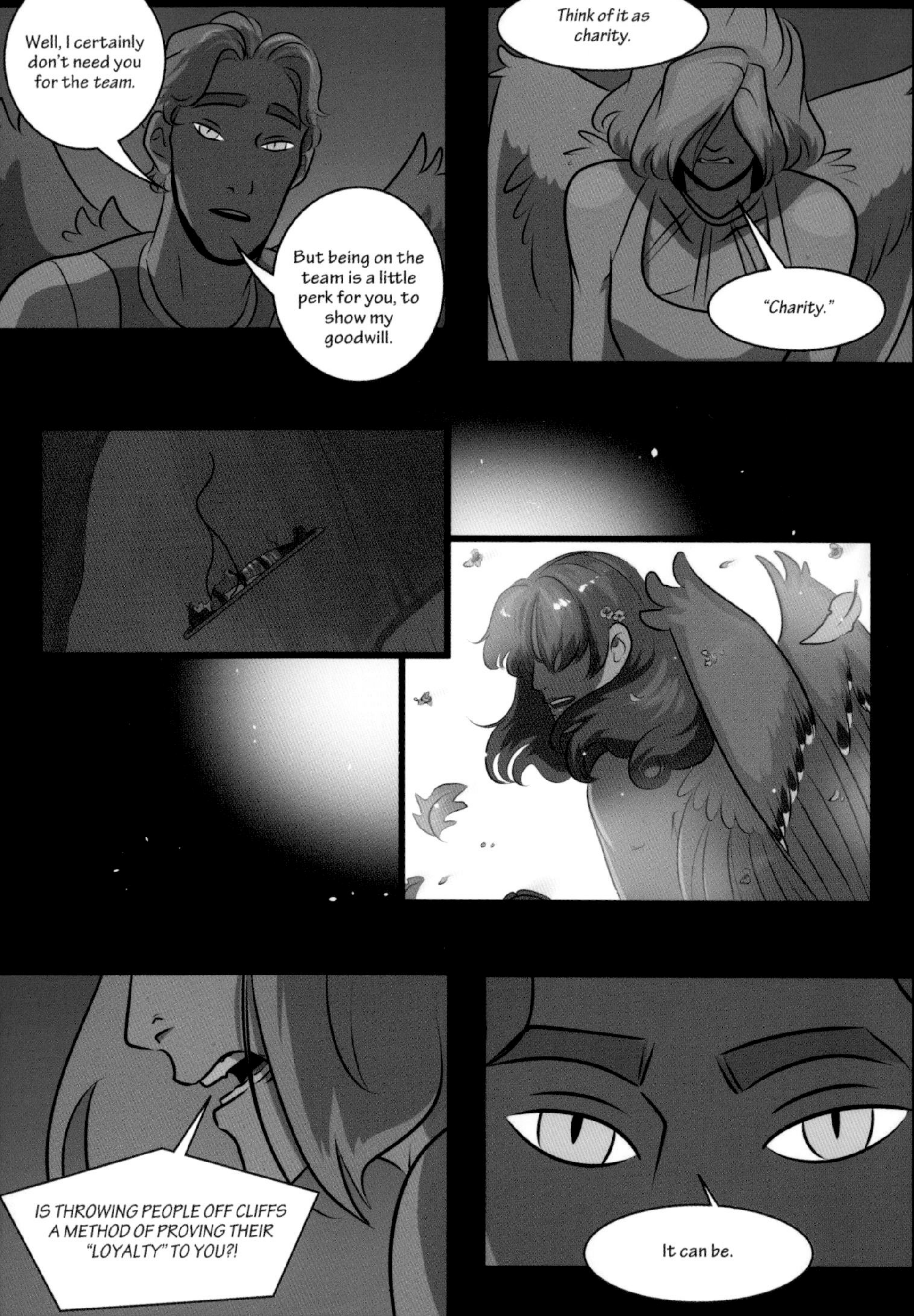
Well, I certainly don't need you for the team.
But being on the team is a little perk for you, to show my goodwill.
Think of it as charity.
"Charity."
IS THROWING PEOPLE OFF CLIFFS A METHOD OF PROVING THEIR "LOYALTY" TO YOU?!
It can be.

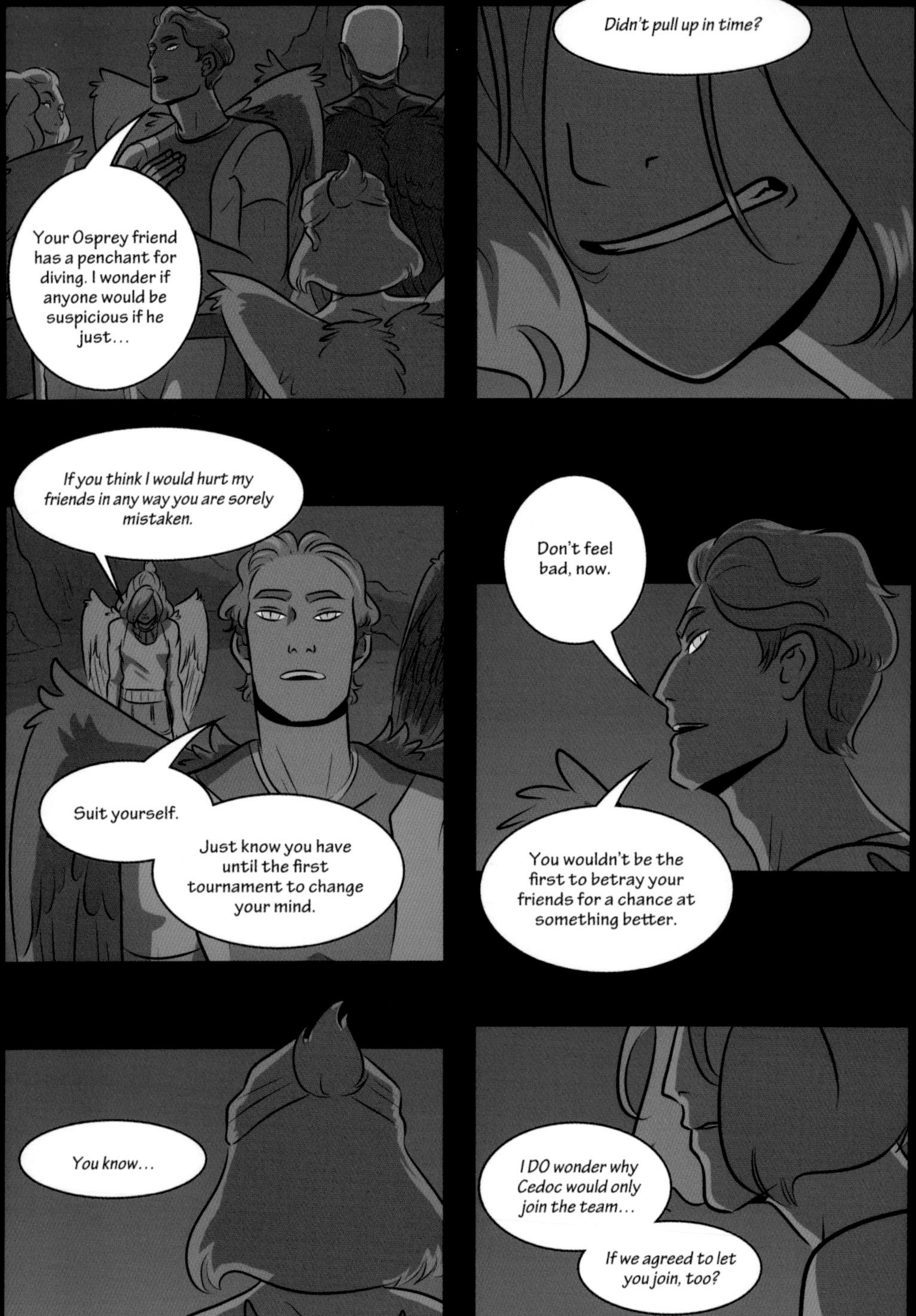

Your Osprey friend has a penchant for diving. I wonder if anyone would be suspicious if he just...
Didn't pull up in time?
If you think I would hurt my friends in any way you are sorely mistaken.
Suit yourself.
Just know you have until the first tournament to change your mind.
Don't feel bad, now.
You wouldn't be the first to betray your friends for a chance at something better.
You know...
I DO wonder why Cedoc would only join the team...
If we agreed to let you join, too?

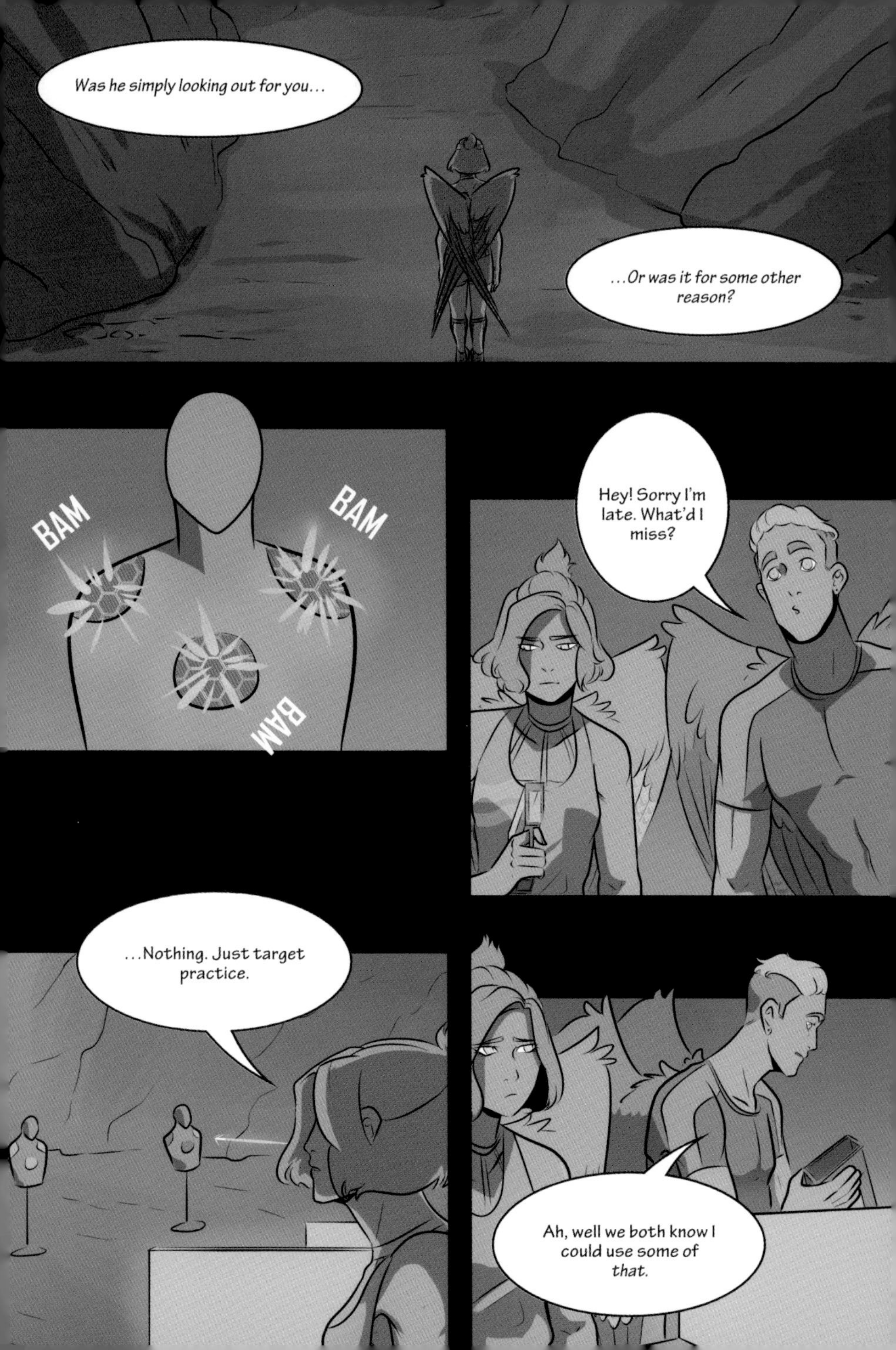
Was he simply looking out for you...
...Or was it for some other reason?
BAM
BAM
BAM
Hey! Sorry I'm late. What'd I miss?
...Nothing. Just target practice.
Ah, well we both know I could use some of that.

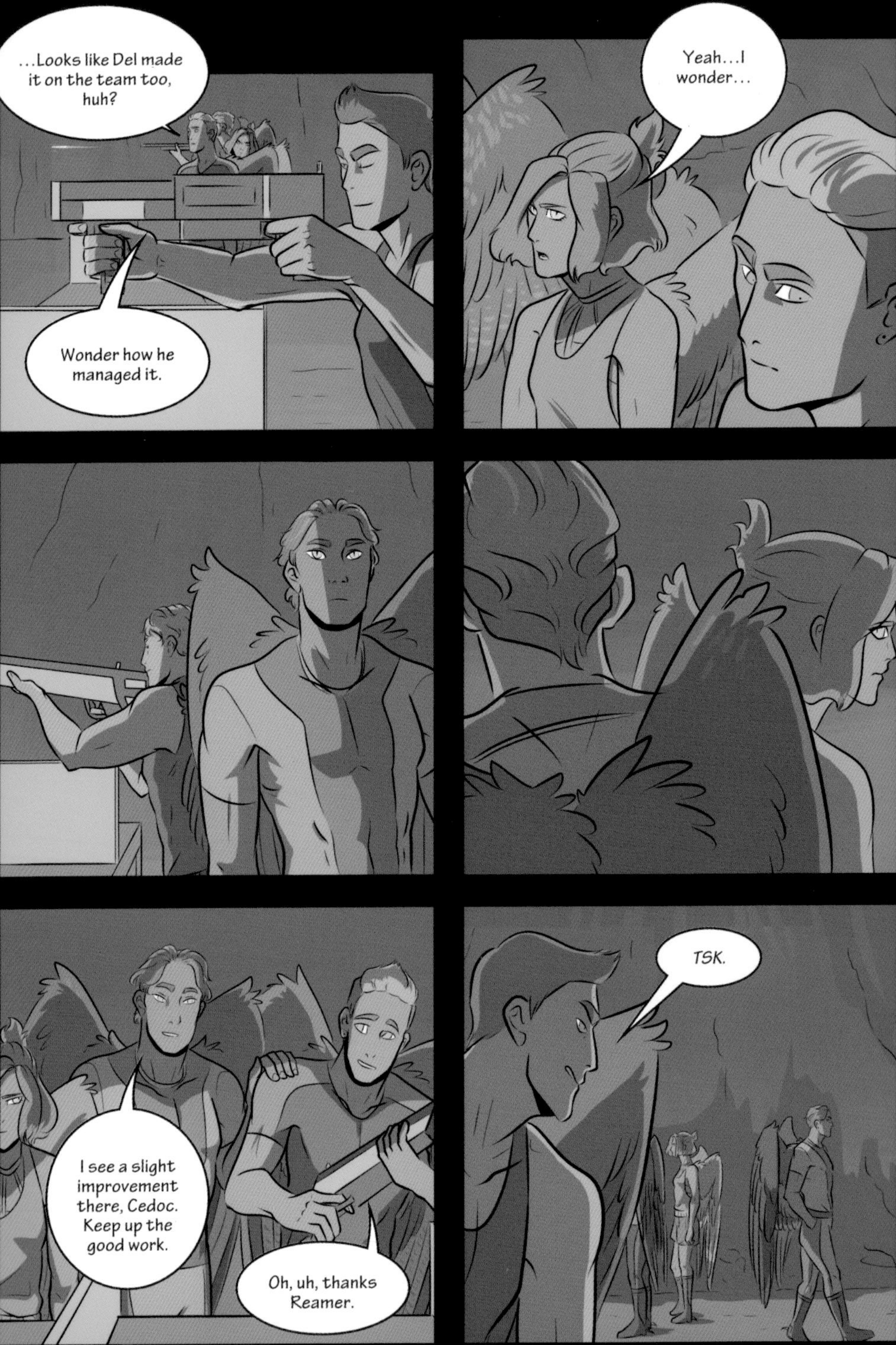
...Looks like Del made it on the team too, huh?
Wonder how he managed it.
Yeah...I wonder...
I see a slight improvement there, Cedoc. Keep up the good work.
Oh, uh, thanks Reamer.
TSK.

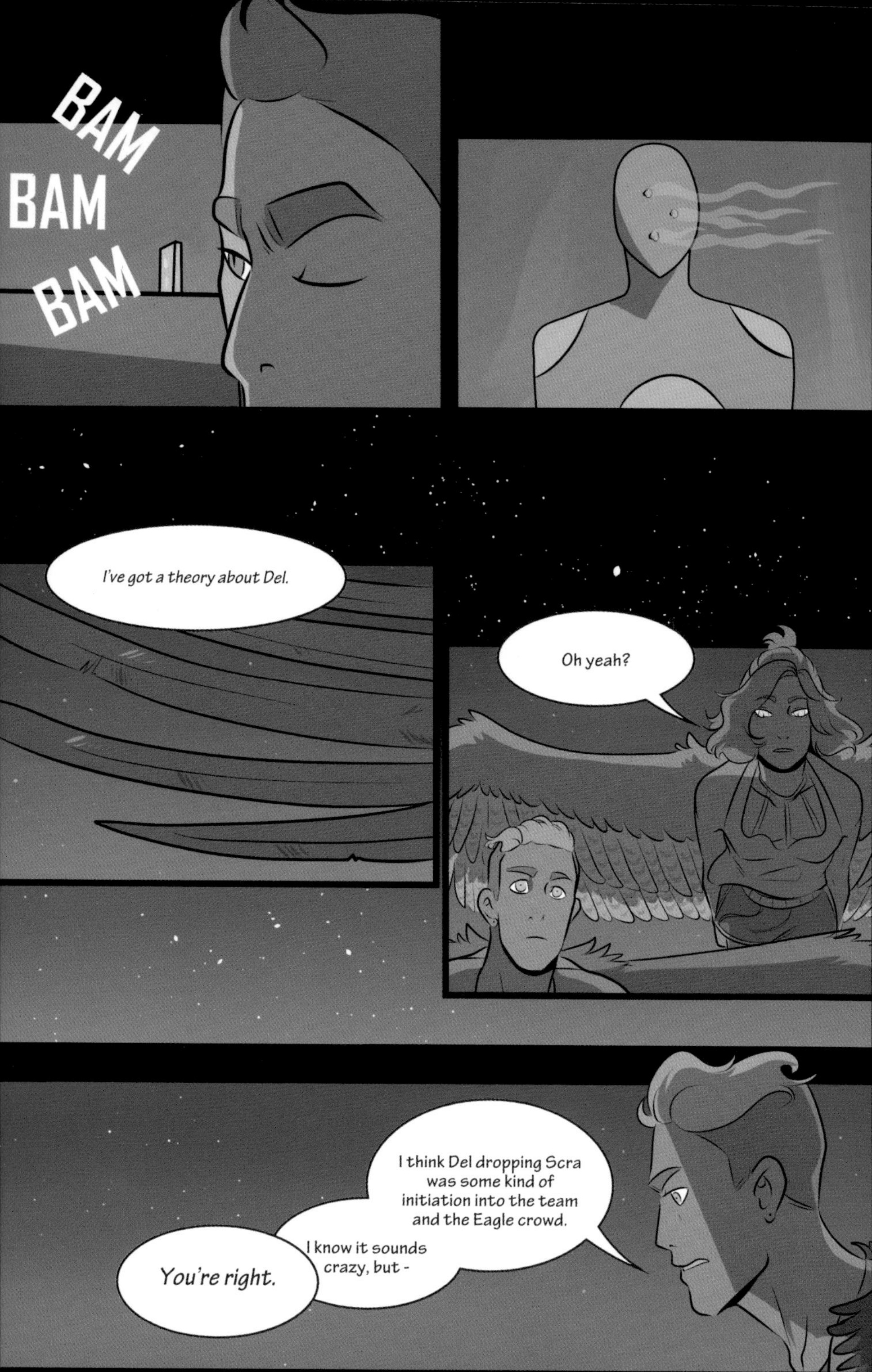
BAM
BAM
BAM
I've got a theory about Del.
Oh yeah?
I think Del dropping Scra was some kind of initiation into the team and the Eagle crowd.
I know it sounds crazy, but -
You're right.

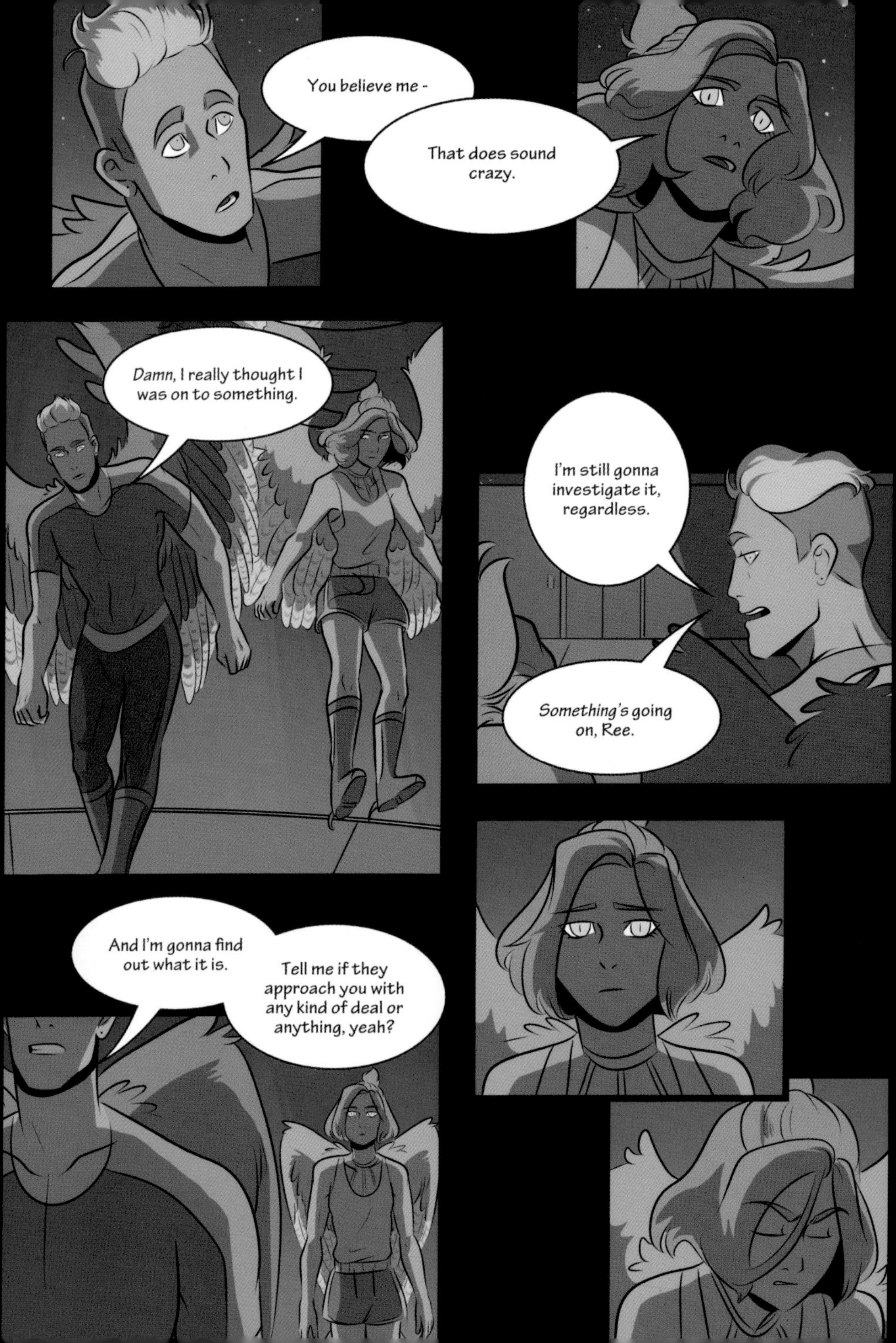
You believe me -
That does sound crazy.
Damn, I really thought I was on to something.
I'm still gonna investigate it, regardless.
Something's going on, Ree.
And I'm gonna find out what it is.
Tell me if they approach you with any kind of deal or anything, yeah?

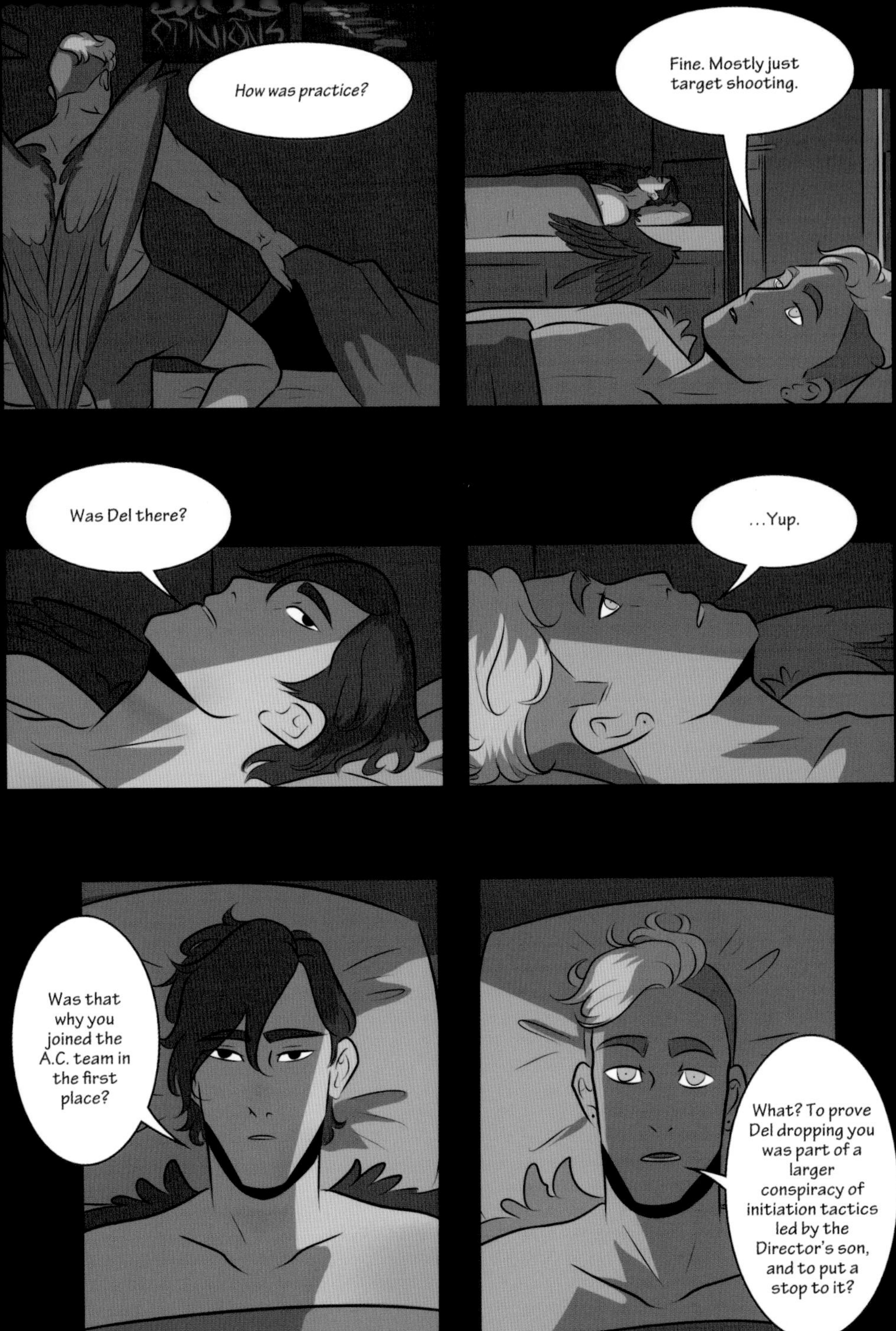

OPINIONS
How was practice?
Fine. Mostly just target shooting.
Was Del there?
...Yup.
Was that why you joined the A.C. team in the first place?
What? To prove Del dropping you was part of a larger conspiracy of initiation tactics led by the Director's son, and to put a stop to it?

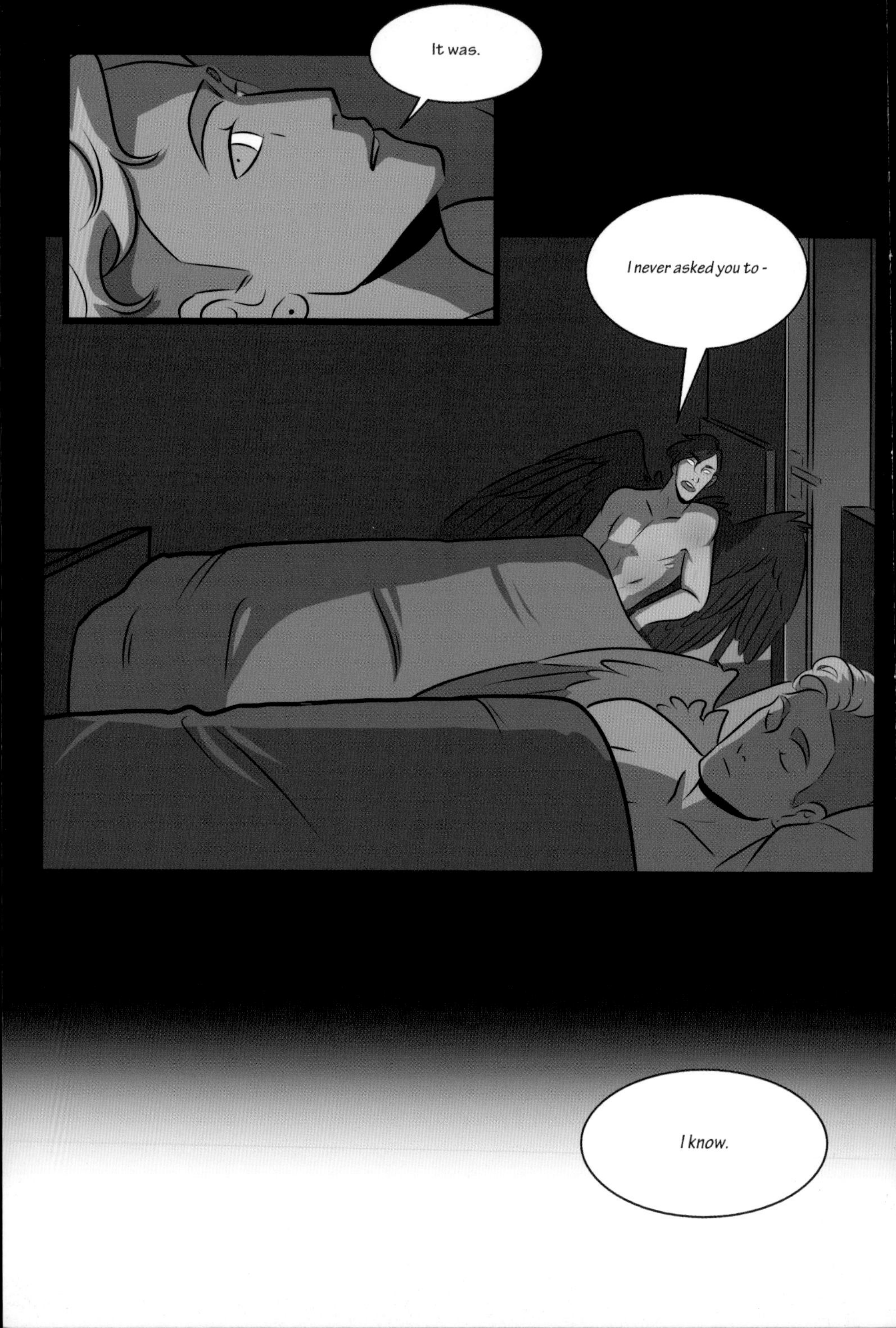
It was.
I never asked you to -
I know.

THE CROAKING

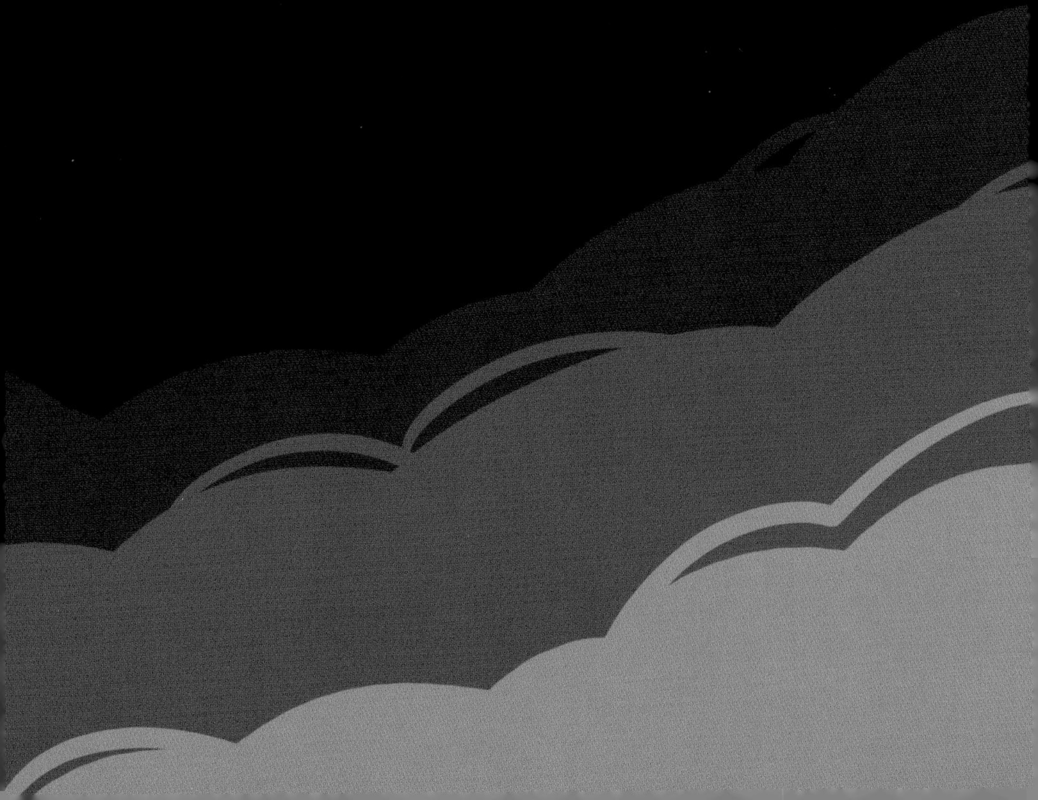

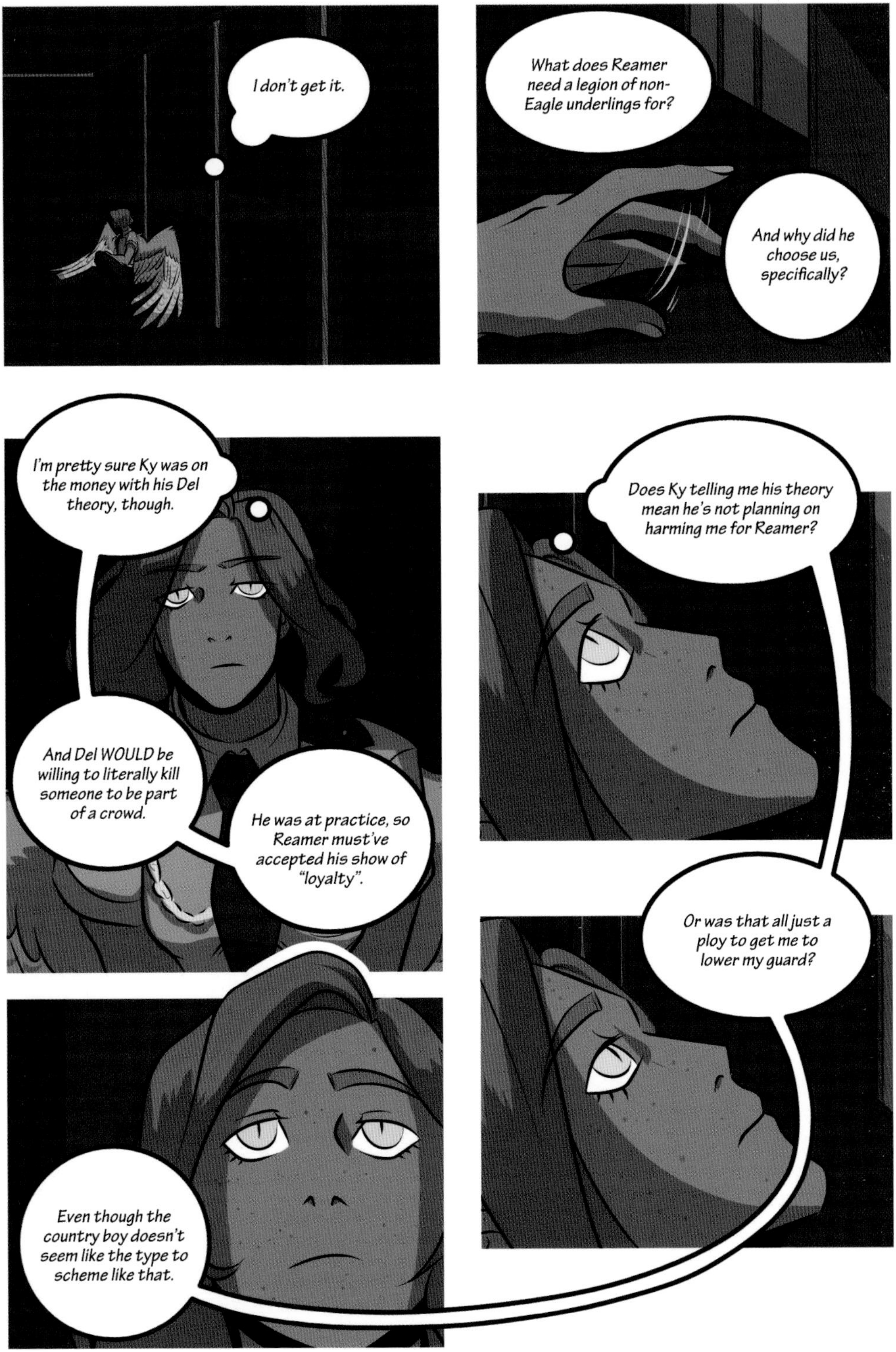
I don't get it.
What does Reamer need a legion of non-Eagle underlings for?
And why did he choose us, specifically?
I'm pretty sure Ky was on the money with his Del theory, though.
And Del WOULD be willing to literally kill someone to be part of a crowd.
He was at practice, so Reamer must've accepted his show of "loyalty".
Does Ky telling me his theory mean he's not planning on harming me for Reamer?
Or was that all just a ploy to get me to lower my guard?
Even though the country boy doesn't seem like the type to scheme like that.

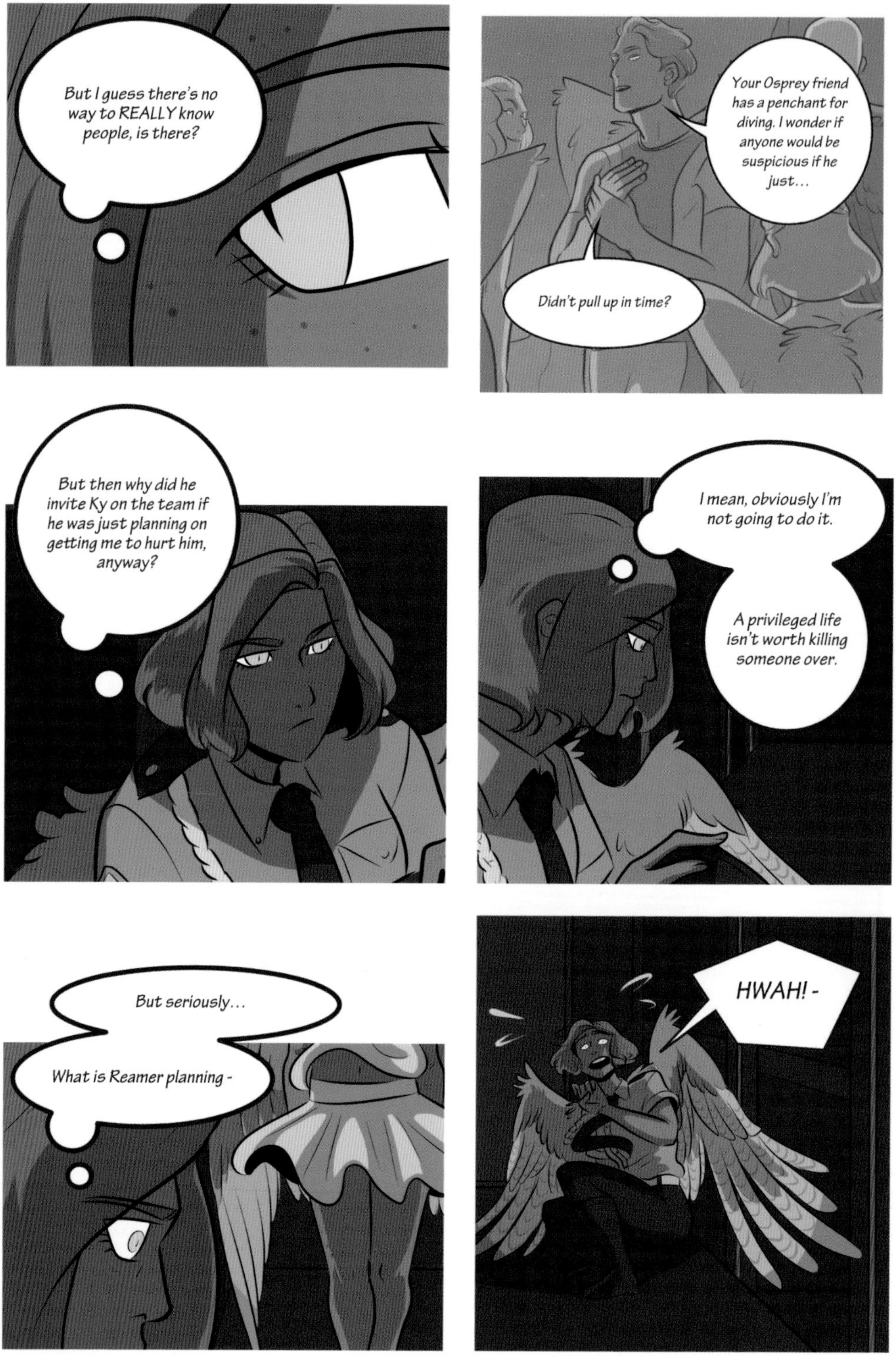
But I guess there's no way to REALLY know people, is there?
Your Osprey friend has a penchant for diving. I wonder if anyone would be suspicious if he just…
Didn't pull up in time?
But then why did he invite Ky on the team if he was just planning on getting me to hurt him, anyway?
I mean, obviously I'm not going to do it.
A privileged life isn't worth killing someone over.
But seriously…
What is Reamer planning -
HWAH! -

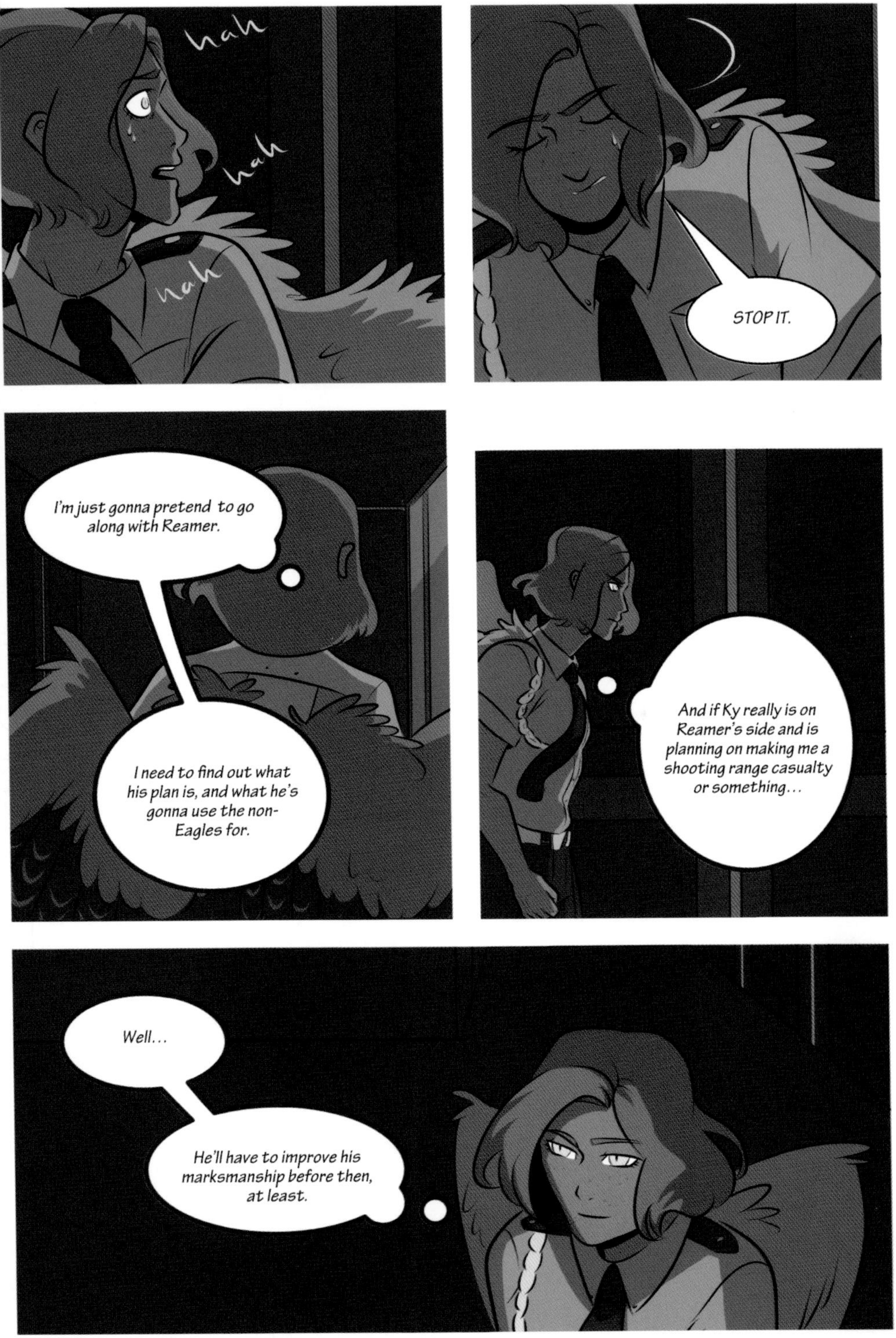
hah
hah
hah
STOP IT.
I'm just gonna pretend to go along with Reamer.
I need to find out what his plan is, and what he's gonna use the non-Eagles for.
And if Ky really is on Reamer's side and is planning on making me a shooting range casualty or something...
Well...
He'll have to improve his marksmanship before then, at least.

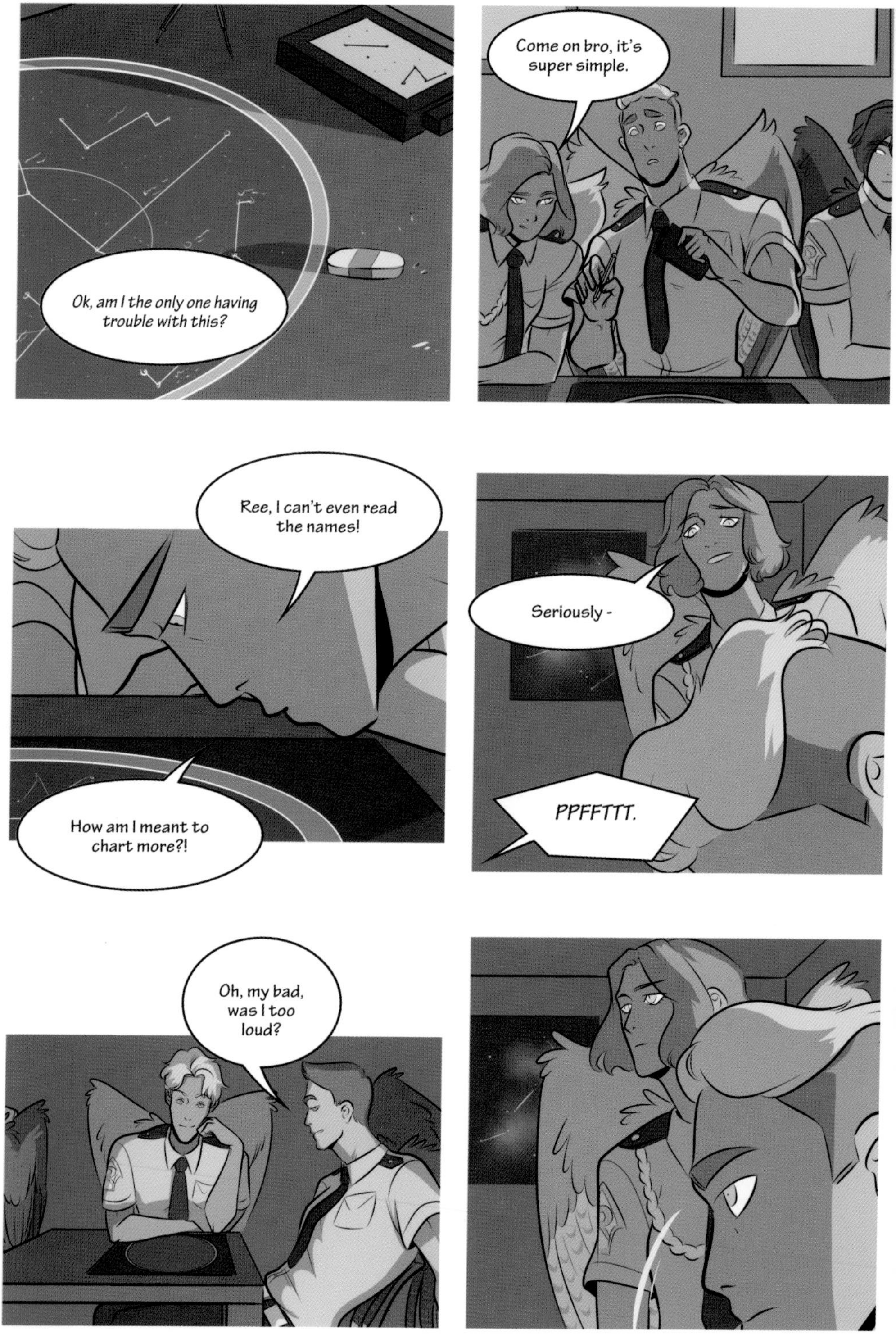
Ok, am I the only one having trouble with this?
Come on bro, it's super simple.
Ree, I can't even read the names!
How am I meant to chart more?!
Seriously -
PPFFTTT.
Oh, my bad, was I too loud?

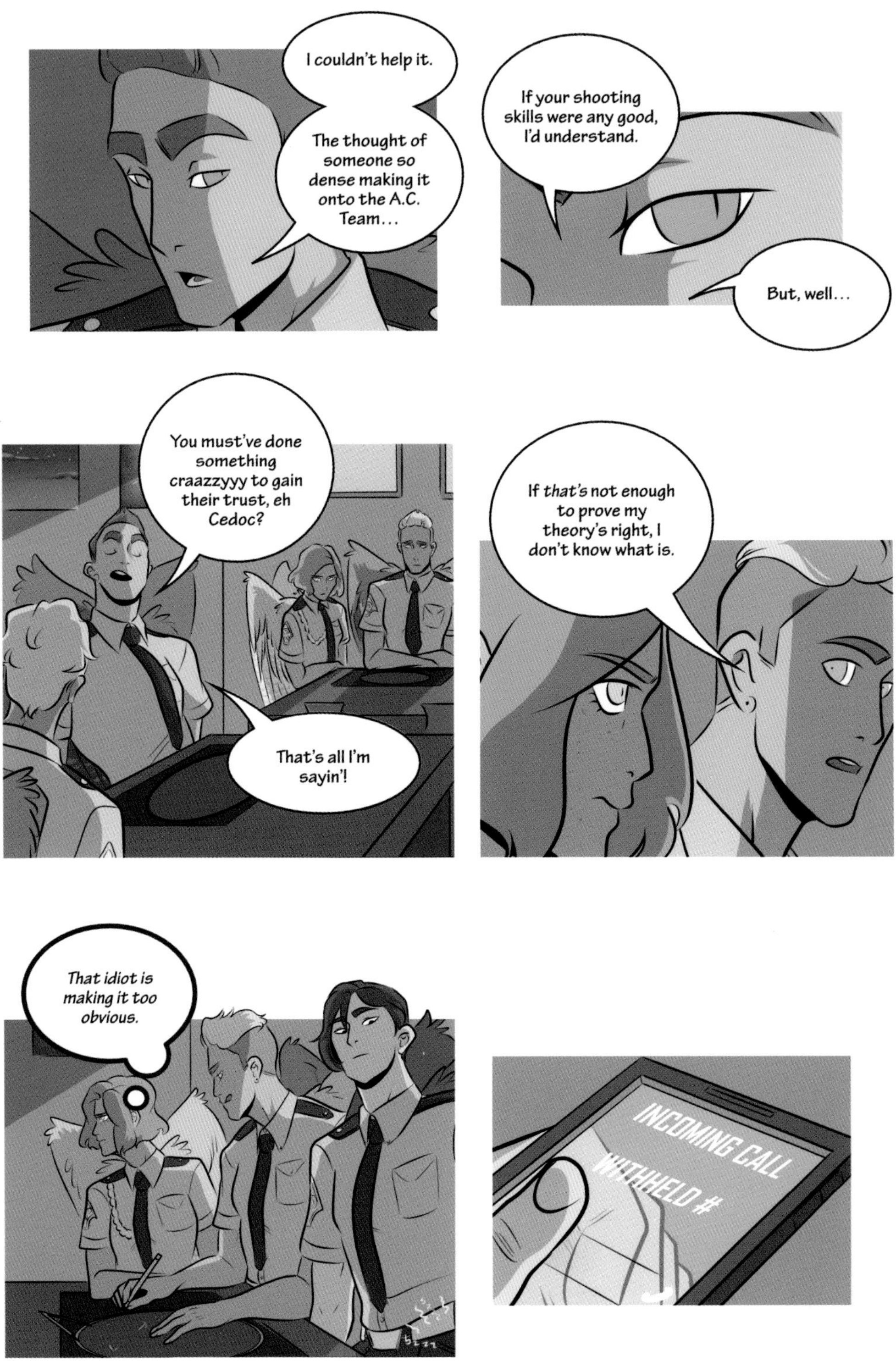
I couldn't help it.
The thought of someone so dense making it onto the A.C. Team…
If your shooting skills were any good, I'd understand.
But, well…
You must've done something craazzyyy to gain their trust, eh Cedoc?
That's all I'm sayin'!
If *that's* not enough to prove my theory's right, I don't know what is.
That idiot is making it too obvious.
INCOMING CALL
WITHHELD #

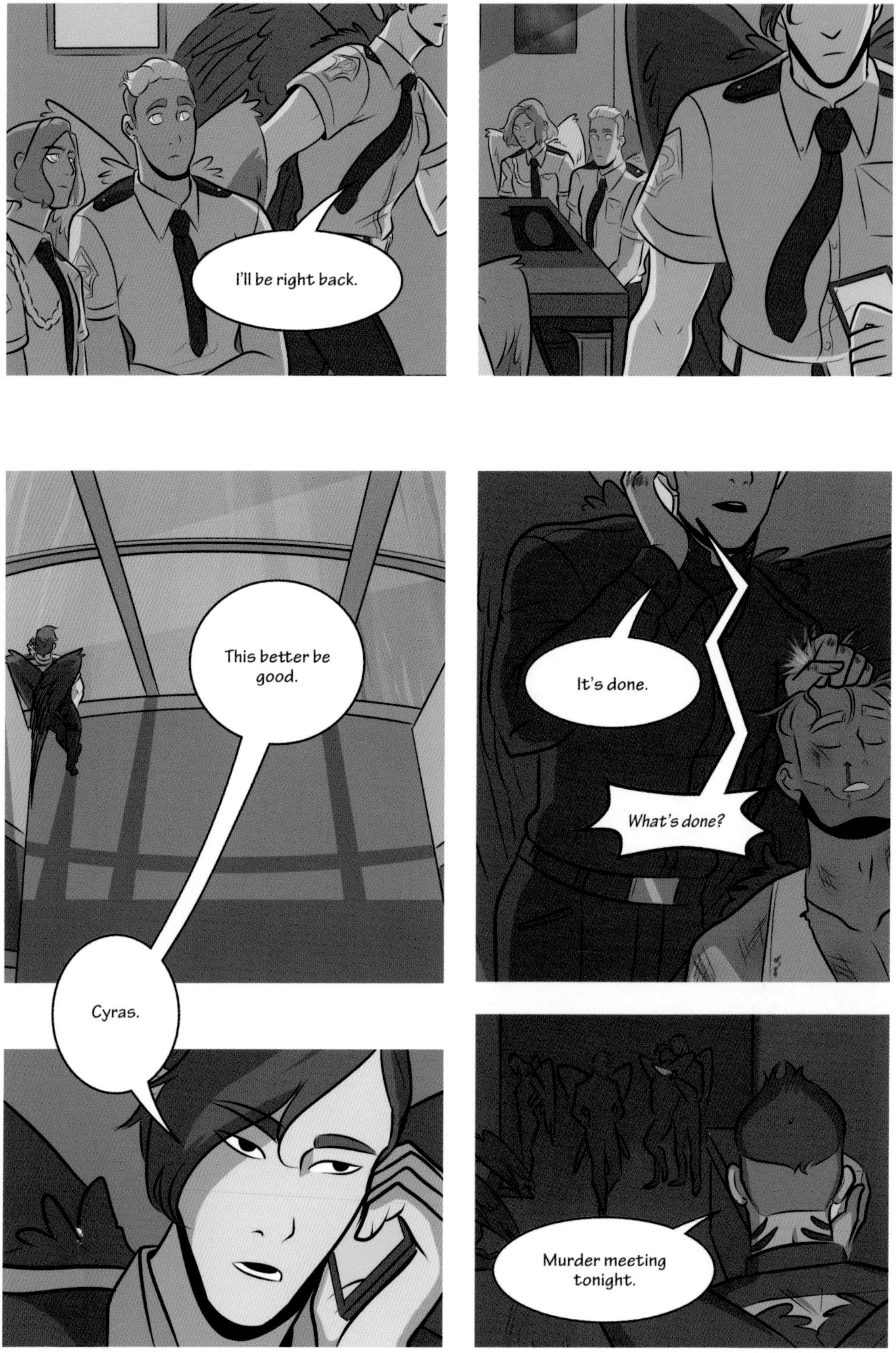
I'll be right back.
This better be good.
It's done.
What's done?
Cyras.
Murder meeting tonight.

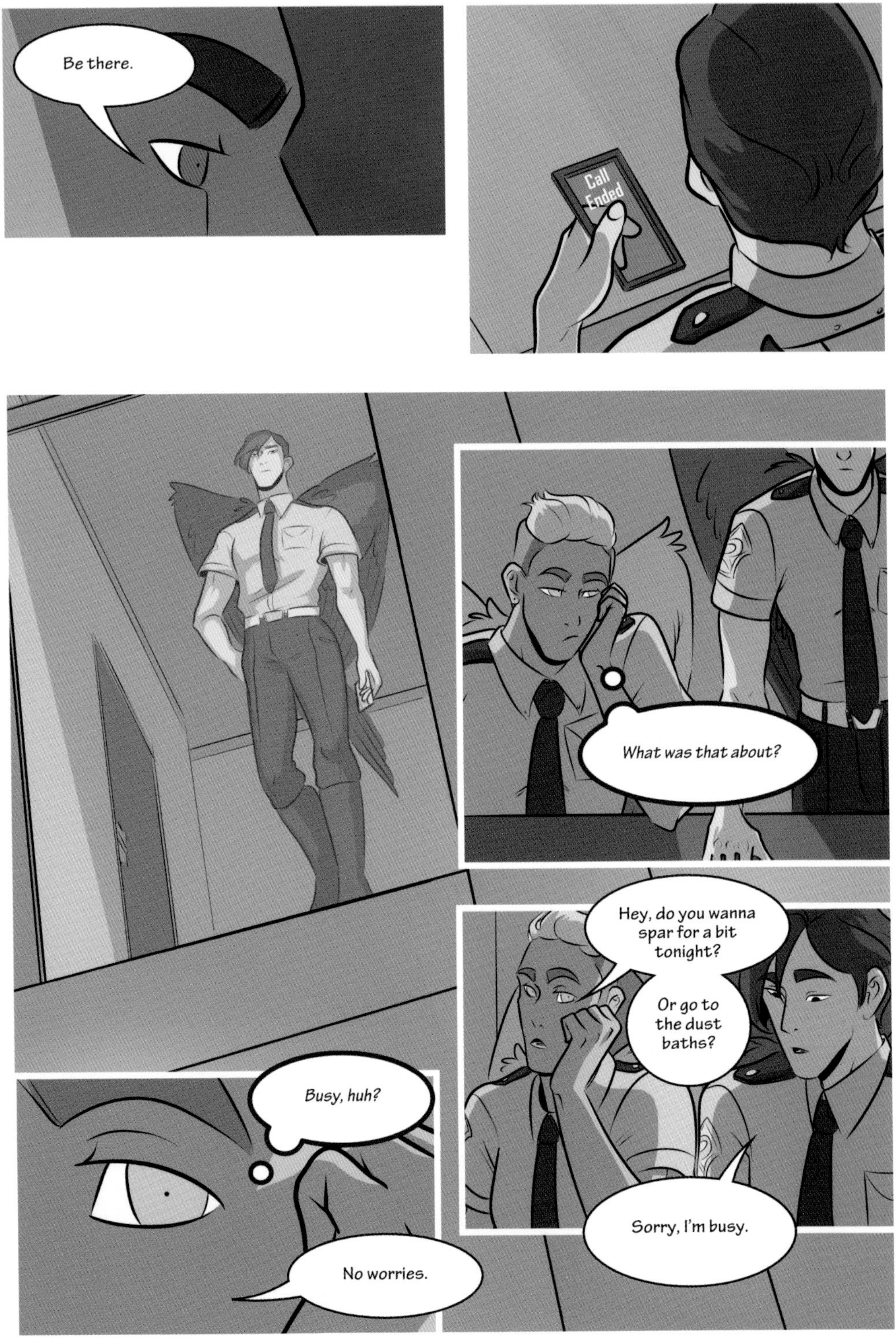
Be there.
Call Ended
What was that about?
Hey, do you wanna spar for a bit tonight?
Or go to the dust baths?
Sorry, I'm busy.
Busy, huh?
No worries.

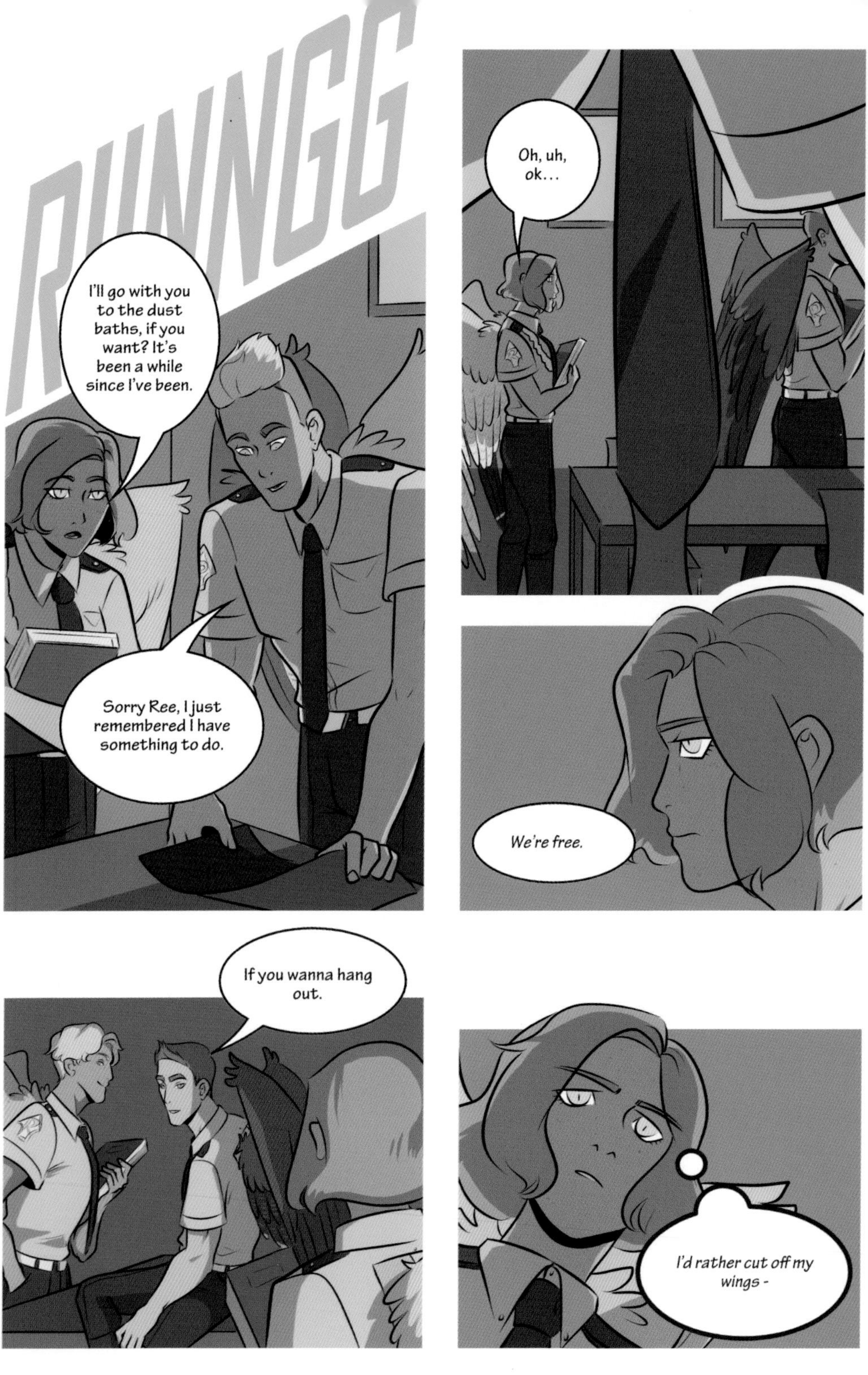
RUNNGG
I'll go with you to the dust baths, if you want? It's been a while since I've been.
Sorry Ree, I just remembered I have something to do.
Oh, uh, ok...
We're free.
If you wanna hang out.
I'd rather cut off my wings -

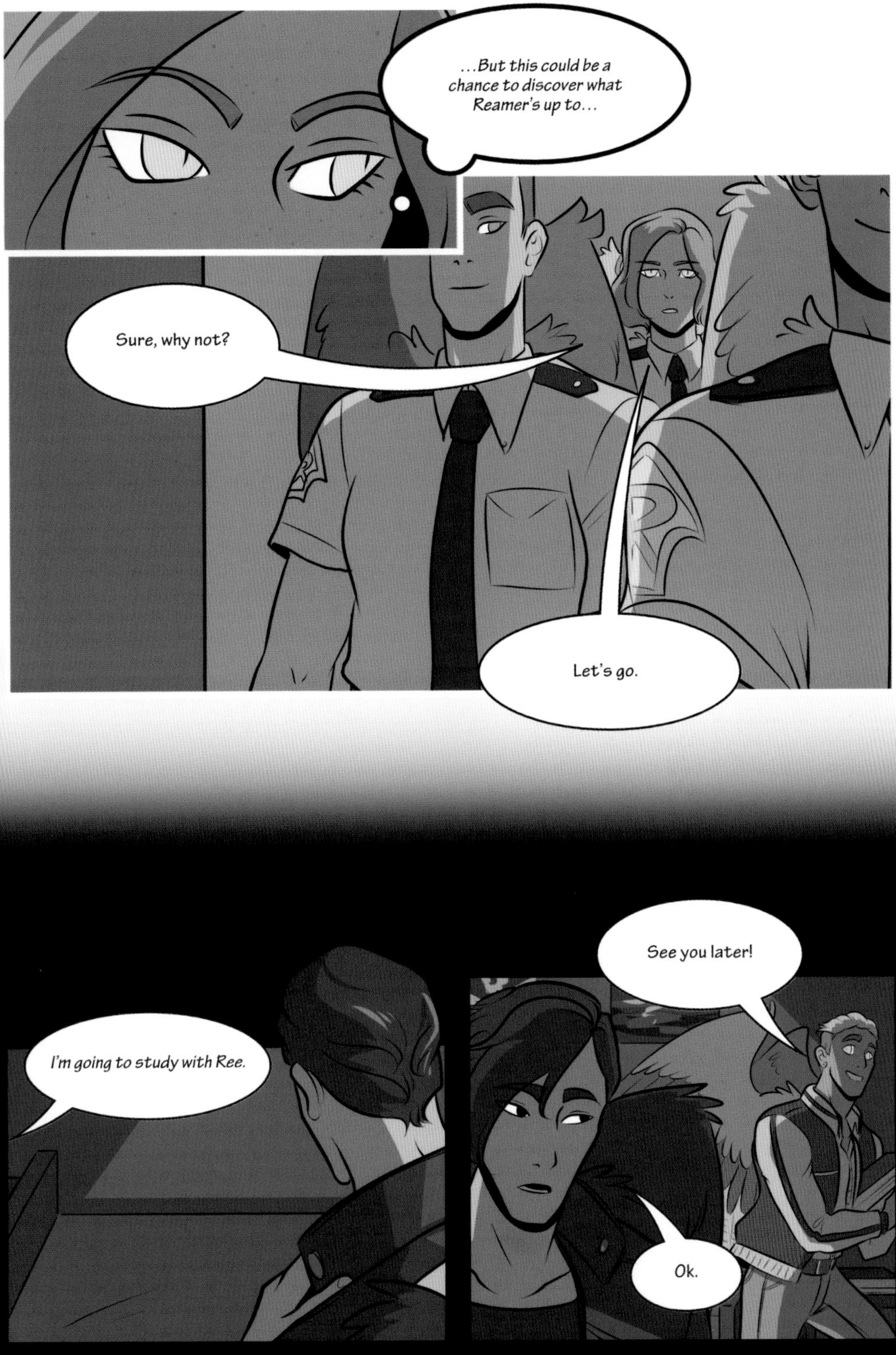
...But this could be a chance to discover what Reamer's up to...
Sure, why not?
Let's go.
See you later!
I'm going to study with Ree.
Ok.

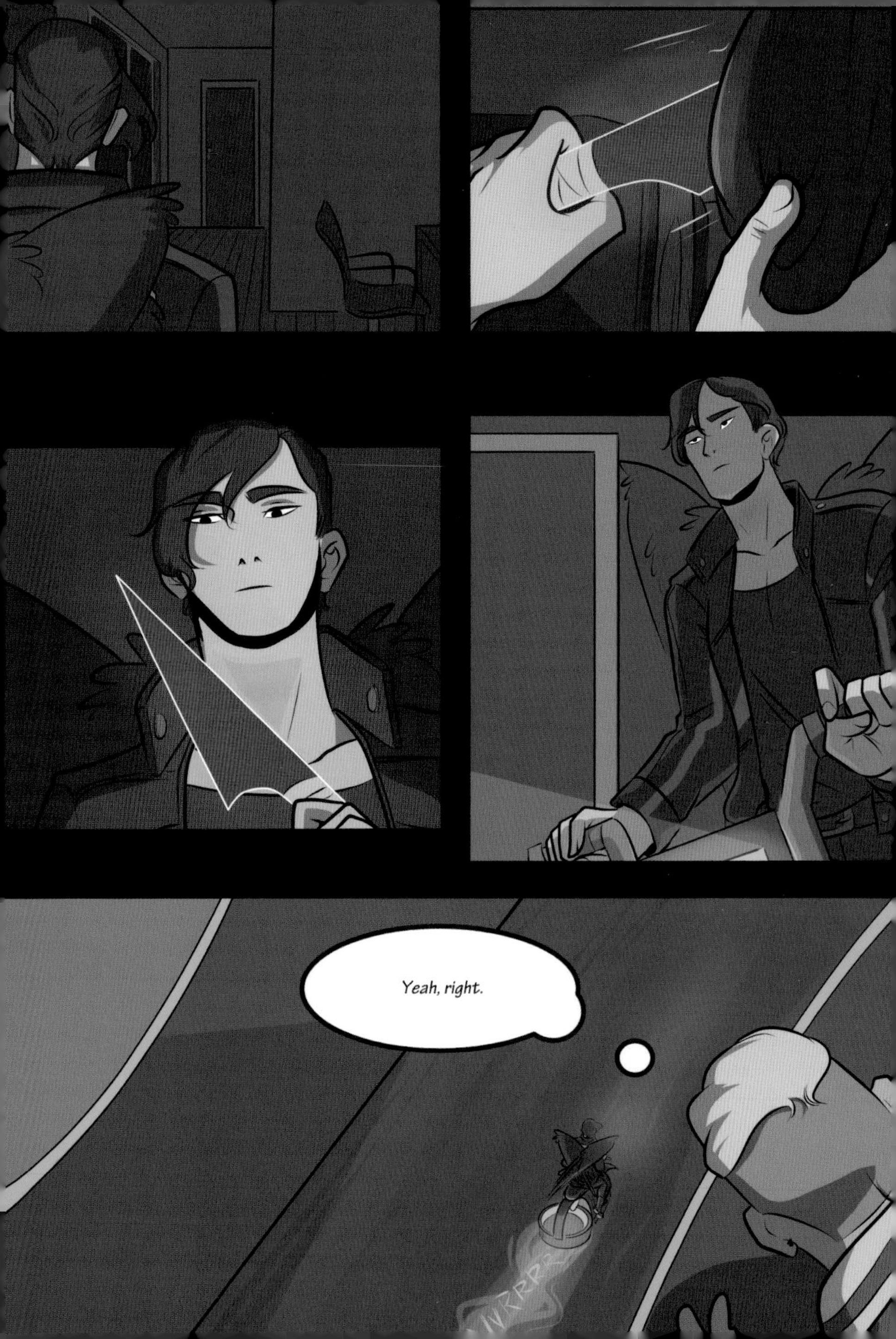
Yeah, right.

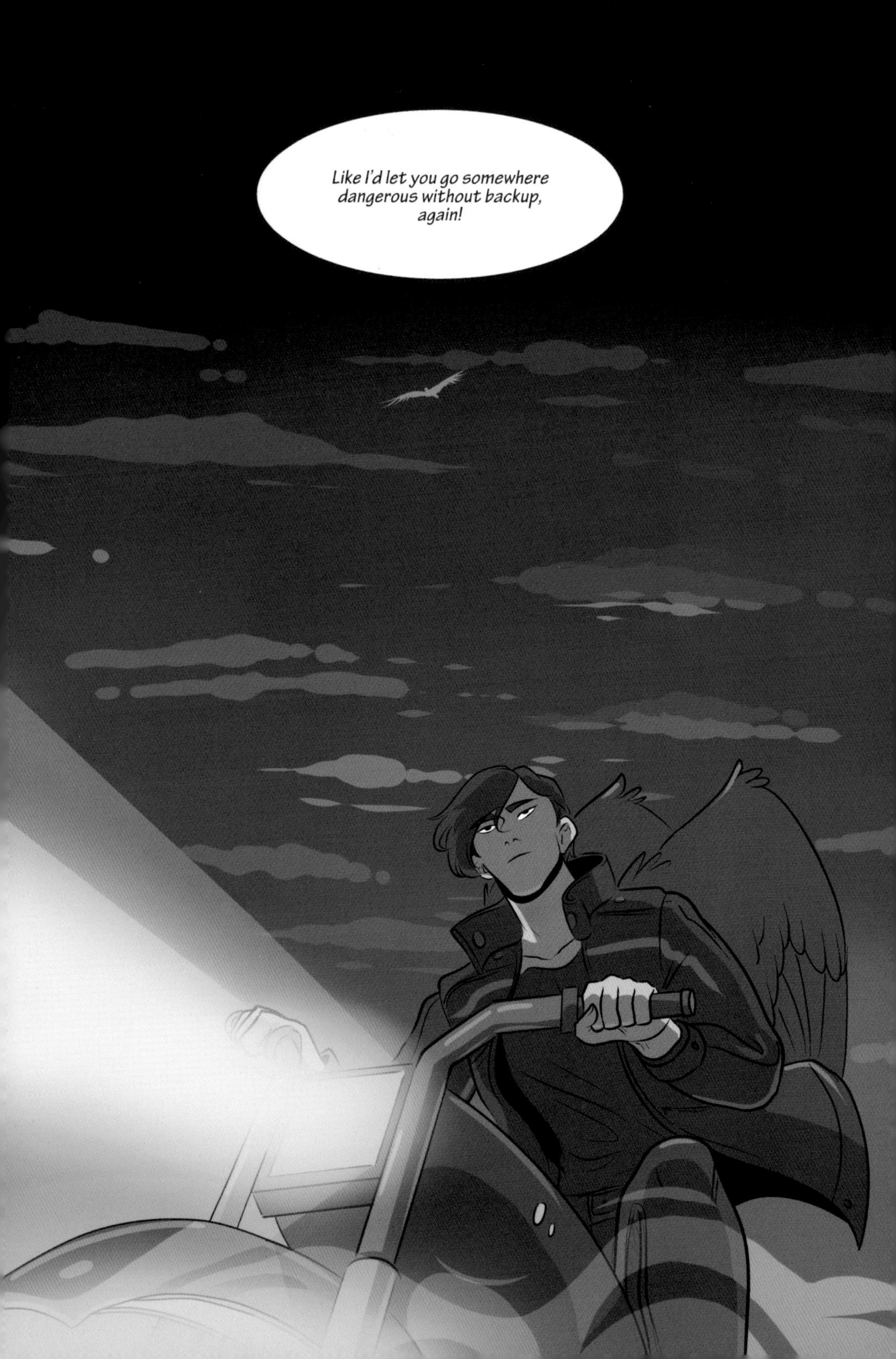
Like I'd let you go somewhere dangerous without backup, again!

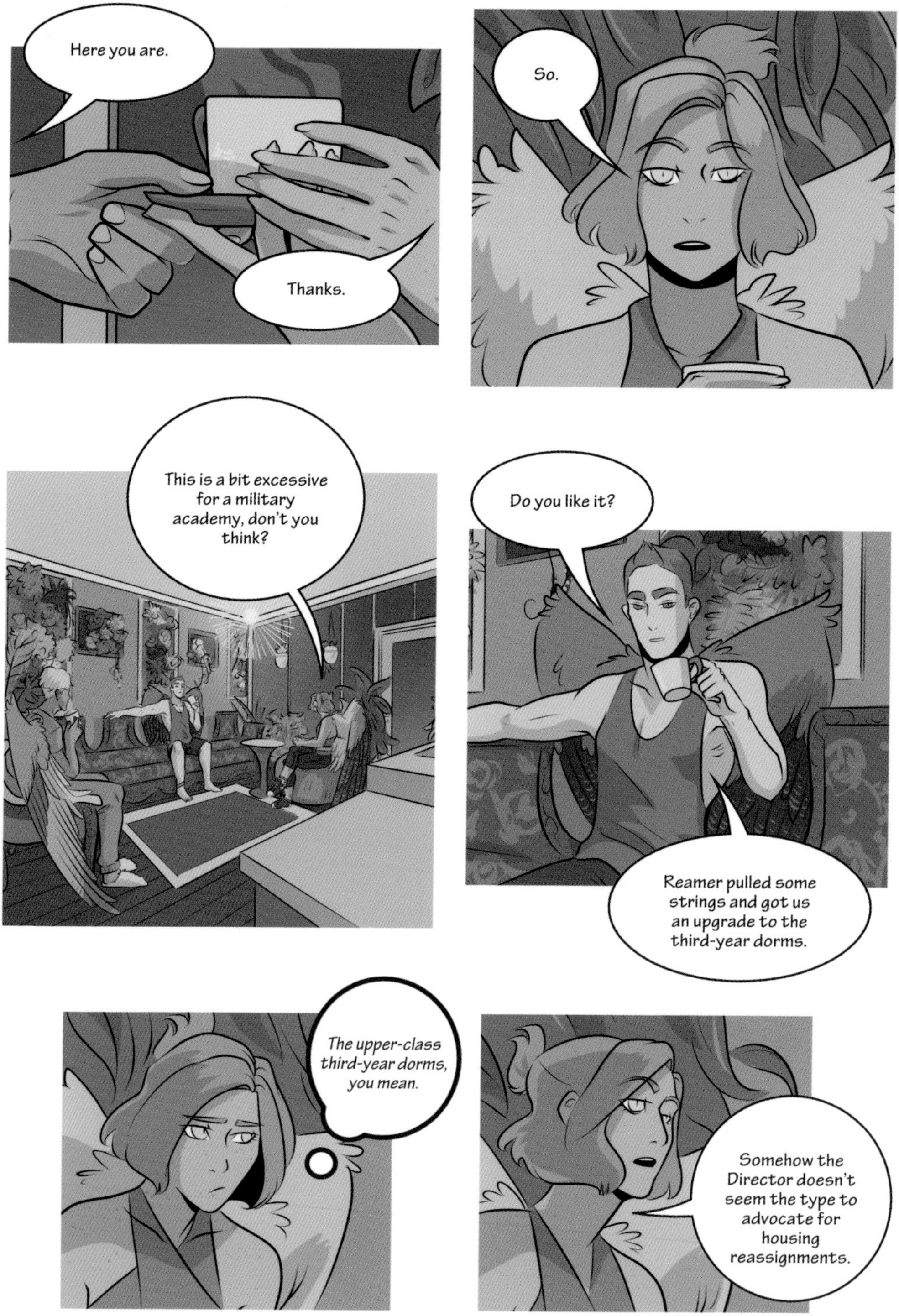
Here you are.
Thanks.
So.
This is a bit excessive for a military academy, don't you think?
Do you like it?
Reamer pulled some strings and got us an upgrade to the third-year dorms.
The upper-class third-year dorms, you mean.
Somehow the Director doesn't seem the type to advocate for housing reassignments.

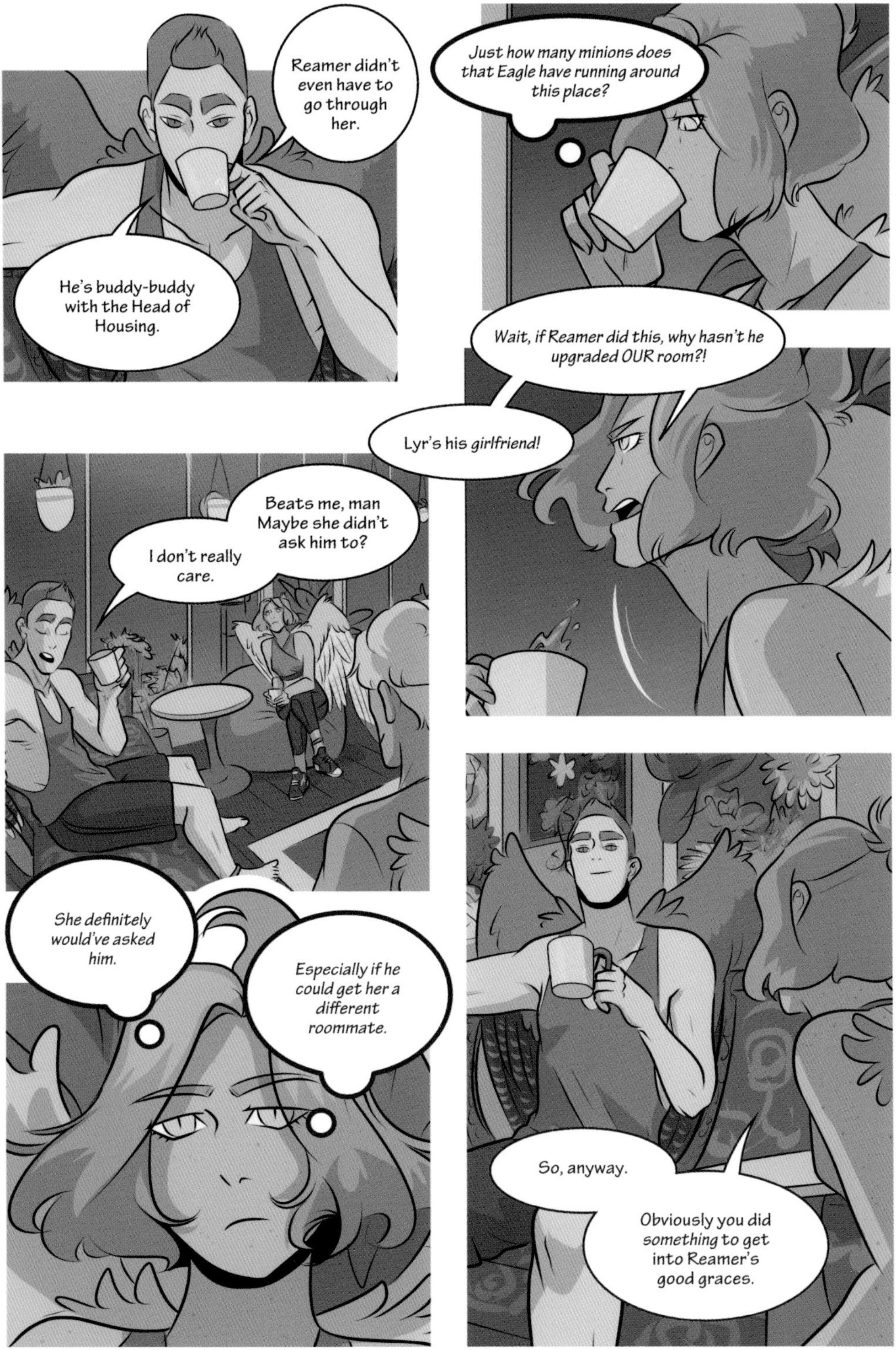
Reamer didn't even have to go through her.
He's buddy-buddy with the Head of Housing.
Just how many minions does that Eagle have running around this place?
Wait, if Reamer did this, why hasn't he upgraded OUR room?!
Lyr's his *girlfriend!*
Beats me, man Maybe she didn't ask him to?
I don't really care.
She definitely would've asked him.
Especially if he could get her a different roommate.
So, anyway.
Obviously you did something to get into Reamer's good graces.

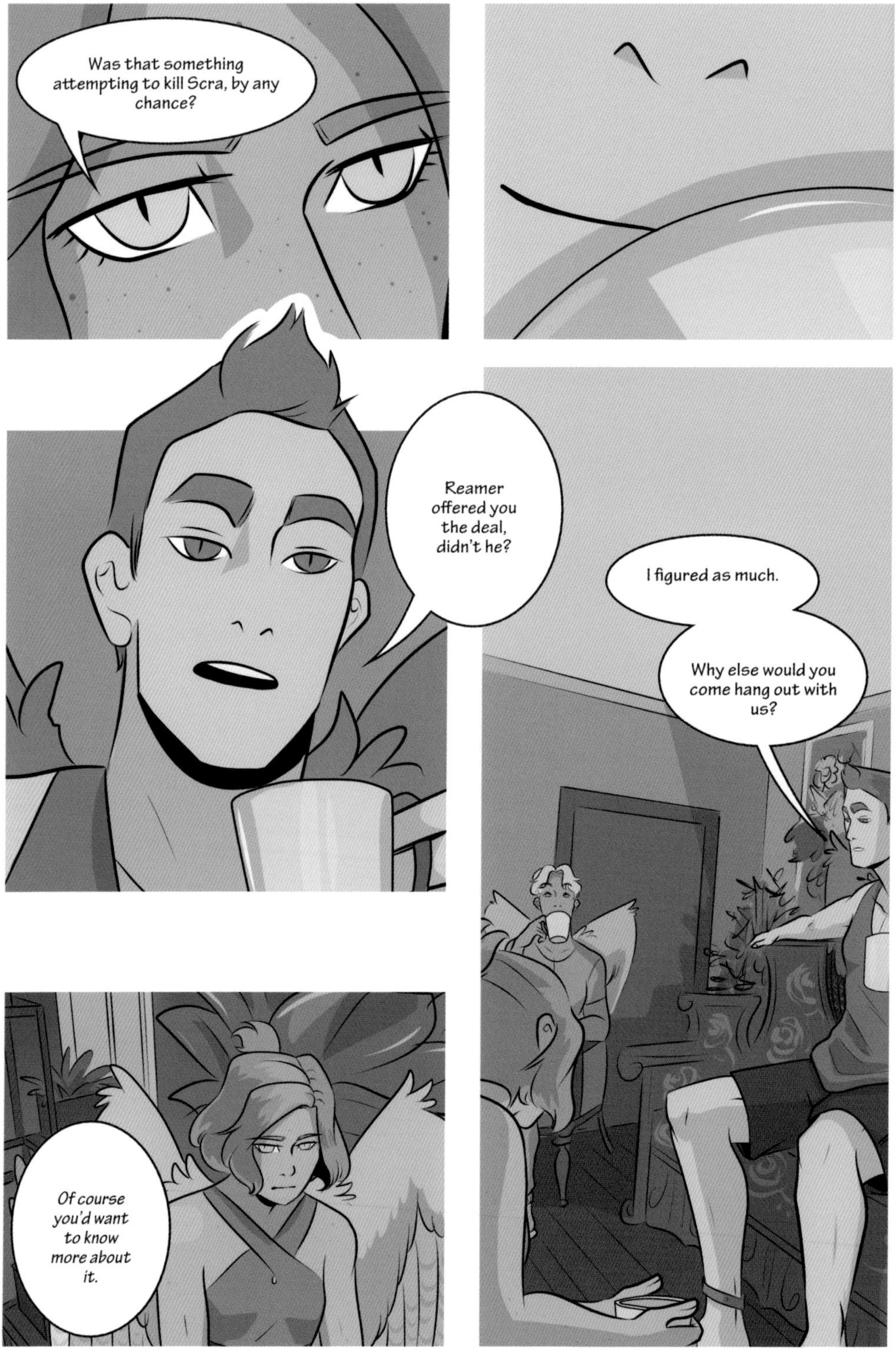
Was that something attempting to kill Scra, by any chance?
Reamer offered you the deal, didn't he?
I figured as much.
Why else would you come hang out with us?
Of course you'd want to know more about it.

Please, I'm not so desperate for a bigger room that I'd kill for it.

It doesn't have to be a room, Vermillioss.

It can literally be anything.

Anything you could want.

I'm not interested.

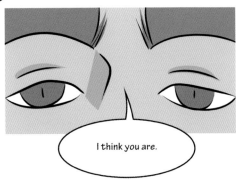

I think you are.

I think there's a part of you that realizes that this is the best shot at a good life you'll ever get.

Regardless of whether you've admitted it to yourself or not.

Why else would you even be asking about it?

If you really weren't interested, you would've just reported him straight away and been done with it.

Probably could've gotten him court-martialed, too.

If his mother didn't protect him. Which you know she would.

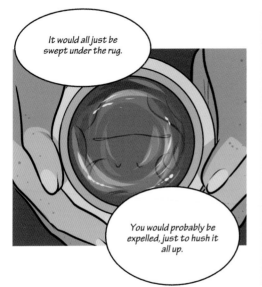

It would all just be swept under the rug.

You would probably be expelled, just to hush it all up.

Wouldn't be the first time that's happened.

Won't be the last, either.

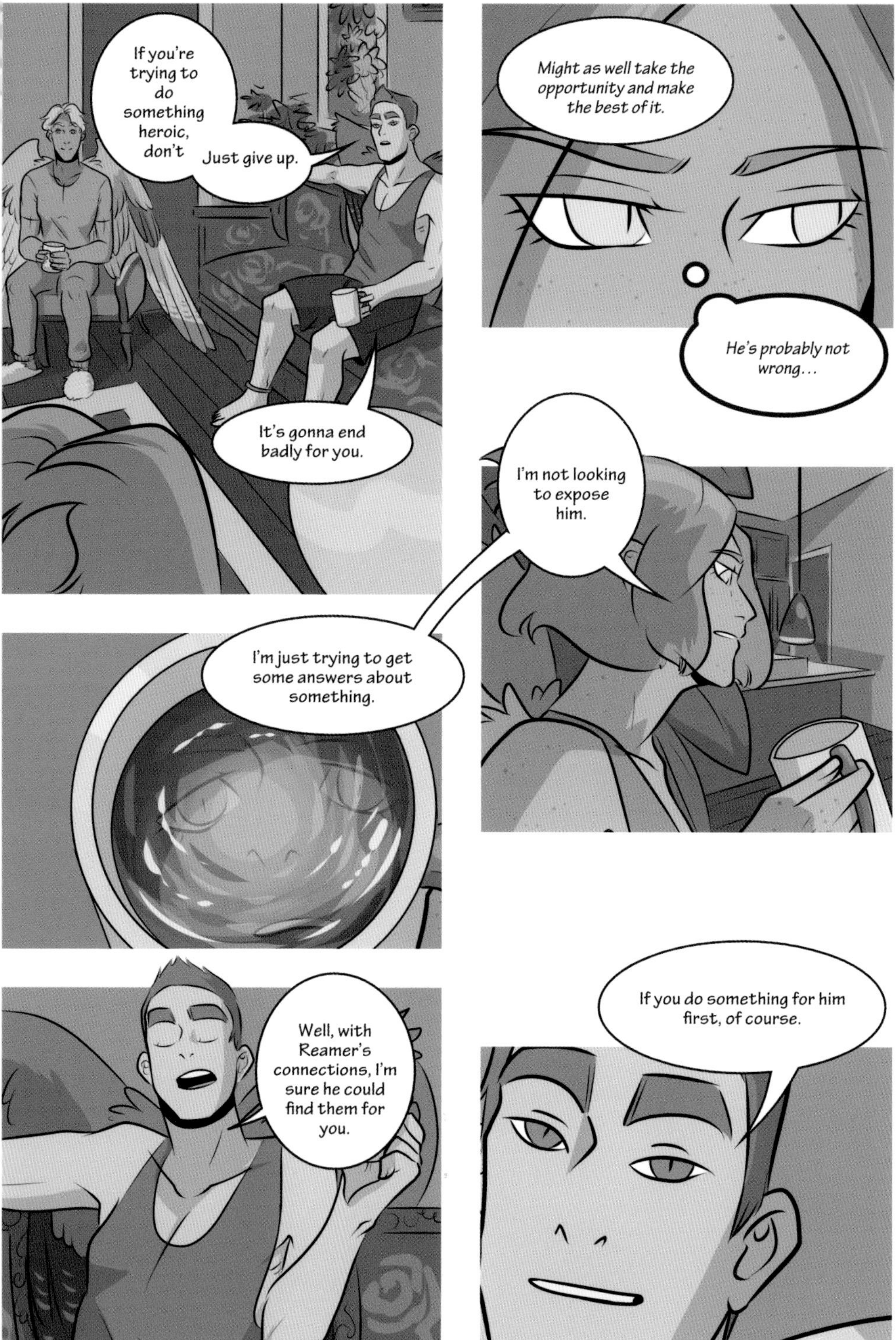
If you're trying to do something heroic, don't
Just give up.
It's gonna end badly for you.
Might as well take the opportunity and make the best of it.
He's probably not wrong…
I'm not looking to expose him.
I'm just trying to get some answers about something.
Well, with Reamer's connections, I'm sure he could find them for you.
If you do something for him first, of course.

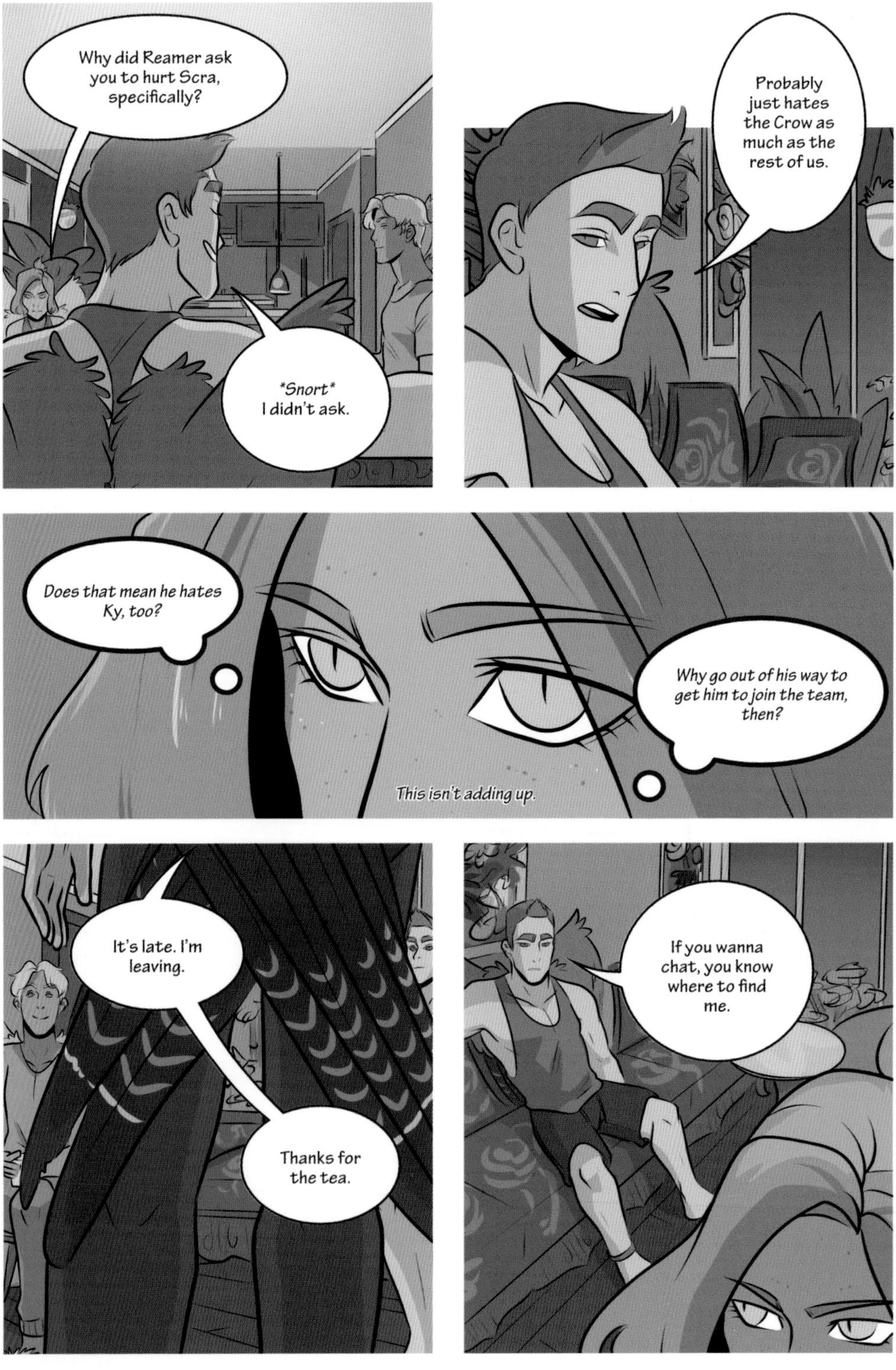
Why did Reamer ask you to hurt Scra, specifically?
Snort I didn't ask.
Probably just hates the Crow as much as the rest of us.
Does that mean he hates Ky, too?
Why go out of his way to get him to join the team, then?
This isn't adding up.
It's late. I'm leaving.
Thanks for the tea.
If you wanna chat, you know where to find me.

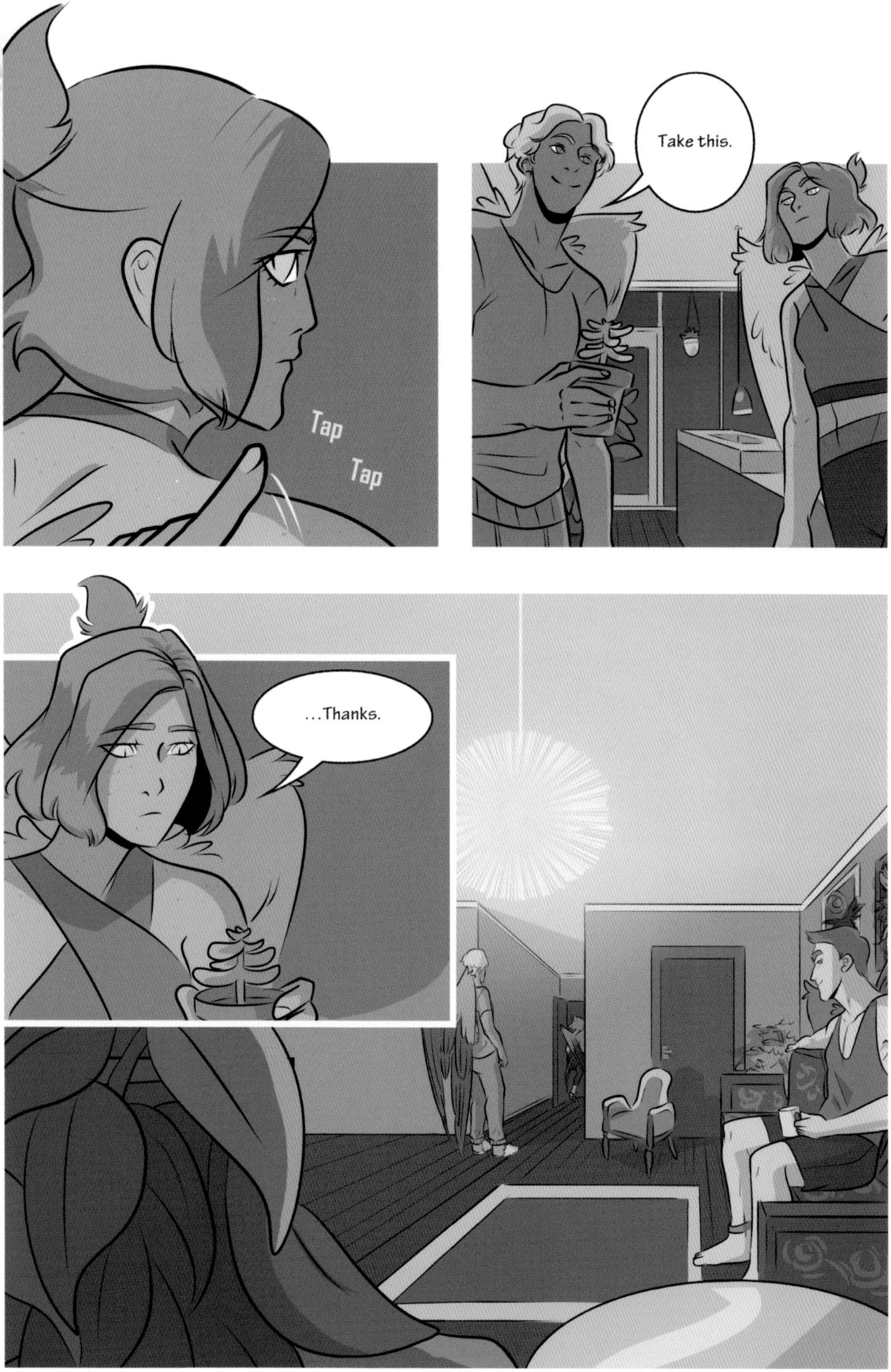

Tap
Tap
Take this.
...Thanks.

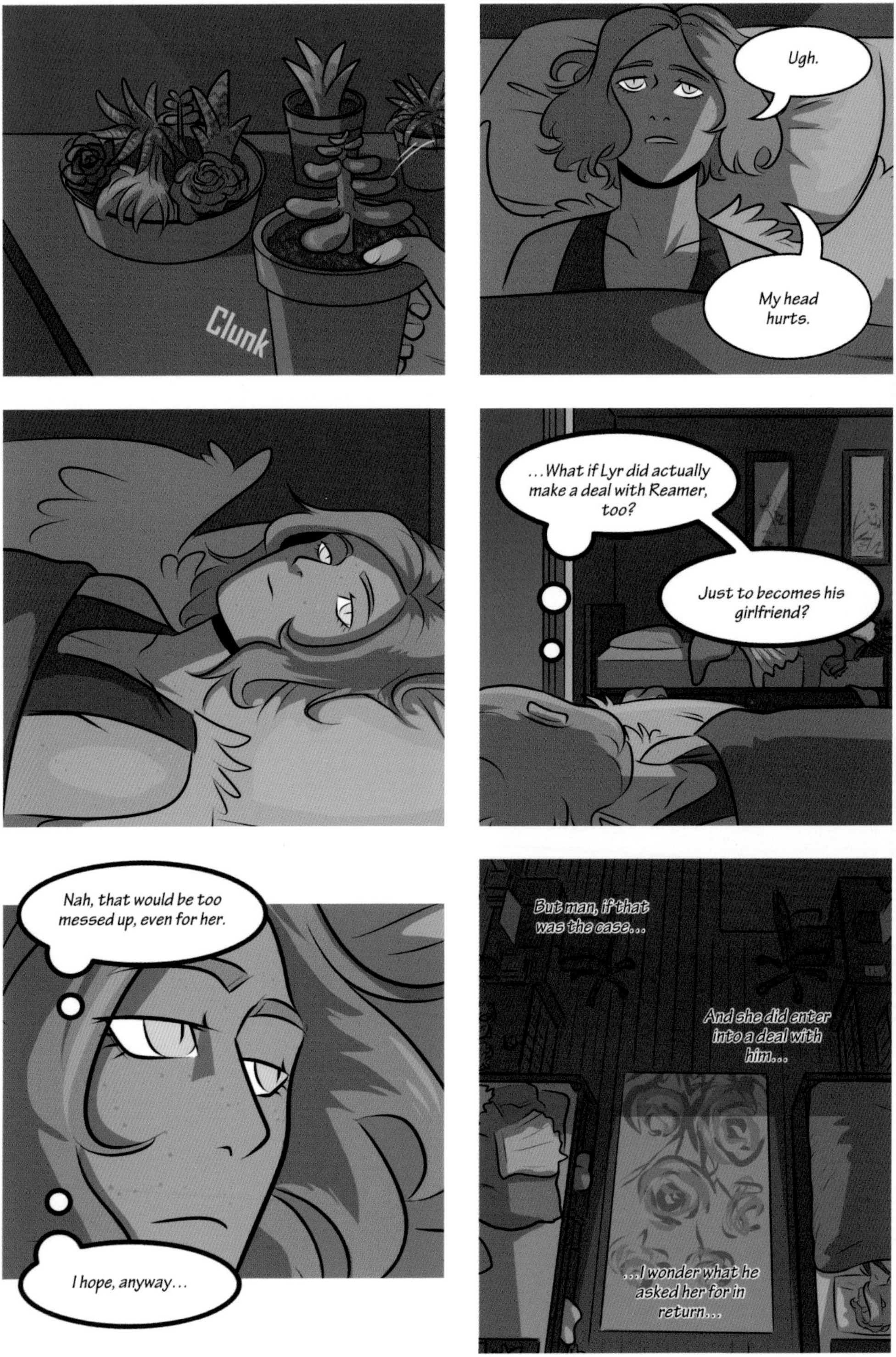
Clunk
Ugh.
My head hurts.
...What if Lyr did actually make a deal with Reamer, too?
Just to becomes his girlfriend?
Nah, that would be too messed up, even for her.
I hope, anyway...
But man, if that was the case...
And she did enter into a deal with him...
...I wonder what he asked her for in return...

THE CROAKING

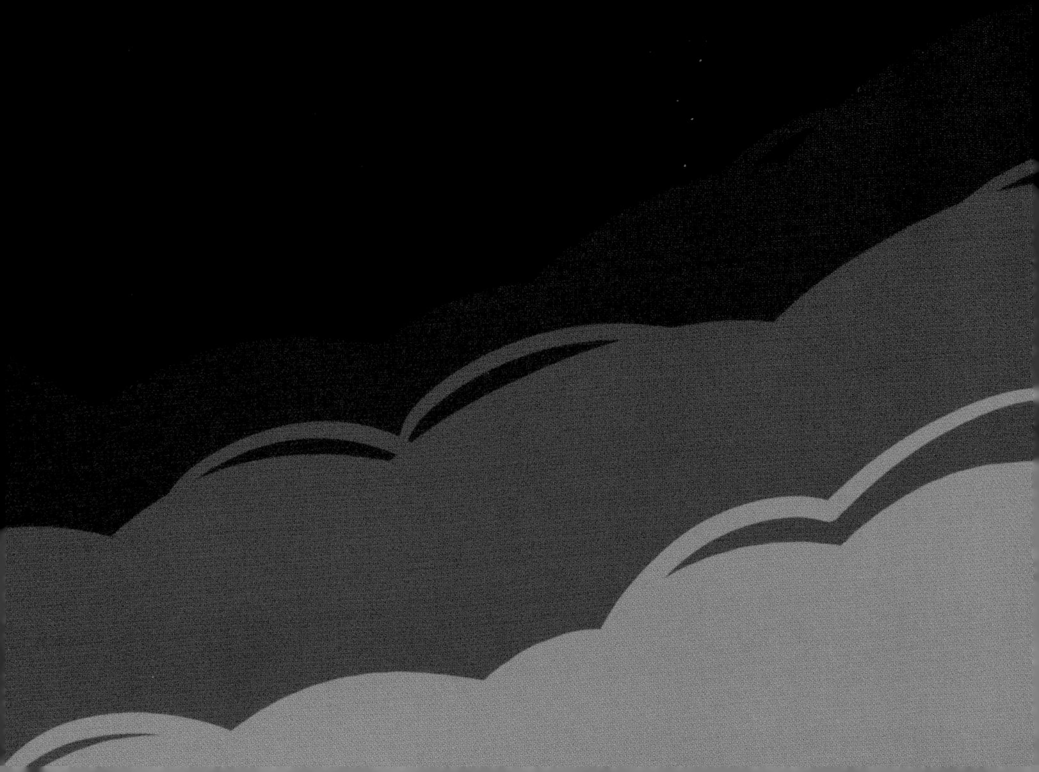

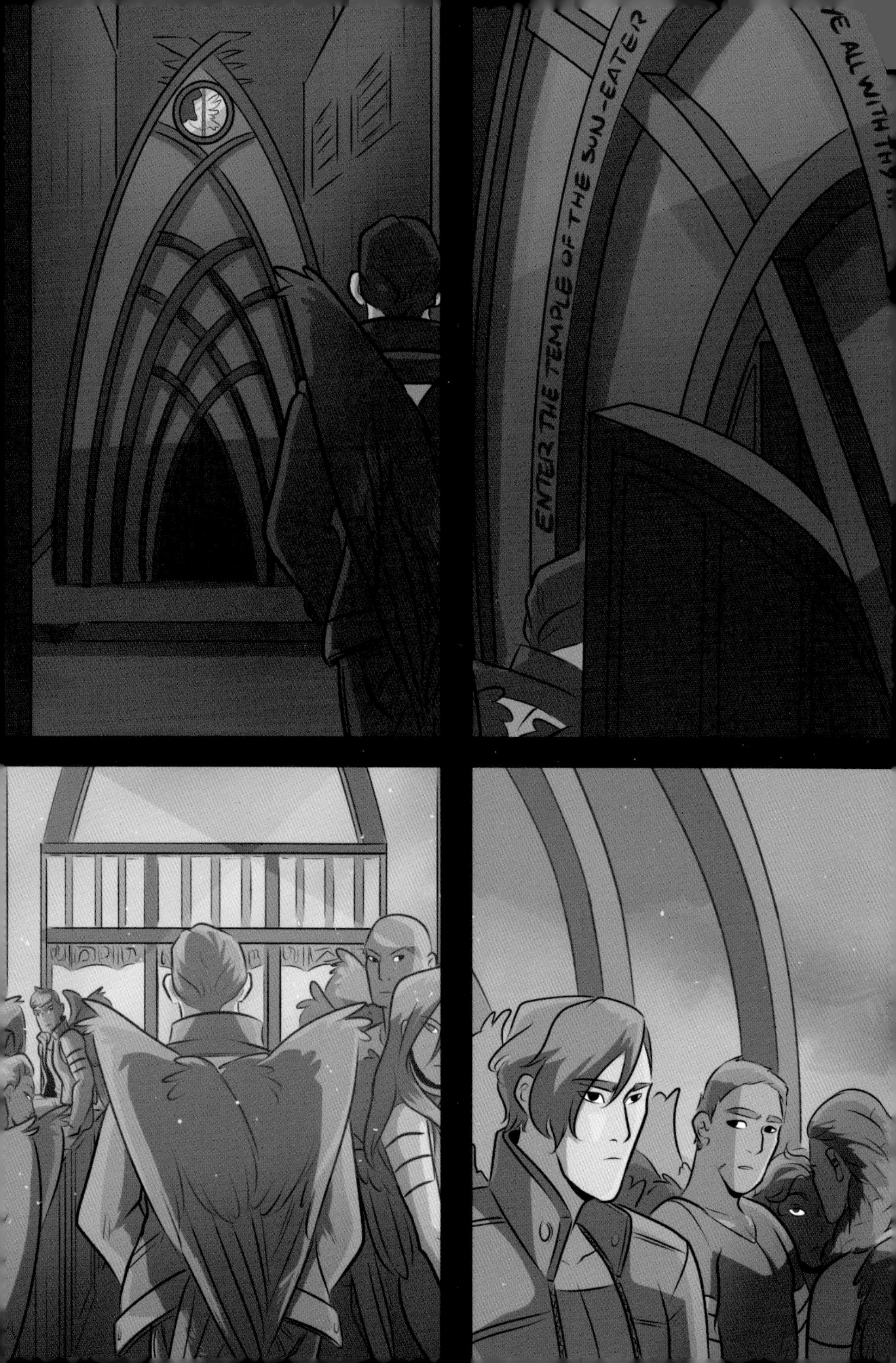

ENTER THE TEMPLE OF THE SUN-EATER
YE ALL WITH THY...

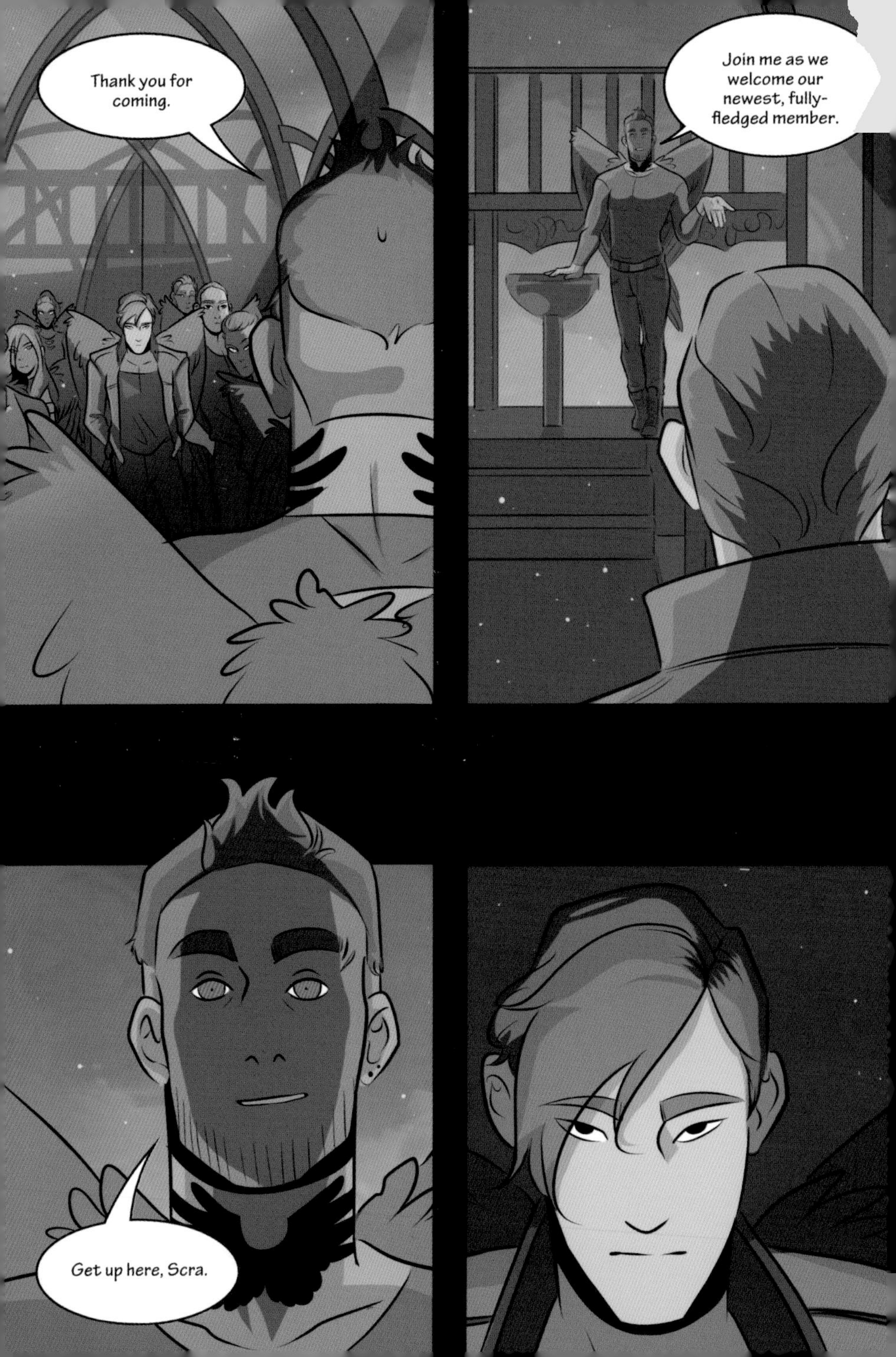
Thank you for coming.
Join me as we welcome our newest, fully-fledged member.
Get up here, Scra.

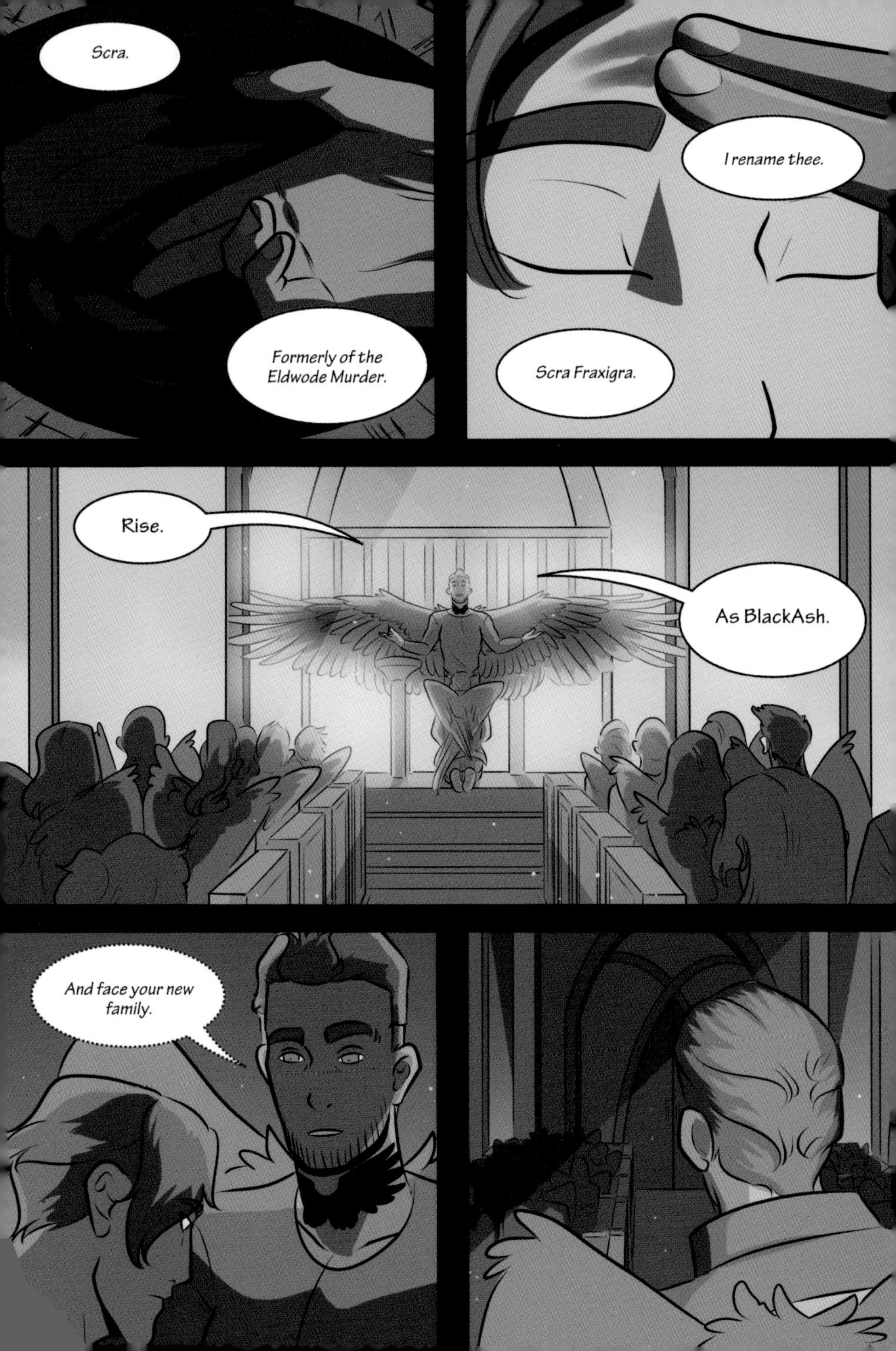
Scra.
Formerly of the Eldwode Murder.
I rename thee.
Scra Fraxigra.
Rise.
As BlackAsh.
And face your new family.

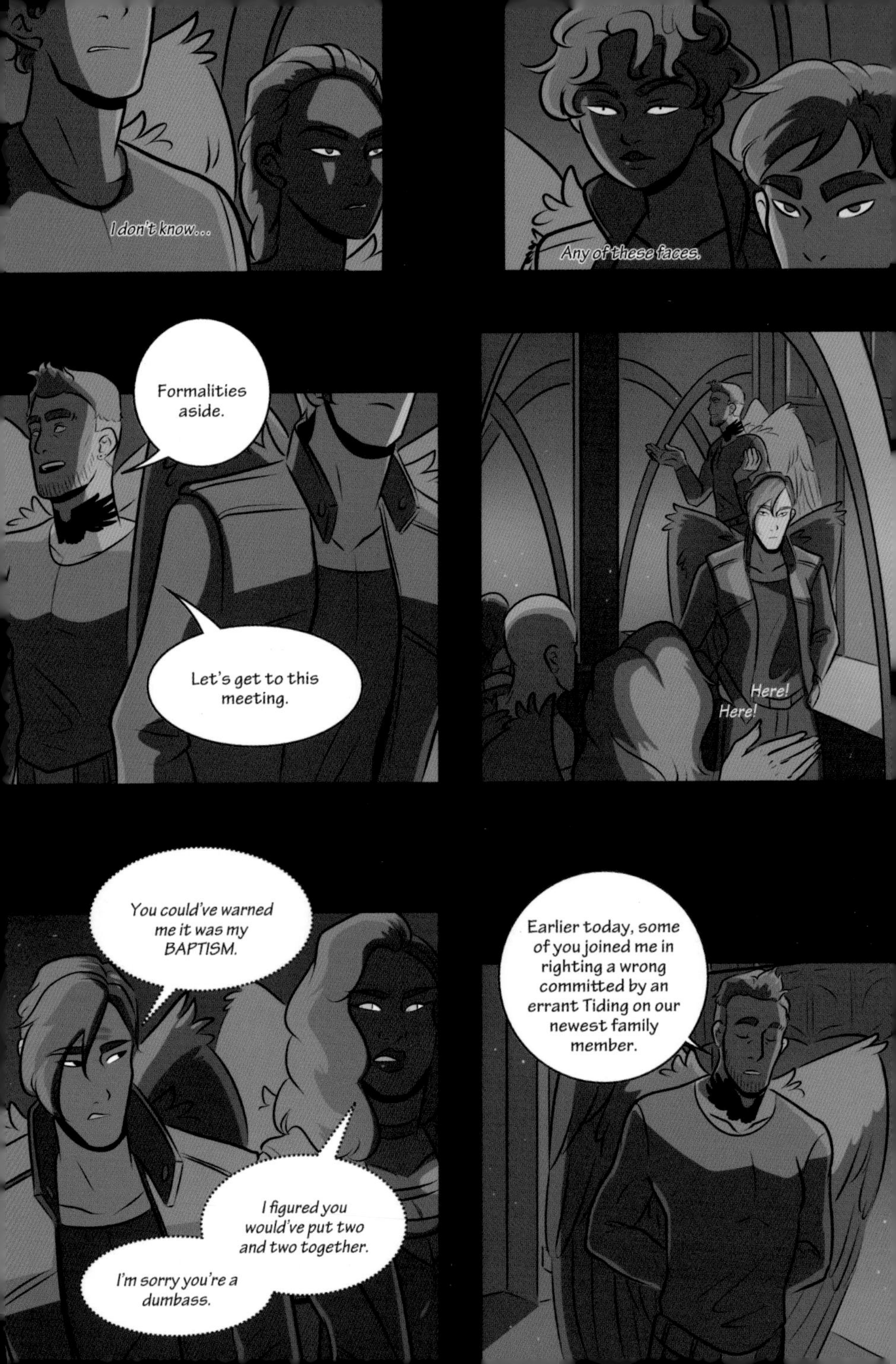
I don't know...
Any of these faces.
Formalities aside.
Let's get to this meeting.
Here!
Here!
You could've warned me it was my BAPTISM.
I figured you would've put two and two together.
I'm sorry you're a dumbass.
Earlier today, some of you joined me in righting a wrong committed by an errant Tiding on our newest family member.

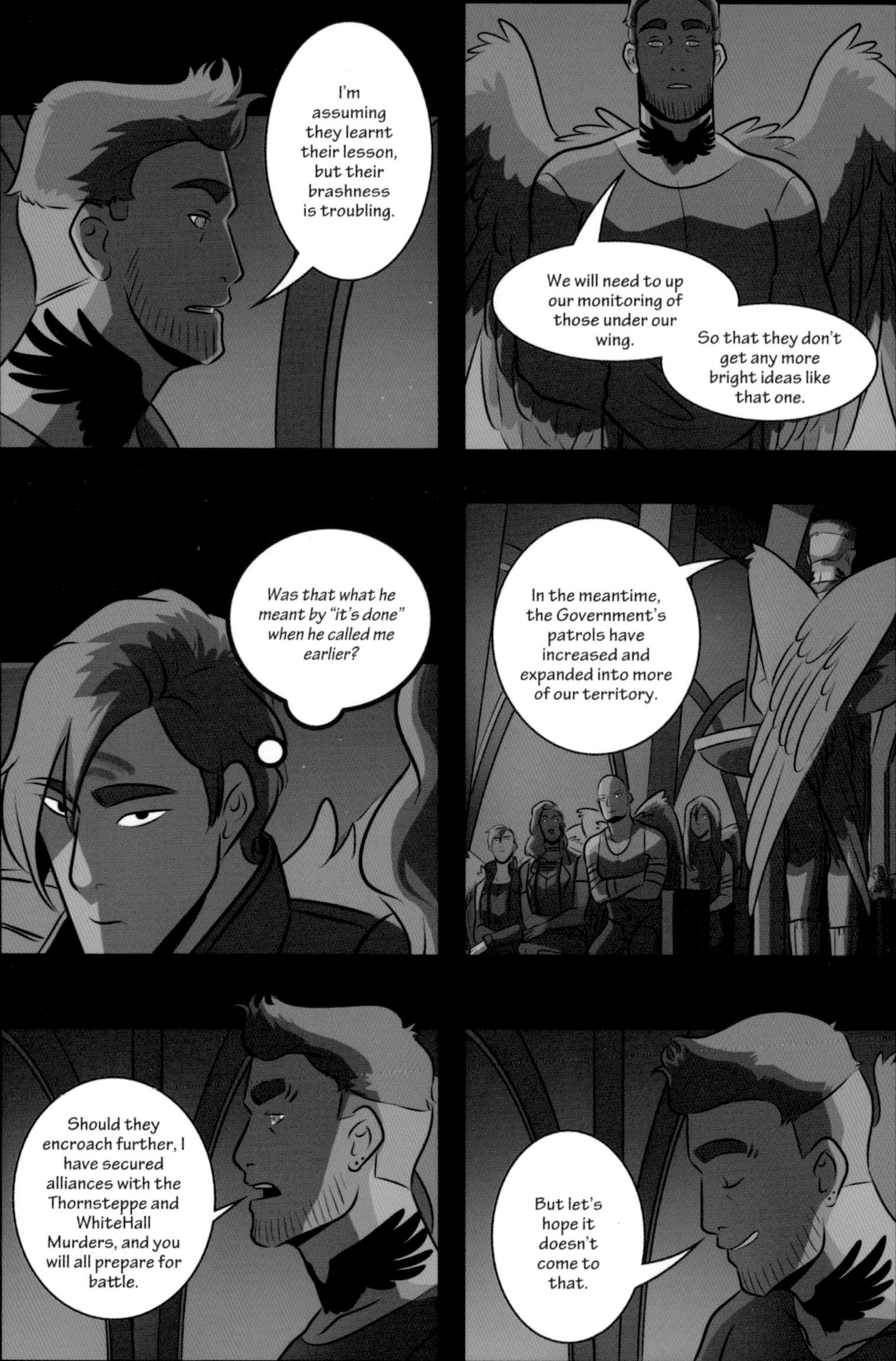
I'm assuming they learnt their lesson, but their brashness is troubling.
We will need to up our monitoring of those under our wing.
So that they don't get any more bright ideas like that one.
Was that what he meant by "it's done" when he called me earlier?
In the meantime, the Government's patrols have increased and expanded into more of our territory.
Should they encroach further, I have secured alliances with the Thornsteppe and WhiteHall Murders, and you will all prepare for battle.
But let's hope it doesn't come to that.

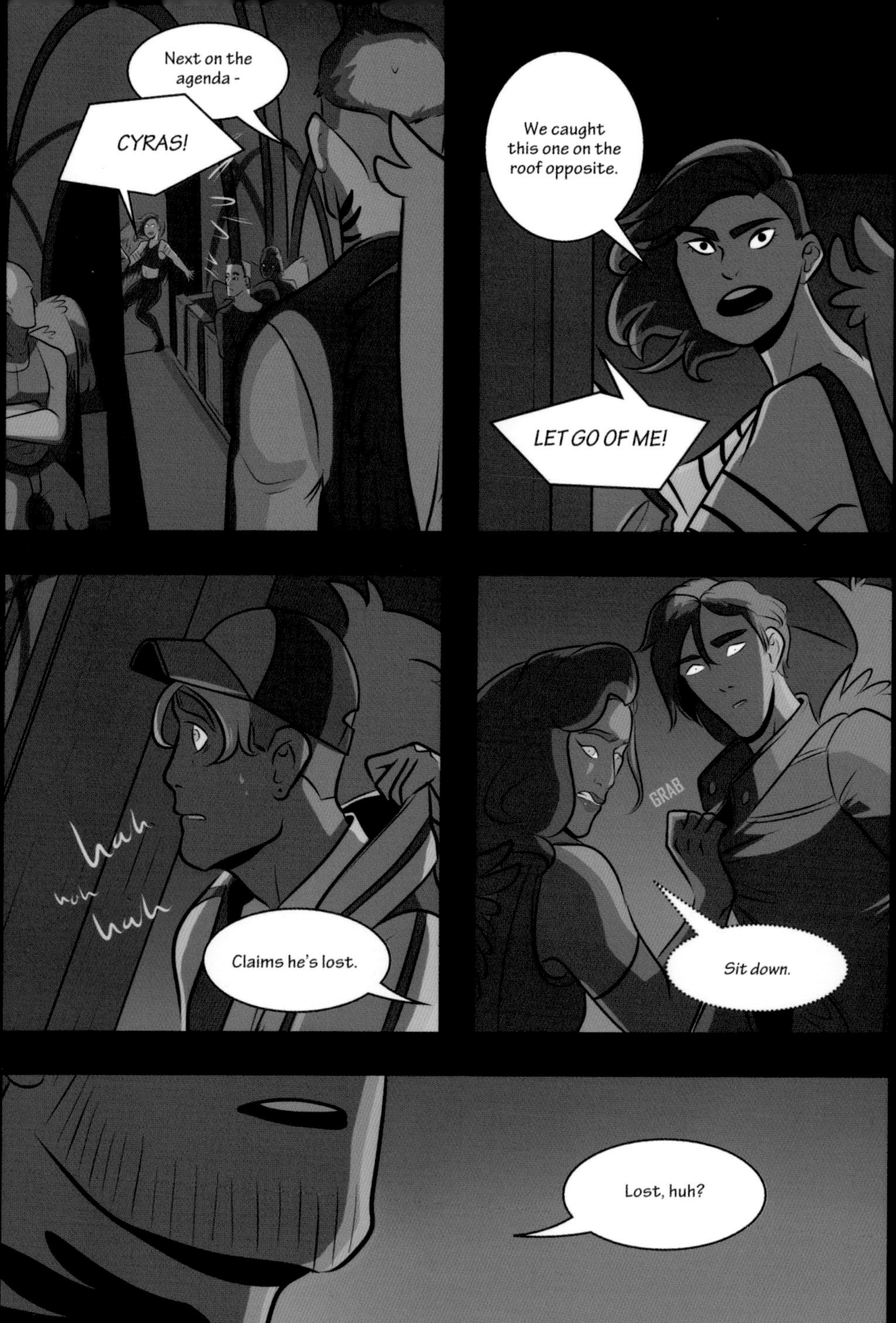
Next on the agenda -
CYRAS!
We caught this one on the roof opposite.
LET GO OF ME!
huh
huh
huh
Claims he's lost.
GRAB
Sit down.
Lost, huh?

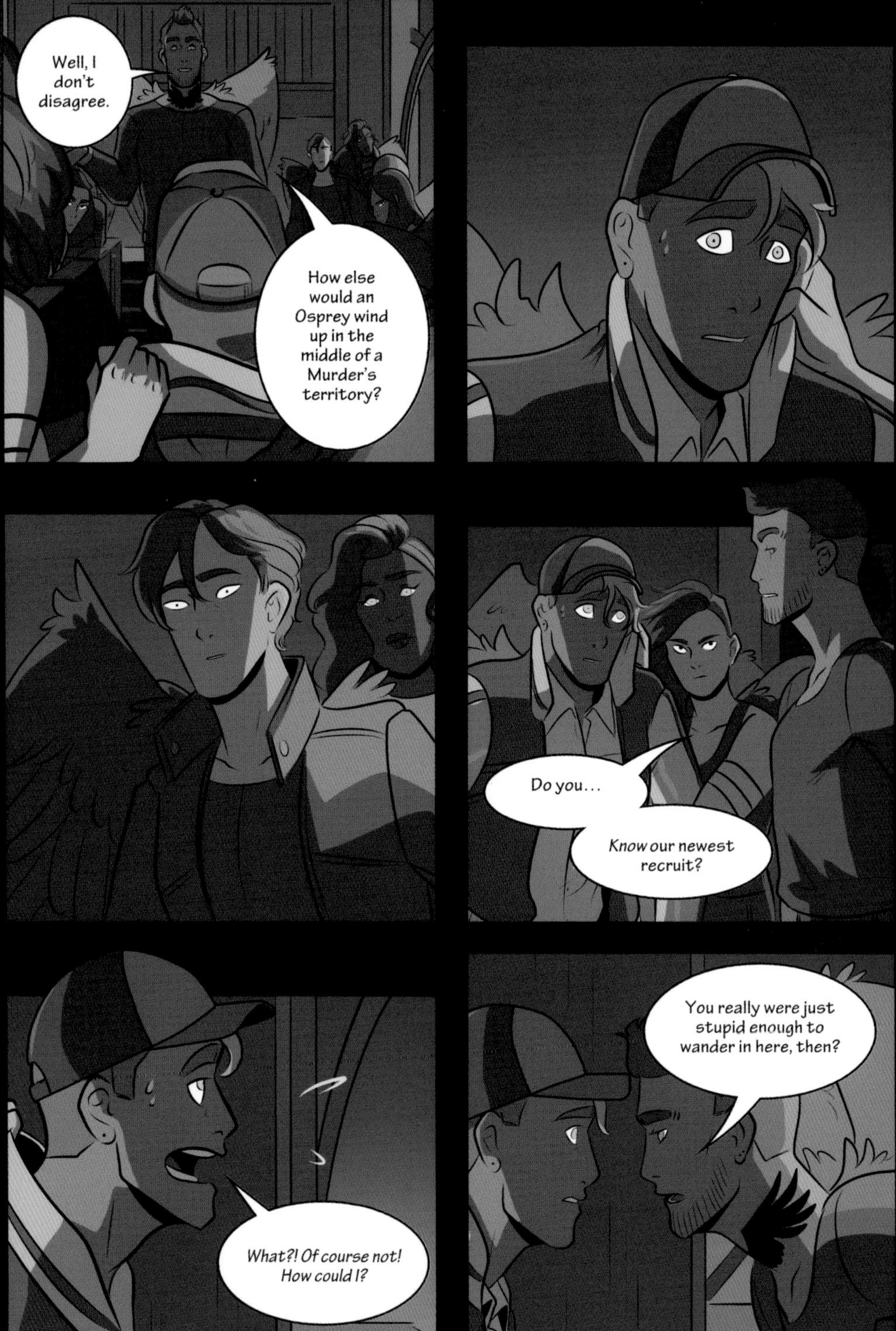
Well, I don't disagree.
How else would an Osprey wind up in the middle of a Murder's territory?
Do you...
Know our newest recruit?
What?! Of course not! How could I?
You really were just stupid enough to wander in here, then?

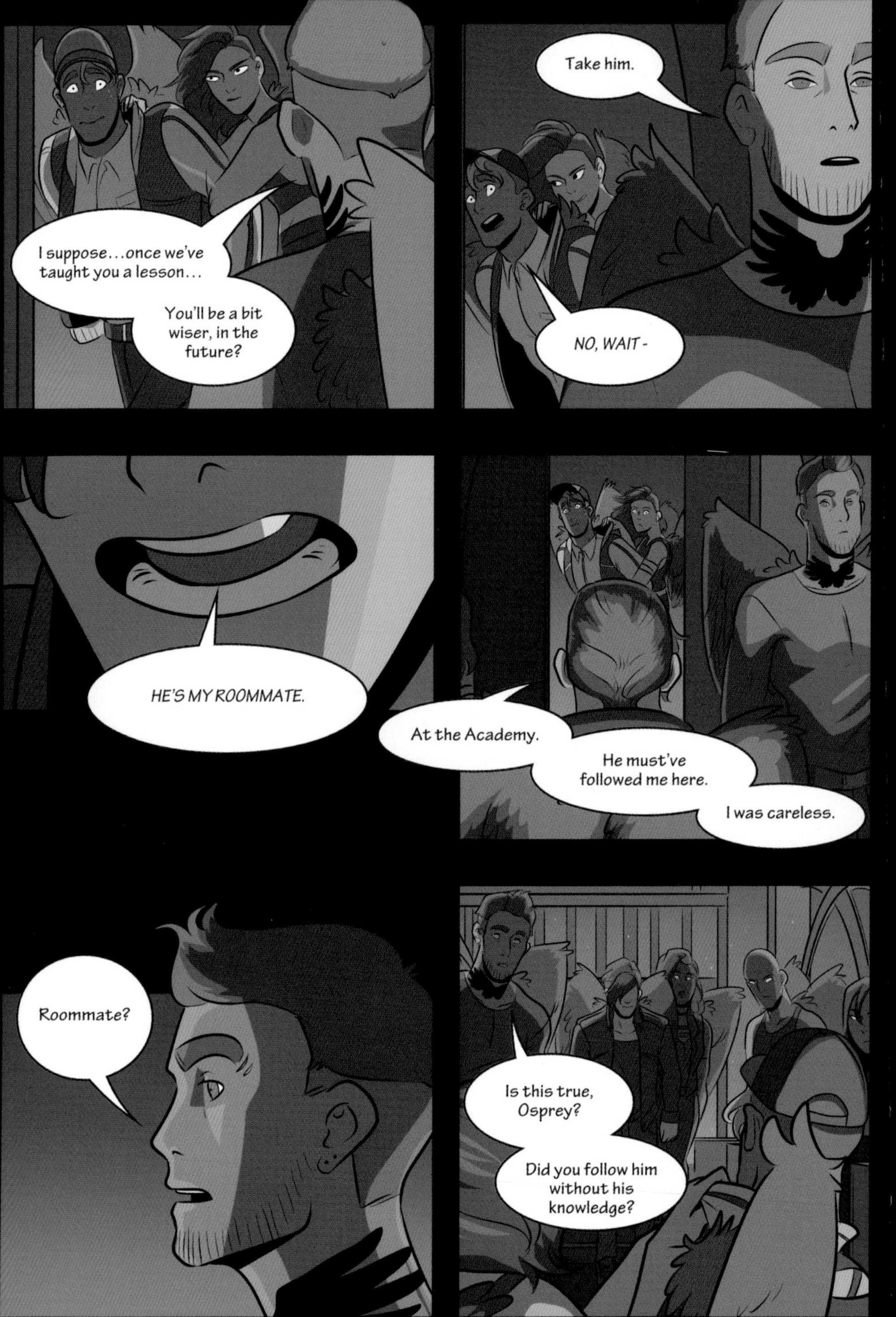
I suppose...once we've taught you a lesson...
You'll be a bit wiser, in the future?
Take him.
NO, WAIT -
HE'S MY ROOMMATE.
At the Academy.
He must've followed me here.
I was careless.
Roommate?
Is this true, Osprey?
Did you follow him without his knowledge?

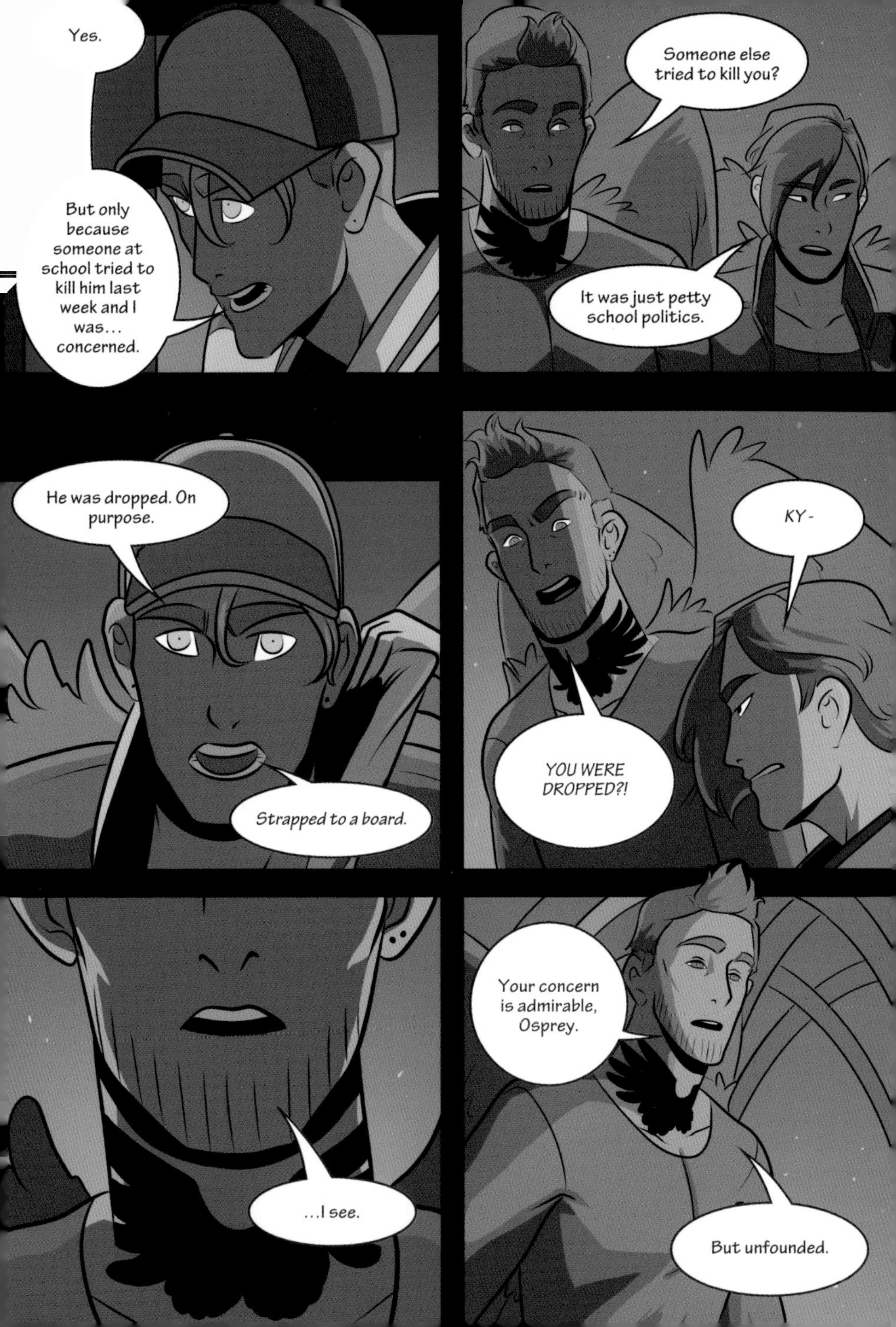
Yes.
But only because someone at school tried to kill him last week and I was… concerned.
Someone else tried to kill you?
It was just petty school politics.
He was dropped. On purpose.
Strapped to a board.
KY-
YOU WERE DROPPED?!
…I see.
Your concern is admirable, Osprey.
But unfounded.

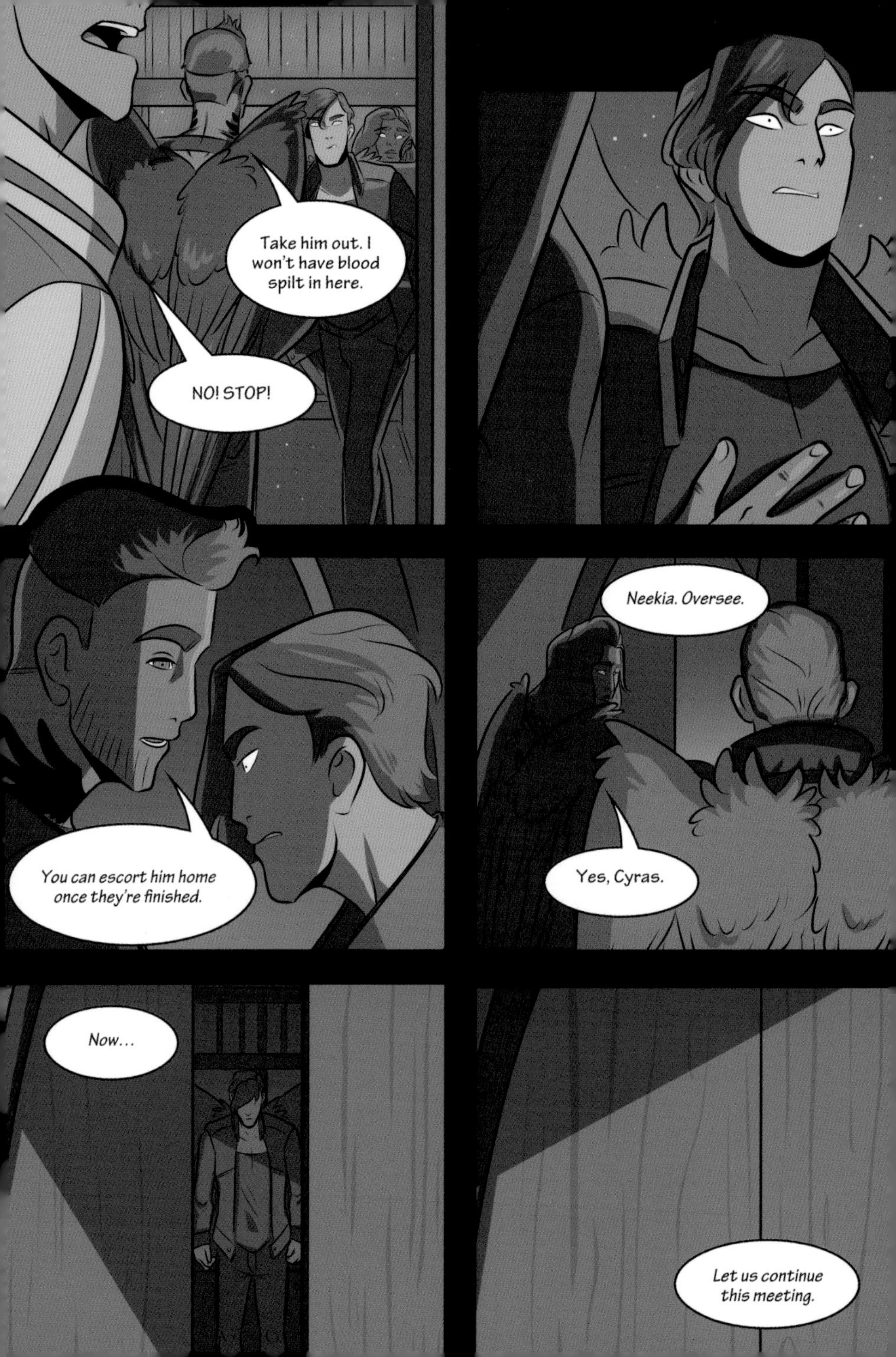
Take him out. I won't have blood spilt in here.
NO! STOP!
You can escort him home once they're finished.
Neekia. Oversee.
Yes, Cyras.
Now...
Let us continue this meeting.

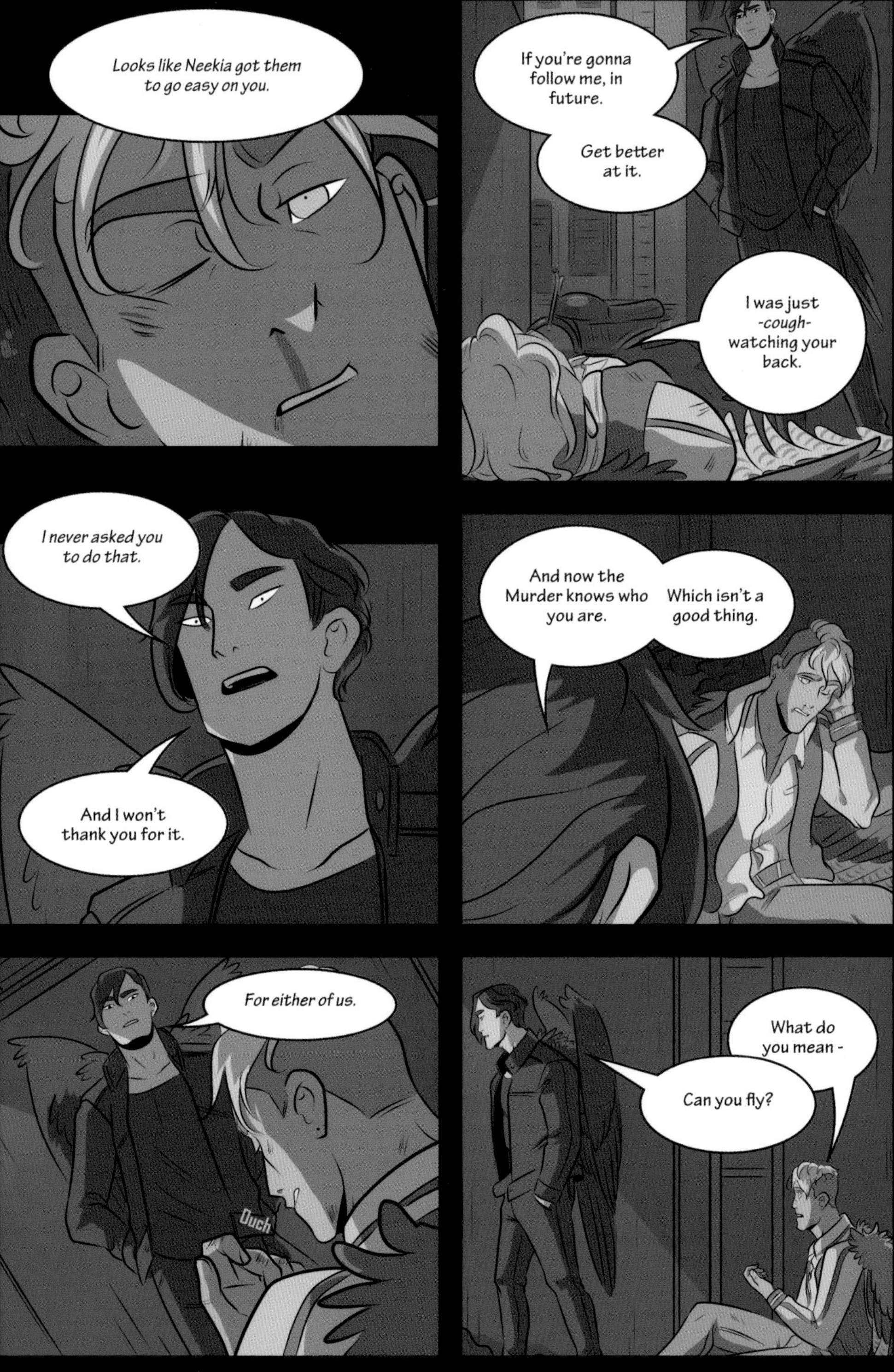
Looks like Neekia got them to go easy on you.
If you're gonna follow me, in future.
Get better at it.
I was just -cough- watching your back.
I never asked you to do that.
And I won't thank you for it.
And now the Murder knows who you are.
Which isn't a good thing.
For either of us.
Ouch
What do you mean -
Can you fly?

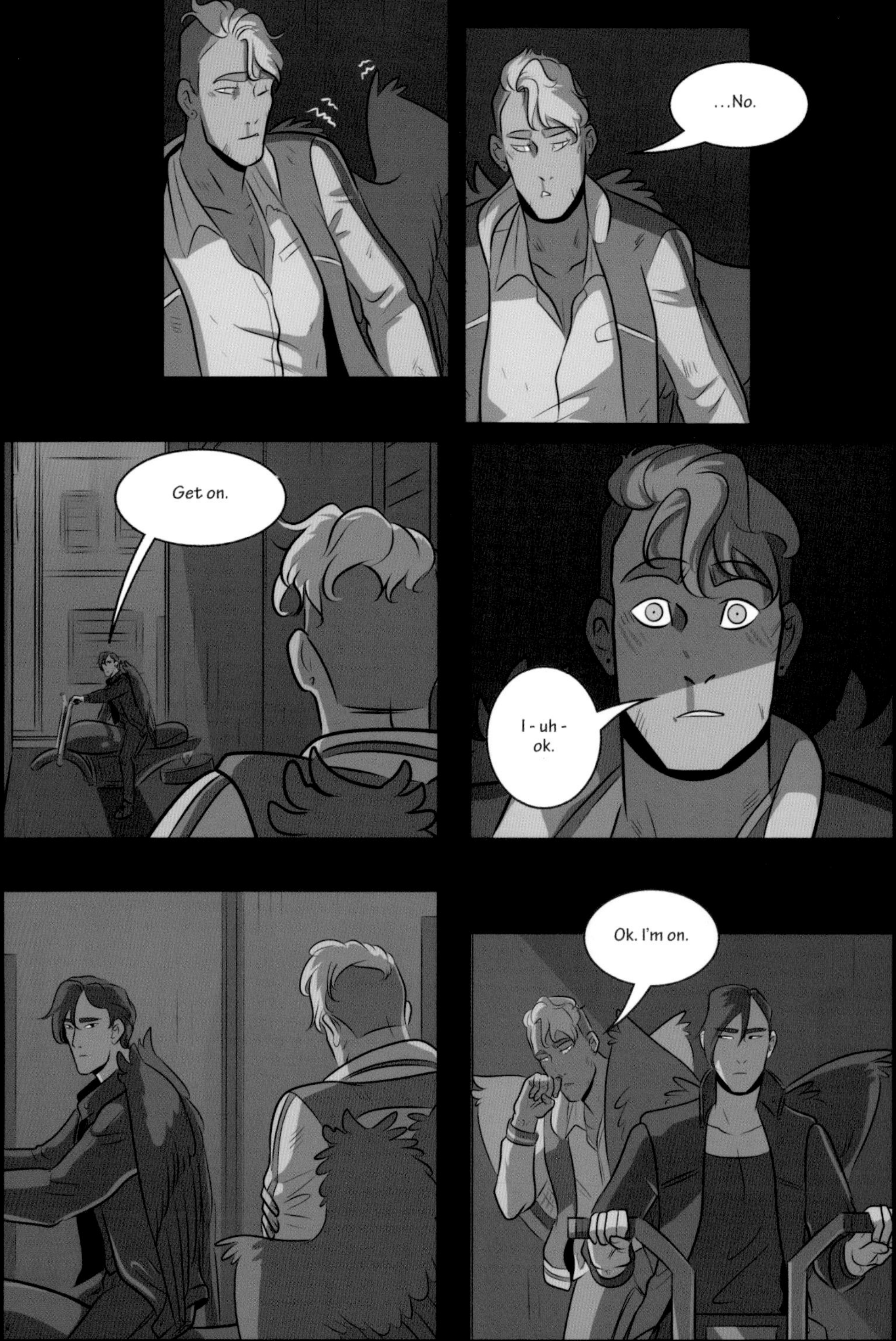
...No.
Get on.
I - uh - ok.
Ok. I'm on.

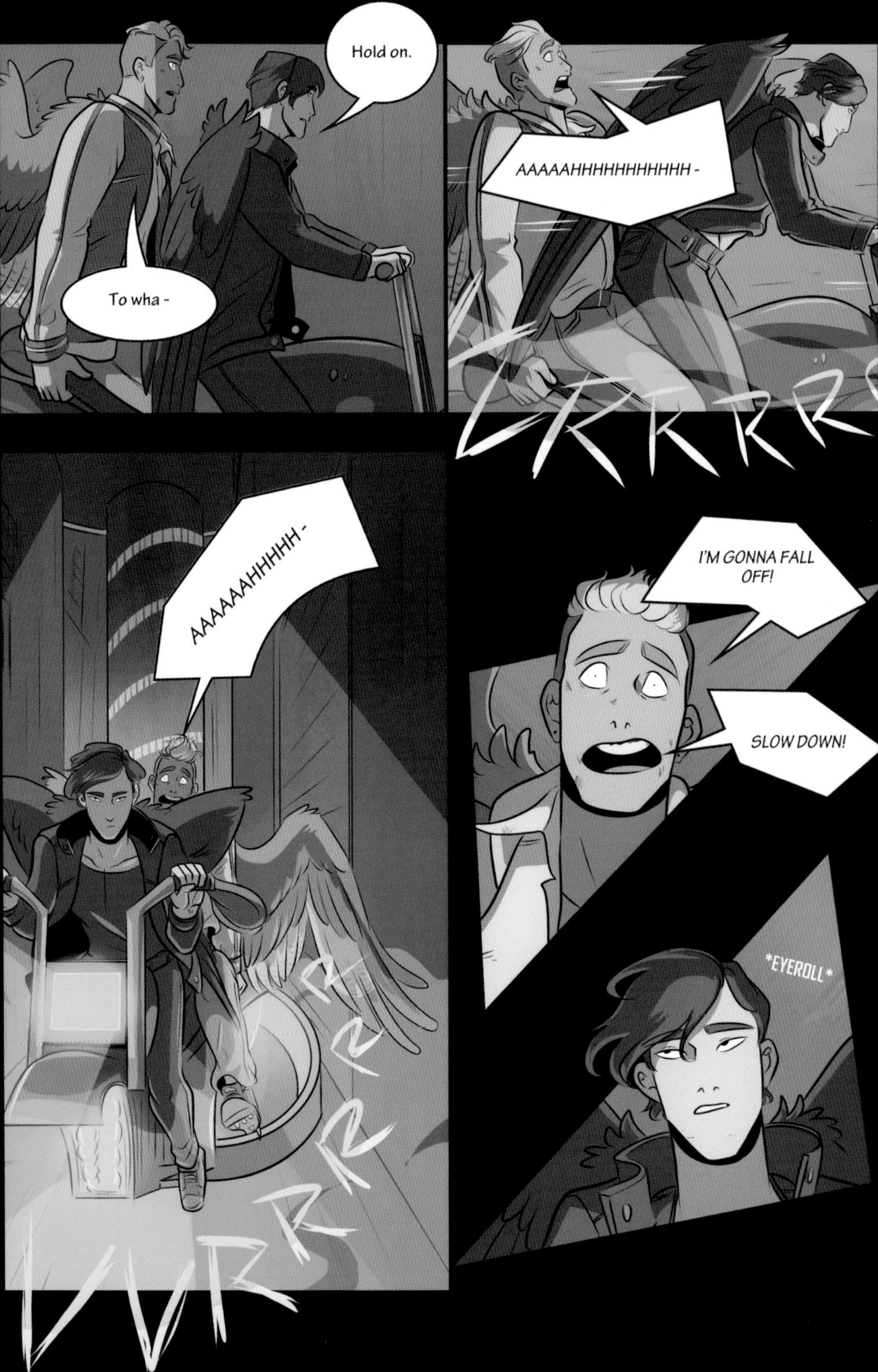
Hold on.
To wha -
AAAAAHHHHHHHHHHH -
AAAAAAHHHH -
I'M GONNA FALL OFF!
SLOW DOWN!
EYEROLL

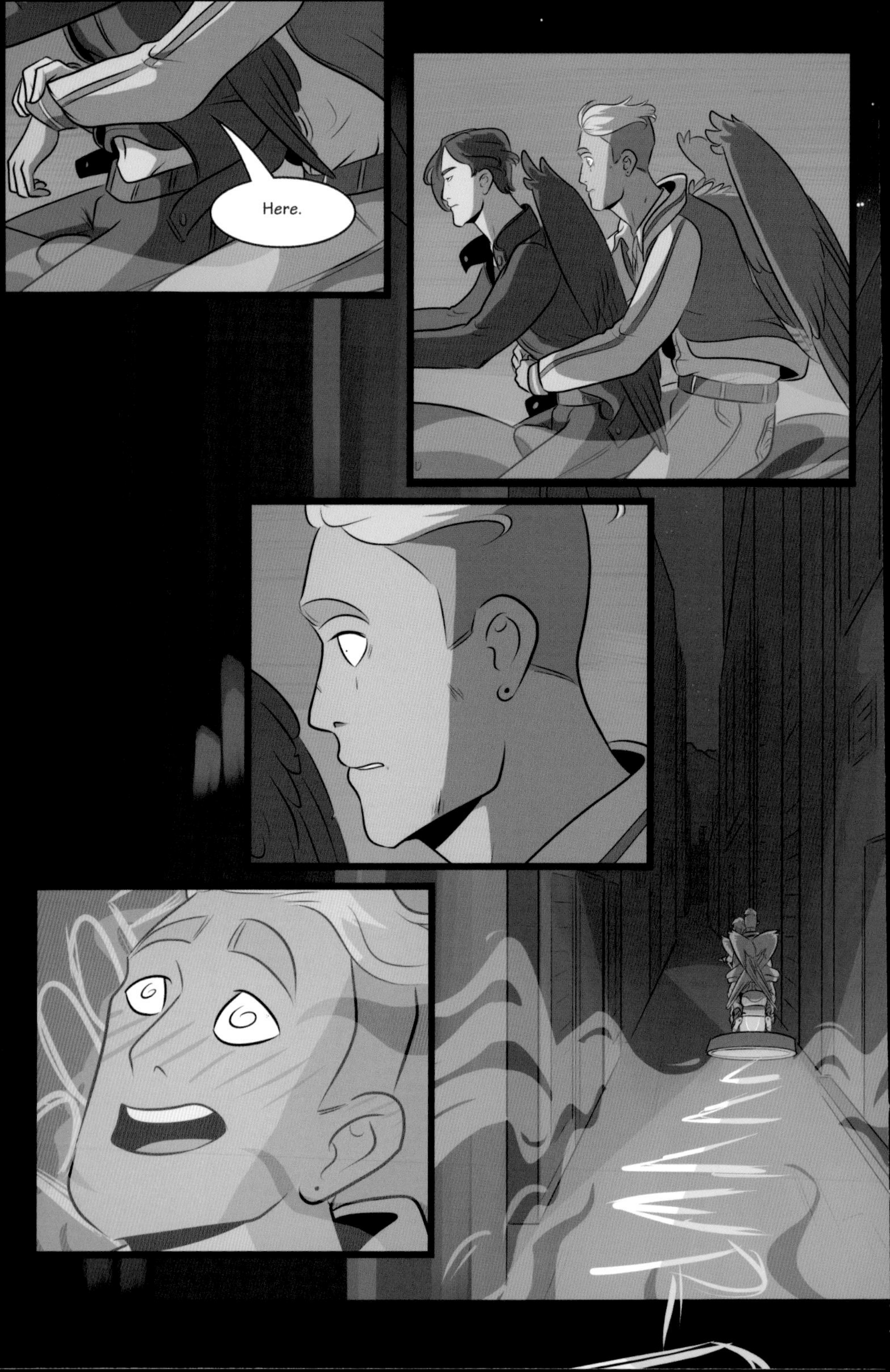
Here.

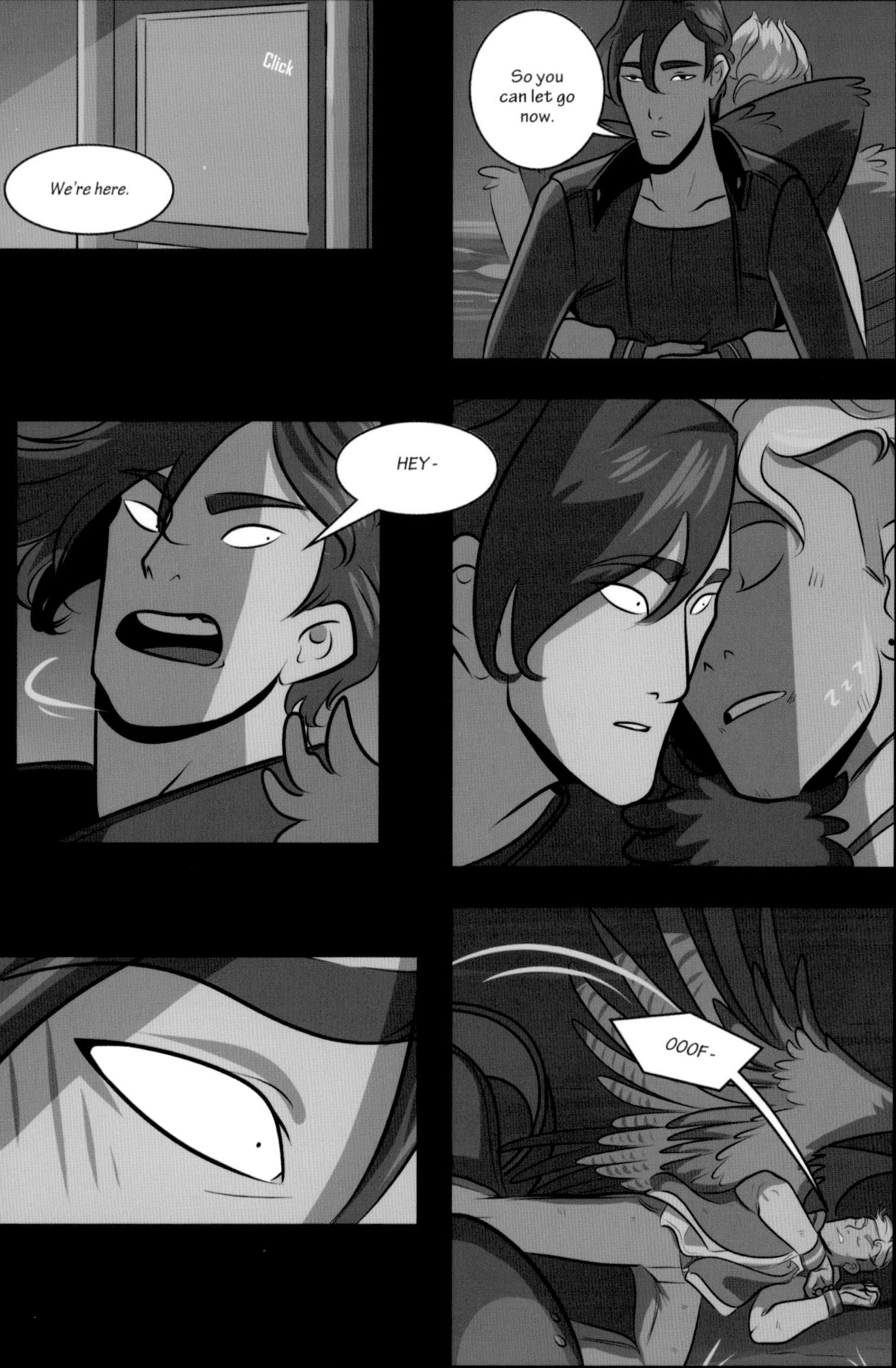
Click
We're here.
So you can let go now.
HEY-
OOOF-

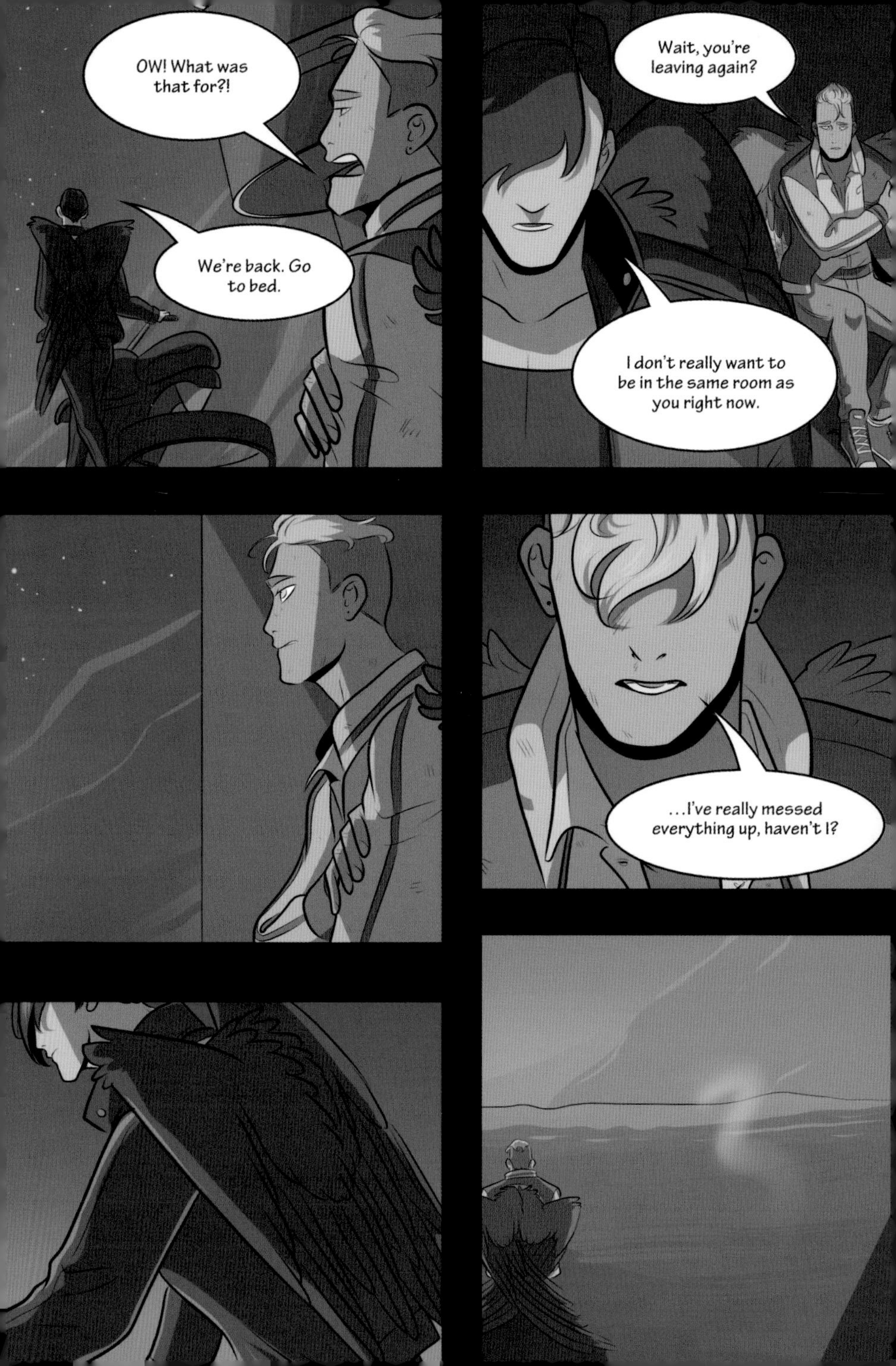
OW! What was that for?!
We're back. Go to bed.
Wait, you're leaving again?
I don't really want to be in the same room as you right now.
...I've really messed everything up, haven't I?

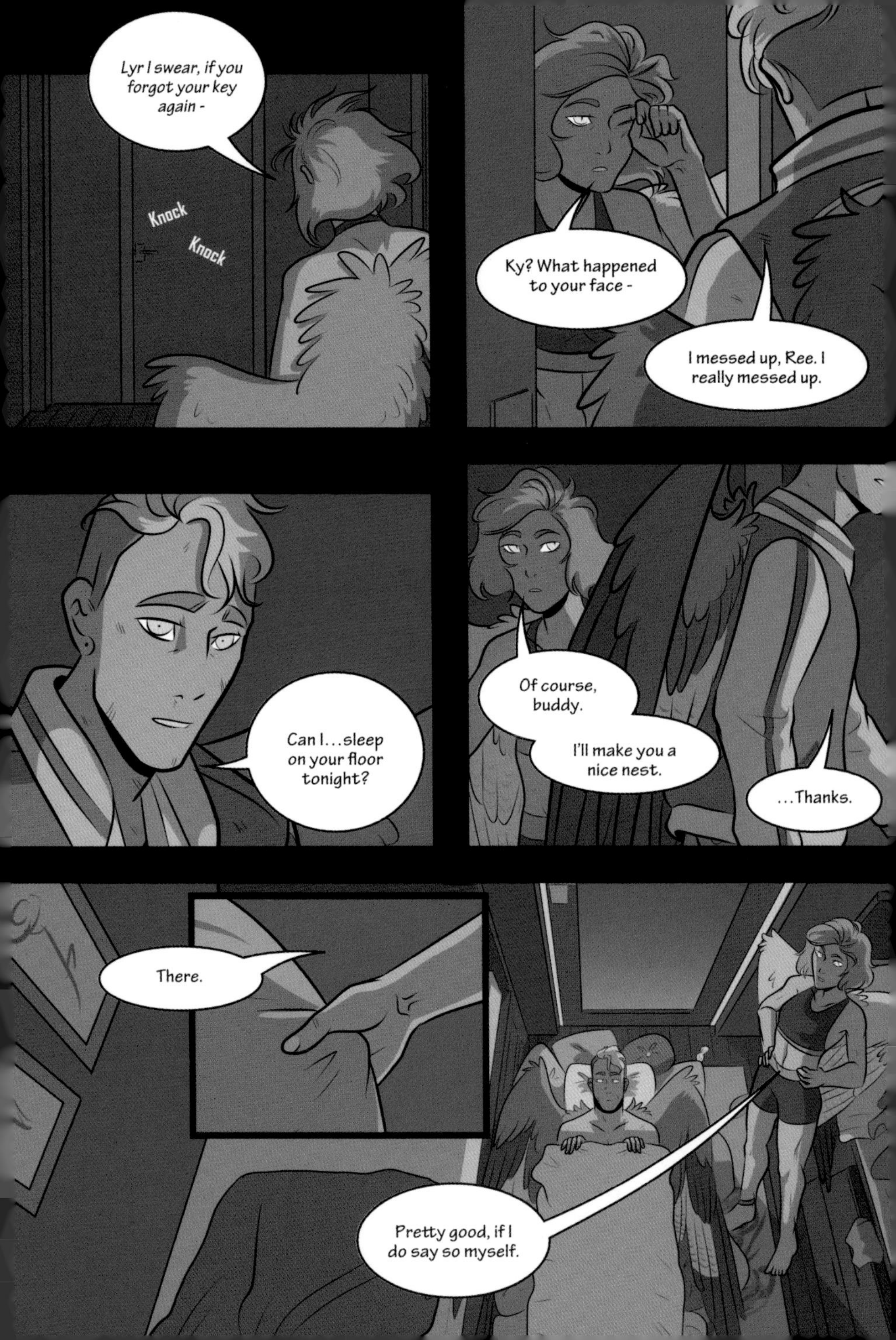
Lyr I swear, if you forgot your key again -
Knock
Knock
Ky? What happened to your face -
I messed up, Ree. I really messed up.
Can I...sleep on your floor tonight?
Of course, buddy.
I'll make you a nice nest.
...Thanks.
There.
Pretty good, if I do say so myself.

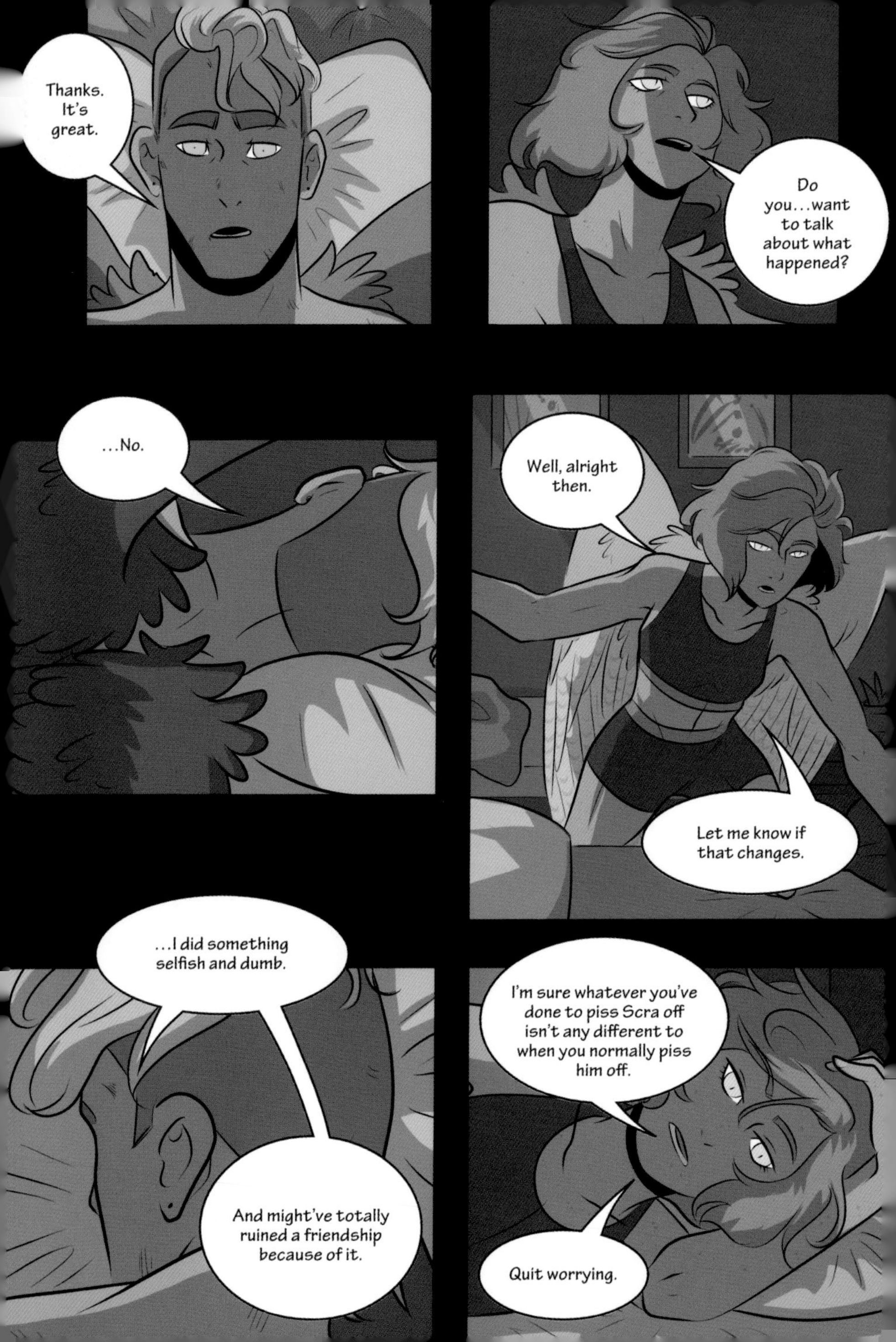
Thanks. It's great.
Do you…want to talk about what happened?
…No.
Well, alright then.
Let me know if that changes.
…I did something selfish and dumb.
And might've totally ruined a friendship because of it.
I'm sure whatever you've done to piss Scra off isn't any different to when you normally piss him off.
Quit worrying.

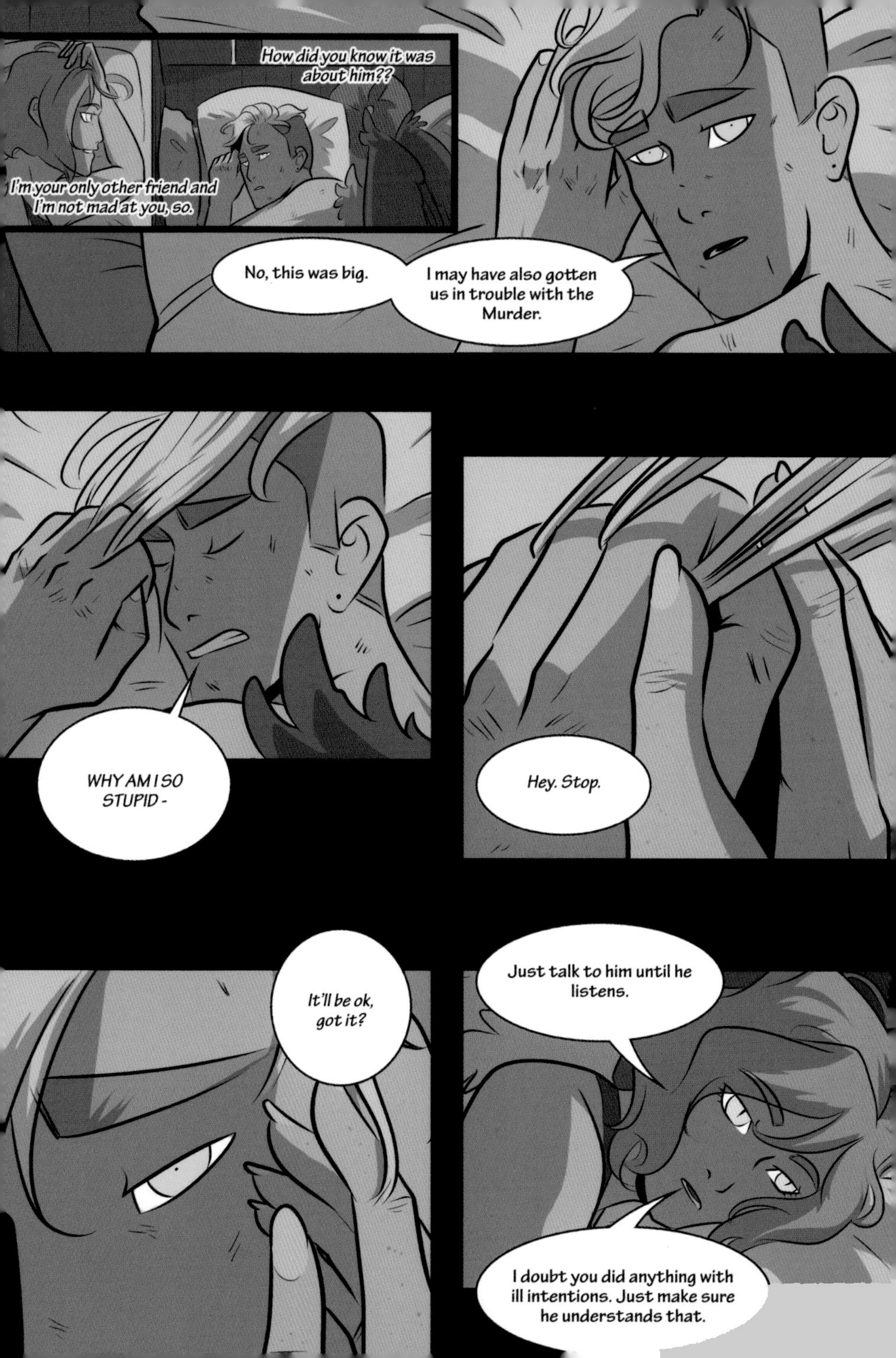
How did you know it was about him??
I'm your only other friend and I'm not mad at you, so.
No, this was big.
I may have also gotten us in trouble with the Murder.
WHY AM I SO STUPID -
Hey. Stop.
It'll be ok, got it?
Just talk to him until he listens.
I doubt you did anything with ill intentions. Just make sure he understands that.

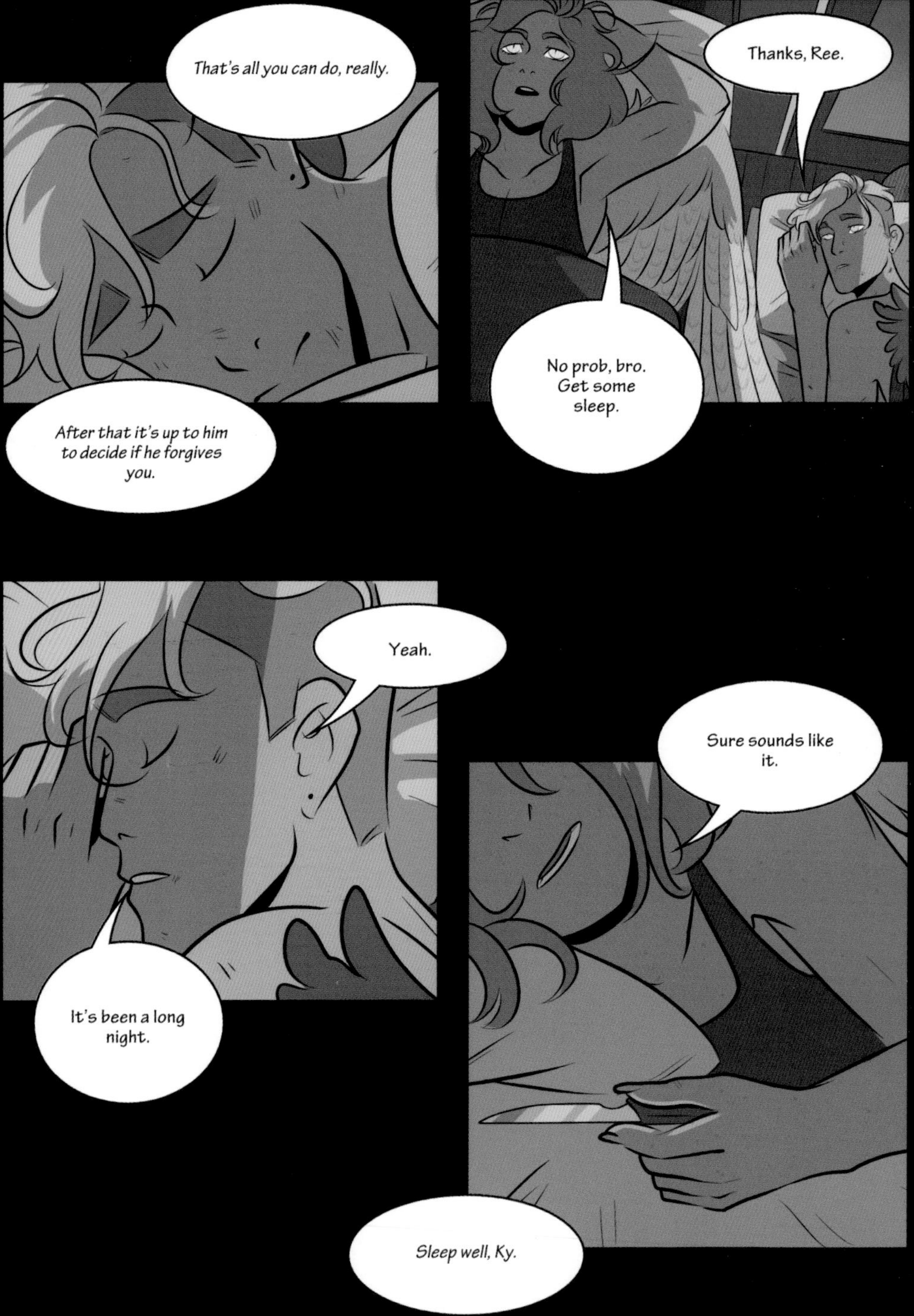

That's all you can do, really.
After that it's up to him to decide if he forgives you.
Thanks, Ree.
No prob, bro. Get some sleep.
Yeah.
It's been a long night.
Sure sounds like it.
Sleep well, Ky.

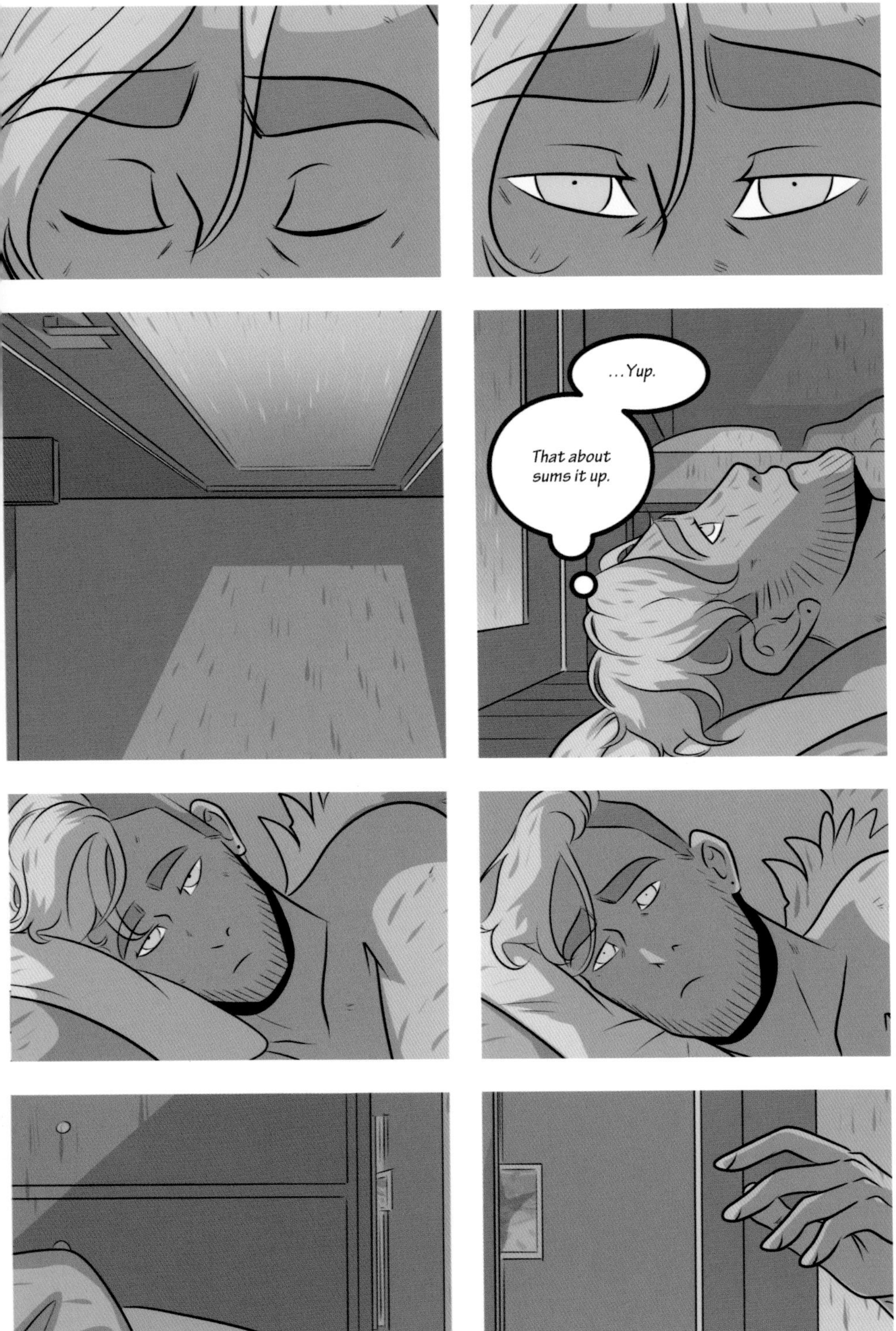
…Yup.
That about sums it up.

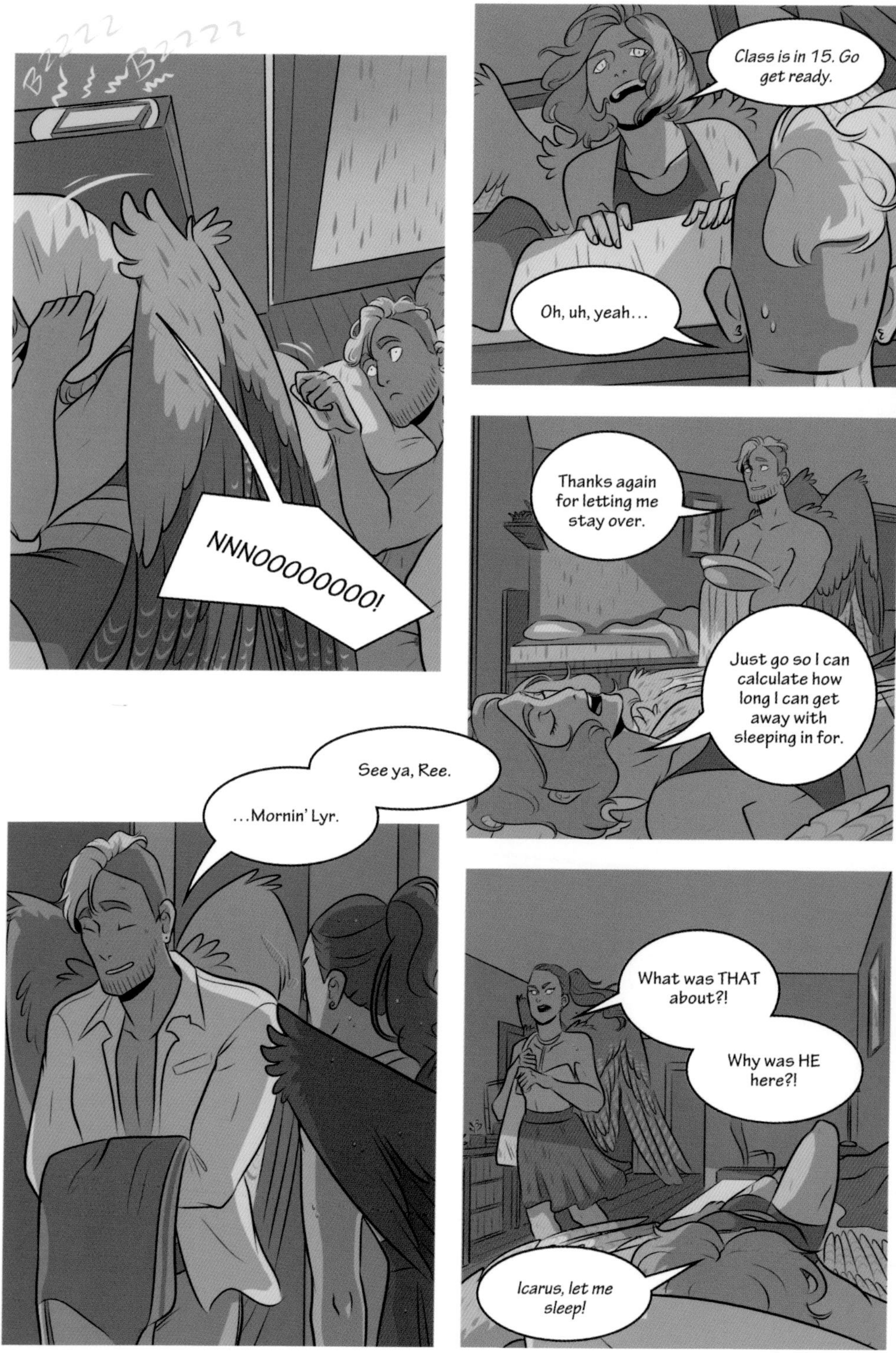
Bzzzz
Bzzzz
NNNOOOOOOOOO!
Class is in 15. Go get ready.
Oh, uh, yeah...
Thanks again for letting me stay over.
Just go so I can calculate how long I can get away with sleeping in for.
See ya, Ree.
...Mornin' Lyr.
What was THAT about?!
Why was HE here?!
Icarus, let me sleep!

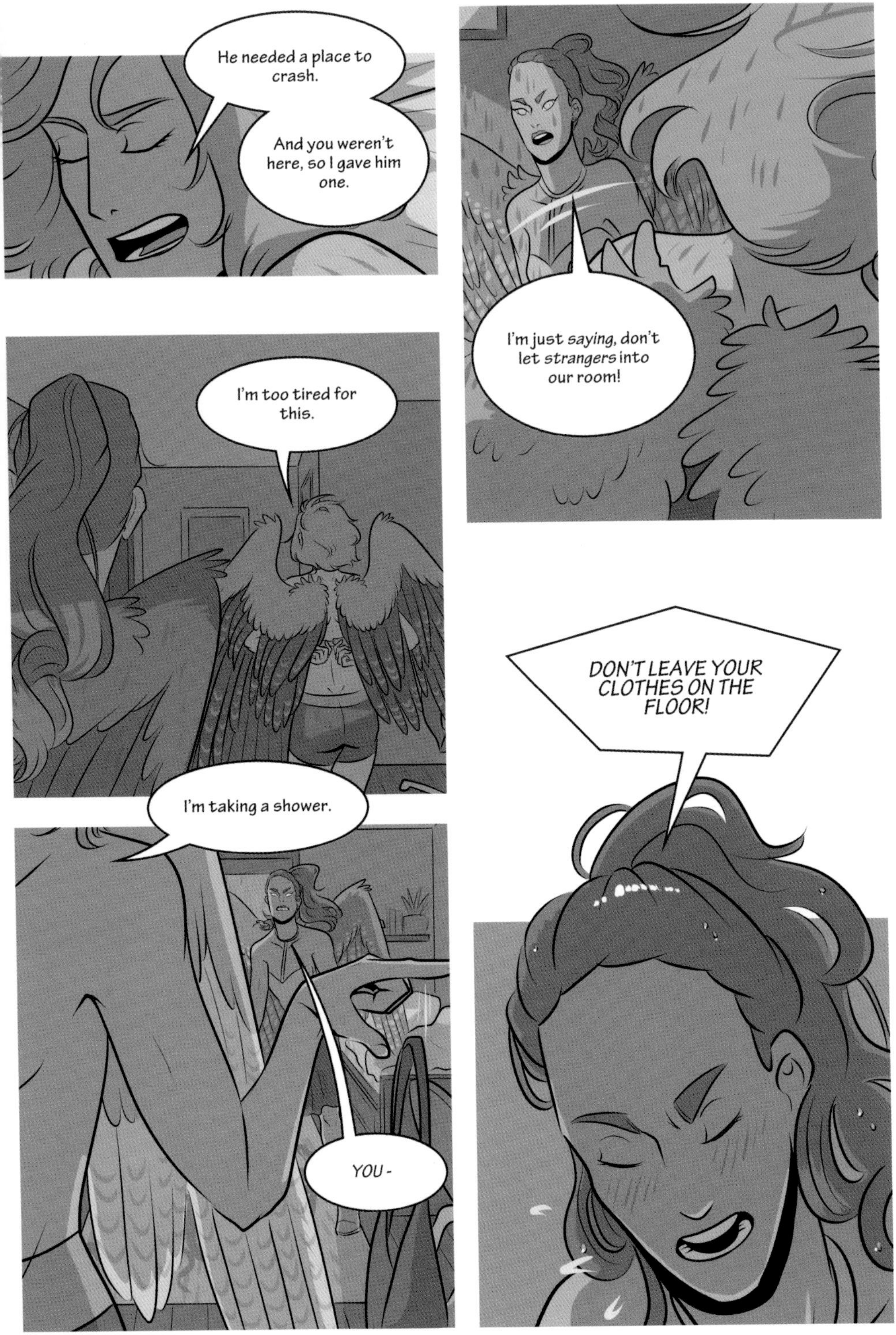
He needed a place to crash.
And you weren't here, so I gave him one.
I'm just *saying*, don't let *strangers* into our room!
I'm too tired for this.
I'm taking a shower.
YOU -
DON'T LEAVE YOUR CLOTHES ON THE FLOOR!

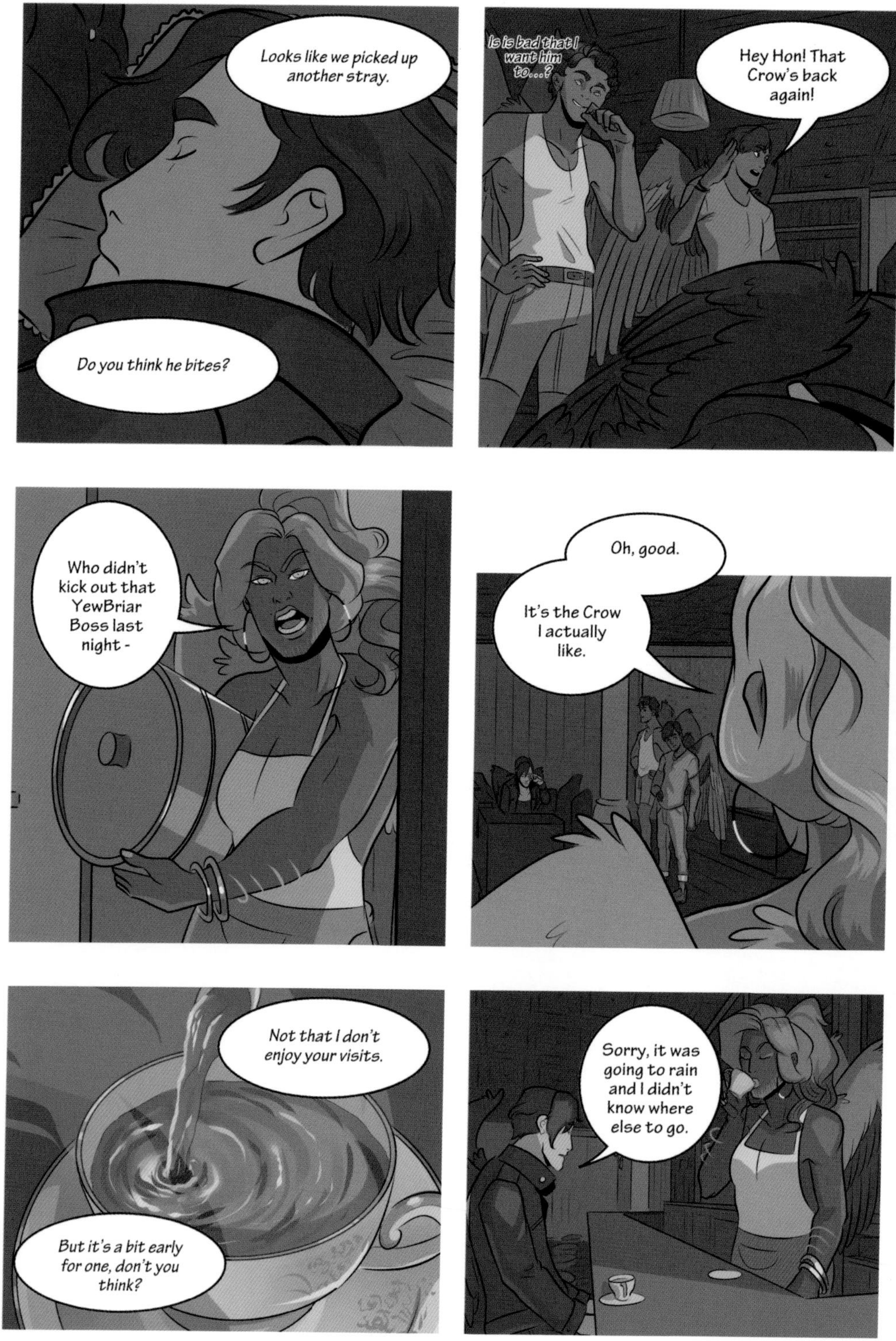
Looks like we picked up another stray.
Do you think he bites?
Is is bad that I want him to...?
Hey Hon! That Crow's back again!
Who didn't kick out that YewBriar Boss last night -
Oh, good.
It's the Crow I actually like.
Not that I don't enjoy your visits.
But it's a bit early for one, don't you think?
Sorry, it was going to rain and I didn't know where else to go.

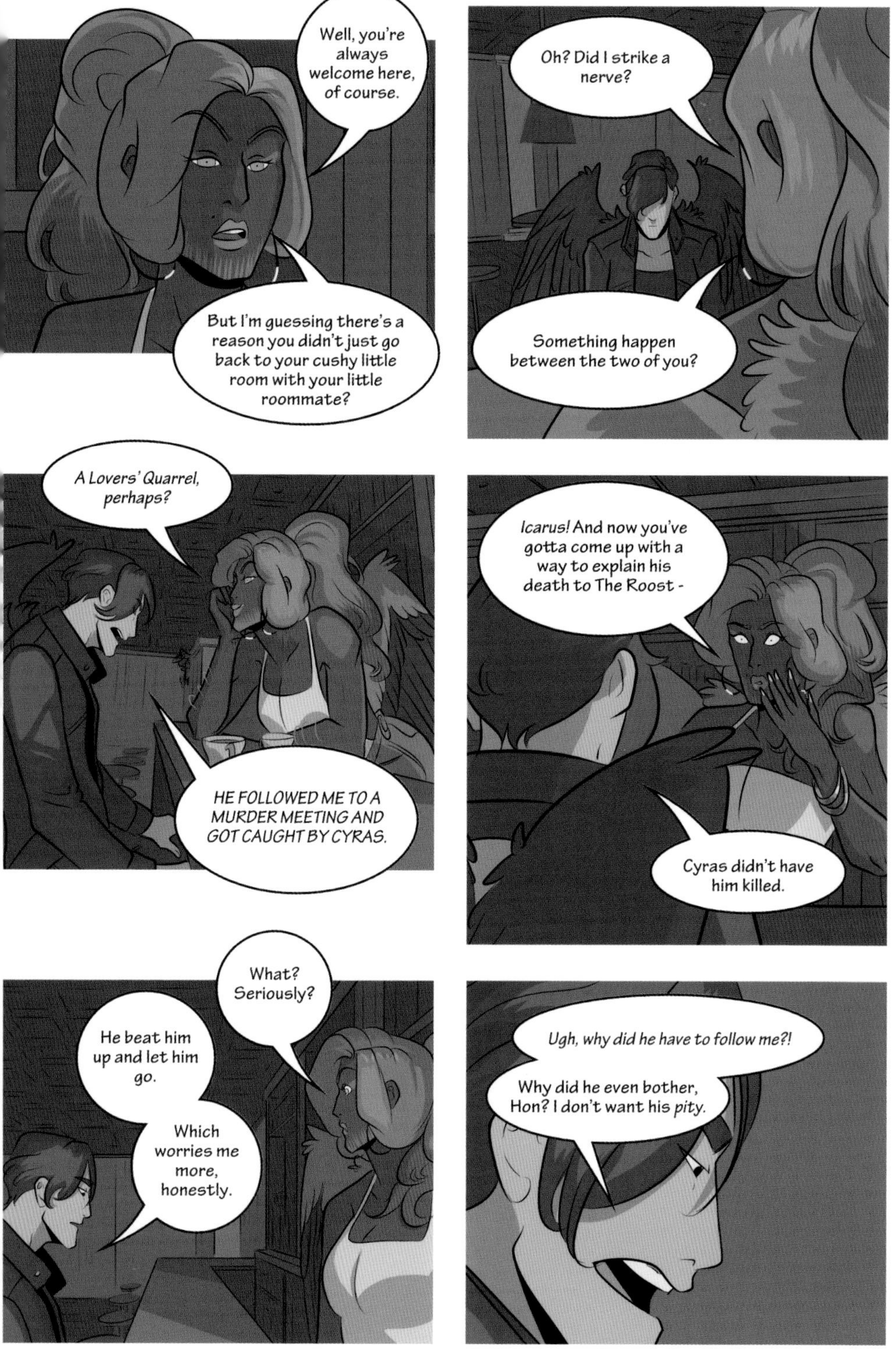
Well, you're always welcome here, of course.
But I'm guessing there's a reason you didn't just go back to your cushy little room with your little roommate?
Oh? Did I strike a nerve?
Something happen between the two of you?
A Lovers' Quarrel, perhaps?
HE FOLLOWED ME TO A MURDER MEETING AND GOT CAUGHT BY CYRAS.
Icarus! And now you've gotta come up with a way to explain his death to The Roost -
Cyras didn't have him killed.
What? Seriously?
He beat him up and let him go.
Which worries me more, honestly.
Ugh, why did he have to follow me?!
Why did he even bother, Hon? I don't want his pity.

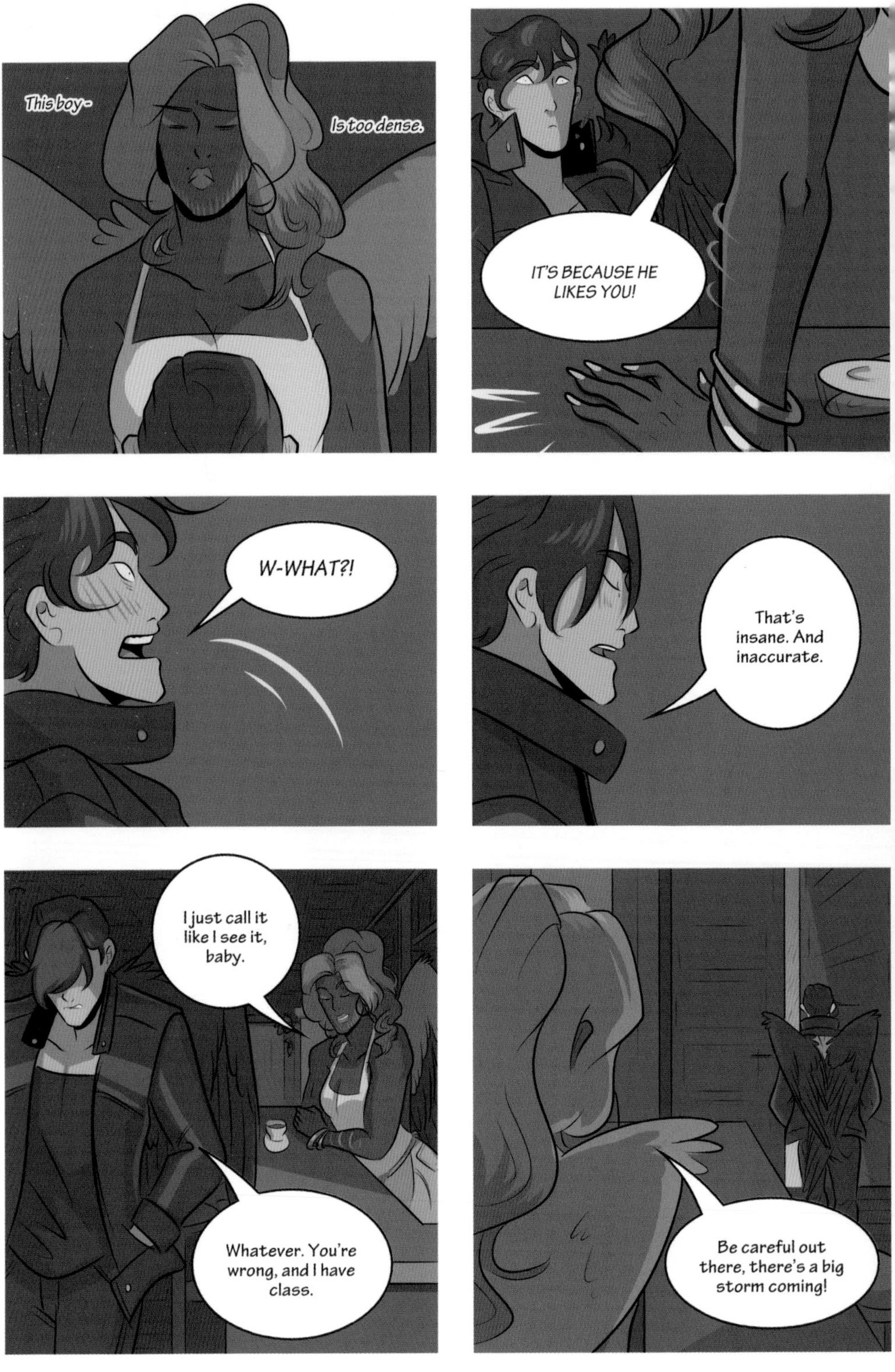

This boy -
Is too dense.
IT'S BECAUSE HE LIKES YOU!
W-WHAT?!
That's insane. And inaccurate.
I just call it like I see it, baby.
Whatever. You're wrong, and I have class.
Be careful out there, there's a big storm coming!

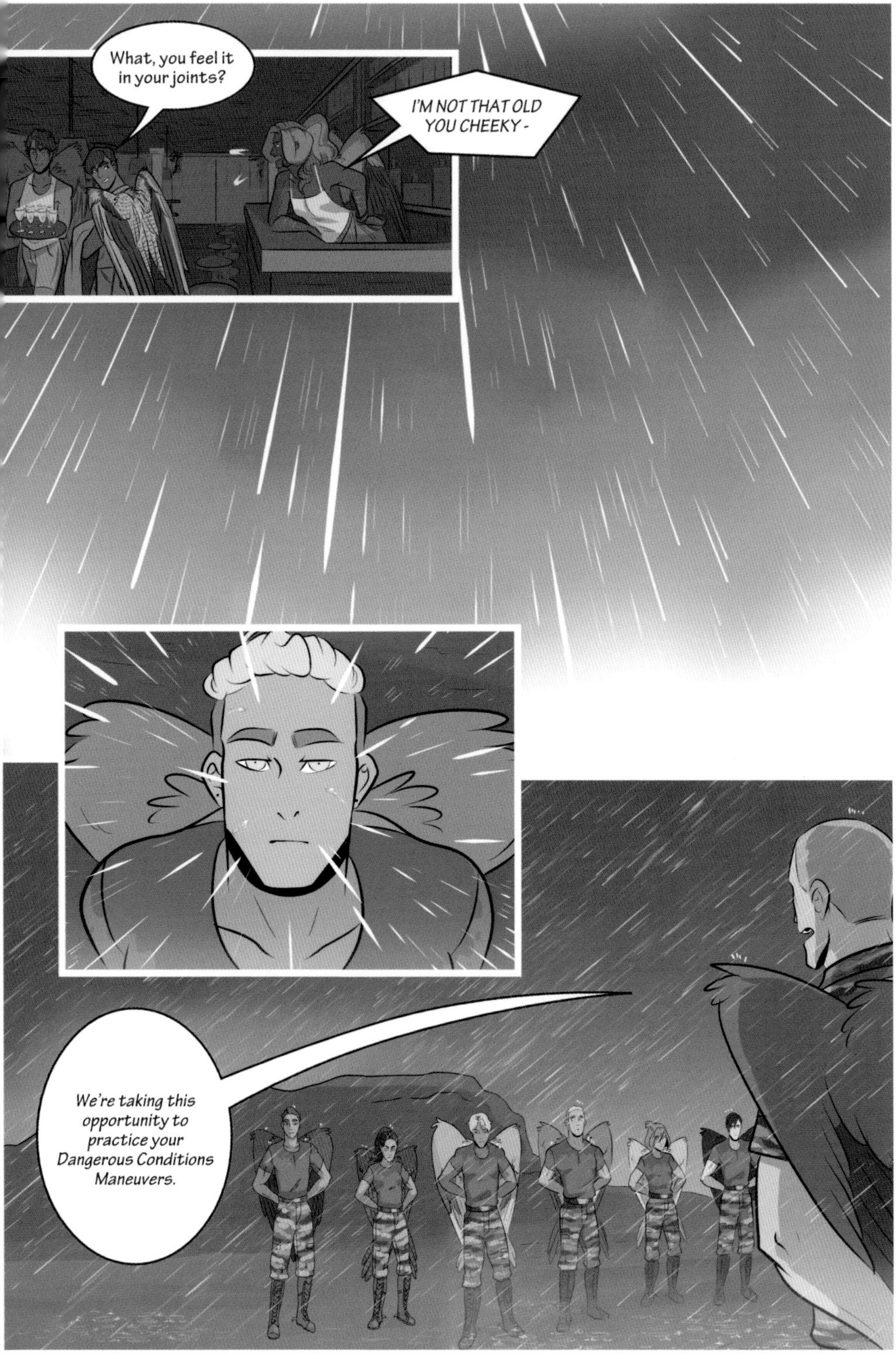
What, you feel it in your joints?
I'M NOT THAT OLD YOU CHEEKY -
We're taking this opportunity to practice your Dangerous Conditions Maneuvers.

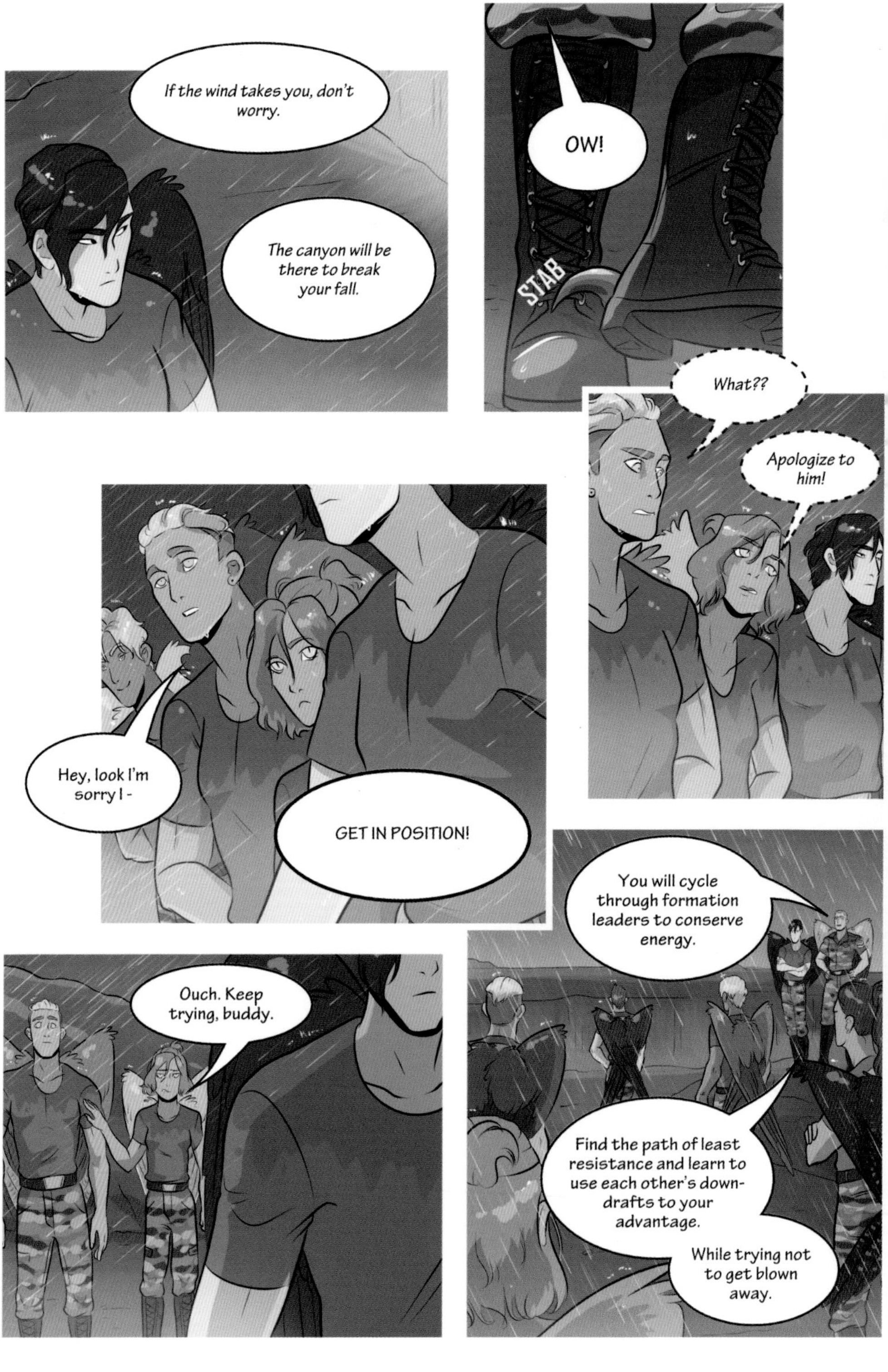
If the wind takes you, don't worry.
The canyon will be there to break your fall.
OW!
STAB
What??
Apologize to him!
Hey, look I'm sorry I -
GET IN POSITION!
Ouch. Keep trying, buddy.
You will cycle through formation leaders to conserve energy.
Find the path of least resistance and learn to use each other's down-drafts to your advantage.
While trying not to get blown away.

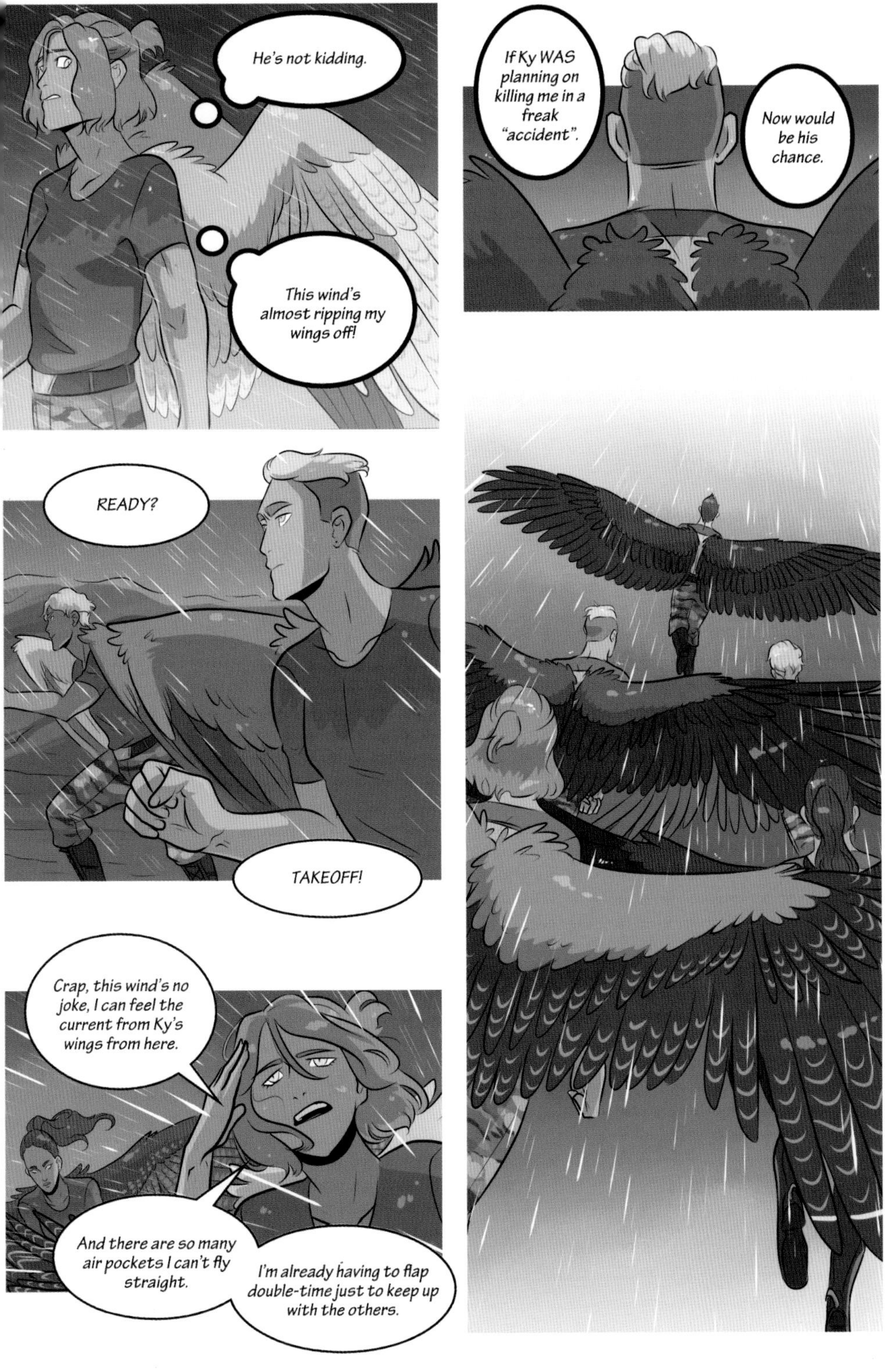
He's not kidding.
This wind's almost ripping my wings off!
If Ky WAS planning on killing me in a freak "accident".
Now would be his chance.
READY?
TAKEOFF!
Crap, this wind's no joke, I can feel the current from Ky's wings from here.
And there are so many air pockets I can't fly straight.
I'm already having to flap double-time just to keep up with the others.

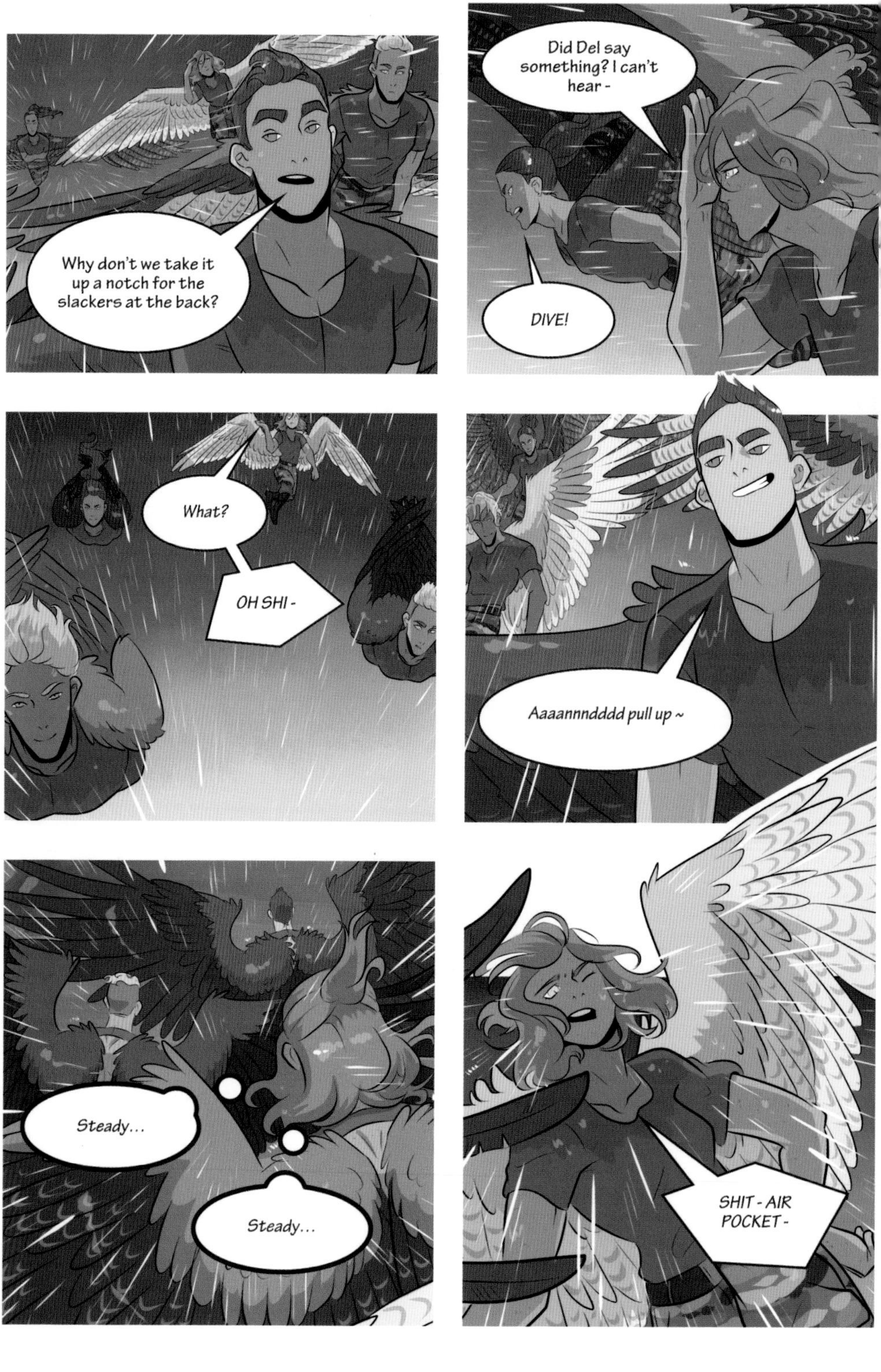
Why don't we take it up a notch for the slackers at the back?
Did Del say something? I can't hear -
DIVE!
What?
OH SHI -
Aaaannndddd pull up ~
Steady...
Steady...
SHIT - AIR POCKET -

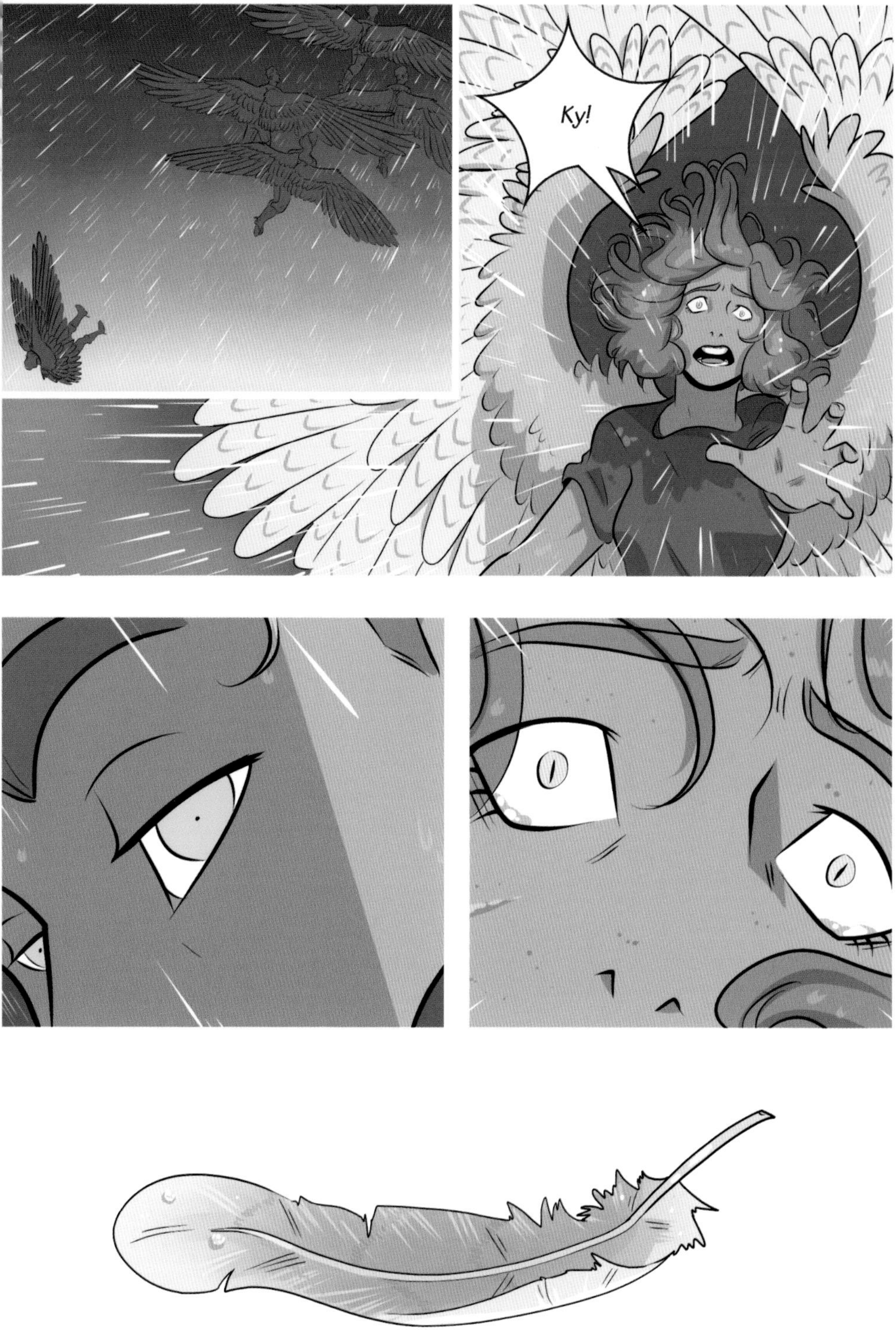
Ky!

THE CROAKING

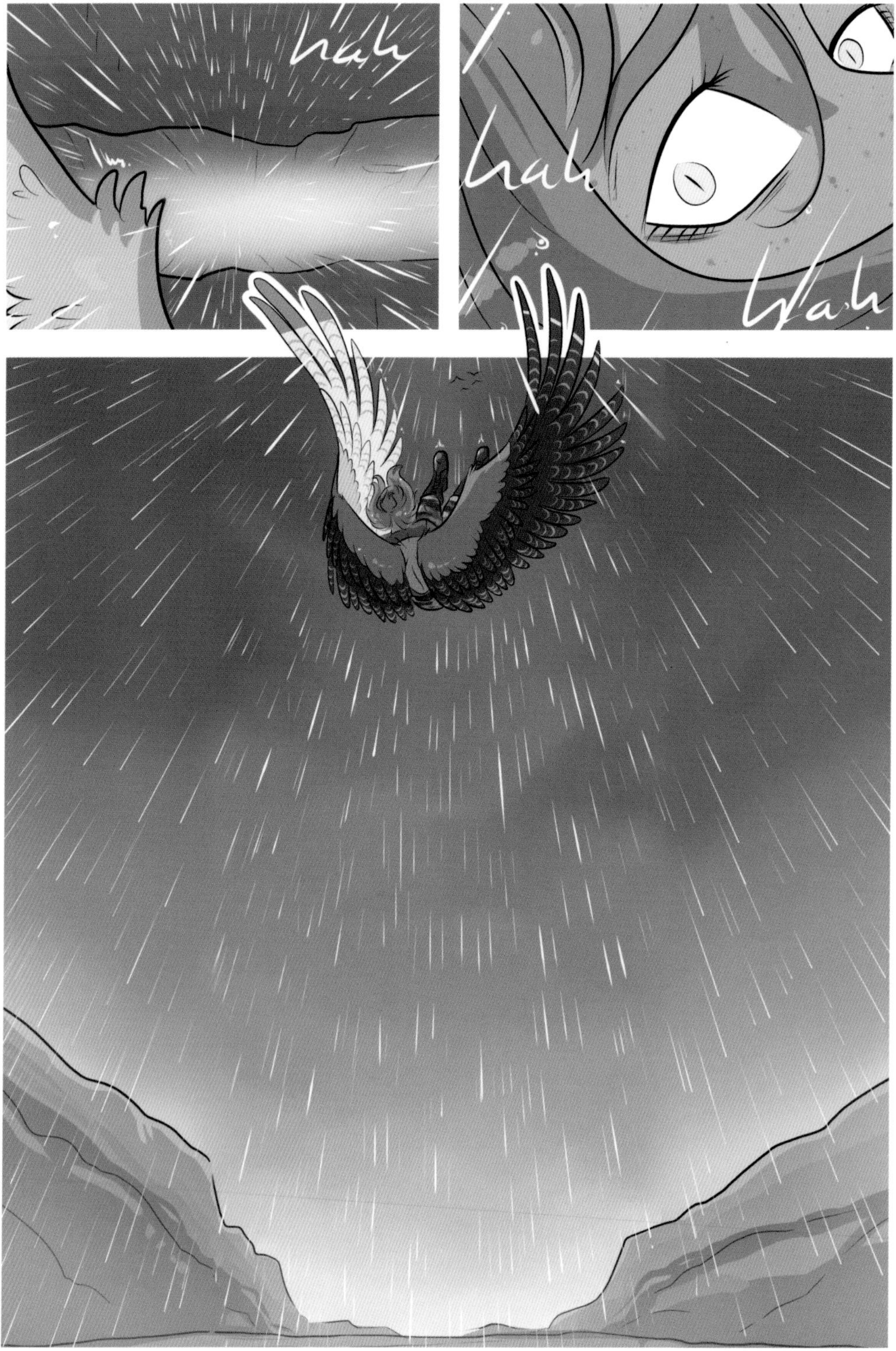
Wah
Wah
Wah

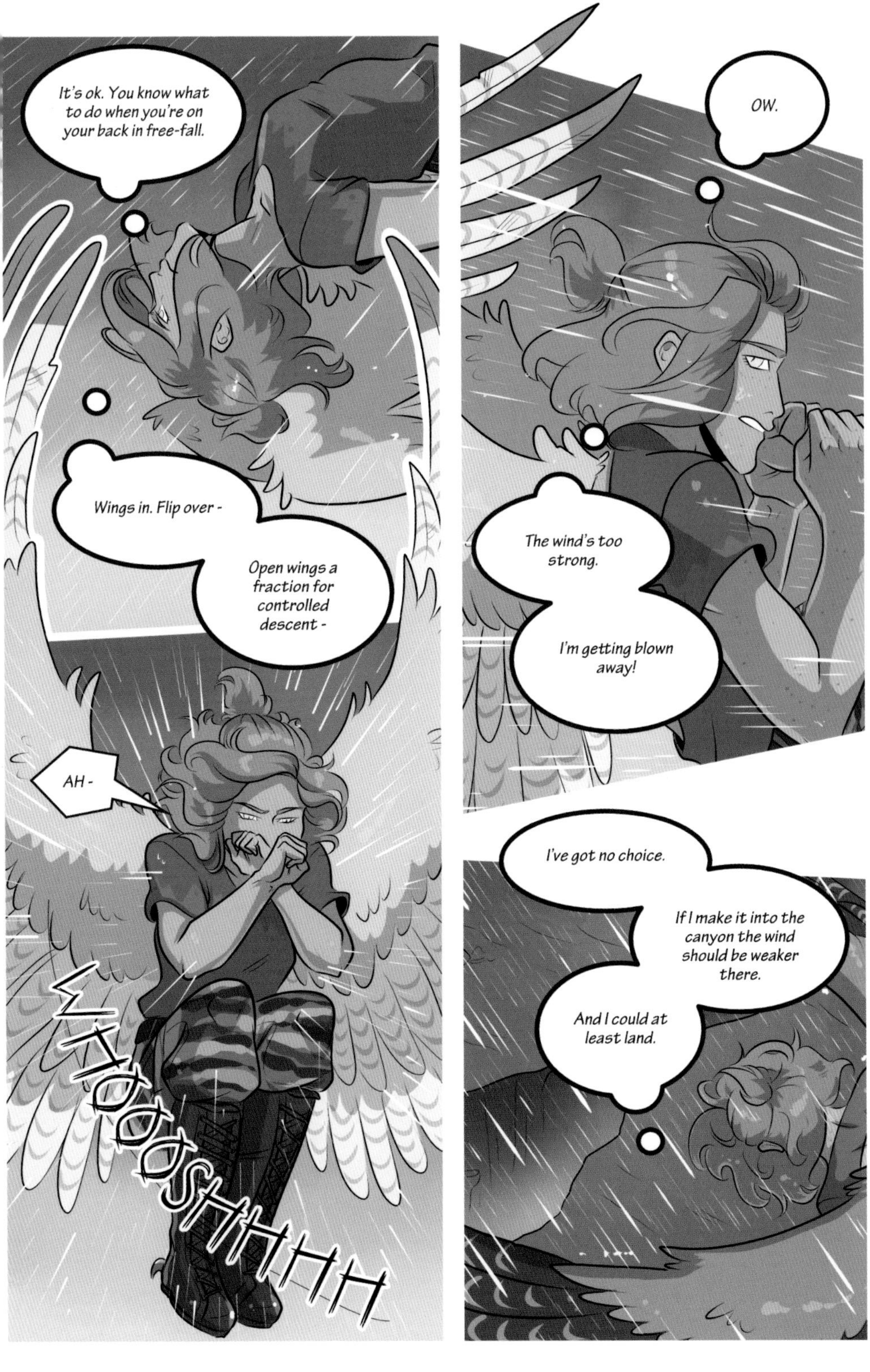
It's ok. You know what to do when you're on your back in free-fall.
Wings in. Flip over -
Open wings a fraction for controlled descent -
AH -
WHOOOSHHHHH
OW.
The wind's too strong.
I'm getting blown away!
I've got no choice.
If I make it into the canyon the wind should be weaker there.
And I could at least land.

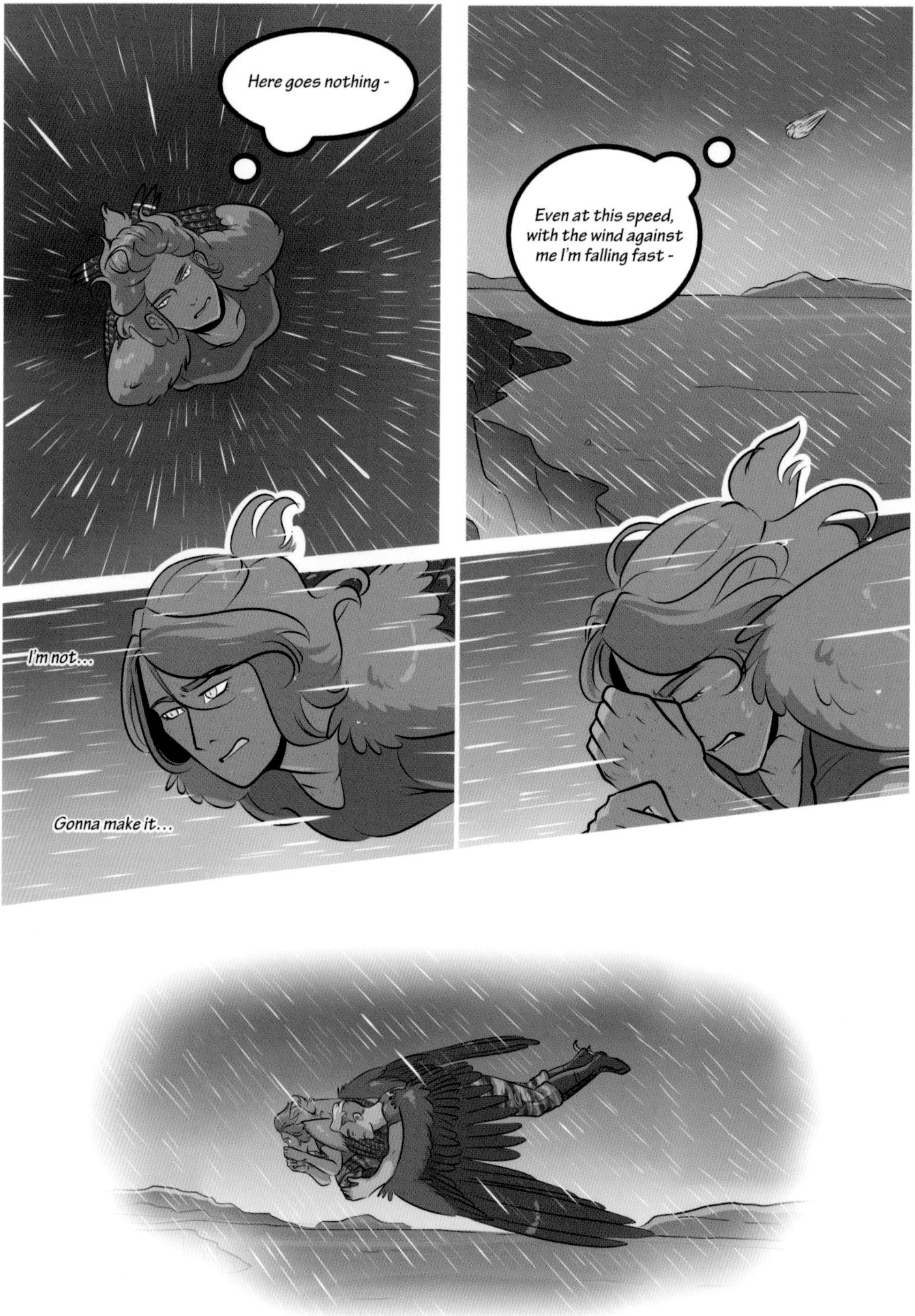
Here goes nothing -
Even at this speed, with the wind against me I'm falling fast -
I'm not...
Gonna make it...

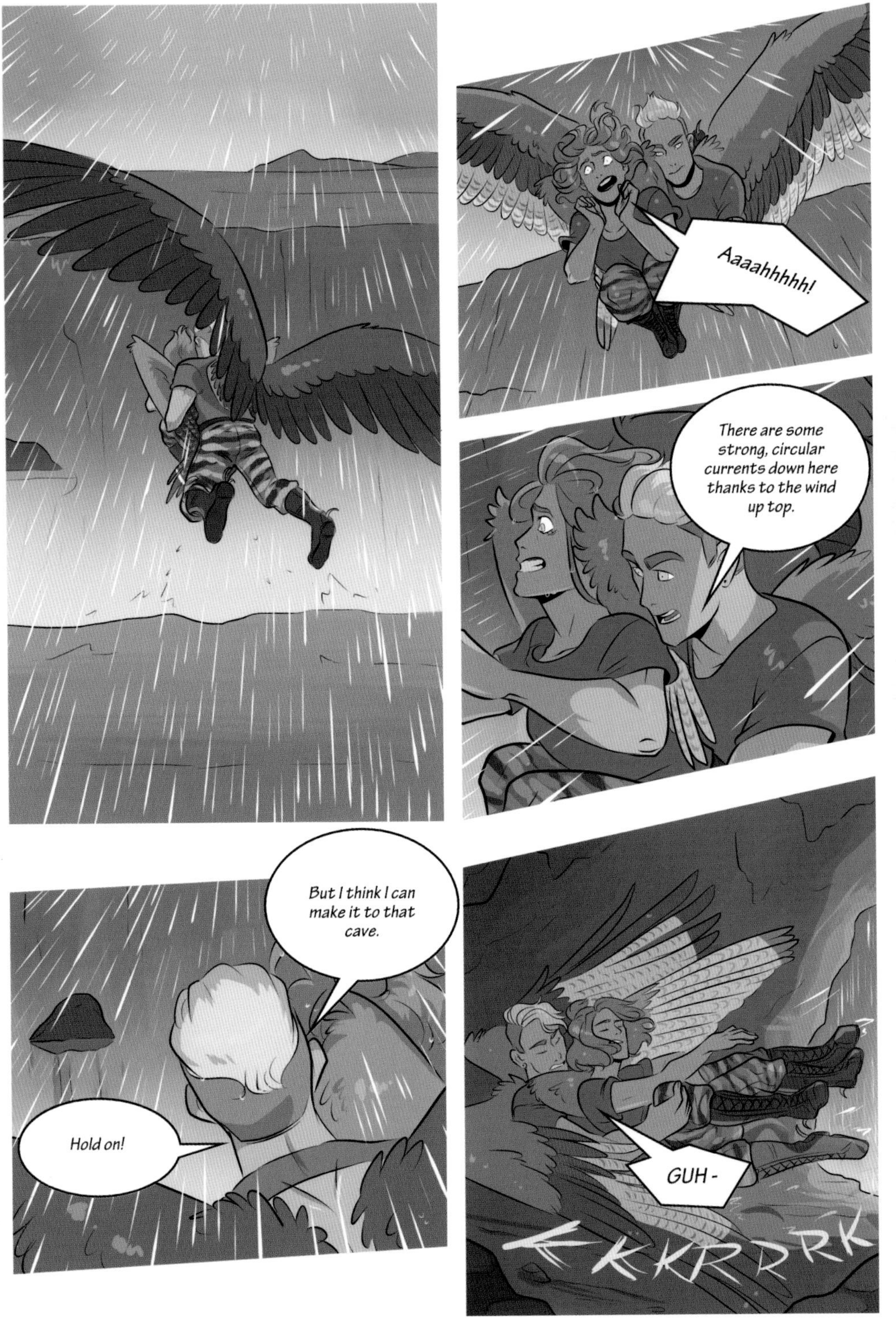
Aaaahhhhh!
There are some strong, circular currents down here thanks to the wind up top.
But I think I can make it to that cave.
Hold on!
GUH -
KKKRRRRK

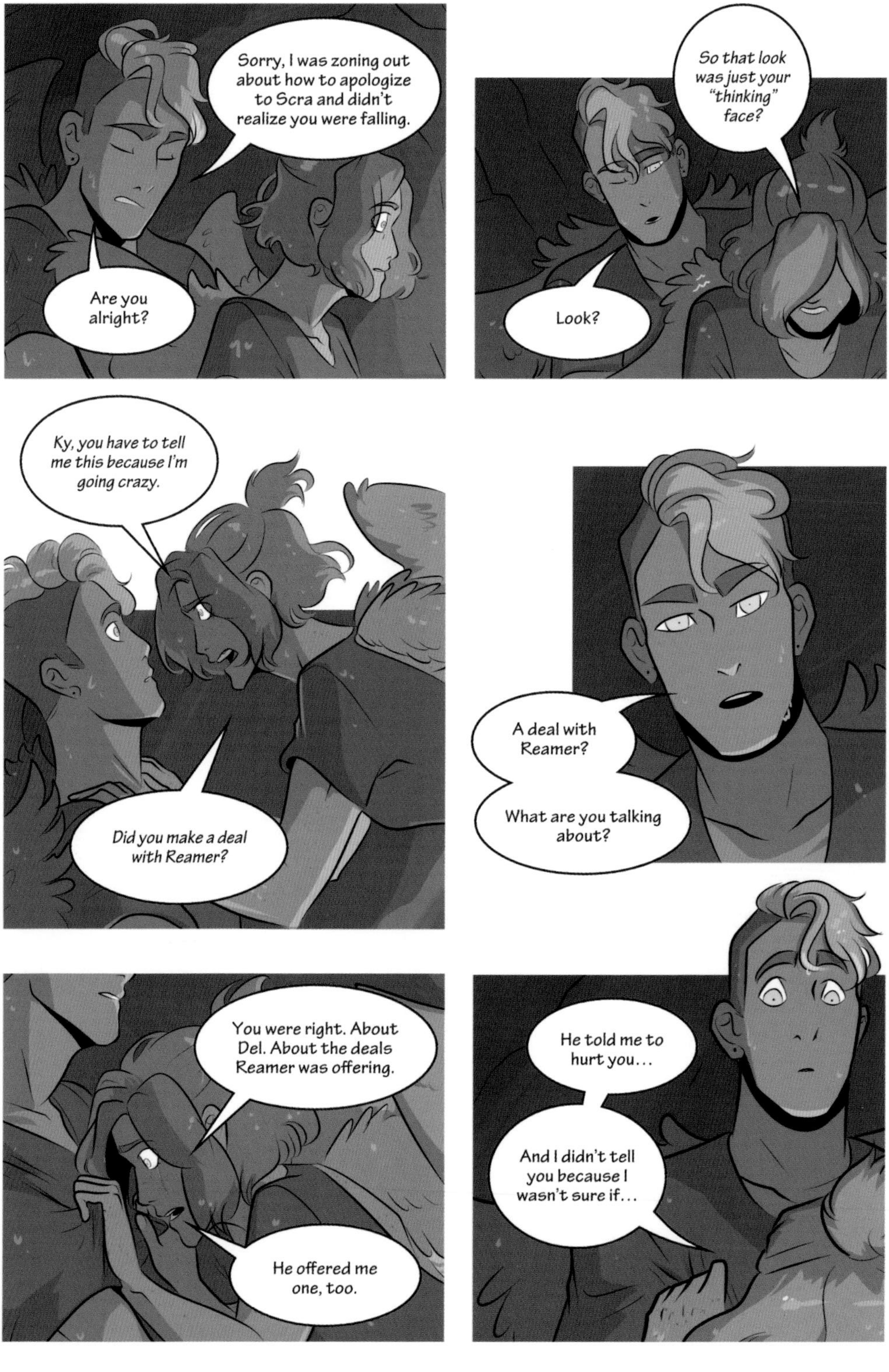
Sorry, I was zoning out about how to apologize to Scra and didn't realize you were falling.
Are you alright?
So that look was just your "thinking" face?
Look?
Ky, you have to tell me this because I'm going crazy.
Did you make a deal with Reamer?
A deal with Reamer?
What are you talking about?
You were right. About Del. About the deals Reamer was offering.
He offered me one, too.
He told me to hurt you...
And I didn't tell you because I wasn't sure if...

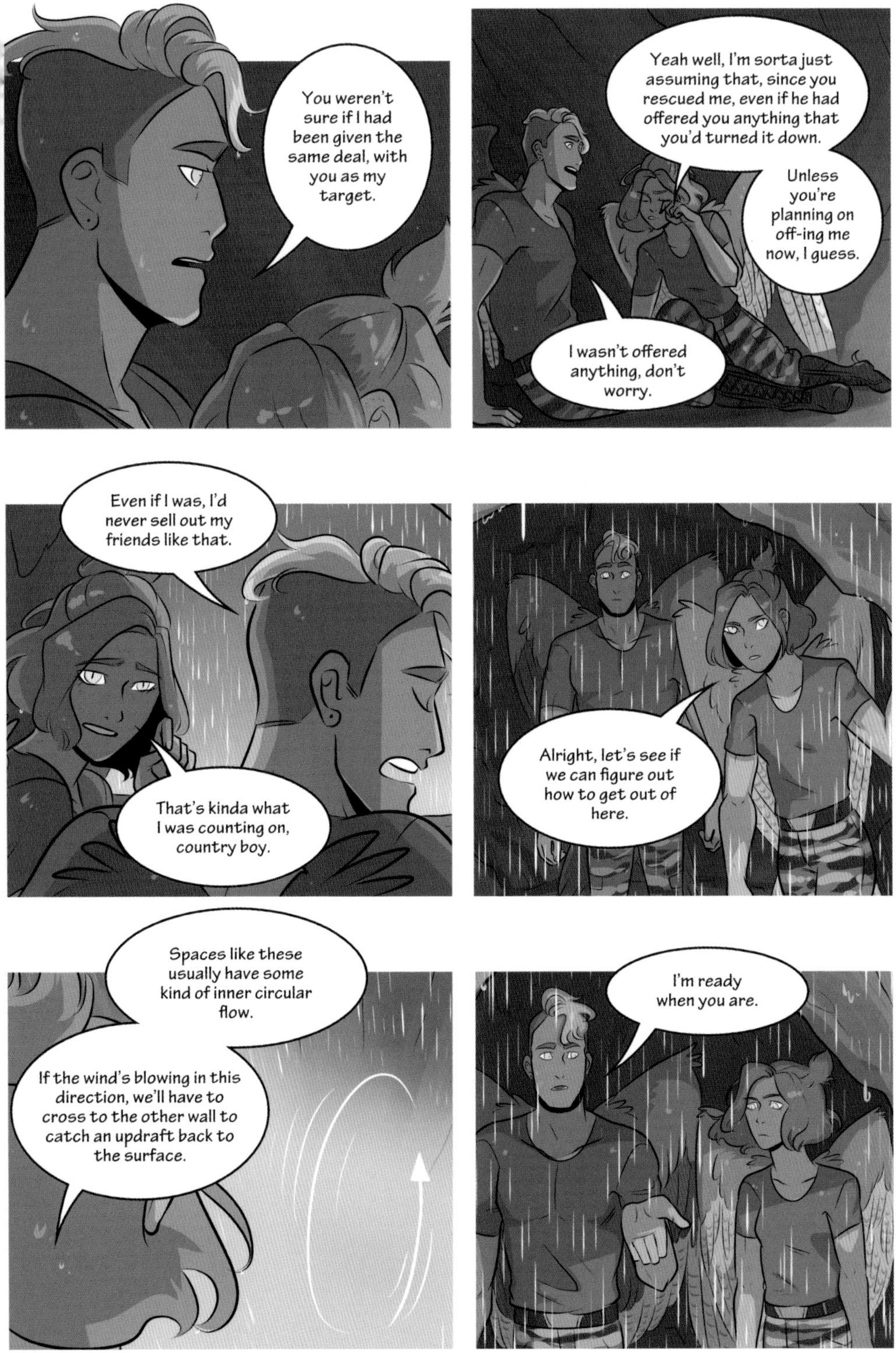
You weren't sure if I had been given the same deal, with you as my target.
Yeah well, I'm sorta just assuming that, since you rescued me, even if he had offered you anything that you'd turned it down.
Unless you're planning on off-ing me now, I guess.
I wasn't offered anything, don't worry.
Even if I was, I'd never sell out my friends like that.
That's kinda what I was counting on, country boy.
Alright, let's see if we can figure out how to get out of here.
Spaces like these usually have some kind of inner circular flow.
If the wind's blowing in this direction, we'll have to cross to the other wall to catch an updraft back to the surface.
I'm ready when you are.

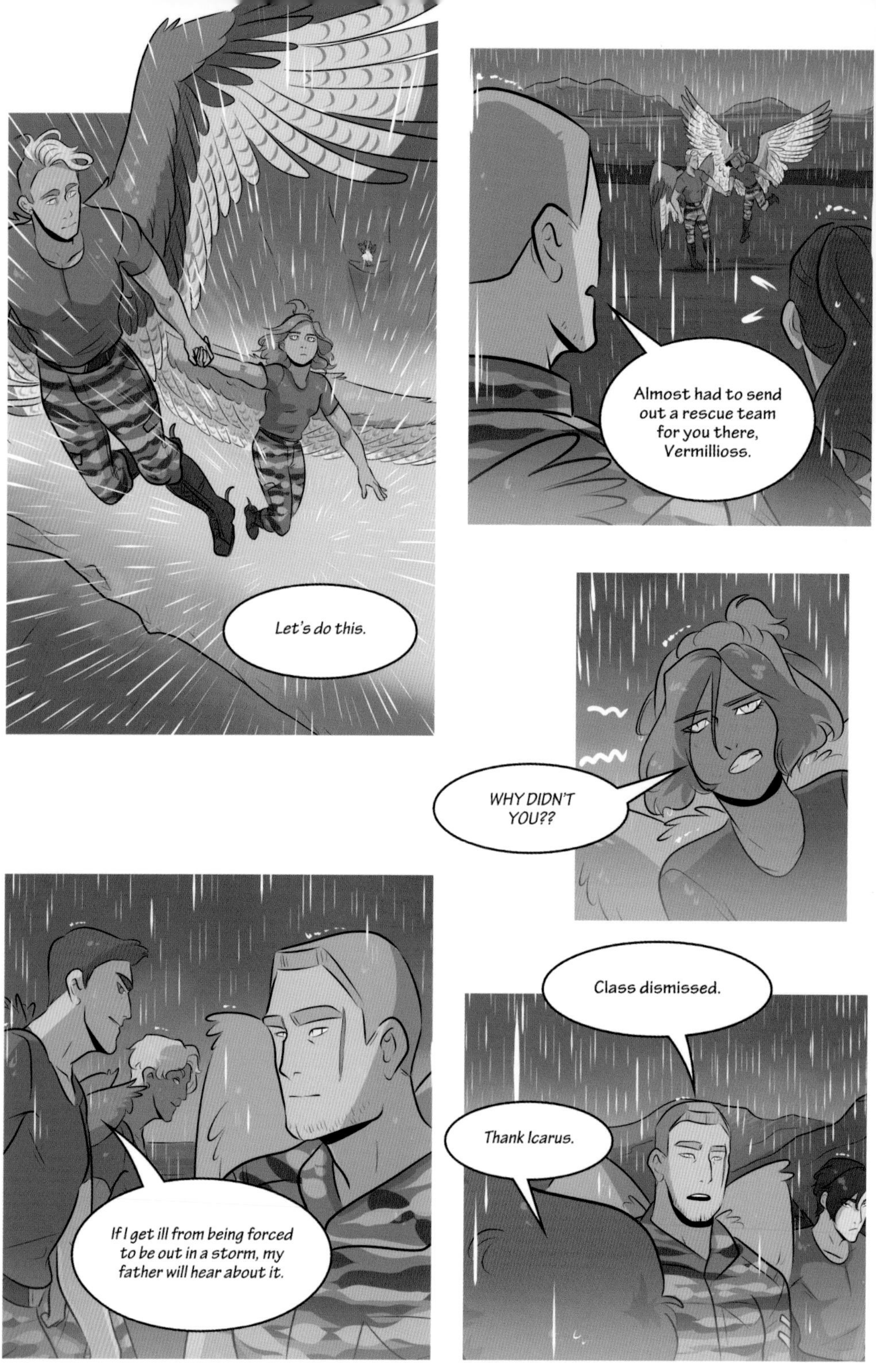
Let's do this.
Almost had to send out a rescue team for you there, Vermillioss.
WHY DIDN'T YOU??
If I get ill from being forced to be out in a storm, my father will hear about it.
Class dismissed.
Thank Icarus.

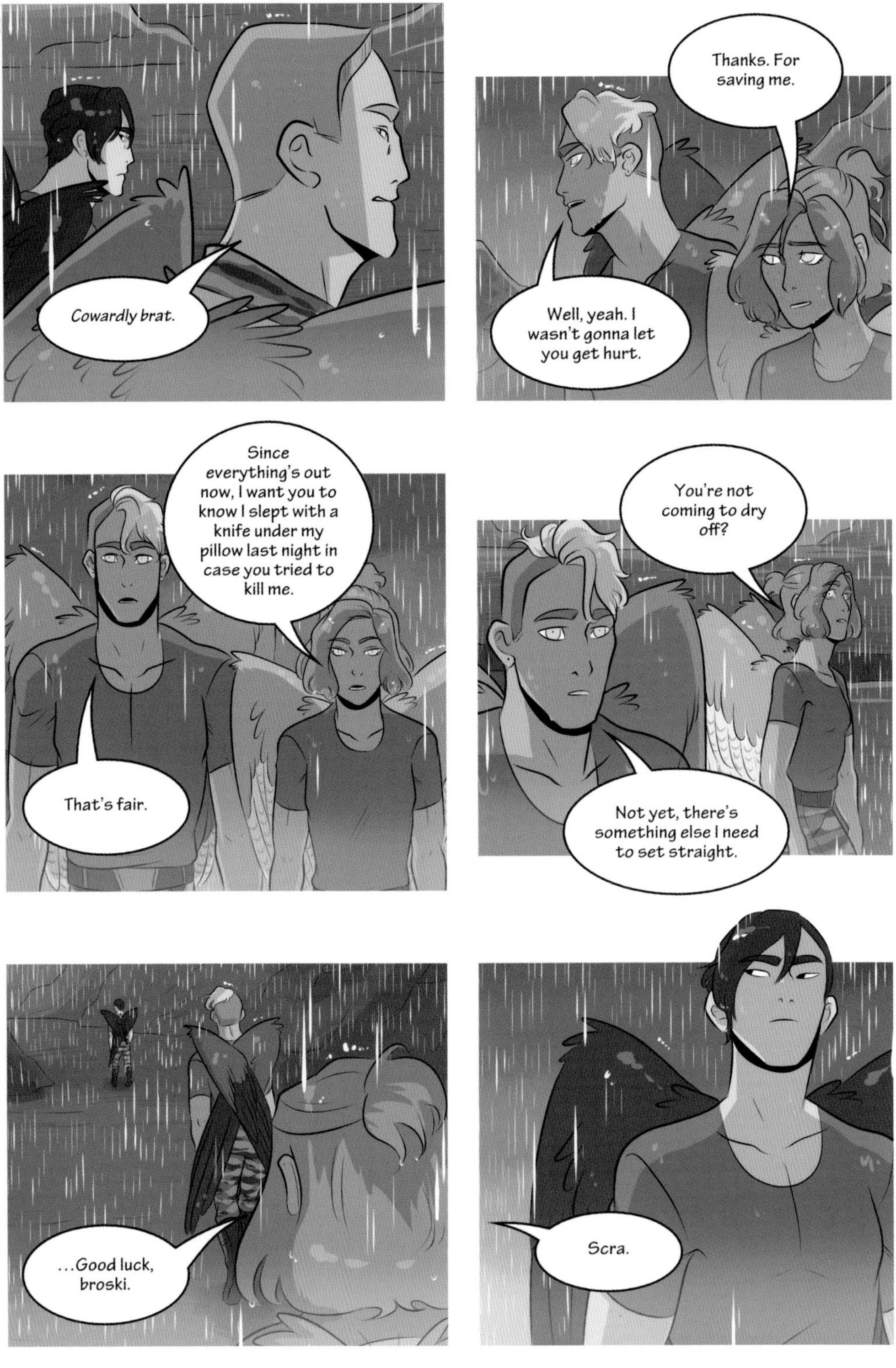
Cowardly brat.
Thanks. For saving me.
Well, yeah. I wasn't gonna let you get hurt.
Since everything's out now, I want you to know I slept with a knife under my pillow last night in case you tried to kill me.
That's fair.
You're not coming to dry off?
Not yet, there's something else I need to set straight.
...Good luck, broski.
Scra.

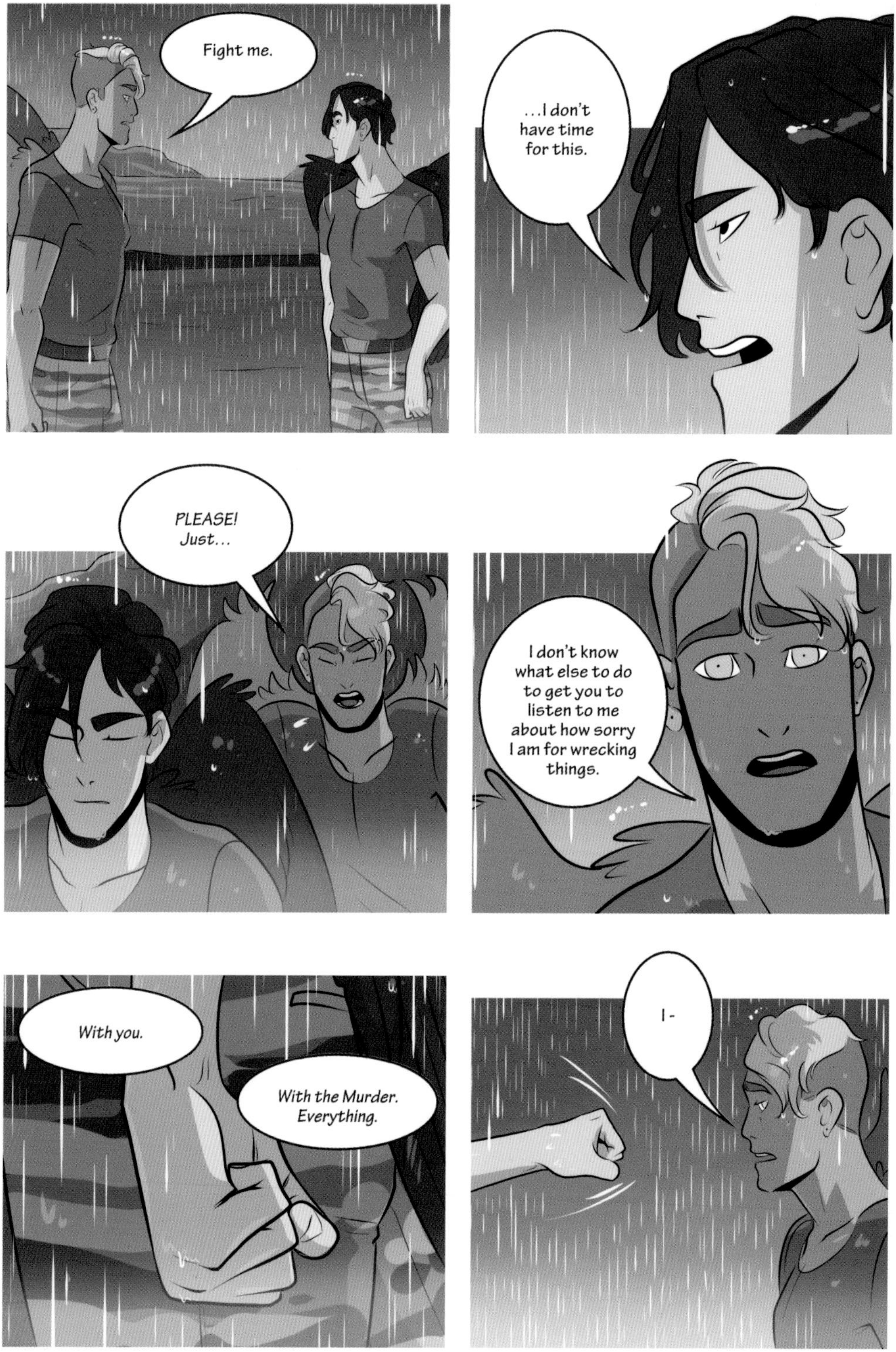
Fight me.
...I don't have time for this.
PLEASE! Just...
I don't know what else to do to get you to listen to me about how sorry I am for wrecking things.
With you.
With the Murder. Everything.
I -

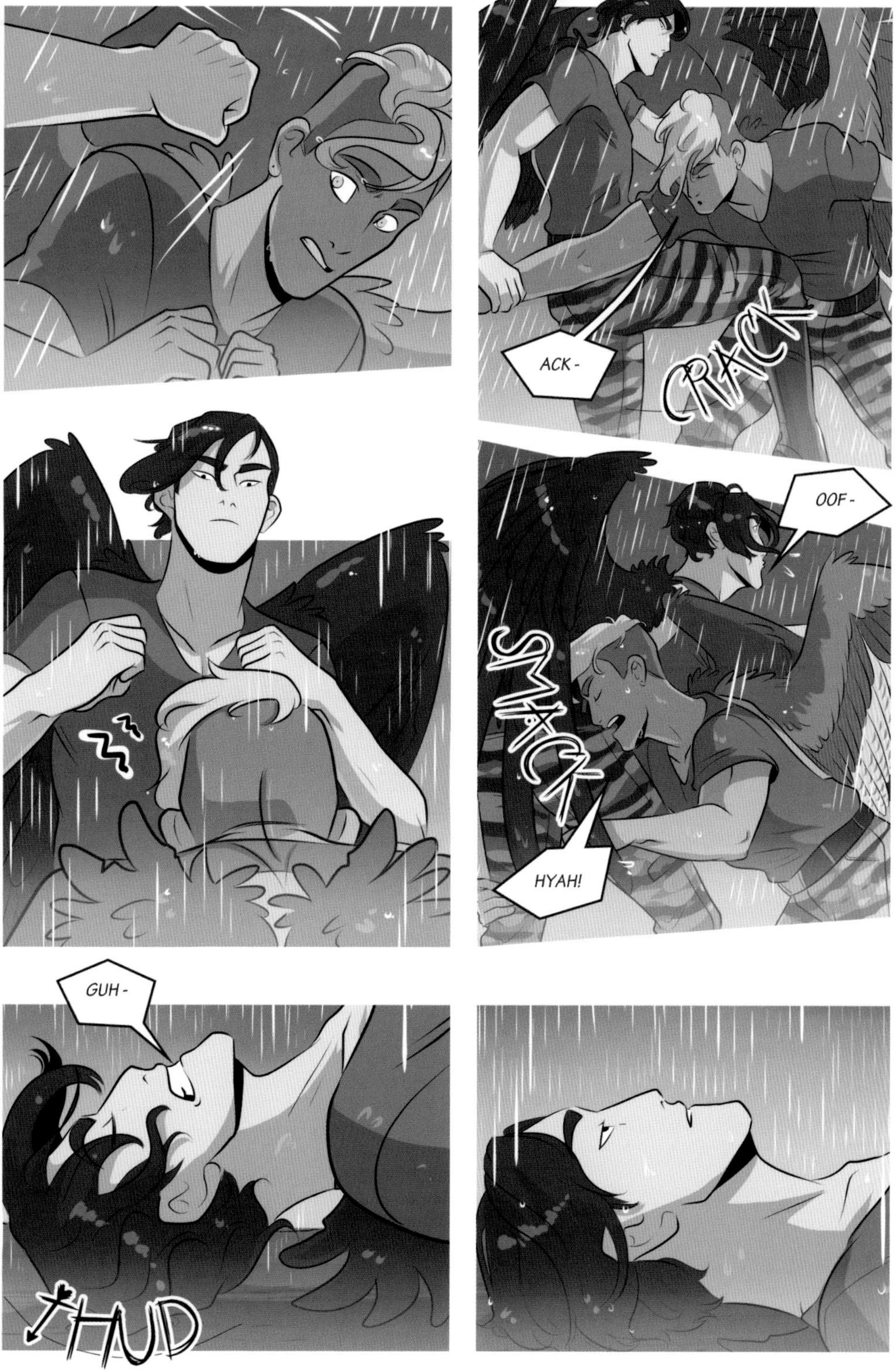

ACK-
CRACK
OOF-
SMACK
HYAH!
GUH-
THUD

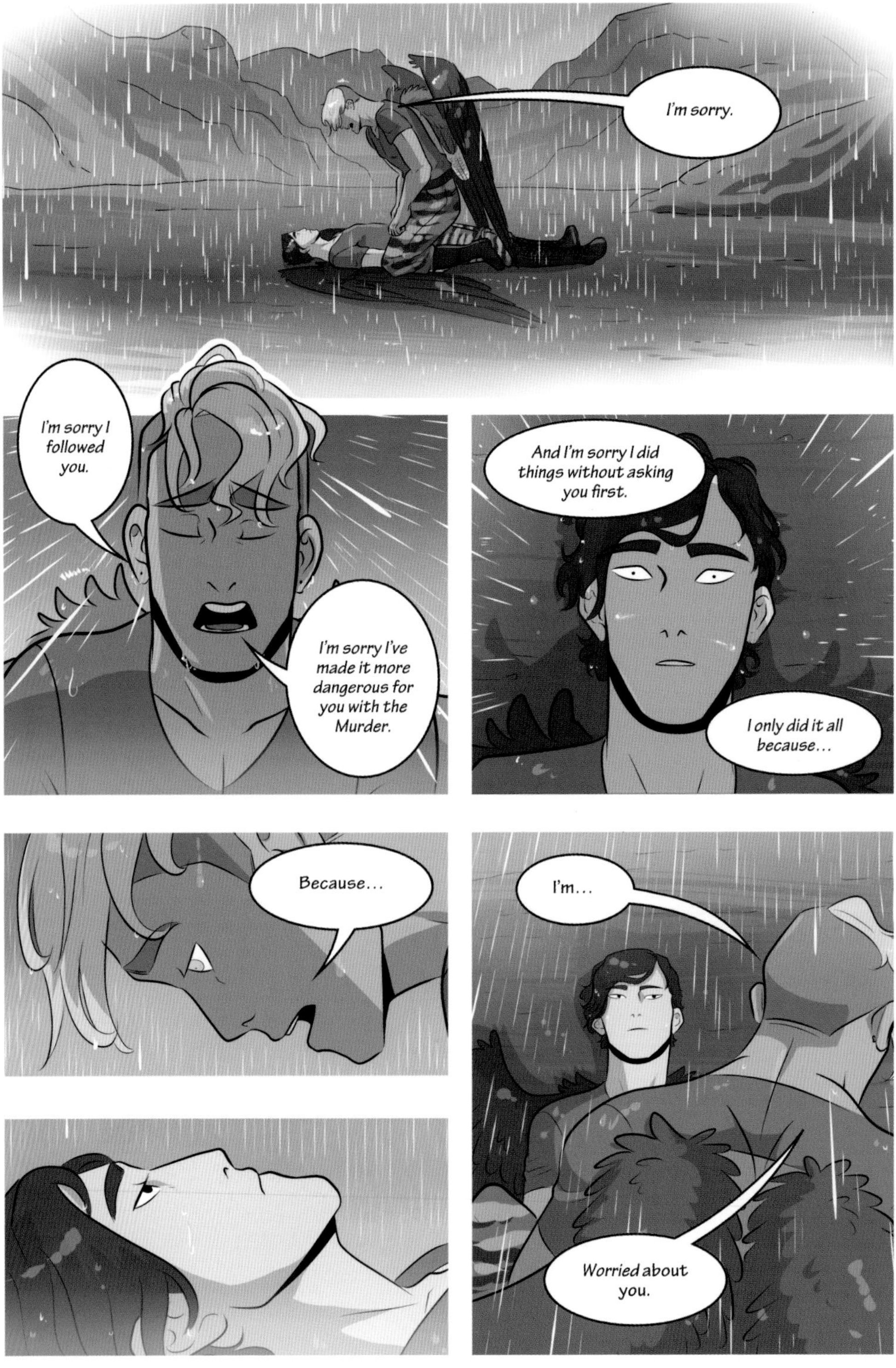
I'm sorry.
I'm sorry I followed you.
I'm sorry I've made it more dangerous for you with the Murder.
And I'm sorry I did things without asking you first.
I only did it all because...
Because...
I'm...
Worried about you.

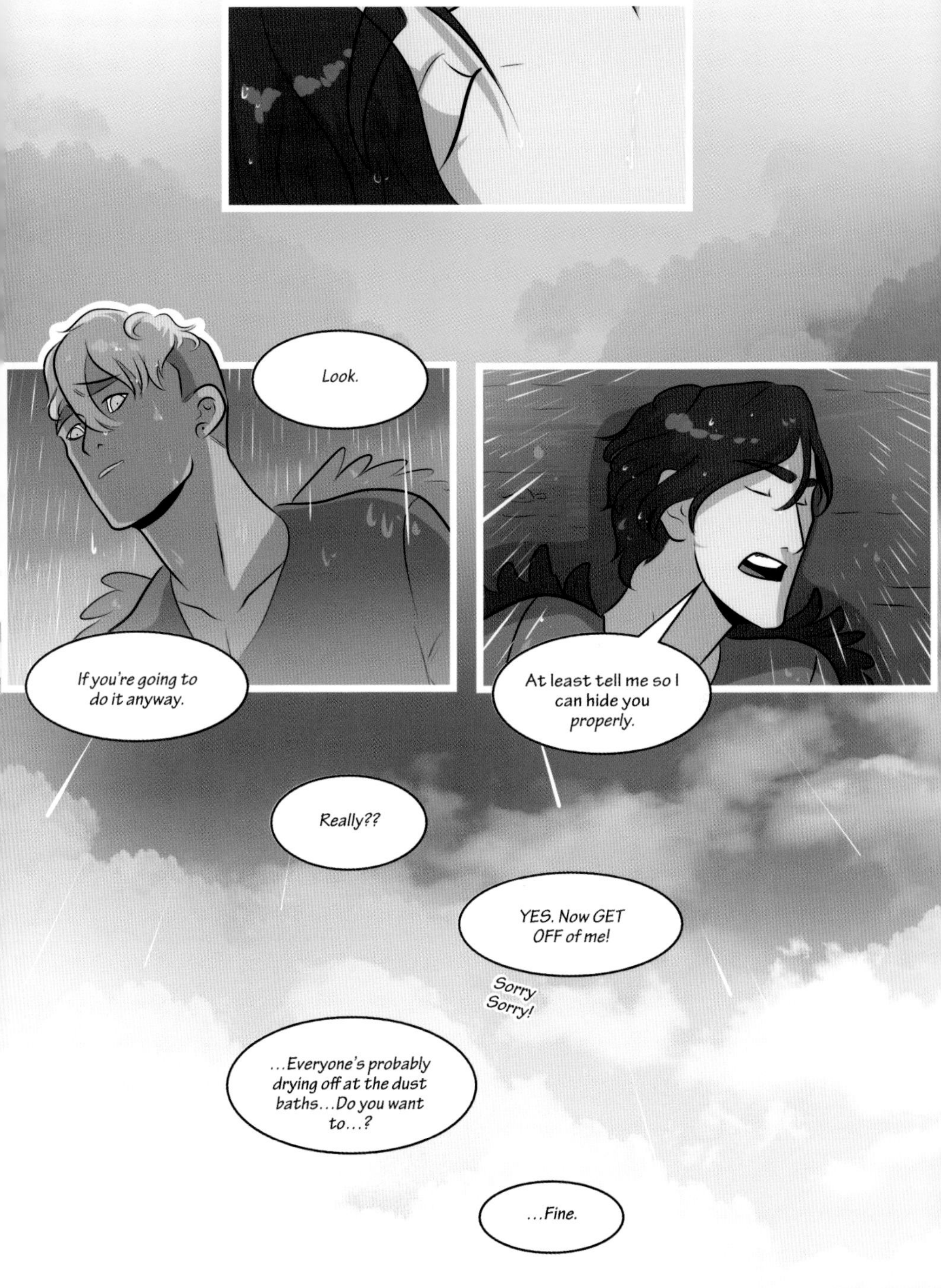
Look.
If you're going to do it anyway.
At least tell me so I can hide you properly.
Really??
YES. Now GET OFF of me!
Sorry Sorry!
...Everyone's probably drying off at the dust baths...Do you want to...?
...Fine.

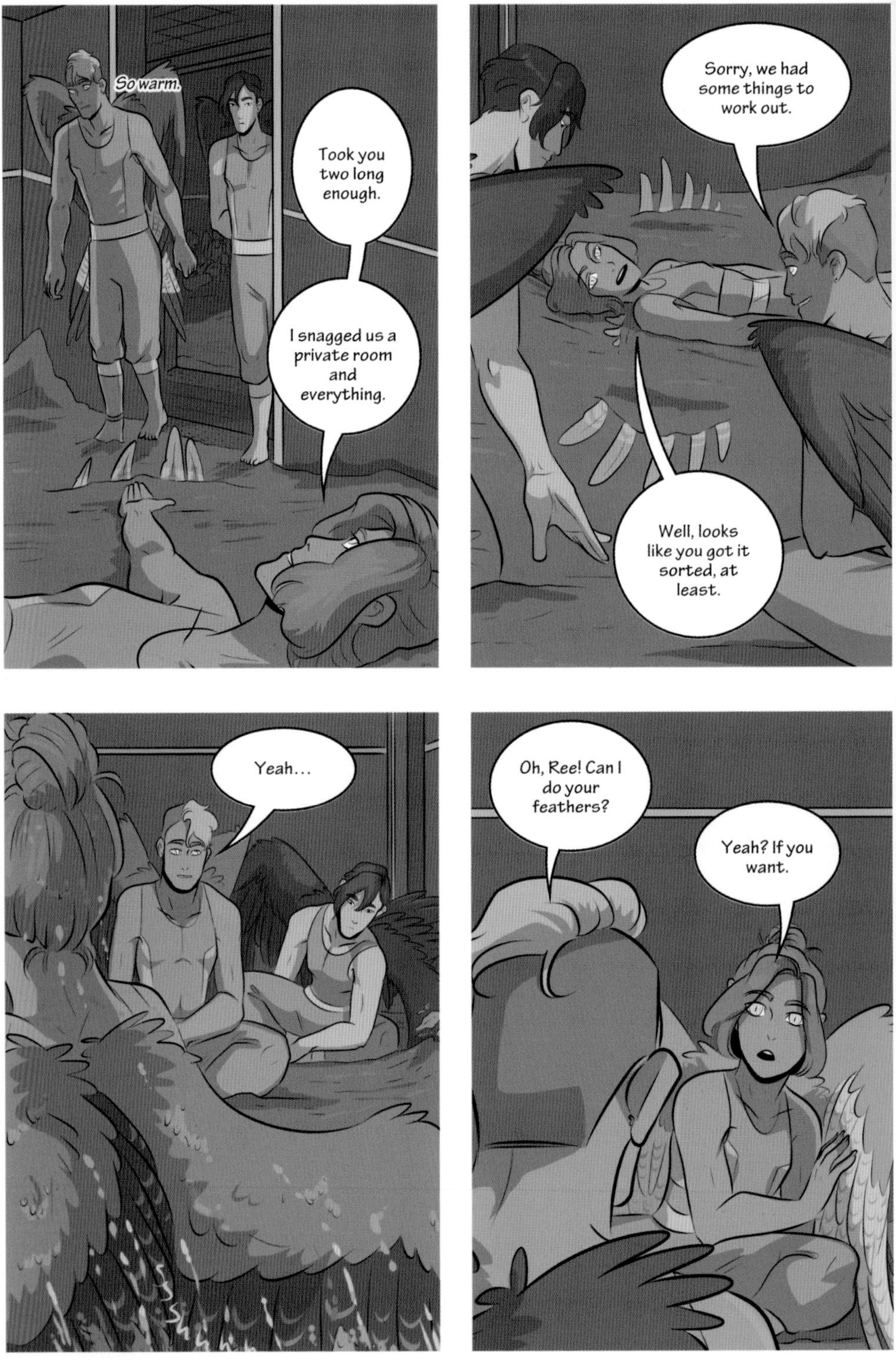
So warm.
Took you two long enough.
I snagged us a private room and everything.
Sorry, we had some things to work out.
Well, looks like you got it sorted, at least.
Yeah...
Oh, Ree! Can I do your feathers?
Yeah? If you want.

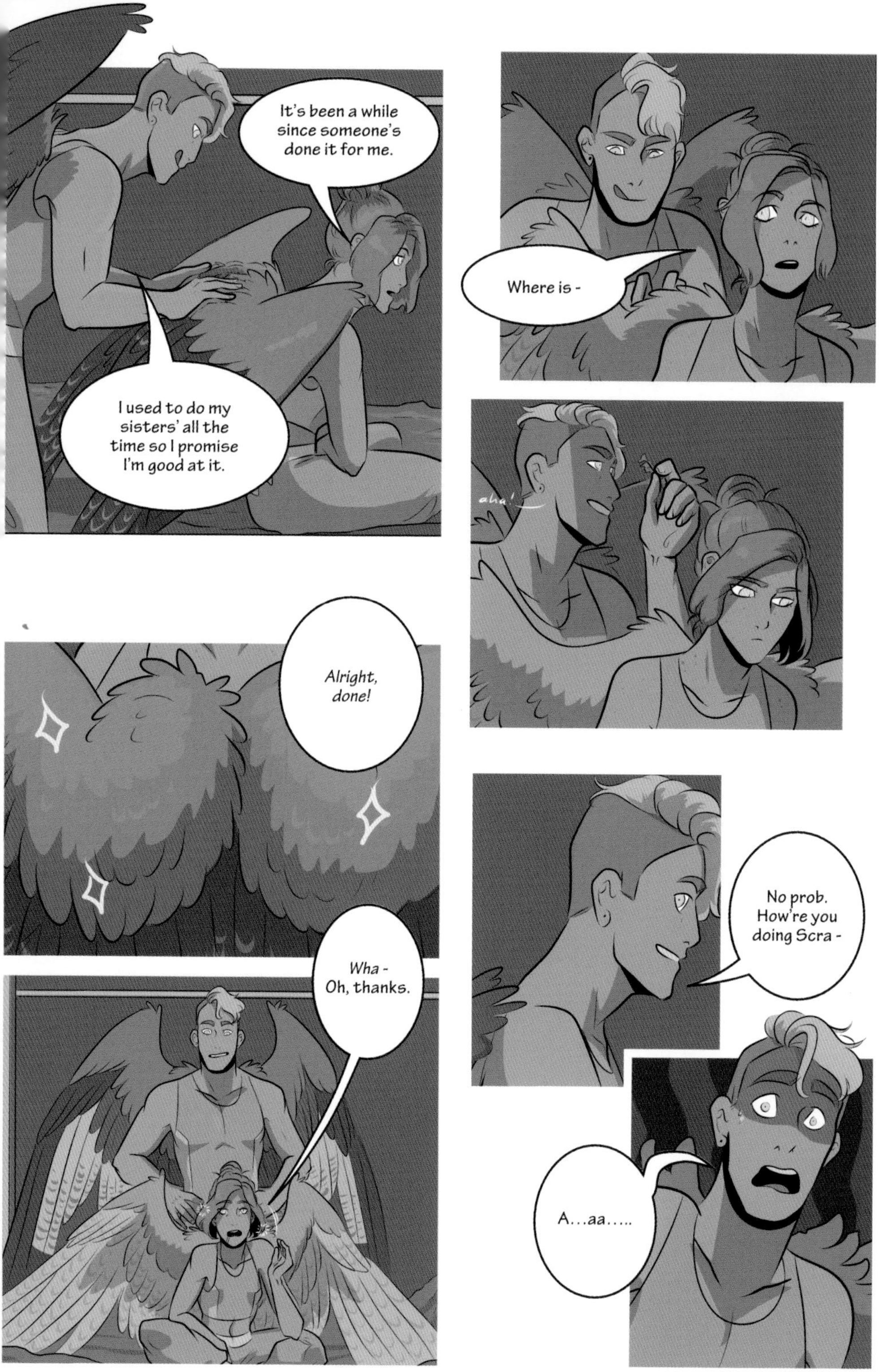
It's been a while since someone's done it for me.
I used to do my sisters' all the time so I promise I'm good at it.
Where is -
aha!
Alright, done!
Wha - Oh, thanks.
No prob. How're you doing Scra -
A...aa.....

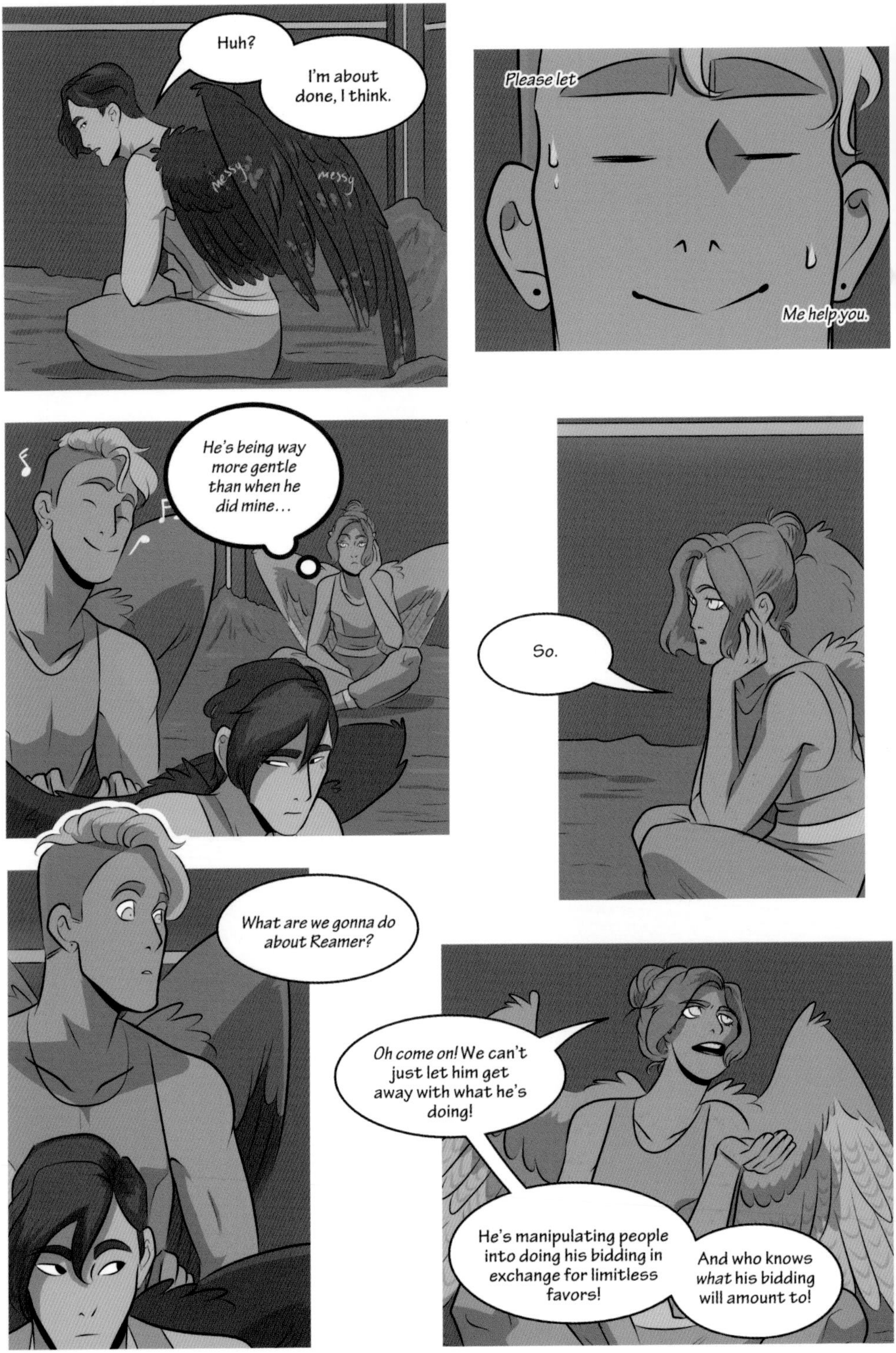
Huh?
I'm about done, I think.
messy
messy
Please let
Me help you.
He's being way more gentle than when he did mine...
So.
What are we gonna do about Reamer?
Oh come on! We can't just let him get away with what he's doing!
He's manipulating people into doing his bidding in exchange for limitless favors!
And who knows *what* his bidding will amount to!

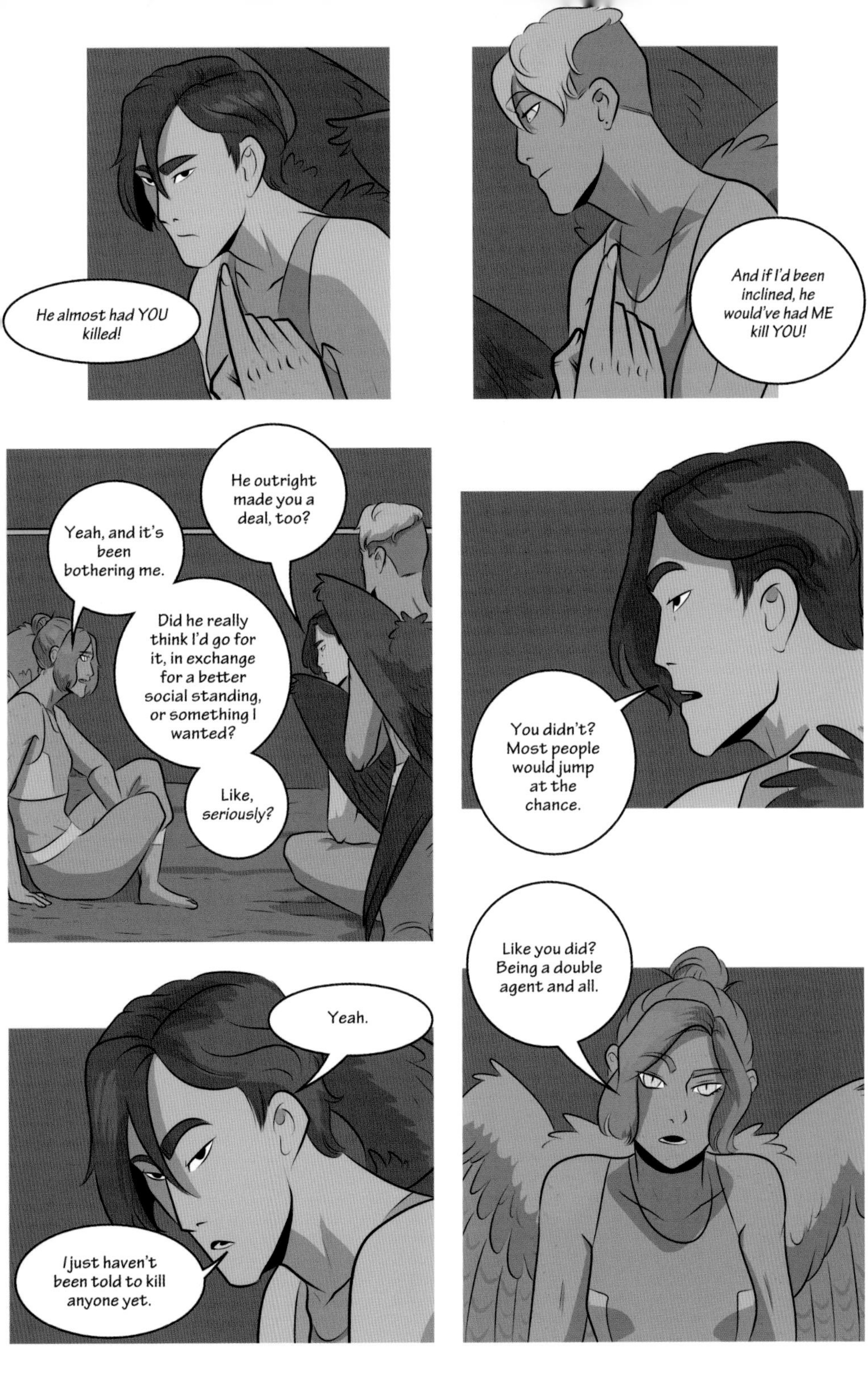
He almost had YOU killed!
And if I'd been inclined, he would've had ME kill YOU!
He outright made you a deal, too?
Yeah, and it's been bothering me.
Did he really think I'd go for it, in exchange for a better social standing, or something I wanted?
Like, seriously?
You didn't? Most people would jump at the chance.
Yeah.
I just haven't been told to kill anyone yet.
Like you did? Being a double agent and all.

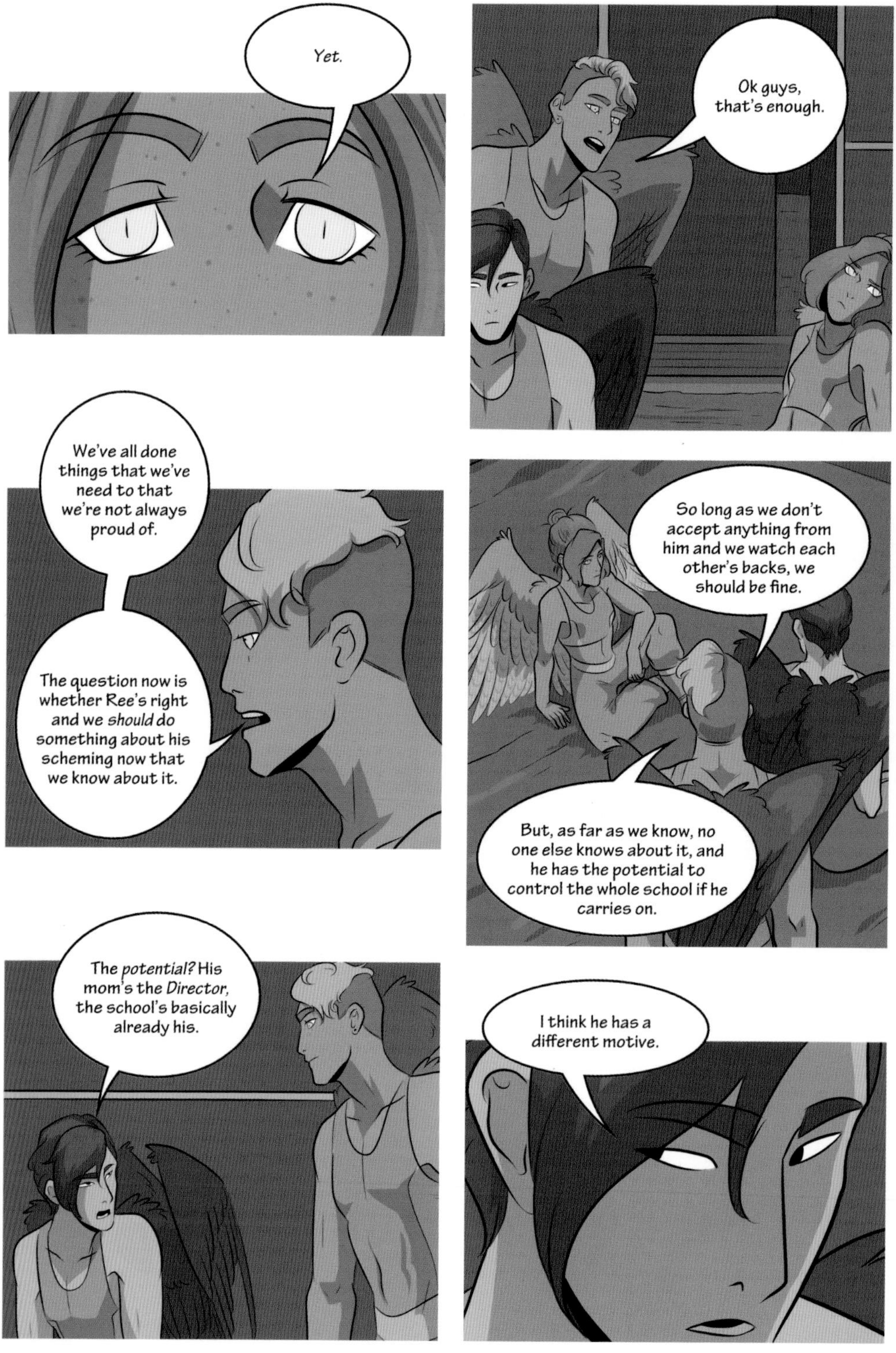
Yet.
Ok guys, that's enough.
We've all done things that we've need to that we're not always proud of.
The question now is whether Ree's right and we *should* do something about his scheming now that we know about it.
So long as we don't accept anything from him and we watch each other's backs, we should be fine.
But, as far as we know, no one else knows about it, and he has the potential to control the whole school if he carries on.
The *potential?* His mom's the *Director*, the school's basically already his.
I think he has a different motive.

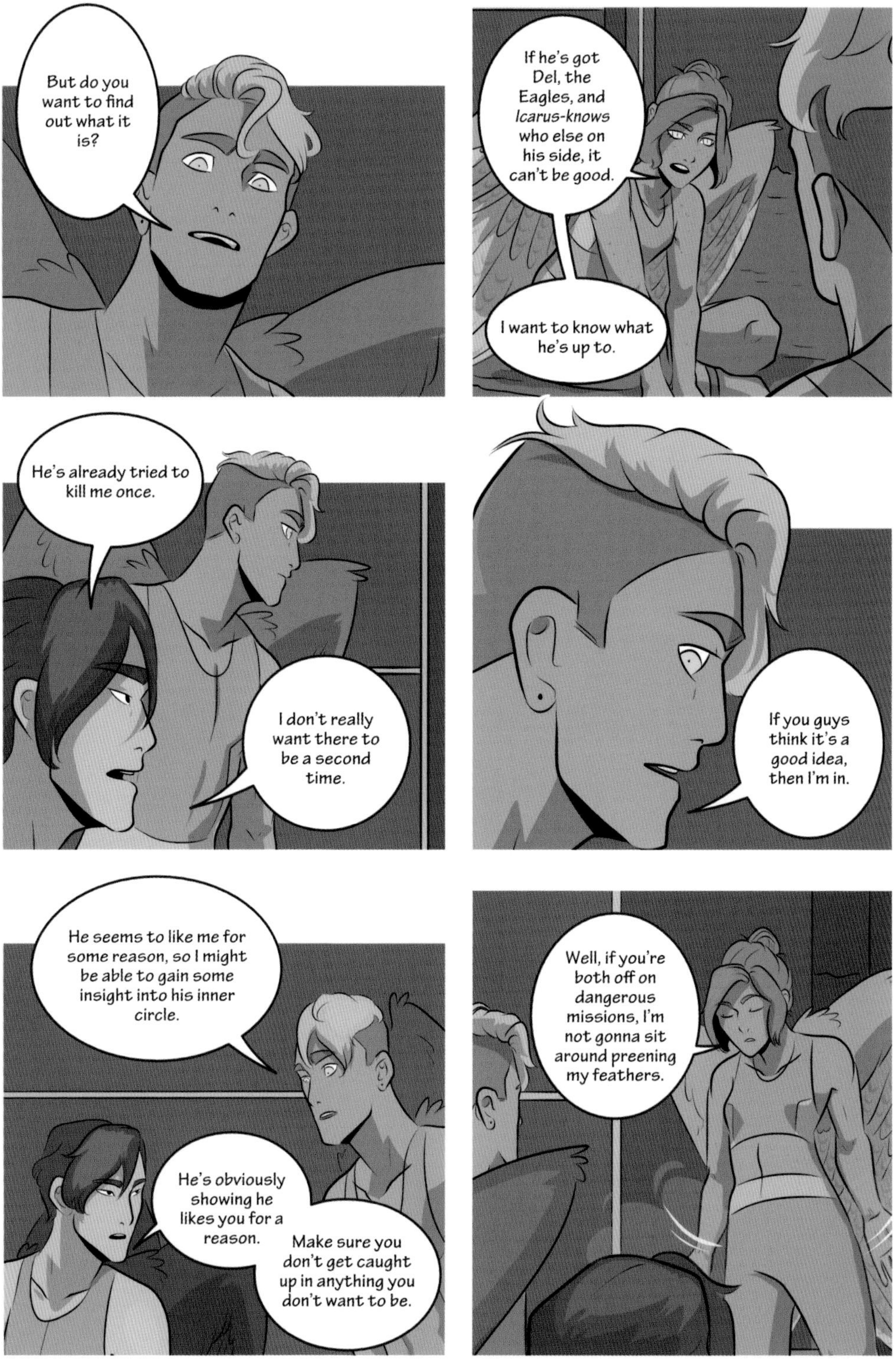
But do you want to find out what it is?
If he's got Del, the Eagles, and *Icarus-knows* who else on his side, it can't be good.
I want to know what he's up to.
He's already tried to kill me once.
I don't really want there to be a second time.
If you guys think it's a good idea, then I'm in.
He seems to like me for some reason, so I might be able to gain some insight into his inner circle.
He's obviously showing he likes you for a reason.
Make sure you don't get caught up in anything you don't want to be.
Well, if you're both off on dangerous missions, I'm not gonna sit around preening my feathers.

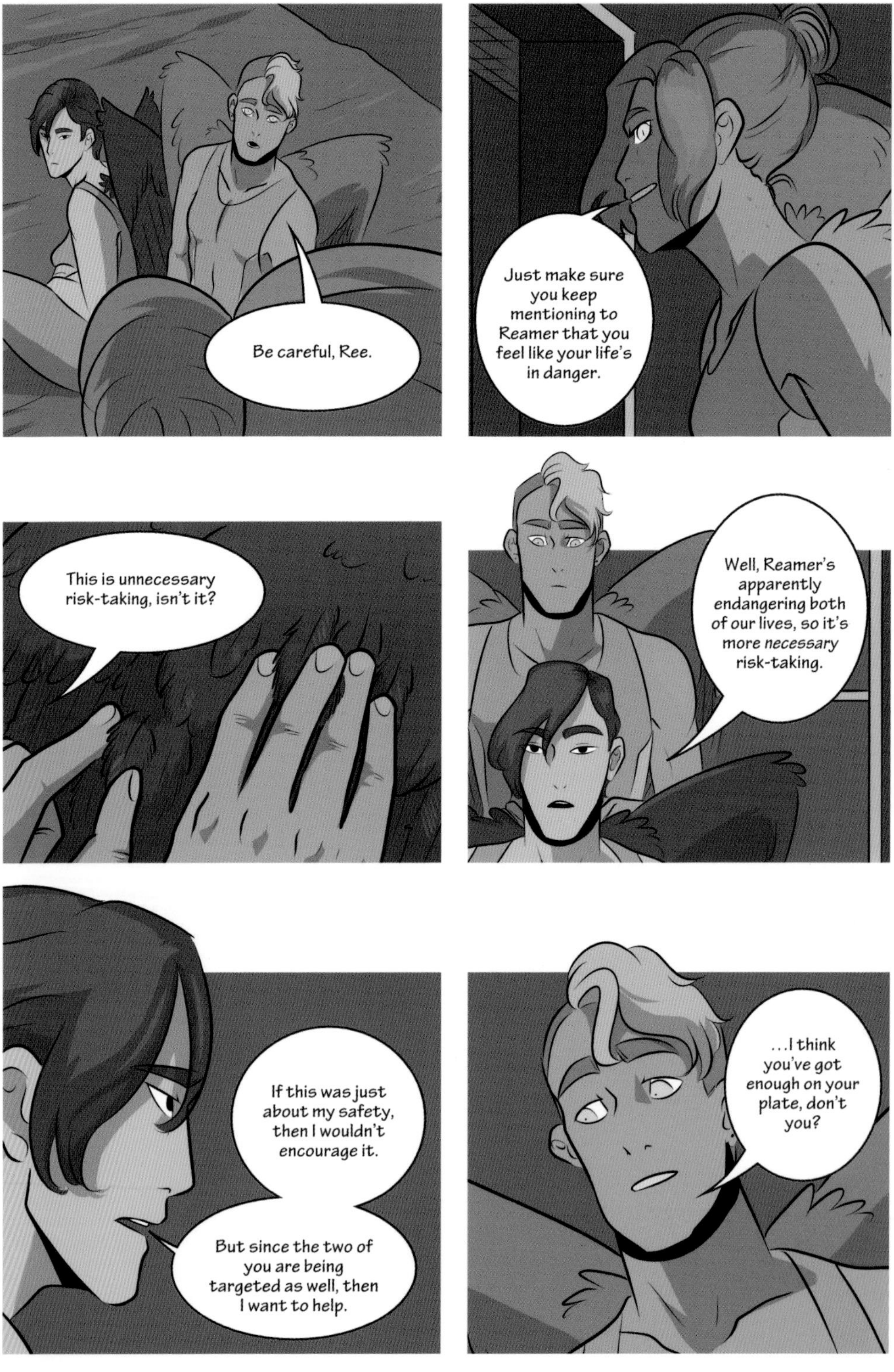
Be careful, Ree.
Just make sure you keep mentioning to Reamer that you feel like your life's in danger.
This is unnecessary risk-taking, isn't it?
Well, Reamer's apparently endangering both of our lives, so it's more *necessary* risk-taking.
If this was just about my safety, then I wouldn't encourage it.
But since the two of you are being targeted as well, then I want to help.
...I think you've got enough on your plate, don't you?

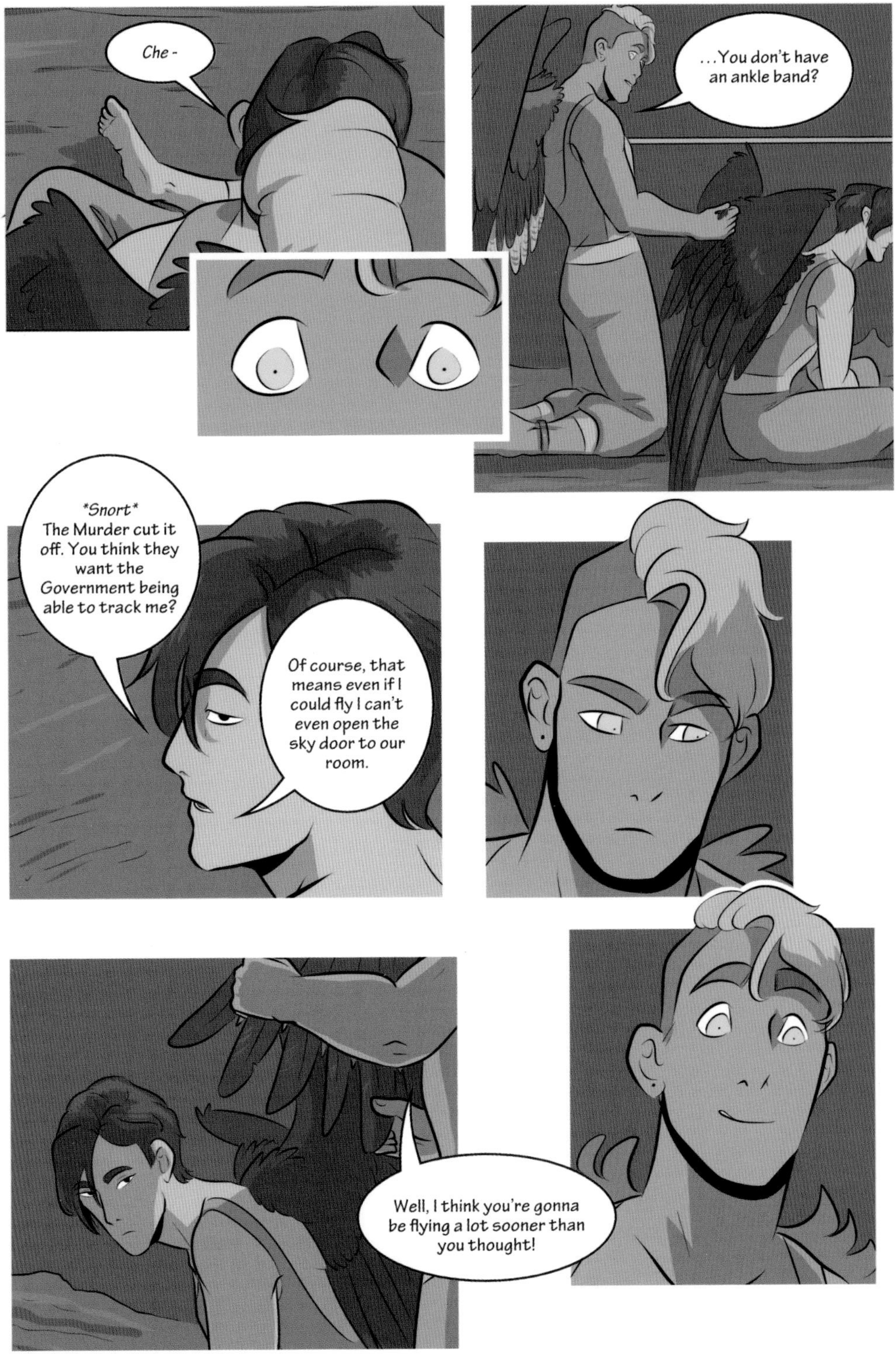
Che -
...You don't have an ankle band?
Snort The Murder cut it off. You think they want the Government being able to track me?
Of course, that means even if I could fly I can't even open the sky door to our room.
Well, I think you're gonna be flying a lot sooner than you thought!

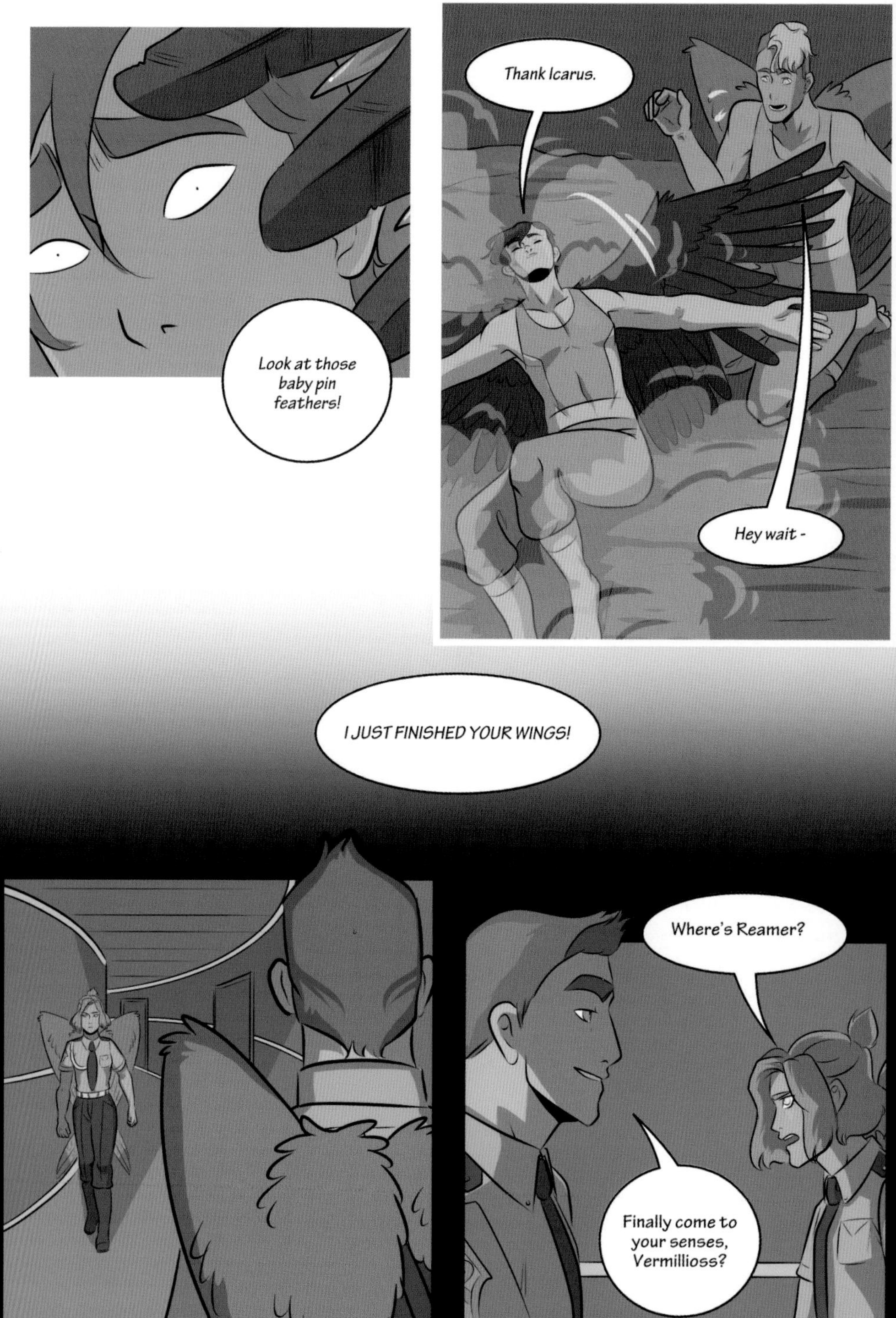
Look at those baby pin feathers!
Thank Icarus.
Hey wait -
I JUST FINISHED YOUR WINGS!
Where's Reamer?
Finally come to your senses, Vermillioss?

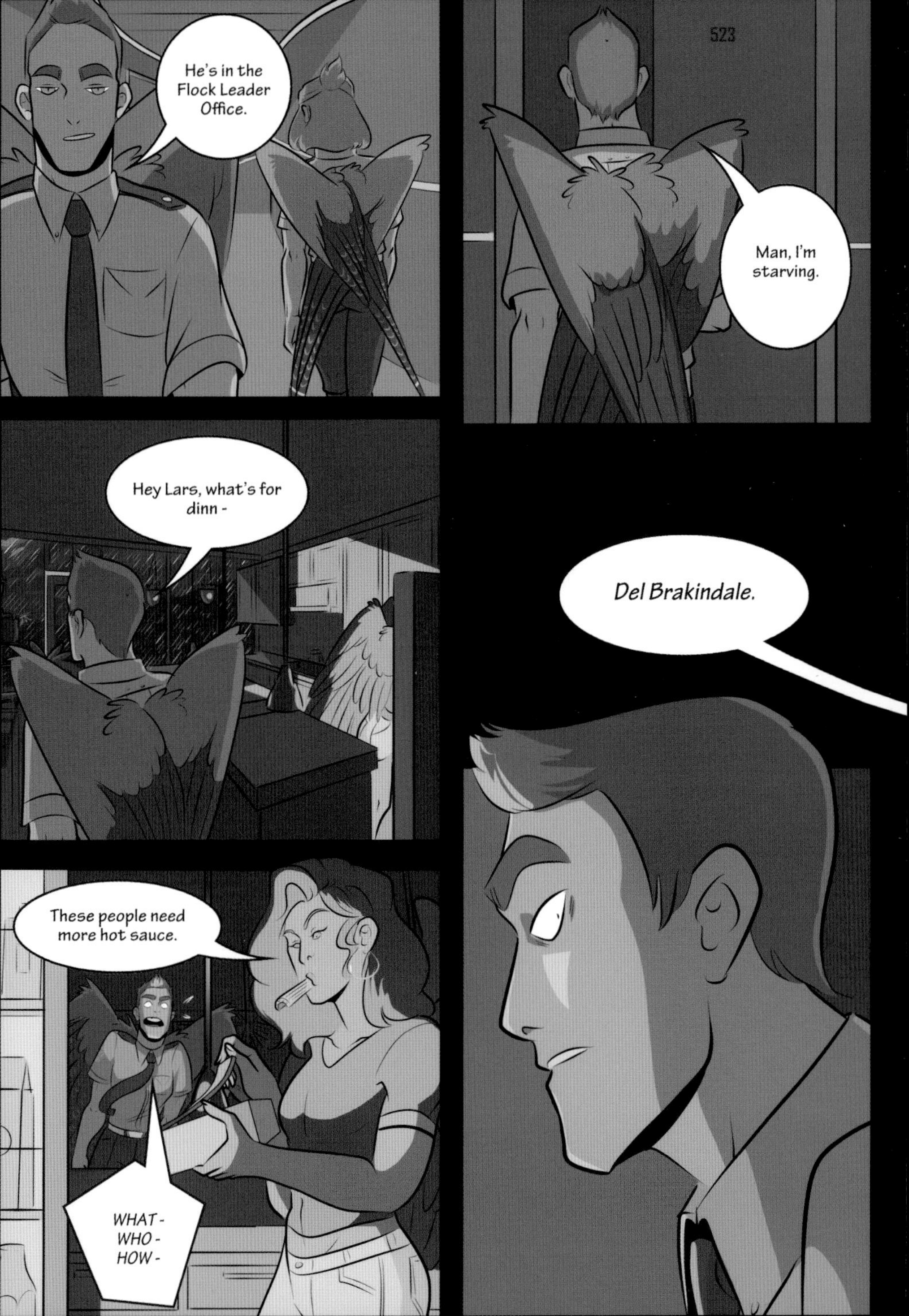
He's in the Flock Leader Office.
Man, I'm starving.
Hey Lars, what's for dinn -
These people need more hot sauce.
WHAT - WHO - HOW -
Del Brakindale.

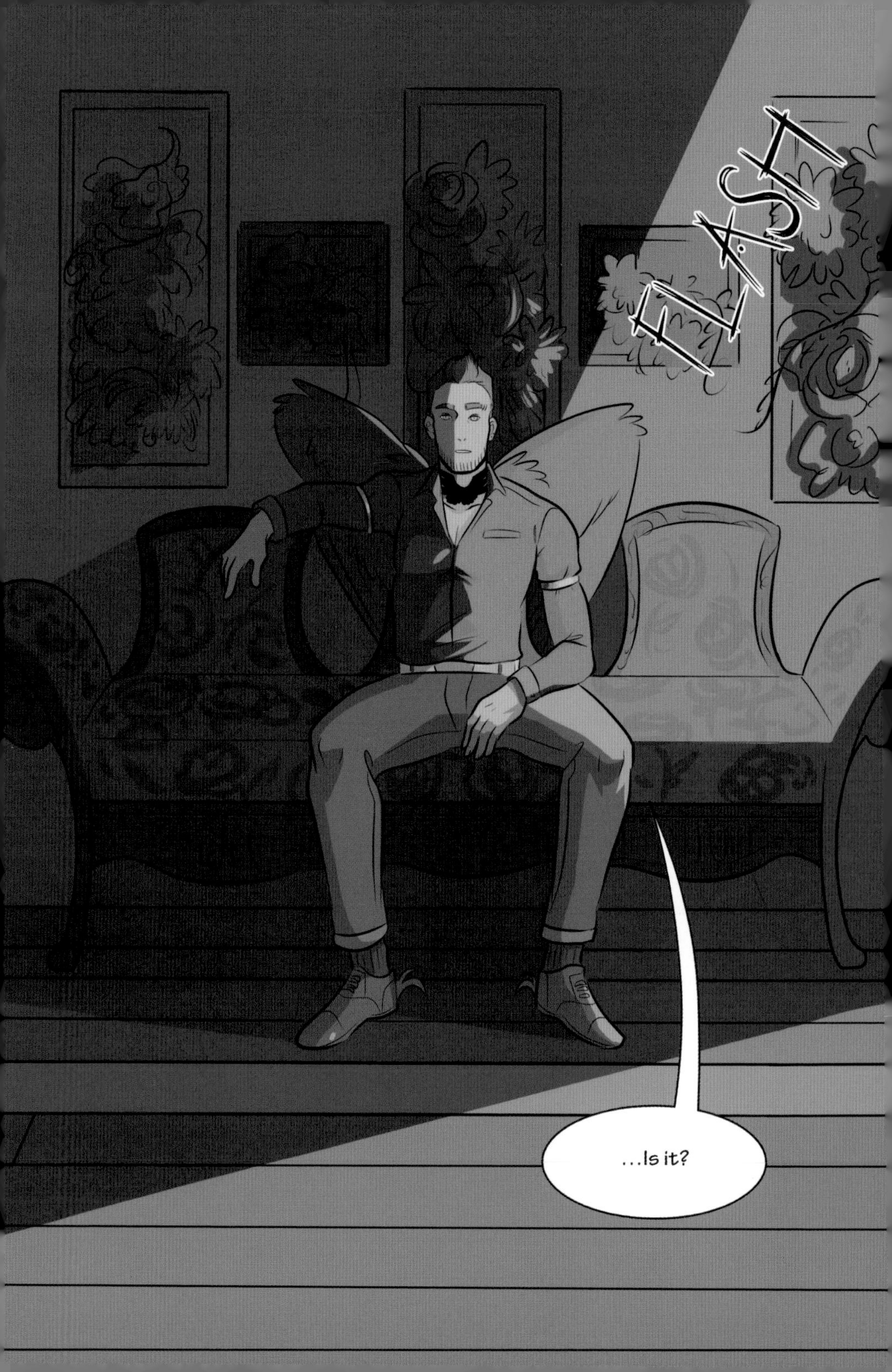
FLASH
...Is it?

THE CROAKING

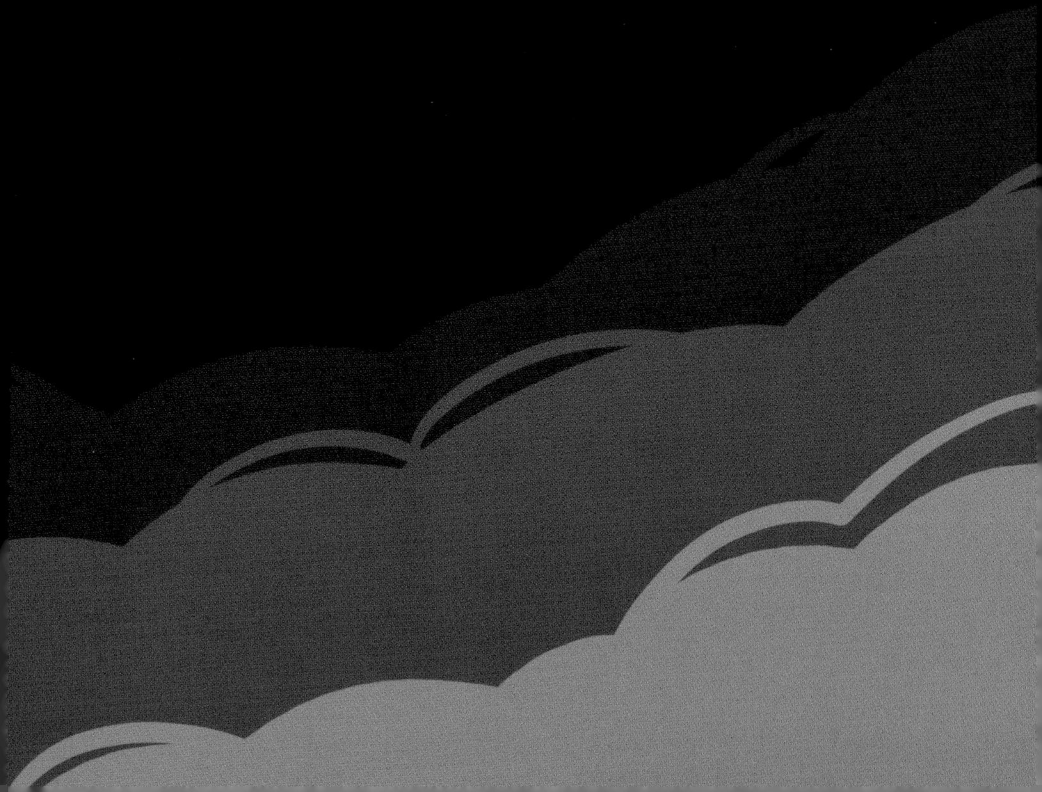

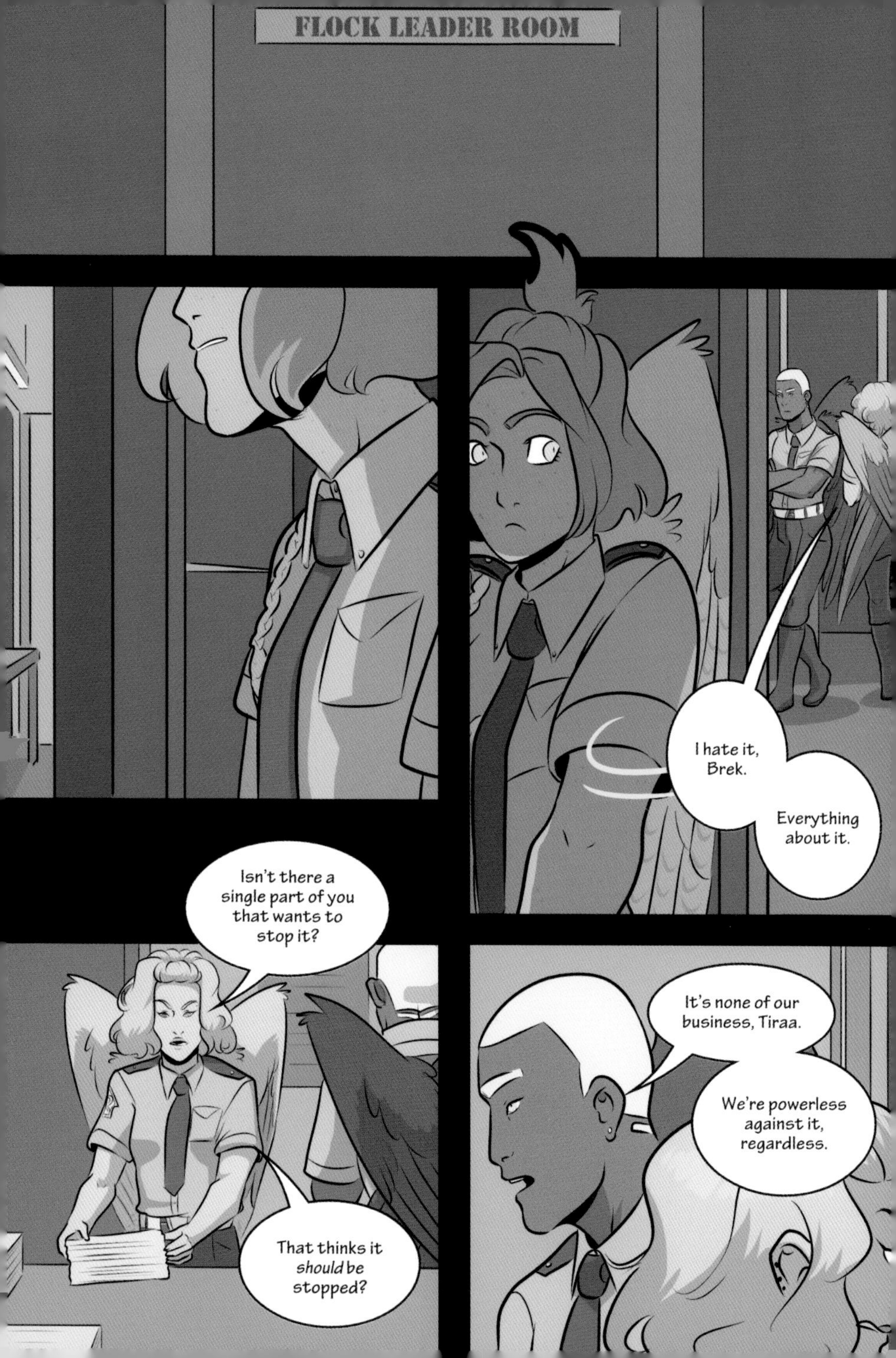
FLOCK LEADER ROOM
I hate it, Brek.
Everything about it.
Isn't there a single part of you that wants to stop it?
That thinks it *should* be stopped?
It's none of our business, Tiraa.
We're powerless against it, regardless.

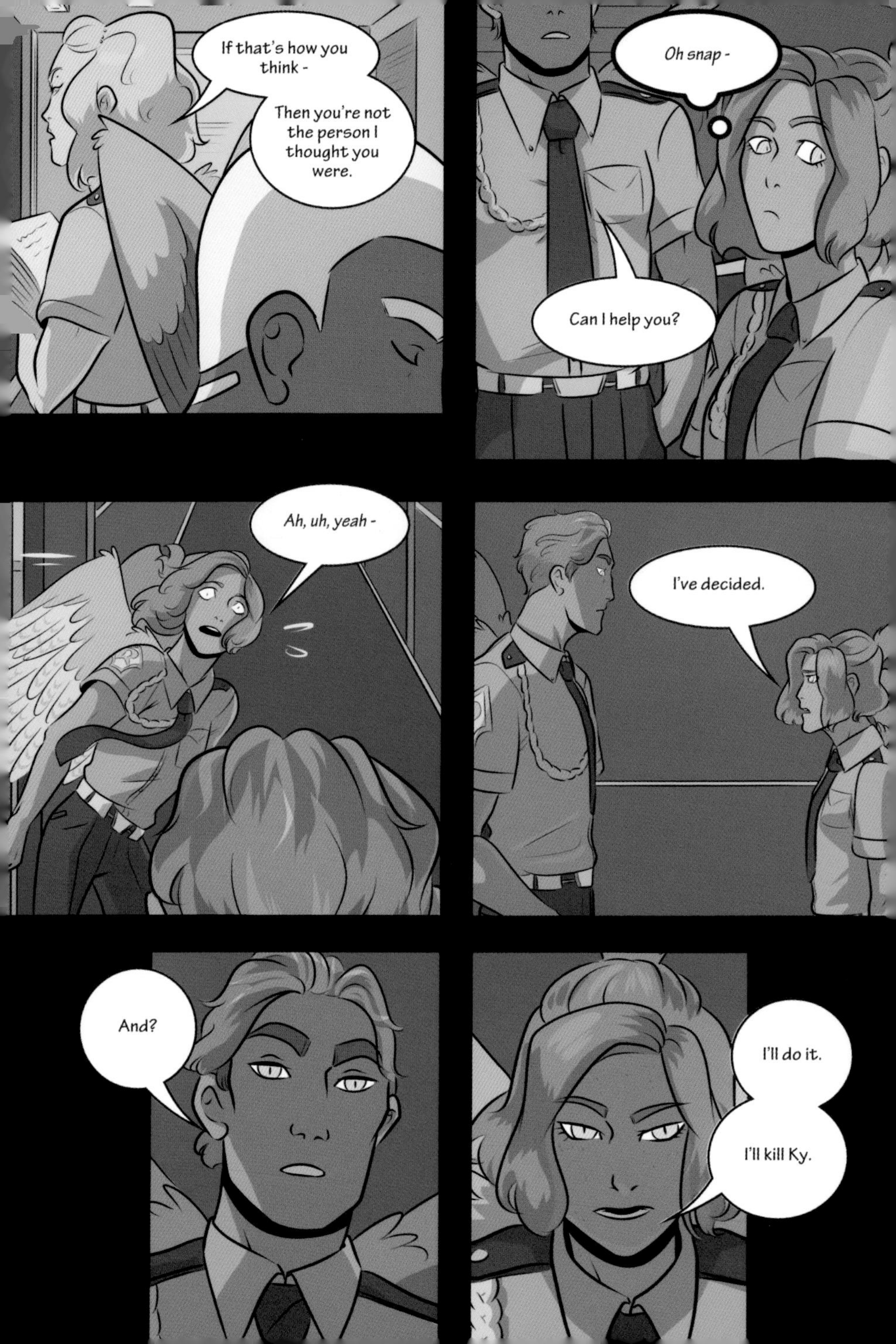
If that's how you think -
Then you're not the person I thought you were.
Oh snap -
Can I help you?
Ah, uh, yeah -
I've decided.
And?
I'll do it.
I'll kill Ky.

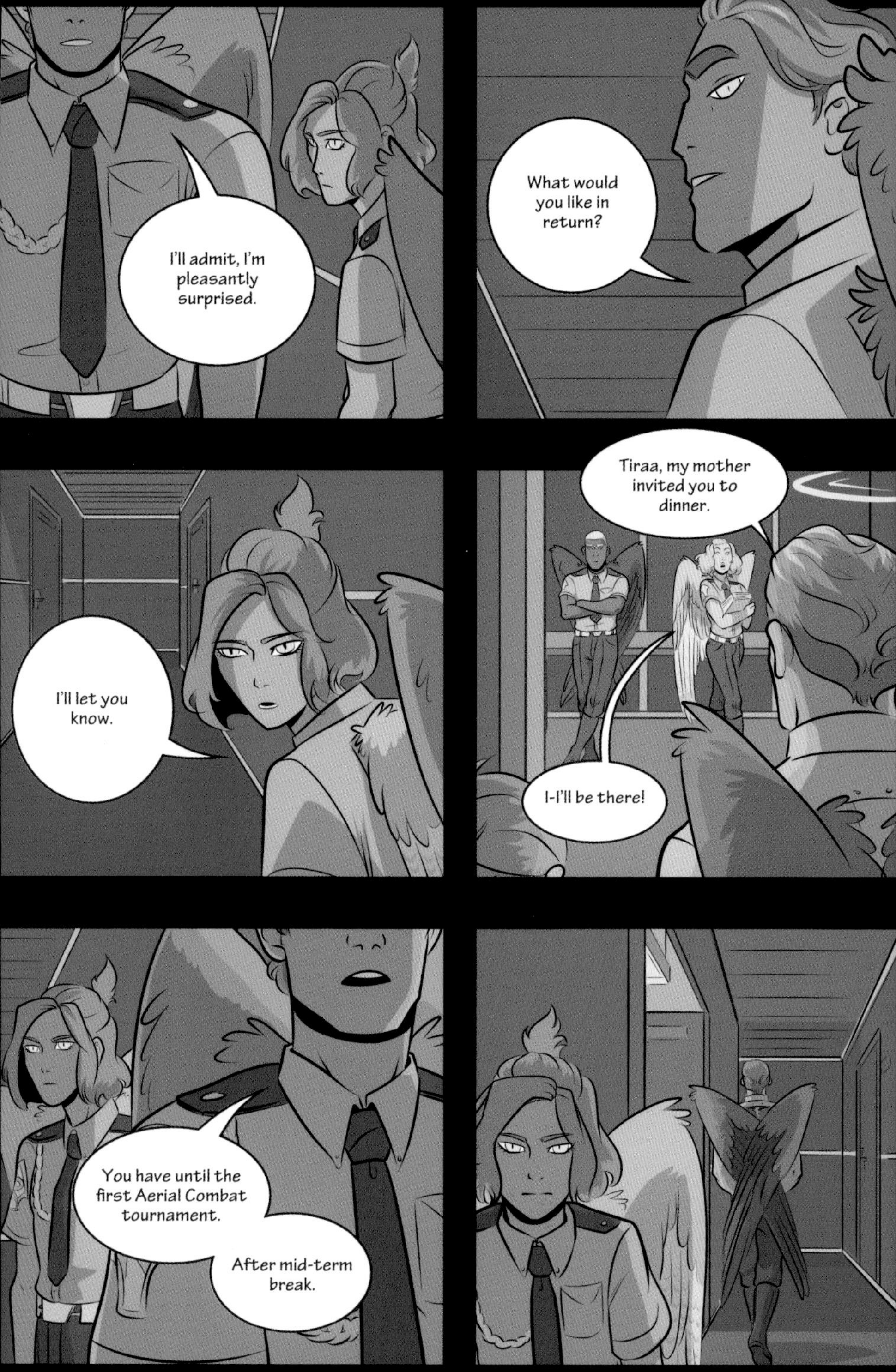
I'll admit, I'm pleasantly surprised.
What would you like in return?
I'll let you know.
Tiraa, my mother invited you to dinner.
I-I'll be there!
You have until the first Aerial Combat tournament.
After mid-term break.

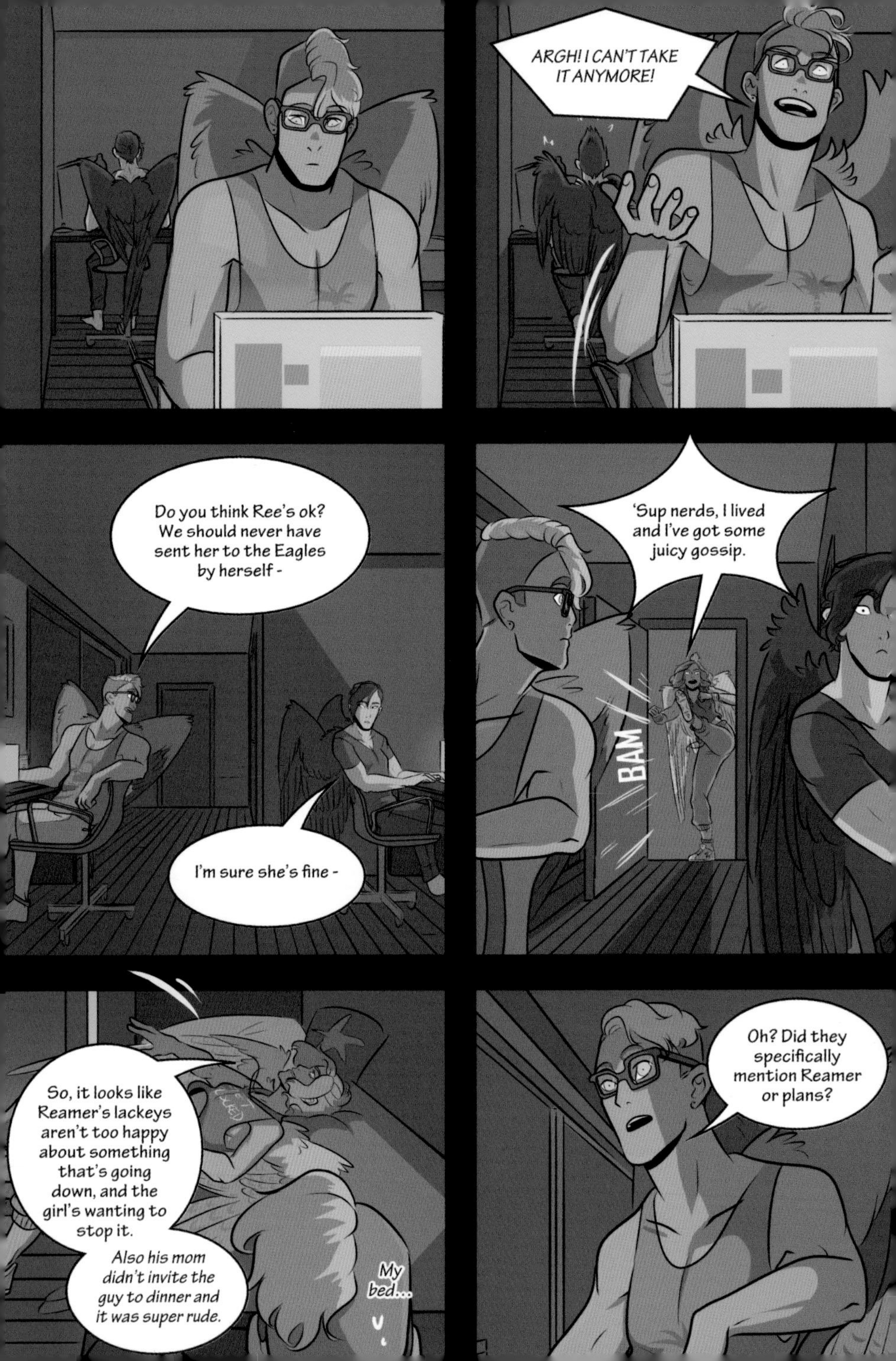
ARGH! I CAN'T TAKE IT ANYMORE!
Do you think Ree's ok? We should never have sent her to the Eagles by herself -
I'm sure she's fine -
'Sup nerds, I lived and I've got some juicy gossip.
BAM
So, it looks like Reamer's lackeys aren't too happy about something that's going down, and the girl's wanting to stop it.
Also his mom didn't invite the guy to dinner and it was super rude.
My bed...
Oh? Did they specifically mention Reamer or plans?

No. But it's a start.

Ree...

Ah. So this was just a waste of time.

I mean, you *could* be on to something.

And if his closest friends are against it, maybe they'll help us.

But right now we sorta need to finish these Crow War papers instead of talking conspiracy theories.

Yeah yeah...

Hey! What'd they teach you about the Crow War growing up, Mr. Crow?

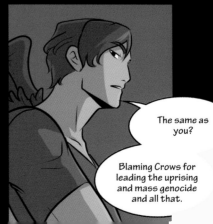

The same as you?

Blaming Crows for leading the uprising and mass genocide and all that.

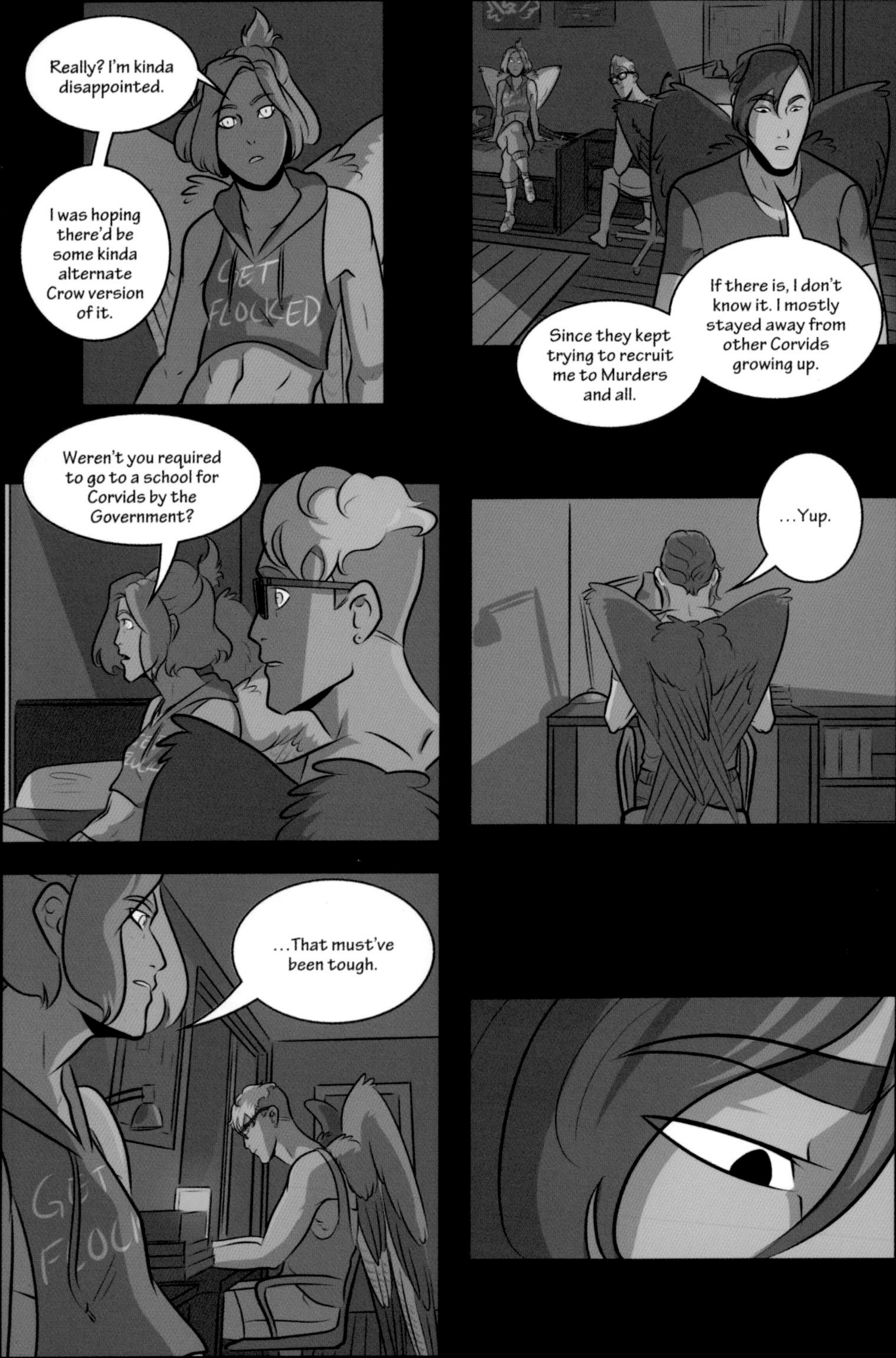
Really? I'm kinda disappointed.
I was hoping there'd be some kinda alternate Crow version of it.
GET FLOCKED
If there is, I don't know it. I mostly stayed away from other Corvids growing up.
Since they kept trying to recruit me to Murders and all.
Weren't you required to go to a school for Corvids by the Government?
...Yup.
...That must've been tough.

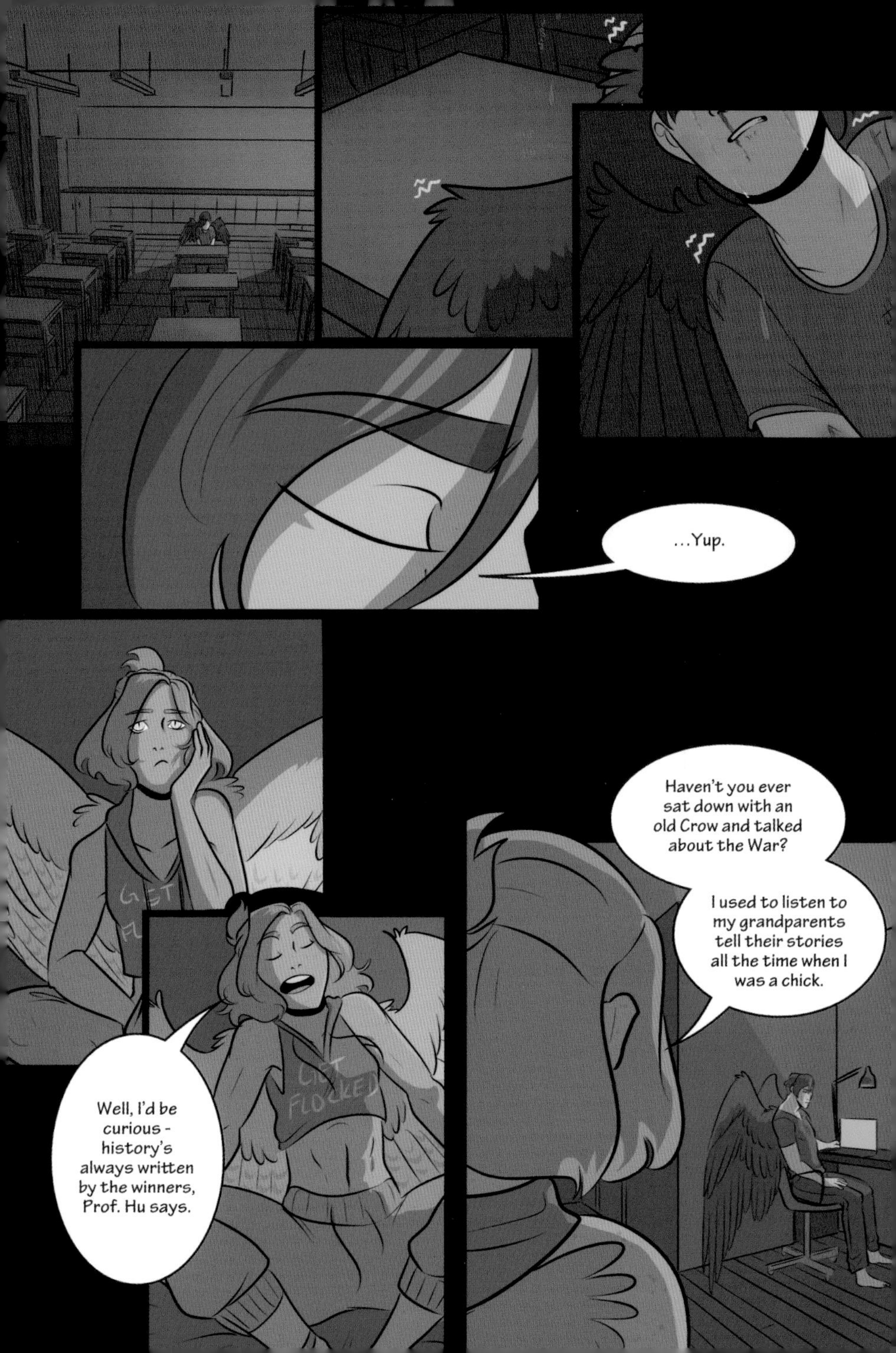
…Yup.
Haven't you ever sat down with an old Crow and talked about the War?
I used to listen to my grandparents tell their stories all the time when I was a chick.
Well, I'd be curious - history's always written by the winners, Prof. Hu says.

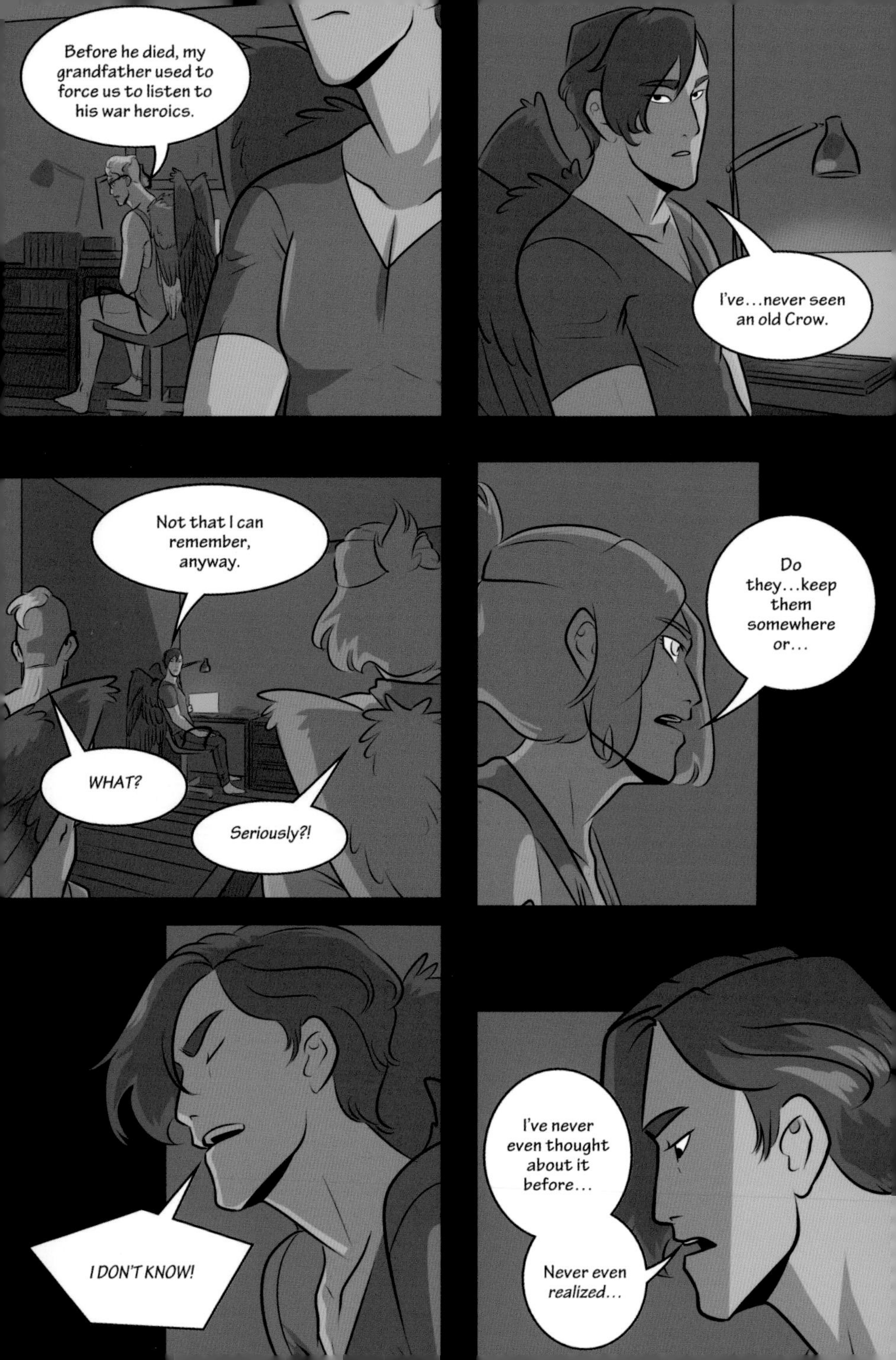
Before he died, my grandfather used to force us to listen to his war heroics.
I've…never seen an old Crow.
Not that I can remember, anyway.
WHAT?
Seriously?!
Do they…keep them somewhere or…
I DON'T KNOW!
I've never even thought about it before…
Never even realized…

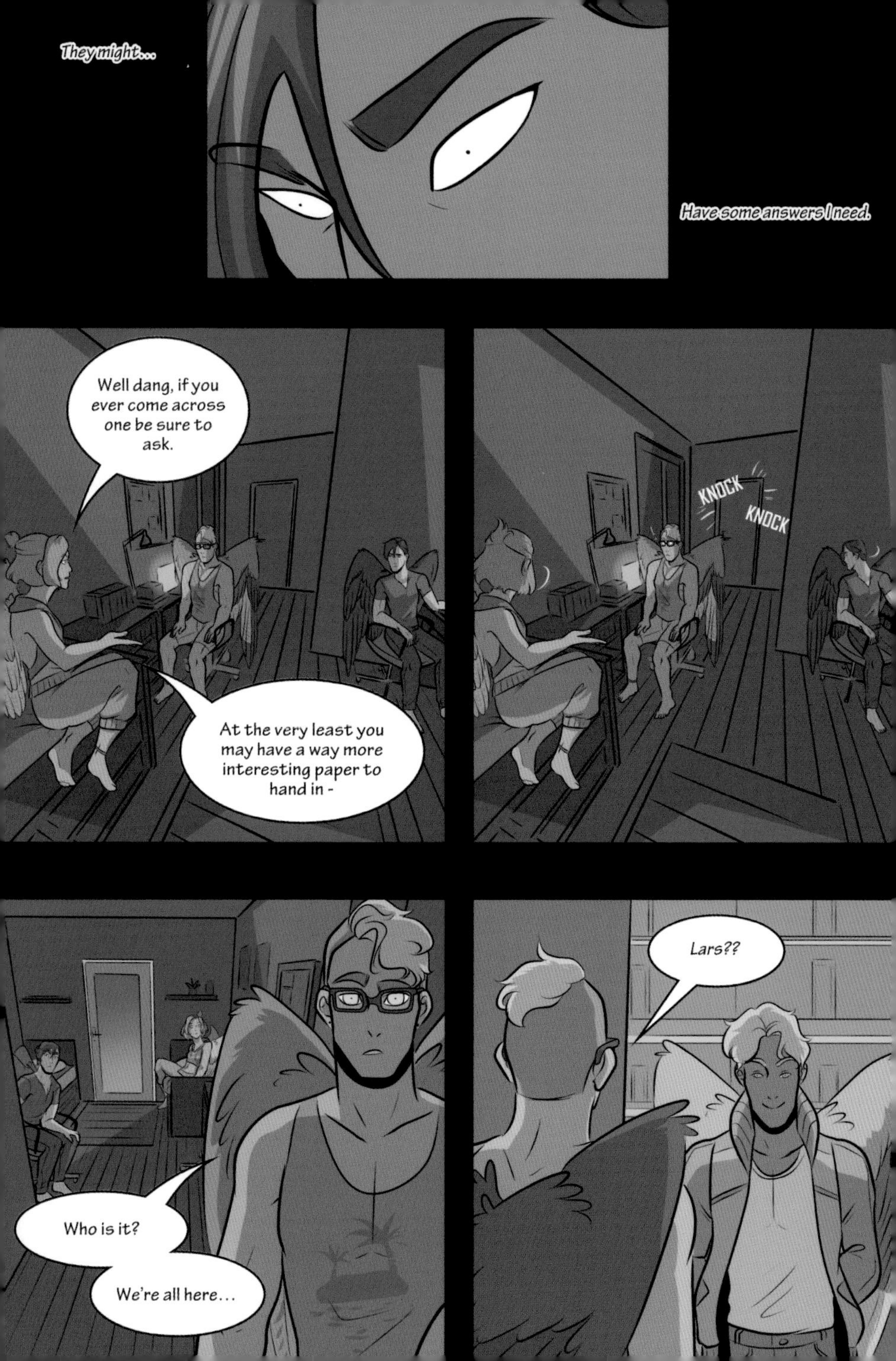
They might...
Have some answers I need.
Well dang, if you ever come across one be sure to ask.
At the very least you may have a way more interesting paper to hand in -
KNOCK
KNOCK
Who is it?
We're all here...
Lars??

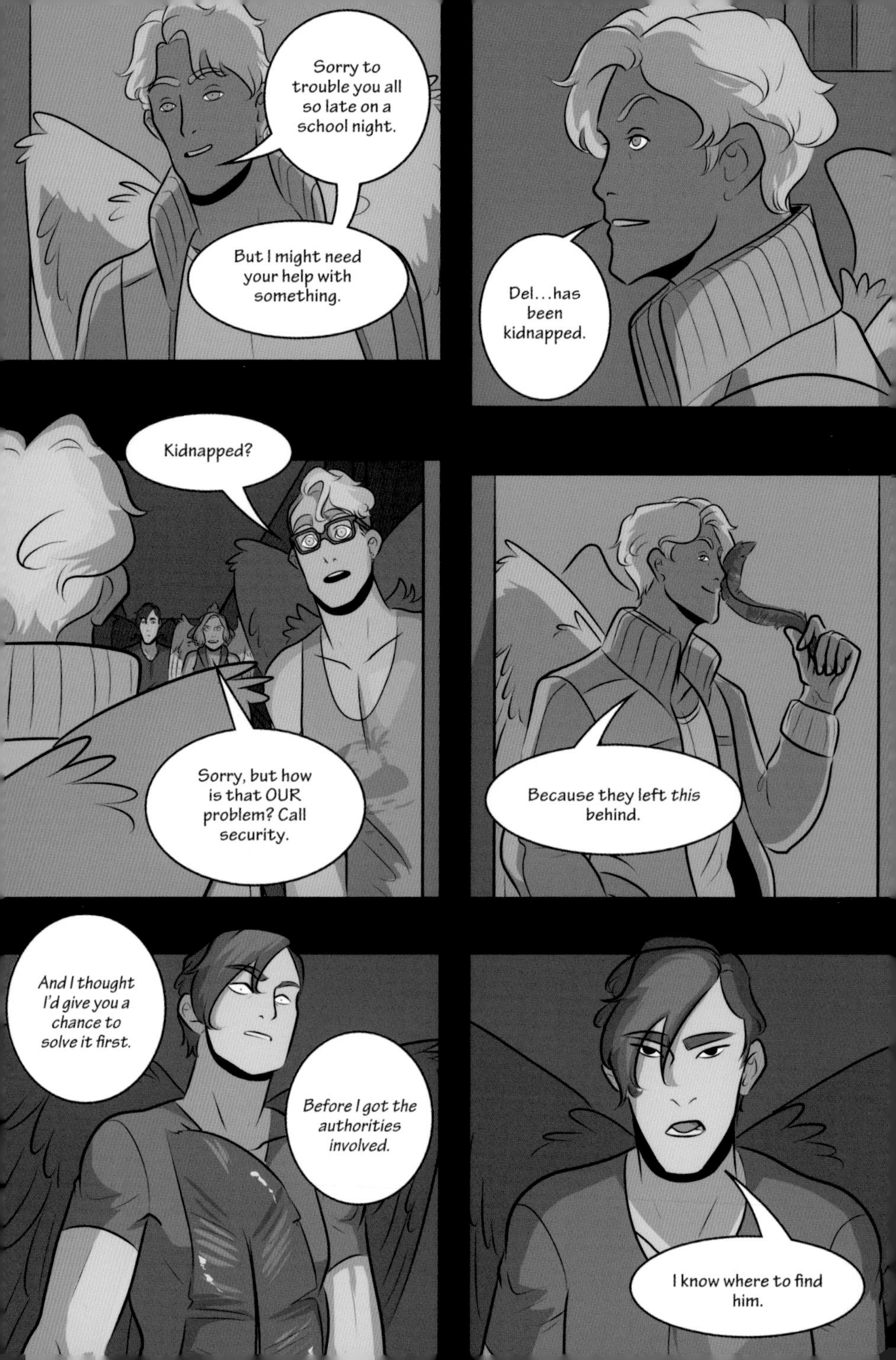
Sorry to trouble you all so late on a school night.
But I might need your help with something.
Del...has been kidnapped.
Kidnapped?
Sorry, but how is that OUR problem? Call security.
Because they left *this* behind.
And I thought I'd give you a chance to solve it first.
Before I got the authorities involved.
I know where to find him.

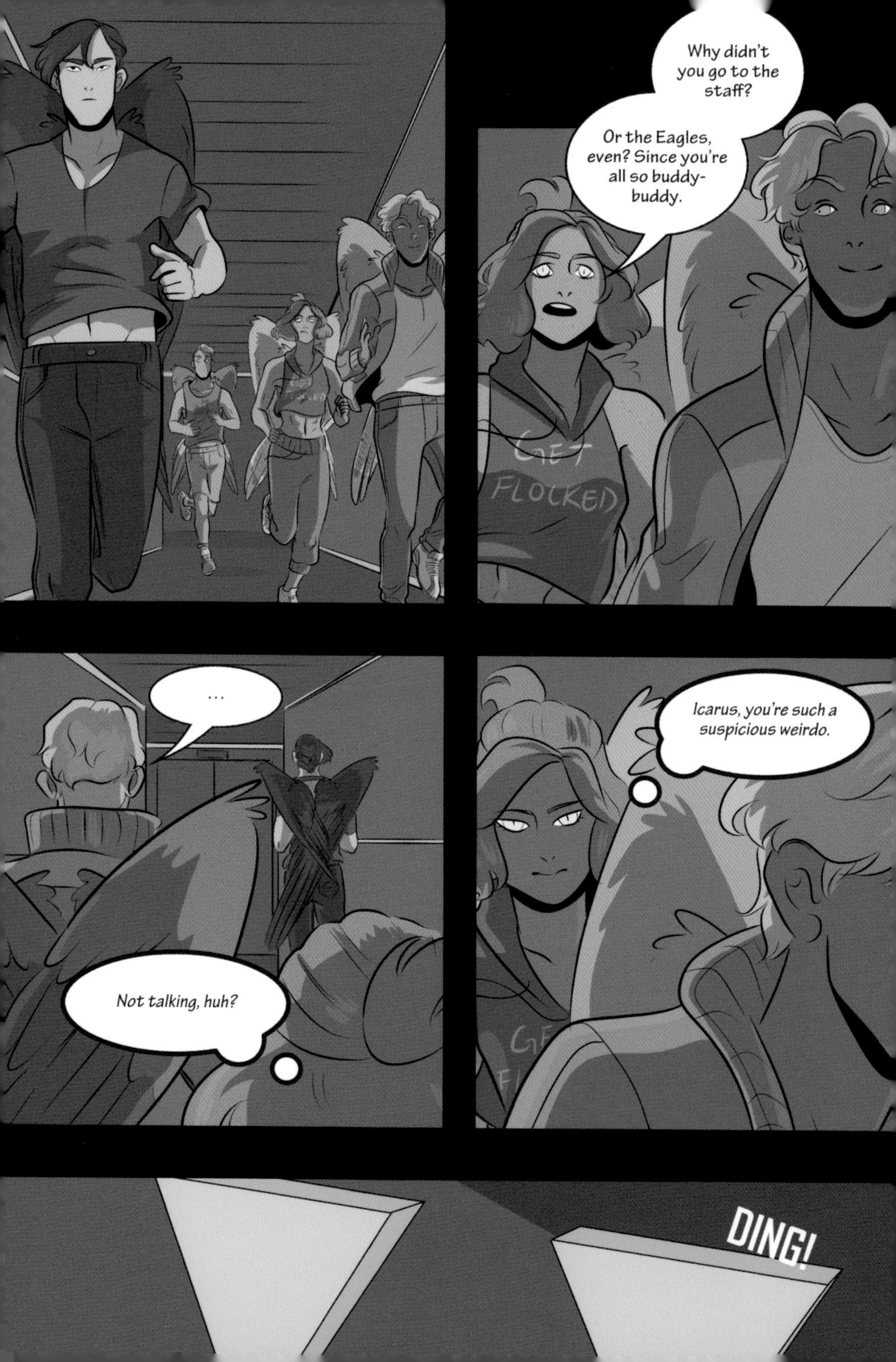

Why didn't you go to the staff?
Or the Eagles, even? Since you're all so buddy-buddy.
GET FLOCKED
...
Not talking, huh?
Icarus, you're such a suspicious weirdo.
DING!

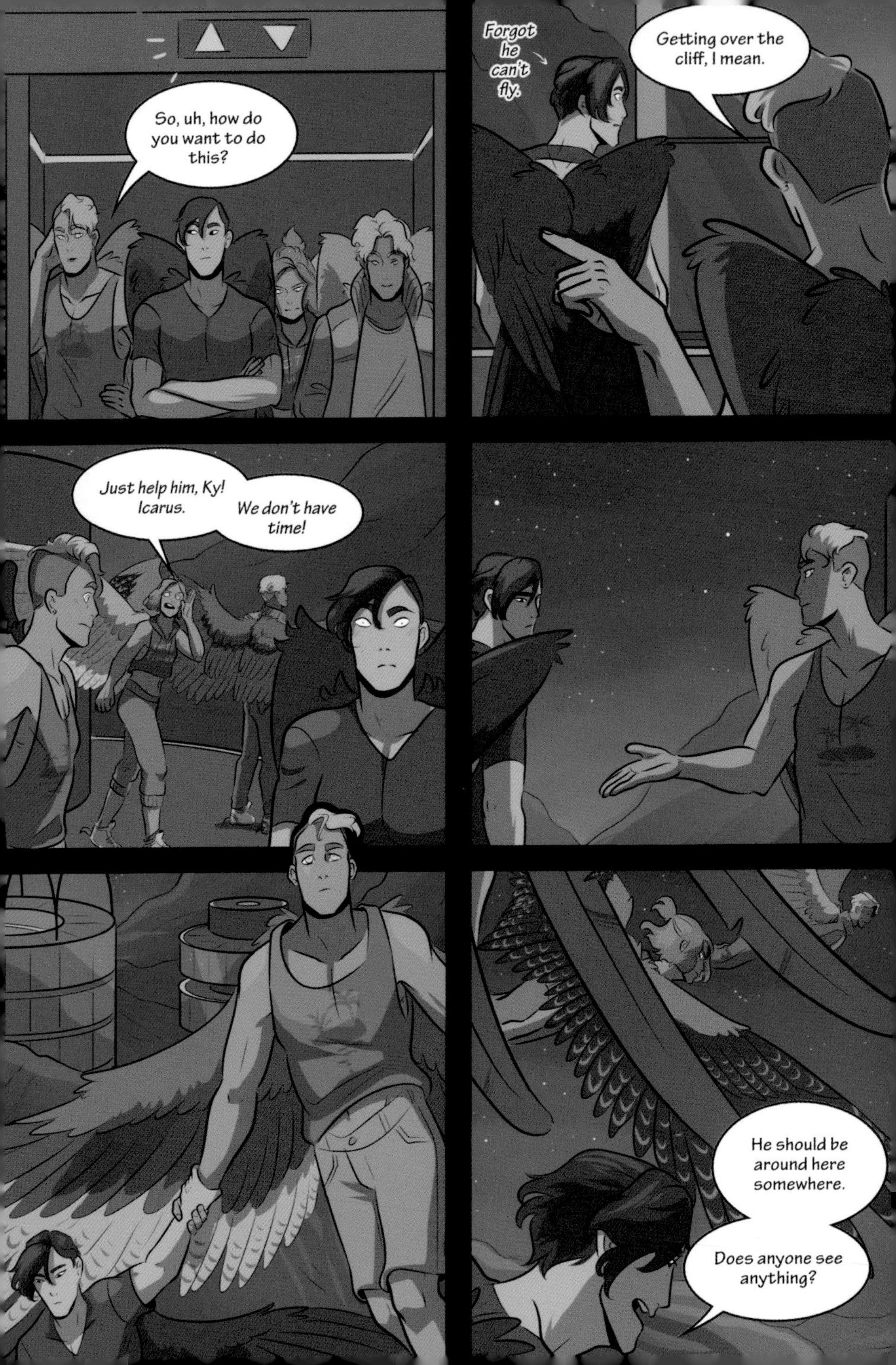
So, uh, how do you want to do this?
Forgot he can't fly.
Getting over the cliff, I mean.
Just help him, Ky! Icarus.
We don't have time!
He should be around here somewhere.
Does anyone see anything?

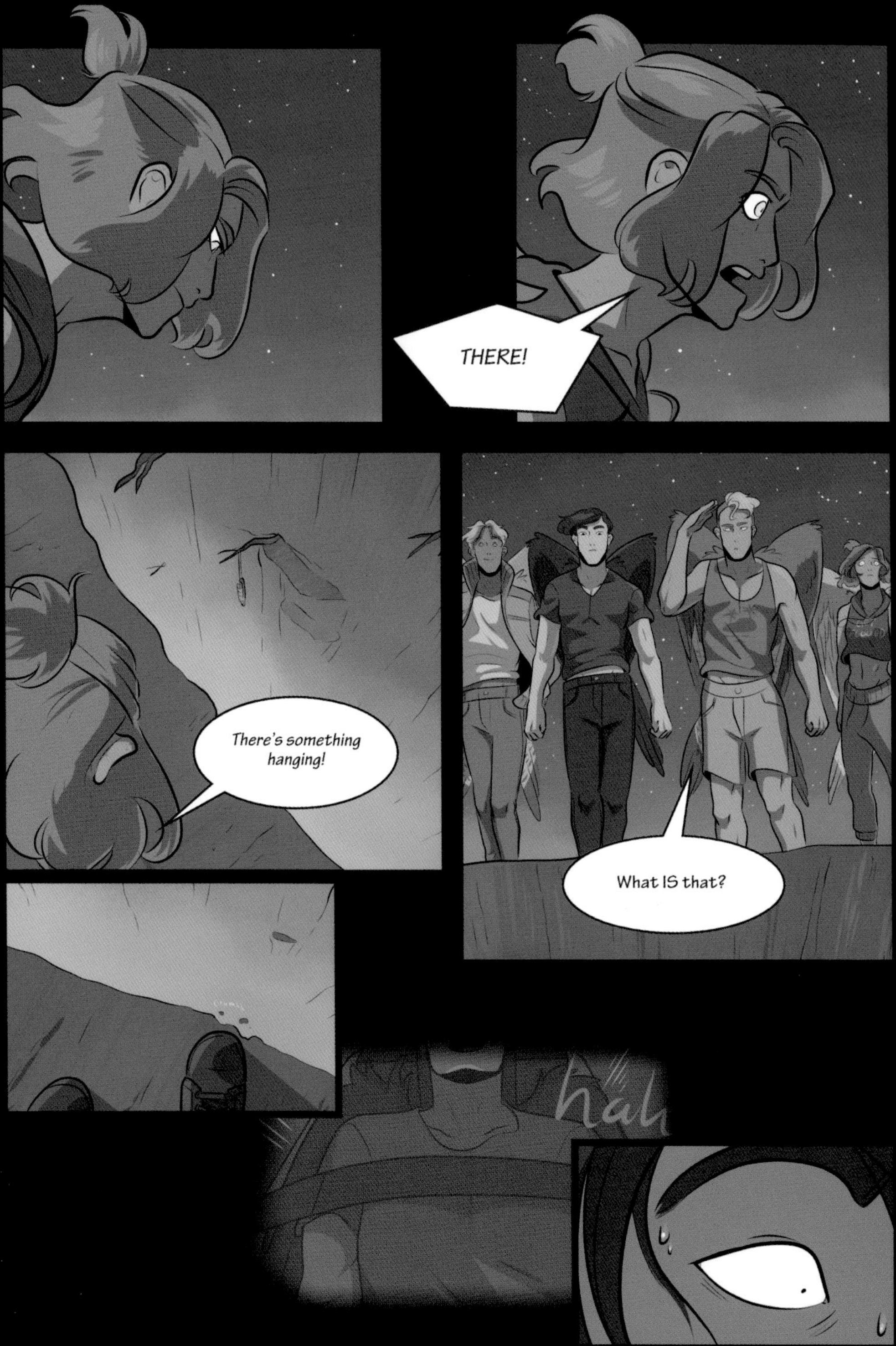
THERE!
There's something hanging!
What IS that?

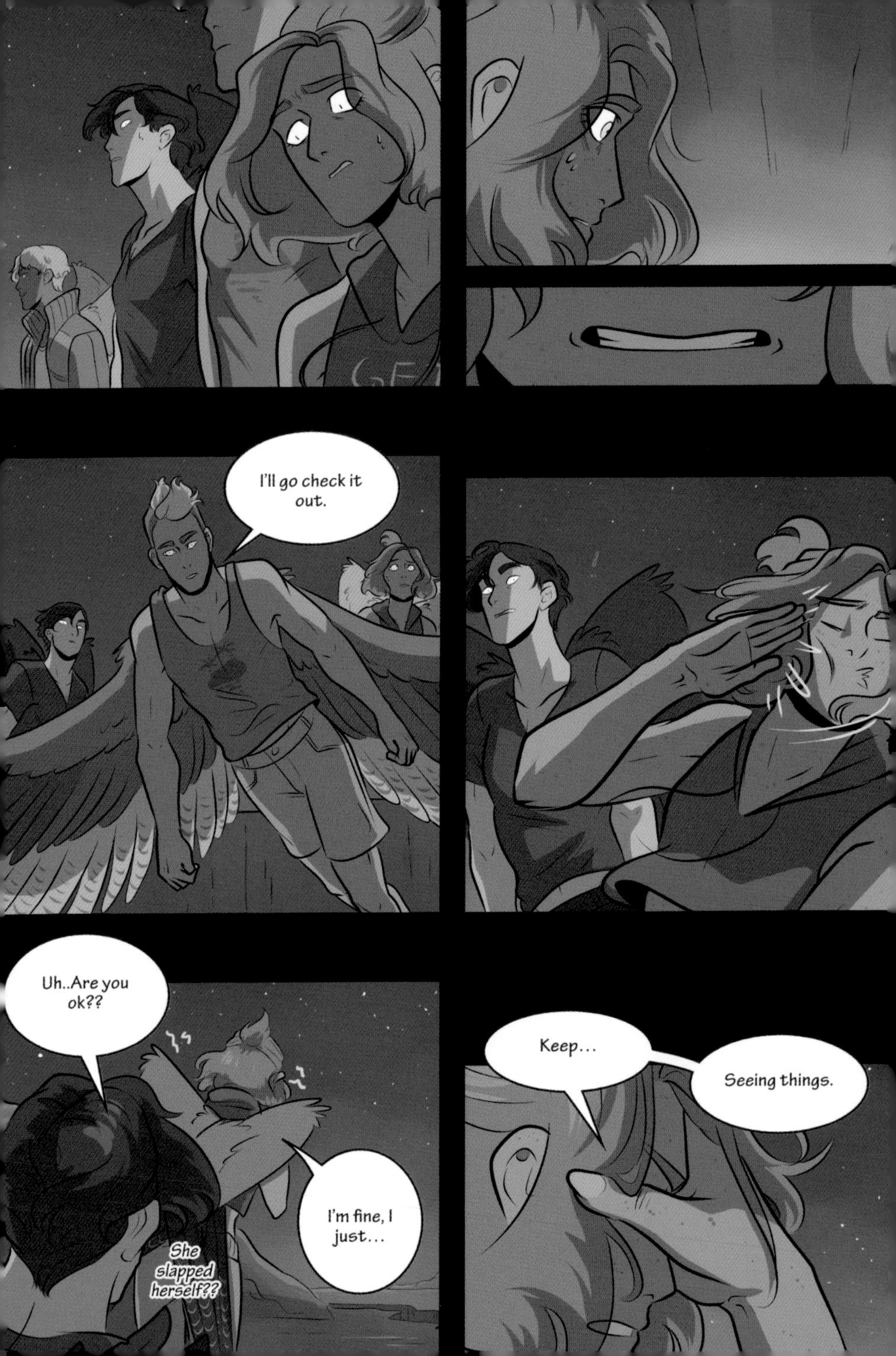
I'll go check it out.
Uh..Are you ok??
She slapped herself??
I'm fine, I just…
Keep…
Seeing things.

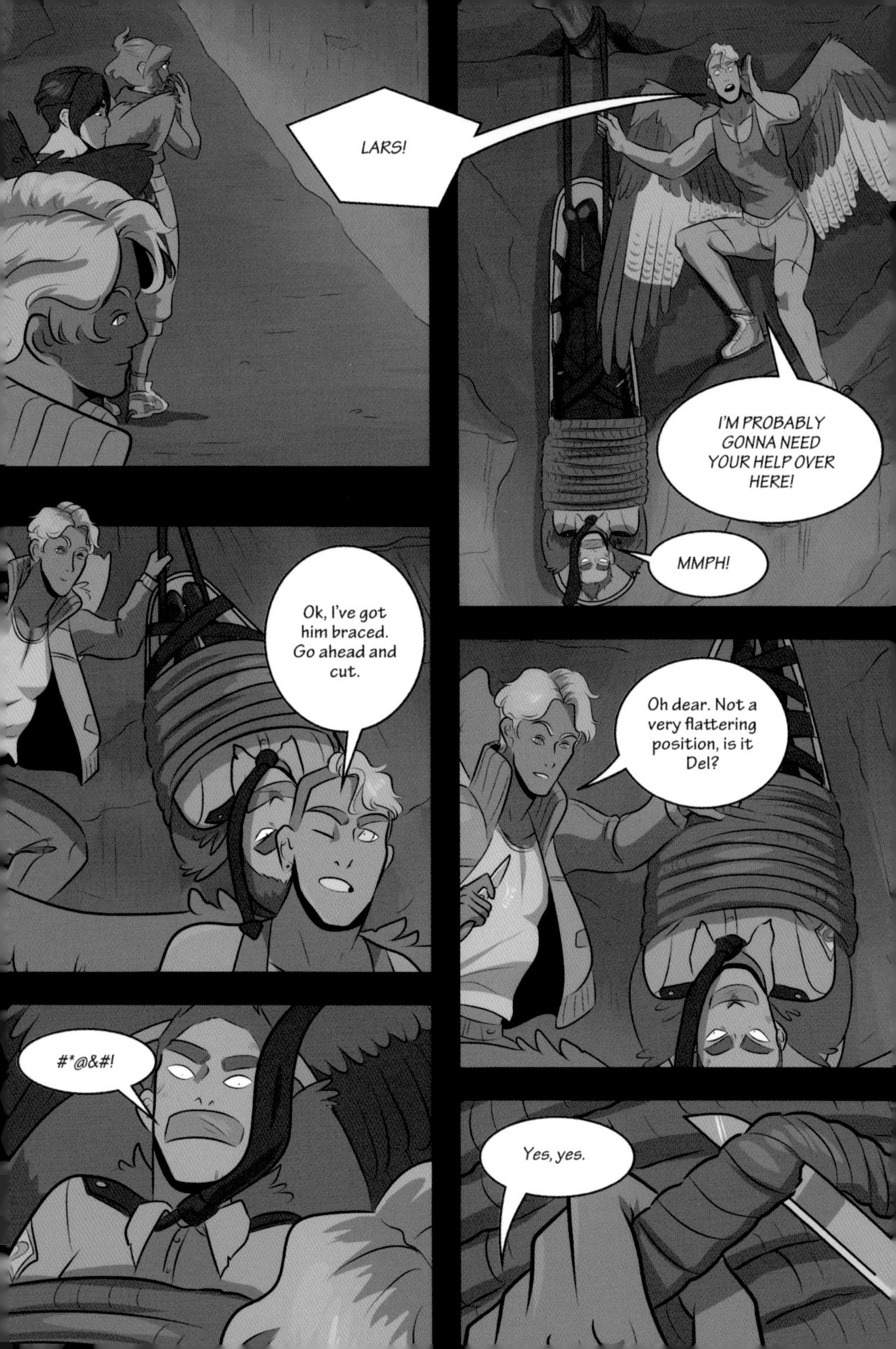
LARS!
I'M PROBABLY GONNA NEED YOUR HELP OVER HERE!
MMPH!
Ok, I've got him braced. Go ahead and cut.
Oh dear. Not a very flattering position, is it Del?
#*@&#!
Yes, yes.

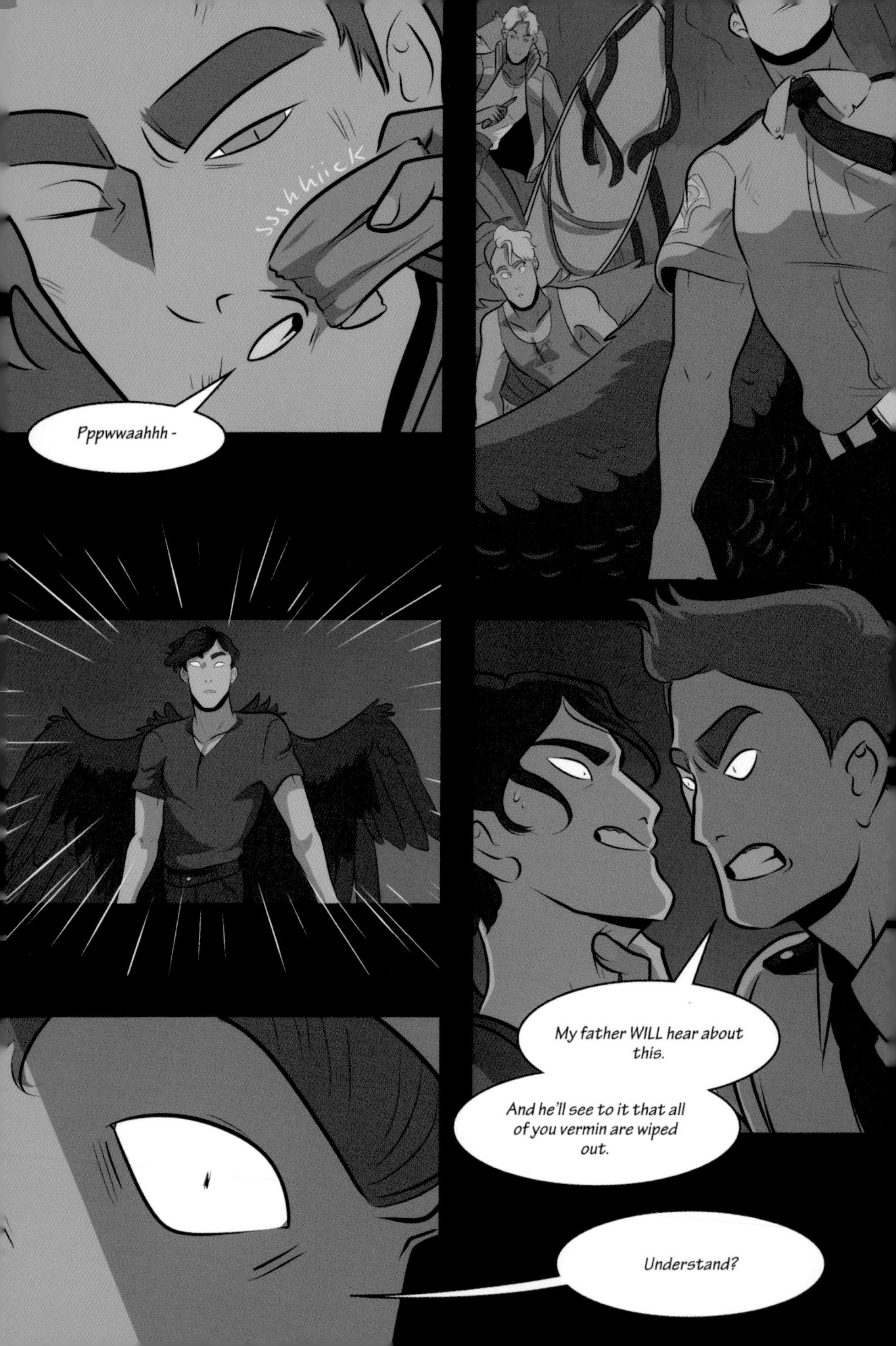
sssshiiick
Pppwwaahhh -
My father WILL hear about this.
And he'll see to it that all of you vermin are wiped out.
Understand?

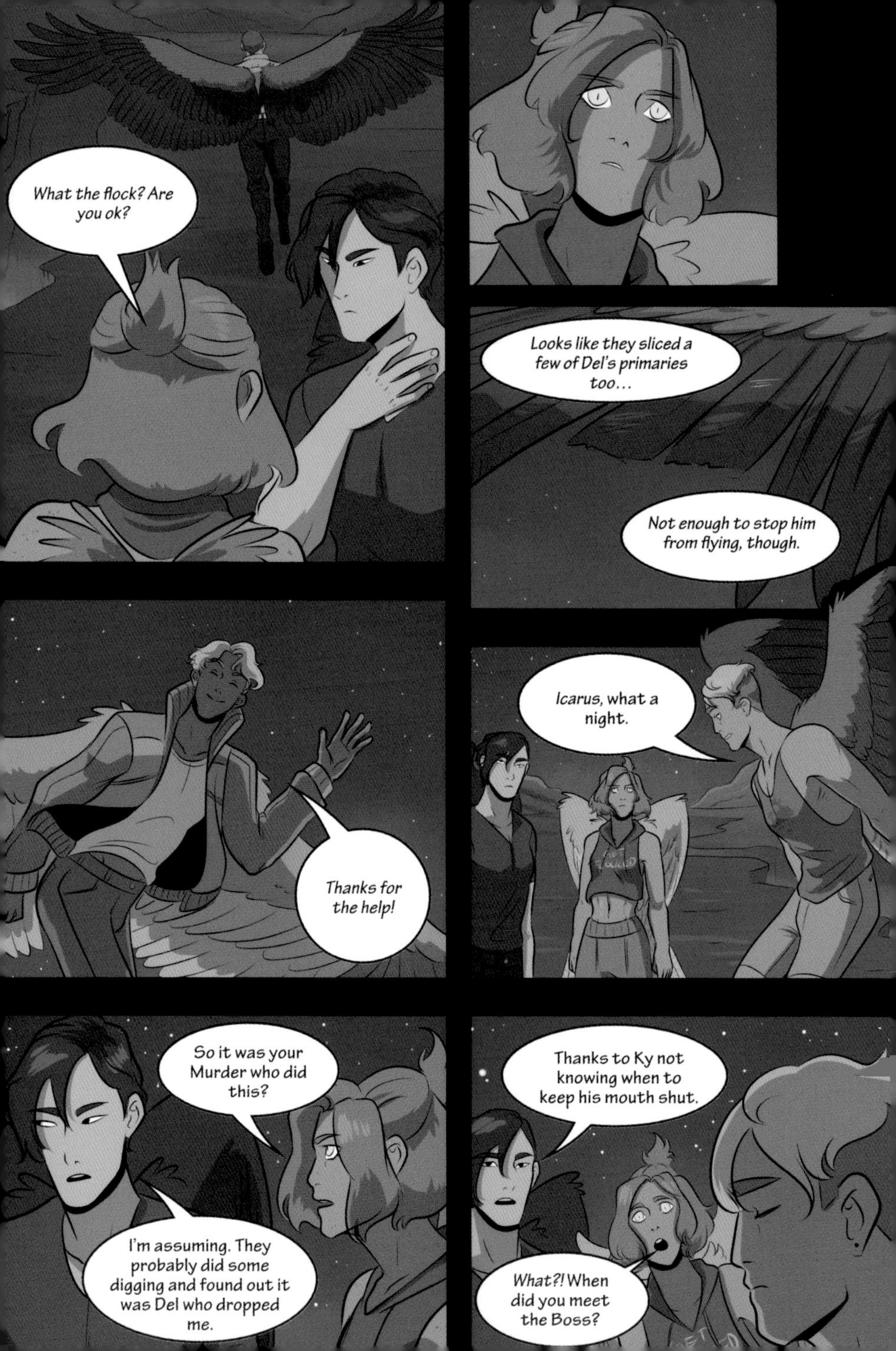
What the flock? Are you ok?
Looks like they sliced a few of Del's primaries too…
Not enough to stop him from flying, though.
Thanks for the help!
Icarus, what a night.
So it was your Murder who did this?
I'm assuming. They probably did some digging and found out it was Del who dropped me.
Thanks to Ky not knowing when to keep his mouth shut.
What?! When did you meet the Boss?

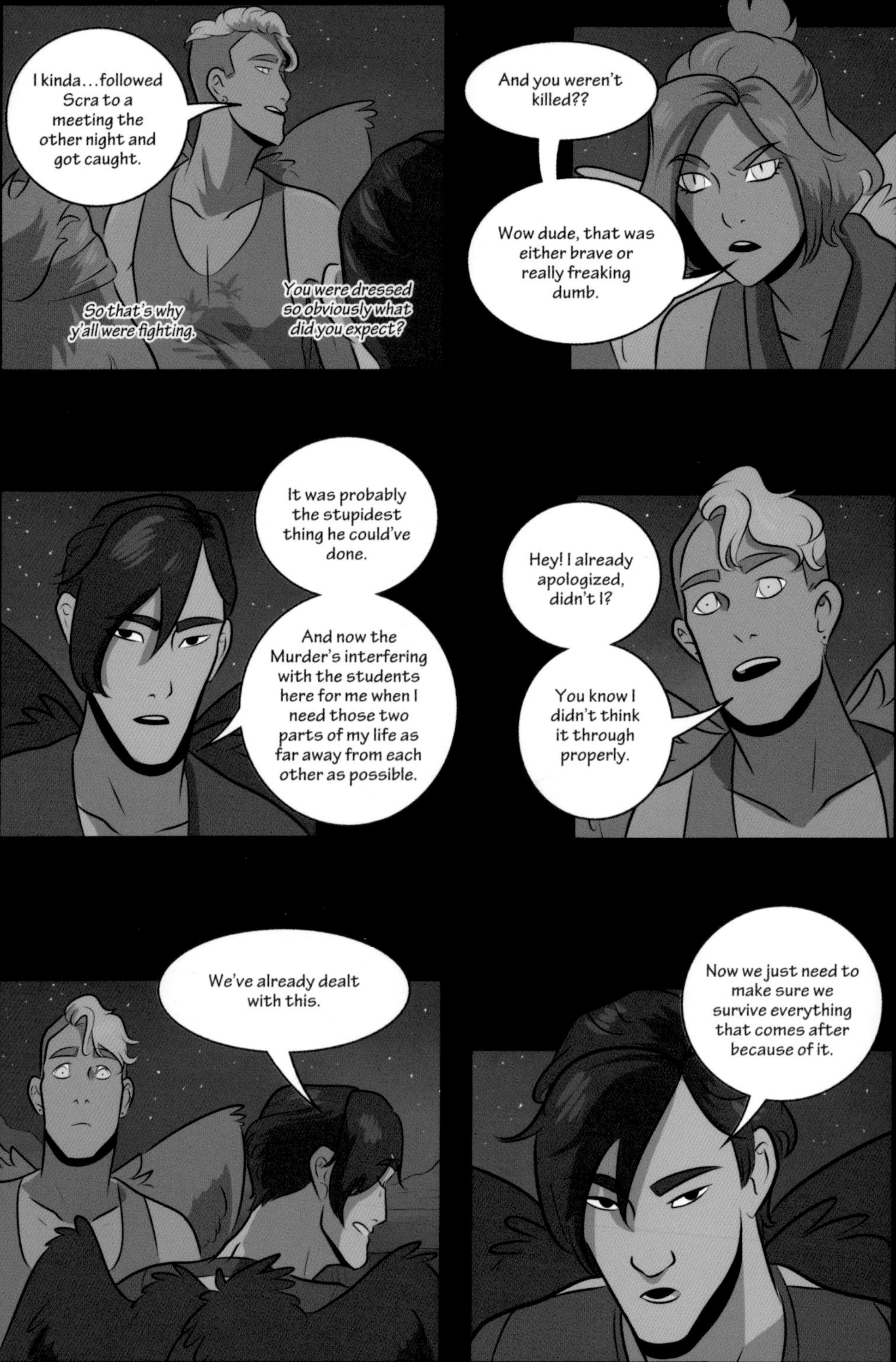
I kinda…followed Scra to a meeting the other night and got caught.
So that's why y'all were fighting.
You were dressed so obviously what did you expect?
And you weren't killed??
Wow dude, that was either brave or really freaking dumb.
It was probably the stupidest thing he could've done.
And now the Murder's interfering with the students here for me when I need those two parts of my life as far away from each other as possible.
Hey! I already apologized, didn't I?
You know I didn't think it through properly.
We've already dealt with this.
Now we just need to make sure we survive everything that comes after because of it.

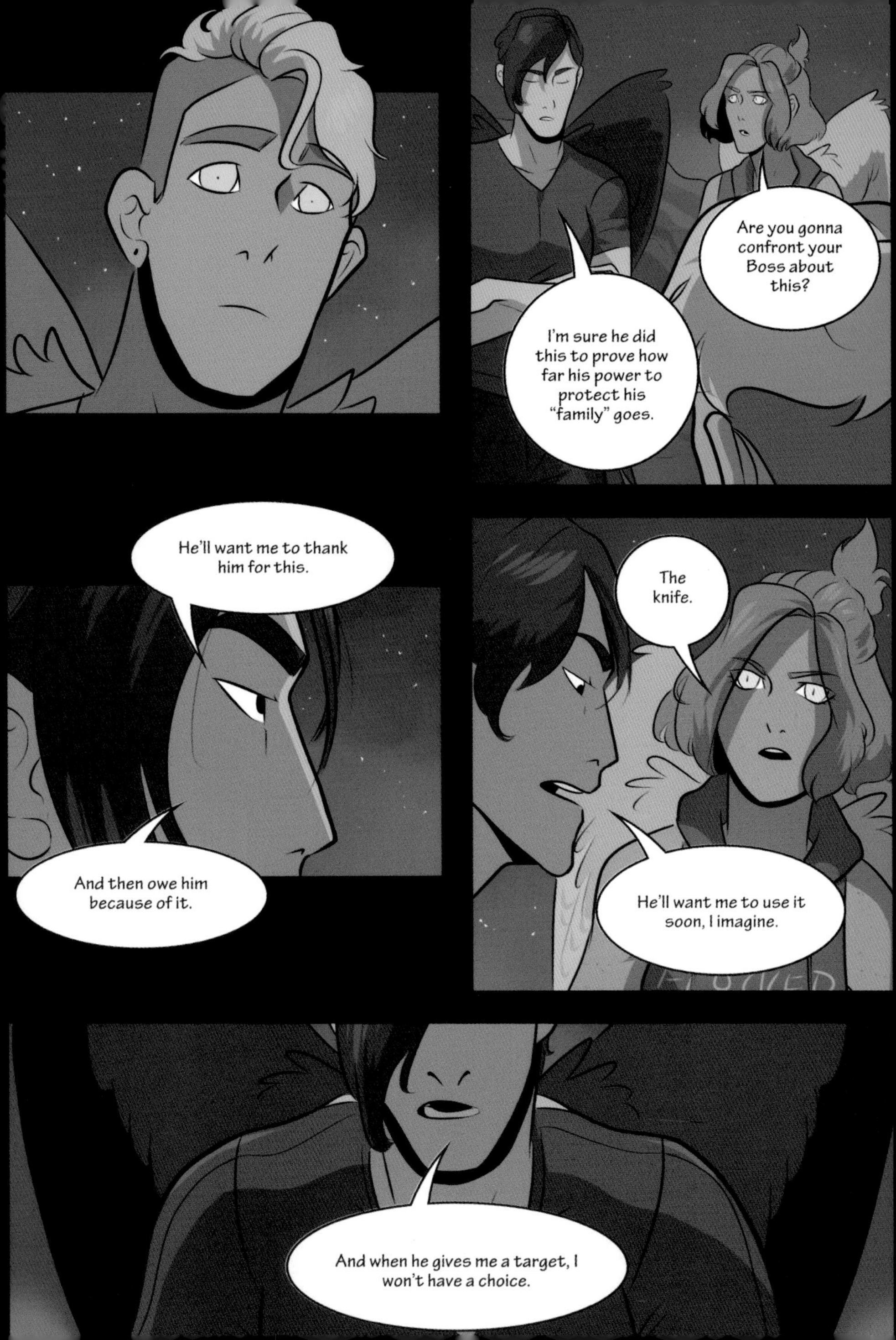
Are you gonna confront your Boss about this?
I'm sure he did this to prove how far his power to protect his "family" goes.
He'll want me to thank him for this.
And then owe him because of it.
The knife.
He'll want me to use it soon, I imagine.
And when he gives me a target, I won't have a choice.

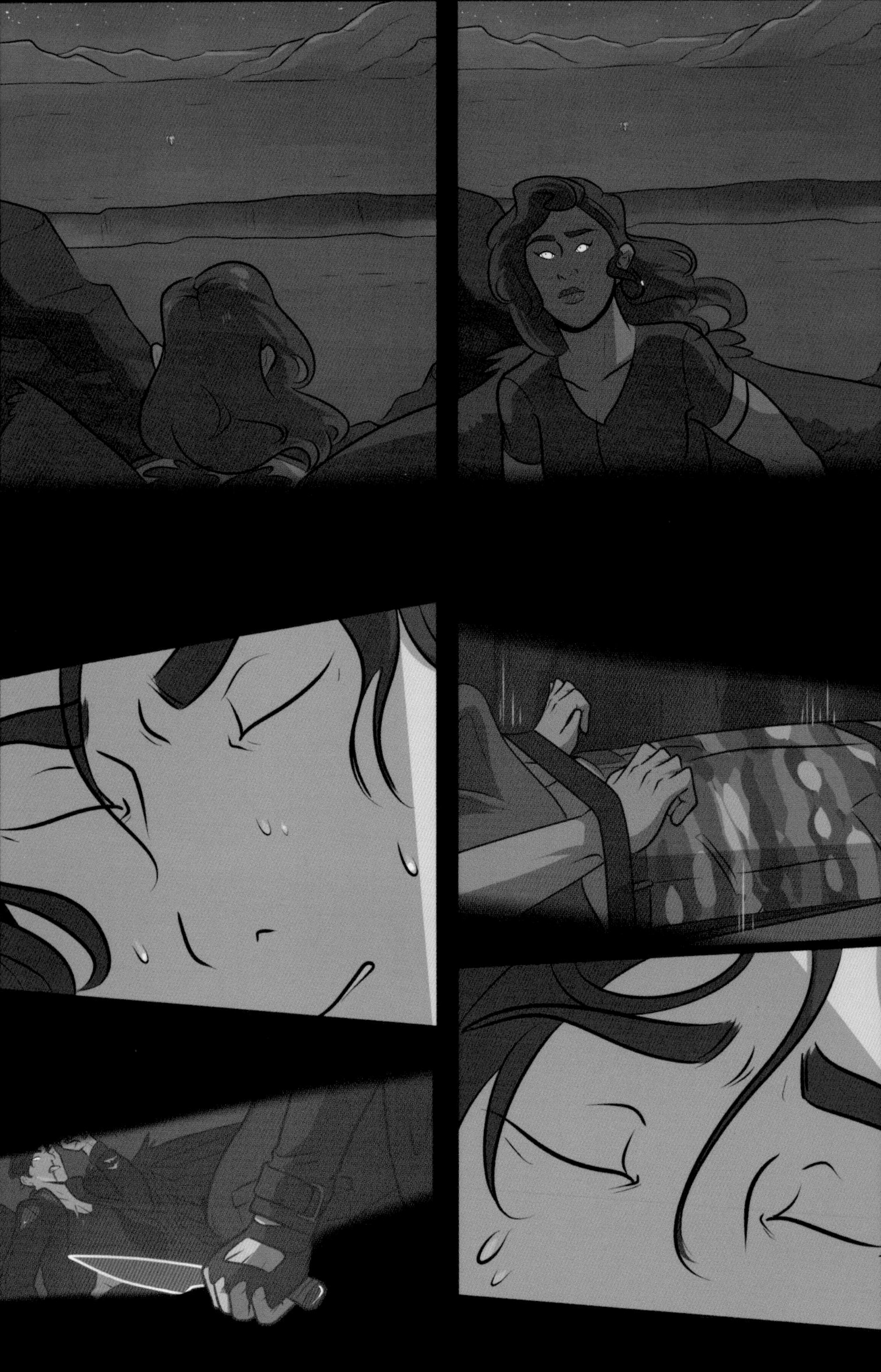

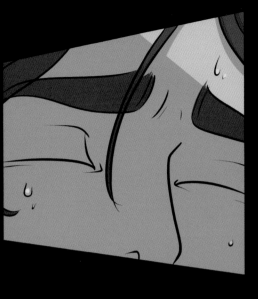

HWAH!

WOAH, HEY -

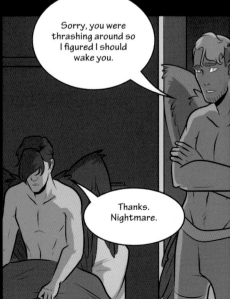

Sorry, you were thrashing around so I figured I should wake you.

Thanks. Nightmare.

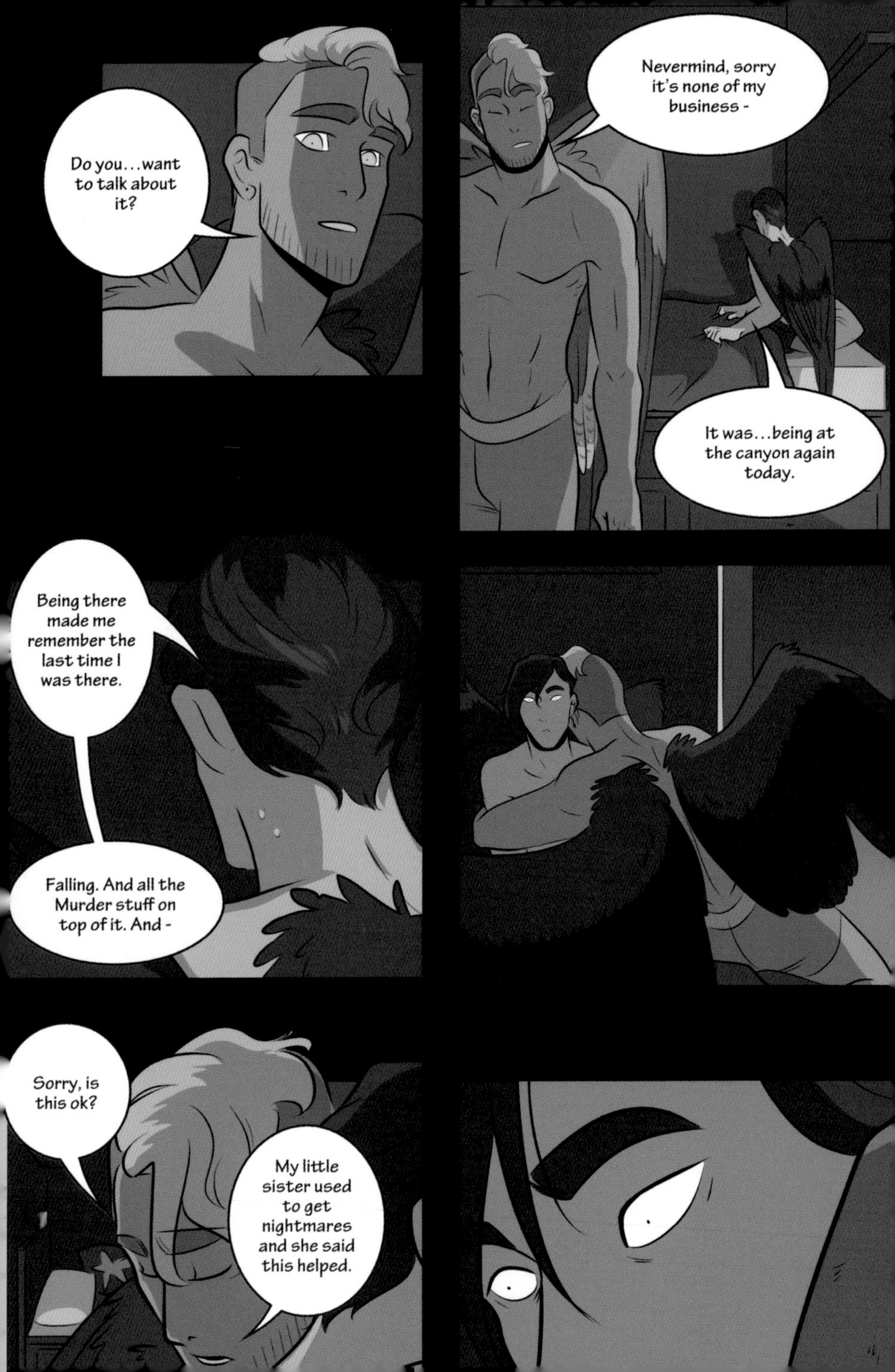
Do you...want to talk about it?
Nevermind, sorry it's none of my business -
It was...being at the canyon again today.
Being there made me remember the last time I was there.
Falling. And all the Murder stuff on top of it. And -
Sorry, is this ok?
My little sister used to get nightmares and she said this helped.

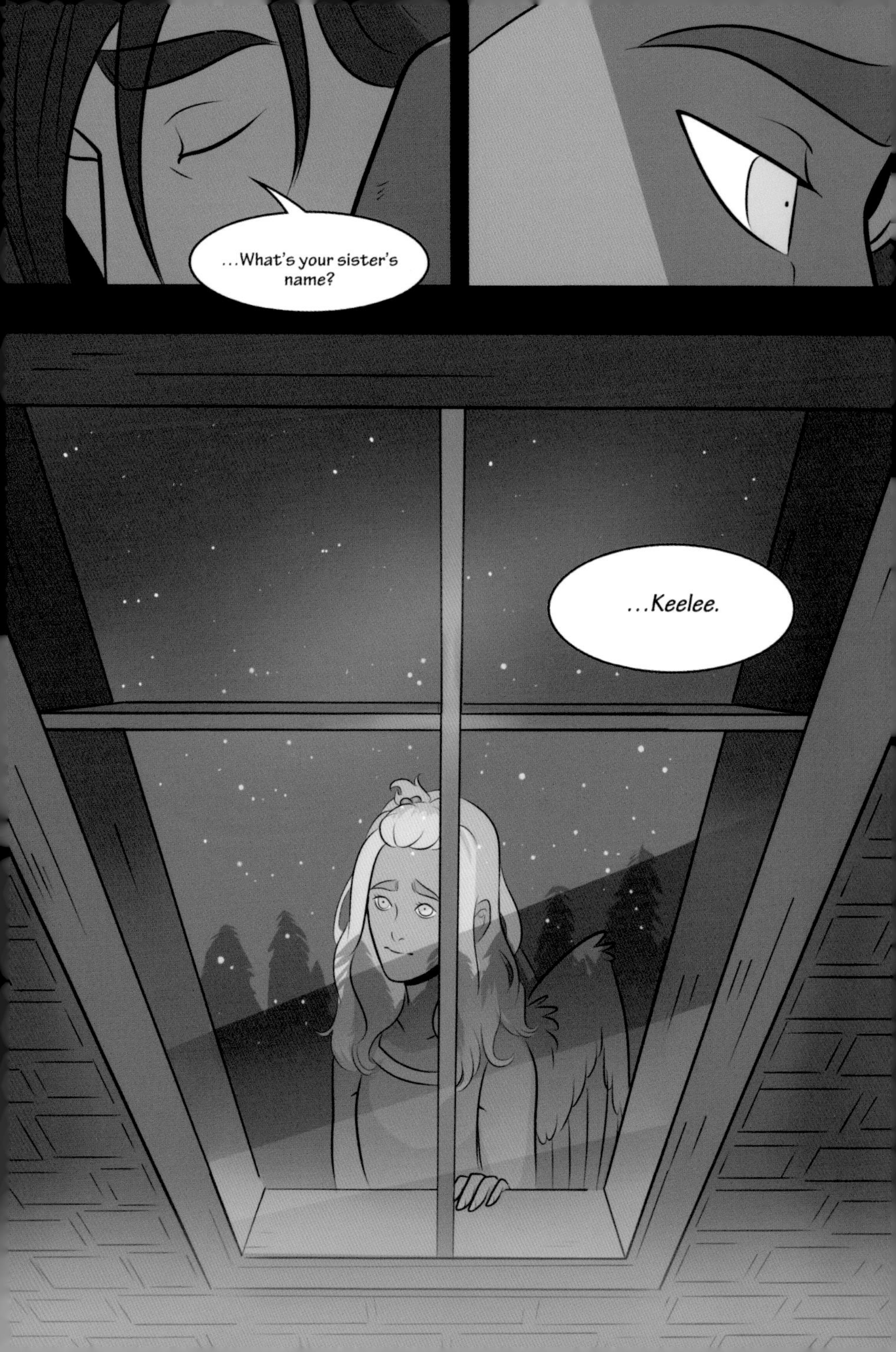
...What's your sister's name?
...Keelee.

THE CROAKING

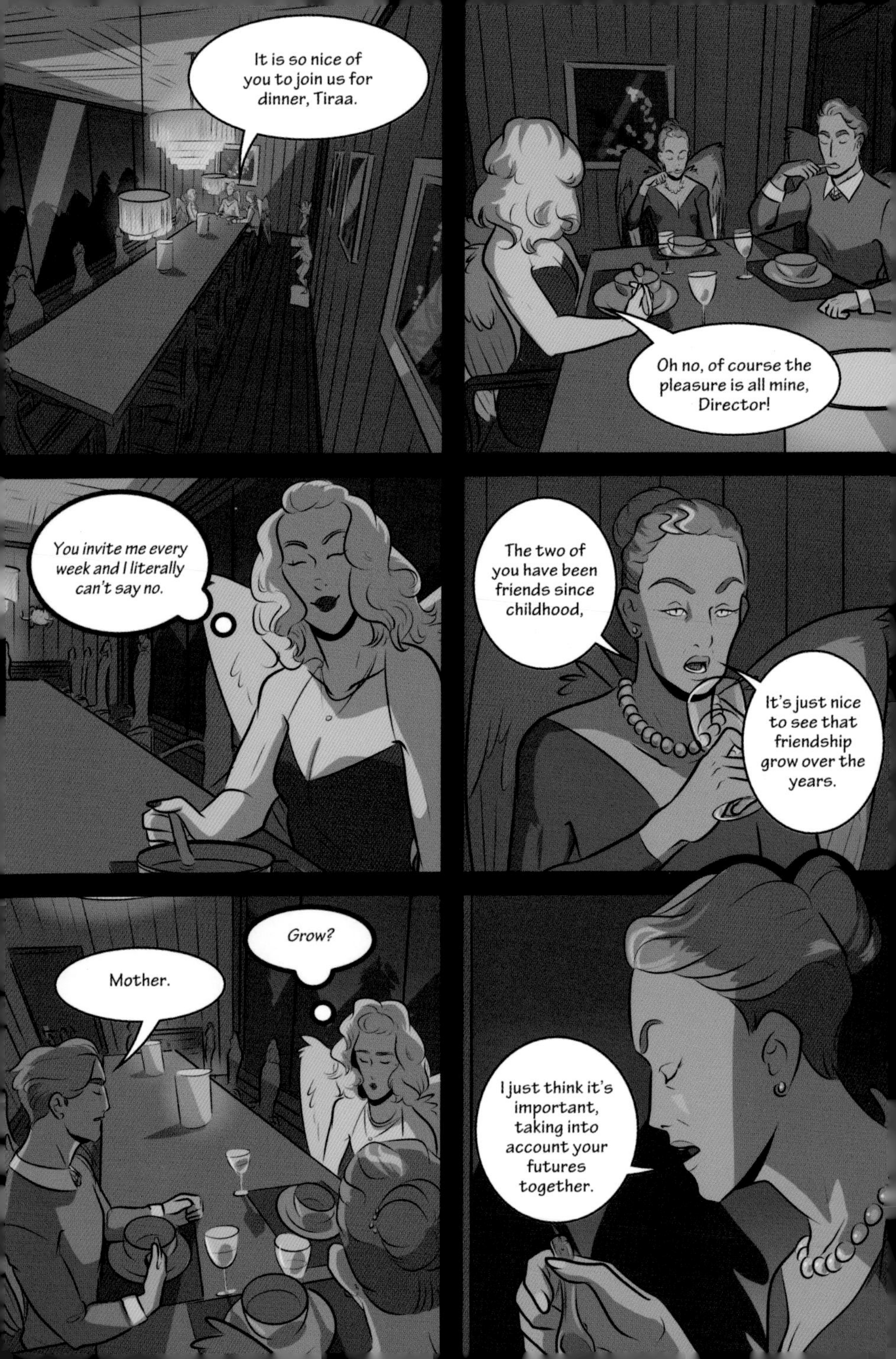
It is so nice of you to join us for dinner, Tiraa.
Oh no, of course the pleasure is all mine, Director!
You invite me every week and I literally can't say no.
The two of you have been friends since childhood,
It's just nice to see that friendship grow over the years.
Mother.
Grow?
I just think it's important, taking into account your futures together.

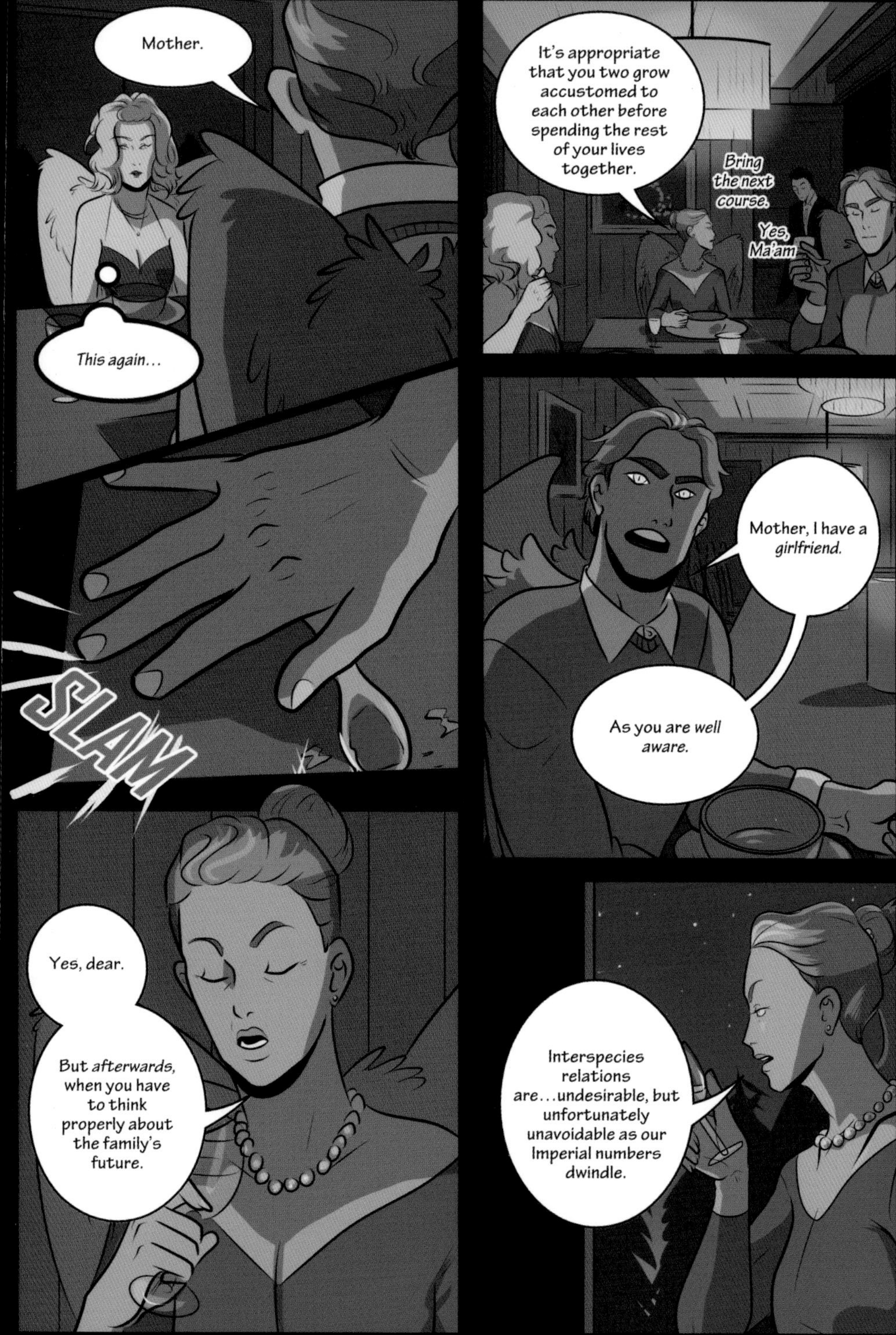

Mother.
This again...
SLAM
It's appropriate that you two grow accustomed to each other before spending the rest of your lives together.
Bring the next course.
Yes, Ma'am
Mother, I have a *girlfriend.*
As you are *well* aware.
Yes, dear.
But *afterwards,* when you have to think properly about the family's future.
Interspecies relations are...undesirable, but unfortunately unavoidable as our Imperial numbers dwindle.

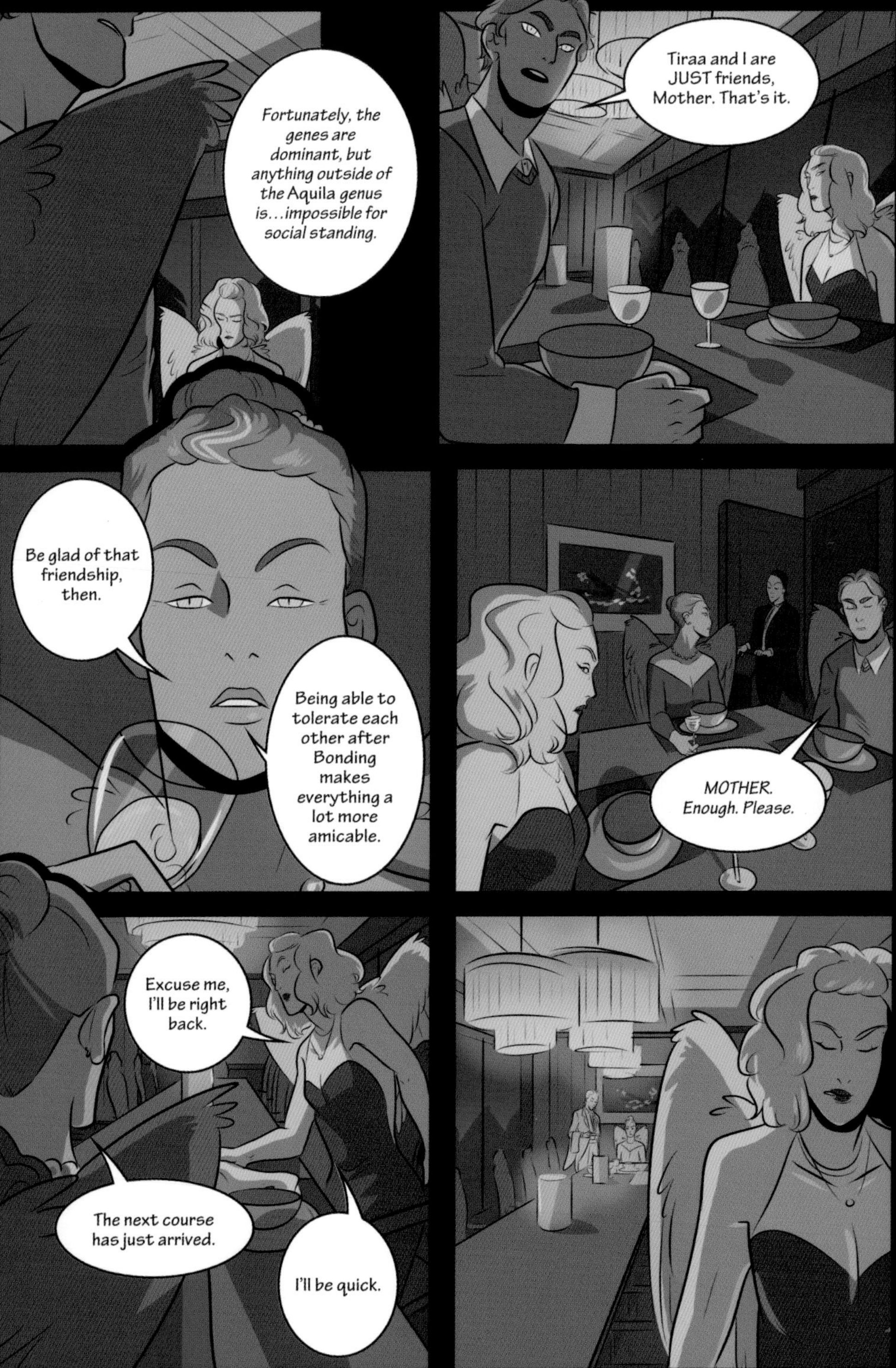
Fortunately, the genes are dominant, but anything outside of the Aquila genus is...impossible for social standing.
Tiraa and I are JUST friends, Mother. That's it.
Be glad of that friendship, then.
Being able to tolerate each other after Bonding makes everything a lot more amicable.
MOTHER. Enough. Please.
Excuse me, I'll be right back.
The next course has just arrived.
I'll be quick.

UGH.

Every week I'm stuck here listening to the same shit.

I knew it was coming for a while.

My mother warned me it would be like this.

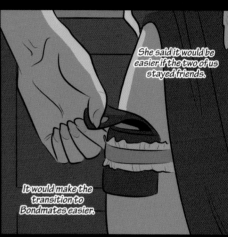

She said it would be easier if the two of us stayed friends.

It would make the transition to Bondmates easier.

Because in the end, getting me Bonded off was all a part of their sick plan.

Flick

It was the reason Reamer and I were even introduced as kids in the first place.

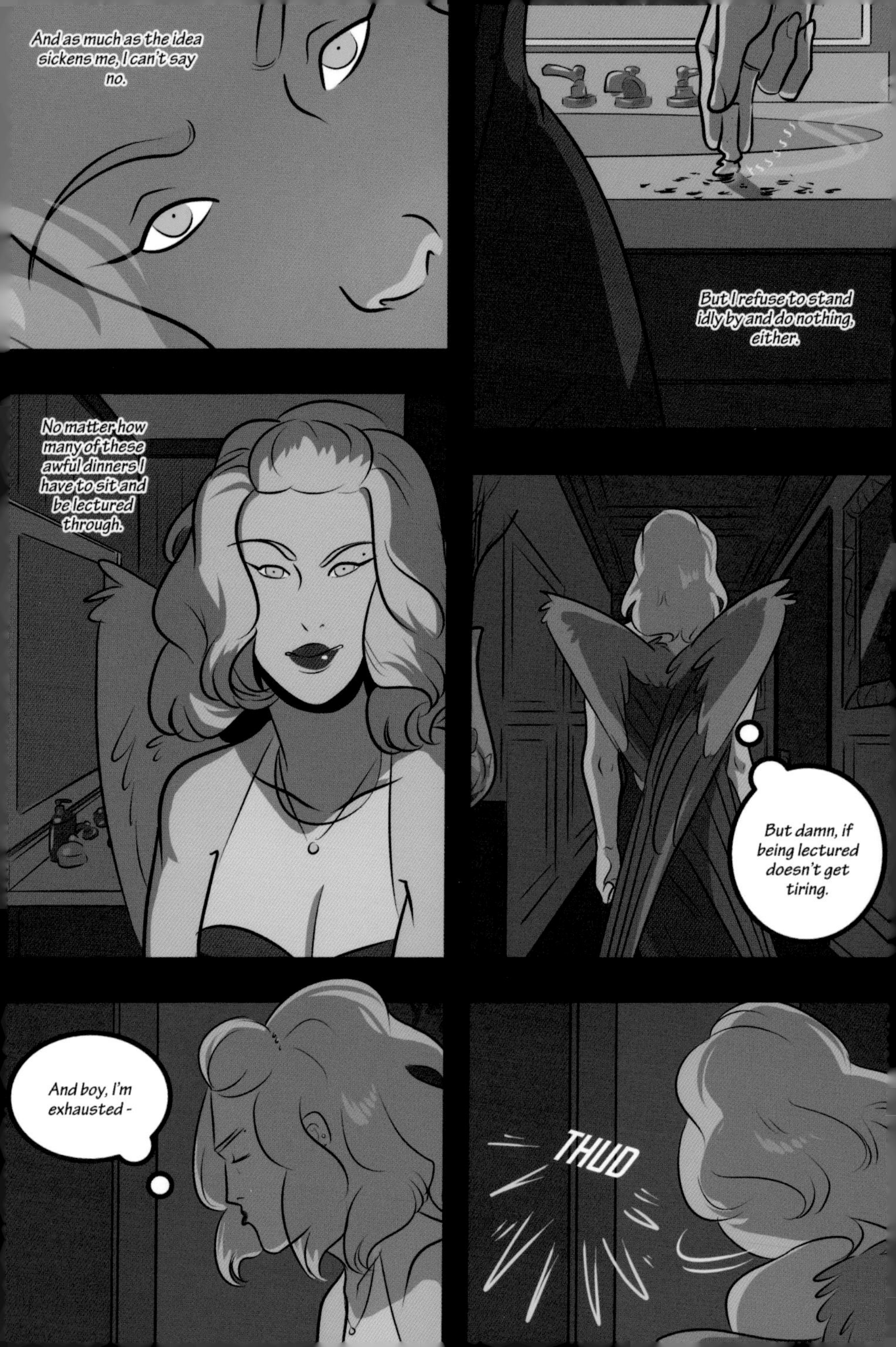

And as much as the idea sickens me, I can't say no.
But I refuse to stand idly by and do nothing, either.
No matter how many of these awful dinners I have to sit and be lectured through.
But damn, if being lectured doesn't get tiring.
And boy, I'm exhausted -
THUD

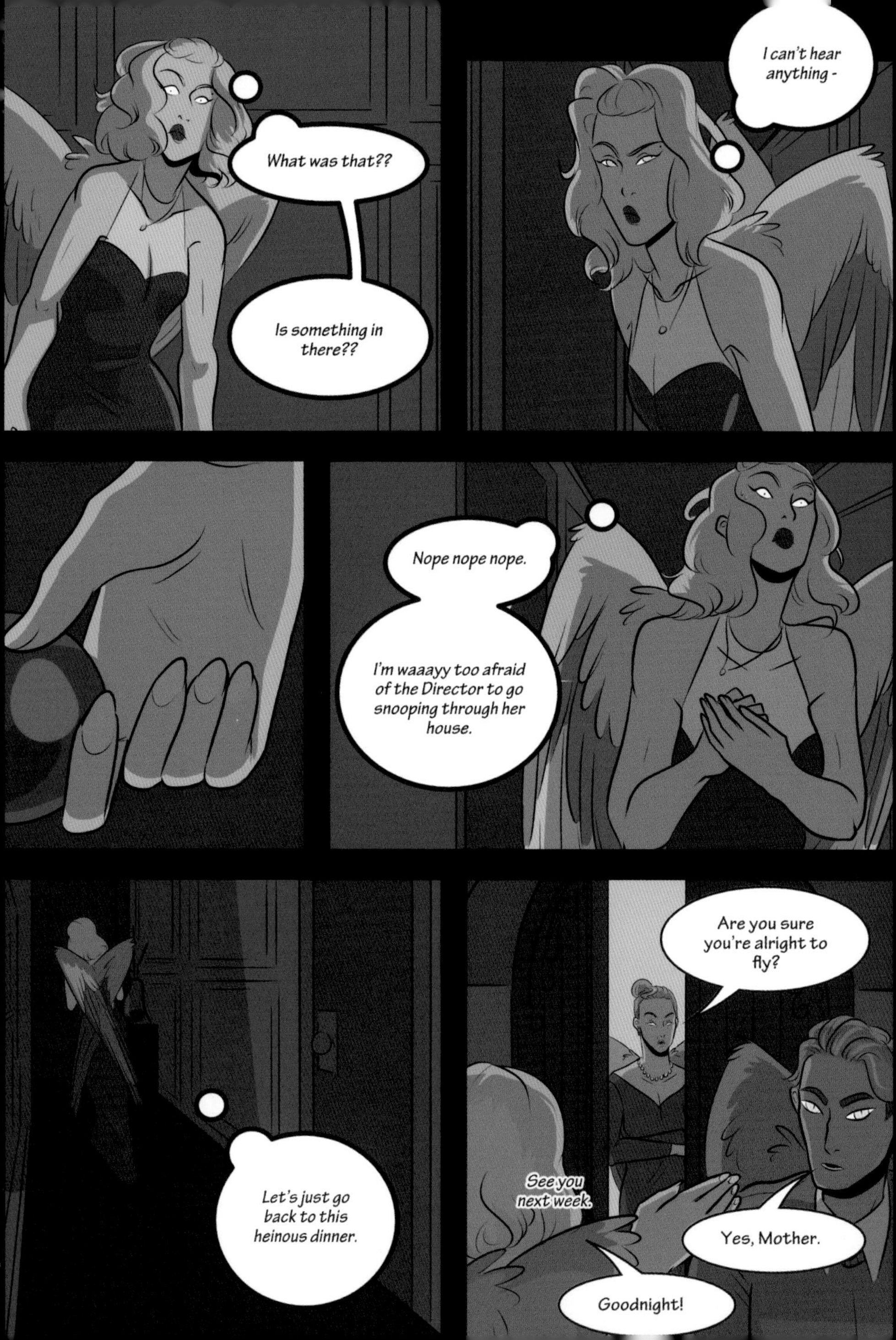
What was that??
Is something in there??
I can't hear anything -
Nope nope nope.
I'm waaayy too afraid of the Director to go snooping through her house.
Let's just go back to this heinous dinner.
Are you sure you're alright to fly?
See you next week.
Yes, Mother.
Goodnight!

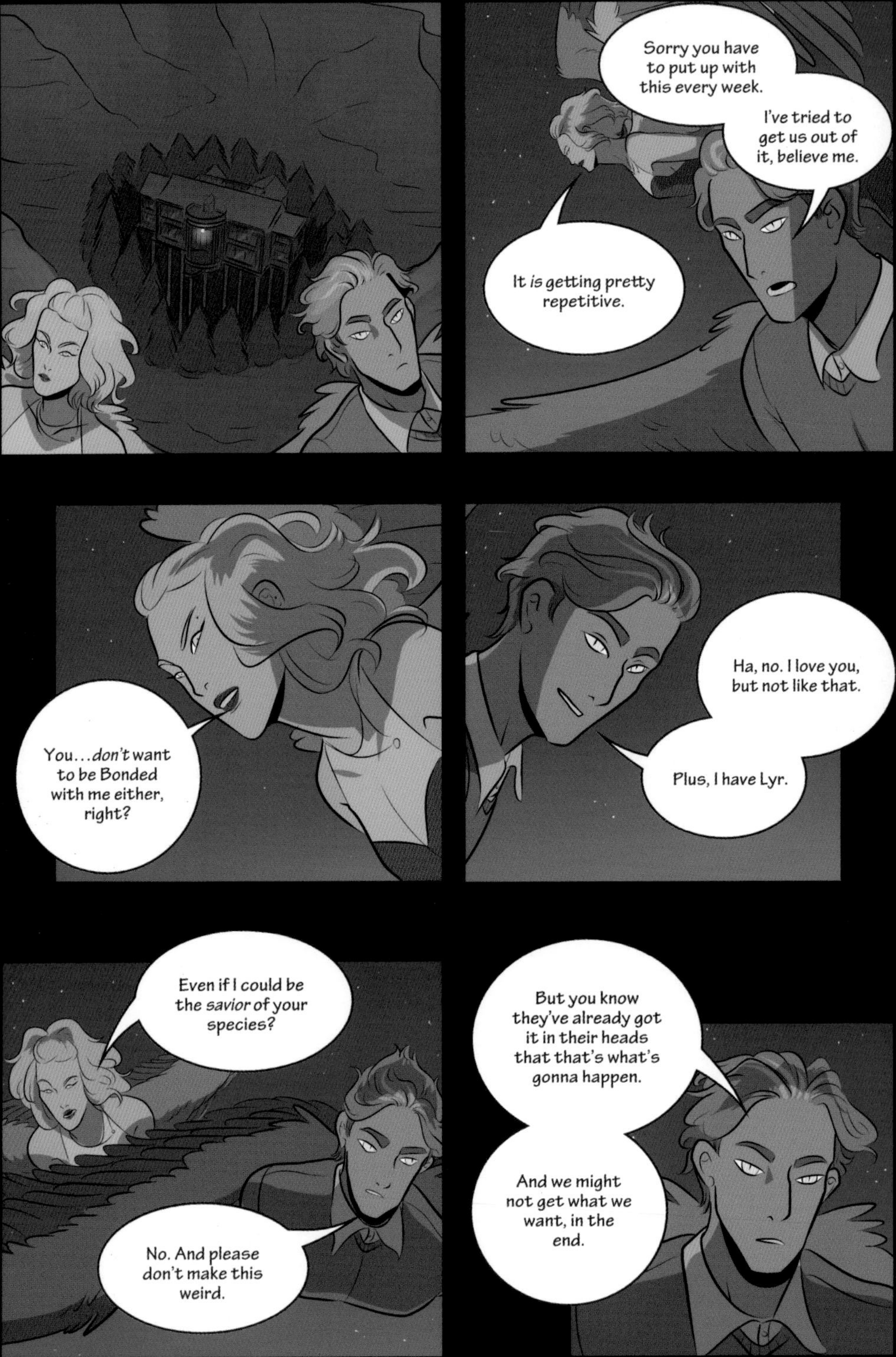
Sorry you have to put up with this every week.
I've tried to get us out of it, believe me.
It *is* getting pretty repetitive.
You...*don't* want to be Bonded with me either, right?
Ha, no. I love you, but not like that.
Plus, I have Lyr.
Even if I could be the *savior* of your species?
No. And please don't make this weird.
But you know they've already got it in their heads that that's what's gonna happen.
And we might not get what we want, in the end.

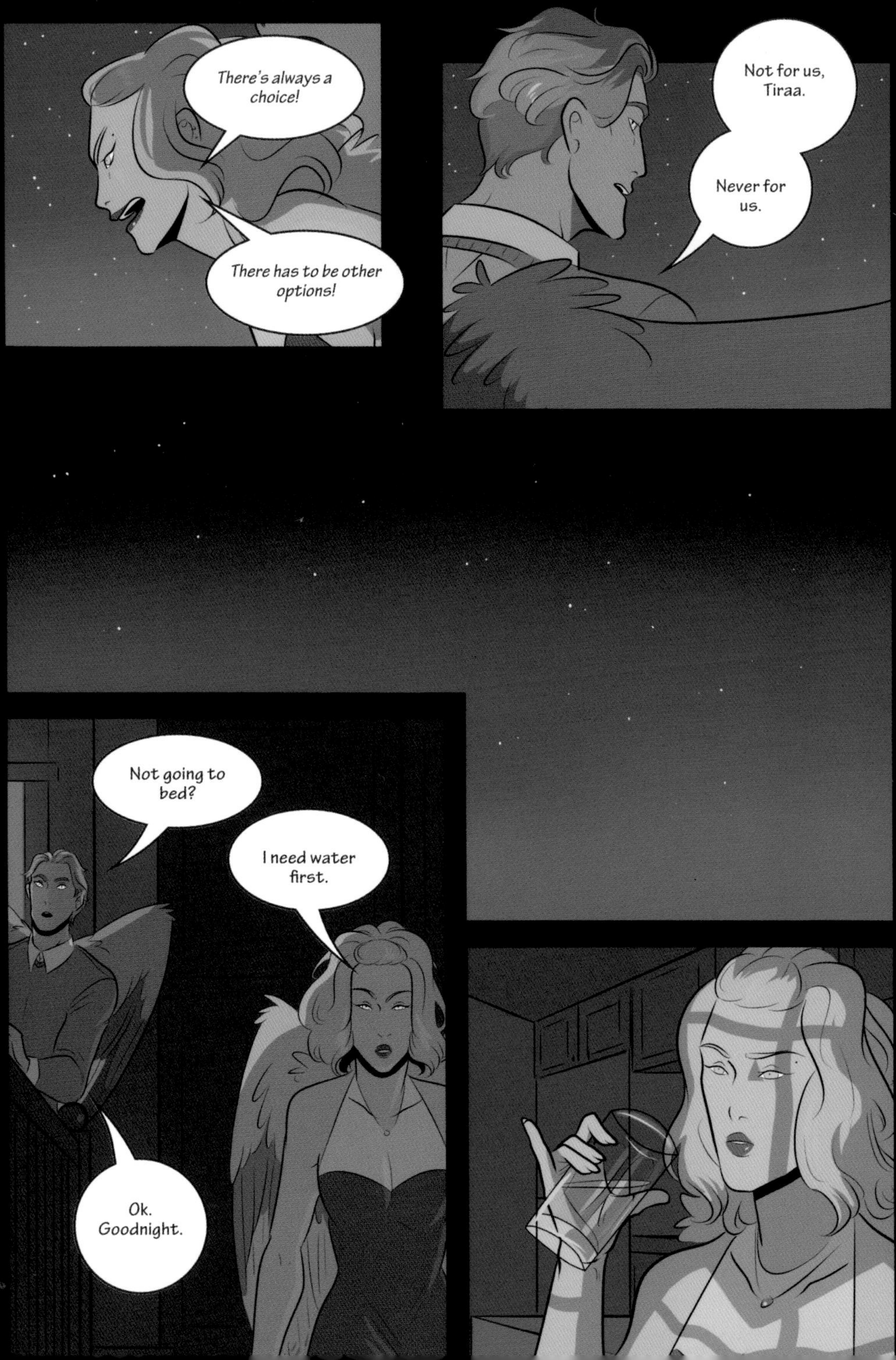
There's always a choice!
There has to be other options!
Not for us, Tiraa.
Never for us.
Not going to bed?
I need water first.
Ok. Goodnight.

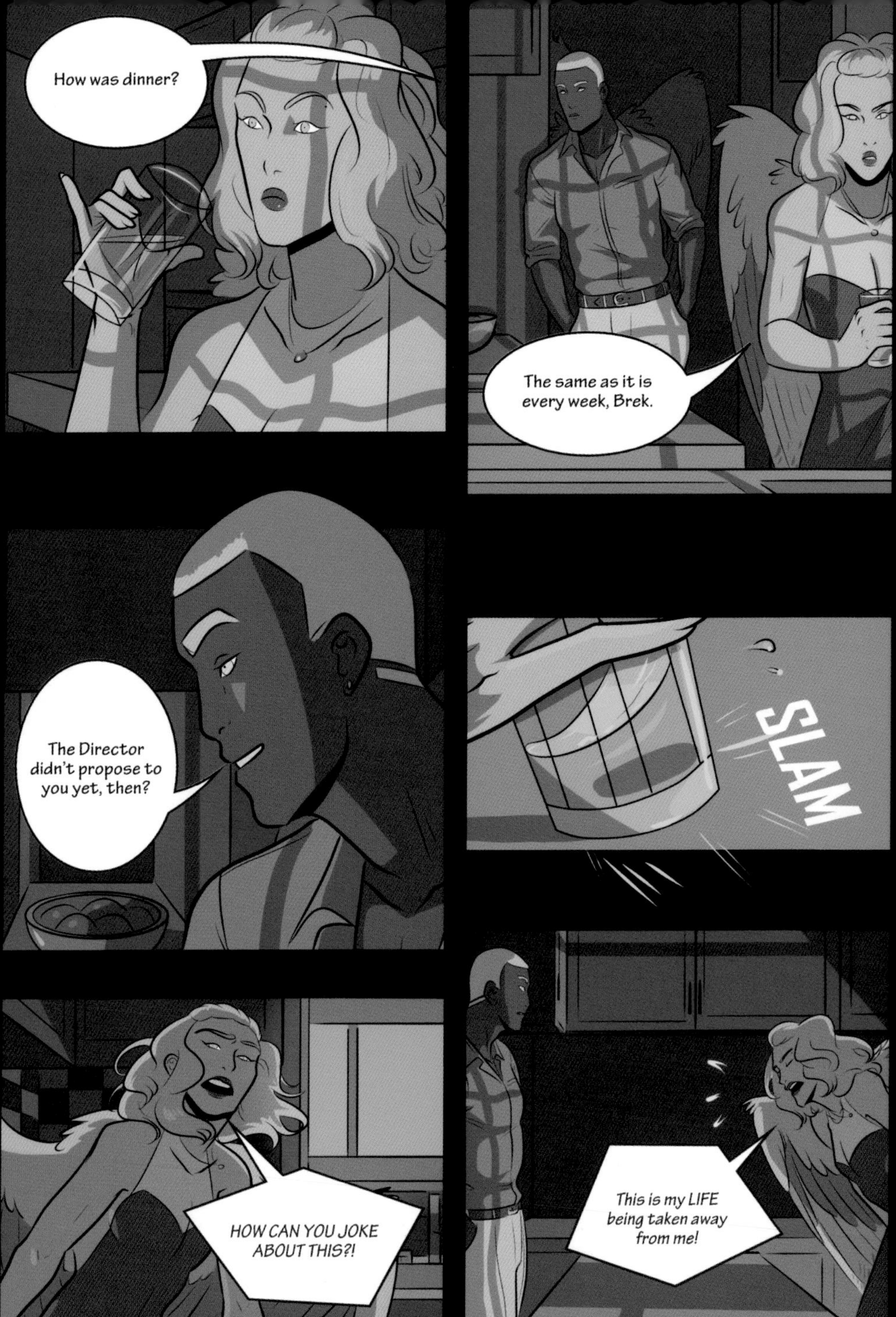
How was dinner?
The same as it is every week, Brek.
The Director didn't propose to you yet, then?
SLAM
HOW CAN YOU JOKE ABOUT THIS?!
This is my LIFE being taken away from me!

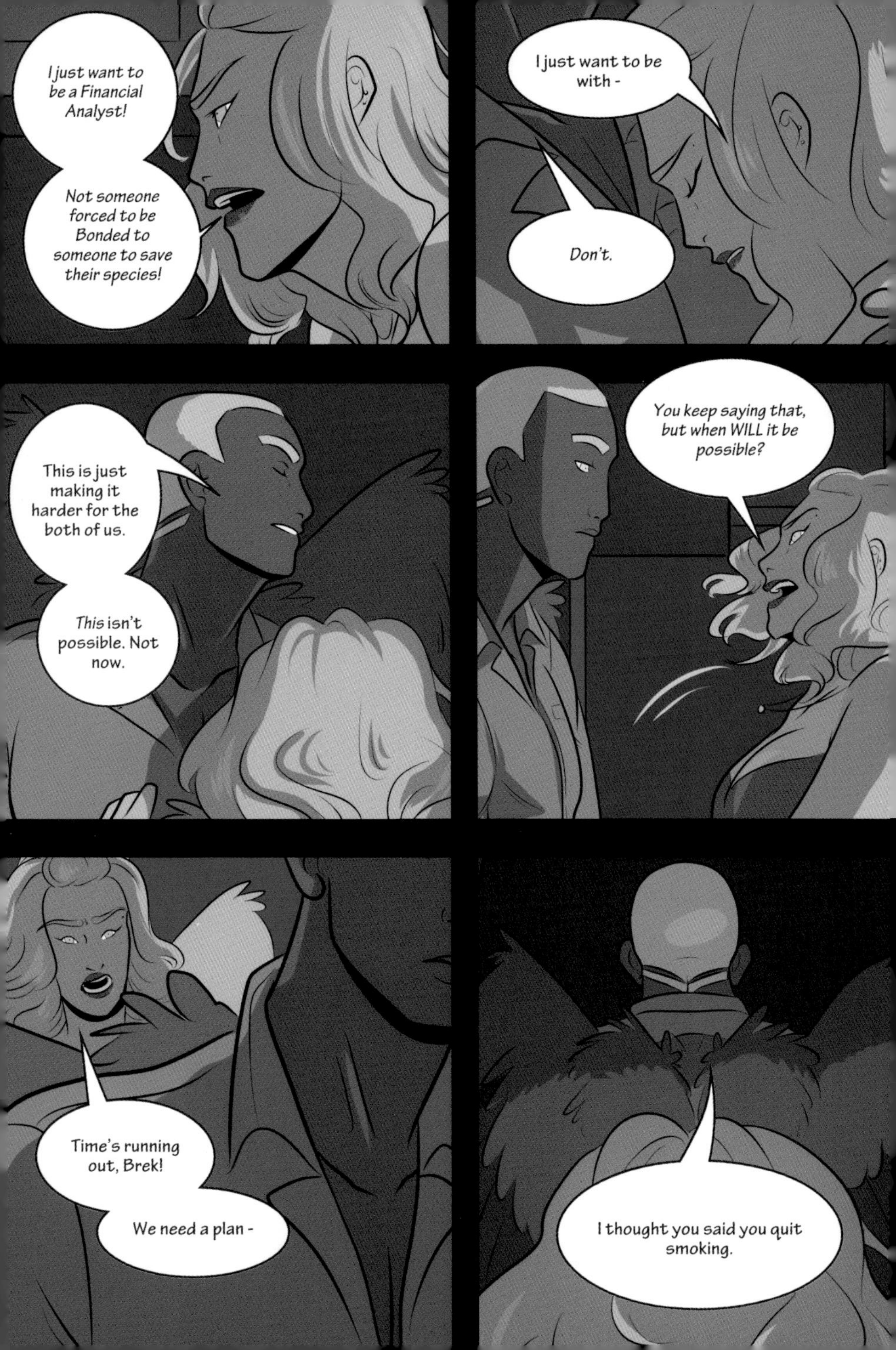
I just want to be a Financial Analyst!
Not someone forced to be Bonded to someone to save their species!
I just want to be with -
Don't.
This is just making it harder for the both of us.
This isn't possible. Not now.
You keep saying that, but when WILL it be possible?
Time's running out, Brek!
We need a plan -
I thought you said you quit smoking.

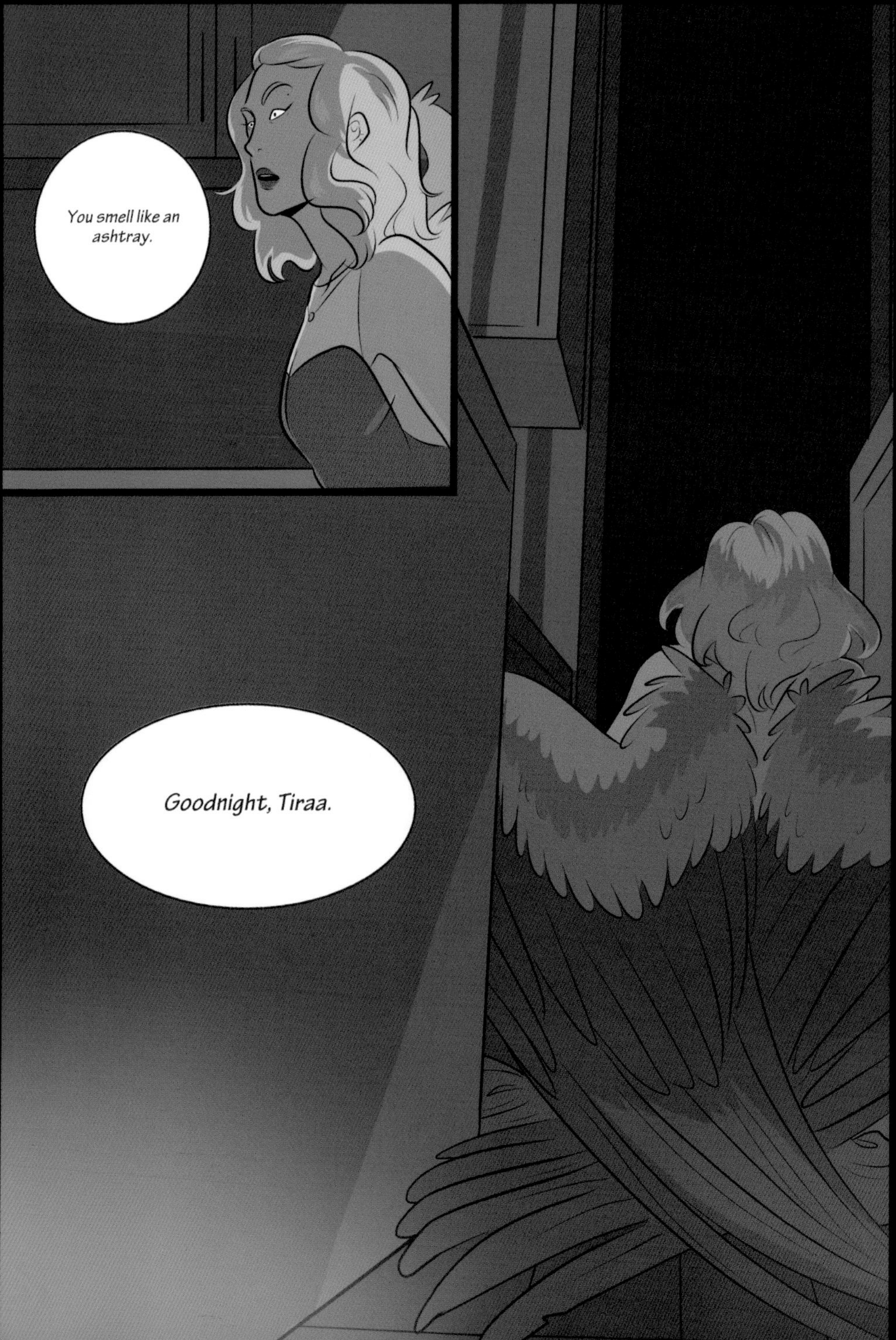
You smell like an ashtray.
Goodnight, Tiraa.

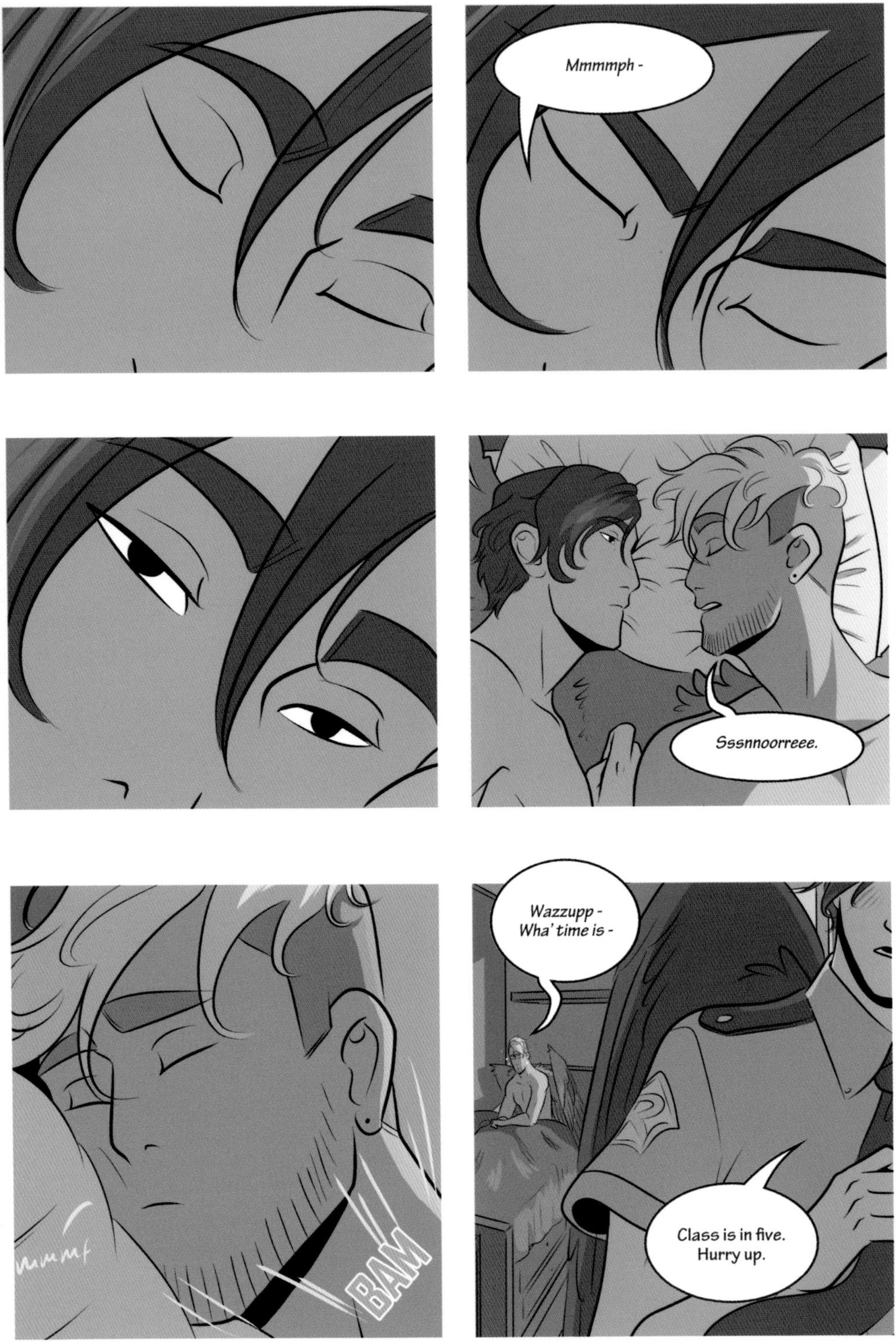
Mmmmph -
Sssnnoorreee.
mmmf
BAM
Wazzupp -
Wha' time is -
Class is in five.
Hurry up.

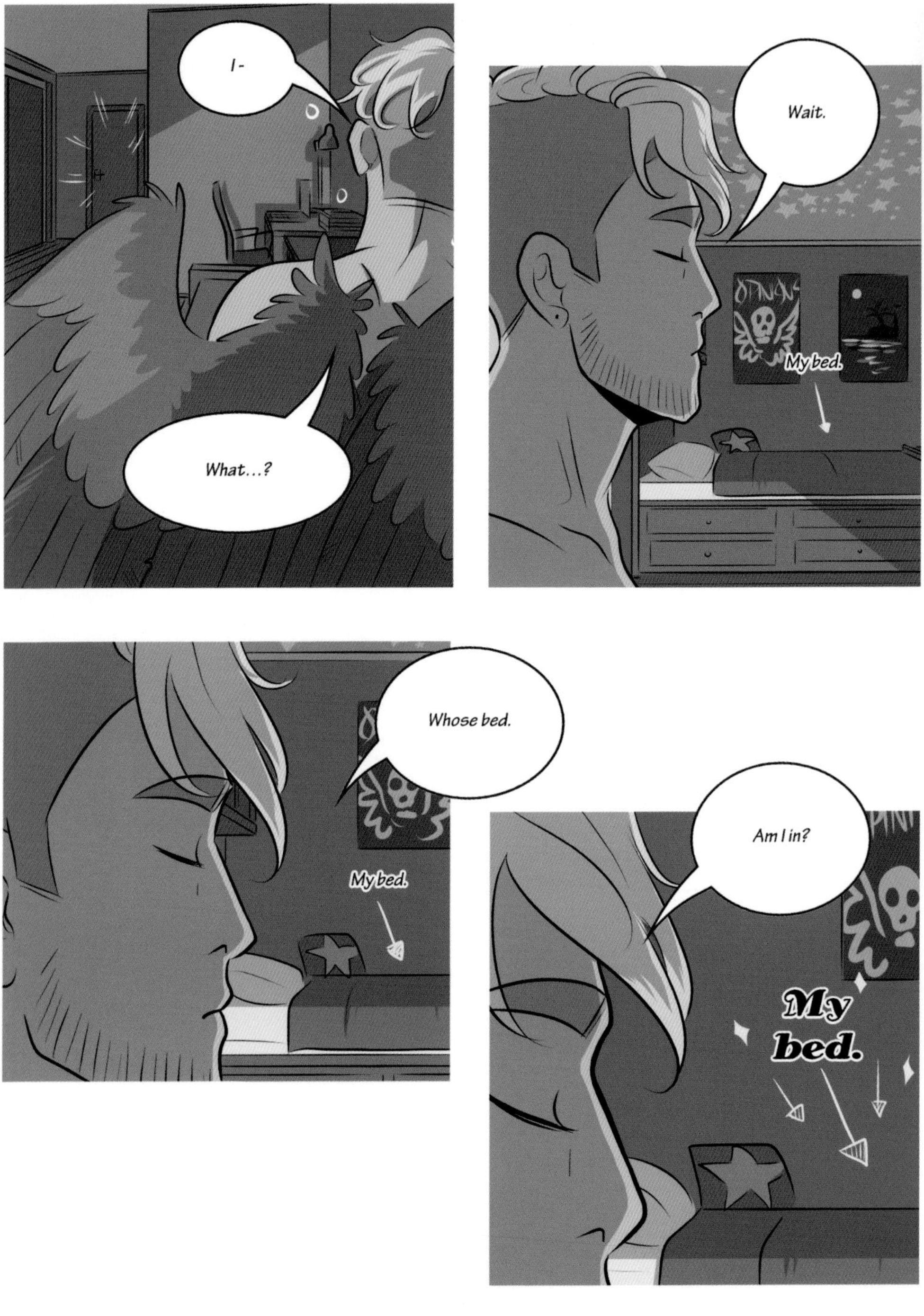
I-
What...?
Wait.
My bed.
Whose bed.
My bed.
Am I in?
My bed.

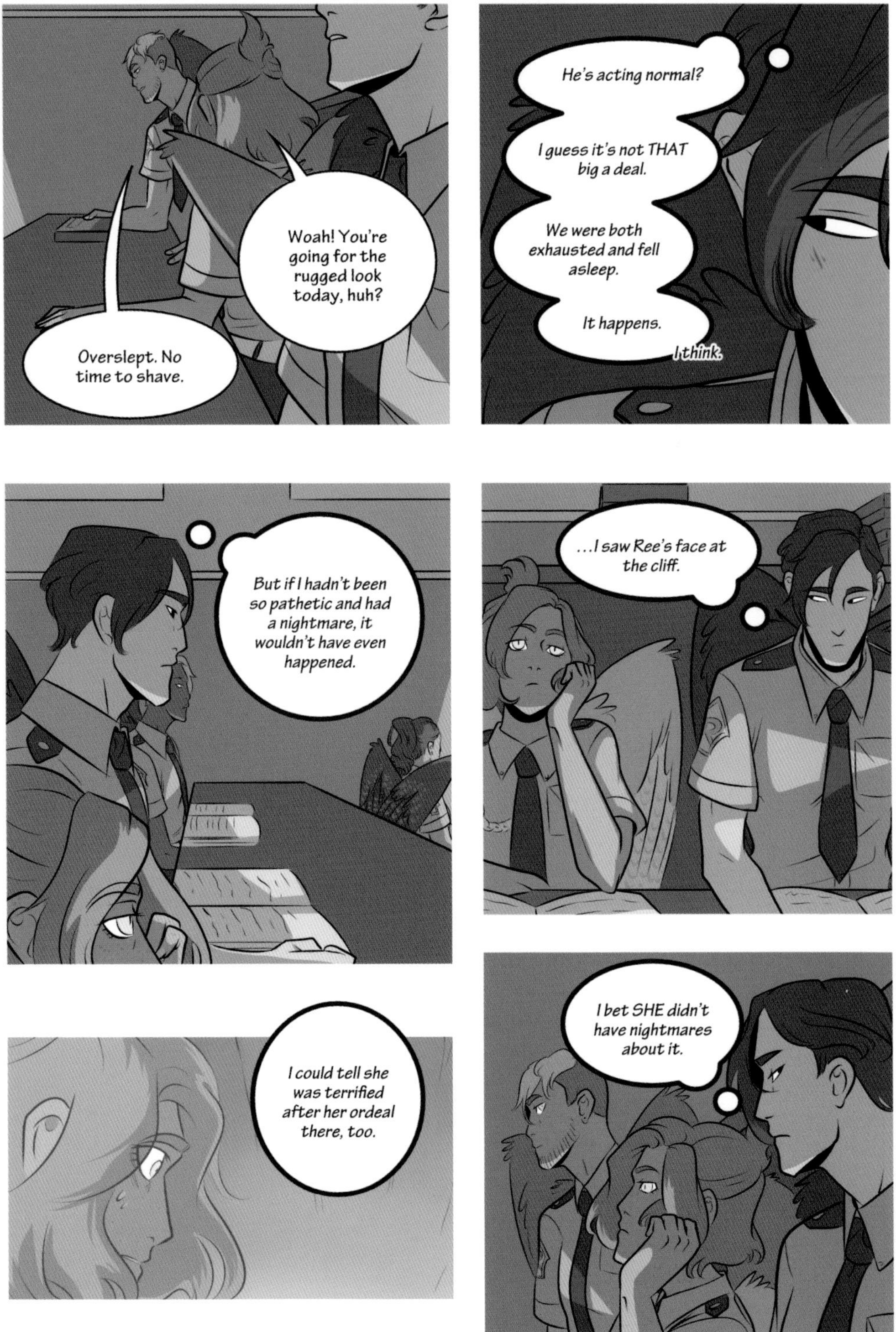
Woah! You're going for the rugged look today, huh?
Overslept. No time to shave.
He's acting normal?
I guess it's not THAT big a deal.
We were both exhausted and fell asleep.
It happens.
I think.
But if I hadn't been so pathetic and had a nightmare, it wouldn't have even happened.
...I saw Ree's face at the cliff.
I could tell she was terrified after her ordeal there, too.
I bet SHE didn't have nightmares about it.

Looks like Del slept last night off well enough.

He's practically his usual asshole self.

Is it bad I'm kinda disappointed he didn't learn any kind of lesson from it?

Ree. Your sadistic side is showing.

And then I was like –

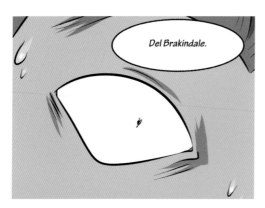

Del Brakindale.

Quiet down. Class is starting.

Y-yes sir –

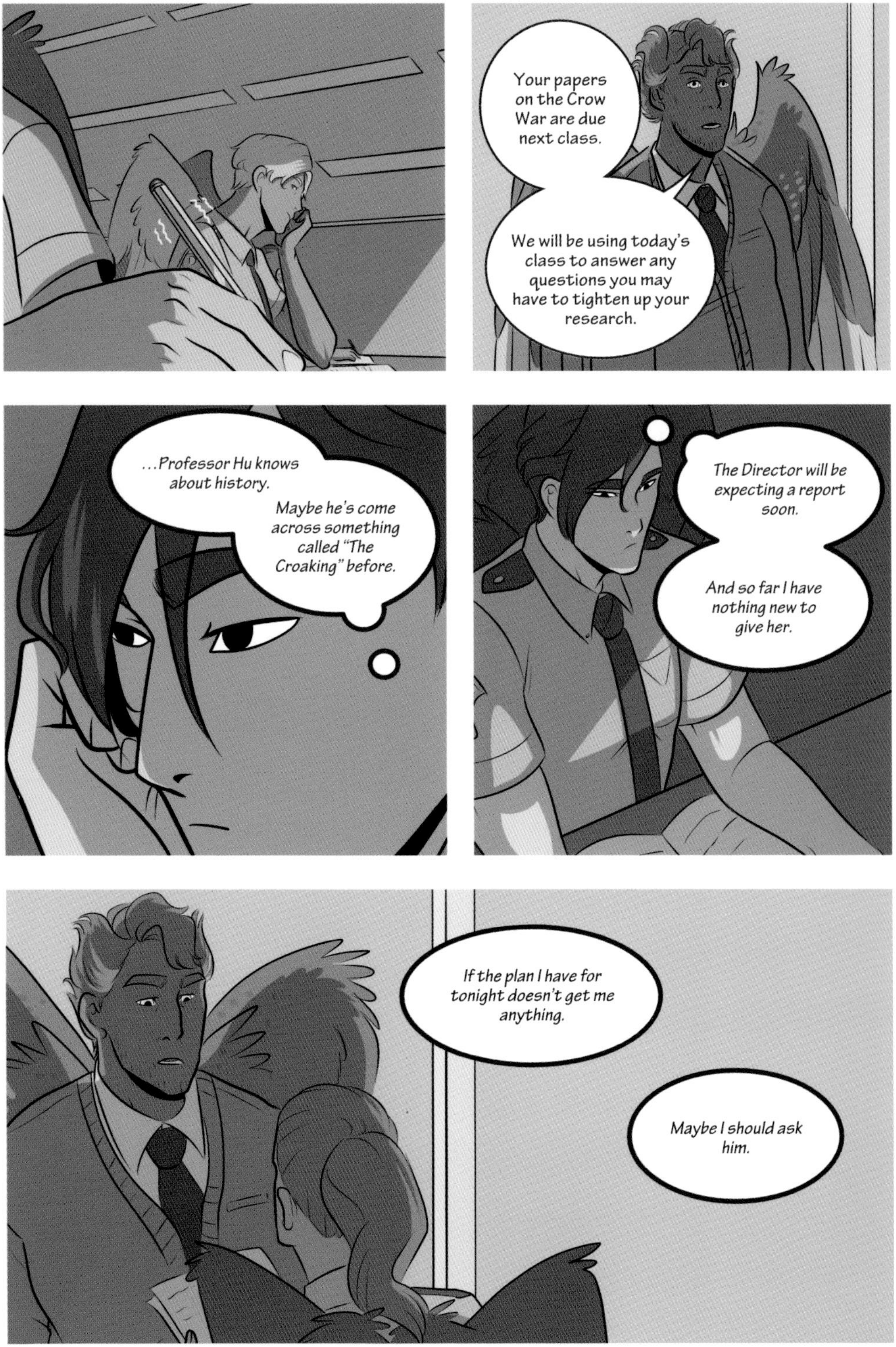
Your papers on the Crow War are due next class.
We will be using today's class to answer any questions you may have to tighten up your research.
...Professor Hu knows about history.
Maybe he's come across something called "The Croaking" before.
The Director will be expecting a report soon.
And so far I have nothing new to give her.
If the plan I have for tonight doesn't get me anything.
Maybe I should ask him.

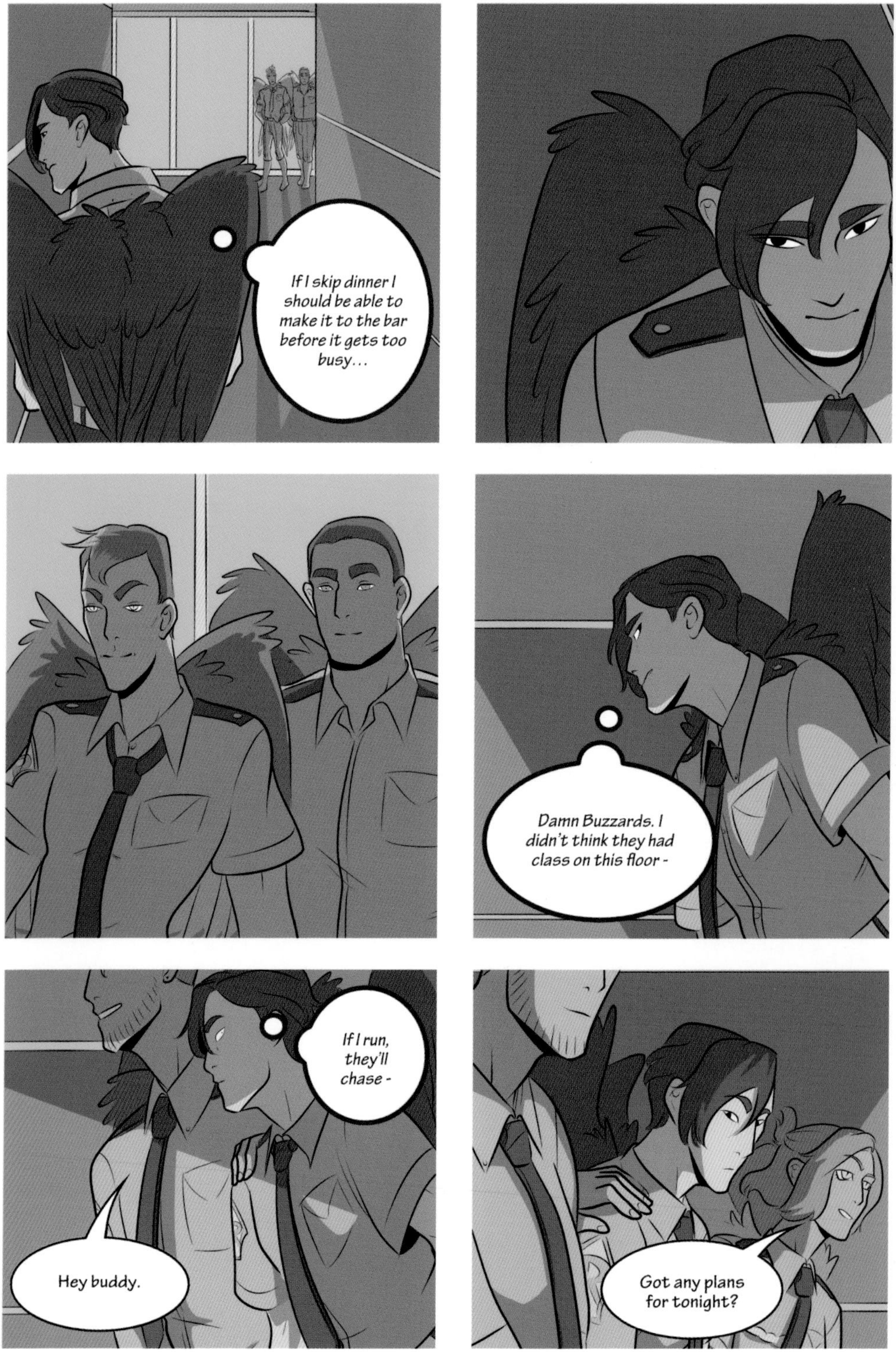
If I skip dinner I should be able to make it to the bar before it gets too busy...
Damn Buzzards. I didn't think they had class on this floor -
If I run, they'll chase -
Hey buddy.
Got any plans for tonight?

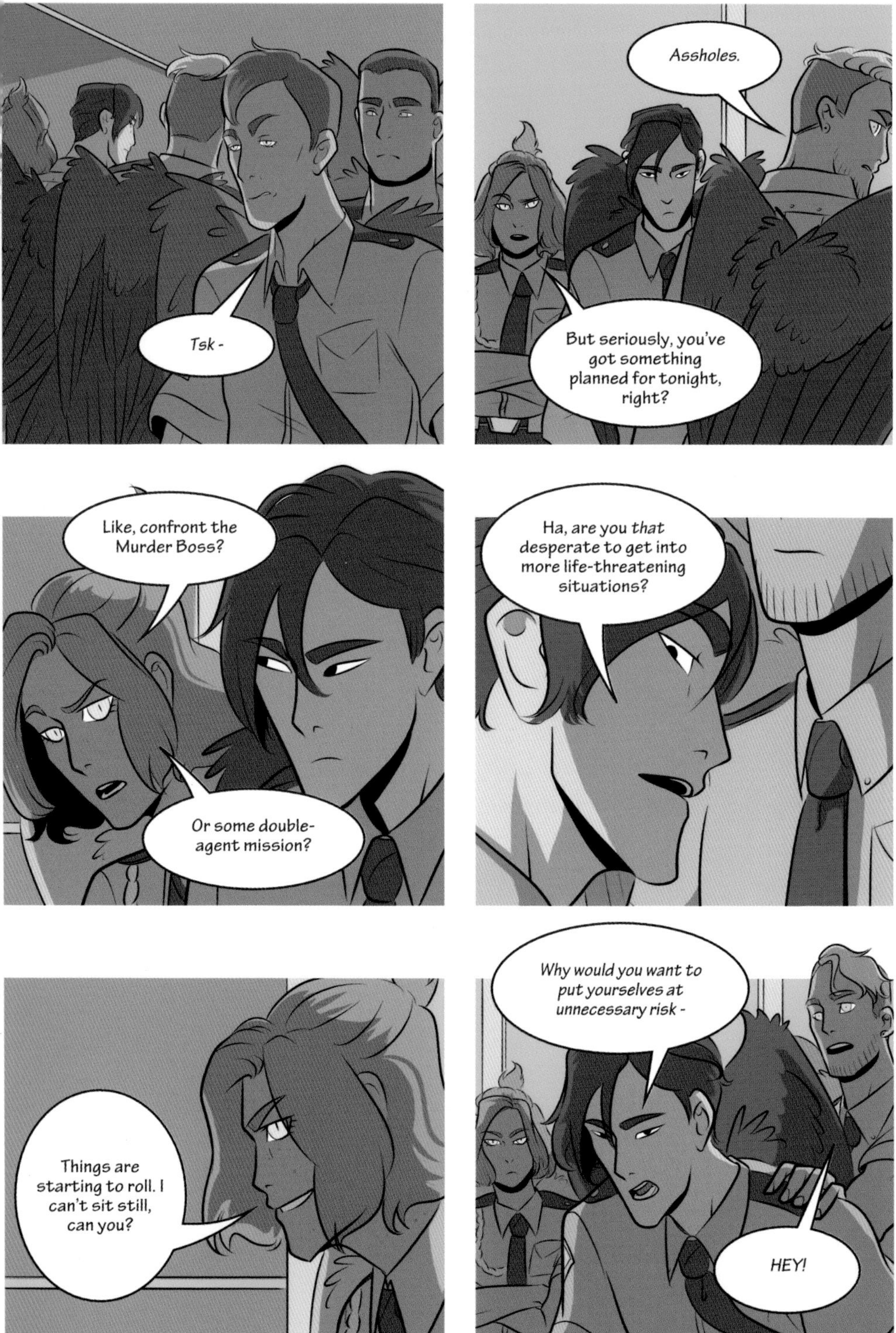
Tsk -
Assholes.
But seriously, you've got something planned for tonight, right?
Like, confront the Murder Boss?
Or some double-agent mission?
Ha, are you *that* desperate to get into more life-threatening situations?
Things are starting to roll. I can't sit still, can you?
Why would you want to put yourselves at unnecessary risk -
HEY!

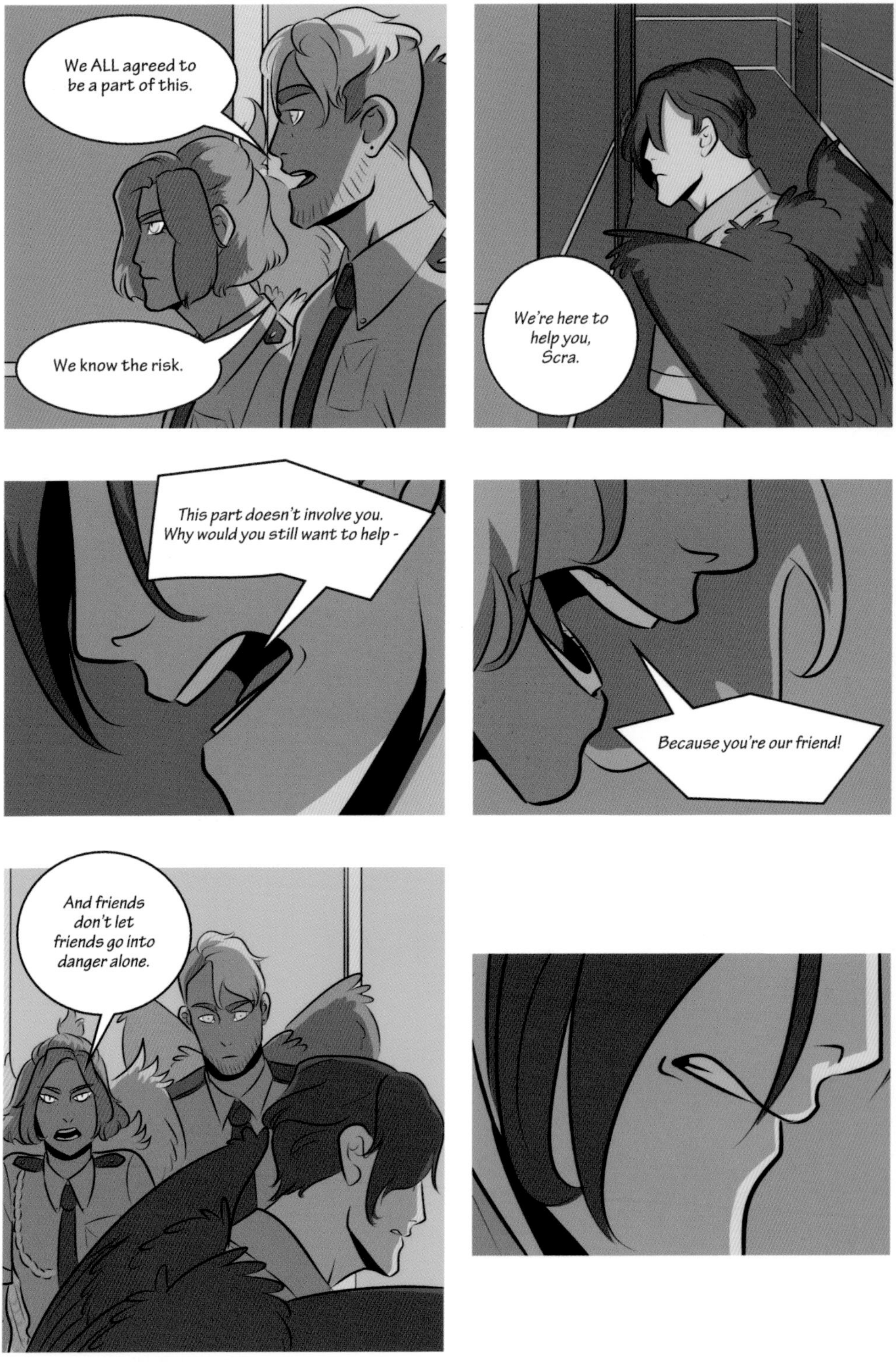
We ALL agreed to be a part of this.
We know the risk.
We're here to help you, Scra.
This part doesn't involve you. Why would you still want to help -
Because you're our friend!
And friends don't let friends go into danger alone.

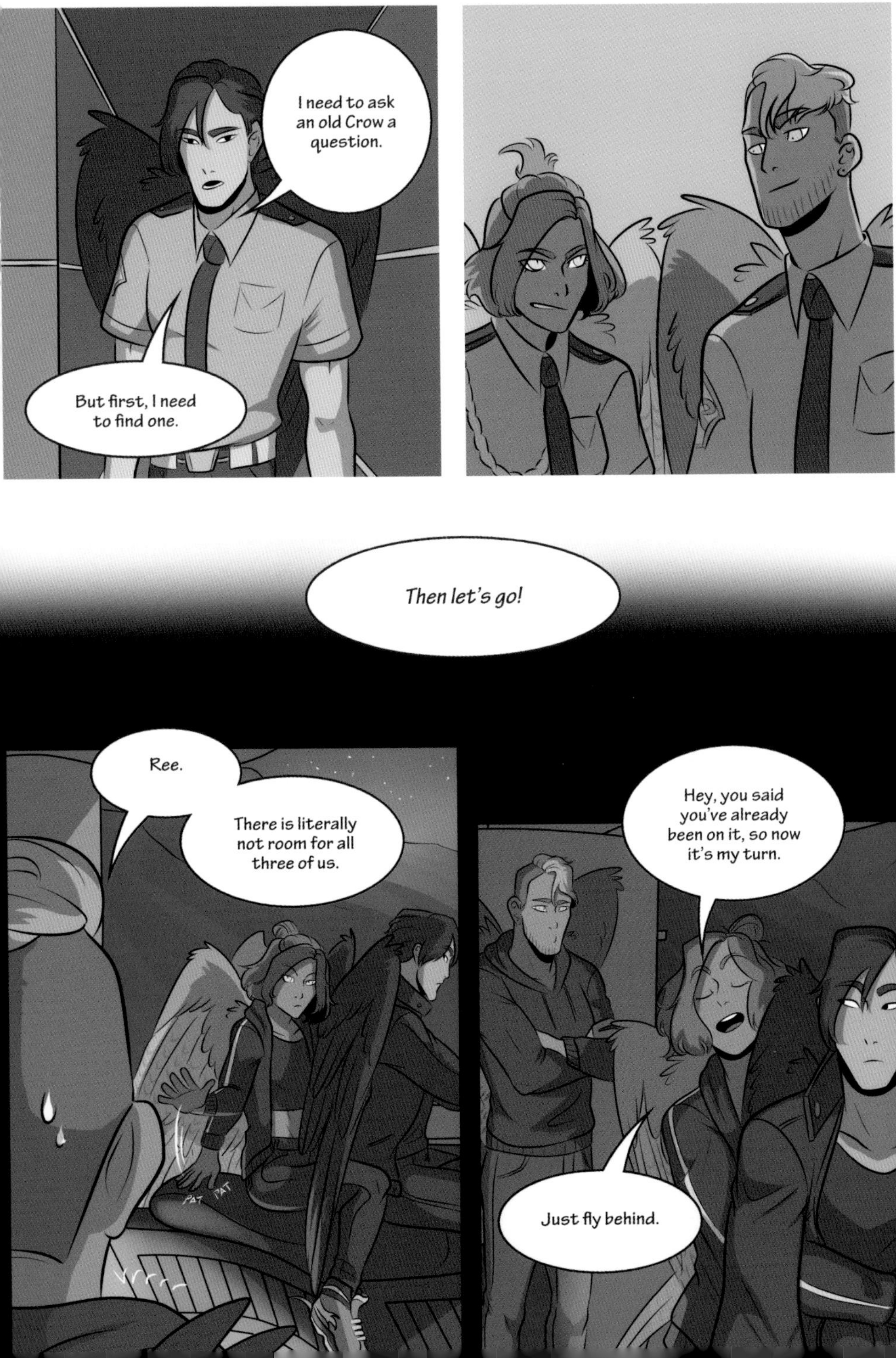
I need to ask an old Crow a question.
But first, I need to find one.
Then let's go!
Ree.
There is literally not room for all three of us.
PAT PAT
Vrrr
Hey, you said you've already been on it, so now it's my turn.
Just fly behind.

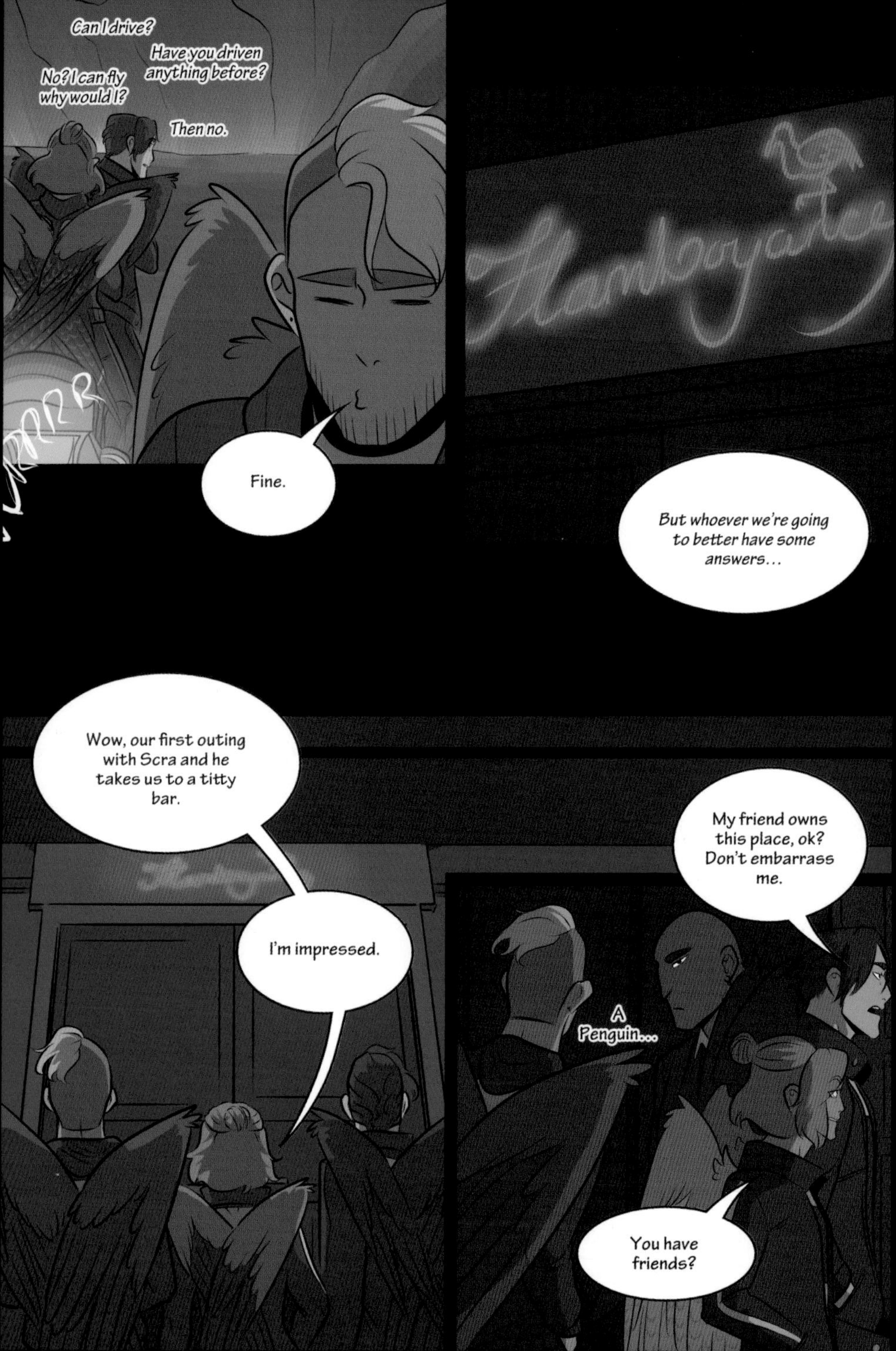
Can I drive?
Have you driven anything before?
No? I can fly why would I?
Then no.
VRRRR
Fine.
But whoever we're going to better have some answers...
Wow, our first outing with Scra and he takes us to a titty bar.
I'm impressed.
My friend owns this place, ok? Don't embarrass me.
A Penguin...
You have friends?

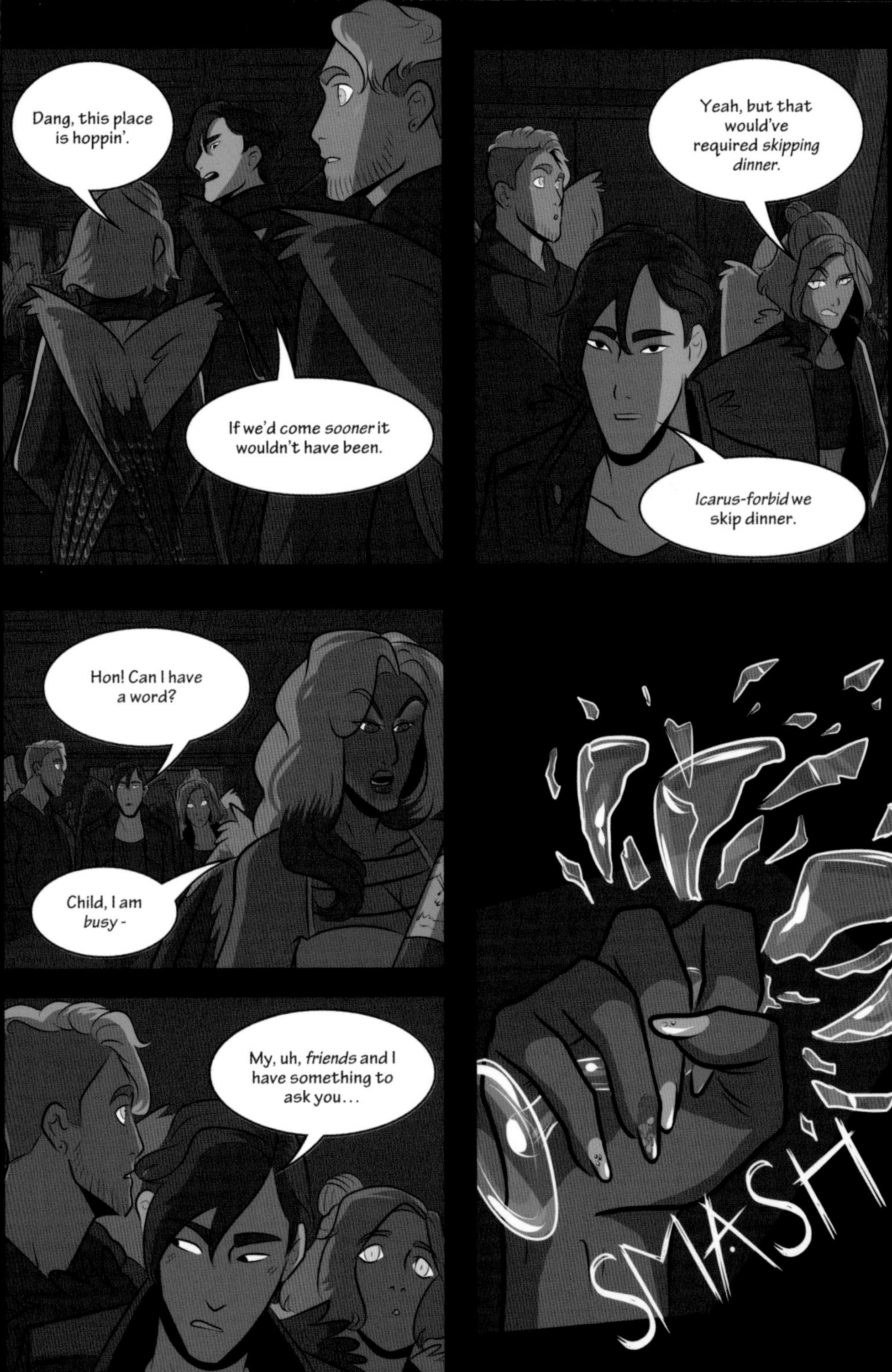
Dang, this place is hoppin'.
If we'd come *sooner* it wouldn't have been.
Yeah, but that would've required *skipping dinner*.
Icarus-forbid we skip dinner.
Hon! Can I have a word?
Child, I am *busy* -
My, uh, *friends* and I have something to ask you...
SMASH

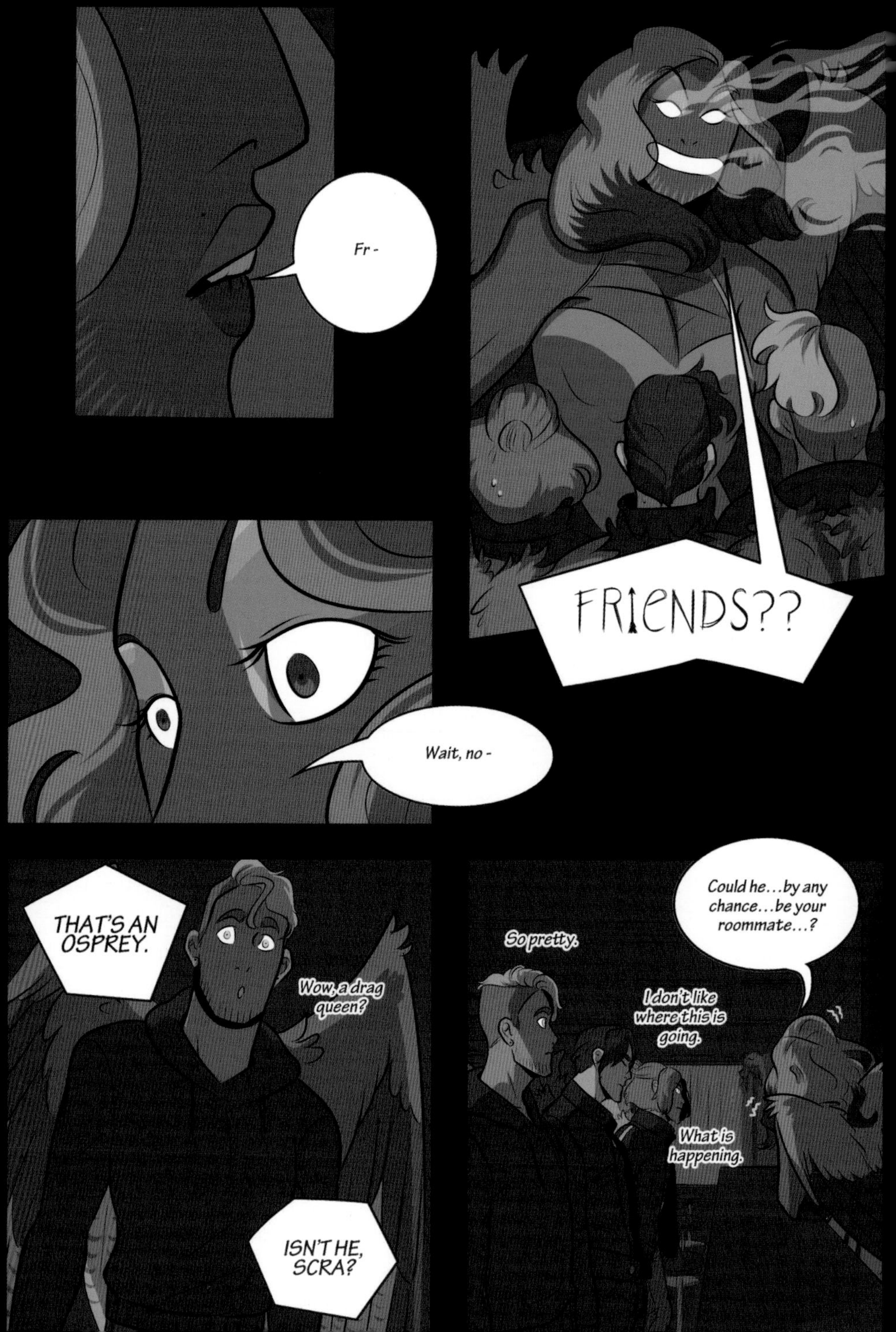
Fr -
FRIENDS??
Wait, no -
THAT'S AN OSPREY.
Wow, a drag queen?
ISN'T HE, SCRA?
So pretty.
I don't like where this is going.
Could he...by any chance...be your roommate...?
What is happening.

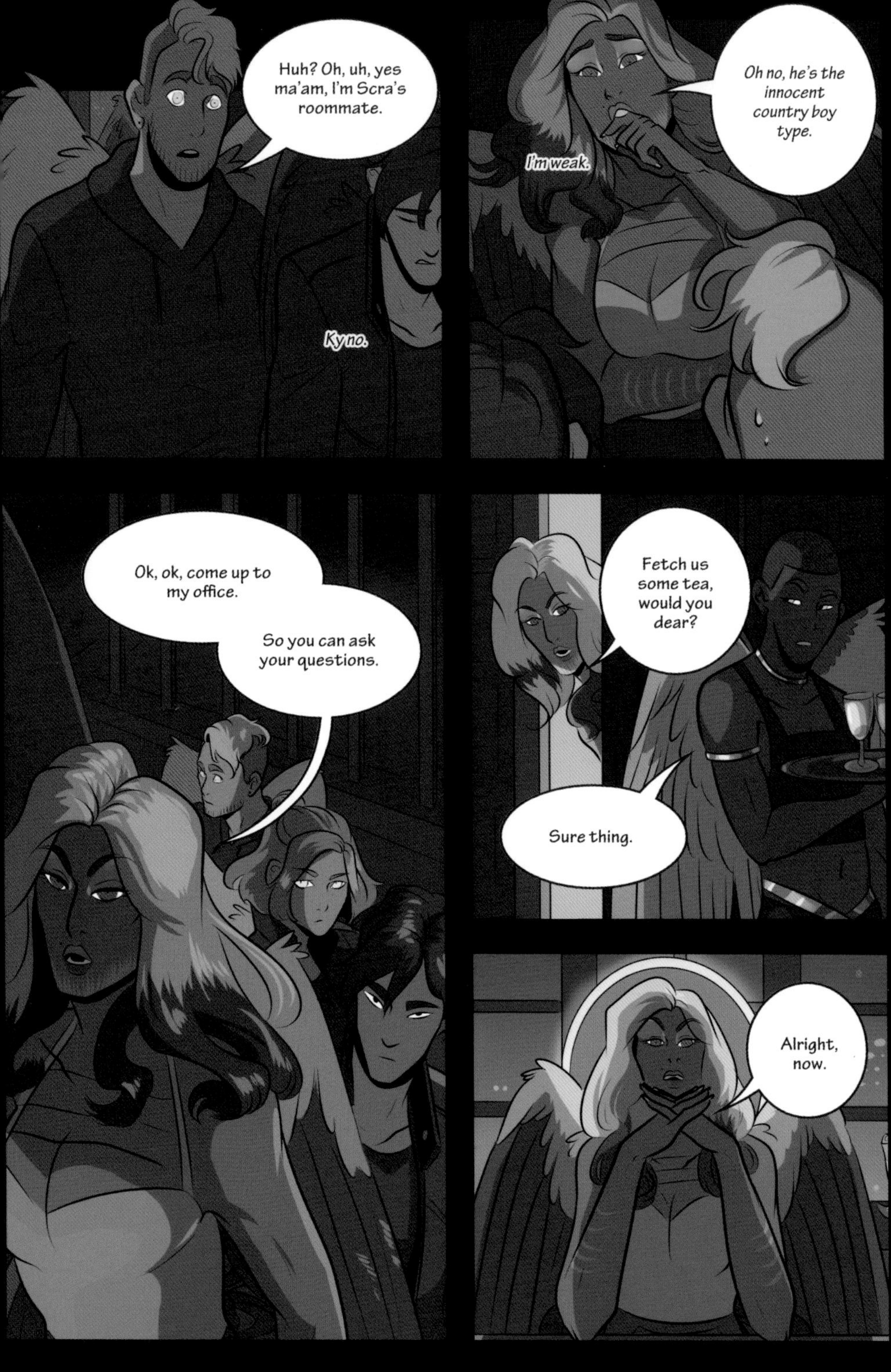
Huh? Oh, uh, yes ma'am, I'm Scra's roommate.
Ky no.
Oh no, he's the innocent country boy type.
I'm weak.
Ok, ok, come up to my office.
So you can ask your questions.
Fetch us some tea, would you dear?
Sure thing.
Alright, now.

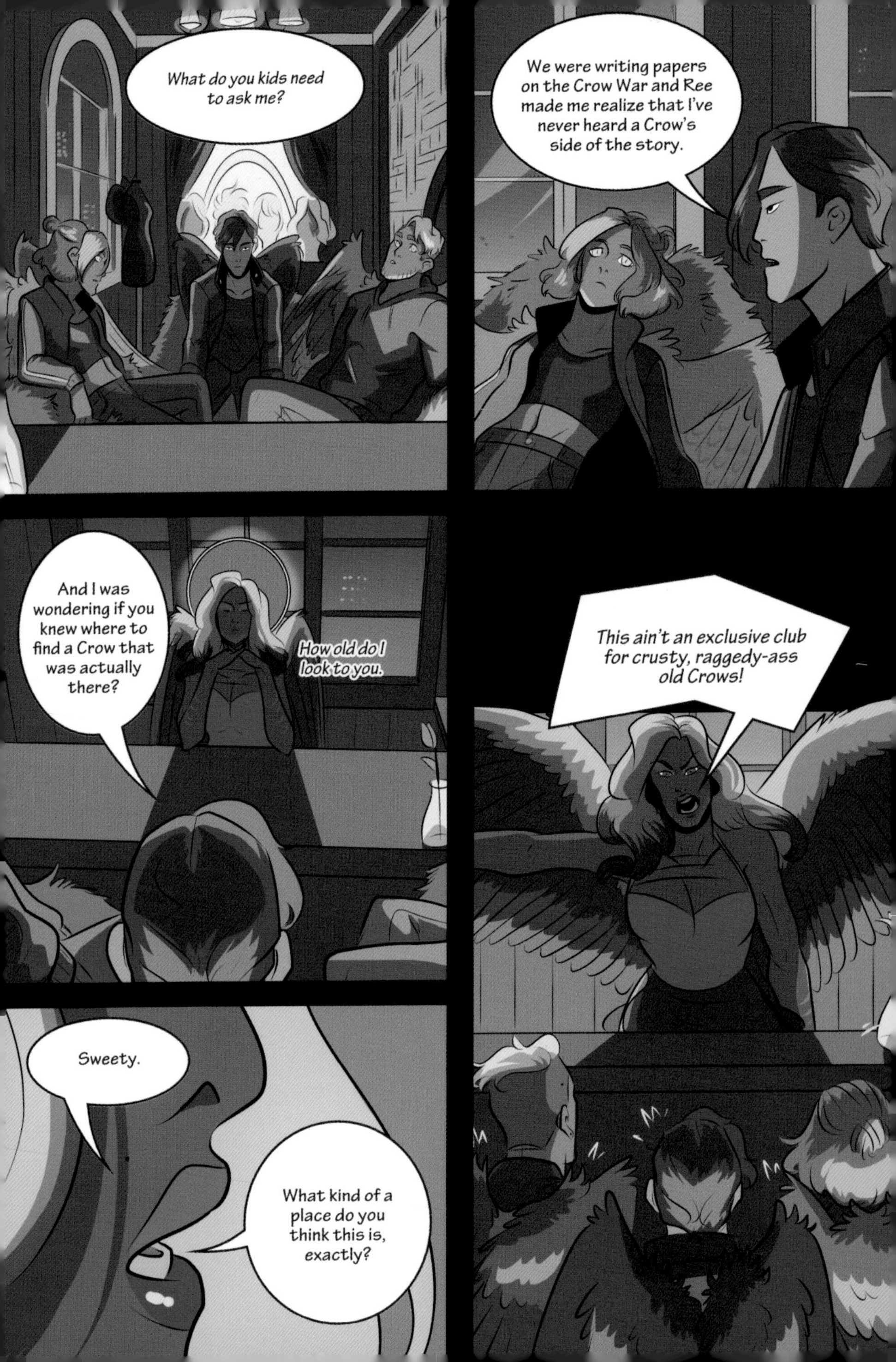
What do you kids need to ask me?
We were writing papers on the Crow War and Ree made me realize that I've never heard a Crow's side of the story.
And I was wondering if you knew where to find a Crow that was actually there?
How old do I look to you.
This ain't an exclusive club for crusty, raggedy-ass old Crows!
Sweety.
What kind of a place do you think this is, exactly?

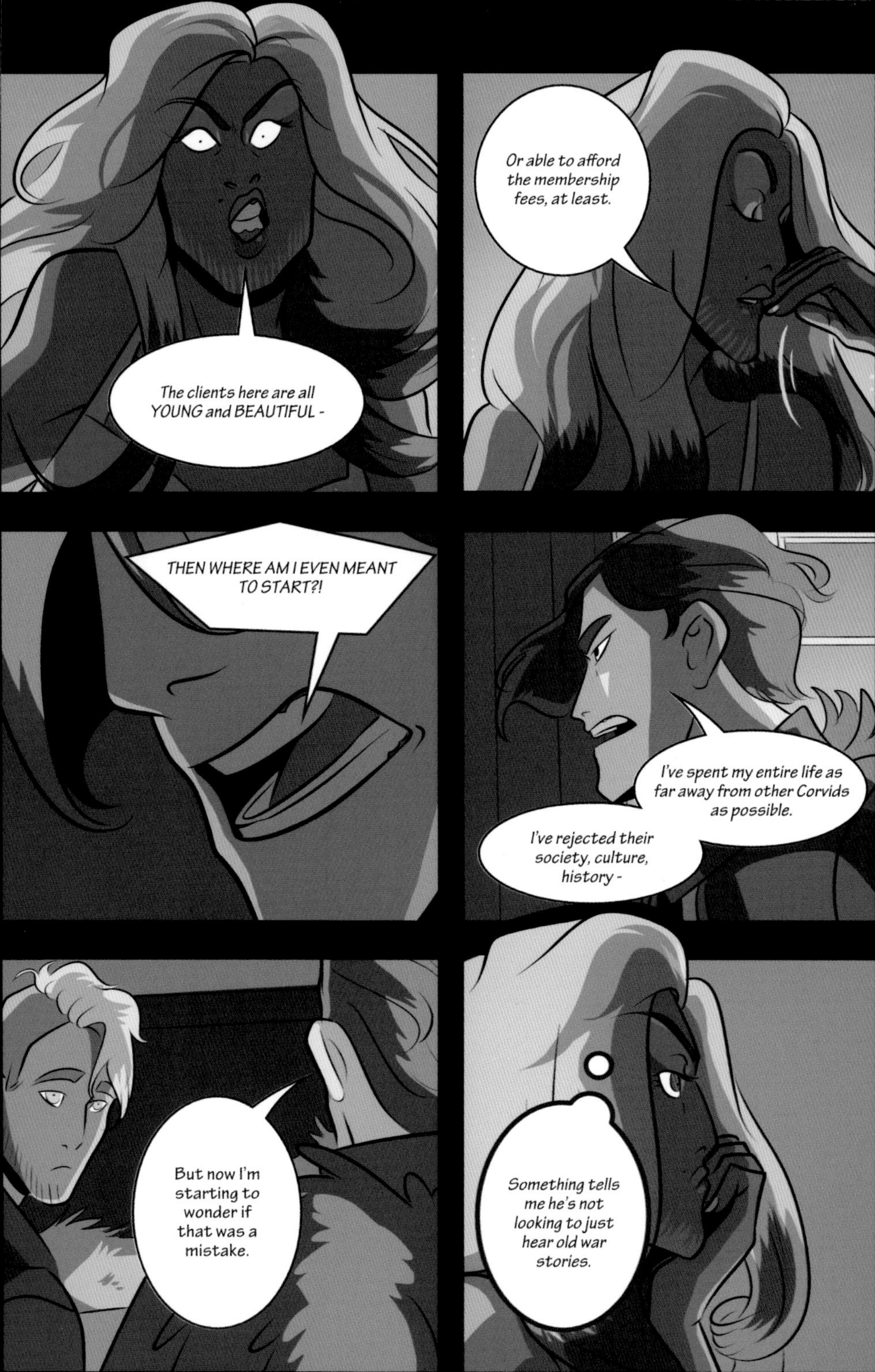
The clients here are all YOUNG and BEAUTIFUL -
Or able to afford the membership fees, at least.
THEN WHERE AM I EVEN MEANT TO START?!
I've spent my entire life as far away from other Corvids as possible.
I've rejected their society, culture, history -
But now I'm starting to wonder if that was a mistake.
Something tells me he's not looking to just hear old war stories.

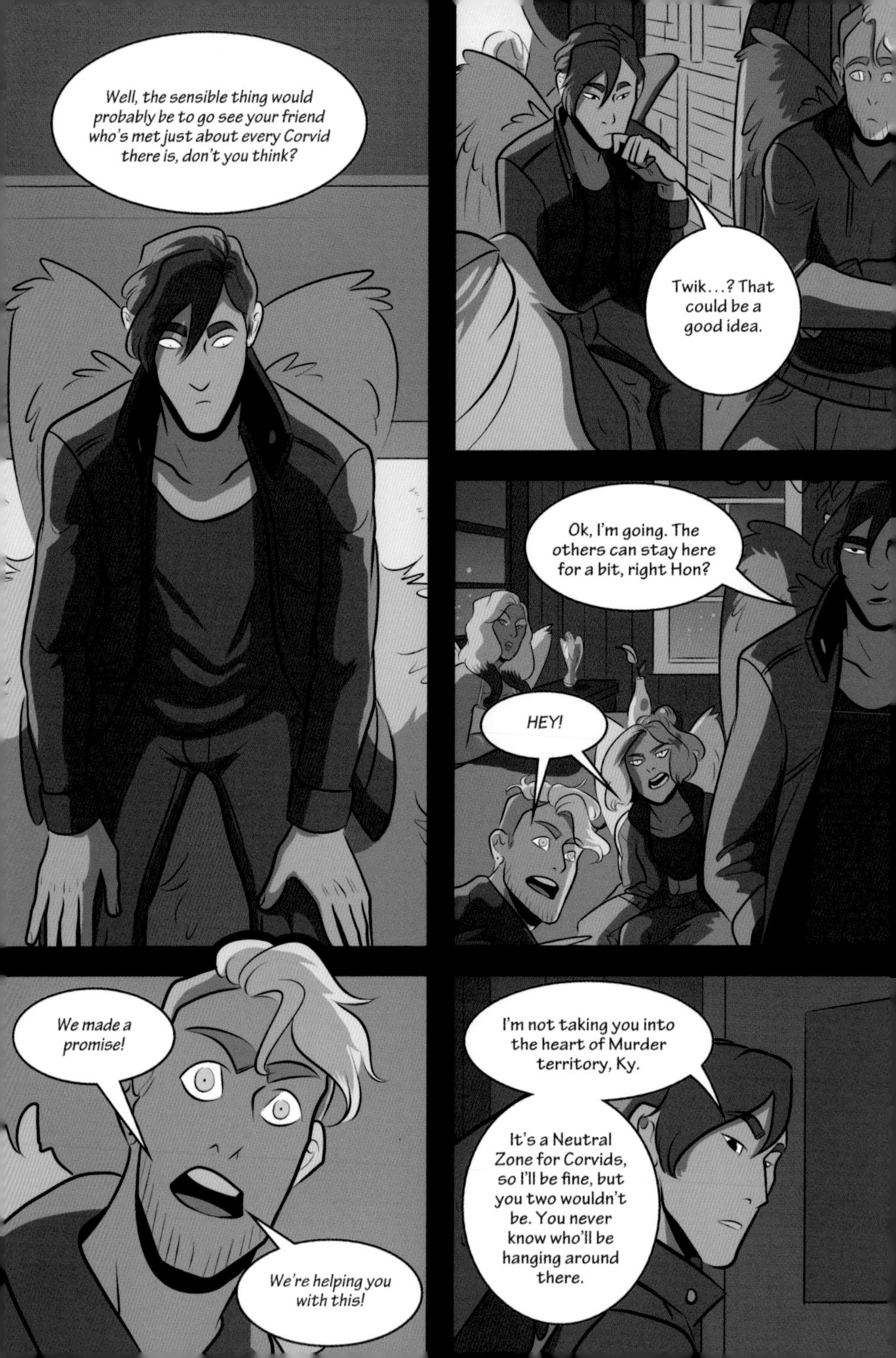
Well, the sensible thing would probably be to go see your friend who's met just about every Corvid there is, don't you think?
Twik…? That could be a good idea.
Ok, I'm going. The others can stay here for a bit, right Hon?
HEY!
We made a promise!
We're helping you with this!
I'm not taking you into the heart of Murder territory, Ky.
It's a Neutral Zone for Corvids, so I'll be fine, but you two wouldn't be. You never know who'll be hanging around there.

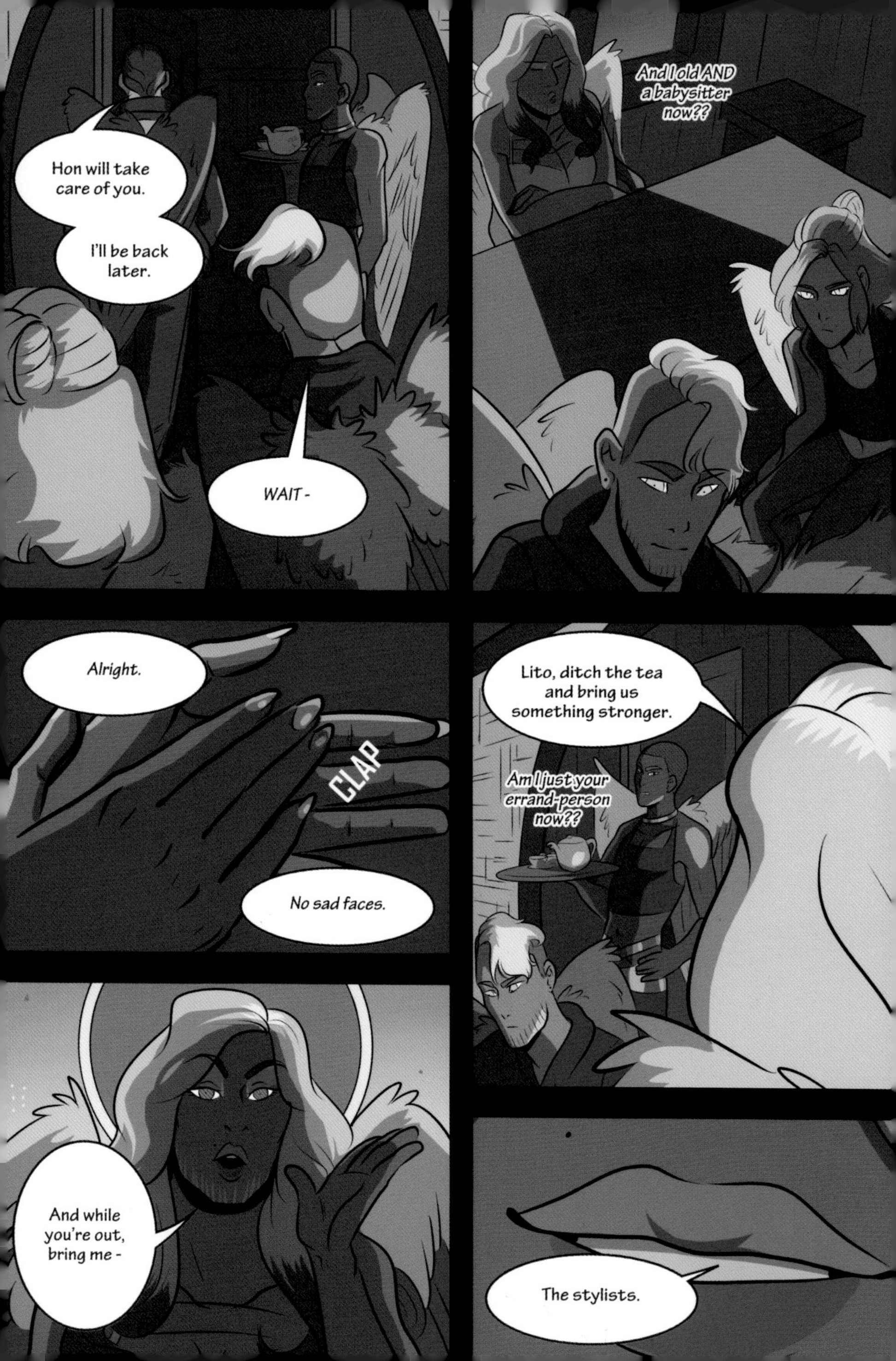
Hon will take care of you.
I'll be back later.
WAIT -
And I old AND a babysitter now??
Alright.
CLAP
No sad faces.
And while you're out, bring me -
Lito, ditch the tea and bring us something stronger.
Am I just your errand-person now??
The stylists.

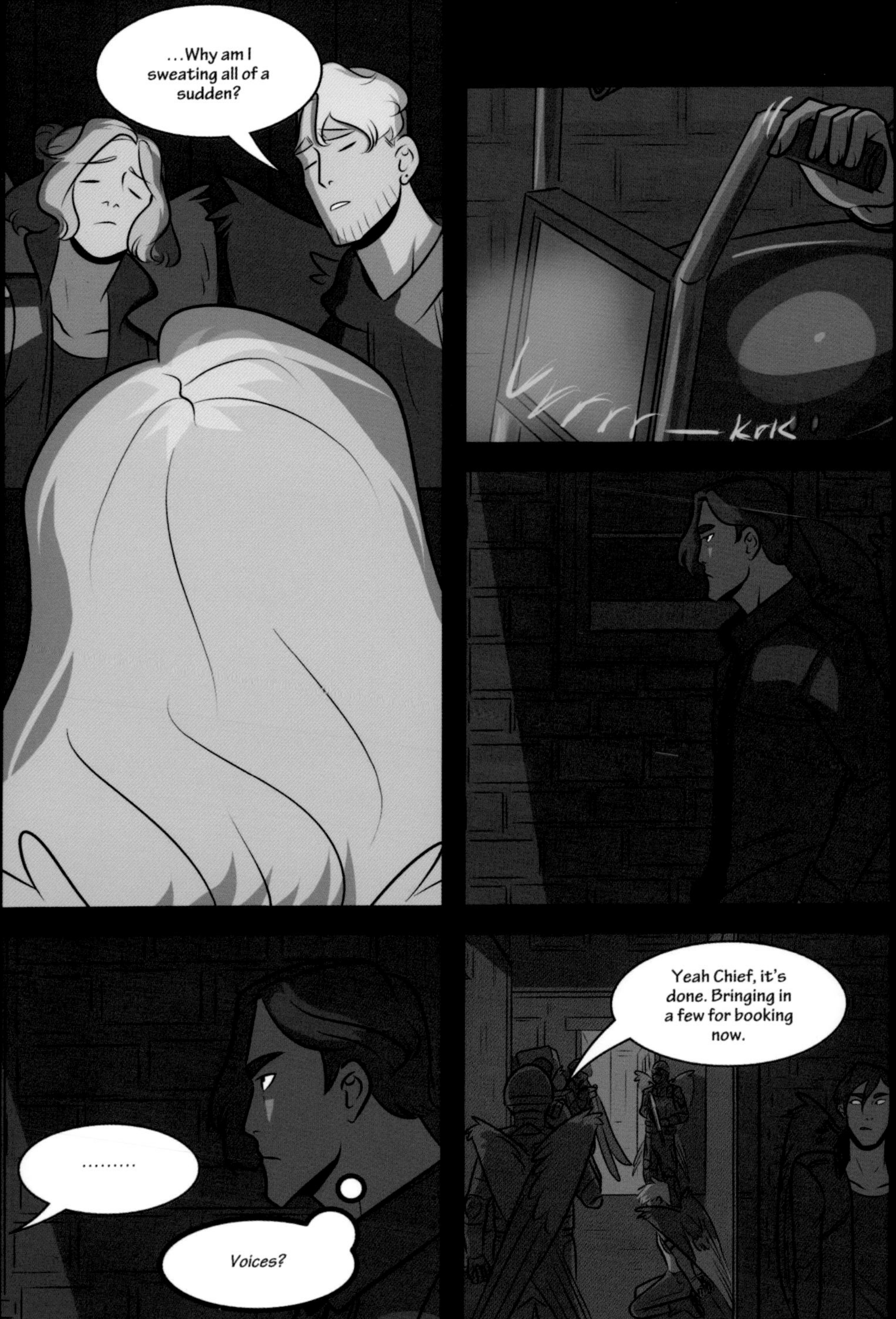
...Why am I sweating all of a sudden?
Vrrrr—krk
....
Voices?
Yeah Chief, it's done. Bringing in a few for booking now.

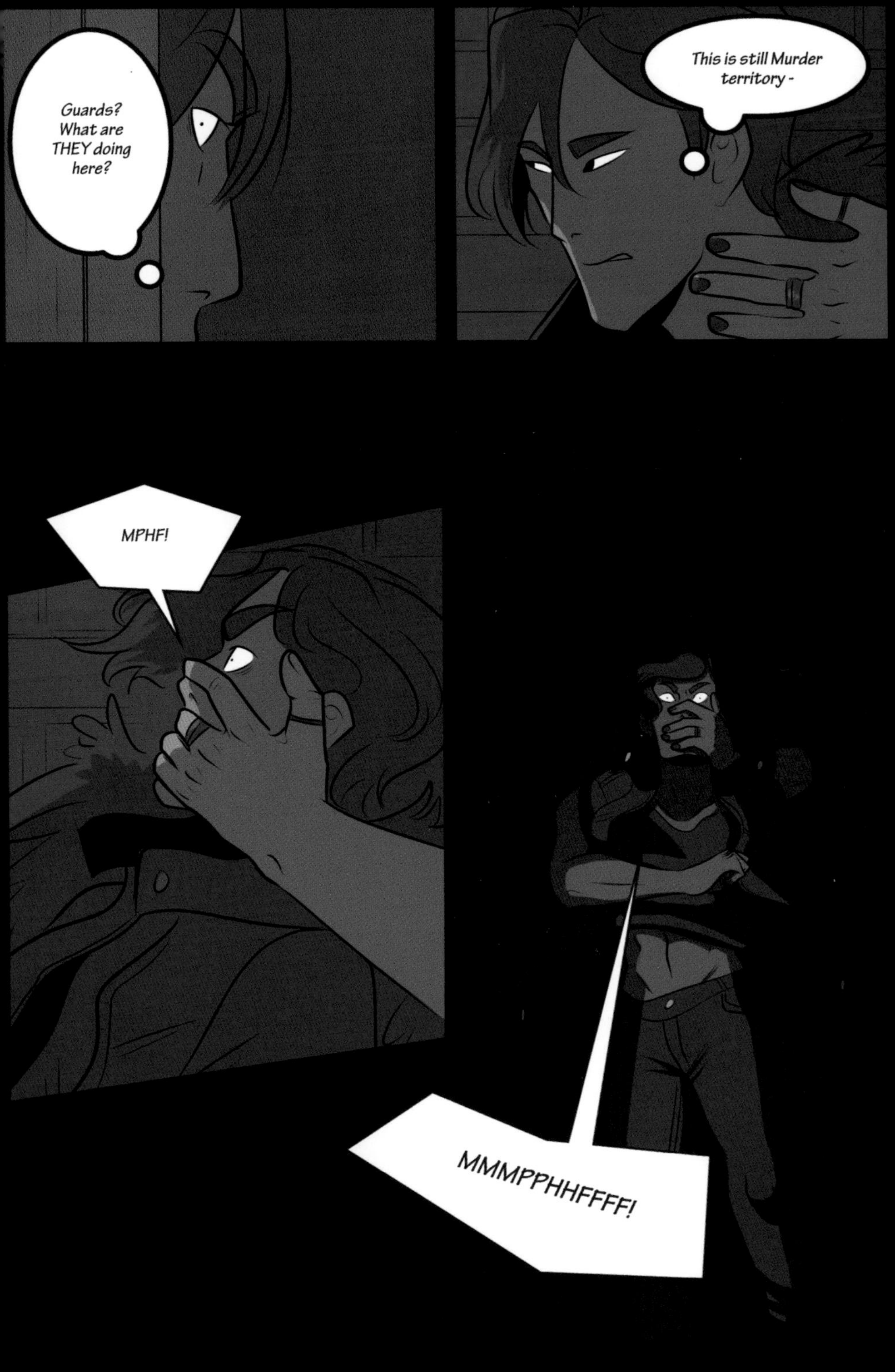
Guards? What are THEY doing here?
This is still Murder territory -
MPHF!
MMMPPHHFFFF!

THE CROAKING

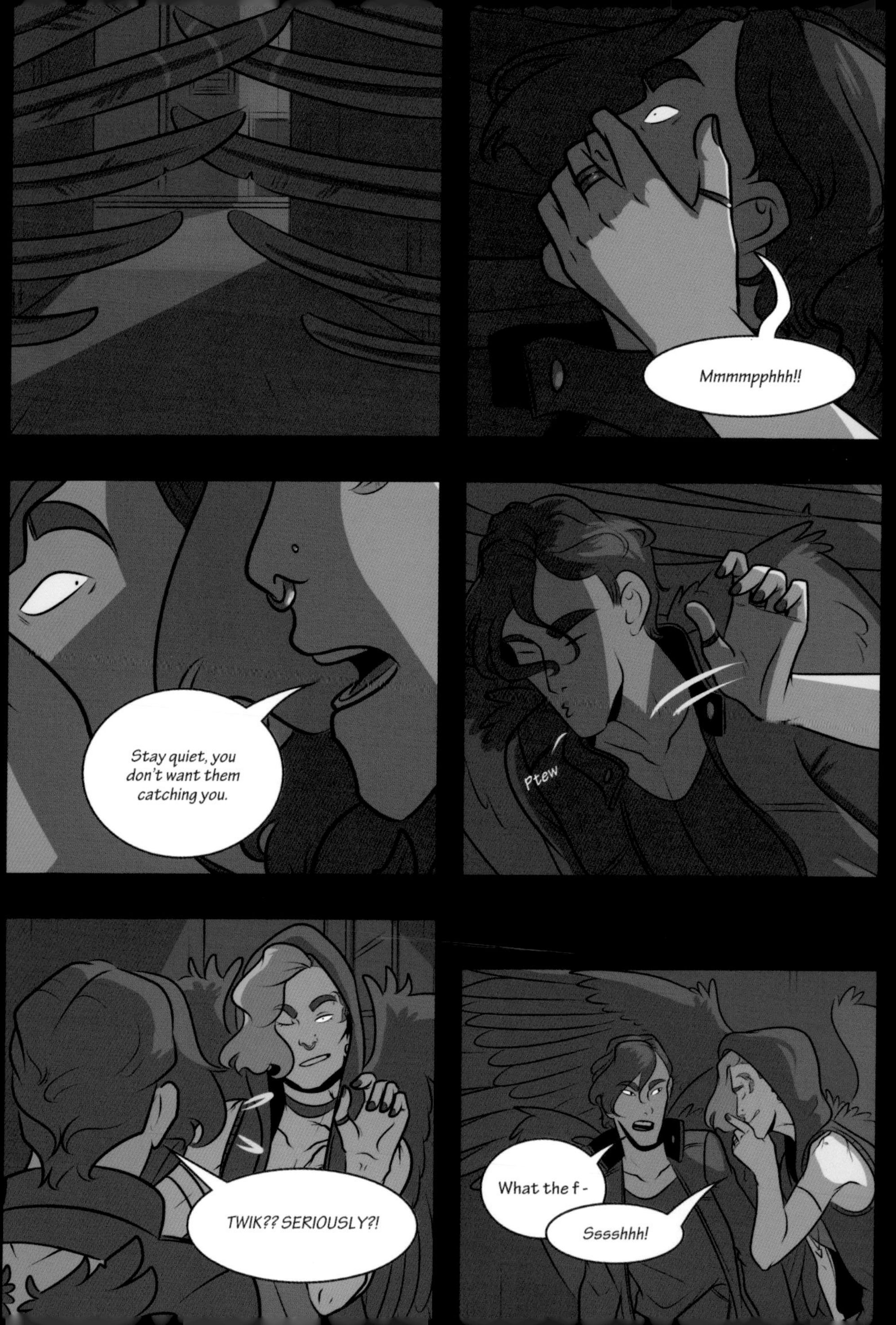
Mmmmpphhh!!
Stay quiet, you don't want them catching you.
Ptew
TWIK?? SERIOUSLY?!
What the f -
Sssshhh!

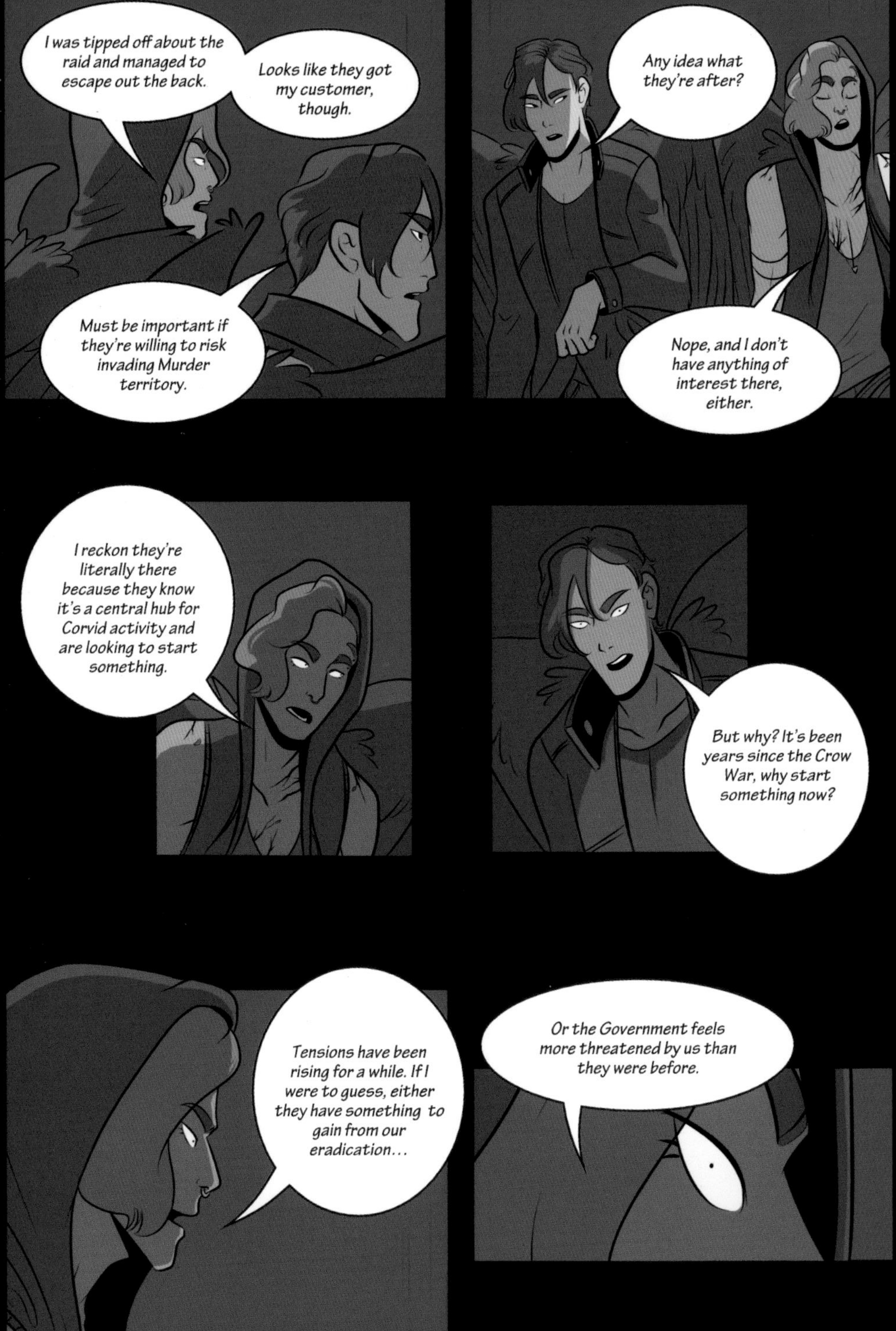
I was tipped off about the raid and managed to escape out the back.
Looks like they got my customer, though.
Must be important if they're willing to risk invading Murder territory.
Any idea what they're after?
Nope, and I don't have anything of interest there, either.
I reckon they're literally there because they know it's a central hub for Corvid activity and are looking to start something.
But why? It's been years since the Crow War, why start something now?
Tensions have been rising for a while. If I were to guess, either they have something to gain from our eradication...
Or the Government feels more threatened by us than they were before.

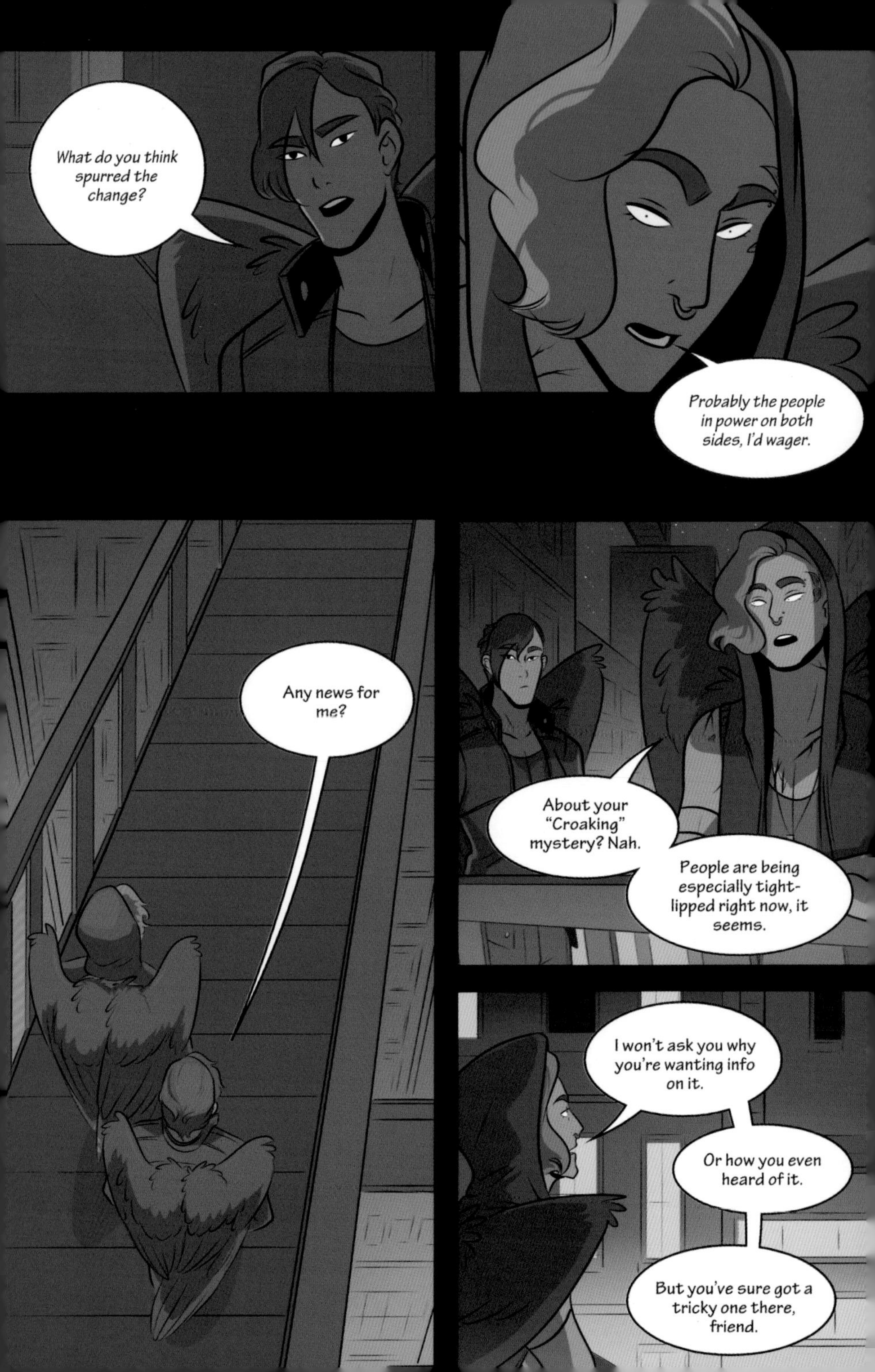
What do you think spurred the change?
Probably the people in power on both sides, I'd wager.
Any news for me?
About your "Croaking" mystery? Nah.
People are being especially tight-lipped right now, it seems.
I won't ask you why you're wanting info on it.
Or how you even heard of it.
But you've sure got a tricky one there, friend.

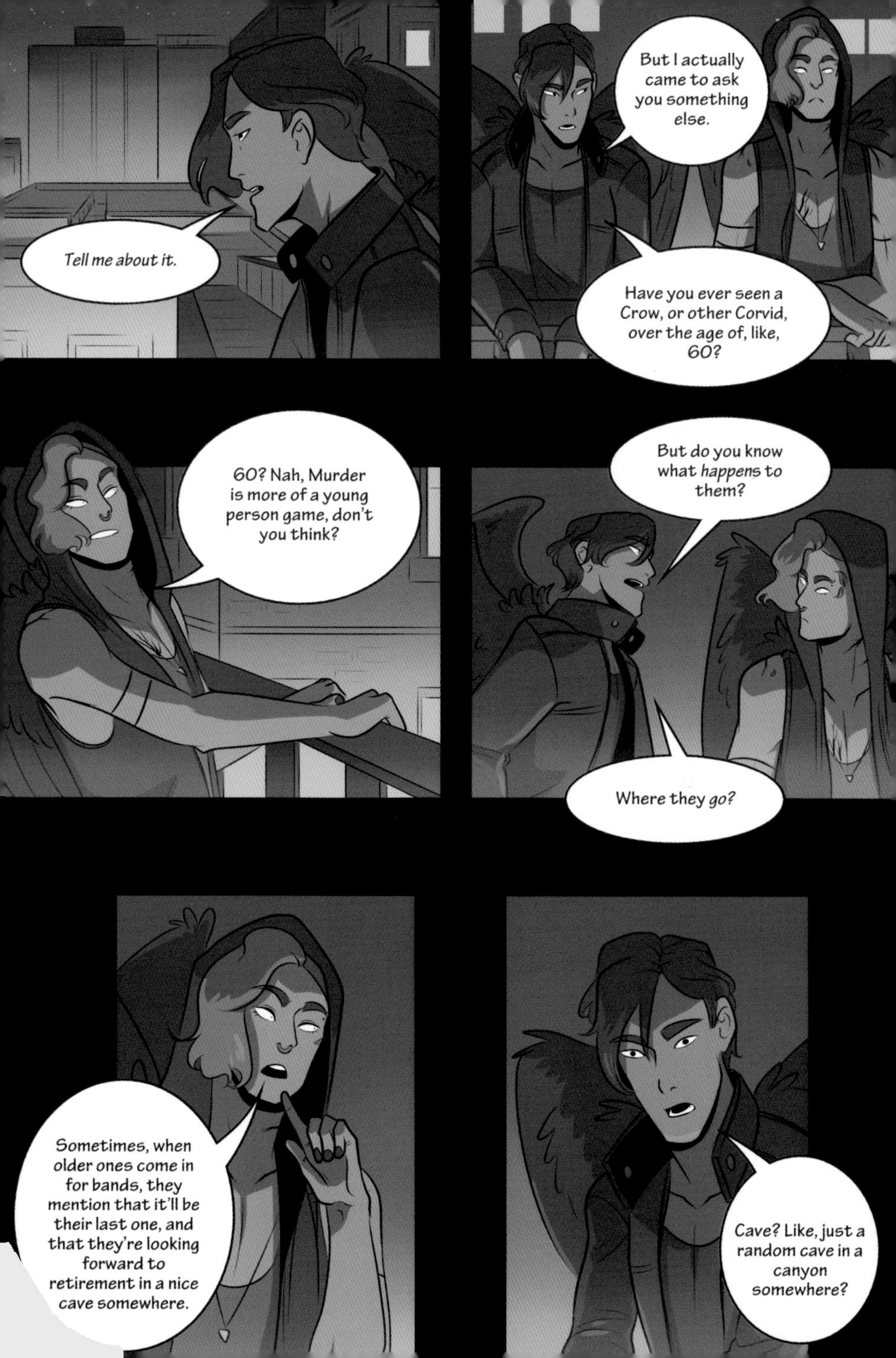

Tell me about it.
But I actually came to ask you something else.
Have you ever seen a Crow, or other Corvid, over the age of, like, 60?
60? Nah, Murder is more of a young person game, don't you think?
But do you know what *happens* to them?
Where they *go*?
Sometimes, when older ones come in for bands, they mention that it'll be their last one, and that they're looking forward to retirement in a nice cave somewhere.
Cave? Like, just a random cave in a canyon somewhere?

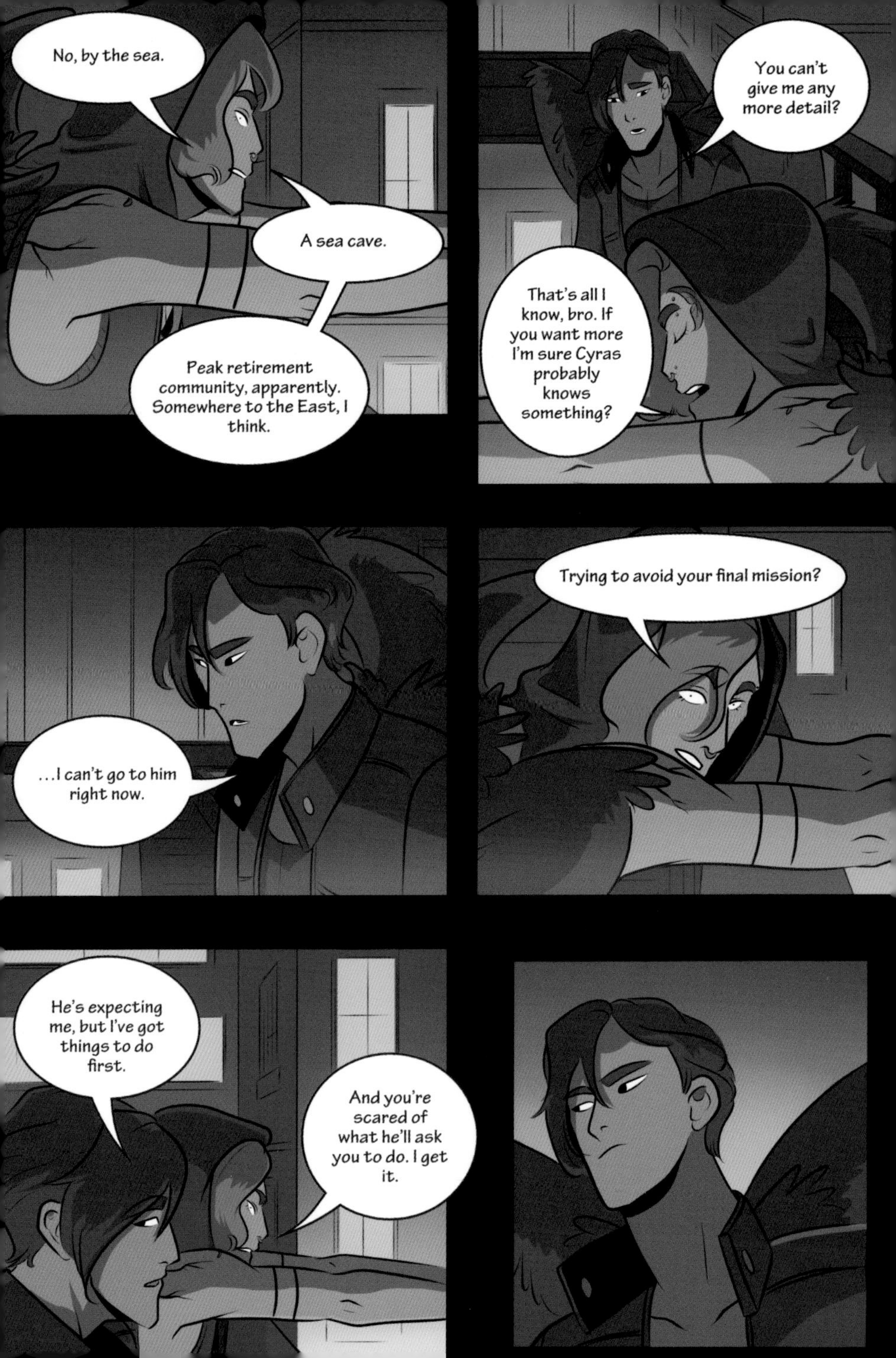
No, by the sea.
A sea cave.
Peak retirement community, apparently. Somewhere to the East, I think.
You can't give me any more detail?
That's all I know, bro. If you want more I'm sure Cyras probably knows something?
...I can't go to him right now.
Trying to avoid your final mission?
He's expecting me, but I've got things to do first.
And you're scared of what he'll ask you to do. I get it.

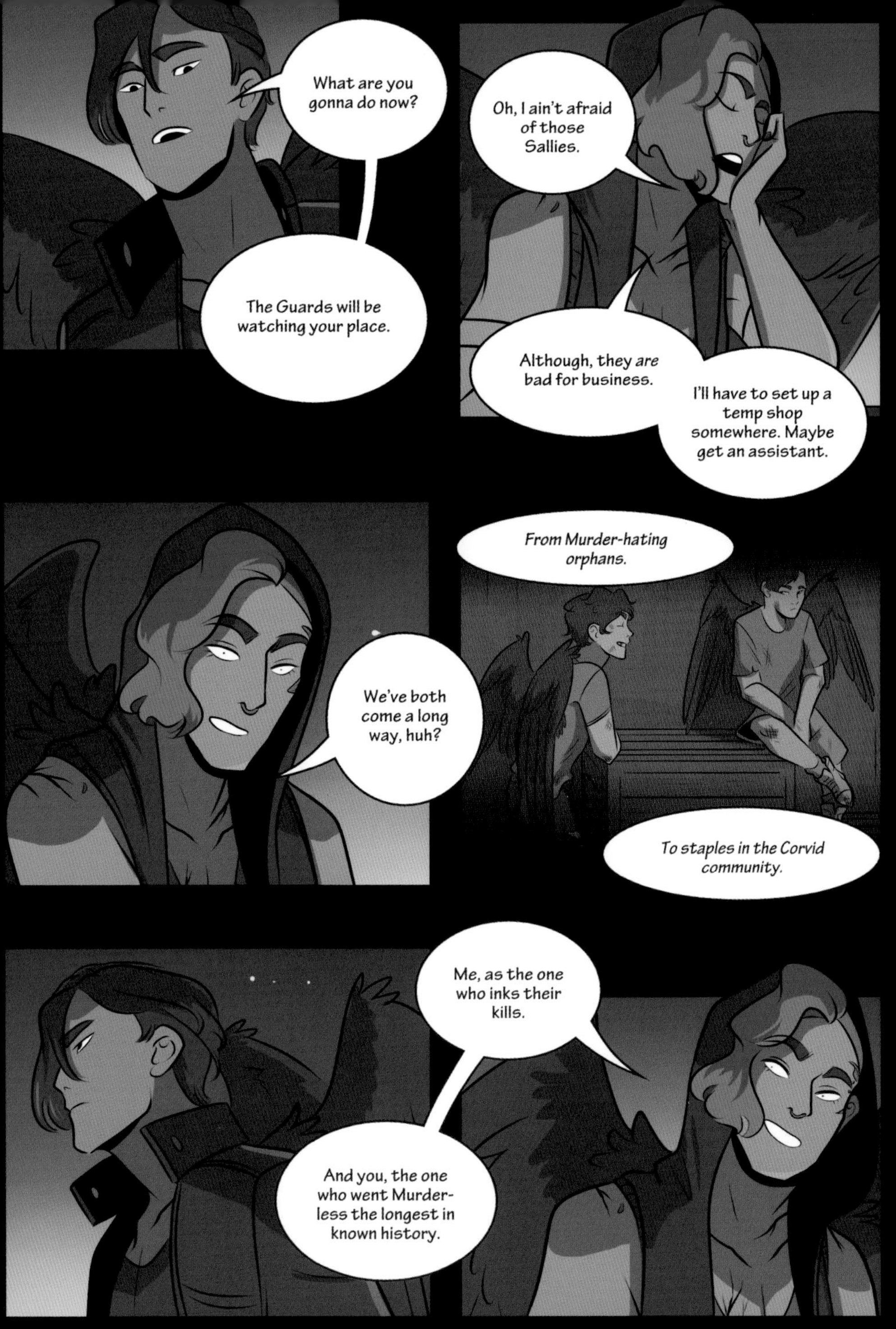
What are you gonna do now?
The Guards will be watching your place.
Oh, I ain't afraid of those Sallies.
Although, they *are* bad for business.
I'll have to set up a temp shop somewhere. Maybe get an assistant.
We've both come a long way, huh?
From Murder-hating orphans.
To staples in the Corvid community.
Me, as the one who inks their kills.
And you, the one who went Murder-less the longest in known history.

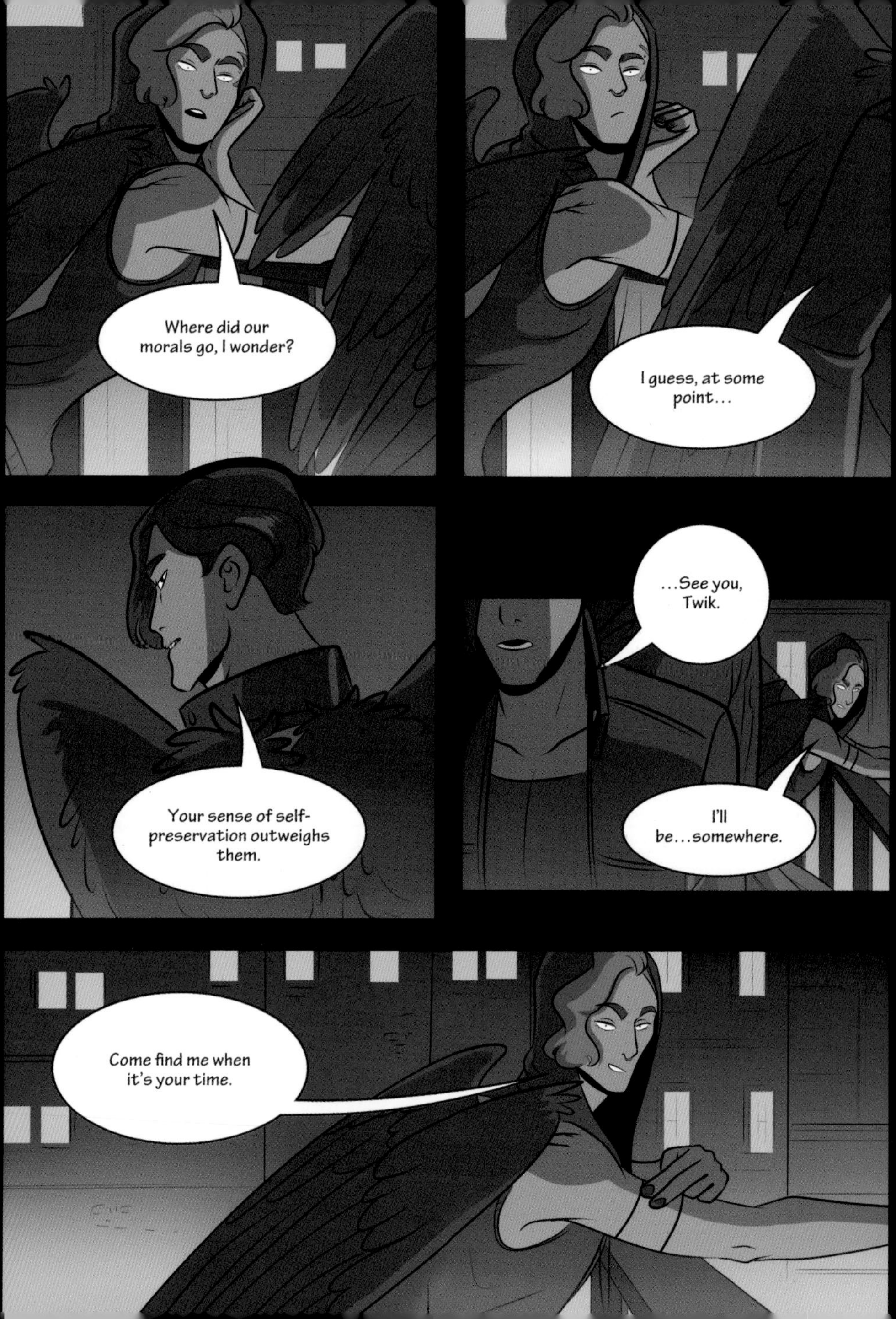
Where did our morals go, I wonder?
I guess, at some point...
Your sense of self-preservation outweighs them.
...See you, Twik.
I'll be...somewhere.
Come find me when it's your time.

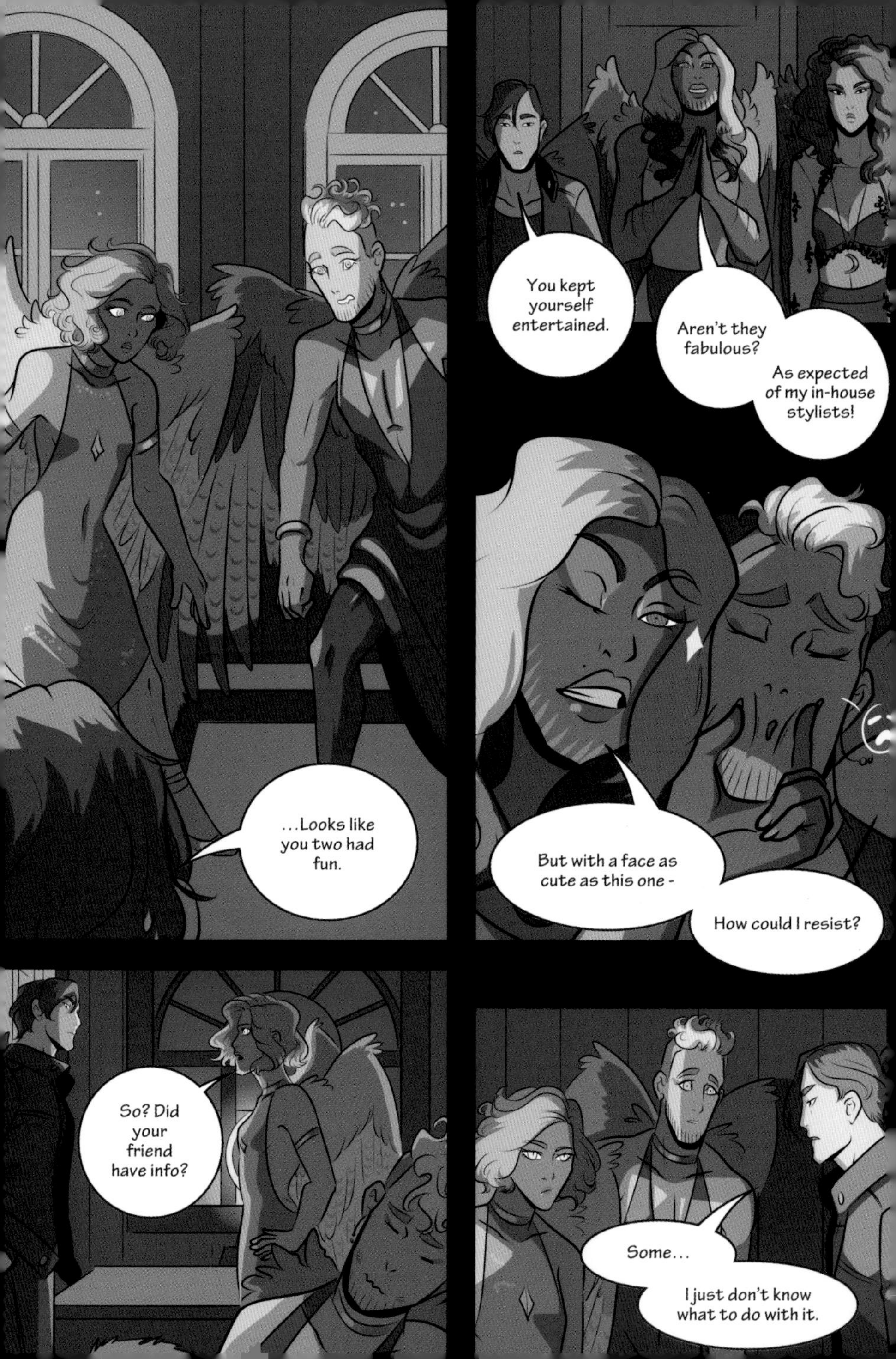
...Looks like you two had fun.
You kept yourself entertained.
Aren't they fabulous?
As expected of my in-house stylists!
But with a face as cute as this one -
How could I resist?
So? Did your friend have info?
Some...
I just don't know what to do with it.

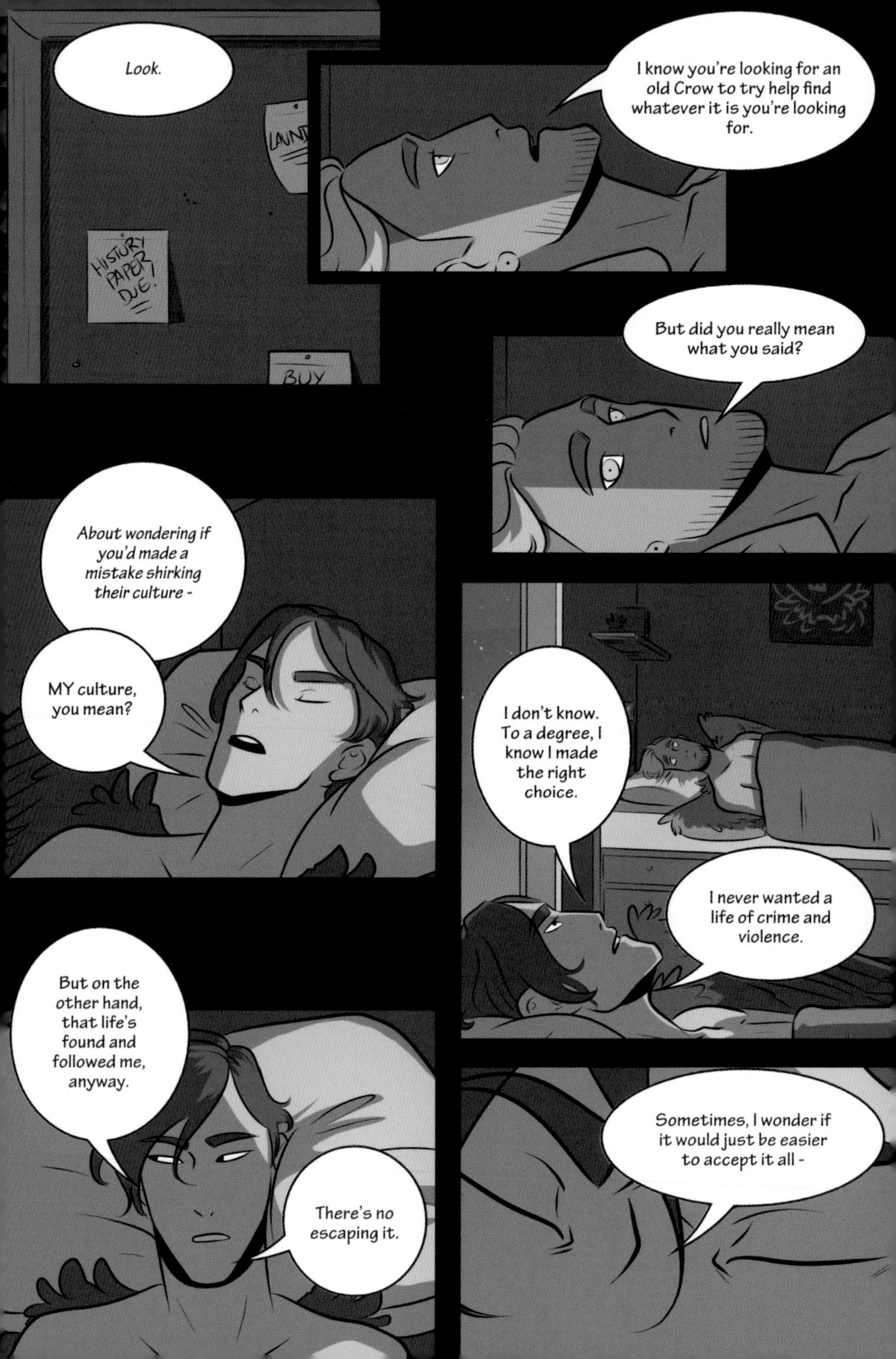
LAUND
HISTORY PAPER DUE!
BUY
Look.
I know you're looking for an old Crow to try help find whatever it is you're looking for.
But did you really mean what you said?
About wondering if you'd made a mistake shirking their culture -
MY culture, you mean?
I don't know. To a degree, I know I made the right choice.
I never wanted a life of crime and violence.
But on the other hand, that life's found and followed me, anyway.
There's no escaping it.
Sometimes, I wonder if it would just be easier to accept it all -

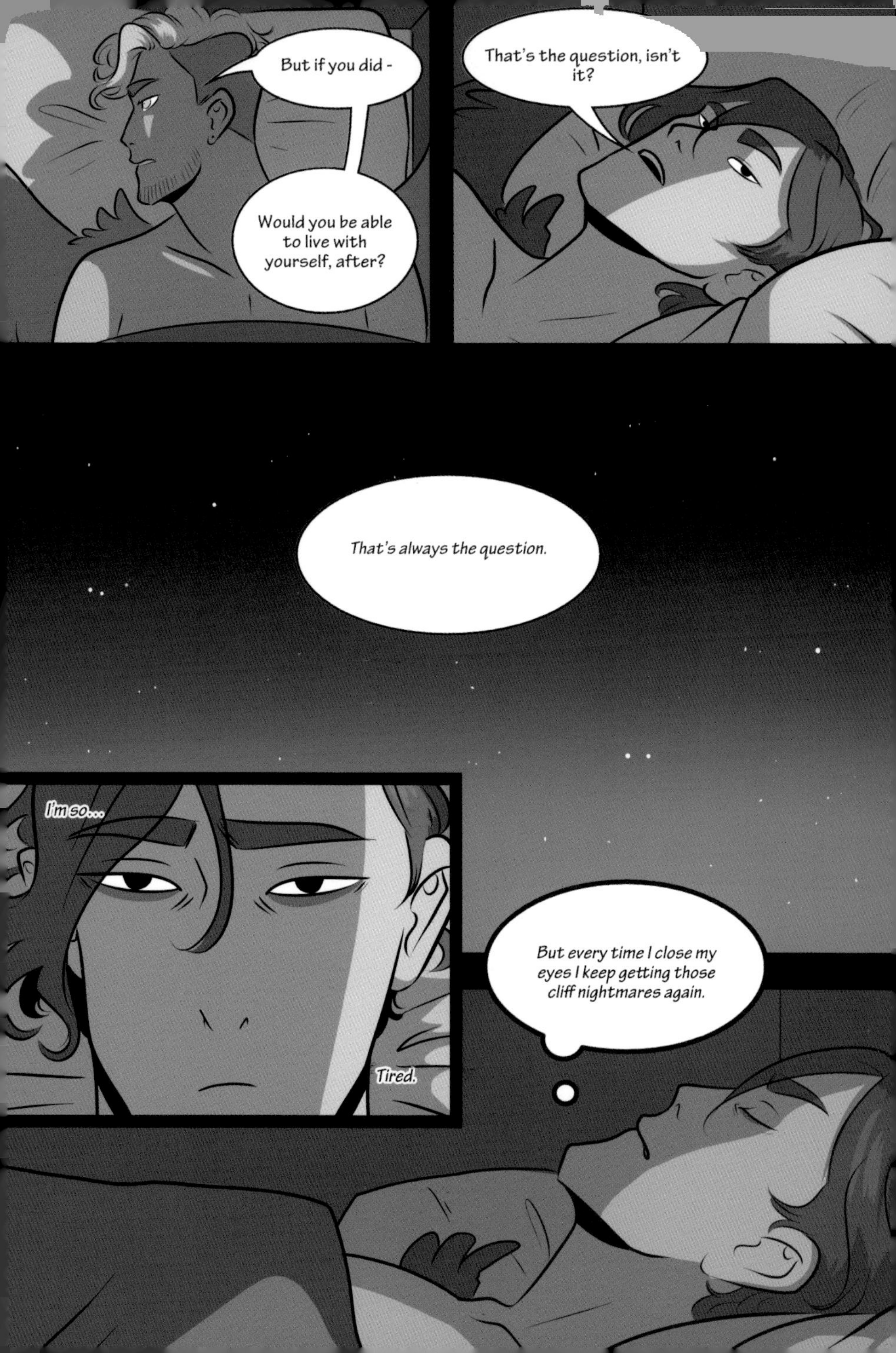
But if you did -
Would you be able to live with yourself, after?
That's the question, isn't it?
That's always the question.
I'm so...
Tired.
But every time I close my eyes I keep getting those cliff nightmares again.

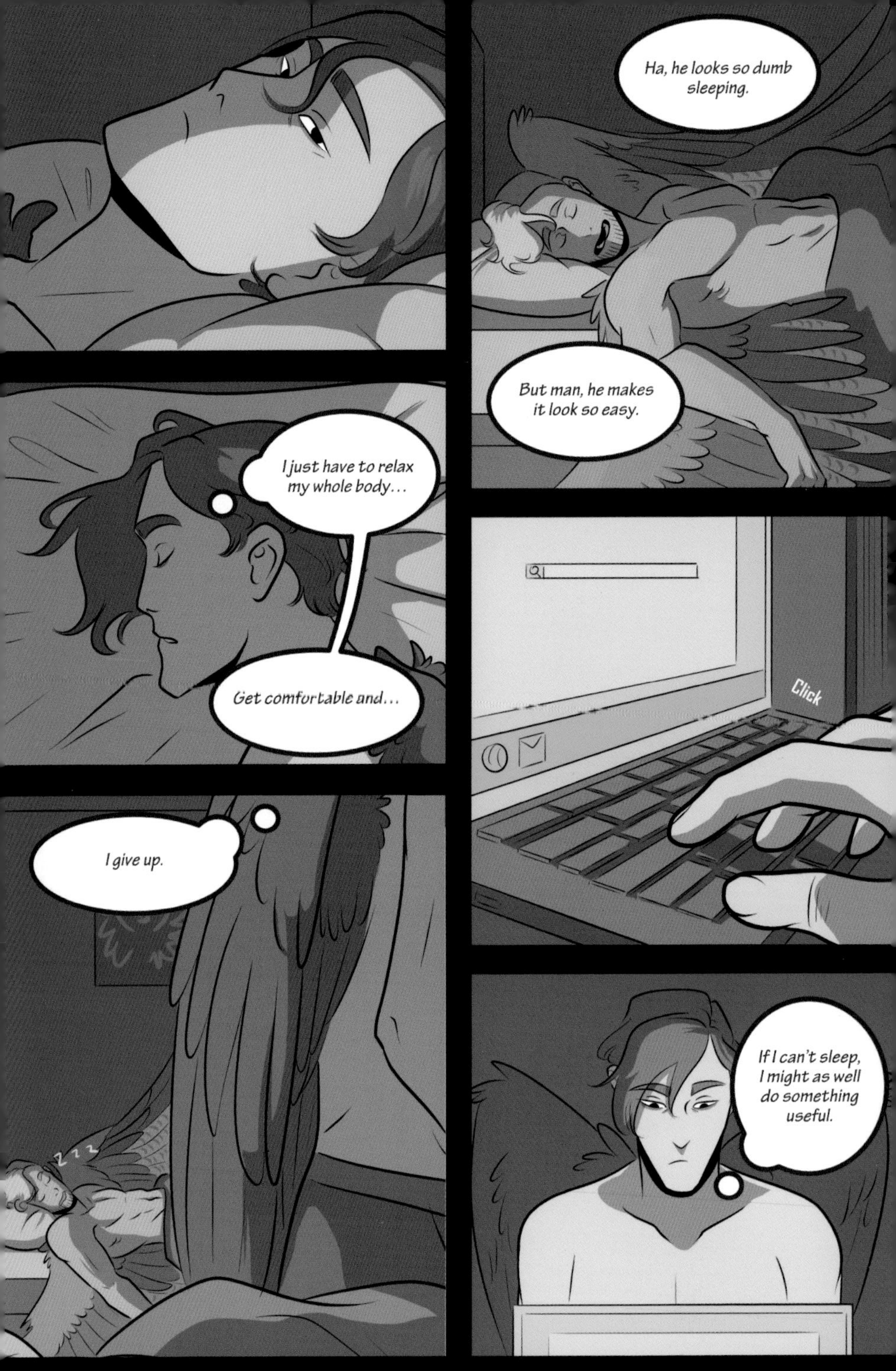
Ha, he looks so dumb sleeping.
But man, he makes it look so easy.
I just have to relax my whole body...
Get comfortable and...
Click
I give up.
If I can't sleep, I might as well do something useful.

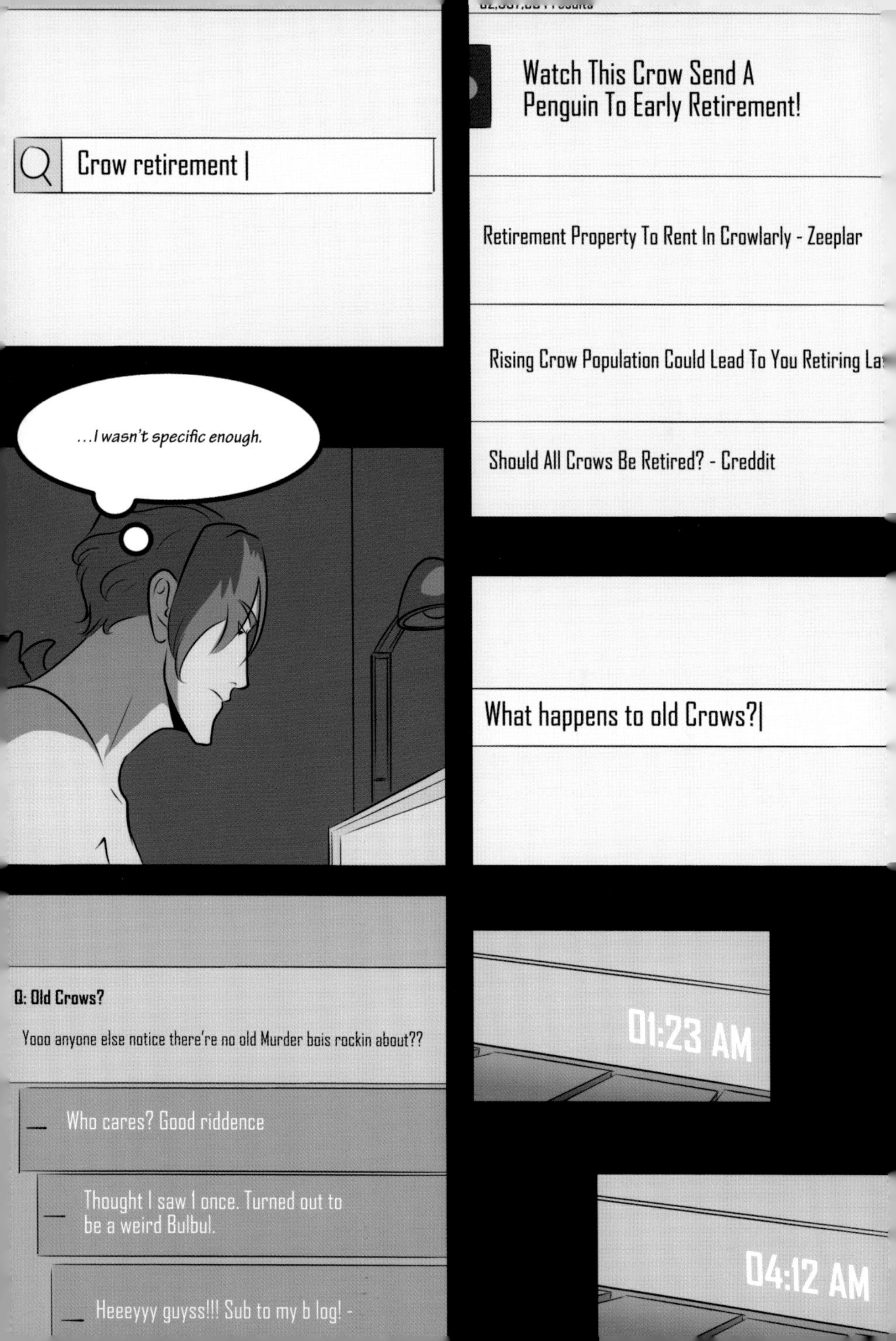

Crow retirement |
Watch This Crow Send A Penguin To Early Retirement!
Retirement Property To Rent In Crowlarly - Zeeplar
Rising Crow Population Could Lead To You Retiring La
Should All Crows Be Retired? - Creddit
...I wasn't specific enough.
What happens to old Crows?|
Q: Old Crows?
Yooo anyone else notice there're no old Murder bois rockin about??
Who cares? Good riddence
Thought I saw 1 once. Turned out to be a weird Bulbul.
Heeeyyy guyss!!! Sub to my b log! -
01:23 AM
04:12 AM

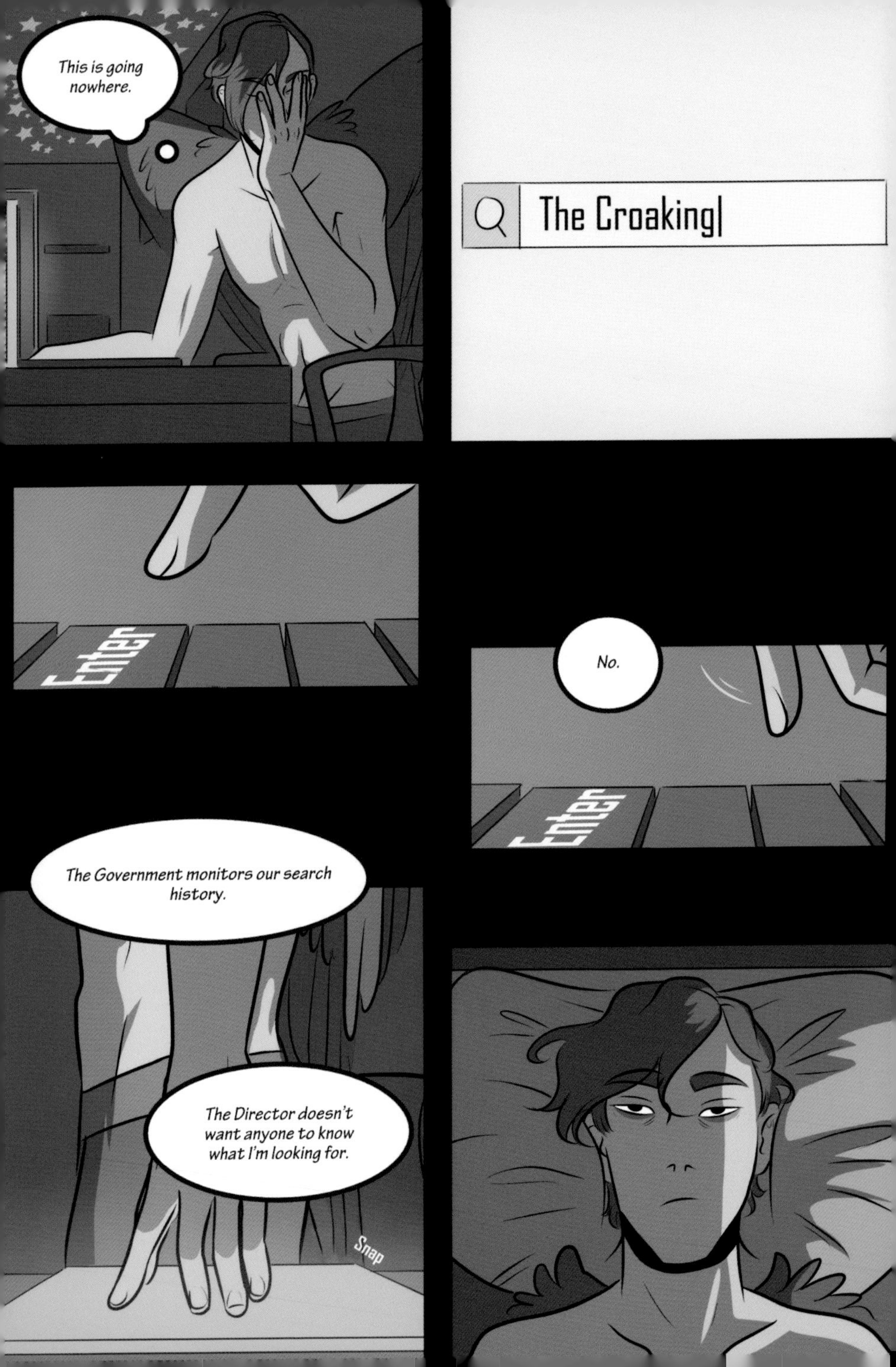
This is going nowhere.
The Croaking|
Enter
No.
Enter
The Government monitors our search history.
The Director doesn't want anyone to know what I'm looking for.
Snap

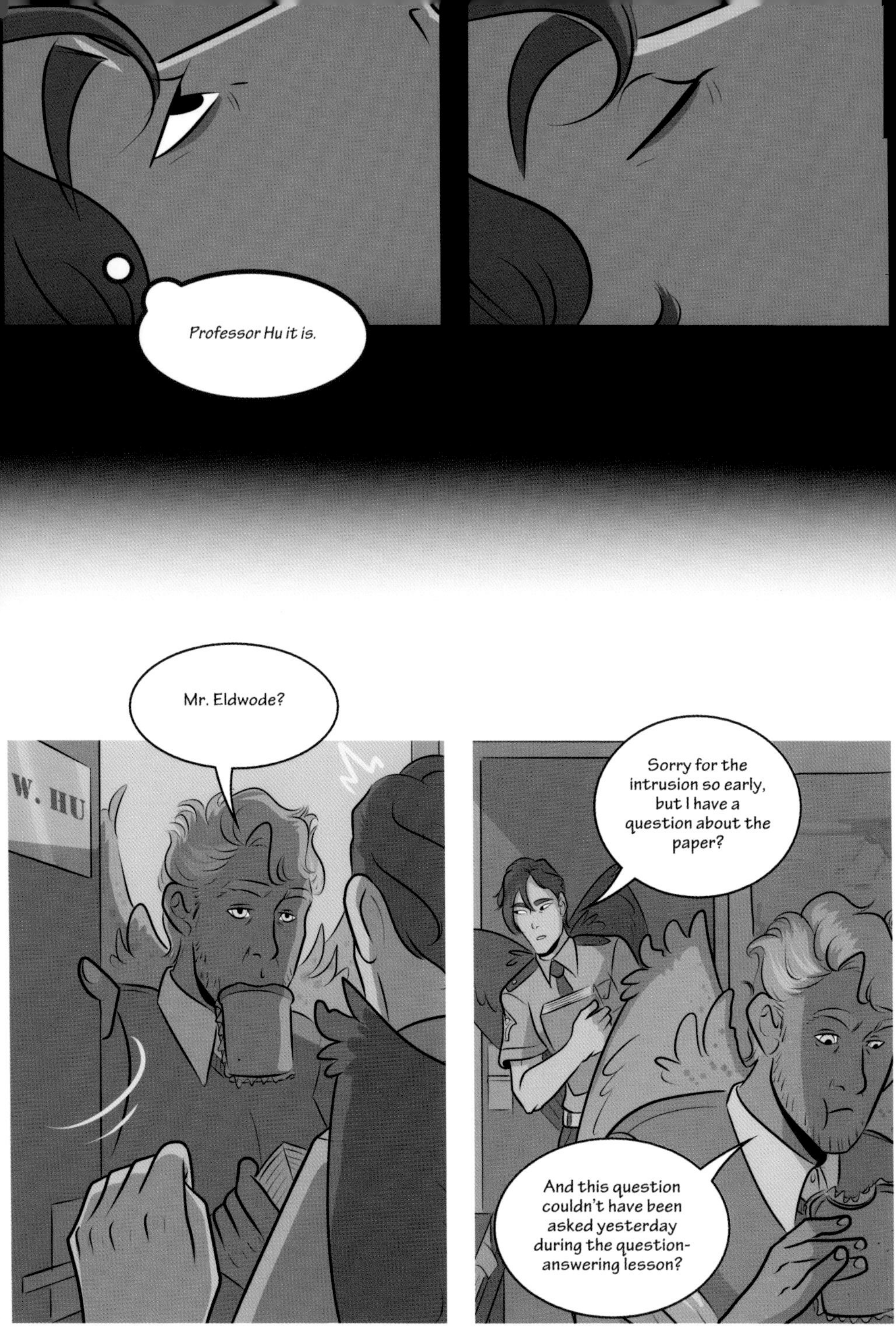
Professor Hu it is.
Mr. Eldwode?
W. HU
Sorry for the intrusion so early, but I have a question about the paper?
And this question couldn't have been asked yesterday during the question-answering lesson?

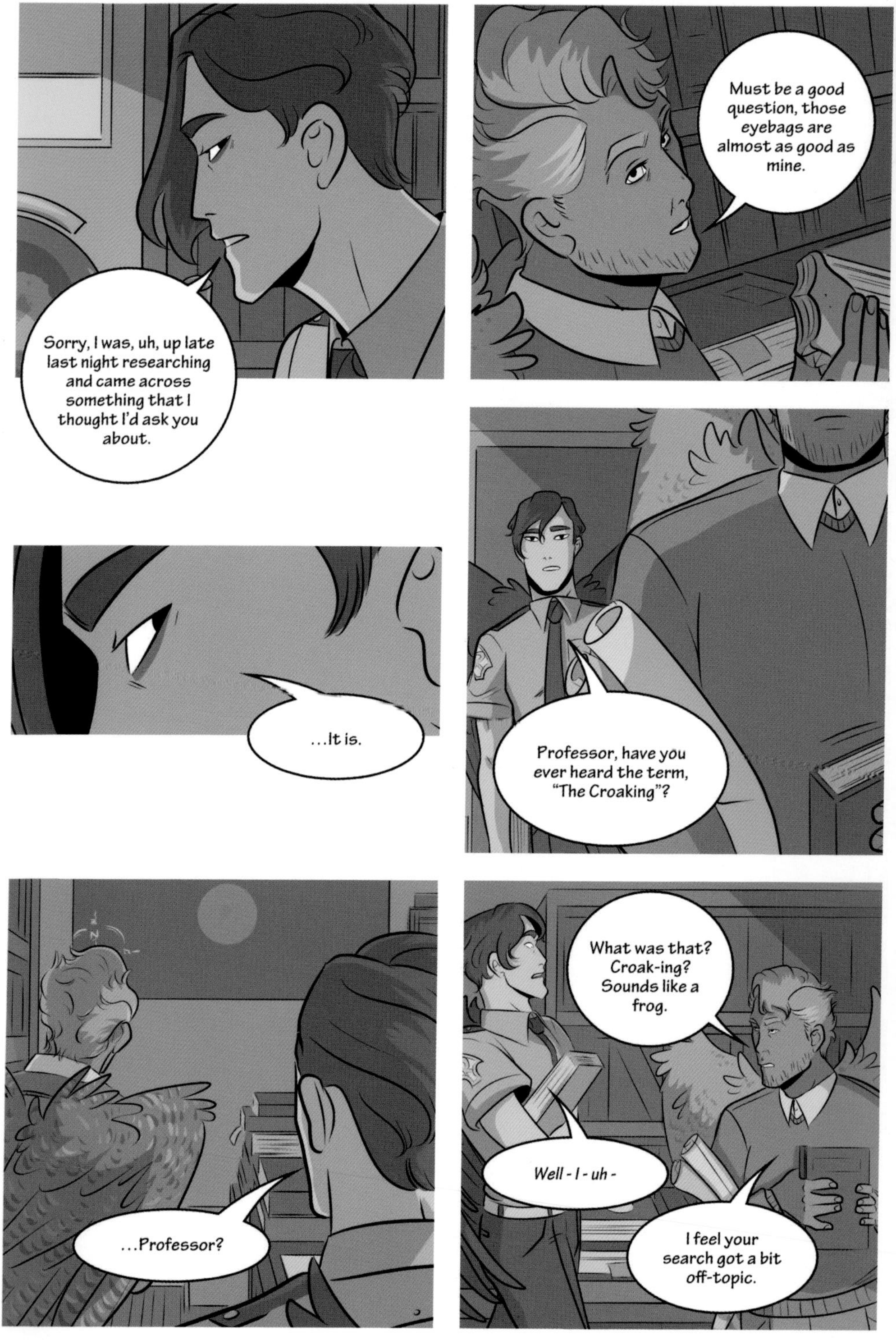
Sorry, I was, uh, up late last night researching and came across something that I thought I'd ask you about.
Must be a good question, those eyebags are almost as good as mine.
...It is.
Professor, have you ever heard the term, "The Croaking"?
...Professor?
What was that? Croak-ing? Sounds like a frog.
Well - I - uh -
I feel your search got a bit off-topic.

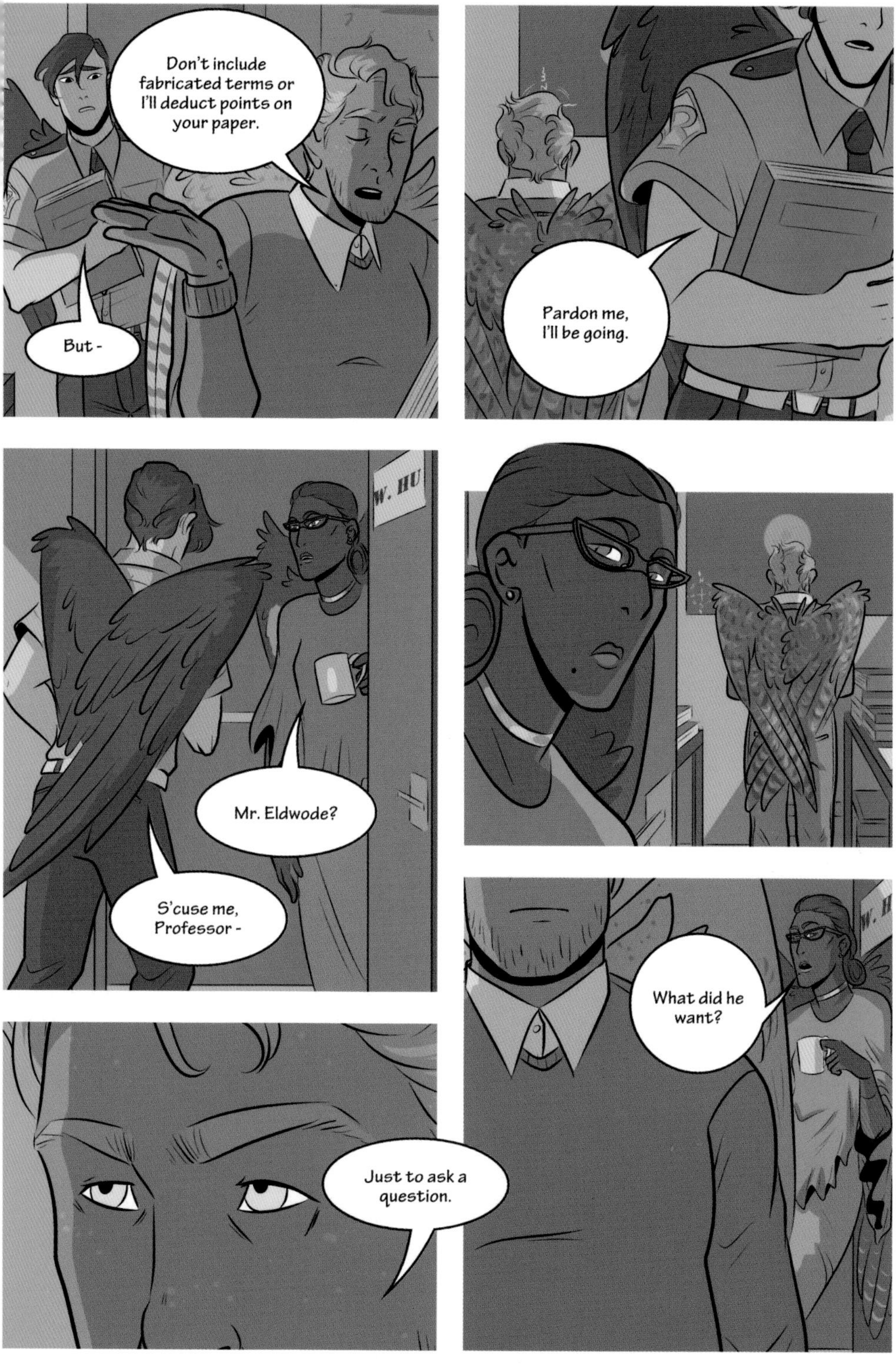
Don't include fabricated terms or I'll deduct points on your paper.
But -
Pardon me, I'll be going.
W. HU
S'cuse me, Professor -
Mr. Eldwode?
What did he want?
Just to ask a question.

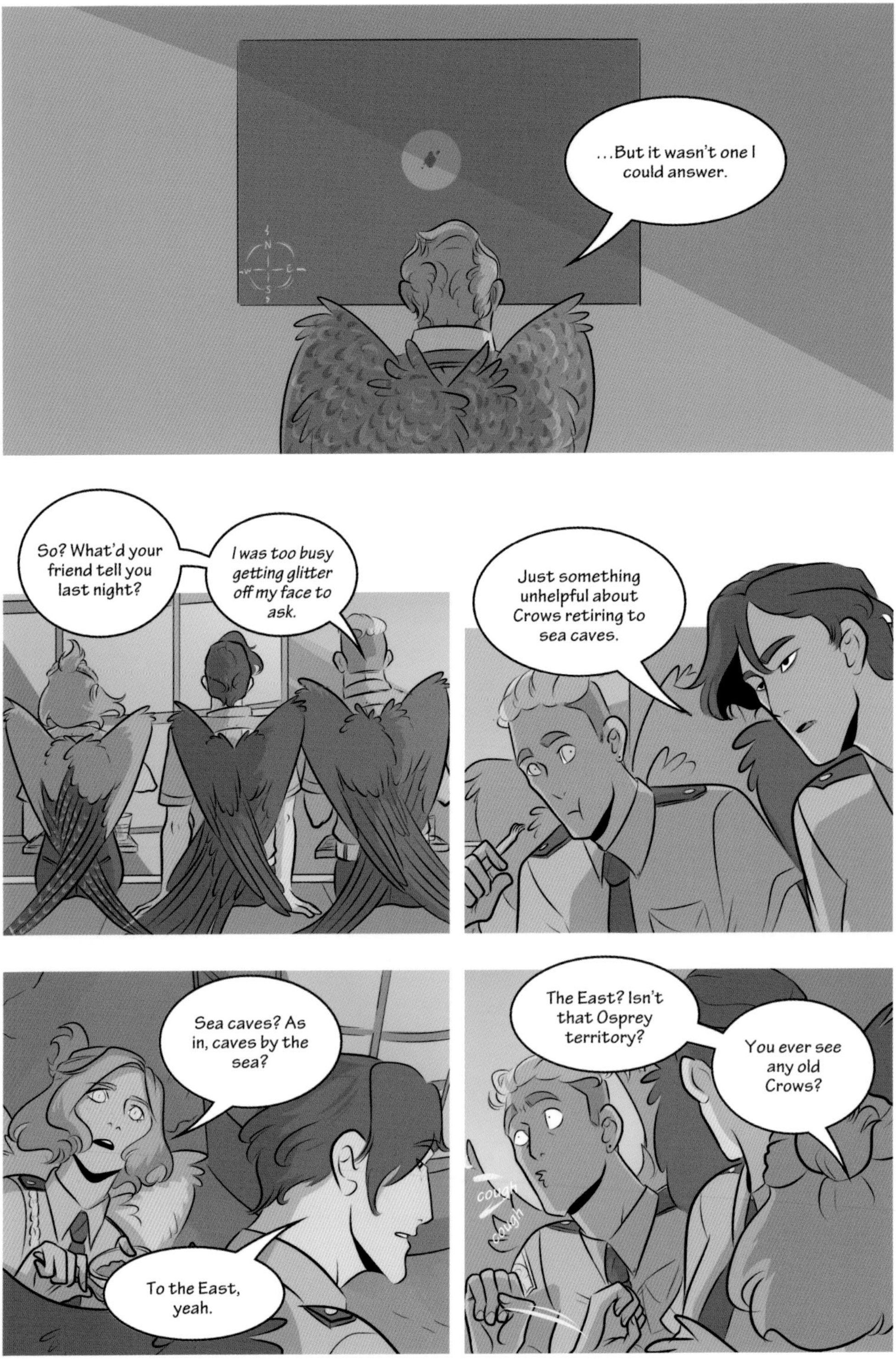
...But it wasn't one I could answer.
So? What'd your friend tell you last night?
I was too busy getting glitter off my face to ask.
Just something unhelpful about Crows retiring to sea caves.
Sea caves? As in, caves by the sea?
To the East, yeah.
The East? Isn't that Osprey territory?
You ever see any old Crows?
cough
cough

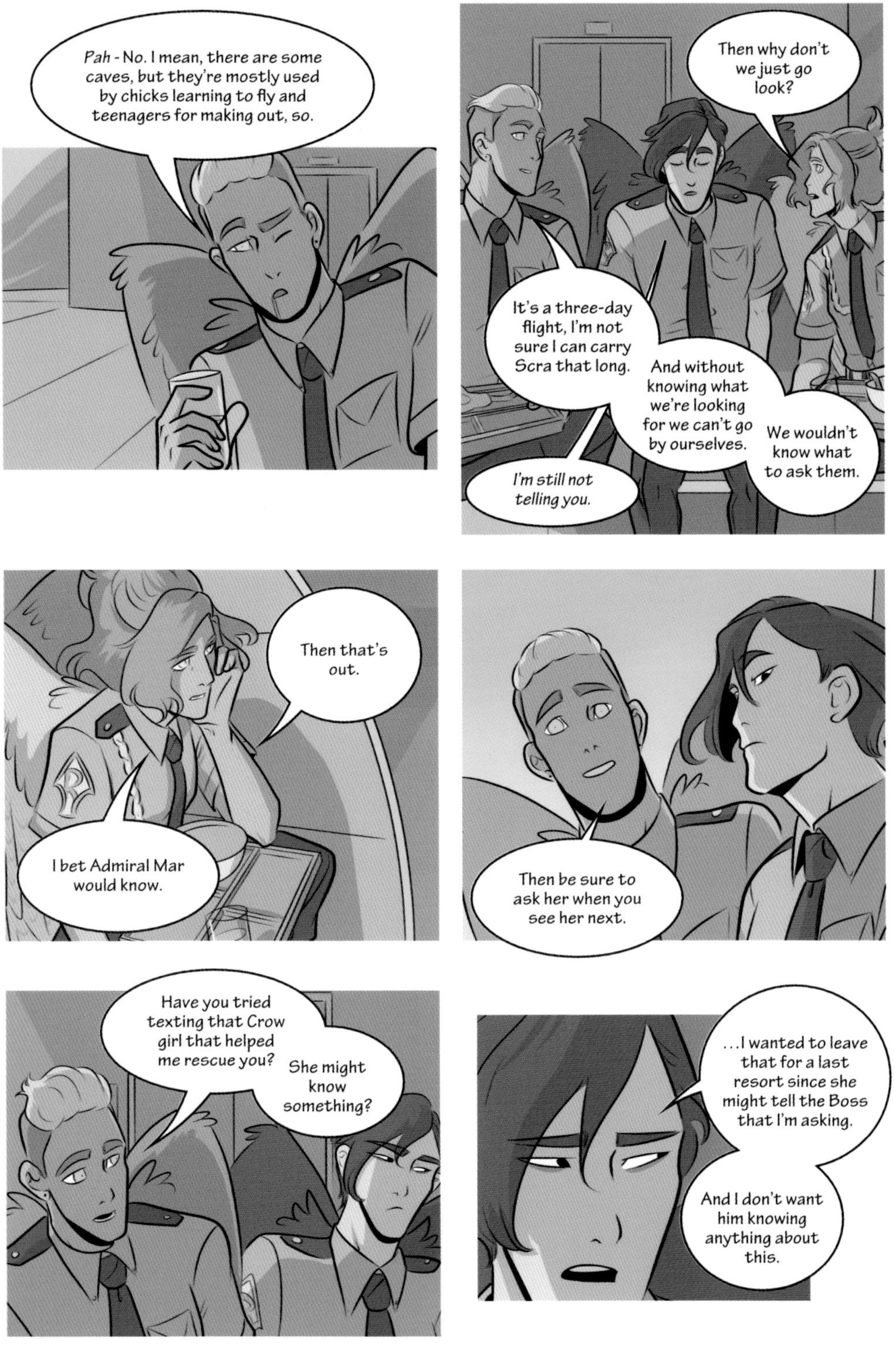

Pah - No. I mean, there are some caves, but they're mostly used by chicks learning to fly and teenagers for making out, so.
Then why don't we just go look?
It's a three-day flight, I'm not sure I can carry Scra that long.
And without knowing what we're looking for we can't go by ourselves.
We wouldn't know what to ask them.
I'm still not telling you.
Then that's out.
I bet Admiral Mar would know.
Then be sure to ask her when you see her next.
Have you tried texting that Crow girl that helped me rescue you?
She might know something?
...I wanted to leave that for a last resort since she might tell the Boss that I'm asking.
And I don't want him knowing anything about this.

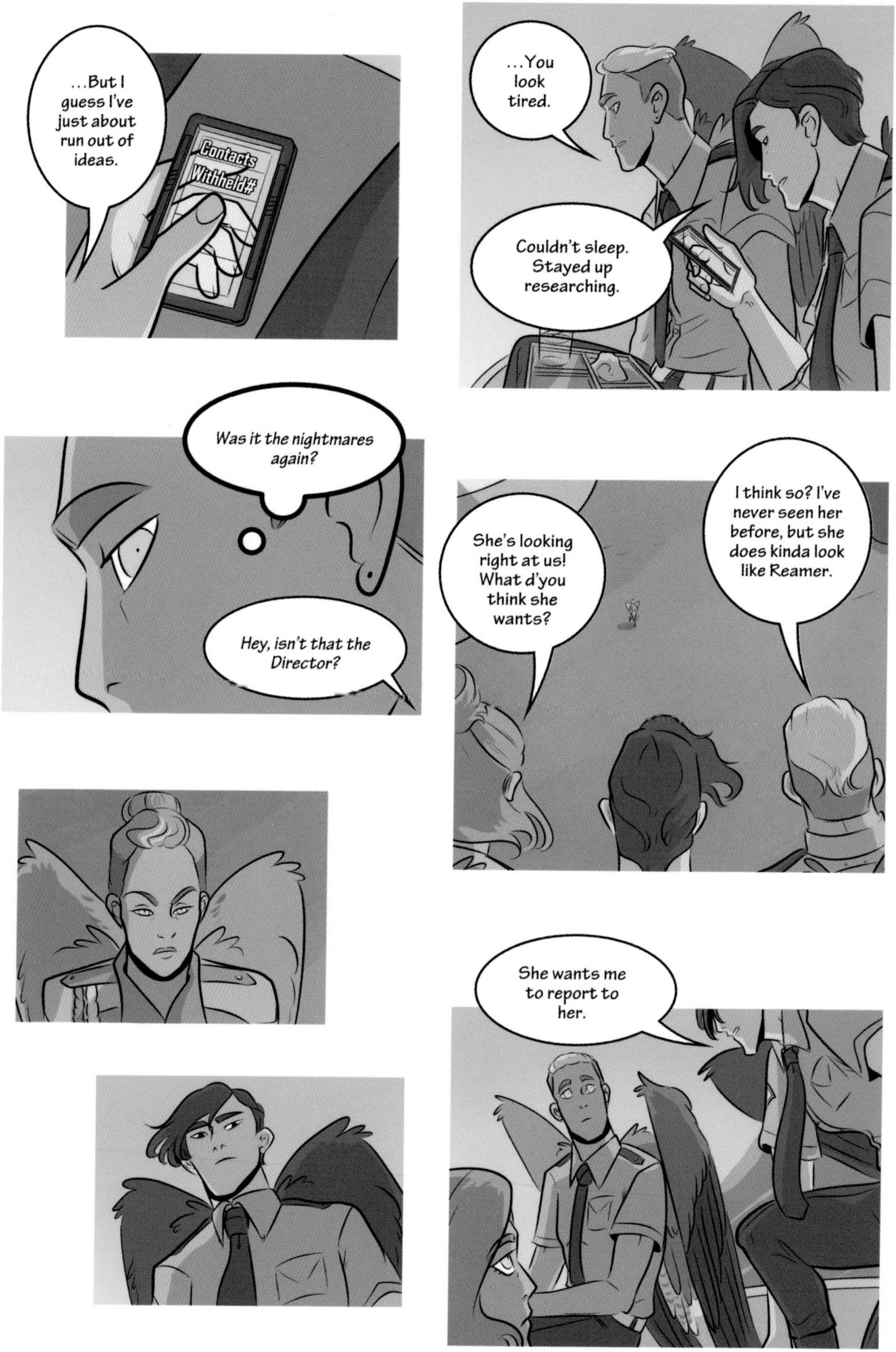

...But I guess I've just about run out of ideas.
Contacts
Withheld#
...You look tired.
Couldn't sleep. Stayed up researching.
Was it the nightmares again?
Hey, isn't that the Director?
She's looking right at us! What d'you think she wants?
I think so? I've never seen her before, but she does kinda look like Reamer.
She wants me to report to her.

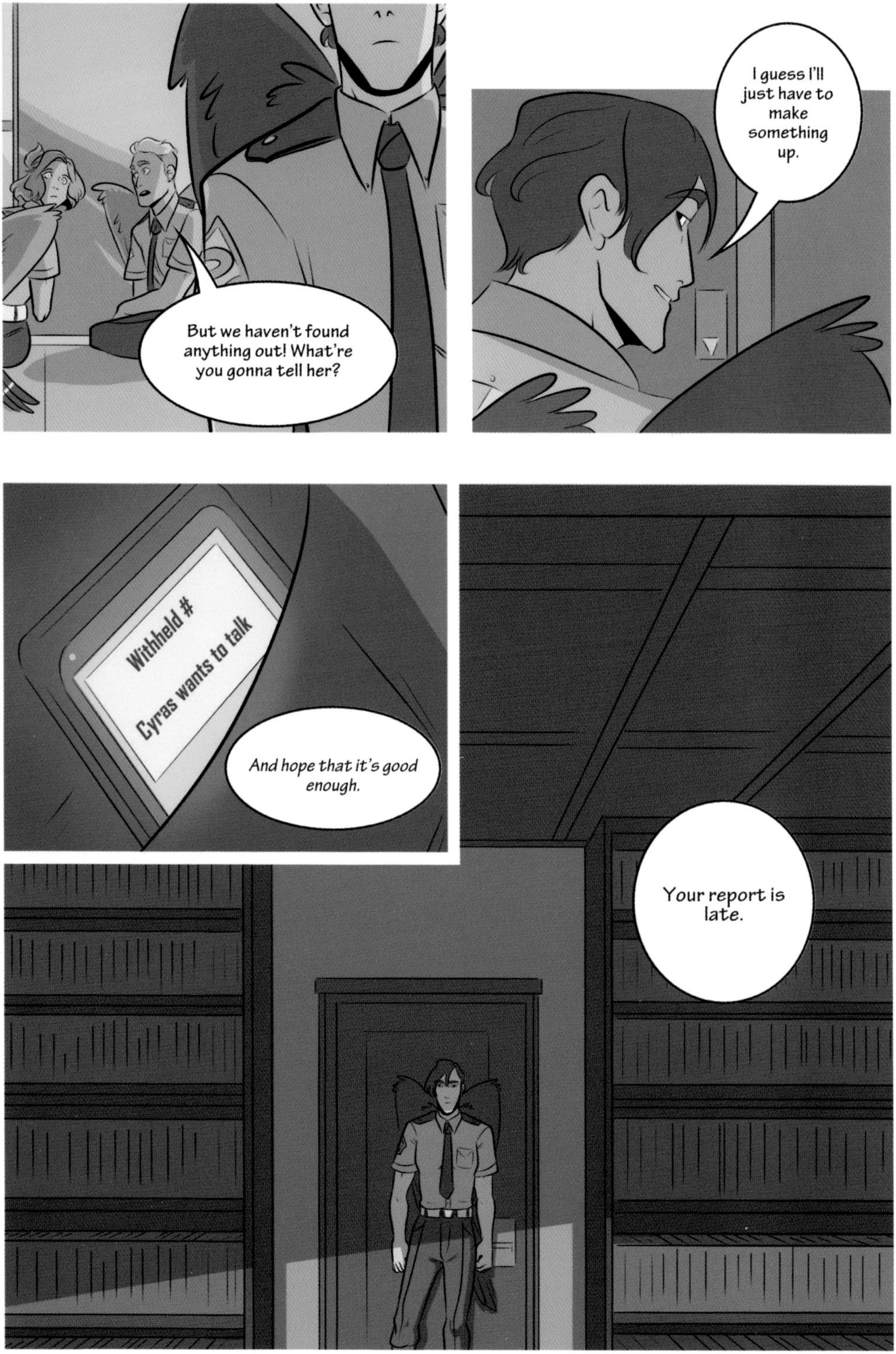
But we haven't found anything out! What're you gonna tell her?
I guess I'll just have to make something up.
Withheld #
Cyras wants to talk
And hope that it's good enough.
Your report is late.

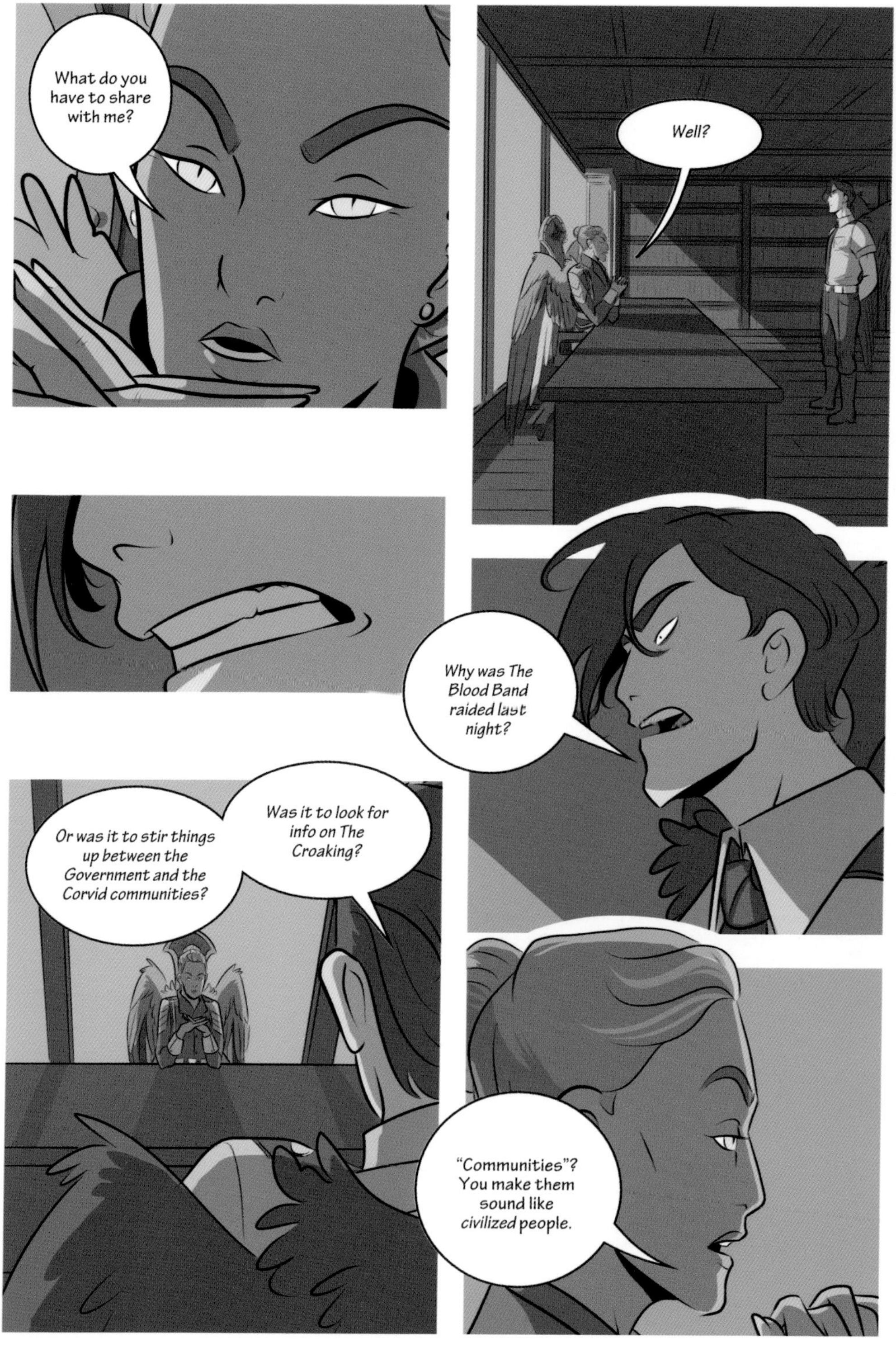
What do you have to share with me?
Well?
Why was The Blood Band raided last night?
Was it to look for info on The Croaking?
Or was it to stir things up between the Government and the Corvid communities?
"Communities"? You make them sound like *civilized* people.

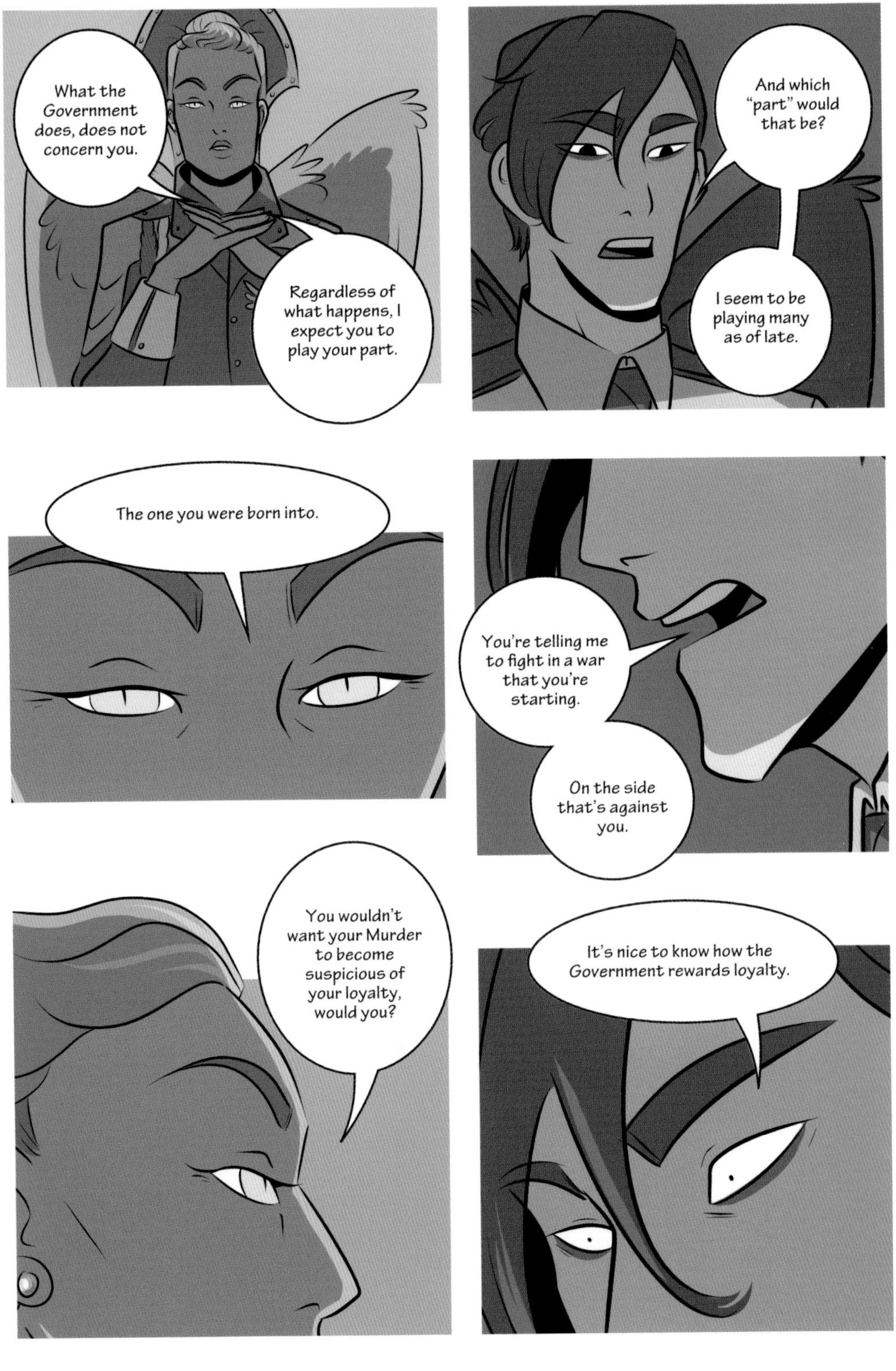
What the Government does, does not concern you.
Regardless of what happens, I expect you to play your part.
And which "part" would that be?
I seem to be playing many as of late.
The one you were born into.
You're telling me to fight in a war that you're starting.
On the side that's against you.
You wouldn't want your Murder to become suspicious of your loyalty, would you?
It's nice to know how the Government rewards loyalty.

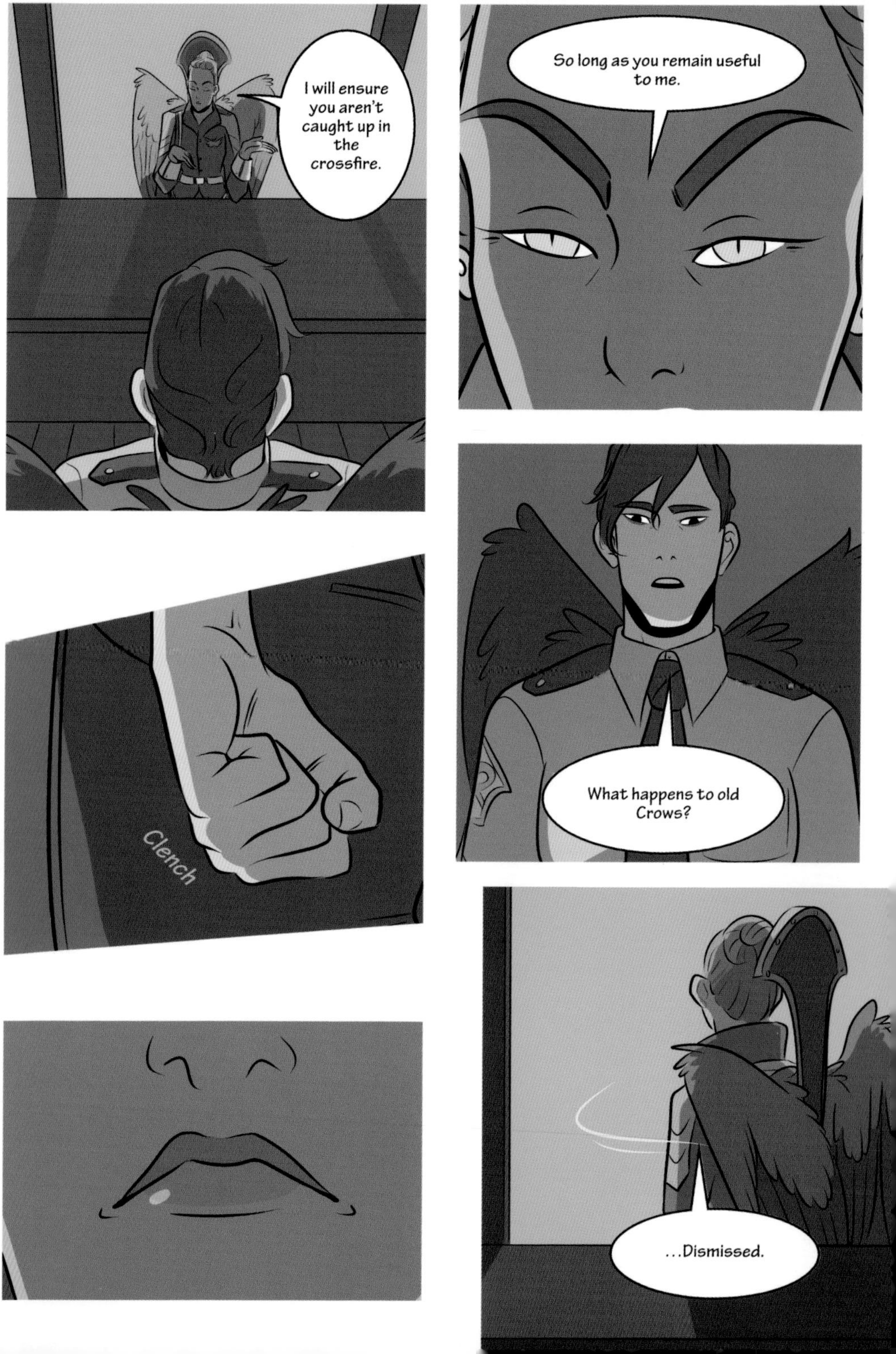

I will ensure you aren't caught up in the crossfire.
So long as you remain useful to me.
Clench
What happens to old Crows?
...Dismissed.

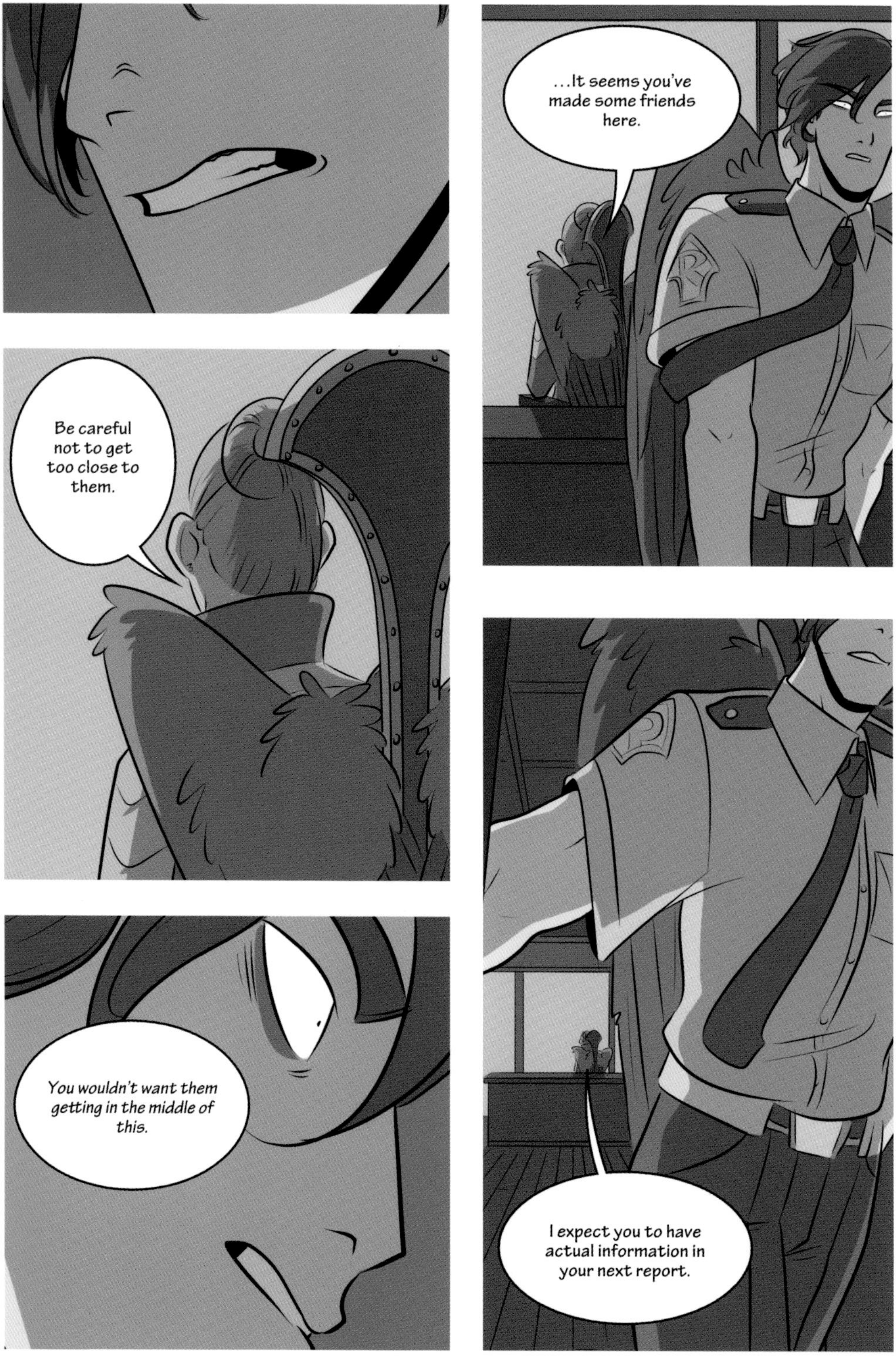

...It seems you've made some friends here.
Be careful not to get too close to them.
You wouldn't want them getting in the middle of this.
I expect you to have actual information in your next report.

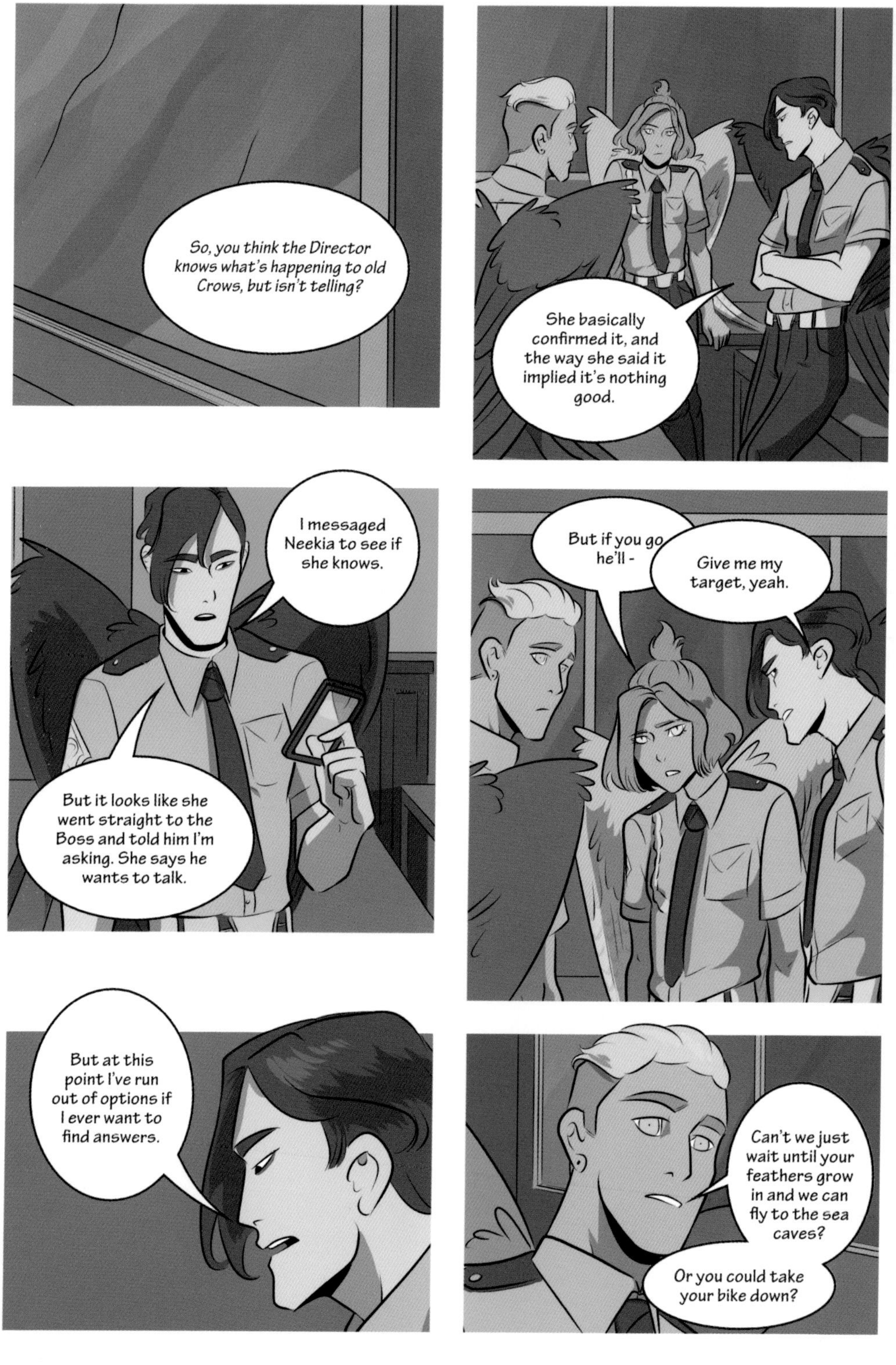
So, you think the Director knows what's happening to old Crows, but isn't telling?
She basically confirmed it, and the way she said it implied it's nothing good.
I messaged Neekia to see if she knows.
But it looks like she went straight to the Boss and told him I'm asking. She says he wants to talk.
But if you go he'll -
Give me my target, yeah.
But at this point I've run out of options if I ever want to find answers.
Can't we just wait until your feathers grow in and we can fly to the sea caves?
Or you could take your bike down?

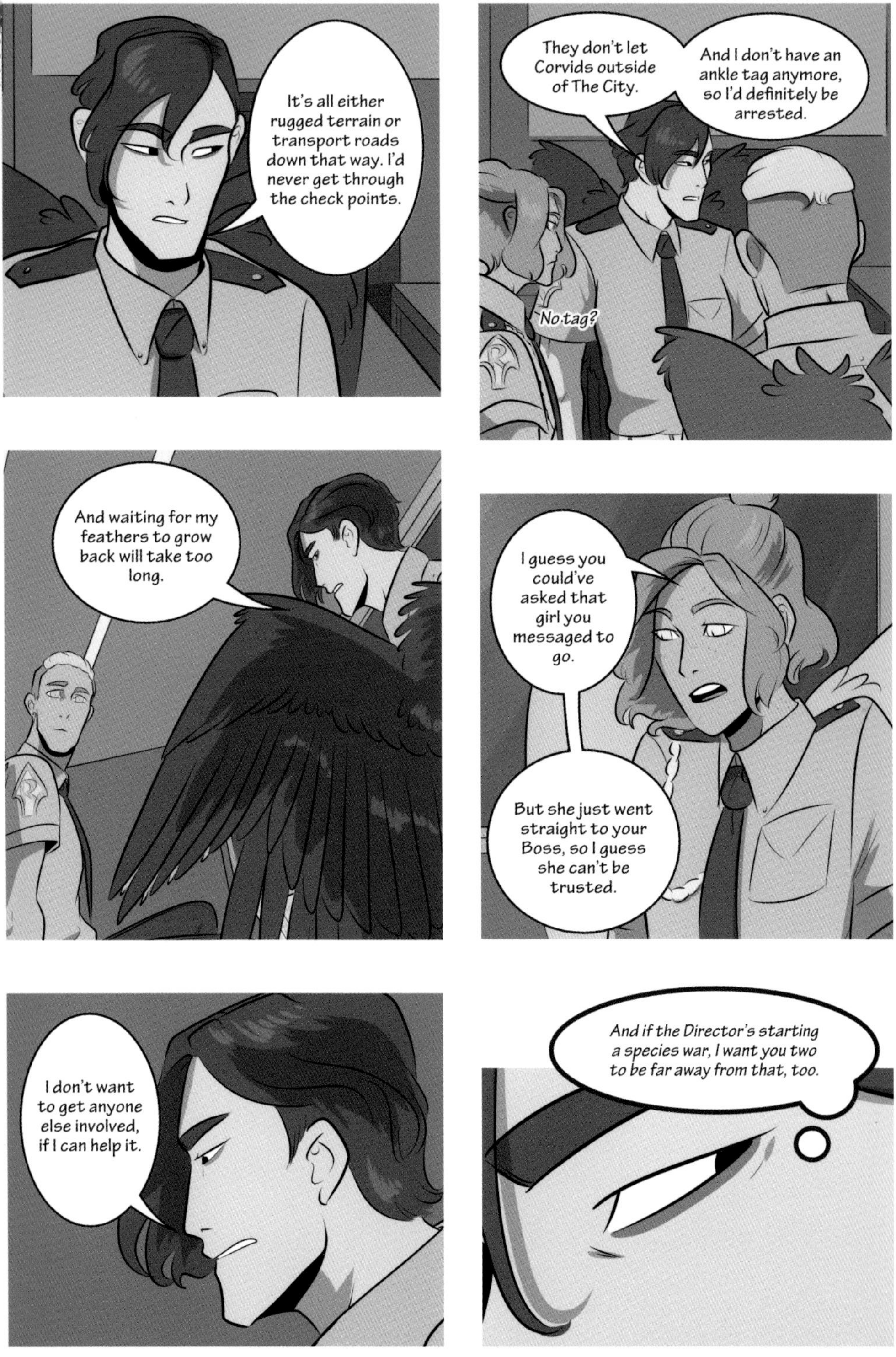
It's all either rugged terrain or transport roads down that way. I'd never get through the check points.
They don't let Corvids outside of The City.
And I don't have an ankle tag anymore, so I'd definitely be arrested.
No tag?
And waiting for my feathers to grow back will take too long.
I guess you could've asked that girl you messaged to go.
But she just went straight to your Boss, so I guess she can't be trusted.
I don't want to get anyone else involved, if I can help it.
And if the Director's starting a species war, I want you two to be far away from that, too.

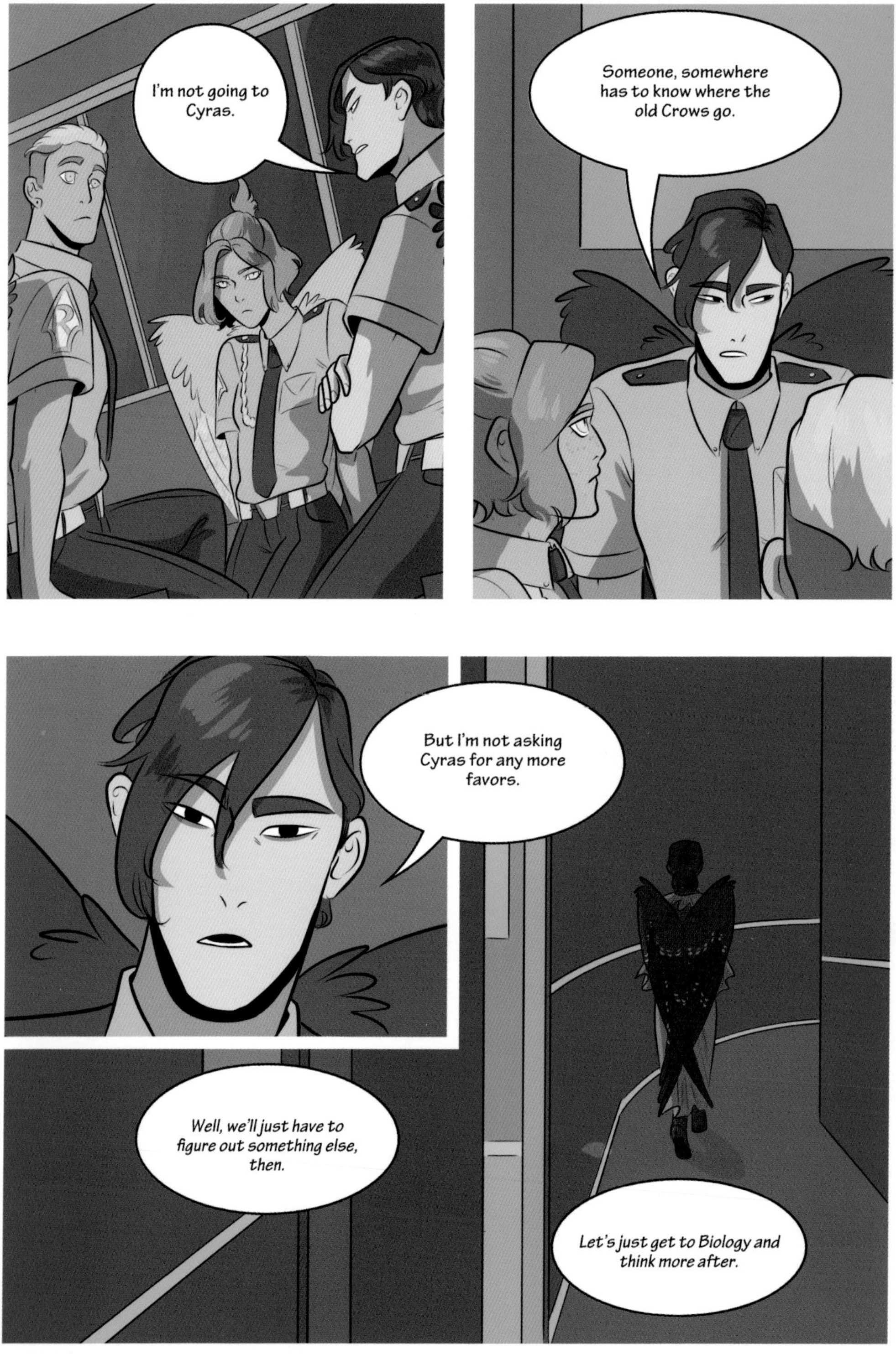
I'm not going to Cyras.
Someone, somewhere has to know where the old Crows go.
But I'm not asking Cyras for any more favors.
Well, we'll just have to figure out something else, then.
Let's just get to Biology and think more after.

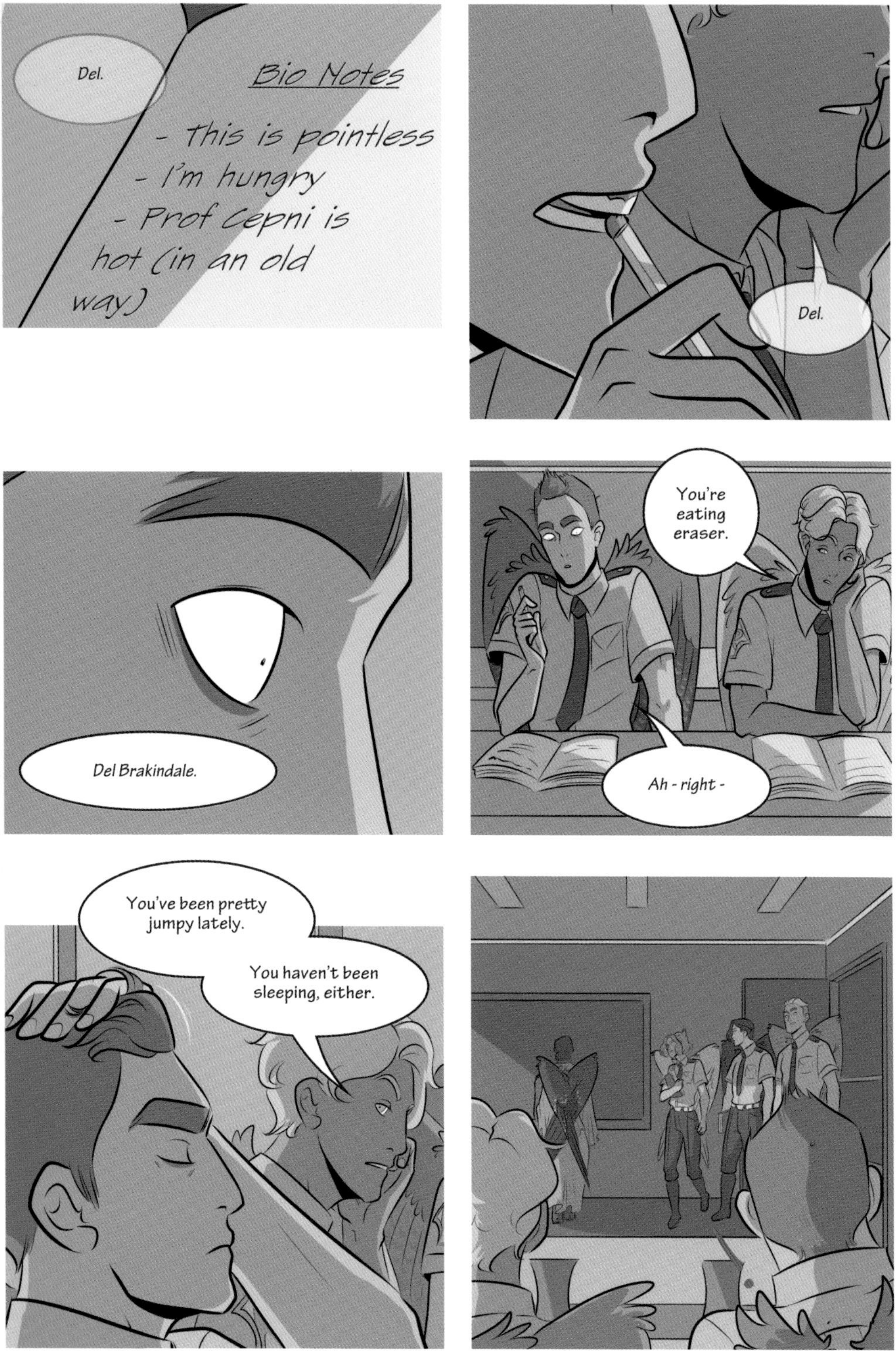
Del.
Bio Notes
- This is pointless
- I'm hungry
- Prof Cepni is hot (in an old way)
Del.
Del Brakindale.
You're eating eraser.
Ah - right -
You've been pretty jumpy lately.
You haven't been sleeping, either.

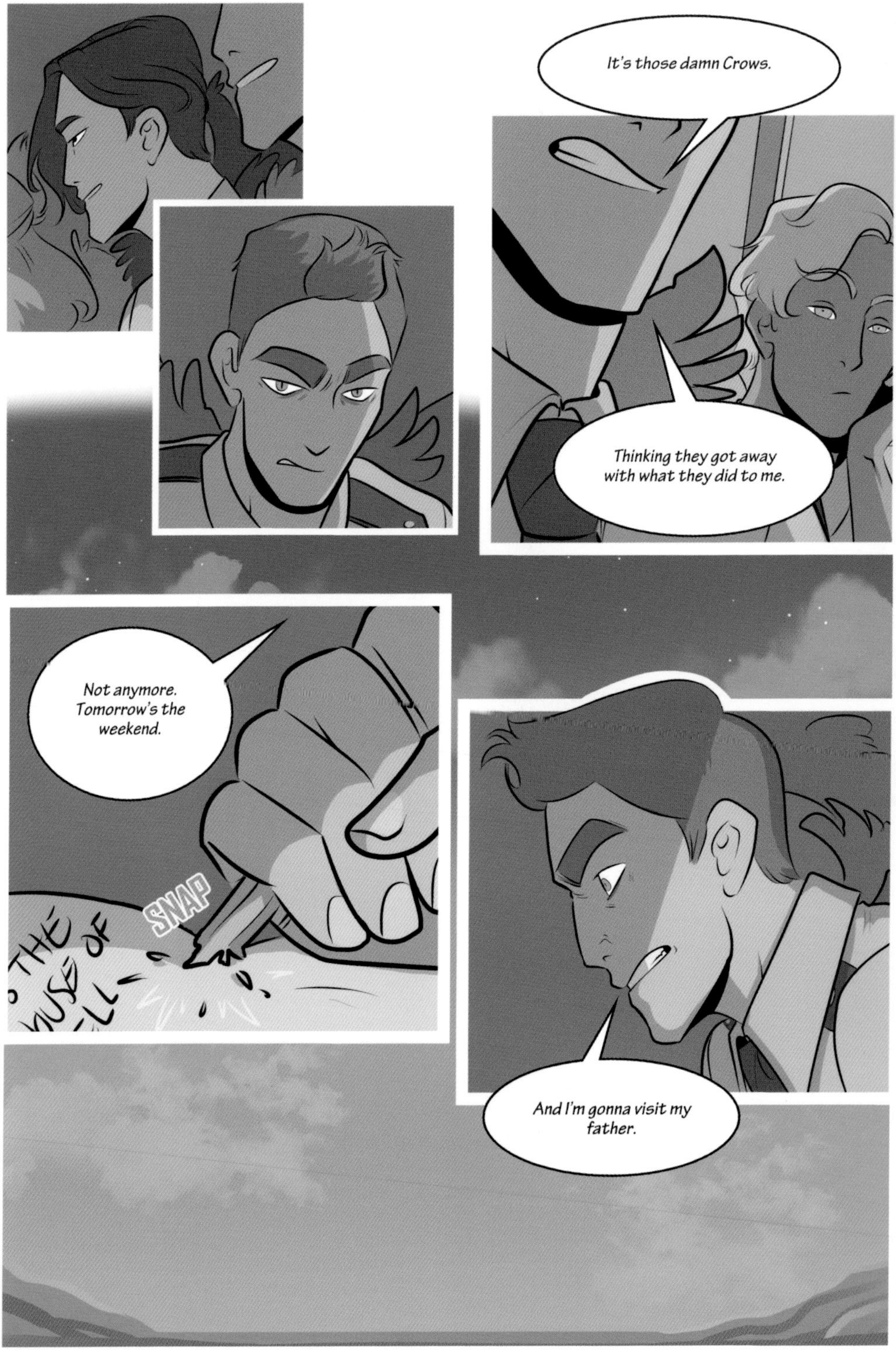

It's those damn Crows.
Thinking they got away with what they did to me.
Not anymore. Tomorrow's the weekend.
SNAP
And I'm gonna visit my father.

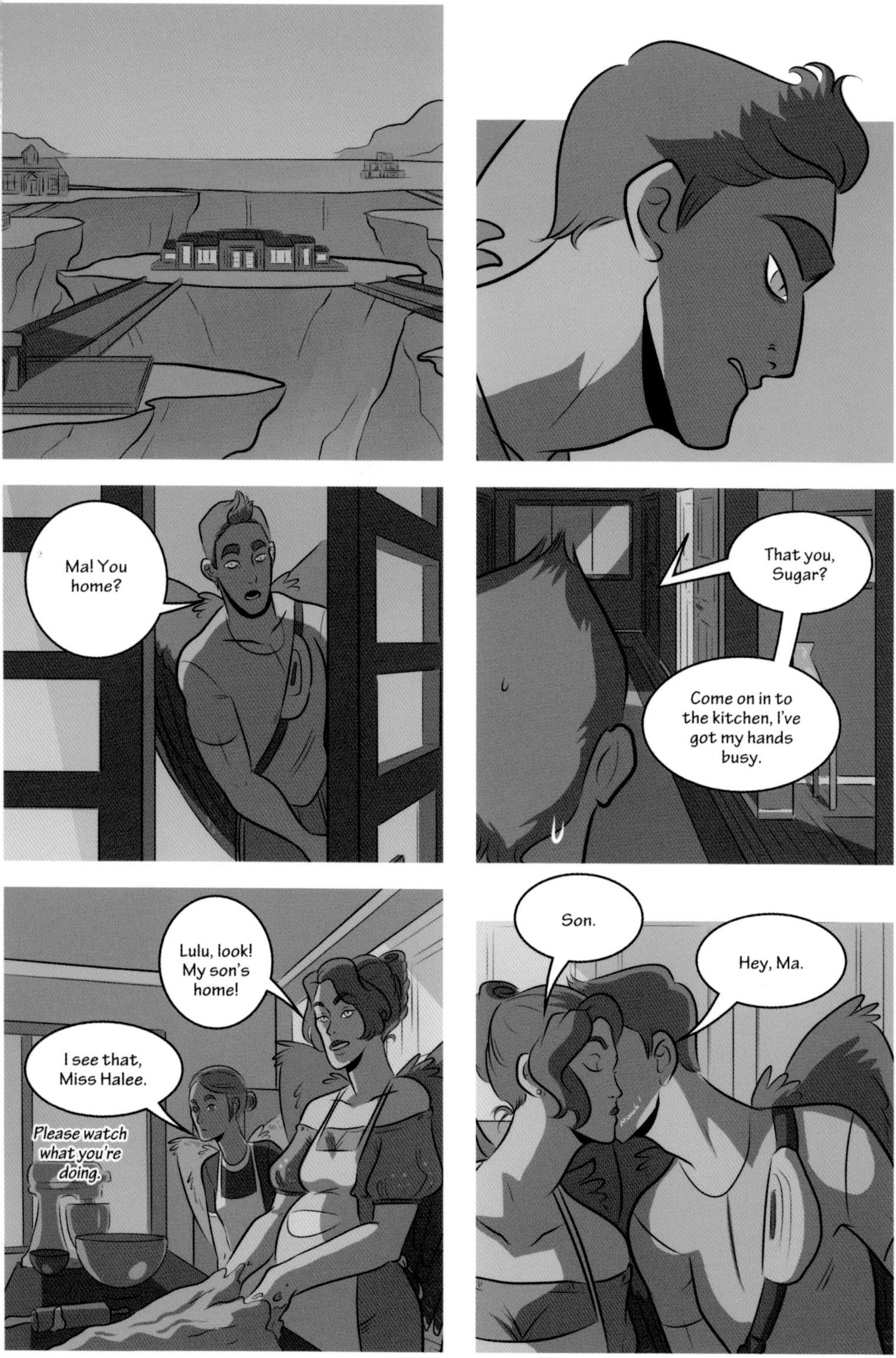
Ma! You home?
That you, Sugar?
Come on in to the kitchen, I've got my hands busy.
Lulu, look! My son's home!
I see that, Miss Halee.
Please watch what you're doing.
Son.
Hey, Ma.

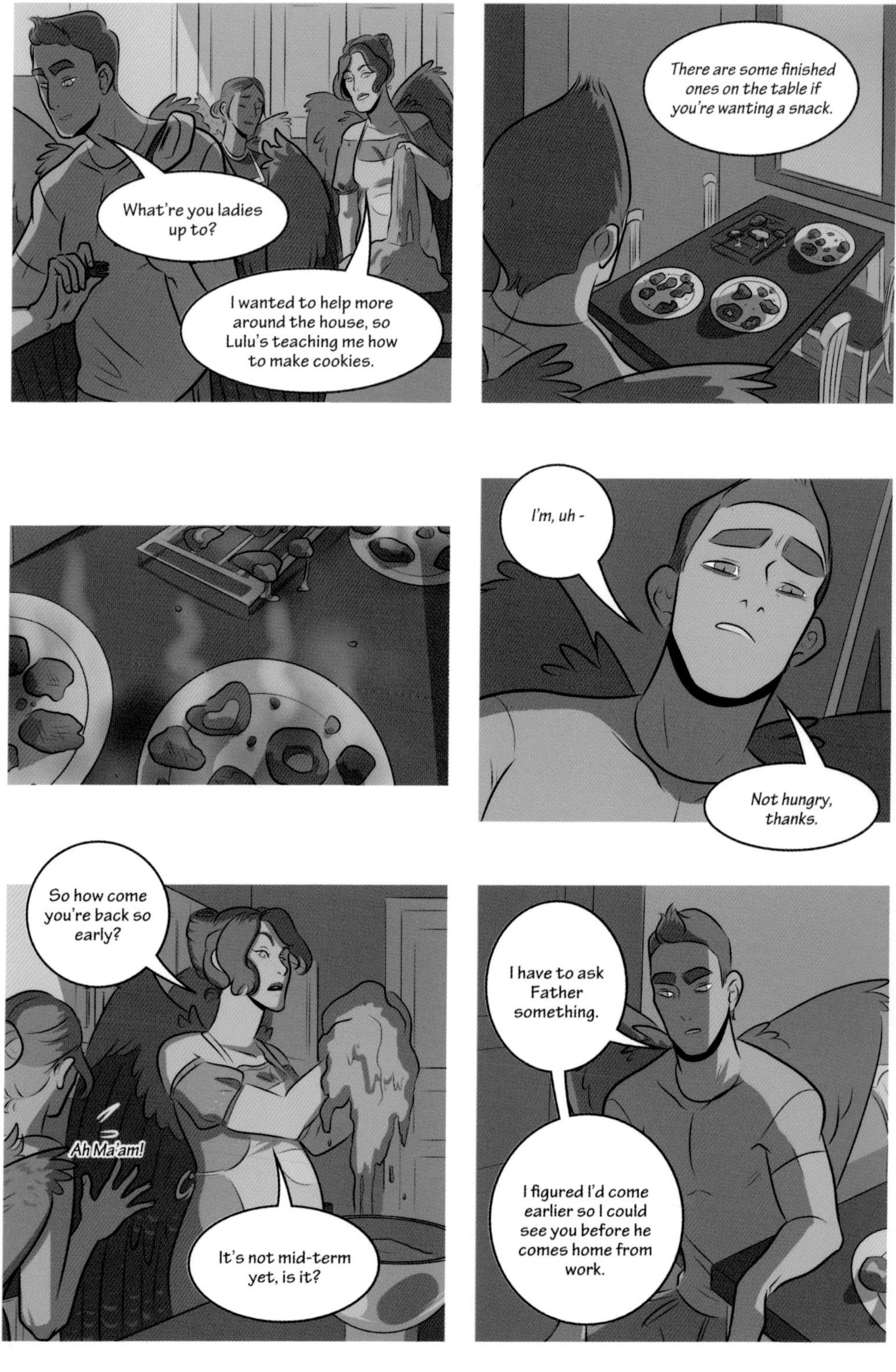
What're you ladies up to?
I wanted to help more around the house, so Lulu's teaching me how to make cookies.
There are some finished ones on the table if you're wanting a snack.
I'm, uh -
Not hungry, thanks.
So how come you're back so early?
Ah Ma'am!
It's not mid-term yet, is it?
I have to ask Father something.
I figured I'd come earlier so I could see you before he comes home from work.

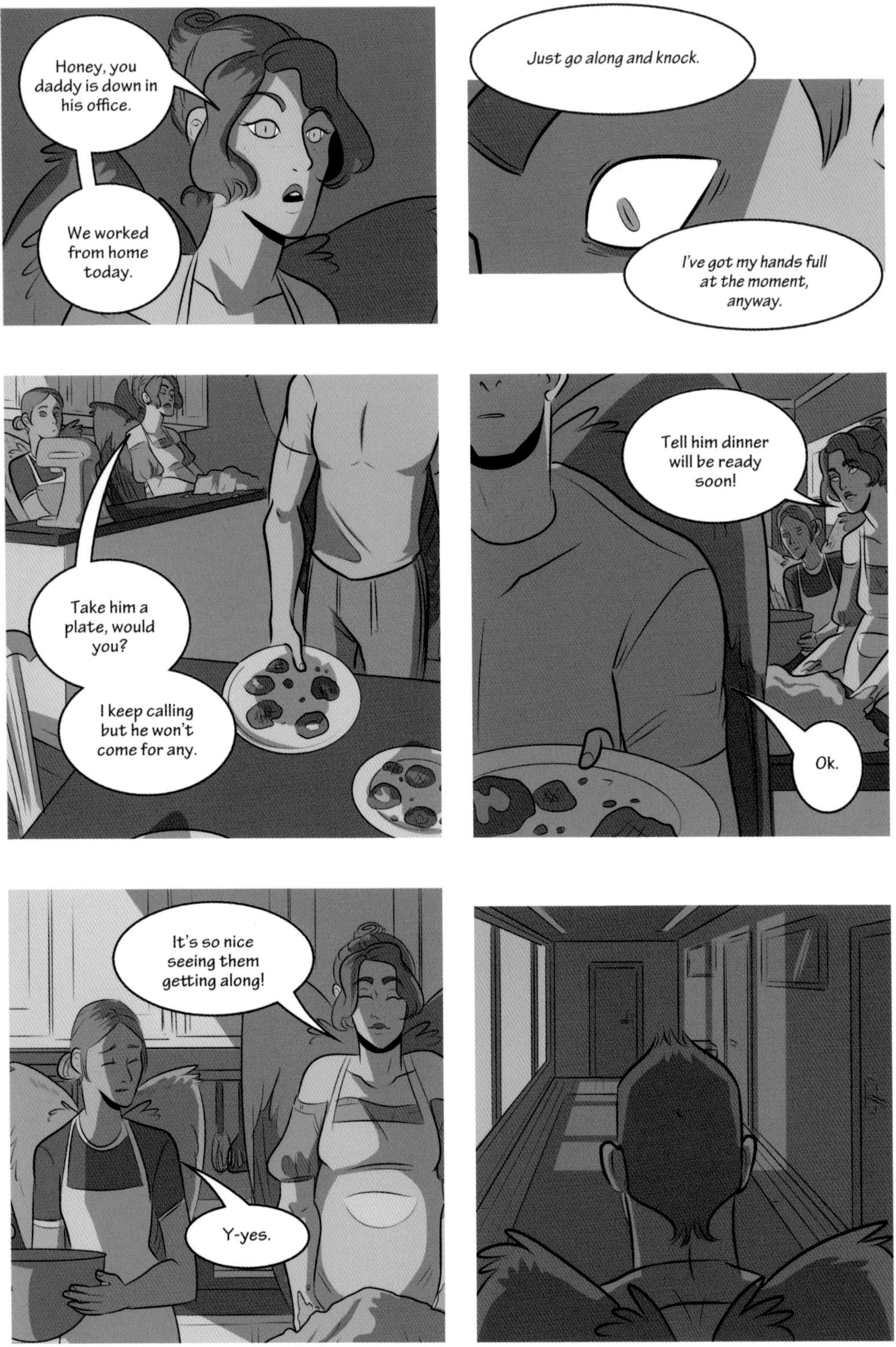
Honey, you daddy is down in his office.
We worked from home today.
Just go along and knock.
I've got my hands full at the moment, anyway.
Take him a plate, would you?
I keep calling but he won't come for any.
Tell him dinner will be ready soon!
Ok.
It's so nice seeing them getting along!
Y-yes.

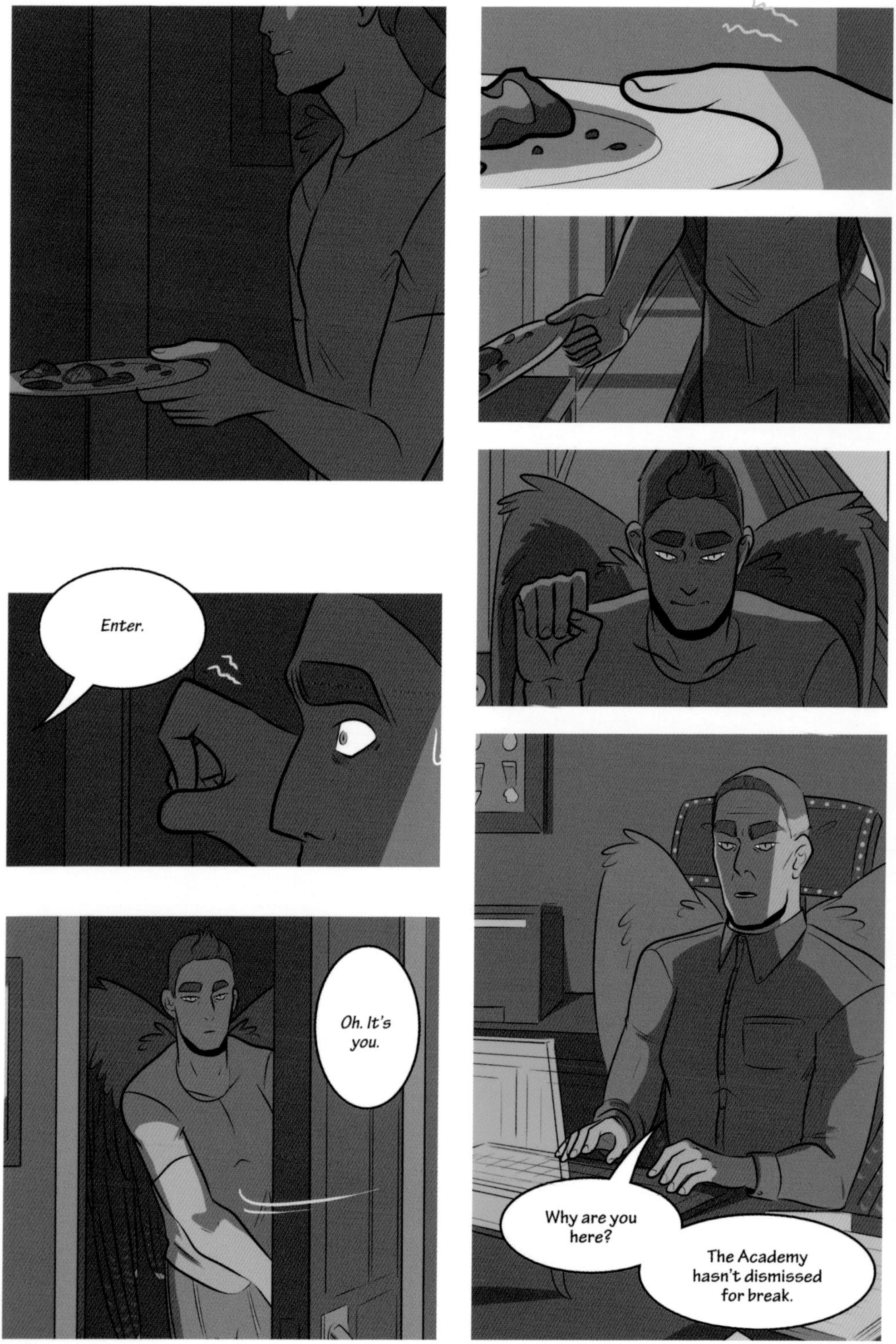
Enter.
Oh. It's you.
Why are you here?
The Academy hasn't dismissed for break.

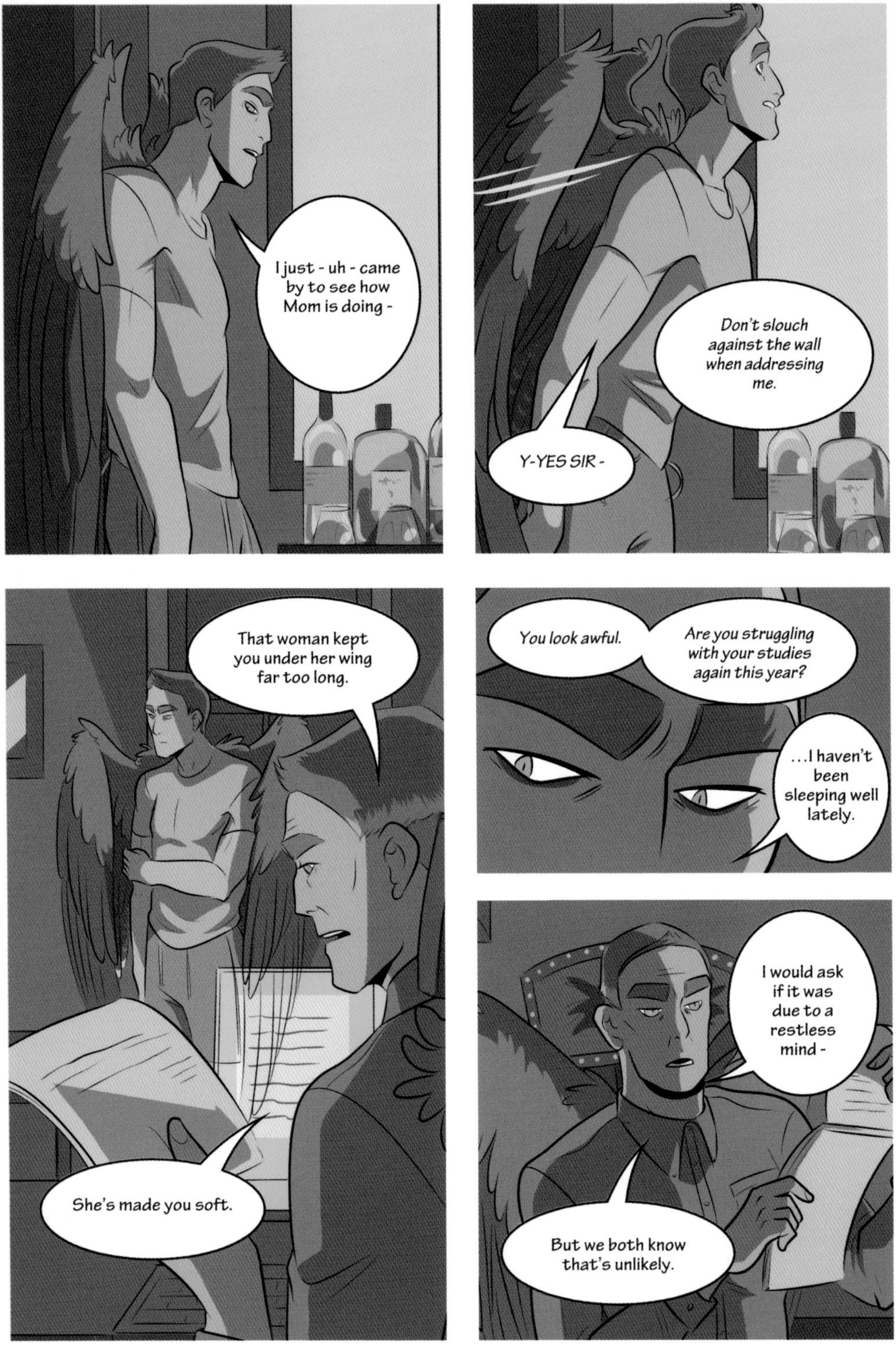
I just - uh - came by to see how Mom is doing -
Don't slouch against the wall when addressing me.
Y-YES SIR -
That woman kept you under her wing far too long.
She's made you soft.
You look awful.
Are you struggling with your studies again this year?
...I haven't been sleeping well lately.
I would ask if it was due to a restless mind -
But we both know that's unlikely.

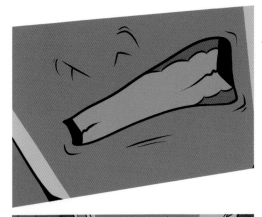

IT'S BECAUSE *YOU* LET A CROW INTO THE ACADEMY!

So this is the real reason for your visit.

As if I need to explain my decisions to the likes of you.

Is that what happened to your feathers?

Did the *Crow* get you?

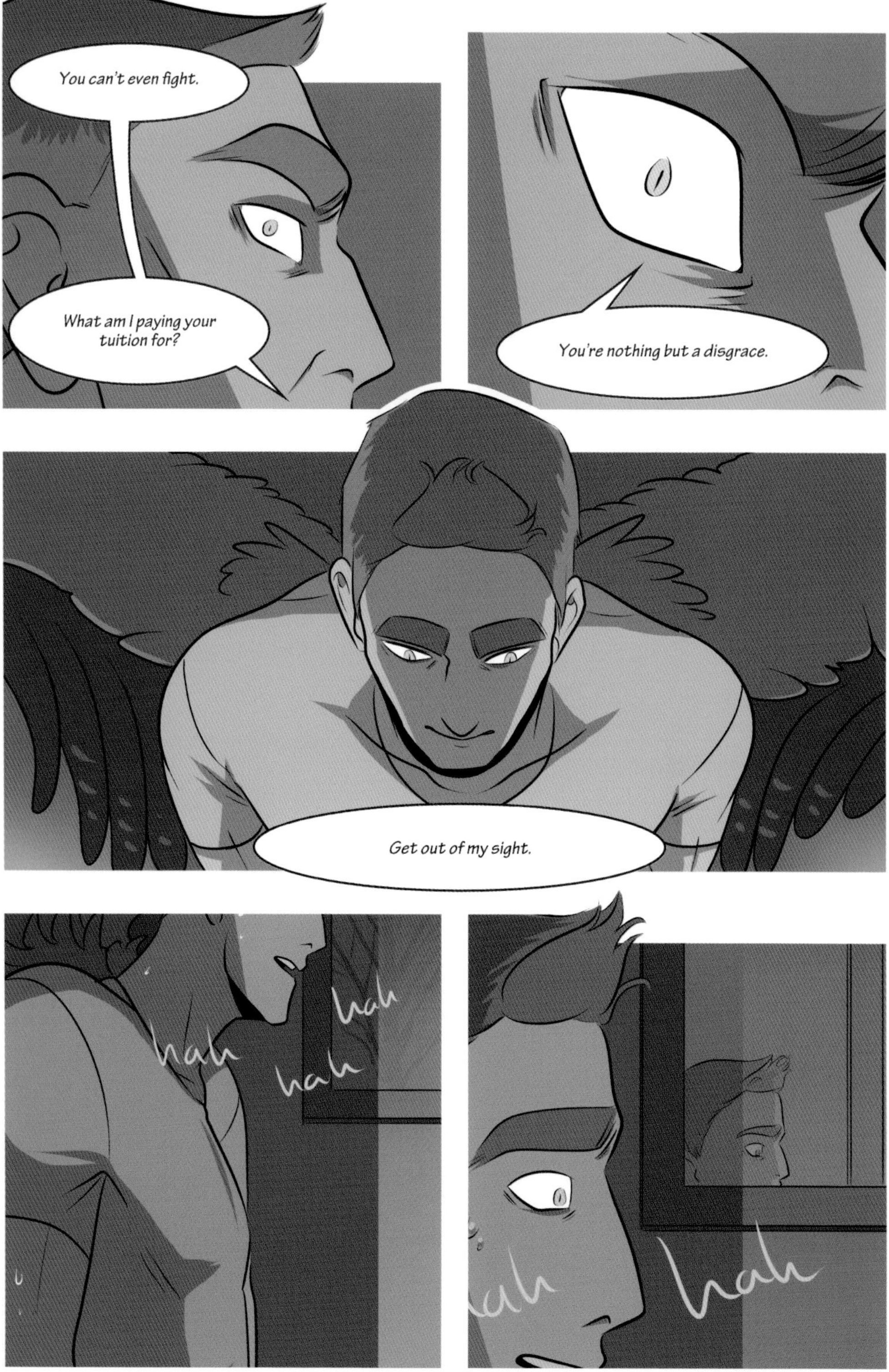
You can't even fight.
What am I paying your tuition for?
You're nothing but a disgrace.
Get out of my sight.
hah
hah
hah
hah
hah

SMASH
Del, honey? What was that noise -
I'm heading back to school.
But dinner!
There's broken glass in the hallway, can you make sure she doesn't step in it, please?

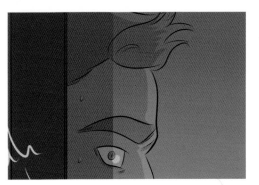

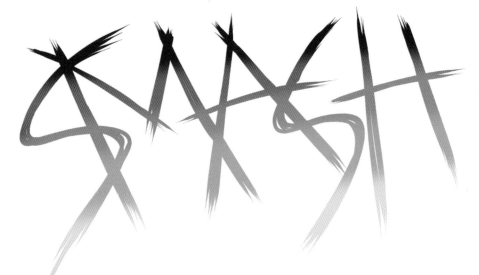

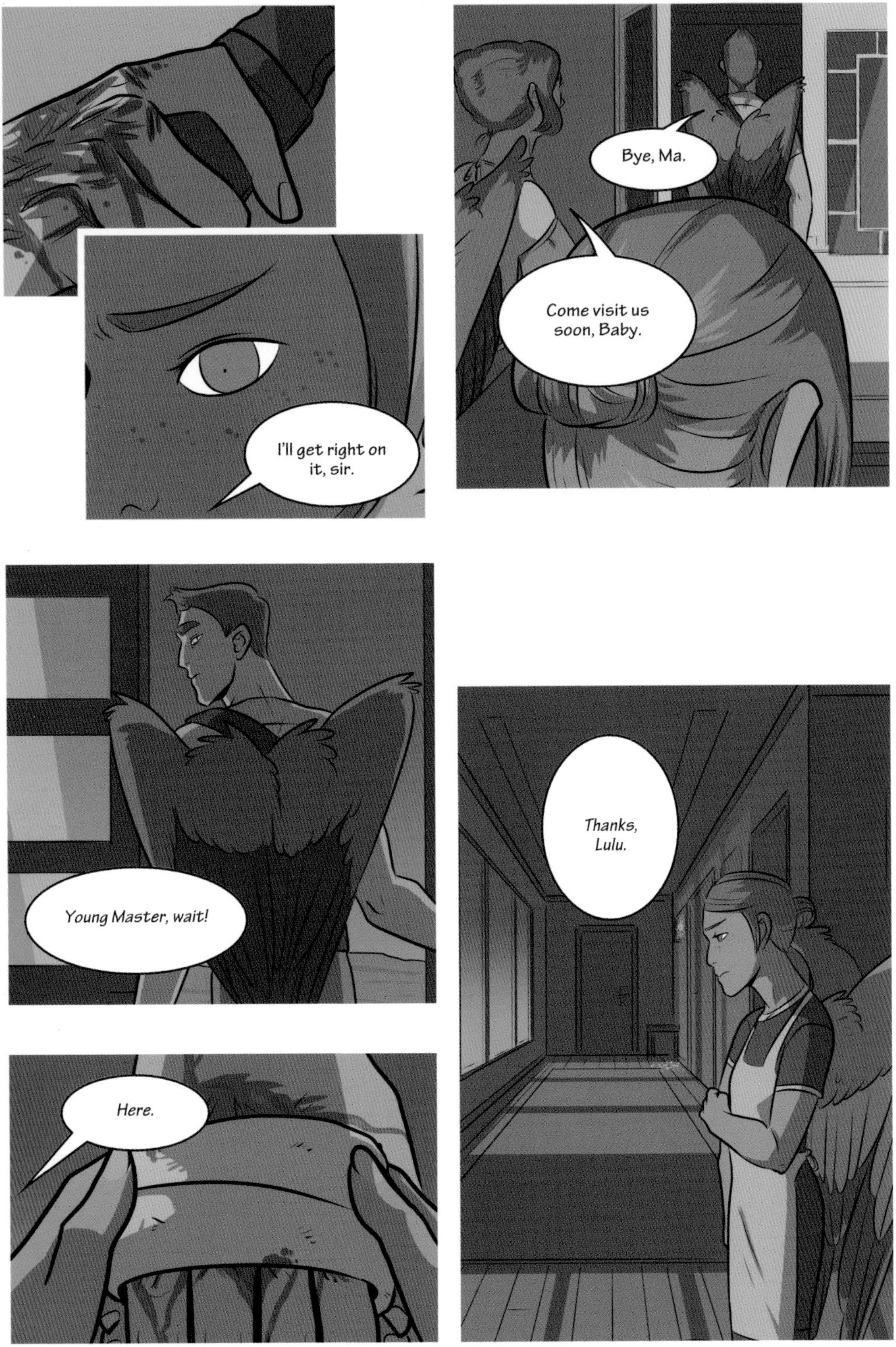
I'll get right on it, sir.
Bye, Ma.
Come visit us soon, Baby.
Young Master, wait!
Here.
Thanks, Lulu.

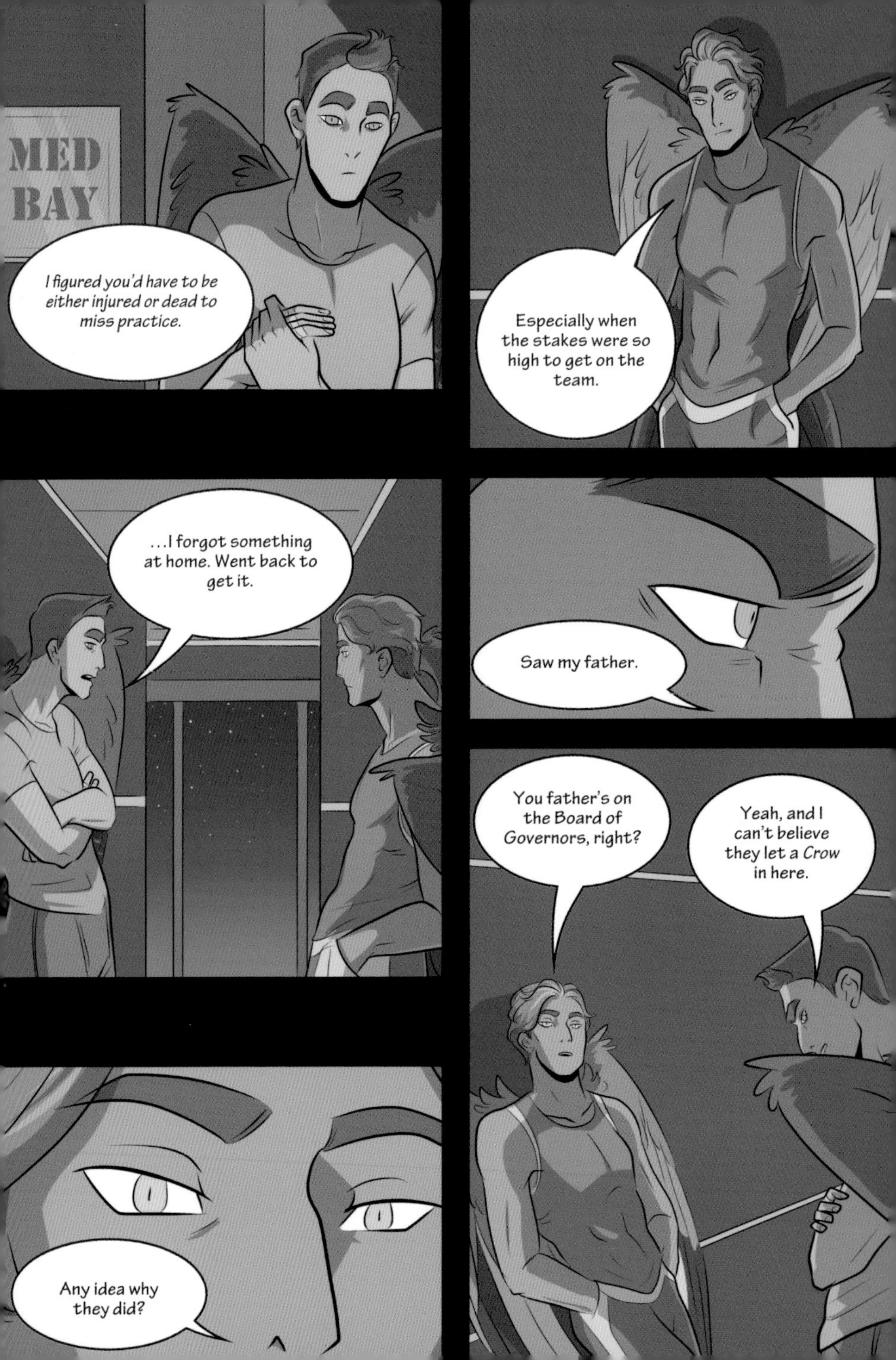
MED BAY
I figured you'd have to be either injured or dead to miss practice.
Especially when the stakes were so high to get on the team.
...I forgot something at home. Went back to get it.
Saw my father.
Any idea why they did?
You father's on the Board of Governors, right?
Yeah, and I can't believe they let a *Crow* in here.

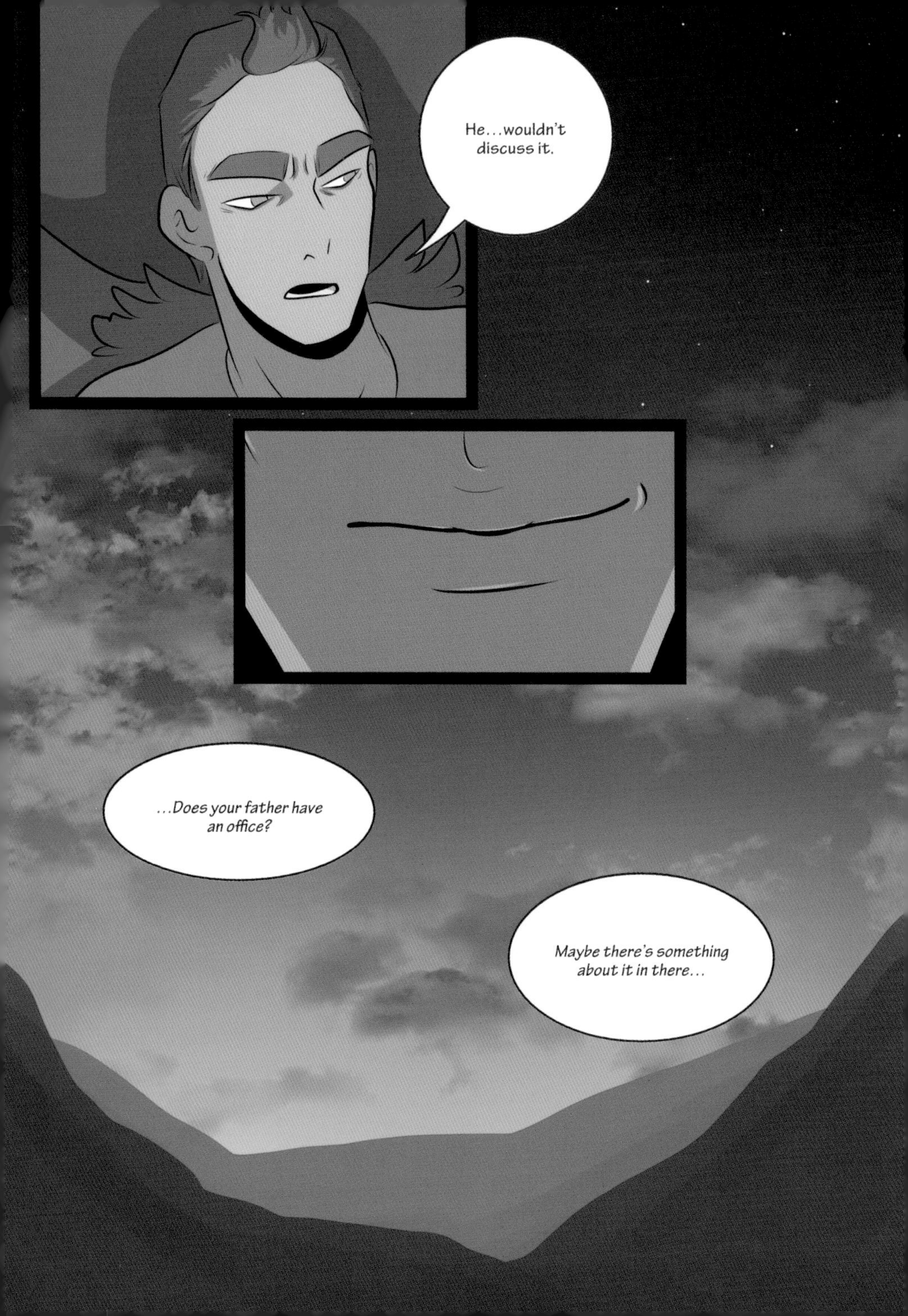
He...wouldn't discuss it.
...Does your father have an office?
Maybe there's something about it in there...

THE CROAKING

Gallery

Featuring selected pin-ups
and covers from this edition.

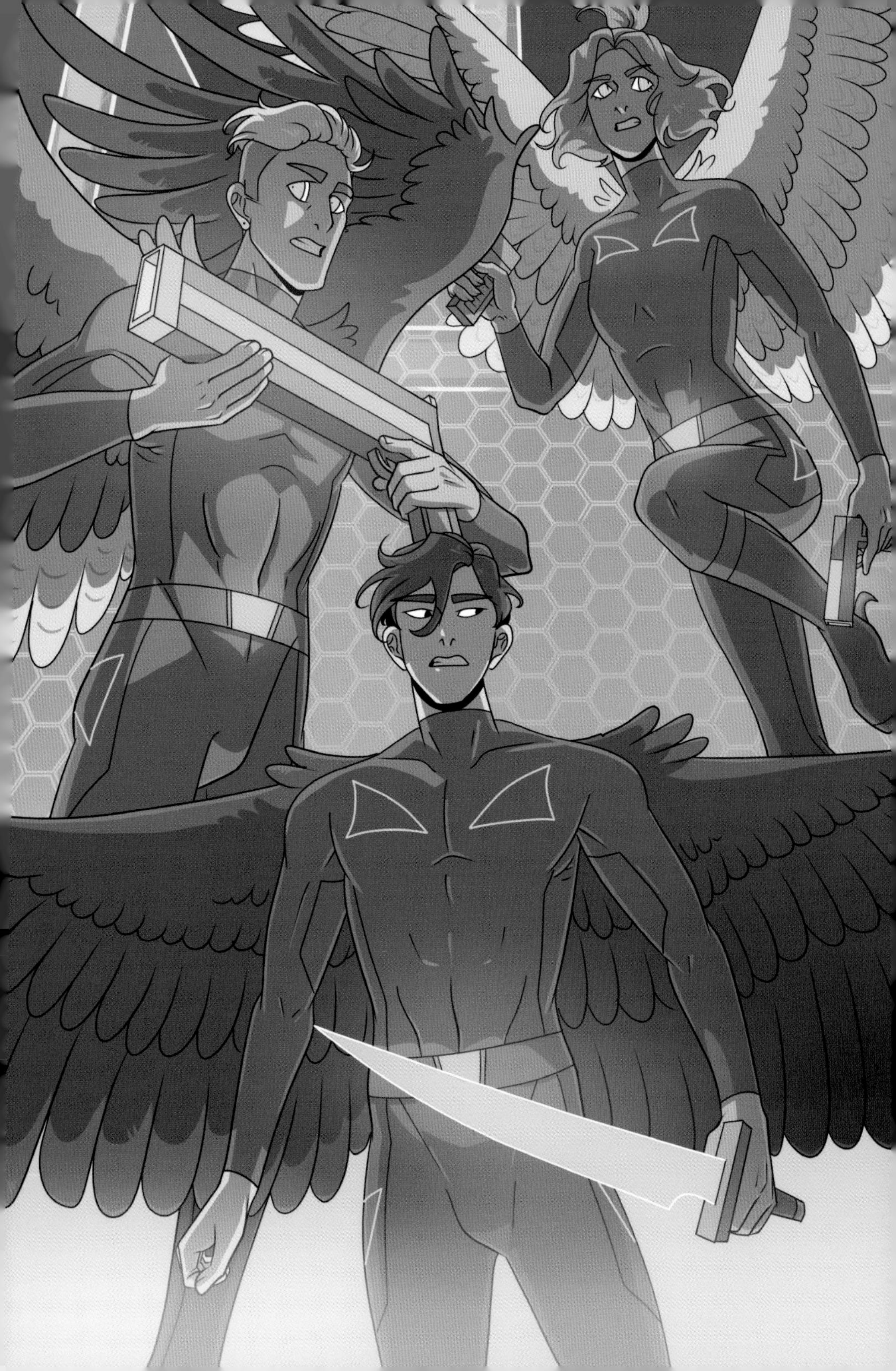

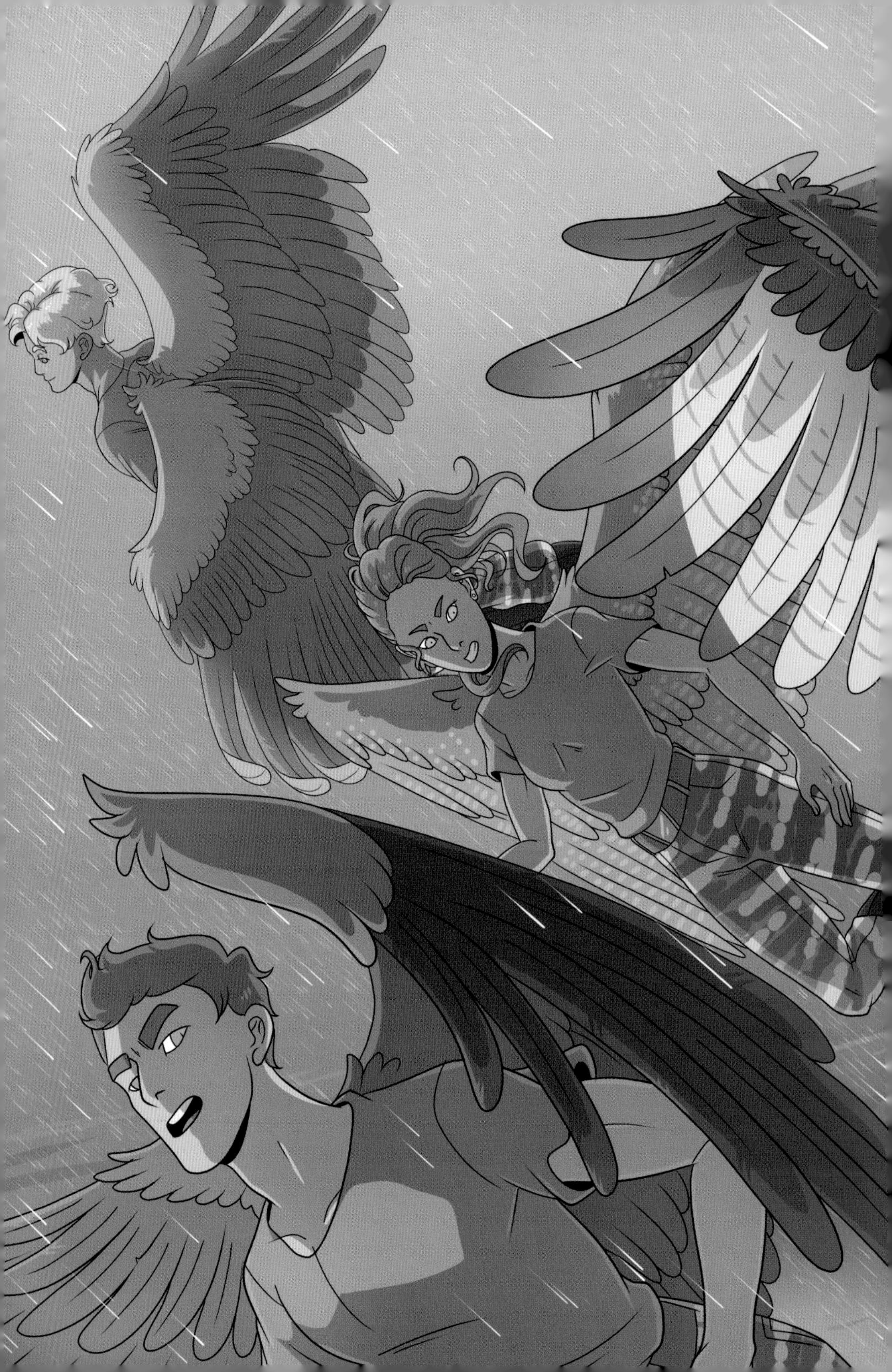

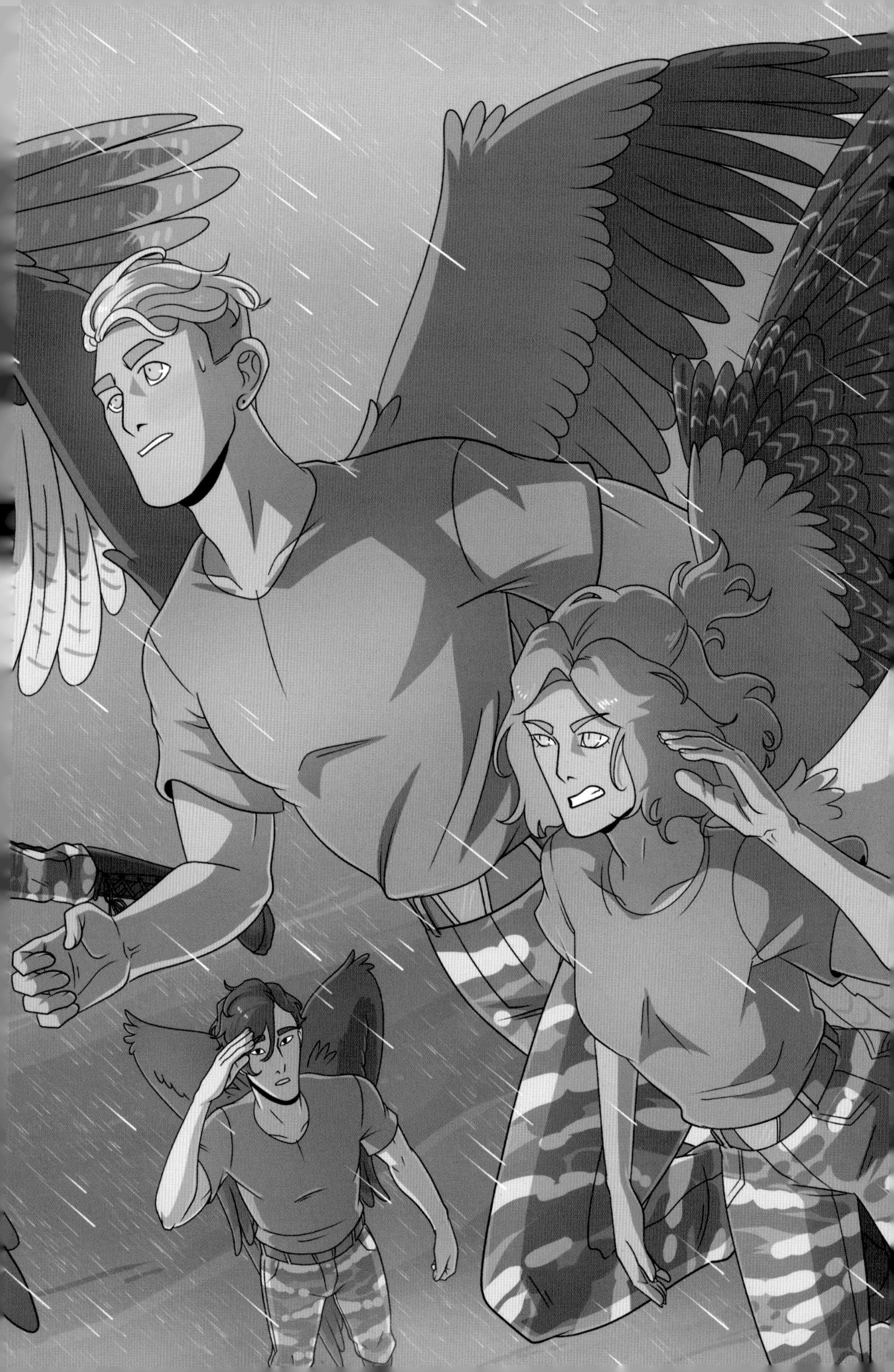

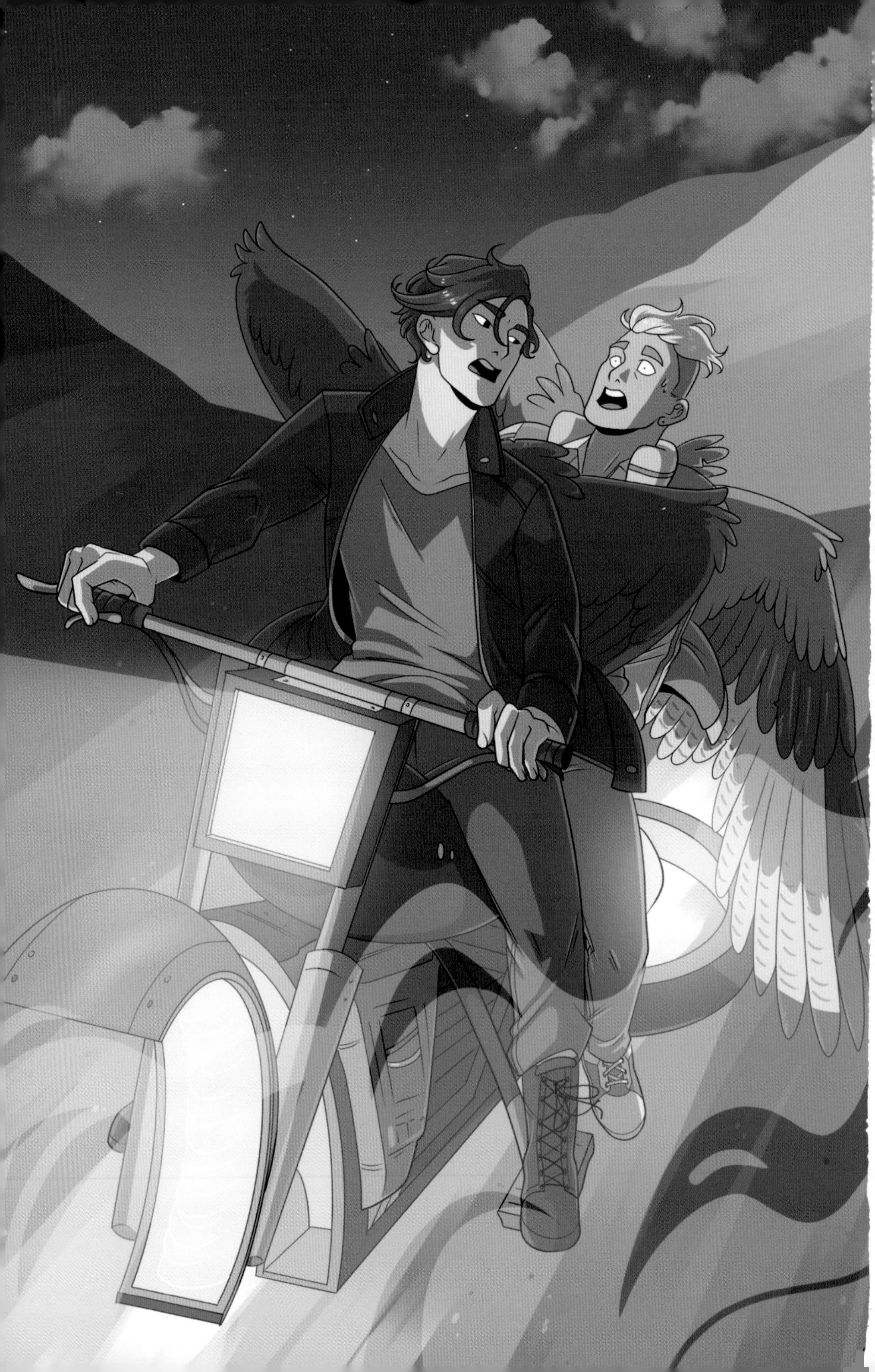

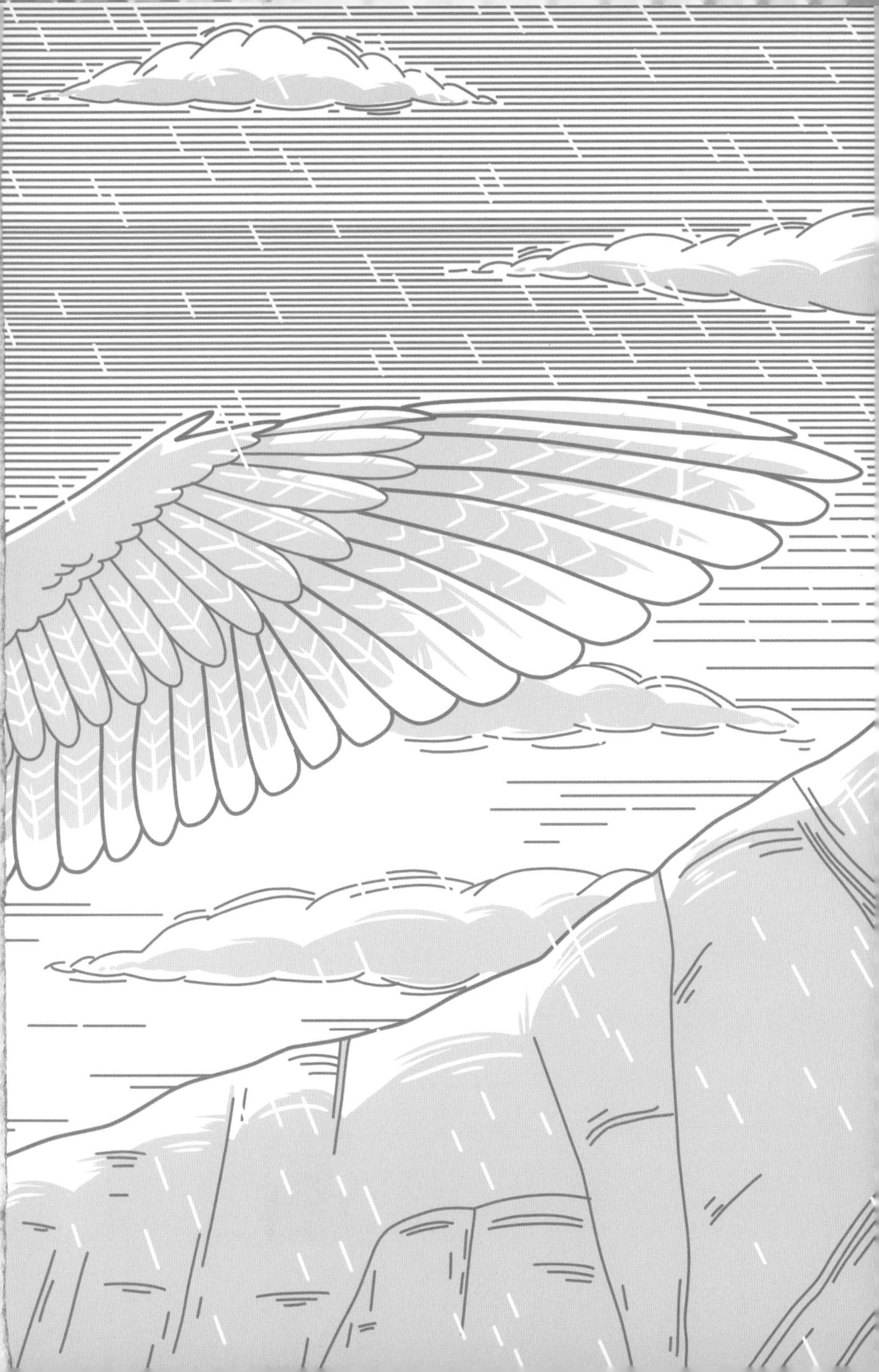

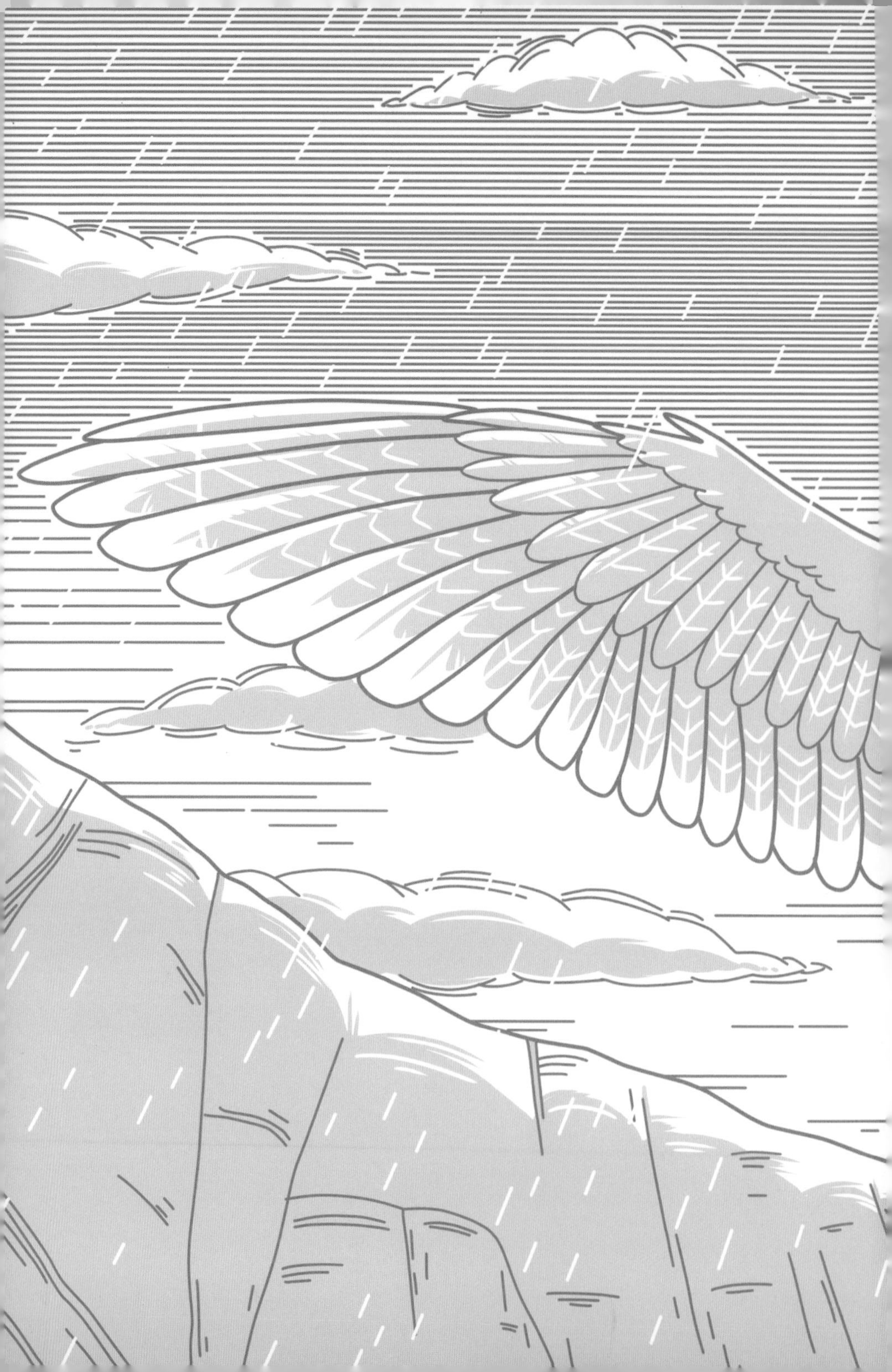